Assistant Army Surgeon Dr. Valentine McGillycuddy, nearing end of horse-meat march to the Black Hills. (*Courtesy Little Bighorn Battlefield National Monument.*)

Posed photo of soldier shooting played-out cavalry horse in march south from Slim Buttes. (*Courtesy Little Bighorn Battlefield National Monument.*)

Miniconjou chief "American Horse" and wife. *(Courtesy South Dakota Historical Society.)*

Buckskin lodge captured at Slim Buttes (note Keogh's I Company guidon recaptured). *(Courtesy Little Bighorn Battlefield National Monument.)*

LAST STAND

Pushing the Sharps lever down, Donegan ejected the empty cartridge, then replanted a live round in the breech. "Seems those warriors dogging our tails was just a little too anxious to close the trap, don't it?"

"Lucky us," grumbled Finerty as he crabbed up to join the three, whining lead following the white men into the timber.

Grouard rolled on his back and found Sibley, then instructed, "Lieutenant, tell your boys not to fire a shot until they got a good target."

"These men have fought before," Sibley snapped.

"Just remind 'em!" Donegan added. "We're going to need every last bullet we have before this day's done."

Nodding, a grim Sibley responded, "All right."

"And . . . Lieutenant," Seamus said, causing the officer to halt in a crouch, "tell your men it's a good idea to keep one last round in their pistols for themselves."

BOOKS BY TERRY C. JOHNSTON

Carry the Wind
BorderLords
One-Eyed Dream

Cry of the Hawk
Winter Rain
Dream Catcher

SONS OF THE PLAINS NOVELS

Long Winter Gone
Seize the Sky
Whisper of the Wolf

THE PLAINSMEN NOVELS

Sioux Dawn
Red Cloud's Revenge
The Stalkers
Black Sun
Devil's Backbone
Shadow Riders
Dying Thunder
Blood Song
Reap the Whirlwind

TRUMPET ON THE LAND

The Sibley Scout, the Skirmish at Warbonnet Creek,
the Battle of Slim Buttes
and Crook's "Horse-Meat March" -
the aftermath of the Custer Massacre

Terry C. Johnston

BANTAM BOOKS
NEW YORK • TORONTO • LONDON • SYDNEY • AUCKLAND

TRUMPET ON THE LAND

A Bantam Book / February 1995

ISBN 0-553-29975-1

Published simultaneously in the United States and Canada

Bantam Books are published by Bantam Books, a division of Bantam
Doubleday Dell Publishing Group, Inc. Its trademark, consisting of the
words "Bantam Books" and the portrayal of a rooster, is Registered in U.S.
Patent and Trademark Office and in other countries. Marca Registrada.
Bantam Books, 1540 Broadway, New York, New York 10036.

PRINTED IN THE UNITED STATES OF AMERICA

OPM   0 9 8 7 6 5 4 3

for all the miles and memories
we have shared together,
this book is affectionately
dedicated to my
Canadian saddle partner,
BRIAN TAYLOR

Cast
of
Characters

Seamus Donegan   Samantha Donegan

Army Scouts

Frank Grouard ("The Grabber," Yugata)
Louis (Louie) Richaud (Reshaw)
Baptiste Pourier ("Big Bat," Left Hand)
William F. Cody
*Charles / James / Jonathan White ("Buffalo Chips Charlie")
Tait / Tate
Baptiste Garnier ("Little Bat")
John Wallace "Captain Jack" Crawford ("The Poet Scout")
"Buckskin Jack" Russell
"Texas Jack" Omohundro

Military

Lieutenant General Philip H. Sheridan—Commander, Division of the Missouri (Chicago)

Brigadier General George C. Crook—commanding Department of the Platte (HQ—Omaha, Nebraska)

General Alfred H. Terry—commanding Department of the Dakota

Colonel Wesley Merritt—Commanding Officer, Fifth Cavalry (Brevet MAJOR GENERAL)

Colonel Nelson A. Miles—Commanding Officer, Fifth Infantry

Lieutenant Colonel William B. Royall—Commanding Officer, Third Cavalry (Brevet COLONEL)

Lieutenant Colonel Eugene A. Carr—Fifth Cavalry (Brevet MAJOR GENERAL)

Lieutenant Colonel James W. "Sandy" Forsyth—headquarters staff, Division of the Missouri

Lieutenant Colonel Joseph Nelson Garland Whistler—Fifth Infantry

Major Edwin F. Townsend—Post Commander, Fort Laramie (Brevet COLONEL)

Major Alexander Chambers—Commanding Officer, Fourth Infantry (Brevet COLONEL)

Major Andrew W. Evans—Second in Command, Third Cavalry (Brevet COLONEL) Battalion Commander

Major John J. Upham—Fifth Cavalry, Battalion Commander

Captain Julius W. Mason—K Troop, Fifth Cavalry (Brevet LIEUTENANT COLONEL) Battalion Commander

Captain William H. Jordan—Ninth Infantry, Commanding Officer, Camp Robinson (Brevet MAJOR)

Captain James "Teddy" Egan—K Troop, Second Cavalry

Captain Emil Adams—C Troop, Fifth Cavalry

Captain Thomas B. Weir—Seventh Cavalry

Captain Edward W. Smith—adjutant to General Alfred Terry

Captain Thaddeus H. Stanton—Paymaster, Department of the Platte, Commander of Volunteers (Brevet MAJOR)

Captain Samuel Munson—C Company, Ninth Infantry

Captain Andrew S. Burt—H Company, Ninth Infantry (Brevet MAJOR)

Captain Gerhard L. Luhn—F Company, Fourth Infantry

Captain Daniel W. Burke—C Company, Fourteenth Infantry

Captain William H. Andrews—I Troop, Third Cavalry

Captain John V. Furey—Expedition Quartermaster, commanding wagon/supply train

Captain Henry E. Noyes—I Troop, Second Cavalry (Brevet MAJOR) Battalion Commander

Captain George M. ("Black Jack") Randall—Chief of Scouts, Twenty-third Infantry (Brevet MAJOR)

Captain William H. Powell—G Company, Fourth Infantry

Captain Anson Mills—M Troop, Third Cavalry (Brevet COLONEL)

Captain Frederick Van Vliet—C Troop, Third Cavalry (Brevet MAJOR)

Captain Alexander Sutorius—E Troop, Third Cavalry

Captain Peter D. Vroom—L Troop, Third Cavalry

Captain Elijah R. Wells—E Troop, Second Cavalry

Captain Samuel S. Sumner—D Troop, Fifth Cavalry (Brevet MAJOR)

Captain Robert H. Montgomery—B Troop, Fifth Cavalry

Captain Sanford C. Kellogg—I Troop, Fifth Cavalry (Brevet LIEUTENANT COLONEL)

Captain George F. Price—E Troop, Fifth Cavalry

Captain Edward M. Hayes—G Troop, Fifth Cavalry

Captain J. Scott Payne—F Troop, Fifth Cavalry

Captain H. J. Nowlan—Seventh Cavalry, acting assistant quartermaster to the Dakota Column

Lieutenant John G. Bourke—aide-de-camp to General Crook

Lieutenant Henry R. Lemly—Regimental Adjutant to Colonel Royall

First Lieutenant William L. Carpenter—G Company, Ninth Infantry

First Lieutenant Adolphus H. Von Luettwitz—E Troop, Third Cavalry

First Lieutenant Augustus C. Paul—M Troop, Third Cavalry

First Lieutenant Edward S. Godfrey—Seventh Cavalry

First Lieutenant Emmet Crawford—G Troop, Third Cavalry

First Lieutenant Henry Seton—D Company, Fourth Infantry

First Lieutenant Joseph Lawson—A Troop, Third Cavalry

First Lieutenant William C. Forbush—Fifth Cavalry, Assistant Adjutant General

First Lieutenant Charles King—Fifth Cavalry, Adjutant

First Lieutenant William P. Hall—Fifth Cavalry, Quartermaster

First Lieutenant Walter S. Schuyler—Fifth Cavalry, aide-de-camp to Crook

First Lieutenant William Philo Clark—I Troop, Second Cavalry, aide-de-camp to General Crook

Second Lieutenant Robert London—A Troop, Fifth Cavalry (after Wilson resigns)

Second Lieutenant Charles M. Rockefeller—H Company, Ninth Infantry

Second Lieutenant Edgar B. Robertson—H Company, Ninth Infantry

Second Lieutenant Henry D. Huntington—D Troop, Second Cavalry

Second Lieutenant Edward L. Keyes—C Troop, Fifth Cavalry

Second Lieutenant J. Hayden Pardee—Twenty-third Infantry, aide-de-camp to Merritt

Lieutenant William C. Hunter—U.S. Navy (Brevet COMMODORE)

Dr. Bennett A. Clements—Surgeon, Expedition Medical Director (oversaw eight medical personnel, assistant surgeons and stewards)

Dr. Albert Hartsuff—Assistant Surgeon

Dr. Julius H. Patzki—Assistant Surgeon

Dr. Charles R. Stephens—Assistant Surgeon

Dr. J. W. Powell—Assistant Surgeon, Fifth Cavalry

Dr. Valentine McGillycuddy—Assistant Surgeon

First Lieutenant Alfred B. Bache—F Troop, Fifth Cavalry

Second Lieutenant Frederick Schwatka—M Troop, Third Cavalry

Second Lieutenant George F. Chase—L Troop, Third Cavalry

First Lieutenant John W. Bubb—Commissary of Subsistence

First Lieutenant Emmet Crawford—G Troop, Third Cavalry

First Lieutenant William B. Rawolle—B Troop, Second Cavalry

Lieutenant Frederick W. Sibley—E Troop, Second Cavalry

Sergeant Oscar Cornwall—Second Cavalry, Sibley Patrol

Sergeant Charles W. Day—Second Cavalry, Sibley Patrol

Sergeant G. P. Harrington—Second Cavalry, Sibley Patrol

†Sergeant Edmund Schreiber—K Troop, Fifth Cavalry

†Sergeant John A. Kirkwood—M Troop, Third Cavalry

†Sergeant Edward Glass—E Troop, Third Cavalry

Corporal Thomas C. Warren—Second Cavalry, Sibley Patrol

Corporal Thomas W. Wilkinson—K Troop, Fifth Cavalry

Corporal J. S. Clanton—B Troop, Fifth Cavalry

Private Valentine Rufus—Second Cavalry, Sibley Patrol

Private Patrick Hasson—Second Cavalry, Sibley Patrol
Private George Rhode—Second Cavalry, Sibley Patrol
Private George Watts—Second Cavalry, Sibley Patrol
Private Henry Collins—Second Cavalry, Sibley Patrol
Private William Evans—E Company, Seventh Infantry
Private Benjamin F. Stewart—E Company, Seventh Infantry
Private James Bell—E Company, Seventh Infantry
Private Christian Madsen—A Troop, Fifth Cavalry
*Private John Wenzel—A Troop, Third Cavalry
Private Albert Glavinski—M Troop, Third Cavalry
†Private Orlando H. Duren—E Troop, Third Cavalry
*Private Edward Kennedy—C Troop, Fifth Cavalry
†Private John M. Stevenson—I Troop, Second Cavalry
†Private August Dorn—D Troop, Fifth Cavalry
Private Cyrus B. Milner—A Troop, Fifth Cavalry
†Private Edward Kiernan—E Troop, Third Cavalry
†Private William B. DuBois—C Troop, Third Cavalry
†Private August Foran—D Troop, Third Cavalry
†Private Charles Foster—B Troop, Third Cavalry

Shoshone Allies

Washakie

Sioux

American Horse   Little Eagle
Dog Necklace   Antelope Tail
Charging Bear   Red Horse
Iron Thunder

Cheyenne

Yellow Hair   Rain Maker

Civilian Characters

John "Trailer Jack" Becker—packer on Sibley Scout
Wilbur Storey—owner/publisher, Chicago Times
Clint Snowden—city editor, Chicago Times
Thomas Moore—Chief of Pack Train
Richard "Uncle Dick" Closter
Grant Marsh—captain, *Far West* steamboat
Dave Campbell—pilot, *Far West* steamboat
†James B. Glover—packer
E. B. Farnum—Mayor of Deadwood
Martha Luhn—officer's wife at Fort Laramie
Elizabeth Burt—officer's wife at Fort Laramie
Robert Strahorn—correspondent, Denver *Rocky Mountain News*, Chicago *Tribune*, Cheyenne *Sun*, and the Omaha *Republican*
John F. Finerty—correspondent, Chicago *Times*
Joe Wasson—correspondent, New York *Tribune*, Philadelphia *Press*, and San Francisco *Alta California*
Reuben B. Davenport—correspondent, New York *Herald*
T. B. MacMillan—correspondent, Chicago *Inter-Ocean*
J. J. Talbot—correspondent, New York *Graphic*
Barbour Lathrop—correspondent, San Francisco *Evening Bulletin*
Cuthbert Mills—New York *Times*
Tom Cosgrove—civilian leader of the Shoshone battalion
Nelson Yarnell—Cosgrove's lieutenant
Yancy Eckles—Cosgrove's sergeant

---

*killed in the battle of Slim Buttes
†wounded at the Battle of Slim Buttes

TRUMPET
ON THE LAND

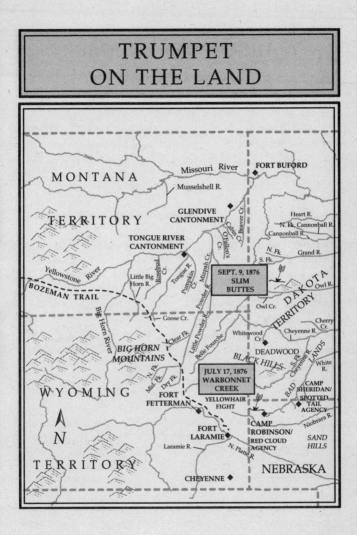

MONTANA

Missouri River

FORT BUFORD

Musselshell R.

TERRITORY

GLENDIVE
CANTONMENT

Heart R.

N. Fk. Cannonball R.

Cannonball R.

TONGUE RIVER
CANTONMENT

N. Fk.   Grand R.

S. Fk.

Yellowstone River

Rosebud Cr.

Little Big Horn R.

SEPT. 9, 1876
SLIM
BUTTES

DAKOTA

BOZEMAN TRAIL

Owl R.

Owl Cr.

TERRITORY

Goose Cr.

Cherry Cr.

BIG HORN
MOUNTAINS

Clear Fk.

Whitewood Cr.

Cheyenne R.

Belle Fourche

BLACK HILLS

DEADWOOD

White R.

WYOMING

N. Fk.

Mid. Fk.

Dry Fk.

FORT
FETTERMAN

JULY 17, 1876
WARBONNET
CREEK

YELLOWHAIR
FIGHT

BAD
LANDS

CAMP
SHERIDAN/
SPOTTED
TAIL
AGENCY

FORT
LARAMIE

CAMP
ROBINSON/
RED CLOUD
AGENCY

Niobrara R.

N

Laramie R.

N. Platte R.

SAND
HILLS

TERRITORY

NEBRASKA

CHEYENNE

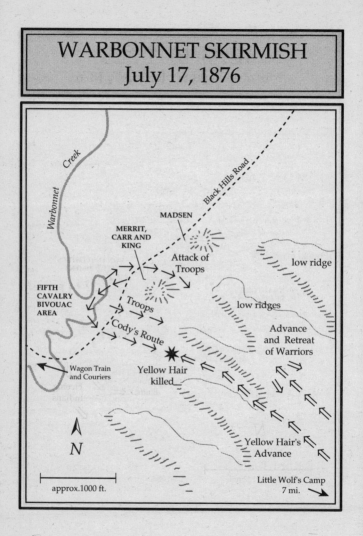

WARBONNET SKIRMISH
July 17, 1876

Creek

Warbonnet

Black Hills Road

MADSEN

MERRIT,
CARR AND
KING

Attack of
Troops

low ridge

FIFTH
CAVALRY
BIVOUAC
AREA

Troops

low ridges

Cody's Route

Advance
and Retreat
of Warriors

Wagon Train
and Couriers

Yellow Hair
killed

N

Yellow Hair's
Advance

approx.1000 ft.

Little Wolf's Camp
7 mi.

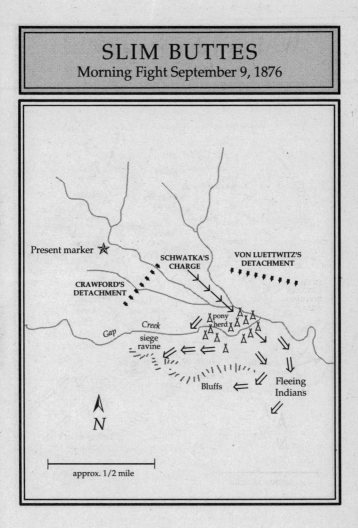

SLIM BUTTES
Morning Fight September 9, 1876

Present marker ☆

SCHWATKA'S CHARGE

VON LUETTWITZ'S DETACHMENT

CRAWFORD'S DETACHMENT

Creek

Gap

pony herd

siege ravine

Bluffs

Fleeing Indians

N

approx. 1/2 mile

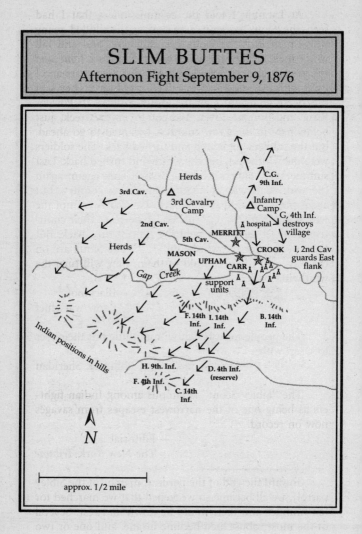

SLIM BUTTES
Afternoon Fight September 9, 1876

3rd Cav.

Herds

3rd Cavalry Camp

C.G. 9th Inf.

Infantry Camp

2nd Cav.

hospital

G, 4th Inf. destroys village

MERRITT

5th Cav.

Herds

CROOK

I, 2nd Cav guards East flank

MASON

UPHAM

CARR

Gap Creek

support units

F. 14th Inf.

I. 14th Inf.

B. 14th Inf.

Indian positions in hills

H. 9th Inf.

F. 4th Inf.

D. 4th Inf. (reserve)

C. 14th Inf.

N

approx. 1/2 mile

At Laramie I told the commissioners that I had seen the Sioux commit a massacre; they killed many white men. But the Sioux are still here, and still kill white men. *When you whites whip the Sioux come and tell us of it.* You are afraid of the Sioux. Two years ago I went with the soldiers; they talked very brave. They said they were going through the Sioux country to Powder River and Tongue River. We got to Pryor Creek, just below here in the Crow country. I wanted to go ahead, but the soldiers got scared and turned back. The soldiers were the whirlwind, but the whirlwind turned back. Last summer the soldiers went to Pryor Creek again; again the whirlwind was going through Sioux country, but again the whirlwind turned back. We Crows are not the whirlwind, but we go to the Sioux; we go to their country; we meet them and fight; we do not turn back. But then *we* are not the whirlwind! . . . The Sioux are on the way, and you are afraid of them; they will turn the whirlwind back.

—Blackfoot
Crow war chief

The people must be left with nothing but their eyes to weep with.
—Lieutenant General Philip H. Sheridan

The "Sibley Scout" is famous among Indian fighters as being one of the narrowest escapes from savages now on record.
—Editorial
The New York *Tribune*

Toward the end of the perilous march [of the Sibley patrol], we all became so weakened that we marched for ten minutes and then would lie down and rest. Several of the most robust men became insane, and one or two never regained their wits.
—Lieutenant Frederick W. Sibley

[The skirmish at Warbonnet Creek] is one of few cases where a large party of Indians was successfully ambushed by troops.

—Don Russell
Campaigning with King

For the Indians who had gloried in the victory of Little Big Horn, Slim Buttes heralded the retaliatory blows that ultimately broke their resistance and forced their submission . . . the actions of September 9 and 10, 1876, commenced the relentless punitive warfare that was to be waged over the next eight months, until the tribesmen either had died or had gone peaceably to the agencies.

—Jerome A. Green
Slim Buttes, 1876

. . . many a suffering stomach gladdened with a welcome change from horse meat, tough and stringy, to rib roasts of pony, grass-fed, sweet, and succulent. There is no such sauce as starvation.

—Lieutenant Charles King
Campaigning with Crook

The terrible persistence with which [Crook] urged his faint, starving, foot-sore, tattered soldiers along the trail, to which he clung with a resolution and determination that nothing could shake, entitles him to the respect and admiration of his countrymen—a respect and admiration, by the way, which was fully accorded him by his gallant and equally desperate foes.

—Cyrus Townsend Brady
Indian Fights and Fighters

Only the brave and fearless can be just.
—Old Lakota proverb

For acting to stop the Cheyennes, [Merritt] was commended by General Sheridan; for delaying the march of the Big Horn and Yellowstone Expedition for a week, he was blamed by General Crook.

—Don Russell
*The Lives and Legends
of Buffalo Bill*

The battle [of Slim Buttes] was one of the most picturesque ever fought in the West. Crook and his officers stood in the camp, the center of a vast amphitheater ringed with fire, up the sides of which the soldiers steadily climbed to get at the Indians, silhouetted in all their war finery against the sky.

—Cyrus Townsend Brady
Indian Fights and Fighters

Slim Buttes was touted as a victory for the army, but it was a shabby victory at best and accomplished nothing beyond angering the Indians. The dawn attack had felled women and children, and when the tribesmen crept back into the village after the military withdrawal, they confronted heartrending scenes. Many of the groups in the vicinity of Slim Buttes, including the one struck by Mills, had intended to surrender at an agency. The sight of women and children maimed or slain by army bullets dampened that impulse.

—Robert M. Utley
The Lance and the Shield

Sitting Bull had warned his people not to take any spoils from the Little Big Horn battle[field], or the soldiers would crush them. The Slim Buttes battle was part of the prophecy which came true.

—Fred H. Werner
The Slim Buttes Battle

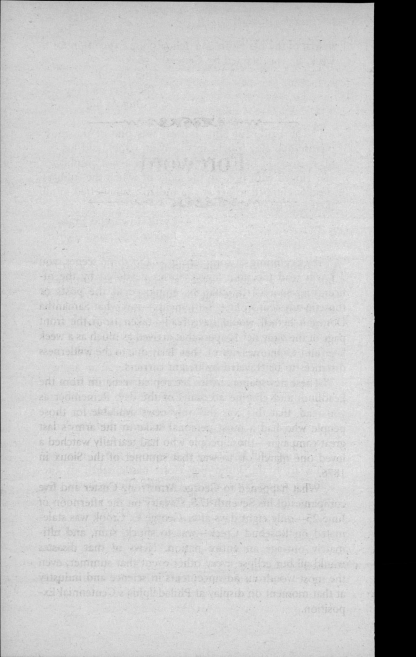

Foreword

At the beginning of some chapters and some scenes, you will read the same news stories devoured by the officers' wives and the civilians employed at the posts or those in adjacent frontier settlements—just what Samantha Donegan herself would have read—taken from the front page of the daily newspapers that arrived as much as a week late (and sometimes more), that delay due to the wilderness distances to be traveled by freight carriers.

These newspaper stories are copied verbatim from the headlines and graphic accounts of the day. Remember as you read, that this was the only news available for those people who had a most personal stake in the army's last great campaign—those people who had tearfully watched a loved one march off to war that summer of the Sioux in 1876.

What happened to George Armstrong Custer and five companies of his Seventh U.S. Cavalry on the afternoon of June 25—only eight days after George C. Crook was stalemated on Rosebud Creek—was to shock, stun, and ultimately outrage an entire nation. News of that disaster would all but eclipse every other event that summer, even the most wondrous advancements in science and industry at that moment on display at Philadelphia's Centennial Exposition.

By starting the chapters and scenes with an article taken right out of the day's headlines, I hope that you will be struck with the immediacy of each day's front page as you finish reading its news—just as Samantha Donegan would have been from the relative safety of Fort Laramie. But, unlike her, you will then find yourself thrust back into the action of an army on the march, an army intent on fulfilling General Philip Sheridan's prophecy that the hostiles of Sitting Bull and Crazy Horse who had destroyed Custer on the Greasy Grass would soon hear a trumpet on the land.

TRUMPET ON
THE LAND

Prologue

20 June 1876

"I hear water's better when you mix it with whiskey."

Upon hearing the quiet interruption of that familiar voice, the Irishman raised his head from the cool grass that flourished along the bank of Little Goose Creek to watch Frank Grouard slide out of his saddle.

"I wouldn't know," Seamus Donegan replied, propped up on one elbow as he kicked his bare feet in the cold water. He had his canvas britches snugged in loose rolls all the way up to his knees to soak in the refreshing current. "You see, I never water down my whiskey."

The half-breed with skin the hue of coffee-tanned leather tied off his army mount, then came over to settle in the shade of a huge cottonwood beside Donegan. "Much as you bellyache about missing your whiskey this trip out, you sure as hell done a lot of soaking in water."

Seamus grinned, then nodded in agreement as he said, "This tends to take a man's mind off his real thirst."

"The sort a man gets when he has a whiskey hunger, eh?"

"Or the kind of hunger what hits a man when he's gone without a woman for too long." Donegan immediately felt bad for the thoughtless words that fell from his tongue. "I'm sorry, Frank. Didn't mean nothing by it. Forgot, is all."

Grouard waved it off with a lukewarm grin and a shrug of his shoulder. "Don't make nothing of it, Irishman. Women been nothing but trouble for me. Whiskey too. Now, a fella like you, he can handle both, I'd wager: all he wants of both. But a man like me gets all buried in a woman, and that makes for trouble with that woman's brother—so that's when I go and get all fall-down and underfoot with some cheap Red River trader's whiskey. . . ."

He heard the head scout's voice fade away while watching the wistful look come over the half-breed's dusky, molasses-colored face. "I figure we ought to talk about what brung you to look me up—"

"It don't matter no more, Seamus," Grouard interrupted. "Something I can talk about now. Hurt for a while. Not so much no more."

"Damn, but you've had your share of dark days. First the trouble with Sitting Bull's Hunkpapas over them whiskey traders. Then you go and get yourself all but scalped and skewered over a woman with Crazy Horse's band."

"Didn't mean for things to turn out so bad with He Dog, that woman's brother, bad with the rest of them Hunkpatila that way."

As much as Crook's chief of scouts might protest otherwise, Seamus could still read the torment of that lost love carved into the lines around Grouard's eyes. Just the way it had to be cut into his very soul. "Never knew a man who lost a woman could honestly claim he was meaning for things to turn out that way, Frank."

Grouard pulled free a long brilliant-green stem from the grass at his side, placed it between his lips, and sucked absently, gazing at the gurgling flow of Little Goose Creek at their feet. Moment by moment the midsummer sun continued its relentless climb toward midsky, easing back the cool, inviting shadows beneath the overhanging cottonwoods like a woman at her morning chores sweeping against a thickening line of dust across her hardwood floor.

"Crook's changed his mind, Irishman," Grouard finally said, sliding the green grass blade from his lips.

"For sure this time?"

He nodded. "When he called off us going on our scout last night like he'd wanted original', I just figured the general wanted time to set his mind on something. But this morning he told me he didn't want to take the chance of losing me, losing any of us right now."

"Don't blame him, do you? What with all but a handful of them Shoshone up and pulling out for home this morning? Why, just two days back even the Crow saw the elephant and left us on the trail so they could hurry back to their villages and have their scalp dances. So now, by God, with the Snakes gone too, the old man's been left stranded." He wagged his head dolefully. "Ain't no wonder that Crook's afraid the enemy could be all around us, now that he ain't got his Injun scouts to be his eyes and ears. But there's no way to know for sure what's out there, all around us now, if we don't go out and scout."

"Them war camps still ain't strong enough to jump us here," Frank replied sourly.

"Maybe they won't jump us, but they sure been making a bunch of trouble for us while we sit and wait. Crook's gotta know that by now."

"General knows."

"So he wants us just to sit on our saddle galls?"

Grouard grinned. "Why the hell you complaining, white man? Looks like you're getting in all the feet soaking you want, Seamus."

"Think about it. While Crook's army sits, what you suppose the Injun camps are doing?"

Grouard's eyes narrowed thoughtfully on the distance, as if he were attempting to measure somehow the sheer heft to all that danger out there. As if he might actually try to divine the enemy's intent across that great gulf in time and space.

"They're hunting."

"Hunting meat?" Seamus replied. "Or hunting soldiers?"

"Both. While they'll hunt for hides and meat to put up for the winter—they damn sure gonna keep an eye on us here. Send scouts down to watch Crook's camp all the time so they'll know if we go to marching north again."

"That has to be a big camp, Grouard. I can't figure 'em staying together for much longer."

"Me neither," Frank agreed, sweeping the grass aside with his fingers so that he could scoop up a palmful of dirt. "That many lodges, that many people, thousands and thousands of ponies—they'll need to break up." With a flick of his wrist he sprayed the dust out from his hand in a wide arc.

Donegan said, "But Crook's got it set firm in his mind he's gonna have to tangle with the whole bunch again."

"He does figure on that—so he don't feel much like moving till he's got more men and bullets."

Donegan rocked off his elbow and eased his head back onto the grass. The sun felt as good as a man could ever want it to feel—every bit as good as he had dreamed the summer sun could feel on his skin while he struggled vainly to stay warm shuddering atop a cold saddle last winter on Reynolds's long march north to the fight on Powder River.*

Here in the heart of summer, Seamus sighed with contentment and said, "If Crook's waiting for men and bullets —then this army of his ain't gonna be marching anytime soon."

"Don't mean you and me won't be working."

At that moment he wanted to crack one of his eyes into a slit so he could weigh the look on the half-breed's face, to see if Grouard was trying to skin him or not. But Seamus fought the sudden impulse down like it were a real thing, not wanting to move at all from this warm, sun-

---

*The Plainsmen Series, Vol. 8, *Blood Song*

drenched creekbank. "Little while back you said Crook's changed his mind."

"He has."

"But?"

Grouard answered, "But it don't mean Crook can't go and change his mind again."

Thinking back on all the generals he had known since 1862, Seamus had to agree. "Seems like that sort of thing just naturally comes with those stars, don't it, Frank? Like it's their duty to up and change your mind. Mither of God! But that's the sole province of a general: this right to change one's mind."

"Crook's the general hereabouts."

"What of those columns off to the north of us?"

Grouard shrugged. "Lots of Injuns between us and them. Like I told you last night: there's a hundred miles stuffed right up to the bunghole with badass Lakota and Shahiyena warriors all wanting white scalps."

"And especially your hair—for you leading sojurs down on them twice now." Donegan brooded a moment, then asked, "What all do you think the Lakota are up to, if them camps really are out to hunt like you say?"

"Figure they have scouts keeping an eye on them other columns too."

"How is it Gibbon's Montana sojurs, or Terry's Dakota column from over at Fort Lincoln, haven't run onto a village that size yet?"

"You asking about Terry's column—that bunch what Crook says is pushing this way with Custer's cavalry riding right out front?"

"Yeah, them. Why hasn't Terry's sojurs run up against that big camp what jumped us three days back?"

Grouard shrugged. "Just lucky, I suppose."

"Naw. It ain't just luck, Frank. Way I see it—them warriors will keep right on doing their best to keep their women and children out of the army's way. Reason they rode south to jump us was they didn't want Crook's army getting anywhere near their village. They'll go and do the same thing with that bunch up north: keep well out of the way of Gibbon and Terry."

He studied Donegan a moment. "Don't think so, Irishman. Way it lays out to me is this: a village that big won't be worried about a damned thing but finding enough grass to feed all their ponies."

"So—what about them sojurs up north of us? You're saying that war camp hit us on the Rosebud just don't give a damn about the three columns closing in on 'em?"

His face a mask of disgust, Grouard slowly brought his two hands together. "Only two columns still closing in now, Irishman."

"So either of them other two expeditions. Why you figure neither of them bumped into that goddamned big village themselves yet?"

With a slow wag of his head Grouard said, "Can't say, Seamus. Only . . . I know one thing's certain as rain: it's just a matter of time before Custer and his men run smack up against more'n they can handle."

Chapter 1

21 June 1876

[The Indian attack on our column] showed that
they anticipated that they were strong enough to
thoroughly defeat the command during the en-
gagement. I tried to throw a strong force through
the canyon, but I was obliged to use it elsewhere
before it had gotten to the supposed location of
the village. The command finally drove the Indians back in great confusion . . . We remained
on the field that night, and having but what each
man could carry himself, we were obliged to return to the train to properly care for the
wounded . . . I expect to find those Indians in
rough places all the time, and so have ordered
five companies of infantry, and shall not probably make any extended movement until they arrive.

George Crook
Brig. Gen.

John Bourke finished the second of two copies he had
made that morning of Crook's letter to General Philip
Sheridan. While one would remain in Bourke's records, as

Crook's longtime aide-de-camp, the original and the second copy would go with two civilian couriers who would ride south separately to Fort Fetterman on the North Platte. There this first report of the Battle of the Rosebud would soon be telegraphed by leapfrog down that string of tiny key stations connected by a thin strand of wire, southeast all the way to Fort Laramie.

From there the electrifying news of Crook's decision to wait at Goose Creek would cause the keys to click and the wires to hum all the way to department headquarters in Omaha, and beyond. Within hours of the letter's arrival at Fetterman, Sheridan would be reading the scrawl of some private's handwriting on the pages of yellow flimsy at Division HQ in Chicago. It wouldn't take that much longer for William Tecumseh Sherman to be studying every one of Crook's carefully chosen words at the War Department in Washington City.

An Irishman himself like Sheridan, Bourke pictured how the bandy-legged hero of the Shenandoah campaign would flush and roar when he read that Crook was electing to sit tight. He would be angry. Nay, furious! After all, no less than Sheridan and Sherman themselves had developed the concept of "total war" waged against an enemy population in those final months of the Civil War.

John had to agree with them. In what he had seen of man's bloodiest sport, war was serious business. If the West was to be won, then he found himself in sympathy with Sherman's views: "Let's be about finishing this matter of the Indians."

While the Confederate officers had practiced a genteel combat against the Union armies, pitting only soldier against soldier, Sherman and Sheridan—as U. S. Grant's right and left arms—refined the concept that mandated an army make war on the entire enemy population, women and children and noncombatants alike. Depriving the enemy of livestock, burning fields and destroying forage, laying waste not only to the enemy's lines of supply, but by making total war on those loved ones the Confederate armies left behind at home, the Union could wreak great spiritual damage to the fighting men of the rebellious South.

"This is taking too long," Bourke said, agreeing with Sherman's impatience over the progress of things out west.

But, then again, that's what this whole Sioux campaign was about, wasn't it? To get the matter settled once and for all?

But instead of clear victories, the army had instead two major engagements that were certainly less than defeats for the enemy. Reynolds had retreated from the Powder River, his men freezing, tormented by empty bellies. And now Crook and the rest had to content themselves with a hollow victory once Crazy Horse retreated with his warriors at the end of that long summer's day of bloody and fierce hand-to-hand fighting across four miles of rolling, rocky hills bordering Rosebud Creek.*

Crook's army held the field at sunset. And buried its dead in the creek bottom that night under cover of darkness. Then started to limp back to Goose Creek the following morning. If the Battle of the Rosebud was ever to live on to Crook's credit, John figured, then either the general would have to follow up with a more stunning victory somewhere in the weeks to come . . . or one of the other columns would have to suffer a more stunning defeat in this summer of the Sioux.

Either way, it would serve to take the dim sheen off what was clearly a dubious victory for Crook's Wyoming column.

Already the newsmen were creating their own slant to that day-long battle. John knew each one of them wrote from his own narrow view of a horrendously complex battle that had raged along a four-mile front. For two days after the fight they had scratched out their stories, the rich ante climbing almost hourly as the reporters bartered for the services of any courier who would dare to carry word of

*The Plainsmen Series, Vol. 9, *Reap the Whirlwind.*

the Rosebud Battle to the nearest telegraph, eventually to end up in the hands of expectant readers both east and west of this Wyoming wilderness.

Along with the wounded loaded in wagons, and an infantry escort Crook was sending south to Fetterman tomorrow morning, would also go T. B. MacMillan, reporter for Chicago's *Inter-Ocean,* a cross-town rival of John Finerty's *Tribune.* Day by day, for weeks now, MacMillan's health had slipped away beneath the onslaught of cold and heat, rain and privation, until even Surgeon Albert Hartsuff had ordered him out of Indian country. Try as the newsman might, valiantly dipping into what reserves the bravest could muster, MacMillan simply did not have what it took to stand up beneath the rigors of the campaign trail. Though he was taking his leave of the Big Horn and Yellowstone Expedition, not one man dared make light of the reporter's pluck and courage during the hottest of the fighting at the Rosebud. Bourke was one of those who had finally convinced "Mac" that he had no business staying on.

"After all," John Finerty said at this morning's fire, "you heard Crook himself say he's planning on sitting pretty right here till he gets him his reinforcements of infantry and cavalry."

"Finerty's right," Robert Strahorn of Denver's *Rocky Mountain News* agreed. "We're going to sit things out until we get more bullets and bacon before we can go chasing after Crazy Horse and Sitting Bull again."

"The summer's going to be all but gone before we move again, Mac," Bourke tried cheering the sickly reporter over strong coffee.

"I'll envy you, I will," Finerty replied with an impish grin. "Knowing you're back in Chicago well ahead of me. While I'm still out here, sitting on my thumbs with nothing to do but fish these creeks, hunt the groves of timber, and eat my fill from the fruit of the land every day. Pretty boring stuff."

"The best place a man could be—Chicago," Bourke

chimed in to help nudge the newsman to relent and head home. "The Indian camps are surely breaking up after the whipping we gave them, so this campaign is all but over, Mac. Only thing left for us to do is eat, sleep, and chase some nonexistent warriors."

"You heard it from the mouth of the general's aide," Finerty said. "The war's over: nothing to do but eat and sleep. Seriously, Mac—I doubt we'll have any more chances to chase warriors."

It would take until the end of summer, but by then all that Bourke and Finerty and the rest of Crook's crippled Big Horn and Yellowstone Expedition would have to eat would be their broken-down, played-out horses as the animals dropped one by one by one into the mud of the northern plains.

That, and Crook's men could always eat their words.

They had a great victory on their shoulders.

So it was that Miniconjou war chief American Horse danced with all the rest in this Moon of Ripening Berries, Wipazuka Waste Wi. At times the Lakota called this the Moon of Making Fat.

Truly, this was a time of great feasting, of living off the fat of the land for the people of American Horse.

"Now the soldiers will stay away!" Dog Necklace growled every bit as tremulously as any grizzly boar as they gathered near one of the many leaping bonfires fed throughout that second night following the great battle against the soldiers, Snake, and Sparrowhawk People. "Surely they know we will never again wait for them to attack our camps of little ones and women."

Red Horse echoed, "They now know we will hunt them down!"

"Yet—what of the great mystic's vision?" asked Iron Thunder.

"Yes," agreed Antelope Tail, worry cracking his voice. "What of Sitting Bull's talk with Wakan Tanka?"

American Horse smiled. He had fought these white

men many, many summers. Even winters too. In fact, thirty winters before his own father, Smoke, had met the famous white man Francis Parkman there beside the white man's Holy Road that paralleled the Buffalo Dung River.*

"The soldiers will return," he told them confidently.

Dog Necklace disagreed, still sour as gall. "The soldiers would not dare try themselves against our strength! As powerful as the mystic's dream was, I nonetheless still find it very hard to believe soldiers will come to fall into our camps now."

"But his vision was so vivid, in such detail," American Horse protested. "The Hunkpatila warrior called He Dog has told me Sitting Bull says we should expect another fight."

"Let us savor this victory first, old one," Red Horse chided the aging war chief.

"Yes," agreed Dog Necklace as he chuckled with disdain. "Even as stupid as the white man is, none of our people can seriously believe the soldiers would still be marching on our villages. Chasing us after the beating we gave them."

"It will be a long, long time before we have to worry about any soldiers marching on us now," Red Horse said.

"Yes. I think they have learned their lesson well and are running away far to the south, never to fight us again this summer," Dog Necklace boasted. "The Great Mystery has taught the soldiers a painful truth: never again come to attack a village of women and children. If they ever try, only death and destruction await them."

"But that's just what the shaman Sitting Bull saw in his vision," American Horse scolded the young warriors for forgetting. "Soon he reminds us—the soldiers will return to fall headfirst like grasshoppers into our camp."

"Never again will we retreat!" Iron Thunder roared.

Antelope Tail joined in. "On the Rosebud we learned a mighty lesson! Never again will we merely fight long

---
*The North Platte River.

enough to cover the retreat of our women and children, protecting those weaker than ourselves!"

Once again American Horse sensed the stirrings of his own warriorhood—as it always stirred when his people were threatened, rising as surely as did the guard hair on the neck of the wild wolf when a challenger presented himself. It had been as Crazy Horse promised them when he led the hundreds south to meet Three Stars. Indeed, it had been a new kind of fighting for the Lakota and their cousins, the Shahiyena of the North. In that one day-long battle with the confused, retreating, frightened soldiers, the Lakota bid farewell to their old way of waging war wherein each man fought on his own for coups and scalps and ponies; each man riding out ahead of the others to perform daring, risky, and often foolish deeds in the face of the white enemy.

There was much talk of how Crazy Horse had orchestrated their great victory over Three Stars and his soldiers. Much talk that from now on the Lakota would never retreat —would instead stand and fight any army come against their villages in this new way Crazy Horse had taught them: to ride knee to knee in massed bunches, swarming together over the white man as the bee flies in swarms that blackened the sky, flinging themselves against the soldier lines in numbers that could not help but roll over every one of the helpless blue-shirted enemy soiling their pants in abject fear.

While most of the warriors turned north with the wounded late in that day of fierce fighting, American Horse and other Lakota, as well as some of the Shahiyena, stayed behind to keep watch on the soldier camp through that first night following the battle. They were as hungry and tired as the rest, for it had been a good day, a great fight, and only one of American Horse's Miniconjou had been wounded seriously enough that he might die.

What a great victory over Three Stars and his soldiers!

The next morning the white men rose early and straggled south out of the valley, finally disappearing among the green hills. With the soldiers gone, the young warriors waiting on either side of American Horse atop a high hill kicked their ponies into motion, racing down to the trampled grass pocked with hundreds of tiny fire smudges, a creek valley dotted with the droppings of so many horses and pack-mules. Here and there they found an abandoned prize: a worn-out hat, a good pair of gloves, a belt pouch, a piece of bloody blue cloth cut from a wounded soldier's trousers or shirt, and even such treasure as some bacon and crackers, along with coffee wrapped in waxed paper packets!

It wasn't long before the young Oglalla called Black Elk after his father discovered the patch of earth the white man had dug up the night before, then trampled with many hooves to hide the digging.

"This is surely the ground where they buried their dead!" Dog Necklace shouted.

Almost at once the two dozen or more fell to their hands and knees, scratching and scraping at the pounded soil, howling like a pack of coyotes expectant of a feast. From the unearthed bodies the warriors took scalps, tore off the thin gray blankets, then stripped clothing and finger rings.

Later that morning they discovered the body of that wounded Lakota butchered by the Sparrowhawk People who scouted for Three Stars as the army retreated out of the valley.

"Wrap our brother warrior in one of those soldier blankets," American Horse demanded angrily as he gazed down at the dismembered remains.

"Not mine!" protested Red Horse, clutching the gray army blanket.

"Then I will use my own," the Miniconjou war chief said. "But I will ask your help."

Three others dismounted to help American Horse gather the scattered flesh and bone of the mutilated warrior identifiable only from the porcupine quillwork decorating shreds of his bloody leggings.

"And you, Red Horse," he said sternly, training his wide-browed glare on the young warrior who had refused to relinquish his army blanket for a death-wrap, "it is you I want to build me a travois so that we can return this man's bones to his family."

By the time American Horse and the others reached the great encampment the following day, most women in the many circles were already at moving camp, dropping smoked hides rich with fragrance from their darkened lodgepoles, loading travois with a family's possessions, with the little ones still too young to walk or ride atop the backs of gentle ponies—travois that might also transport the aged whose numberless winters prevented them from walking or riding. Camp was being moved downstream a few more miles west toward the Greasy Grass.

There the great gathering of circles would have nothing more to worry about than where to find the buffalo and antelope the young men would hunt for meat and hides to put up against the coming winter. Winter always came to this land, and with its arrival always came the retreat of the soldiers. American Horse hoped that by whipping Three Stars and his men on Rosebud Creek, the soldiers would abandon Lakota hunting ground even sooner this season.

From the valley of the Greasy Grass the villages would move slowly southwest toward the Big Horn Mountains, where the hunting was always good. In those days to come the camp circles would slowly break apart, warrior bands and family clans drifting off on the four winds as the summer season slowly aged.

Just as a man aged with the seasons of his own life.

Across the seasons the Miniconjou had known him first as American Horse, later as Iron Plume and Iron Shield, later still as Black Shield because of a dream in which a spirit told him to make a shield he should paint black so that it would protect him from bullets. But even though he was nowhere near so well-known to the whites as Rain-in-the-Face or Gall; American Horse was well regarded among his own Miniconjou for his unquestioned bravery in battle and his steadfast protection of his people.

For a moment American Horse turned to look back at the lone tepee his people were leaving behind as they migrated a few miles farther down the creek toward the valley of the Greasy Grass. A mourning family left it standing in the summer sun as a tribute to the warrior whose body lay inside—a warrior wounded grievously in the hips during the fight against Three Stars, one of those returned on travois to die among his kinsmen. With its smoke flaps wrapped tightly one over the other and the lodge door sewn shut against the elements, none who respected the dead would dare enter. Beside the body within the darkness lay the warrior's favorite weapons—his true wealth in life—as well as his pipe and tobacco pouch, along with some venison soup to feed him on his journey toward the Star Road.

The past two days had witnessed even more new arrivals reaching the great encampment as the immense village eased down toward the Greasy Grass. Summer roamers, these late arrivals were called. Like American Horse's band of some three dozen lodges, the summer roamers were those who fled the reservations when spring warmth caressed the northern plains, where they intended to hunt in the ancient way until autumn turned the buffalo herds south, when the clans would again turn back to the agencies to suffer through another winter.

Already there was much talk that this was to be the last great hunt, perhaps the greatest of all summers for the seven campfires of the Lakota Nation. *Washtay!* Hadn't they defeated Three Stars and sent his soldiers scurrying south with their tails between their legs like whipped dogs? The hunting had never been better here in the timbered valleys among the Wolf Mountains.

With all that, they still had Sitting Bull's prophetic vision yet to come!

American Horse was glad he had urged his people off the reservation early this year, happy to be included in the great strength all Lakota felt this summer. If what Sitting Bull and Crazy Horse and the rest said was true—this Season of Making Fat might well hold the last great fight they would have with the white man.

And forever after the soldiers would dare not enter Lakota hunting ground.

Forever after the white man would stay far away.

No more would American Horse's Miniconjou have to return to their agency to eat the white man's moldy flour and rancid pig meat.

Life would be as it once was when American Horse was but a boy and he saw his first white man along the Holy Road.

Life would be so good again, with the *wasichu* gone forever and ever, gone forevermore.

Chapter 2

Late June
1876

G od! But the air out here smelled better than it did in those closed-in places back east.

William F. Cody drank deep of it this summer morning, chest swelling as he drew it into his lungs as one would drink a life-giving elixir. With that prairie air seeping through his body, Bill remembered his youth as teamster, those months as mail rider for the pony express, and finally his years as army scout. All of that adventure and fun, all that unfettered *life* crammed into his youth before he had gone and followed the siren song of fame and fortune, pursuing a career on the stage.

Now, as he led General Philip Sheridan and his headquarters staff toward Camp Robinson near the Sioux's Red Cloud Agency in the heart of these Central Plains, his keen eyes squinting into the distance from beneath the expanse of his broad-brimmed sombrero, searching the horizon for smoke, or dust, or the dippling of human forms atop fleet ponies breaking the skyline at the crest of some hilltop, Bill Cody couldn't for the life of him remember what had been so damned seductive about that career on the boards before the footlights that it had lured him away from the West. Away from these wide and open places.

Lord, but he loved *this* life! A good horse beneath him, his favorite rifle—the one he had long ago affectionately named Lucretia Borgia—stuffed securely in the saddle pocket across the pommel, and the sweet smell of the tall grass trammeled beneath his buckskin's hooves. This had to be the essence of living! Something few men would ever experience, or so Bill had long ago determined.

Leaving behind Lieutenant Colonel Eugene Carr's Fifth Cavalry at Fort Laramie for a few days before the regiment would once again begin searching these hills and swales like an inland sea of grass, looking for any Indians trying to make it north to join the roaming hostiles, Cody itched to be shed of Phil Sheridan. He wanted to be back with the Fifth as they scoured this land for warriors fleeing the reservations. But not just any warriors. This summer they were hunting the young fighting men who were jumping the reservations to the south: the hotbloods who were stirring things up as they fled the agencies and rode out for the northern camps of those winter roamers, to join Crazy Horse and Sitting Bull.

Maybe Custer would get his chance, Bill thought. Maybe ol' Yellow Hair will finish off those Sioux hostiles in one fell swoop like everyone back east thought only Custer would. Damn, but Bill wanted Carr's Fifth to be the outfit that would have a crack at the action before this Indian war was nothing more than a few footnotes in dusty history books schoolboys would be reading in the decades to come.

God, how he hoped Custer and the rest of them up north left some of the fighting for the Fifth Cavalry.

He looked at the sky, wondering about God. If He really did listen to man. To a lone individual, anyway. Bill thought he'd pray, just in case God was listening right then and wasn't too busy with other matters of more pressing concern. Out here, Cody had found, it was about as easy to pray as breathing. Out here it was damn sure as easy as breathing to know down in his marrow that there was for certain-sure a God. Just to look around him in all directions, why—a man had to realize some great hand had been at work here.

So Bill prayed, not at all embarrassed that he asked the Almighty to leave some of the hostiles for the Fifth Cavalry to fight.

After all, Bill figured—the Fifth Cavalry always had been an Injun-fighting outfit. And no matter where life might lead William F. Cody, no man—nor woman—would ever be able to take the magic of these plains from him.

He had been twenty-three years old that fall of eighteen and sixty-nine, following the summer he led the Fifth down on Tall Bull's village of Cheyenne Dog Soldiers at Summit Springs. That first year of scouting for the army was crammed chock-full of adventure and even some downright belly-busting fun—like that time he had talked Wild Bill and that gray-eyed Irishman into stealing a shipment of Mexican beer bound for another regiment wandering the Staked Plain of the Texas Panhandle in search of Cheyenne and Comanche. After hijacking the load of foamy brew, the trio of scouts instead took their contraband back to their own camp and immediately set up shop for the boys of Carr's Fifth Cavalry.

But now . . . well, now he couldn't dare get away with such a stunt. Now that Buffalo Bill was the darling of the boards and theater lights back east. But Wild Bill? Well, Cody had heard Hickok had become quite the army scout before he turned lawman down in Abilene, Kansas, then finally had retired to become a knight of the green felt: ofttimes making his day's wages over a single turn of the cards. And Donegan? Damn—Bill didn't know what had ever become of the Irishman after that evening he plucked Donegan's hash from the fire back behind the sutler's bar at Fort McPherson in November sixty-nine.

For some reason it seemed most reasonable to think Seamus Donegan could not possibly still be alive, not the way that man lived. But in the next moment Bill decided that it was every bit as reasonable to believe that the Irish-

man would still be very much alive. A man who pushed out
at the edges of his life with as much vitality and zest as did
that Irishman—why, you didn't easily kill off that sort of
man.

Not the sort of man as was William F. Cody.

Likely, it was Edward Zane Carroll Judson who got the
whole damn thing started what had pulled Cody off the
plains to begin with. The stocky little prairie cock called
himself Ned Buntline. Whatever name he wanted to use, in
whatever company, it had been that fall of sixty-nine Cody
first ran onto the dime novelist who was out to write the
glories of the opening of the West. Bill instantly took a
liking to that Buntline fella who had been hanged of a time,
but the rope broke; some said the rope was cut by an ac-
complice. Still, it took some stewing, Buntline's ideas did,
before Bill seriously considered leaving these plains. But
that chance meeting with Buntline that fall of sixty-nine
was to come back to haunt Cody more than once. The first
time was that very Christmas when an officer at Fort Mc-
Pherson ran over to show him a copy of Buntline's latest
dime novel just arrived with a shipment of tinware at the
sutler's: *Buffalo Bill, the King of the Border Men.*

Cody promptly bought up what all copies the sutler
had and gave them away over whiskey and cigars for a
chuckle or two, along with the feeling it gave him to see his
very own name in print. To think of it! Buffalo Bill in print
back east—even though Buntline's story was nothing short
of pure horse pucky—to think that his name in that tale
was being read by thousands of eyes. Thousands upon
thousands!

The Fifth Cavalry had only one Indian fight in all of
1870—things quieting down after the drubbing they had
given the warrior bands, so it seemed. So it was that following winter of seventy, seventy-one that an eager Bill Cody
jumped at the request made of him to guide for the British
sportsman, the Earl of Dunraven. There followed hunting
expeditions for the Grand Duke Alexis in seventy-two—the
hunt when Bill got to meet George Armstrong Custer, the

Seventh Cavalry's hero of the Washita—as well as later expeditions guiding ornithologists and all manner of scientists out beneath this great open sky, into the midst of hundreds upon hundreds of intoxicating miles of absolutely nothing.

Again the following campaign season of seventy-one the Fifth had but one Indian skirmish. Nonetheless, he was developing a personal style mixed with a generous mix of charisma and electrifying dash that would make him truly memorable when he finally took that first step behind the smoky footlights of an eastern theater. Then in November of seventy-one, with little happening on the Central Plains, the Fifth was reassigned to the Apache war in Arizona. They were leaving Bill Cody behind at McPherson, bound for Fort McDowell.

No less than Phil Sheridan himself had instructed the regiment's commanding officer to leave Bill at McPherson because he knew nothing of the Apache, and perhaps even less of the new terrain. The Fifth was ordered "not to take Cody."

The Third Cavalry would be coming to take the place of the Fifth. Sheridan informed Cody he would never have a better chance to accept those numerous invitations to visit New York City. Bill went east. And his life was never to be the same again.

Dividing his time between newspaper publisher James Gordon Bennett and Ned Buntline, Bill got a real taste of the high life that only New York could offer. And he got to see himself played by an actor on opening night at the Bowery Theater for Fred Maeder's production of Buntline's story, *Buffalo Bill: The King of Border Men.* At intermission the theater manager learned that no less than the real William F. Cody was in the audience, so after he made the announcement to the audience, the crowd prevailed upon the scout to make his way reluctantly to the stage, where he said little if anything—frightened to death, and frozen speechless.

Staring at a half-dozen painted, screaming warriors,

each waving a rifle or war club as they charged down on him . . . why, that was one thing. But staring out at hundreds of theatergoers, all expecting him to entertain them merely by opening his mouth and saying something worthwhile? Now, that was a polecat of a whole different color!

Buffalo Bill made the one and only retreat in his life that night as he ducked through the side curtains—but was immediately cornered backstage by the theater manager, who offered him five hundred dollars a week to play the part of Buffalo Bill himself.

Five hundred dollars a week!

At the time Cody believed the man had to be mad, or merely addlebrained. No one could make that sort of money playacting, pretending, simply having fun. So Bill begged off, wanting nothing more than to escape the place as fast as he could get out of there.

"I never was one to talk to a crowd of people like that," he told the group that had him cornered backstage. "Even if it was to save my neck. You might as well try to make an actor out of a government mule."

And with that Bill ducked out a back door into the dark of a New York alley where he made good his hairbreadth escape, back none too soon on his beloved plains, assigned to Colonel John J. Reynolds's Third Cavalry.

The next month, April of seventy-two, Cody guided Captain Charles Meinhold's B Company on the trail of a war party that had killed three soldiers and run off some cavalry mounts a mere half-dozen miles from Fort McPherson itself. Two days later on the evening of the twenty-sixth as the entire company went into camp, Cody led Sergeant Foley and six men out to reconnoiter the immediate area before settling in for the night. No more than a mile from their bivouac Bill discovered a small Indian camp and a nearby pony herd, which included some of those stolen army horses. Cody and Foley decided to attack—killing three of the horse thieves. In the brief fight Bill found himself alone among the warriors, facing some daunting odds —yet stayed cool long enough to shoot his way out of the fix while the remaining horse thieves made good their escape before the rest of the company came up on the run.

For that bravery shown along the South Fork of the Loup River in Nebraska, Bill was awarded the Medal of Honor. And he thought on that now, touching his gloved fingers to his breast for a moment here in the warm morning sun—remembering how damned proud Louisa had been to slip that ribbon over his neck, remembering how the medal felt against the hammer of his heart. Recalling how he so enjoyed the long, joyous rolls of deafening applause from those in attendance as they clambered to their feet, their approbation ringing from those walls and rolling over and over him.

That same spring some of his McPherson friends secured Bill's nomination by the Democratic party to represent the twenty-sixth district in the Nebraska legislature. He won by the slim margin of forty-four votes. When Bill had pressing matters with the army and did not show up at Lincoln on the specified date to be sworn in and to claim his seat, a suit was filed on behalf of his opponent, stating that some votes had been improperly returned.

Despite a questionable recount, Bill accepted the new figures, which gave D. P. Ashburn the election. Cody went on with his life.

Following his return to McPherson from the skirmish on the Loup River, Bill received the first of what would be many letters sent him by Buntline, every one of them urging, cajoling, begging Bill to go on stage to play himself.

"I still remember that dreadful night at the Bowery Theater," he wrote Buntline.

"You'll get over it," the novelist wrote back. "Any man as brave as you can learn to overcome an enemy so weak as shyness."

But Colonel Reynolds distrusted the self-promoter Buntline. "I advise against you going, Cody," he told Bill. "You have a good job with us. A good future. Think of your family. Three children now?"

Yes. Two daughters and his beloved Kit Carson Cody.

He had wavered, gazing again across the plains that surrounded McPherson. Who was he fooling, anyway? To think about becoming a showman, a traveling actor? He was a frontiersman. A scout. He didn't have what it took to make a go of that theater stuff.

Then Buntline's bluntest letter arrived late that November. Ned cut right to Cody's quick. "There's money in it. Big money."

Cody remembered the money. Most of all, the money. Five hundred dollars a week, by damned. What that kind of money could do for his family! For Lulu and the three babies.

By that time Louisa was anxious to visit her family in St. Louis, so they started Bill's trip east right there. A journey that would last more than three and a half years before he got back here to the plains. Fact was, he hadn't been off the army's payroll since he made that first ride for General Sheridan back to September of sixty-eight . . . right on through to that December of seventy-two when he resigned, went east with the family, and began a whole new life.

Again now Bill's eyes all but closed as he drank deep of the air, feeling the stiff breeze against his face. He turned in the saddle to find Sheridan's escort column far behind him, inching along like a dark serpent wending its way through the broken country. Far out on either side rode a few flankers. But he was out front. Alone. The way he so enjoyed. Just him and the horse. Him and the horse, and by God these plains he had forsaken for theater lights.

On the eighteenth of December, 1872, he made his first appearance in Ned's production of *Buffalo Bill* at Nixon's Amphitheater in Chicago, starring in a play Buntline called *The Real Buffalo Bill!* By the time the curtain dropped that night, Cody was able to savor his first success on the boards.

"There's no backing out now," he told Buntline later that night at a bar as they celebrated their take from the door.

Ned promptly set about writing a whole new play he would coproduce with Bill, *The Scouts of the Prairie*. Wherever they opened to packed houses, reviewers praised the show: "The Indian mode of warfare, their hideous dances, the method they adopt to 'raise the hair' of their antagonists, following the trail, etc., or in the way their enemies deal with them, manner of throwing the lasso, &c., are forcibly exhibited, and this portion of the entertainment alone is worth the price of admission."

Another waxed, "Those who delight in sensations of the most exciting order will not fail to see the distinguished visitors from the western plains before they leave."

And the Boston *Journal* even told its readers, "The play itself is an extraordinary production with more wild Indians, scalping knives, and gunpowder to the square inch than any drama ever before heard of."

Soon even the New York *Times*'s theater critic declared, "It is only just to say that the representation was attended by torrents of what seemed thoroughly spontaneous applause; and that whatever faults close criticism may detect, there is a certain flavor of realism and of nationality about the play well calculated to gratify a general audience."

From Chicago to Cincinnati, on to Boston, New York, Rochester, and Buffalo, he and Buntline moved the production company, consistently grossing more than sixteen thousand dollars a week!

"I promised you there'd be money in this!" Buntline reminded him one evening after the performance as they were taking their leisure over a brandy and a good cigar.

"You've kept your word to me, Ned. And I'm thankful to have you to trust."

For the moment there was no turning back.

From the first hint of autumn to the last vestige of spring each year, Bill toured the eastern theaters with his troupe of actors, moving through the steps of a newly inspired Buntline melodrama every season. Why, in the fall of seventy-three Cody even invited his old friend Wild Bill to come take a stab at the easy money of playacting. But Hickok didn't take to it the way Bill had, and he muffed his lines and missed his cues—making for a rub between the two old friends from army days. It didn't take long for the savvy Hickok to realize he was out of his element. Wild Bill quit to go back out west. Cody got Hickok paid off proper, with a thousand-dollar bonus to boot, and they shook—promising to meet again one day, out here on the prairie.

It was a promise Bill prayed they both would keep.

Since that winter when Wild Bill left for the frontier, hints and rumors floated back east. Cody learned that his friend finally ended up in Cheyenne, where he gambled his nights away through the intervening years, at least until he met the widow Mrs. Agnes Thatcher Lake, a circus performer Hickok had met years before while serving as city marshal in Abilene. Then this past March, Bill telegraphed Hickok his heartiest congratulations the moment he read of Wild Bill's marriage to Mrs. Lake in the eastern papers. He figured Hickok would be following the circus in its travels from now on—sawdust show business! To think of Wild Bill Hickok giving up the saloons and keno tables, forsaking the lamplit fan-spread of cards laid out before each player as the last card is dealt in a high-stakes game of stud!

Surely something would eventually lure Wild Bill away from his intoxicating widow and that traveling circus. Something seductive, something far west of the hundredth meridian.

The following spring Cody was asked to act as guide for a group of rich Englishmen headed west for a Nebraska hunting expedition. Late summer found him guiding Captain Anson Mills, who led five companies of the Third Cavalry and two of infantry on a fruitless search for warrior bands making for trouble in the hill country surrounding Rawlins Station in Wyoming Territory. Besides packers and teamsters, also along were four Pawnee scouts who remembered Cody from the summer campaign of sixty-nine, and a young scout named Charlie White.

An excellent horseman who had served with General

J. E. B. Stuart's Confederate cavalry during the war, White had come in to McPherson to have a leg wound treated by army surgeons that fall. When the physicians refused to treat the civilian because he had no money and no visible means of support, Cody intervened, saying he would pay White's bill. Some twenty-four or twenty-five years old, the pockmarked Confederate veteran promptly latched on to the famous Cody, eager to prove himself an excellent marksman. In fact, that very fall White began to grow his hair into long curls in fond imitation of Buffalo Bill's flowing brown mane, as well as coming to dress, walk, and talk in the manner of the great frontier scout.

The gentle, soft-spoken White was proud in every way to be compared to the famous Buffalo Bill and soon earned his very own, if unflattering, nickname: "Buffalo Chips."

For the next year and a half Bill stayed back east, reorganizing his troupe of players and relaxing at his new home in Rochester. Then come this past spring, just a month after Hickok's wedding, on a terrible, rainy April night, a telegram caught up to him in Springfield, Massachusetts, where *Scouts* was playing.

> Kit Carson Cody seriously ill. Stop.
> Please come home at once. Stop. Your
> son needs you. Stop. I need you
> desperately. Stop. Please, Bill.
>
> Louisa

Cody choked down the sour taste that remembrance brought him and stared into the bright summer sunlight reflected off the endless brilliance of these grassy plains, blinking away the sting of tears the loss welled up within him. Kitty, his only son, so ill with scarlet fever the night Bill made it home to Rochester, flung open that front door and left it hanging in the wind as he leaped up those stairs two and three at a time to reach the boy's room. He had held young Kit Carson tightly, so tightly, against his breast as his son took his last breath.

Perhaps it was that, he thought now as he turned around once again and peered back at the short, snaking serpent of a column far behind him among the verdant hills, the grass bending and rising in undulating swells beneath the omnipresent breeze. Perhaps it was his dear Kitty's death as much as the barrage of letters he received all last spring from Colonel Anson Mills, urging Cody to return to the frontier, to return to service for the army—saying this was surely to be the last great fight every frontiersman knew would one day come to these plains.

It took him six long weeks after they had laid the cold sod over his beloved five-year-old son for Bill finally to wrestle a decision out of himself. On the night of June 3, while playing Wilmington, Delaware, he told his audience that he was through with playacting and off to the Indian wars.

Making his way west that Centennial summer at the same time the entire nation's eyes were beginning to turn east, focusing on the grand Exposition in Philadelphia, Cody stopped at Sheridan's Division Headquarters in Chicago, where the lieutenant general inquired as to the scout's plan as he shuffled through a stack of correspondence that day in early June.

"I'm headed to Cheyenne, from there to make my way on to join Colonel Anson Mill's Third Cavalry."

"He's with Crook's column, just marched away from Fort Fetterman—bound for the villages of Crazy Horse and Sitting Bull, I'd daresay. Yes, I daresay Crook will strike the hostiles very, very soon."

"Damn, I was hoping—"

"Don't get yourself disappointed just yet, Bill."

Cody had been, couldn't help it. "I was wanting to attach myself to Colonel Mills and the Third."

"Ah, yes—here it is," Sheridan exclaimed as he yanked out a telegraph flimsy. "General Carr has asked for you: 'Your old position open to you. Join us here.'"

"The Fifth?"

"Yes."

"I thought they were in Arizona."

"Lord, no!" Sheridan said, beaming. "Carr's got them marching off to fight the Sioux as we speak."

"C-carr wants me to guide for the Fifth?" Cody's voice rose.

"Your old outfit, Bill. Since the regiment's been reassigned to the plains, Carr's written here twice, inquiring as to your whereabouts."

"He wants me?"

"Bloody right he does," Sheridan replied. "I'll see you have orders written before you leave this office. You can meet your old regiment by taking that same train to Cheyenne City."

Four days later, Bill had stepped off the Union Pacific onto the platform at Cheyenne, Wyoming Territory, to shake hands with Lieutenant Charles King of the Fifth Cavalry . . . whereupon Bill had promptly smelled the air.

Knowing in his heart, in every fiber of his being, that he had returned home.

Chapter 3

Late June
1876

In the saddle out here on the Central Plains with the Fifth
Cavalry in pursuit of warriors jumping their reservations,
Lieutenant Charles King didn't figure Brigadier General
John Pope had gotten much better at predicting future
events than he had been when he was in command of
Union forces at Second Bull Run.

Late this past spring Pope confidently proclaimed his
assertion that there would be no Indian campaign in seventy-six.

But here they were, pushing north by east about as
hard as Lieutenant Colonel Eugene Carr could push these
eight companies of hardened troopers—once more ordered
to do the near impossible. Still, as Carr's regimental adjutant, at least this time King wouldn't have to ride back in
column somewhere. The lieutenant loped along with headquarters, in the lead. Only the scouts and a handful of
flankers were out front this warm summer's day.

Earlier in the month King's K Company, Fifth U.S.
Cavalry, was ordered west from their comfortable barracks
at Fort Riley, Kansas, hauled by rail to pitch their tents

beside the Smoky Hill at Fort Hays, in preparation for something. What, they did not know at first. But, one thing was certain—the army did not move troops about on trains unless something big was afoot, and they needed those troops somewhere in a hurry. Yet that was still only a matter of speculation, of hushed rumor.

A smallish, wiry man, built on the short side and just barely tall enough out of his boots to meet the army's required height, Lieutenant King had been out on a three-day hunt on the first of June hoping to round up stampeded horses north along the Saline River when the official word came.

Regimental commander Eugene Carr looked up from the three-page dispatch when King rode up to join the other officers gathered in the lieutenant colonel's office. Outside, the sun was setting in a clear Kansas sky as the regiment's band encircled the flagpole for retreat, raising the brassy strains of "Soldaten Lieder" as the Stars and Stripes came down. Some couples interrupted their croquet game on the parade to take up the waltz amid children in their bright dresses and knee britches playing blindman's buff or rolling hoops along the graveled walks.

Carr grinned toothily, much satisfied with himself. "What did I tell you, gentlemen?"

With his ruddy skin drawn tightly over his cheekbones, King asked, "News from the front?"

Carr rattled the pages with eagerness, saying, "I told you Crook would need the Fifth!"

"Hurrah!" was the immediate cheer raised right then and on through that night in all the barracks and officers' quarters, sounded with the most proper John Bull, or Irish, or German accents. "We're going for to join Crook!"

The next morning the lieutenant colonel had fired off a telegram requesting of Sheridan, "Please authorize me Wm. F. Cody at Cheyenne. Could I get Pawnees as Indian Scouts; I had them in sixty-nine."

Sheridan promptly wired back, "You can employ Cody. Will try to obtain Pawnees, but doubt success."

On the night of 5 June Companies A, B, D, and K departed Fort Hays, railed west to Denver, then north to Cheyenne, where on the seventh Major John J. Upham met them with his battalion of Companies I, C, and G ordered up from Fort Gibson and Camp Supply in Indian Territory. A day later M Company arrived from Fort Lyon, Colorado Territory. Then on the ninth King was asked to ride in to Cheyenne rail station, there to await the arrival of no less than Buffalo Bill Cody himself, expected on the semiweekly westbound. What a joyous stir that reunion had caused for the veterans of the sixty-nine campaign in the regiment to see the famous scout and their beloved regimental commander side by side once more.

"With them two together," cheered one of the old noncoms, "the Fighting Fifth is ready to get the jump on all the Sitting Bulls and Crazy Horses in the hull danged Sioux tribe!"

Two days later eight companies of mounted troopers set away for Fort Laramie, where they were told they would receive orders from Division Headquarters.

King hadn't fought the Sioux or Cheyenne before, only Apache in the southwestern deserts of Arizona Territory, a land of cactus and centipede, where he was seriously wounded and narrowly escaped capture during a fierce skirmish at Sunset Pass. Without question, to a veteran Indian fighter like the lieutenant, the campaign trail was far preferable to fort duty.

This was a fighting outfit, the Fifth Cavalry. First organized in 1855, the regiment saw its initial Indian service across the arid plains of west Texas, fighting Lipan, Tonkawa, and the fierce Comanche until the outbreak of the rebellion in the South.

In 1866 when Albany-born and Milwaukee-raised King graduated from West Point, he was carrying on for his famous father, Rufus King, himself a member of the class of thirty-three. With the first shot fired at Fort Sumter in the Civil War, the senior King quickly set about organizing the legendary Iron Brigade, of which he became major general following the regiment's defense of Washington City. Young Charles accompanied his father in those early months of the war as a mounted orderly, a volunteer position without pay. Firsthand he watched the formation of the famous Army of the Potomac, but before he could become a part of it, young King received his appointment to the U.S. Military Academy from President Lincoln. He was bound and determined to make something of himself, coming from such a distinguished bloodline: Grandfather King, another Charles, served as president of Columbia College, and Great-grandfather had been a signer of the Constitution of the United States and the last candidate of the Federalist party for President.

On Reconstruction duty in the South after graduation, King's battery of light artillery was often called out to quell riots. The mere arrival of his platoon with their Gatling guns never failed to disperse the noisy crowds of rabble. Three years later he was assigned to recruiting duty in Cincinnati, where in off-duty hours he played with the Red Stockings, a pioneer professional baseball team.

In 1870 he was promoted to first lieutenant and assigned to the Fifth Cavalry, then stationed at Fort McPherson, where he first saw the famous scout Bill Cody. It was while he was serving in detached duty in New Orleans that King married Adelaide Lavender Yorke. In seventy-four Charles rejoined his regiment at Camp Verde in Arizona. Many were the times he remembered the fierce fights at Diamond Butte and Black Mesa, but nothing awoke him at night like nightmares he suffered remembering that fight at Sunset Pass on the first day of November 1874. If Sergeant Bernard Taylor hadn't pulled King over his shoulder and carried the lieutenant out of those rocks . . .

Charles tried hard to think on other things when those vivid, black memories returned to haunt him. The wound kept King from active duty for more than a year, but at least he survived.

About the time he returned to his K Company, the Fifth was being transferred back to the plains, and by the time King arrived back in Kansas, Carr appointed him regimental adjutant as the nation began to murmur rumors of one final campaign to end the Indian troubles on the northern plains.

Now, here at Laramie, in the midst of so many officers' wives with their husbands already off to the north with Crook, Charles dwelt that much more often on his sweet Adelaide, who had elected to stay behind with her parents in New Orleans. How his heart yearned to walk across this parade with her, to sit beside her, to hold her hand and gaze into her eyes with that longing only youth can know.

How his heart burned to have her with him now, more painfully than ever. Charles knew it would be a long, long while before this business with the hostile bands was wrapped up and put behind them. Something told him that warm evening late in June that this would not be a short summer's campaign.

Something like a whisper, haunting Charles King. And sitting here in these evening shadows at Fort Laramie, the lieutenant began to fear their business with the Sioux and Cheyenne would not only boil over into the fall and on into the winter, but that the mess it caused would be very, very nasty indeed.

Already Bill missed Lulu, the warm sun causing his skin to sweat beneath the thin shirt. Any breeze at all cooled him as he led the column of fours on and on across the rolling wilderness.

Cody thought on her as he squinted into the sun-drenched distance, remembering land like this from that summer they caught Tall Bull at Summit Springs.* Lulu looked so damned good under a sunbonnet, a parasol coyly laid over her shoulder where she could spin it, cocking her head to the side and making him fall in love with her all over again. He remembered the sight of all those children

---

*The Plainsmen Series, Vol. 4, *Black Sun*.

dashing across the Fort Laramie parade, scurrying all about officers' quarters and Bedlam too, changed from bachelor officers' quarters to housing the wives and families of men already off to war with Crook's Wyoming column. Young children made him think on Kitty, wondering if he could have done something different, if he hadn't been away from home so much, if . . . but he had to admit that even if he had been around more, he doubted there was much a father could do to protect his only son from the scourge of scarlet fever.

Out here Bill Cody could do something, perhaps even something heroic. But when it came to saving young Kit Carson Cody in those final hours and minutes before he stopped breathing in his father's arms—William F. Cody would have to live with that failure for the rest of his life.

"There's a feeder trail, Cody," Sheridan explained days ago, hunched over the map table where Carr and many of the Fifth's officers had circled in tight-lipped conference.

"A trail that I imagine goes right from here, and over here," Bill had replied that fourteenth day of June, jabbing a finger at the Red Cloud and Spotted Tail agencies, then dragging the finger dramatically across the sepia-toned paper, "all the way north to the hostiles raising hell in the Powder River and Rosebud country, right there."

"General Carr," Sheridan said, using the lieutenant colonel's brevet rank awarded for bravery in battle during the civil war, as he straightened, "I'm wanting to use your Fifth to block that trail north."

Carr appeared dismayed, asking, "But you're not sending us north to unite with General Crook?"

"No. Jordan down at Red Cloud has been hammering out reports to me every day on his situation there. I want to use your force to block this trail to the Powder River country. I've already sent Crook a dispatch detailing my plans to use you to the east of him. You are, after all, the commander of an entirely new district in my department, the District of the Black Hills."

"Yes," Carr replied.

In recent days Sheridan had indeed carved out a new military district for Carr and the Fifth Cavalry: embracing portions of western Nebraska and Dakota, along with a slice of eastern Wyoming Territory that ran up to but did not include Fort Fetterman. Carr's primary task would be protection of the settlers pouring into the Black Hills townships now that the government was seriously going about the business of reclaiming the sacred Paha Sapa from the Sioux and Cheyenne.

"Schuyler?"

"Yes, General?" said Walter S. Schuyler.

Sheridan stood even taller that afternoon days ago, still the shortest man there in that assembly of officers. "Read General Carr my orders."

"Yes, sir," the lieutenant replied, opening up the folded orders pulled from a thin leather valise he carried over one shoulder. Turning to Carr, Schuyler read, "The lieutenant general commanding directs you to proceed, with the eight companies of the Fifth Cavalry, on the road from Fort Laramie to Custer City until you reach the crossing of the main Powder River trail leading from the vicinity of Red Cloud Agency westward to Powder and Yellowstone rivers. Arriving at that point, you will follow the trail westward, proceeding such distances as your judgment and the amount of supplies which you carry will warrant. As little is known about the country over which you will operate, the lieutenant general . . . does not wish to hamper you with any official instructions, but will leave you to operate in accordance with your best judgment."

As Schuyler refolded the orders and presented them to Carr, Sheridan asked, "You have any questions, General?"

"None, sir."

"You understand I don't want to tie your hands with the letter of these orders."

"Understood, sir."

"I want you and Cody to figure out where the hell the hostiles are and strike them—just like the two of you did in sixty-nine."

For a moment Carr glanced at his civilian scout before turning back to the commander of the entire division that was erupting into full-scale war. "Make no mistake, General. We will accomplish our objective."

"Very well," Sheridan replied. "Let's cut off Sitting Bull and Crazy Horse from all hope of reinforcements."

Outfitted with rations for thirty-seven days, Carr's column had pulled away from its huge camp pitched a mile east of Fort Laramie on 22 June. In their ten days at the post, trader John S. Collins did a land-office business with those reinforcements about to push off to war. Cody pulled up the corner of the long bandanna he had loosely knotted around his neck and swiped at his forehead, dragging it across his eyes, then blinked into the shimmering distance once more.

Recalling that first day after riding up from Cheyenne with Lieutenant King, striding over to the post trader's to see if Collins had some little something he could not live without.

The hushed but excited voices trailed the buckskinned scout across the parade.

"That's Bill Cody!" was one not-so-muffled whisper.

"Buffalo Bill?"

"That's him!"

"I heard he's here to guide for the Fifth!"

Inside the cool shadows of the sutler's store, Bill had busied himself studying the cases of all things essential here on frontier duty as the hubbub grew behind him, more and more people squeezing through the door to take a look for themselves, young children forced to crowd through adult legs to take a peek and gawk at him for themselves.

"Mr. Cody?"

He straightened and turned immediately at the soft, feminine song to the voice, sweeping his broad-brimmed hat from his head gallantly, his eyes as quickly sweeping across the woman's beautiful face, the doelike eyes, those high cheekbones brushed with a natural blush, her full lips exposing but a hint of straight teeth, all atop that long, white neck. Bill felt the natural pull that for but an instant gave him desire to flirt with this beauty. That is, until his eyes dropped from the neck, past the rounded bosom, and he saw the expanse of her belly.

"M-ma'am?" he stuttered. "It is *ma'am*, isn't it?"

She held out her hand. "Yes."

Good, he thought. After all, the woman was with child. An officer's wife, sitting out her pregnancy in this frontier post. He congratulated himself for suffering Lulu through only one of her three pregnancies at Fort McPherson.

"You are William F. Cody?"

"I am."

"You are the scout who served with the Fifth Cavalry during the summer of sixty-nine when you discovered Tall Bull's village of Dog Soldiers at Summit Springs in Colorado Territory?"

His eyes narrowed a bit as the hushed room inched closer about them both, anxious to overhear every bit of conversation. "Yes?"

"Then you are the scout who rescued one of the two women held captive by that rogue band of warriors."

Swallowing, Bill could think of nothing more to do but nod, then again answered, "Y-yes?"

She suddenly smiled, those teeth and those eyes lighting up that tiny, shady trading post, re-presenting him her hand.

He took it, held it, mystified at it all, until she explained.

"I am so very pleased to meet you, Mr. Cody. My husband has told me so very much about his time with you —chasing horse thieves all the way north to the Elephant Corral in Denver City. When we ourselves visited Denver last fall, he showed me that very same place and explained how you got the jump on the criminals."

"E-elephant Corral . . . he was with me?"

"All the way through for the Summit Springs fight."

"Your name . . . I'm afraid I didn't catch it, ma'am."

"Oh, dear. Now it's my turn to apologize," she said, removing her hand from his and holding it flat against her bosom. "It's only that I suppose I felt I know you already, sir—why, the way Seamus has talked and talked and talked about you so."

"S-seamus?"

"I'm Samantha Donegan."

"S-samantha . . . Seamus Donegan?" he gasped. "You're . . . he's . . . don't tell me he . . . gone and got married, has he?"

"Last summer," she replied, then patted her swollen belly. "And now this. With Seamus gone north to scout for General Crook—"

Cody roared. "Ain't that just like an Irishman now? To marry as beautiful a woman as there ever was on the plains . . . then go galloping off to the Indian wars once he's got her with child!"

Chapter 4

22–24 June
1876

"Samantha!"

She heard her name called out and leaped to peer down from the tiny window in her upstairs room. Across the Fort Laramie parade hurried Elizabeth Burt, wife of Captain Andrew S. Burt of the Ninth Infantry, waving a sheaf of yellow papers in the breeze like a bright clutch of radiant sunflowers as she dashed over the green lawn, her skirts and petticoats maddeningly a'swirl at her ankles like sea foam.

"Oh, dear God," Sam prayed aloud, "don't let this be . . . bad news," then cradled her hands atop her swelling belly.

"Samantha!"

Sam turned back to the window, looking down on Elizabeth again, flagging the handful of yellow telegraph flimsies at the end of her arm. And she calmed herself, thinking that Mrs. Burt wouldn't be hurrying so, shouting out at her, if it was bad news she carried.

With a swallow Samantha turned and gazed down at her belly, patting her bulk reassuringly a moment before she dashed from the room and lumbered ungainly down the narrow stairs to the landing, where more than a dozen women poured through the front door onto the porch in an eager crush of skirts and bodices, all swishing below a cacophony of voices excited yet etched with dread.

For a moment Sam held at the last step, gripping the newel in her right hand, wishing him back here with all her might. She licked her lip as the others flooded onto the porch, where Elizabeth Burt began passing out the telegram pages on which the key operator had scrawled each message.

Word from the war.

They already knew there had been a big fight—something on the order of a week ago now. By the time word of that battle reached Fort Fetterman and was relayed down the telegraph wire to Fort Laramie, already the Indians camped all about the post spoke of hearing on the moccasin telegraph of a great fight wherein the army was bested. Those rumors were only whispered, conveyed in hushed tones, until Crook's official report of the fight reached Laramie, disproving the worst fears that the Big Horn and Yellowstone Expedition had suffered a massacre. From that moment on it was only a matter of waiting out the agonizing days until each wife learned if her husband would be among the cold, sterile numbers Crook listed for Sheridan's headquarters: was a loved one among the dead or wounded, a casualty of that great fight?

Taking a moment at the landing to tug down her bodice, Samantha straightened the apron over her belly and quartered through the open doorway as if she were bigger than she really was. More and more every week it seemed she was having to learn all over again how to move around in a body that always seemed to conspire against her.

"Here's yours, Samantha," Elizabeth said, rattling the yellow page aloft over others' shoulders. "Oh, dear," she said, sudden worry in her voice as she moved through the crush toward Samantha. "It's good news! Trust me—he's all right."

Sam crumpled the flimsy telegram to her breast, daring not to read it just yet. Wanting to trust in Elizabeth's eyes, those eyes that peered into Sam's at this moment. "He's . . . Seamus is all right?"

"Read it yourself. They can't say much. None of them, not even my Andrew, an officer, dear Lord—not a single one is allowed to say much to us. But Seamus says there's a letter coming, Sam," she reassured, her finger tapping that flimsy that Sam held against her breast. "Read it and see he's fine. Just fine."

"F-fine?"

"He'll be coming back here before your little one makes his debut at Fort Laramie. You can count on that, Sam."

"Yes, I want to count on that," she murmured softly as she turned away into the crush of women and Elizabeth was once more swallowed by anxious wives and clamoring voices.

At the edge of the porch Samantha stopped, pulled the yellow page from her breast, and smoothed it in her hands, then held the paper up to the sunlight, squinting at the telegrapher's crude scrawl. In the open space that comprised nearly two thirds of the telegraph.

As Sam's eyes misted, she brought the crumpled page to her breast and finally breathed one long sigh. She didn't think she had breathed since she first heard Elizabeth call out from parade ground below her window. But now, at last, she could breathe again. As she did, Samantha felt the baby turn, a foot, a hand, or an elbow jabbing up beneath her ribs. And that sudden blow took her breath away a moment. She had to smile at that.

"Yes, little boy—your father is unharmed. And he says he'll be coming home to us both real soon."

Smoothing that pale-yellow paper again, instead of looking at the telegrapher's handwriting, this time she peered at the printed form.

THE WESTERN UNION TELEGRAPH COMPANY

The rules of the Company require that all messages received for transmission shall be written on the message blanks of the Company, under and subject to the conditions printed thereon, which conditions have been agreed to by the sender of the following message.

ANSON STAGER, Gen'l Sup't,   }   WILLIAM ORTON, Pres't,   } New York.
Chicago, Ill.   GEO. H. MUMFORD, Sec'y.

Date *Bank of South Fork Tongue River,
20th inst 1876*
Received of *Via Fort Fetterman 23rd*
To *Mrs. Seamus Donegan, Fort Laramie*

*I am not hurt. Casualties light.
Be coming home when this business
is done. Letter to follow.*

S. Donegan

Then she read a third, and finally a fourth time before finding she could really trust the words. After all, it wasn't Seamus's handwriting. And he was so very far away. So scared was she that she discovered she couldn't overcome the doubt. She feared the worst—a dreadful hoax played on them all . . . yet she began to fight down the sob growing in her chest just in reading the terse message over and over again. She mentally replayed Elizabeth Burt's assertion that the men of Crook's command were never allowed to say too much in their brief telegrams to loved ones waiting back home.

Home.

This wasn't home. Home was up there on the South Fork of the Tongue River. Or wherever in hell Seamus was at this moment. Home was with him. Whether it was in that barn of Sharp Grover's down in the Texas Panhandle country, perhaps in some Denver or Cheyenne hotel, or only beneath a few yards of canvas he had stretched inelegantly over some willow or plum brush to give her some shade on their trip north through Kansas and Colorado and now to Sioux country . . . home was with Seamus Donegan.

For some time she had known home wasn't four walls and a roof over her head to keep out the snow and rain, wind and sun. *Home* was his arms, the security and shelter and sanctuary of that embrace.

So now the two of them would wait for his letter to come down from Fort Fetterman by courier, brought there by another courier riding south out of the land of the Sioux and the Cheyenne, where Seamus was risking his life.

"Dear God, dear God, dear God," Sam whispered, turning again to the commotion on the porch as women screeched and giggled, hugged and patted one another on the back, congratulating one another on the good fortune of their husbands to this date in this summer of the Sioux.

"Watch over that man for me," Sam whispered, dabbing the corners of her wet eyes with that yellow flimsy that meant more to her at that moment than all the gold they could dig out of the Black Hills.

"Just—bring—him—home—to—us."

At four A.M. on Thursday, 22 June, buglers raised the shrill notes of reveille up and down that camp the Fifth Cavalry had pitched about a mile from Fort Laramie near the confluence of the North Platte and Laramie rivers.

By first light Lieutenant Charles King heard the throaty sergeants bawl, "Prepare to mount!" Then came that long-anticipated order, "Mount!" and seven companies crossed the river on a new iron bridge and were setting off on the chase. They were ordered due north toward Custer City in Dakota to intercept the trail being used by hundreds of warriors riding north to join the summer roamers known to be in the unceded hunting grounds of the Powder River–Rosebud country. For the time being

Captain Robert H. Montgomery's B Company would remain behind in post, with orders to catch up with the main
column in four days.

After only two miles the column passed the charred
ruins of Rawhide Station, telegraph link between Fort Fetterman and Fort Laramie, burned by hostiles as little as ten
days before. The Fifth pushed on with that vivid reminder
seared into their consciousness, marching into an austere
land carved with majestic buttes and dry coulees, covered
by only sage and cactus.

Before he had left Laramie on an inspection trip to
Captain William H. Jordan's Camp Robinson and its
nearby agency at Red Cloud, District Commander Philip
Sheridan had ordered Lieutenant Colonel Carr to take his
Fifth and close down that trail. But at the same time, Sheridan had drafted Bill Cody to ride along eastward as guide
for his own escort, which included a Beecher Island veteran, now a member of Sheridan's personal staff, Lieutenant Colonel James W. "Sandy" Forsyth. Left behind to
guide temporarily for Carr's Fifth Cavalry were Cody's
friend, Charles "Buffalo Chips" White, and Baptiste "Little
Bat" Garnier, the half-breed interpreter Crook had assigned to Fort Laramie after Colonel Joseph Reynolds's disastrous Powder River campaign.

After a march of something on the order of thirty
miles that Thursday, the regiment went into camp on the
South Fork of Rawhide Creek, where water and grass could
be found in abundance, but firewood was in short supply.

With another day's march behind them, the third
morning the regiment pulled away from its camp at the
Cardinal's Chair,* a well-known geographical rock formation situated on the headwaters of the Niobrara River, at
daylight on the twenty-fourth. By noon Lieutenant King,
riding with Carr's staff at the head of the column, entered
the valley of what frontiersmen lovingly called the "Old
Woman's Fork" of the South Cheyenne River. There were

_____
*Near present-day Lusk, Wyoming.

shouts, voices leapfrogging from behind them, farther back along the column until the call reached the front.

"Rider approaching!"

Squinting his eyes into the bright summer's light, King turned to watch the lone courier, still better than a quarter mile back along the dusty column, sprinting up on his lathered horse, his mount raising rooster tails of golden spray that shimmered with the waves of heat rising off the land.

"Colonel Carr?"

"You found him," the lieutenant colonel answered.

The young courier saluted, licking his dry lips. Alkali dust caked his face, and foam at the horse's bit, tail-root and at the edges of the blanket. "Dispatches from Fort Laramie, sir. General Sheridan."

"Give 'em over."

King watched the man's impassive face as he read over the three pages of handwritten documents.

Carr asked, "Sheridan's returned to Laramie?"

"No, sir. He telegraphed these from Camp Robinson."

The lieutenant colonel nodded, saying nothing more, then read over the dispatches one more time. When he looked up, he blinked, pursed his lips a long moment, then asked the courier, "You've been ordered to return, Private?"

"Yes, sir. As soon as I've delivered those to you, General."

Carr saluted. "Back there a couple of miles, you passed a spring. Get that mount watered, then rest him an hour before you ride back. Is that understood, soldier?"

"Yes, General."

"And—one other thing, Private. By God, keep your eyes moving all the time."

The youngster grinned, cracking the sweat-plastered powder caking his face, swiping his hand across the sweat and grime on his chin. With a salute he turned and was pushing his mount back down the column.

"Gentlemen, we've had a small change in our plans."

King asked, "We're not going to unite with Crook, General Carr?"

"No. At least not for the time being, Lieutenant."

King felt disappointment, curiosity mixed. "Where to?"

"We're to continue on north along the Custer City Road, but once we hit the Powder River trail the war bands are reported using, instead of following it into their hunting grounds—we're supposed to halt there and await further orders."

"Further orders?" squealed Major Julius W. Mason nearby. "Are we ever going to get into this war or not?"

"I don't know about you fellas," Carr told them as he reined his mount around so its nose once more pointed north, "but something tells this old horse soldier that we might just bump into some action before we even join up with Crook."

Then he pointed into the distance. "How far to that line of trees would you gauge, Mr. King?"

"Less than a mile, General."

"Very good," Carr replied. "Inform the company commanders we're going to take a short rest there, and tell the officers I expect to have a conference with them in some of that shade up there."

King raised his face into the heat of the noonday sun. The tender flesh along the inner sides of his thighs chafed with sweat, rubbed against the rough wool and unforgiving saddle tree of his McClellan until they felt as if they were on fire. "Yes, sir."

"Damn right, King. If I know what you're thinking. But trust me—it's even hotter to an old soldier like me. Now, you ride on ahead and bring those two scouts in. I want their latest report on the ground ahead at the officers' meeting."

Minutes later Little Bat and Buffalo Chips were back in what shade the stubby, rustling cottonwoods offered, joining that ring of officers. Carr listened to what the half-breed scout had to tell them about the country to the north, and what Indian sign the two of them had crossed since daybreak. The regiment's commander didn't take long in deciding his course of action.

"Major Stanton," Carr said, addressing the department's paymaster, "I've decided to send you ahead on our trail with a company in reconnaissance."

"Which one, sir?" asked Captain Thaddeus Stanton, Sheridan's own emissary riding with the Fifth.

"C. That'd be yours, Lieutenant Keyes."

Edward L. Keyes straightened. "Yes, General."

Stanton turned to Carr. "General, I'd like to request that you send King with me."

Carr looked at his young adjutant. "Lieutenant? How's that sound to a veteran Apache fighter like you?"

King grinned, glancing at Stanton. "By all means, sir!"

Stanton stood, dusting the back of his wool britches. "When do you want us to detach, General?"

Carr turned to Keyes. "When can you have C Troop ready, Lieutenant?"

"Half an hour, sir."

"Make it fifteen minutes, Lieutenant."

Keyes saluted and was gone, trotting off toward the horses tethered nearby.

Carr turned back to Stanton, but for a moment his eyes connected with King's meaningfully. "I'm giving you Little Bat as guide. White will stay with me. Gentlemen, it is crucial that you reach the Cheyenne River as quickly as possible. Sheridan wired down from Red Cloud that the warrior bands are abandoning the agency en masse. I need you on the Cheyenne, and I need you there as fast as you can cover that ground."

"Understood, General," Stanton said, tapping the sawed-off blunderbuss of a rifle he carried on a sling looped over his left shoulder.

Minutes later, as King stood in a narrow patch of noonday shade tightening his cinch, Carr strode over. The lieutenant colonel spoke softly, almost fatherly.

"Lieutenant—I feel I must warn you: these Indians of

the plains aren't like those Apache we fought down in Arizona."

"Yes, sir."

"These are horse warriors. Nothing against the Apache, but those renegade Chiricahua could move faster on foot in those rugged mountains of theirs than a man on horseback."

"How well I remember."

"Yes, of course you do," Carr replied, glancing at King's shoulder. "But these Sioux and Cheyenne, Lieutenant—never underestimate them when they climb on the back of a pony. Watch yourself."

King slipped the big curb bit back into his horse's mouth. "I will, General."

"See that Keyes doesn't get rattled, either."

"No, sir."

"And by all means—keep the company together. If these horse warriors get the troops scattered in a running fight of it—they'll eat you alive."

Swallowing hard, the lieutenant saluted. "I'll remember, sir."

"Have at them, Mr. King. Have at them."

Two hours later, having crossed one wide valley after another in that unforgiving country, reaching ridge after naked ridge, Baptiste Garnier finally signaled to halt the column of forty men. King, Stanton, and Keyes came forward on foot to see what the scout had discovered.

"That's the first war trail of the campaign," Thaddeus Stanton cheered, pulling his hat from his head to swipe a damp bandanna across his broad forehead.

"Lead on, Mr. Garnier," Keyes ordered as the group got to their feet there above the troubled, flaky earth where more than a hundred unshod ponies had crossed the bare ground.

The tracks led straight down the valley. Heading north for the Mini Pusa, the Cheyenne River. C Troop rode on into the afternoon's waning light. Every hour it seemed more and more small groups of Indian ponies joined up, uniting with the main band as it continued north.

While the sun settled off to their left, the lone company noticed a single column of signal smoke climbing into the clear summer sky far to the north in the direction of Pumpkin Buttes. In less than ten minutes another signal column rose off to the west.

"If that ain't the damnedest luck," Stanton growled. "Looks like they know we're coming."

"I don't think it will do them a bit of good to try hitting us, Major," King advised. He pointed off into the distance. "We're in open country. Not a tree or bush to hide them sneaking in on us."

"You're right, Lieutenant," the old workhorse replied. "Absolutely right. Besides—we're not stopping until we're at the Cheyenne, fellas."

In the lengthening, indigo shadows of twilight, as the breezes stiffened and cooled, King caught sight of Little Bat five hundred yards in the lead, circling his horse to the left.

"Mr. King," Stanton said, "go see what he's found this time."

Charles knelt alongside the scout over the newer tracks—even more warriors crossing the wide valley, their trail disappearing to the northwest. "How many more?" he asked.

"Maybe this many," Garnier said, opening and closing both hands five times. "Going the shortcut to the Big Horns."

King stared off to the north. "How far till we reach the Cheyenne?"

Little Bat shrugged. "Two. No, three hours, maybe."

"You keep on, Little Bat," the lieutenant said. "I'm going back to the column so they can put out flankers."

"Tell every one of them keep his eyes open," Garnier advised before he turned away and was gone.

Stanton and Keyes quickly dispatched outriders to cover the side and rear flanks of the company—choosing old soldiers who were veterans to this country, and to this sort of Indian chasing. On and on the company column moved as quickly as their jaded horses allowed them, shadows creeping longer and longer until the whole land was eventually swallowed up by dusk and the first stars began to wink into sight overhead.

At last in the distance King saw Little Bat loping his mount back toward them. As he came up, the scout shouted.

"Over that ridge! We done it. Mini Pusa over that ridge!"

"You heard him, fellas," Stanton rasped, his throat sounding as dry as a file drawn across rusty iron. "We made it to the Cheyenne River. And that's where Sheridan figures we'll make contact with the red sons of a buck."

At twilight atop the ridge Garnier pointed out the darker line of trees and willows and thick vegetation that indicated the banks of the Cheyenne below them, meandering its way across a wide valley where the troopers found water only in scanty pools trapped among the smooth rocks in the streambed. They paused only long enough to fill their canteens, then let the horses drink, the iron shoes clattering and scraping the rounded stones. This sorely parched country hadn't received the blessing of rain for more than a month.

A mile beyond the Cheyenne, at the base of some low bluffs to the north, King and Garnier found a basin where enough grass grew to please the animals they picketed and hobbled for the night. There was ample wood for the coffee fires they buried in the ground as these veteran horse soldiers stretched their legs and lit their pipes in this stolen moment of relaxation in a horse soldier's day. Keyes deployed a dozen men as pickets to surround the camp, assigning a rotation throughout the moonlit night. As darkness squeezed on down upon the Cheyenne River patrol, in the distance they couldn't help but see the faraway glow of signal fires at five different points.

"They're talking about us, aren't they, Major?" King asked Stanton.

"Damn right they are. And those red-bellies'd jump us if they had the nerve."

"They won't: we've got pickets out," Keyes said.

"It's not us they're afraid of particularly, Lieutenant," Stanton replied. "Trust me—them sonsabitches know Carr and the rest aren't far behind us. No sense in making the jump on us since they figure we can hold 'em off till the rest of the boys make it up."

The lieutenant's eyes began to droop, what with a bellyful of coffee, hardtack, and fried bacon, as well as his aching muscles screaming for rest after the long day's march. A grin cracked his bristling, dust-caked face as his head sank back onto his McClellan, tugged the saddle blanket over his shoulders, and listened to the quiet, rinsed-crystal-clear tenor of one of the cavalrymen singing nearby at one of the tiny fires.

"The ring of a bridle, the stamp of a hoof,
    Stars above and the wind in the tree;
A bush for a billet, a rock for a roof,
    Outpost duty's the duty for me.
    Listen! A stir in the valley below—
The valley below is with riflemen crammed,
    Cov'ring the column and watching the foe;
    Trumpet-Major! Sound and be damned!"

King was just sliding down into that warm place where the exhausted can flee when the nearby gunshot cracked his sleeping shell.

In a heartbeat the entire bivouac came alive, men thrashing out of their blankets, others kicking sprays of dirt into the deep fire pits, some scurrying toward the patch of grass where they had their horses picketed. Above the rumble of curses and warnings, Keyes and Stanton barked orders and hollered their anxious questions at the perplexed sergeant of the guard.

Down in a crouch the old file halted halfway between bivouac and his outlying pickets, grumbling loudly from his hands and knees. "What chucklehead fired that god-damned shot?"

"I-I did sir," piped the youthful answer from the darkness.

The sergeant asked, "That you, Sullivan?"

"Yes . . . yes, sir."

"What'd you see, soldier?" Keyes demanded.

"Something . . . something was crawling right up out of that holler over there, Lieutenant," the soldier answered his company commander. "So I challenged—and he didn't answer—that's when I fired."

"Did you hit him, by damned?" the sergeant asked.

"I think so . . . ah, hell! I don't know, Sarge."

"There!" King said suddenly, rising off his knees.

The others studied the moonlit nearness of the hollow the hapless picket had been watching. There for one and all to see a four-legged intruder loped up the side of the coulee to the top of the plain, where he halted to survey the men below him with no little disdain. After a moment the night visitor turned away in indignation and disappeared over the hill, rump, tail, and all.

Climbing out of the dirt, the sergeant bawled at his picket, "You walleyed guttersnipe! Your own grandmother would have known that was nothing but a goddamned coyote!"

With that loud and definitive declaration, the bivouac erupted with laughter and good-natured backslapping that accompanied the crude jokes at picket Sullivan's expense.

"Hey, Sully," bawled a voice out of the darkness, "if it was *two* coyotes, would you advance the senior or the junior with the countersign, eh?"

On and on, back and forth the joking went for close to half an hour before the troopers settled back in for their night beside the Cheyenne River.

No more coyotes were to visit the company's bivouac as the sky lights whirled overhead.

Then just past moonset—three o'clock, as King noted on his turnip pocket watch when the alarm went up—

pickets on the lieutenant's side of camp heard the distant passing of many hoofbeats as they faded into the distance.

That eerie echo of unshod pony hooves galloping north in the dark—headed safely around C Troop and making for the last great hunting ground of the Sioux and the Cheyenne.

Chapter 5

Sunday
25 June 1876

Two hours later the Cheyenne River patrol arose in the cold darkness that greeted those who crossed the high plains even at the height of summer. There would be no breakfast this fateful Sunday morning for Company C, Fifth Cavalry.

Without much said the troopers saddled their mounts, formed up in a column of twos, and set off behind Baptiste Garnier, bearing north up a broadening valley before the horizon to the east even hinted at turning gray.

A half mile from camp the half-breed scout had discovered a flood of pony tracks. In sweeping around the edge of C Troop's bivouac, the enemy had ventured closer than he had ever come before. This was to be a day that would live on and on in history.

Come the arrival of that same false dawn, some two hundred miles farther to the north as the far-seeing golden eagle might fly, Crow scouts were singing their death songs among some tall rocks on the crest of the Wolf Mountains called the Crow's Nest. They peered down into the faraway valley of the Greasy Grass and saw the smoke of many,

many lodge fires, the dust raised by thousands upon thousands of pony hooves.

But here in Wyoming Territory, Little Bat was making for the Dry Fork of the Cheyenne.

After a march of some six miles they reached the stream that had disappeared beneath its dry bed. Its sandy, rippled course wound lazily through stands of old cottonwood and willow, their roots forced to reach deep for that underground water. Yet deadfall lay matted against the trunks and among the brush, testament to the force and fury of mountain runoff that past spring.

"First of May, I figure we could barely ford this valley," Stanton said.

"And look at it now," King replied. "Dry as a bone."

"Got to find some water, fellas," Keyes ordered, sending a small detachment upstream, Stanton and a handful choosing to ride downstream.

It was the old crusty major's call that rallied Company C as well as any bugle could. They found Stanton squatting underneath a steep, overhanging bank shaded by stunted cottonwood and a profusion of willows.

"Better'n nothing at all," the major cheered, submerging his canteen.

Stanton's mount stood up to its fetlocks in what clearly had once been a big pool. But at this late season the water was warm and decidedly alkaline, even a bit soapy to the taste. Nonetheless, their thirsty horses did not balk when they were led to the pool two or three at a time to drink their fill.

"We find better by night come," Little Bat reassured them in his broken English as he mounted up and set out so that he could ride some distance ahead of the company column.

King didn't see much of the half-breed for the rest of that morning, only glimpses of the horse and rider caught briefly on the crest of a hill as Garnier watched the soldiers coming on, then disappeared again from view, remaining far in the front. One after another, hill after valley then on again, until they finally clambered into the rugged country northeast of the Mini Pusa. This was the land where Sheridan's intelligence said they would find the great Indian trail —here, where it would cross the valley of the South Cheyenne some distance west of the Beaver River, very near its confluence with the Mini Pusa itself.

Then at noon, as the sun hung hot and sultry, sulled like a wild mule's eyeball in that great pale sky of summer's best, King spotted him again. Garnier was coming back across a ridgetop. Once in plain sight of Keyes's column, he stopped and circled his horse again, ripping his hat from his head and waving it wildly.

"He's bringing us on, boys," Stanton observed.

"What you think he's found?" King asked.

The old major snorted. "If it were Injuns—that half-breed son of a red-belly would be hightailing it back here instead of signaling us on."

Keyes turned in the saddle and issued orders for the rest of the column to proceed at its pace, then turned to go on up the trail at a lope with Stanton, King, and two others. Garnier led them down into a wide swale, where he quickly leaped from his mount.

"Every man get off," Little Bat said. "Leave horses with holder. Him." He pointed to one of their number.

Keyes nodded to the soldier Garnier had indicated. "You can rest here."

The half-breed said, "Come with me and see."

King followed the others trailing out behind the scout, who was clambering on foot up the side of the ridge, making the best purchase he could with his boots in the flaky soil and loose rock gone too long without rain. Time and again they slid, grabbed hold with their hands, and kept on up the slope. Just short of the crest Little Bat signaled for the rest to wait while he peered over.

Taking a few minutes to satisfy himself while the others caught their breath, Garnier finally signaled them on up. At the top the others blew just like horses after a climb, huffing in the midday heat of another scorcher on the plains.

"Take your glasses," Garnier directed. "Look there. Right over there."

Keyes and Stanton were slow in getting their looking glasses out. King was the first to peer off to the southeast.

"You see?"

"By damn, I do!" King replied.

Even at this distance it was clearly visible: a broad, beaten trail leading down to the riverbed—pony hooves and travois scouring the fragile earth in a track as broad as anything the young lieutenant could ever hope to see.

"It's a goddamned highway," Stanton cursed behind his field glasses.

"And with no sign of 'em anywhere," Keyes added, slowly swinging his glasses to all points from the north of east, clear down to the south of east—where the warriors would be found fleeing from the reservations.

"Silent and still," King observed with disappointment, sensing the eerie emptiness of that landscape. "Maybe we're too late."

"We better not be," Stanton growled. "If we are—then maybe Crook, or even Custer himself, will have more on their hands than they bargained for."

"I can't help but wonder how Sheridan knew we'd find this big trail right here, right where he said it would be," King said with no little amazement.

Stanton looked at him. "You mean you don't know how he figured it out?"

King wagged his head. "Not sitting back there in his office in Chicago, no. Only the Sioux and Cheyenne could know this ground very well."

"You're right there, Lieutenant," Stanton agreed. "But here—watch."

And with a twig he snapped off some dry sage, the major drew some quick landmarks in the dust.

"This here's the Big Horns. Where Crook put his base camp, and he's marching north of there as we speak—

going to strike the enemy villages. Now, down here to the southeast"—and he drew a couple of circles—"is Red Cloud and Camp Robinson. Here's Spotted Tail and Camp Sheridan, you see. So if you draw the Beaver and the Cheyenne and its South Fork on the map like so"—and Stanton scratched in those east-west flowing rivers there in the middle of his map—"where do you think those red-bellies are going to go if they're of a mind to jump the reservation?"

"I suppose they'd go north toward the Rosebud and the Big Horns, where the rest of the hostiles are, right?" asked Keyes.

"Right, Lieutenant. Now draw me a line from the agencies to that hostile hunting ground Crook and Custer are closing in on."

King watched Keyes take the twig and draw a straight line heading northwest from reservations.

"That's right, fellas. That's how Sheridan knew. On any map you can do the same goddamned thing. Whether it's a map in Chicago, or a map at Fort Laramie. That line the lieutenant here drew in the dirt crosses right there, by doggy! You look right over there and you'll see that very same spot—where Little Bat here found us that big trail." Again he jabbed with the point of his twig as he emphasized, "Simple enough: you want to get from there to there, you got to cross right *here.*"

The small band with Garnier kept their horses under cover as they pushed on one ridge more, reaching a crest where they were greeted with an even wider panorama, able to make out the great sweep of the valley of the South Cheyenne for more than fifty miles as it flowed toward the north by east into the dim, timbered rise of tumbled ground that indicated just how close they were to the Black Hills.

"I'll stay here with Mr. King," Stanton told Keyes. "I figure you should return to the rest of the company and retrace your steps back to the timber along the Mini Pusa. Loosen cinches, but don't unsaddle, Lieutenant."

"You're going to keep an eye on the trail, Major?" Keyes inquired.

"And you can post a man with a looking glass to keep an eye on us," Stanton replied. "If we see anything, we can signal and he can alert you. The company can be on its way here in a matter of seconds."

"Very good, sir," Keyes said, saluted, and turned down the slope to take two soldiers on the backtrail with him.

The sun stalled there in the sky, seeming to refuse to move at all as the minutes crawled by, every one of them more torture than the last as the growing heat seemed to rise with fiery intensity right out of the ground. Here at midday the air refused to stir, waves of heat shimmering in the middistance. Sometime past one o'clock King was rubbing the kinks out of his leg and watching to the south and west when he noticed a far-off column of dust spiraling high into the air—another sign that this land was without any breeze today.

"Slow but steady, Carr's bringing 'em on," King observed dryly. "I'm sure glad I'm not riding with that bunch."

Stanton turned, training his glasses on the distant dust cloud. "They're eating their forty acres today."

Looking into the sky, the lieutenant said, "What I wouldn't give for a little rain, Major."

Licking his cracked lips as he turned back to watch the Indian trail, Stanton said, "Me too, Lieutenant. A little rain would do this ground and this army some real good."

Through the next few hours King imagined he dozed off and on, catching himself nodding, then blinking to stay awake, squirming and shifting positions in the heat of the sun as he kept staring at the unmoving, unchanging, austere horizon where nothing stirred, not even a distant swirl of dust. Minute by minute, ultimately hour by hour. Made harder still knowing the rest of Company C was likely sleeping out the shank of their afternoon down in the shade of the South Fork's cottonwoods and willows.

As quiet at it was on the Mini Pusa that hot Sunday

afternoon, two hundred miles farther to the north an entire regiment was embroiled in a fight for its very life.

But here it was as quiet as it would be at the bottom of a freshly dug grave. Somewhere to the southeast the Indians would be coming, eager and on their way to join Crazy Horse and Sitting Bull. Over to the southwest Carr was bringing on the rest of the Fighting Fifth. It was only a matter of time now, King knew. Wouldn't be long before the regiment had its hands full.

"I don't think there's a damned red-belly stirring today," grumbled the major. He slapped his glasses against his dusty britches, disgusted.

King continued to peer through his, for a few minutes content to watch the distant flight of a hawk, perhaps a golden eagle, sailing against the cloudless summer blue far to the northeast. Wondering if that bird of astounding eyesight could look down on Crook's column as it chased Crazy Horse. Wondering if it peered down on the fairhaired Custer as the gallant Seventh Cavalry narrowed the noose around old Sitting Bull himself.

King watched that bird fly far above the hot land, not knowing that somewhere below its wide wings men fell and bled. And lay still in the tall grass, dreaming of eternity's reward.

Throughout that night and into the morning of the twenty-sixth they kept up their watch over the nearby Indian trail without success. Then, near noon, the head of Carr's column hoved into sight, which made for a joyous rendezvous in the valley of the Cheyenne. Here Sheridan had ordered them to set up their base of operations and await further instructions while keeping an eye on any warrior activity. Near sundown the lieutenant colonel dispatched Captain Sanford C. Kellogg with his I Company to explore the well-beaten warrior trail behind Little Bat while the other seven troops picketed and hobbled their horses, making camp, and while they set about relaxing for this first of many days of waiting.

And waiting.

Five long, hot summer days of waiting.

On 1 July dust was spotted rising to the southwest, below it a dark column of twos. It was Captain Montgomery's B Company, bringing the Fighting Fifth up to eight full troops of strength. As well, a courier sent out from Major E. F. Townsend, Laramie's commander, to explain that Townsend would send supplies along as soon as he could guarantee wagon transportation for them. At the earliest, it would be 6 July before a supply train could depart the North Platte.

There were also dispatches from Sheridan, one notifying Carr of Crook's predicament, his disappointing affair on the Rosebud, and his present stalemate far to the north, that same dispatch reporting that Terry and Gibbon planned to probe south of the Yellowstone using their cavalry—and what better cavalry to use than Custer's Seventh? So for the time being Sheridan was recommending the Fifth sit tight on the trail and keep a wary eye open. At the moment, the lieutenant general was not sending the Fifth in to reinforce Crook. Not just yet.

Yet for all the momentous news come from Indian country, it was nonetheless the arrival of a single man that caused the most stir there in the valley of the Mini Pusa. Charles King could see that Eugene Carr immediately recognized the old soldier riding at the head of Montgomery's company as the troops came to a dusty halt beneath its snapping guidon.

The lieutenant colonel stopped by the officer's horse and saluted, his eyes squinting into the bright light. "General Merritt, Lieutenant Colonel Eugene Carr, sir. Welcome."

Wesley Merritt returned the salute and slid out of his saddle, yanking his sweaty gauntlets from his hands. "Colonel Carr. It's good to see you again."

Carr's face was a study of stony impassivity as he asked, "By your presence here, am I to understand that General Emory has retired, sir?"

"He has. I am come to take over the Fifth."

Suddenly snapping his back straight, as rigid as any fighting man's, Carr saluted again. "Yes, sir, General Merritt. May I be given the opportunity to introduce you to your officer corps?"

"By all means, General Carr," Merritt replied, using Carr's brevet grade earned during the Civil War. "I can't tell you how proud I am to be leading this outfit."

King watched the pair stroll off, followed by Merritt's aides and a dog-robber who was there to fetch anything the new commander of the Fifth Cavalry should desire. Then the young lieutenant wagged his head.

"What's wrong, Mr. King?" Stanton asked as he strode up.

"Shouldn't happen this way."

"You mean Merritt riding in to take over the regiment?"

"Right, Major. Not in the field like this."

Stanton nodded. "Carr resents Merritt already, don't he?"

"No," King answered firmly. "I don't think he does. He figured Merritt was up for the post. After all, for a long time Merritt's been part of Sheridan's Chicago staff. Carr knew he wouldn't get it himself—even though the man deserves it, many times over . . . but that's not the way things work back in Washington City, do they? Not even the way things work back with Sheridan in Chicago, either. But this, taking over in the field like this. Yanking the field command right out of Carr's hands when he's led the Fifth against every kind of fighting Injun you can imagine—"

"A colonel's not a fighting position, is it?"

King looked at Stanton squarely. "You tell me, Major. With old man Emory as this regiment's colonel, Carr's had actual fighting and field command of the Fifth since 1868. Seems to me the government's going to spend a hell of a lot of money and get a bunch of soldiers killed teaching all these armchair generals like Crook and Terry and Merritt how to fight. But what have you got to say, Major? You were with Reynolds on the Powder River yourself. Reynolds is a colonel. So you tell me, sir. Should Reynolds have been in charge on the Powder . . . or should he have left the fighting to the men who know how to fight Injuns?"

Turning on his heel, King stomped off, feeling the anger rising in himself like a boil, sensing what he was sure had to be Carr's own great personal disappointment at being stripped of field command of the Fighting Fifth, here as his beloved regiment stood on the brink of jumping into the Sioux War with both boots.

Chapter 6

26 June
1876

"What do you figure that is?" Seamus asked the half-breed scout, who was stretched on his belly beside the Irishman atop a hill a few miles north of Crook's Goose Creek base camp early that Monday afternoon.

Frank Grouard squinted, rubbed his eyes, blinked them repeatedly, and stared into the sunlit distance marred only by a few high, thin clouds. "Could be dust from that village we was about to bump into a week back."

"There, along the horizon," Donegan said, pointing north by east, "looks to be it's darker than dust raised by a pony herd—even a big one."

"They'll have lots of drags," Grouard said. "Bound to stir up a lot of dust moving a village that big."

With a shake of his head Donegan replied, "That's smoke."

The half-breed appeared to weigh the heft of that a moment. "You figure they're firing the grass behind them, eh? Maybe so, Irishman."

"Crook will want to know."

"He's got hunting on his mind," Grouard replied. "Thinking of heading into the Big Horns in a week or so."

"With that enemy camp escaping, moving north?"

Grouard looked at Donegan. "How you so sure they're moving north?"

His gray eyes danced impishly. "I just figured they would be skedaddling in the opposite direction from us."

"How far you make it to be?"

This time Seamus calculated, slowly chewing a cracked lower lip that oozed from sunburn. "Less than a hundred miles from here."

"Naw. Closer to sixty, maybe seventy at the most, I'd make it. That's how far it would be to the Greasy Grass."

"Greasy Grass?"

"What the Injins call the Little Bighorn River. A favorite camping place as they wander every summer toward the Big Horn Mountains to cut lodgepoles."

Seamus slapped Grouard on the back. "See? I told you! Those Injins ain't headed south, they're going west toward the mountains."

Frank stared into the distance again, then said, "Could be they're moving this way—to keep away from that army north of 'em."

"Gibbon and Terry's bunch?"

"And Long Hair Custer's Seventh Cavalry too," the half-breed said. "C'mon, Irishman. Let's go see if Crook figures now is the time for you and me to go sniff around to the north."

As the fates would have it, George Crook was off hunting in the foothills for the day, and Lieutenant Bourke did not think the general would return with his party until late in the afternoon. Seamus waited nearby as Frank told his story to Crook's aide, as well as to some of the other officers and newsmen who quickly gathered to hear the half-breed's report of telltale smoke along the northern horizon.

"Indian signals?" sniffed Reuben Davenport, reporter for the New York *Herald*. "What of them?"

"No such a thing," declared Captain Henry E. Noyes of the Second Cavalry. "Balderdash."

"Where are you going, Grouard?" Bourke asked the moment the rest of the group began laughing at the scout's assertions, causing Frank to turn on his heel and stomp off in Donegan's direction.

All the half-breed did was whirl about and point.

Seamus said, "We're riding north, Johnny."

Bourke asked, "So you're in on this cold-hatched scheme too?"

"I saw the smoke with me own eyes."

Grouard turned away again, prodding Donegan off. "Let's go, Irishman."

"Tell the general we'll have a report for him when we get back," Seamus said over his shoulder as he moved off with Grouard, each of them pulling his horse behind him.

"Get back? From where?"

"North!" Grouard growled.

Donegan added, "Where the wild Injins play, Johnny. Where the Montana and Dakota columns are having all the fun . . . up on the Greasy Grass where the wild Injins play!"

"You'll watch yourself, Seamus?"

"Indeed I will, Lieutenant!"

The pair had their mounts quickly grained while they rolled up blankets inside gum ponchos, packed a little coffee, salt pork, and hardtack into the saddlebags already heavy with ammunition for their rifles, plus a pair of belt weapons apiece—those .45-caliber 1873 long-barreled single-action Army Colt's revolvers. While Grouard favored the .45/70-caliber Springfield carbine, that shorter cavalry model, Donegan had grown quite attached to the eleven-pound Sharps single-shot cartridge rifle sold him by teamster Dick Closter immediately following their fight with Crazy Horse on the Rosebud. Seamus had given the ten-year-old Henry repeater a fitting burial after dark that night before Crook began his retreat south: burning the battered stock in his coffee fire to finish the destruction begun in the furious hand-to-hand fighting. A redeeming end for the weapon that had seen the Irishman through a decade of Indian fighting.

With each of them tying a small sack of oats to the back of his saddle, the two scouts mounted up and moved north by east along Goose Creek, striking the Tongue River itself by late afternoon. With every mile they put behind them, Donegan became more acutely aware that they were drawing another mile closer to what all evidence was showing had to be the biggest gathering of hostiles ever assembled on the plains. They hugged the timber where they could. But when their route lay across open ground, they left horses tied in sheltered coulees as they bellied up to the crest of hilltops to examine the country they were about to traverse. And never did they take their eyes off that cloud of smoke and dust thickening to the north. Occasionally Seamus would test the caliber of the wind, sniffing to see if he could smell grass smoke. Figuring that when he got his first good whiff of it, he and Grouard would be nearing the thick of things.

Leaving the Tongue, they had struck out overland, almost due north for the Wolf Mountains far in the distance, by and large following the expedition's line of march toward Rosebud Creek better than eight days before. The sun was in its final quadrant of the western sky by the time they reached the army's creekside camp the morning of 17 June, to discover that the bodies of those soldiers killed in the battle had been dug up.

"Looks like predators," Donegan said as they looked down on the shallow graves, the whole scene carpeted with paw prints.

"The Wolf Mountains up ahead," Grouard replied as he knelt to have himself a closer look at the ground. "What else would you expect in this country?"

"Damn them! Can't even give a sojur-boy a decent resting place but the carrion eaters won't dig a body up and drag it off from its final sleep."

"Maybe not all wolves," Frank added sourly as he leaned back on his haunches.

"Injins?"

"Might be."

"Sonsabitches!" he swore with quiet force, slapping a glove across his pommel. "Godless savage h'athens—"

"Don't you remember what Crook's soldiers done to ever' scaffold we come across so far?"

Donegan pursed his lips. Yes, he could remember how the soldiers had desecrated the Lakota burial platforms, searching for souvenirs, taking what they wanted before gleefully dumping the bones in nearby creeks or perhaps leaving the rotting remains to whatever four-legged or winged predator might be attracted by the wind-borne odor of death.

His gray eyes narrowed, bright with an anger he could not direct at any one enemy for the moment. "You made your point, Frank."

"We best be getting."

Seamus nodded and urged his horse away with a tap of his heels. Then glanced once more at the torn earth clawed up and sniffed over. "Wolf Mountains, you say?"

Grouard nodded. "Chetish. Injun name for them."

"Ain't no Injins gonna camp in the mountains."

"You're right, Irishman. But by moving down the Rosebud to keep out of sight of any wandering scouts they may have out—it means we'll eventually have to cross over them low mountains."

"Then that big camp is west, ain't it?" Donegan replied. "Like you said: in the valley of that Greasy Grass."

"See the sun on them clouds?"

Donegan peered west, gazing at the distant haze laced with the first tendrils of a sunset's delicate light painted a golden rose but underlaid with an angry belly of blood-hued crimson. "That's smoke, Grouard."

"Your turn to be right, Irishman."

Seamus said, "Covering their tracks, ain't they?"

"Burning the grass because something's for sure driving them south."

"Terry's army, by God," Seamus replied. "Crook'll wanna know."

"Yes, Terry—maybe even Custer's Seventh," Grouard said all too quietly, "herding Crazy Horse and my old friend Sitting Bull right down into Crook's lap."

"I suppose we ought to go see for ourselves, Frank." Seamus nudged the big horse toward the timber bordering the hillside once more. "Go see if Sitting Bull's coming for Crook."

What a glorious day it had been!

Here in the final days of Wicokannanji, the Lakotas' middle moon, Wakan Tanka had showered his people with honor, blessing all Lakota for all time!

For all time to come, the white man would cease to trouble American Horse's people.

Indeed, the soldiers had come. Soldiers had fallen into camp! Exactly as Sitting Bull's vision had disclosed. It was almost more than an aging warrior could ever hope would happen—yet American Horse had seen it with his own eyes. In his ears had echoed the screams and wails of dying soldiers, the war cries of the Lakota and Shahiyena so driven in fury that their bodies still trembled volcanically for hours after the battle. Yes, and he had seen the first of the white men fall there near the river, then more along the southern end of the ridge. And with his own eyes he had watched as Wakan Tanka touched some of the soldiers with the moon, for there was no other reason that could explain why the white men turned their guns on themselves all along the length of that terribly hot ridge.

No other explanation for a simple man like him to understand how or why the soldiers would take their own lives. It was something American Horse finally turned over to the Great Mystery, only because there was no other way for his heart and mind to deal with the overwhelming power of it.

Wakan Tanka had promised those soldiers to the Lakota. In no more time than it took for the sun to move from one lodgepole to the next, the Great Mystery had kept His promise to His people. This was not for man to wonder, but to accept.

American Horse would accept.

For days the nomadic camps had known about the soldiers to the north camped along the Elk River.* Scouts rode out from the villages daily to shoot at the soldiers, and to steal ponies from the Sparrowhawk People,† the scouts working for the Limping Soldier.‡ Some of the Lakota scouts even brought back word that white men traveled in smoking houses that walked on water!**

Then in those first days following their great fight on the Rosebud, when the camps were ever watchful of the soldiers to the north, Crow King arrived with his many lodges. The following day the mighty Gall rode in with his people, welcomed by the shouts of the thousands. Yes! Every warrior, from the youngest and untried, to the oldest scarred veteran of Harney's fight on the Blue Water—they vowed they would all be ready when the Great Mystery delivered them the soldiers of Sitting Bull's vision.

Then came that sleepy morning after so much singing and dancing, courting and feasting—that warm sunny morning when the first reports came that soldiers had been spotted far away near the crest of the Chetish Mountains. Sitting Bull, Gall, and the rest promptly doubled their *akicita*, the camp police, in a fierce attempt to keep all the eager, fire-blooded young men from racing out for glory.

"No man must make contact with the white man away from this camp," demanded Sitting Bull, the Hunkpapa mystic.

Gall spoke even more fiercely. "The coming fight must

---

*The Yellowstone River.
†The Crow Indians.
‡Colonel John Gibbon, commanding, Montana column.
**Paddle-wheel steamboats supplying the army's river depots.

not be started anywhere but here among this great gathering!"

How important it was to all Wakan Tanka's people that the prophecy be ordained on this day!

What glory the fight had been for them all, American Horse thought now as he moved south with the great cavalcade, astride his pony moving slowly down the west side of the immense procession that stretched for miles, spread up to a mile in width, as they plodded toward the White Mountains* to harvest lodgepoles. He, like most of the other warriors, rode the flanks of the colorful parade, ever watchful for signs of the enemy—whether that proved to be those soldiers said to be hurrying down from the north, or perhaps some of the Sparrowhawk People or more Corn Indians,† like those who had scouted for the soldiers who fell into their camp the day before. American Horse wanted to believe—really believe—that there would no longer be any danger from soldiers hunting for Lakota and Shahiyena villages. How he wanted to believe they would live and hunt, laugh and love in peace from now on.

The way his father, Smoke, had said it was for a long time before the white man began pushing west along the Holy Road that took him to the land where the sun went to bed each night. The way it was before then . . . the way it could be again now.

How American Horse prayed it to be so.

---

*The Big Horn Mountains.
†The Arikara or Ree Indians.

Chapter 7

26 June
1876

Dusk was falling as they stumbled across that wide, well-beaten trail crossing the divide between the Rosebud and the Little Bighorn. Even in the lengthening shadows, Donegan and Grouard could read the story of the encampment's passing many days before, the earth tracked and chewed by thousands of lodgepoles dragged behind more ponies than any man could possibly imagine.

Yet . . . atop that trail of unshod hooves and moccasin prints lay another of iron-shoed horses and peg-booted men. An army on the move.

The pair found the column's first campsite not that far west of the Rosebud on the trail up the divide, then ran across a second some distance down from the crest—where the troops had stopped and started coffee fires, smoked their pipes and slept, curled up in the trampled grass and dust.

"Didn't they have any idea what they were marching into?" Seamus asked.

"Only a blind man would fail to see what waited for them down there," Grouard answered just past sunset as they reached the top of the divide and gazed upon the valley of the Greasy Grass.

There in the west, shoved clear up against the deep indigo and purple of the foothills and benchlands on the far side of the distant river, lay a pall of smoke, its belly underlit in orange-tinted hues from the tongues of miles upon miles of grass fires.

"That ain't lodge smoke," Donegan grumbled quietly as they moved down from that high place, down the banks of Ash Creek toward the valley of the Greasy Grass.

"I'll give you this one, Irishman. Were it a game of cards, I'd gambled against you and lost. But you were right —them Injuns are firing the grass behind 'em as they go."

Above the thick layer of roiling grass smoke the summer sky remained pale, almost translucent, for the longest time of that evening, and when the moon came out behind the scouts, and the stars finally winked wakefully in a scatter across that darkening sky, the entire canvas allowed just enough light for an experienced plainsman to continue down, down into the valley as they followed that great churned trail the thousands upon thousands had followed.

Some distance from the Greasy Grass they came upon the place where it appeared the soldiers had divided, some of the regiment moving off to the left, gone to the southwest. The rest continued on down toward the Little Bighorn. A short time later they found the trail divided again —this time more of the regiment crossed to the left side of the creek and continued toward the bluffs hiding the Greasy Grass. It was here that Frank chose to steer them north.

Seamus asked, "Why don't we just follow this trail down to the river? Find out what come of this bunch?"

Grouard shook his head, peering into the darkness, as if divining something no more than a handful of miles away. "The river is bordered on this side by rough, high bluffs. This much I remember from this old camping spot of the Lakota. We will go north, moving around that bad stretch of country."

Donegan watched the half-breed move his horse away silently in the coming cool of that summer night as darkness and silence swallowed them both. And he wondered if Frank Grouard was feeling like he was a Hunkpapa or Hunkpatila warrior again, sensing something unseen out there in the darkness, even miles away yet. Something mystical that pulled the half-breed on. Something that might have been pulling Frank Grouard onward ever since last winter when the scout performed the impossible in the middle of a high-plains snowstorm and brought Colonel John Reynolds's cavalry across a rugged divide and right down on an enemy village nestled along the Powder River.

If Frank Grouard could do that, there was something uncanny about the man. Maybe something even unholy.

And that made Seamus Donegan shiver as he put his own horse in motion, following the half-breed into the deepening darkness of that summer night.

He had grown up Catholic, learned his catechism early at his mother's knee, then later beneath the thick leather strop of a series of stern priests who ruled the village school with an iron Celtic hand. Growing up Catholic in Ireland had come to mean that he too was superstitious. There were the legends of the first nomadic Celts and the mystical druids and, of course, tales of the Little People. Damn right, Seamus grew up every bit as superstitious as these savage heathens he'd been fighting for a full bloody decade come this very summer.

Ten years ago. There at the Crazy Woman Crossing it had been—when he watched that first warrior racing in atop his pony, all painted up, hair and a cock's comb of feathers all a'spray in the wind, the look on that dark, contorted face like no other he had seen since . . . why, since he saw the etching in the ancient book one of the old Irishmen in the village had shown all the interested young lads. It was the face of a banshee, the like of those what came to wail out of the dark places in the forests, to frighten off but lure at the same time—banshees that would suck the very life from a man's body if ever they got their hands on you.

Donegan swallowed hard, remembering that very first warrior he had dropped with the Henry repeater. In the dust and sage and sunlight there on the top of a bluff near the Crazy Woman Crossing. For so long he hadn't believed it had been an Indian at all. No. By the Blessed Virgin—in his sights Seamus had beheld an unholy banshee galloping right out from the bowels of the earth when he pulled the Henry's trigger.

So was he a Christian? he asked himself now this night. And eventually, as darkness shrouded them while he followed Frank Grouard into the rugged badlands east of the Greasy Grass, in the footsteps of a doomed command riding to its death—Seamus admitted he was not a Christian. Instead, he was what his mother and the priests had made of him: a Catholic. And an Irish Catholic at that.

He had been ever since he had known enough to cross himself and mutter the prayers of his childhood catechism whenever evil lurked just out of reach, as it did throughout that dark ride north into the unknown.

Within an hour the breeze came up and thin veils of clouds wafted in from the west. A few drops fell, big ones the size of tobacco wads. Cold they were. But a few heavy drops were all the sky had in it while the temperature plunged, chilling Donegan as he followed the half-breed. Overhead the moon rose to midsky behind the graying pall of pewter-tinted clouds scurrying east. As if even they knew better than to tarry above this ground forever touched by death's foul hand.

Then, as they were beginning to climb the dark foreground of a slope that appeared as if it would take them out of a wide saddle toward the top of a long ridge, Grouard's horse suddenly snorted, jerking its head to the left as if to avoid bumping into something that had loomed right out of the darkness.

Seamus had his hand on the butt of a pistol, half out of its holster, when he demanded in a hush, "What is it?"

"Don't know," Grouard growled, fighting the black-coated animal until it settled and came to a rest. "Never knowed this horse to act this way. To get scared at anything."

"You see what it shied at?"

"No," he replied, dropping from the saddle. Standing on the ground, he handed the reins to Donegan. "But I'm fixing to find out."

As Seamus watched, the half-breed crouched forward, bent nearly on all fours. Grouard had barely gone ten feet when he jerked to an abrupt halt. In the darkness it appeared the scout inched sideways, his arms out, feeling something with both hands.

Swallowing, he quickly glanced around him at the darkness seeming to swell around him. Donegan asked nervously, "What'd you find?"

"Shit!" Grouard squealed, and fell backward on his rump.

"What the hell is it?" Seamus demanded, his raspy voice louder now as he forced the question from a throat constricted in fear. Maybe the gruff edge he could bring to his words would scare away the ancient demons haunting him ever since the fall of darkness.

"It's a goddamned body."

"A body?" Donegan asked, dropping immediately to the ground. His own horse caught the scent of the corpse, yanking at the reins. "Man?"

"Yeah."

He joined the half-breed as Grouard knelt a second time over the dark shape. In what murky light the rind of moon and starlight could strain through the oilcloth covering of clouds, Seamus finally made out the unmistakable human form beneath them. Pale. Naked. White as the dust itself.

"His arms—" Grouard said.

"I see. They been cut off."

"When I put my hand out first time, I found his head."

"Ain't much left of it, is there?"

"No," the half-breed replied. "Scalped, and they smashed his face in."

"War club does a pretty job of that, don't it?" Donegan asked grimly. "A white man?"

"My bet'd be this fella was a soldier."

"Yeah. One of them what made the trail we been following." Seamus stood stiffly, feeling the pull in his legs after going so long in the saddle. Up and down the length of his thighs he rubbed with his palms in the way of a horseman gone afoot after hours of crossing rough country, working those leg and rump muscles in partnership with the animal below him.

Grouard stood slowly as well.

"Let's go," Donegan said hollowly, holding out Grouard's rein.

The half-breed's only answer was to take up the leather strap and fling himself into the saddle without using the stirrup from the off-hand side. With a sudden jerk he yanked the animal's head about to the north and set off once more into the darkness, straight up the long slope at the end of that narrow ridge running parallel with the river.

Twenty feet from the crest of the ridge Grouard's horse shied again, snorting, wheeling, once more fighting the bit. Frank brought it under control as Donegan came up, both scouts peering down at a second body, white as paste among the dust beneath that cloudy moonlight.

"We get up on top there," Frank whispered, "we likely won't run onto any more of 'em."

As much death as he had seen—men torn limb from limb by canister and grapeshot during the war, men wounded not by bullets but struck by the flying pieces of bone from other bodies torn apart by concussion shot, as well as the finest in mutilation handiwork practiced by the native inhabitants of the high plains—Seamus nevertheless found his heart beginning to hammer more loudly with its every beat thundering in his ears. All too soon he began to realize that what they had stumbled across wasn't a battle-field.

It was a slaughterhouse.

And when the cool breeze of the prairie night shifted to come out of the north, again carrying the promise of moisture on it as that breeze scurried beneath the thin clouds, Donegan caught the first whiff of decay. Mortifying flesh left to molder and rot, exposed to sun and time, left to bloat beneath the flight and crawl of countless insects already about their devilish work.

This . . . this was like Gettysburg.

"Frank, you smell that?"

"Yes," Grouard said, struggling to keep his mount pointed to the north, moving a bit west as he kicked the animal's coal-black flanks to leap up the last few yards to the very spine of that ridge.

As the two scouts reached the crest, those thin, ghostly clouds parted like the opening of a veil, casting a sudden, eerie light on the silvery ribbon of river below them.

"The Greasy Grass."

"Yeah," Seamus replied. "The Little Bighorn."

And as the clouds scudded back from the quarter rind of moon even more, the jumble of ridge and coulee, the cut and slash of ravines that fingered up from the east bank of the river, all revealed themselves to the horsemen. Exposing the dark clumps of four-legged beasts left moldering against the pale hue of ground and trampled grass. Among those huge carcasses lay the stark, ghostly white of crumpled human forms. Unstirred at this interruption to their sleep, never again to move. Left here beneath this hallowed sky to await another day of searing heat, and more bloating, and perhaps the coming of all the more predators to finish the work of life's great eternal circle.

Dust to bloody goddamned dust, Seamus thought, coughing with the sour taste at the back of his tongue as his nose came alive each time the breeze stiffened in his face. Just like rotting meat.

For as far as Seamus could see in the silvery light of

what star and moonshine had been allowed through the wispy, inky shreds of clouds speeding over their heads, the four-legged carcasses dotted both sides of the long ridge. And clustered here and there, everywhere for as far as he could see to the north, lay those pale, fish-bellied bodies. Much more than a hundred of them. More than two hundred ghosts.

"W-white men," Donegan muttered.

"They're soldiers," Grouard said. "*Were* soldiers."

"Blessed Virgin Mither of Christ," the Irishman whispered, crossing himself suddenly. His skin crawled. His eyes darted here, then there. Knowing he could never fight something he could not see. "I got to get out of here."

"I'm with you," the half-breed agreed, heeling his horse north along the hogback ridge.

Side by side they walked their horses, casting their eyes at times down to the bright sheen of that river ribboned below them, clear to the far bank, where the thick stands of tall cottonwoods revealed abandoned wickiup frames among a few pale cones—lodges for some reason left behind in the great village's departure.

Off to the left a coyote yipped in warning, snarled in anger, then snapped its jaws angrily at the riders and their horses before it tucked its tail and led a half-dozen others in loping long-legged down toward a deep ravine, where Donegan could hear the distant throat-gurgle, that distinctive canine growl of animals contesting one another over spoils. Some of the soldiers must have tried making it to the river.

And now the beasts were already working over the dead of this army.

For what seemed like hours they plodded their way north along the top of that ridge above the Greasy Grass, the oppressive, sickeningly sweetish stench of mortifying flesh mingled with the aroma of burned grass that was carried up from the valley floor and benchland west of the river by the breezes. This seemed to be a land laid to waste. Nothing left alive except the predators, both four-legged

and hard-shelled, at work on the bloated, gassy flesh. Nothing else alive, except for two intruders who had stumbled
onto this ridge where the two hundred would tomorrow
again lie beneath a blistering canopy of high-plains summer heat.

Yet by the time Grouard and Donegan reached the
northern end of the ridge where more than forty, perhaps
as many as fifty, bodies lay bunched a few yards down the
western slope, Seamus realized that even though their ride
along that hogback had seemed to take endless hours, it
had taken less than a dozen minutes as their horses nosed
their way through the stiff-legged carcasses and fish-bellied
corpses. Both horses had fought their bits, bobbing their
heads in disgust at the smell of decay every step of that
journey through this killing ground.

This had to be the same bunch that caught Crook's
army flat-footed on the Rosebud, Seamus thought. Had to
be. The big village was camped on the Rosebud—that
much they knew. Between then and now they crossed over
the mountains. Which meant that the same bunch that
came close to wiping out Crook a week later wiped out
these soldiers.

Injins what had me and the Snake scout surrounded
and all but dead . . . finished the job on these . . . these
men.

For longer than he dared remember, his mouth had
been painfully dry. With this slaughterhouse of death
around him, it was becoming harder and harder still to
concentrate on how he breathed—having to remind himself to inhale through his mouth and not through his nose.
Feeling the rotting stench like a crawling, wriggling, living
thing on the back of his tongue instead of smelling it.

What made that big man shudder in abject fear there
in the dark, there in the utter silence of that unmarked
graveyard, was that these had been the Indians he had
fought on the Rosebud, come face-to-face with, the warriors who almost killed him.

A few feet ahead Grouard halted his mount down the

slope from the northernmost end of that long ridge of death. He patted the animal's sleek black neck and said, "We better cross and see where the village is headed."

Seamus swallowed, shuddering unconsciously as he remembered standing over that soldier's fallen body when Royall began his retreat near the Rosebud, swinging his empty Henry against the onrushing red horde for what seemed like an eternity spent in hell.

Then he forced himself to say, "We both know where they're headed, Frank. There's no mistaking it."

"S'pose you're right," Grouard replied. "Moving south."

Donegan peered off into the eerie blackness at the dark humps of the hills that lost themselves as they thrust up against the cast-iron underbelly of the night sky. "Moving south . . . and heading straight for Crook's army."

It wasn't until that first graying of dawn shortly after moonset that Donegan and Grouard got themselves a good look at the immense trail heading toward the Bighorn Mountains. Less than an hour later they both caught the aroma of wood smoke on the wind.

"You said you know this country pretty good, Frank?"

Grouard nodded. "Lakota come to this ground to hunt last few years, yes."

"Where you figure they're going to be camped?"

"Maybe on up there, I suppose. Yes. On Pass Creek. Maybe down to the mouth of Twin Creek on what some call the Big Flat."

Donegan sighed, troubled. "Then if you know that much about the ground between us and them, you're gonna keep us as far away from them h'athens as you can—right?"

"Wrong, Irishman."

"Wrong?" he squeaked, his throat constricting, remembering that slaughterhouse along the bluff above the Little Bighorn.

"We gotta get close enough to figure out for sure what

they're gonna do, where they're headed for certain. Crook'll wanna know."

"Yeah, yeah. Crook'll wanna know. Blessed Mither of God, Grouard. I come along thinking this was going to be an Injin *scout*. Not a God-blame-ed Injin *fight*!"

"No fighting to do if you stick with me, Irishman."

"I'll remember you said that," Seamus growled. Then he eventually smiled. "And if there's fighting to do—by God, I'll make you eat your words, you half-breed son of a bitch."

Grouard grinned as he led off. Seamus could do nothing more than shake his head, and follow.

Now there were Indians between them and Crook's camp at Goose Creek. Enough Indians to slaughter more than two hundred pony soldiers back there on that ridge above the Greasy Grass.

More than enough to take care of two army scouts.

Chapter 8

27–28 June
1876

"You can't be serious about going over there to talk with that old man!" Seamus squealed, his throat cords constricting in surprise.

Grouard nodded, not even looking at the Irishman. Instead he continued to peer through the thick brush at the ancient Indian, who at that moment was driving some ponies from the fringe of a crowded lodge circle down to Twin Creek for water that early morning. "This is the first Lakota camp we come on. Maybe I can find out where they're heading—something."

"You're crazier'n I ever thought, Grouard."

"I figure that's got to be a compliment, coming from you, Irishman." He grinned. "Just make yourself small here till I get back."

"I'm gonna make myself real small, you half-witted son of a bitch. Damned small—what with you walking into the biggest goddamned Injin camp ever there was."

"Ain't walking in there," Grouard whispered back raspily. "Just gonna go dust off my Lakota some with that ol' man."

Unlashing his bedroll behind his saddle, Grouard pulled his old red blanket from its gum poncho and draped it over his head and shoulders, holding it together with one hand, while beneath the blanket he concealed the pistol he slipped from its holster. Through the thick brush and out onto a flat, it wasn't long before the half-breed caught up to the ponies that shied at first with the intruder's appearance, then settled and moseyed on toward the creekbank behind the lead horse.

Donegan couldn't make out either of the voices as Grouard hailed the old man, but he did hear a dog howl, then others bark, somewhere in that nearest Indian camp. After bumping into those four-legged predators on that battle ridge last night, just the sound of those Sioux canines was enough to raise the hair on the back of his neck, to make him shudder as he sat there in that thick brush drenched by the cold gray light of dawn in this valley of the Greasy Grass.

Seamus had turned, warily watching for any signs of movement off to his right in the direction of the first camp circle, when he heard the old Indian's frightened squawk. By the time Donegan jerked around to look, Grouard's blanket was off his head and shoulders, gathered in a clump under one arm as he sprinted back toward Donegan, yelling. The half-breed's voice was drowned out by the old man's continued warning cry as the Indian herder fled in the opposite direction from Grouard—down the creekbank and across the water toward the village.

"Get the goddamned horses!"

By the time he finally made out what Grouard was yelling, Donegan was up and moving himself. "You bet I'll get the bleeming horses!"

Yanking the animals out of the brush toward Grouard just as Frank came huffing up, Seamus vaulted onto the horse's back using only the saddle's big horn. The half-breed flung the red blanket at Donegan as he swept up the reins to the big black he rode.

"Where?" Donegan asked in a panic, gathering the old blanket across the saddle in front of him. "Which way?"

Sawing his mount's head around in a tight circle, Grouard answered, "Anywhere there ain't Injuns, you idiot!"

In the rosy hint of dawn together they kicked muscled flanks and dashed up Twin Creek, making for the western foothills lit with the first pale pink of the sun's rising, foothills that promised about the only cover available for their escape south, back to the Tongue River.

After two miles at a punishing gallop, Seamus finally asked, "What the hell you do to that old man?"

Grouard shrugged. "Just asked him some questions."

"Looks like you asked him the wrong questions," he growled.

"Wasn't that. Trouble started when he asked who I was and what camp I come from—then I told him my name."

"Jesus and Mary!" Seamus exclaimed, wagging his head. "You didn't tell him you were the *Grabber,* did you?"

Like a contrite, apologetic child, the half-breed answered, "Only thing I could think of was my Lakota name."

"By the saints! You're an idiot, Grouard! The whole Lakota nation knows Crazy Horse and Sitting Bull both want the Grabber real bad because they figure you betrayed them—and you go and tell him just who the hell you are!"

"Just ride, goddammit. No talk, Irishman. Just ride!"

On they raced another half-dozen miles, twisting in the saddle from time to time to look over their backtrail, before Donegan spotted any pursuers. By then the sun had come up, splashing not only the grassy slopes with summer's most golden radiance, but the lower valley as well. Hunters and hunted alike stood out on the rolling tumble of hill and coulee.

With each rise and fall of the land, Seamus measured the gait of the hard-muscled animal beneath him, sensing what he could of its every weakness as the horse slid down a slope, every imperceptible falter as the animal clambered back up the far side, then rolled again into a ground-eating gallop. He had to know if the mount was going to weaken, or slow, or just plain give out. If that was going to be the way of things, then he needed to know soon enough to choose a good place to make his stand, some spot with plenty of trees and rocks around. Somewhere he would make it hard on his hunters. A piece of ground where he could take as many of them as he could before they got to him.

But as the sun climbed higher into that cornflower-blue sky and he began to sweat like the heaving, lathered animal beneath him, Seamus began to allow himself the luxury of thinking they just might make it. As strong and well fed as those Sioux ponies were, they still weren't making up for the jump the two scouts had on their pursuers. At long last the sun fell from midsky and began to tumble ever so slowly into the western quadrant. Then, near dusk, Donegan finally recognized the land that stretched for miles ahead of them. Familiar ground.

He turned around in the saddle, finding that the hunters were still coming. They hadn't given up after a long day's chase over rugged, broken country.

Up ahead now that familiar land was almost like seeing home, it was. Home to a man who had been away for too damned long. Up there—how he wanted to hope—but that sure as hell looked like the Tongue River.

"There," Grouard said, the evening wind whipping his long black hair across his face as he turned to speak to Donegan. He pointed up the valley, indicating the timber-and-brush border of a stream that meandered toward the faraway Tongue.

"That creek bottom?"

The half-breed nodded. "Soldier Creek."

Down the long, long slope they raced as the sun back-lit the nearby Big Horns with a reddish-purple glow, washing away all but the heartiest of shadows. Time and again

Seamus turned to peer at their backtrail. Not sure if he could allow himself to hope any more than he already did. Not sure if that would hex what he hoped for most.

"They gave up," Grouard finally said it.

"I ain't seen 'em either, not in a long time."

"Maybe saving their ponies is all. They'll still hunt us," the half-breed sighed. "But maybe the hard chase is over."

"These horses could stand some rest, Grouard."

"Maybe we can take the chance—come dark."

Down in the brushy bottom of Soldier Creek they unsaddled their horses. After watering them, both men yanked up tufts of the tall grass and rubbed down the damp, glossy coats as the animals ate their fill.

"You sleep first, Irishman. I'll wake you later and you keep watch."

Seamus did not argue. He curled an arm under his head, pulled his lone blanket over his head, and didn't think of a thing until he felt Grouard nudging him, whispering.

"Your watch."

"For how long?"

"Rest of the night. Wake me before dawn," Grouard said wearily. "Now it's my turn to snore enough to wake the dead, just like you was doing."

"Wake the dead, did I?" Seamus grumbled as he sat up to rub the grit from his eyes.

Staying awake that night proved to be one of the hardest things he had ever had to do, what with having no sleep the night before when they stumbled onto that hallowed ground where so many good soldiers had given their greatest sacrifice. Throughout that long night and into the ashen, predawn gray of the twenty-eighth, the Irishman thought on those nameless ones, men unburied, left where they had fallen to a stronger foe.

And he thought on that long slope of Lodge Trail Ridge ten years gone, littered with the grotesque, frozen dead finally returned to Fort Phil Kearny, where they were consigned everlasting to God's hand and that Dakota soil.*

There were more, those fallen near that narrow, brushy island in the middle of an unnamed riverbed after those nine hot summer days fighting off Cheyenne.•

Then he thought on the soldiers who were killed in that desperate fight in the sulfurous no-man's-land of Black Mesa by the Modoc, who wanted only to live on the ground where they had buried their ancestors. And he remembered how the warriors had pulled back and disappeared—when they could have come in to finish the wounded. It would have been no hard task, after all, for those who weren't wounded and incapable of fighting were dead.†

Back in seventy-four the buffalo hunters he had thrown in with had buried their own right there in the sod beside the Myers and Leonard hide yard, after Quanah Parker had given up the bloody fight at Adobe Walls after five days, after discovering that their medicine man's power wasn't strong enough to protect them when they charged into the maw of those big-bore buffalo guns.‡

And he brooded on the bodies of the soldiers Colonel Reynolds ordered his Third Cavalry to leave behind after the subzero fight beside the thick ice crusted over Powder River.** More good men who would never know a grave. More families who would never be able to visit the final resting place of a fallen father, or husband, or son. The very same tragedy visited upon the loved ones of those brave men who had breathed their last beside Rosebud Creek a scant week before.†† Some child's father, some woman's husband, some parent's son.

So it was that he thought on Samantha, and how he

---

*The Plainsmen Series, Vol. 1, *Sioux Dawn.*
•The Plainsmen Series, Vol. 3, *The Stalkers.*
†The Plainsmen Series, Vol. 5, *Devil's Backbone.*
‡The Plainsmen Series, Vol. 7, *Dying Thunder.*
**The Plainsmen Series, Vol. 8, *Blood Song.*
††The Plainsmen Series, Vol. 9, *Reap the Whirlwind.*

missed her so terribly. Right down to the marrow of him. Sitting here in the darkness, in the middle of this last great hunting ground of the Sioux. Surrounded by thousands of warriors who had just finished off some army sent to defeat the roaming bands, sent to drive them back to their reservations. How he thought on her, and their child. The babe that Sam claimed would be Seamus's firstborn son.

"May he never know war," Donegan whispered to the silent night wind. "Dear God—if you ever answer a prayer of mine, answer this one. That this son of mine may never know war."

In the first coming of day's light Seamus shook Grouard awake, holding a finger to his lips. The half-breed's eyes widened as he heard the voices; then he nodded.

In the beginning Donegan had thought he caught himself dozing, dreaming, hearing voices as he slept. But no —he was awake, and those were men's voices he heard in the gray coming of morning. Trouble was, they spoke Sioux.

Leaving their horses in that clump of brush where they had spent the night, Grouard and Donegan crawled out on their bellies a few yards toward the voices—and discovered where their pursuers were camped. Not five hundred yards away.

Already up and stirring, the two dozen or so warriors were completing their toilet, freshening war paint, retying braids, and bringing their ponies into camp as they prepared to set off as soon as enough light let them follow a pair of tracks once more.

Grouard signaled with a thumb, indicating they should back up into the thick brush, where they savagely yanked their horses' heads to the side at the same time they heaved their shoulders into the animals to throw the mounts onto the ground. With some strips of thick latigo, on each animal they lashed three legs together, which would prevent the horses from rising. That done, they tied strips of blanket over the wide nostrils so the animals would not scent the war ponies. Then the men backed off through the brush.

Scrambling farther up the hillside, Grouard discovered an outcrop of sandstone that made for a narrow cave, where the two of them were forced to slide in feet first. From their rocky fortress that reminded a gloomy Donegan of an early grave, the pair kept an anxious watch on the valley floor as well as on that long slope below them, all the way down to the timber where they had cached the horses, throughout that summer's morning and into the hot afternoon, long after the war party finally departed, riding off to the southeast, away from the foothills.

It wasn't until after the sun had set behind them that the two dragged themselves from their narrow hole and rubbed sore, stiff muscles. Down in the timber they untied their horses, resaddled, and set off at moonrise. Angling away from the valley where the warriors had headed, Grouard and Donegan decided their only choice was to hug the foothills, making for a longer trail back to Crook's Camp Cloud Peak.

"Still say that was a damned-fool stunt you pulled back there at the Injin village," Donegan grumbled late that night after the stars came out.

"What stunt?"

"Going down to talk to that old Injin," Seamus replied. "Why didn't we just ride around that village?"

"You know how big that son of a bitch was?"

With a shrug Donegan complained, "So—I'm still waiting for you to tell me why you went and told that old man what your Injin name was."

Grinning, Grouard replied, "I only claimed I was one of the best scouts on the northern plains, Irishman. Never said I could think fast on my feet."

With the return of Frank Grouard and the Irishman, rumors began to run as deep and swift as runoff in spring through the army's camp. Most doubted the pair's claim concerning their nighttime journey through the battlefield littered with dead soldiers—the very same skeptics who doubted both the size of the enemy village as well as the number of hostile warriors the two scouts were estimating for the general.

As the object of so much jovial banter, if not downright derision, Grouard and Donegan kept to themselves after reaching the Goose Creek camp, refusing even to say anything about their adventures to John Finerty.

"Not even to tell your story to a fellow Patlander?" the reporter prodded Donegan.

"Go away, Finerty," the scout growled, pulling his hat back over his face.

For a moment more John stared down at Donegan, the tall scout stretched out in a respectable piece of shade that Saturday morning, his ankles crossed and flicking a finger now and then at an annoying deerfly.

One last time the newsman asked, "Maybe you'll want to tell me by the time I get back, eh?"

"Good-bye, Finerty."

"Only gonna be gone just a few days with Crook."

"You already told me," Donegan said, his words muffled beneath the crown of the wide-brimmed hat pulled fully over his face. "So be off with you."

"Hunting's said to be good up there. Sure you don't want to join us and enjoy yourself after your harrowing experiences?"

"I'll skin you myself if you don't leave me be," Seamus grumped.

"Suit yourself, Seamus."

When the Irishman did not reply, Finerty turned and strode back through the cavalry camp toward Crook's headquarters, leading his mount, all packed and ready for the general's hunt into the recesses of the Big Horn Mountains. He wasn't the only correspondent making the sojourn: Joe Wasson, correspondent not only for the New York *Tribune* but for the Philadelphia *Press* and the San Francisco *Alta California,* along with Robert Strahorn of Denver's *Rocky Mountain News,* and Reuben Davenport of the New York *Herald* were going along as well, all four of them invited by Crook to join him and a party of officers on their leisurely excursion. As curious as any man could be, but cursed because he was more prone to boredom than most, the restive reporter for the Chicago *Times* jumped at the chance to flee the army's camp and do something, any-thing.

Anything after a week and a half of lounging about in a place with so many men and not a single woman—not even that dish-faced Calamity Jane Cannary—not to men-tion that out of a thousand soldiers there was very, very little money to be won at cards. Why, the officers were down to wagering tins of peaches or tomatoes on horse- and footraces, perhaps even placing bets on who would catch the most or the biggest fish each day. Fishing was a pleasant enough sport, as long as a man could practice its fine arts from a patch of shade. While the evenings were delightfully cool, the days had a stifling sameness to them: by eleven o'clock the heat had become unbearable, lasting until well past five. In those same hours of torment, horse-flies, deerflies, all sorts of biting, buzzing, winged torture—including the omnipresent mosquitoes—drove the men and animals mad with their incessant cruelty.

At long last came the respite of each evening, times when Finerty repeatedly pressed John Bourke to regale them all with tales of his adventures with Crook in the Arizona campaigns, at least when the newsman couldn't lay his hands on one of those well-traveled paperback books so many were borrowing from the small personal library of Captain Peter D. Vroom or Lieutenant Augustus C. Paul, both of the Third Cavalry. Oh, to have even a dime novel to read! A poem by Walt Whitman! Even a reading tract of a temperance lecture delivered by Deacon Bross or one of Brother Moody's uplifting speeches on his spiritual hope for mankind!

Driven to collecting gossip and what bits of news he could glean from those thirty Montana miners who had wandered into camp from over on the Tongue River before the Rosebud fight—none of it kept Finerty interested for all that long. It damned well all had a way of wearing pretty thin on a young, outgoing fellow from the sociable streets of Chicago. Why, in that lazy camp there wasn't so much as a glass of warm beer to be had, much less the numbing taste of strong whiskey—not so much as a cigar! A man had to content himself with government tobacco, sold by the plug or pouch.

Even Sundays no longer held their special significance for him: his one day off back in Chicago. Here by the Big Horns, Sunday was just one of the seven every one of them had to endure, one after another until Crook decided they would march again. Deep in the cold of last winter he figured he would be home by spring—the Sioux campaign over and the hostiles driven back to their agencies. After Reynolds's debacle on the Powder, Finerty revised his thinking and figured that it might take one more campaign —this time with more killing and less driving. But after their fight on the Rosebud, Crook limped back here to lick his wounds.

And now, by God—it looked like this was going to be a summer campaign. If not longer!

Came the times when John wished he had packed it in with the cough-racked MacMillan, who'd gone south with the wagons for resupply at Fetterman. If nothing else, Finerty figured he could fight boredom by spending a few hours at Kid Slaymaker's Hog Ranch across the river from the post before the teamsters would have everything loaded and be turning about for a return trip to the camp at Goose Creek. Ah, just a little heady potheen to drink and the sweet fragrance of a moist, fleshy woman.

So it would be a trip to the mountains for him and the general. After the excitement of getting his story of the Crazy Horse fight written with a dateline of 17 June, "Banks of the Rosebud," then finding a suitable courier who would accept pay to carry John's dispatch down to Fetterman so that it could be telegraphed back to Chicago, things all too quickly had become ho-hum. Now after a week and a half of waiting to learn if his story had made it back to his editor, Finerty was growing more and more convinced no courier could be trusted. They were vermin, nothing more than an annoyance to a war correspondent.

But what ate at Finerty the most was that he had come to the conclusion that Crook was now intending to make an entire summer's campaign out of this—something no man, officer, soldier, or civilian had expected back in May when they'd put Fort Fetterman at their backs.

With the Big Horns scraping the clouds south and west of the camp, a grouping of wall tents pitched on the flats along the north bank of Goose Creek indicated the headquarters of Crook's Big Horn and Yellowstone Expedition. For hundreds of yards on either side of the general's camp stretched row upon row upon row of the small A-tents pitched by the infantry. Across the creek the horse soldiers had raised their neat rows of identical dog tents.

As pleasing as the scene was to his newsman's eye, John Finerty was more than ready to flee to the mountains. Why, the way he was feeling, he might even accept something a bit more strenuous than a mere hunt in the Big Horns—he might even welcome another chance to pit himself against the hostiles.

Just as long as it ended as the Rosebud fight had— with Crazy Horse turning tail and running at the end of the day.

Sure enough, Finerty thought as he halted his loaded horses near John Bourke, William B. Royall, and the rest who would accompany Crook into the mountains—he might just welcome another good fight of it.

Even that, simply to fend off the boredom.

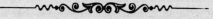

Chapter 9

First Days of July
1876

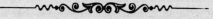

There was no way John Bourke would have stayed in camp and not gone to the mountains with the general. Only a team of Tom Moore's most ornery, stubborn mules could have held him back.

Besides the four reporters, Crook had invited Lieutenant Colonel William B. Royall, commanding officer of the Third Cavalry; Royall's adjutant, Lieutenant Henry R. Lemly; Captain Andrew S. Burt of the Ninth Infantry; Captain Anson Mills of the Third Cavalry; Lieutenant William L. Carpenter of the Ninth Infantry; and Lieutenant Walter S. Schuyler, on detached service from the Fifth Cavalry and serving as one of Crook's aides. To handle the packing chores, Tom Moore had selected a man named Young, one of his assistant packers, to ramrod a half-dozen civilians who accompanied the general's party out of camp that Saturday, the first of July. Mounted entirely on mules, each man in the group carried provisions for four days.

After a two-hour ride that morning through forests bristling with pine and fir, following the trail the Shoshone Indians had taken upon departing for their Wind River

Reservation back on the nineteenth of June, the hunting party reached a grassy plateau watered by several icy streams that ran right out of the glaciers poised above them, a meadow delightfully carpeted with countless species of mountain wildflowers. After a short stop to rest the mules, the group pushed on, finding the narrow trail growing increasingly difficult.

"I thought an Indian always picked the easiest route," complained Joe Wasson as they lumbered ever upward in single file.

"Not when those Indians figure the Sioux might follow them," instructed Captain Mills. "The Snakes took the hardest trail they could because they know the enemy might soon be in these hills to cut lodgepoles and run across their trail."

"Will you look at that, gentlemen?" Crook said a few minutes later, stopping his mule and turning in the saddle to take in the entire panorama that lay before them.

"Utterly beautiful," John Finerty offered.

Bourke himself was struck speechless for the moment, looking down upon the view fanned out below their feet. From the headwaters of the Little Bighorn River far to their left, all the way to the ocher mounds of Pumpkin Buttes out on the broken plains, on south to the land of the Crazy Woman and Clear creeks, the lieutenant could not remember seeing anything more beautiful than what he beheld at that moment.

Crook took his time surveying the country to the north of their base camp with his field glasses before he sighed disgustedly and snapped them shut in the leather case he had strapped over his shoulder.

Royall inquired, "You see anything at all of the enemy, General?"

"Not a damned thing."

"No smoke, not even some telltale dust, sir?" asked Mills.

Shaking his head, Crook replied, "I must admit I'm more than disappointed. I'm damn well depressed. Here I was hoping that by coming up here on this hunt, I'd discover more than just a few days of relaxation. By damned—I was figuring on seeing some clue as to Terry's whereabouts."

"Maybe he's got the hostiles cornered on the Yellowstone, General," suggested Burt.

Finerty chuckled, saying, "Better that we don't see a damned thing, General Crook, than find that huge village headed our way."

"Always the optimist you are, Mr. Finerty," Crook said with a wry grin. "Damn, but aren't you Irishmen always the optimists!"

With every mile's climb growing tougher on the mules, by midafternoon Crook called it quits in a beautiful meadow on the headwaters of a branch of Goose Creek itself. All about them lay trees long ago uprooted by the force of winter gales, and in every direction ran spidery-thin game trails, although not one man among them had seen anything to shoot for their supper kettle. With trout breaking the surface of a nearby stream, a few attempted some fishing but could not lure a single cutthroat or brown to what they used for bait. Not until the shadows had lengthened did Crook return to camp with a black-tailed deer.

"From up on top," the general said, pointing upslope with his rifle after he had pulled the carcass from his mule's back, "the whole range is dotted with tiny lakes just like those we passed in the last hour or so of our climb."

Against appetites whetted by the strenuous work, the fresh meat from that one deer, along with strips of bacon and fresh-baked pan bread, all quickly disappeared before the men leaned back onto their beds of pine boughs cut for fragrant mattresses and lit their pipes. As the sun went down on the far side of the snowy granite peaks just above them, the men began to huddle ever closer to the fires, pulling their blankets more snugly about their shoulders. It startled Bourke just how cold it could get in the mountains here in the heart of summer.

Setting off the next morning, the hunters climbed ever upward on a trail of their own making, every few yards crossing tiny rivulets of freezing runoff that spilled from snowbanks still found here and there back in the deepest shadows of thick timber. Wild flax grew in abundance, as well as a profusion of harebells, forget-me-nots, sunflowers, and the wild rose they already discovered on the plains below, along the creek that bore its name. It would be a case of their finding the beauty before the unbearable.

By midmorning their climb had become a torturous exercise in endurance. The stands of fir and pine thinned as they neared timberline, making for a growing number of alpine meadows crisscrossed by so many icy streams that they were forced to slog through virtual bogs. Man and mule struggled onward with the greatest exertion, stumbling across what first looked like solid ground but was quickly discovered as being nothing more than a thick layer of decaying pine needles crusted over an icy pond. Time and again they all fell, climbing back out of the cold, muddy bogs to shiver as they planted another sucking foot or hoof in front of the last still buried up to the ankle, or deeper yet, in the pasty ooze. Everywhere deadfall and huge outcrops of smooth-faced granite the size of railroad cars impeded their path. Above their struggles loomed the immensity of Cloud Peak itself, dwarfing everything below it, especially a dozen puny men and their pack-train.

At long last they struggled out of the final vestiges of dwarf pine and juniper to stand above timberline itself, struggling those last few hundred years in the thin air to reach the shore of a narrow, crystalline mountain lake that fed both the Tongue River on the east, as well as the Big Horn and Grey Bull to the west. Huge bobbing cakes of thick ice marred its wind-furred surface. At the edges of the slowly retreating banks of crusty snow along the lake's shore raised the tiny blue heads of the dainty forget-me-nots. Off to the west and northwest they could make out still higher ranges likewise covered with a mantle of white even at this late season.

"I must admit," Mills said, huffing slightly with the rest, "I have traveled some in Europe and have seen many a gorgeous landscape in my years—but I will tell you here and now that I have never laid my eyes on anything quite as beautiful as this."

His heart pounding with its cry as his lungs drank deep with every breath, Bourke could not believe he had actually made it there, where it seemed they stood on top of the world. Below lay the last great hunting ground the hostiles were mightily set upon defending to the death. Far to the east came that rush of civilization ever westward, with the army as their spear point. But for these ageless forests and these huge granite spires towering against this sky since time immemorial, for the earth where the lieutenant stood at this very moment, such events of war and the clash of cultures meant little.

As tired as his legs were, Bourke stood gazing slack-jawed at it all for the longest time before he sat upon an icy snowbank and made notes in his journal. Before he put the journal away in his wool coat, the lieutenant thought to pick some of the tiny flowers, pressing them carefully between the blank pages of his book.

After halting atop that windy crest for half an hour, Crook pushed on west, across another divide, where they one and all marveled at the distant Wind River Range before beginning a slow, arduous descent to timberline, on through another forest thick with pine and spruce, noisy with foamy cascades and beautified with glass-topped pools and bubbling springs, until the sun began to fall toward its western bed. While the rest went into bivouac, Crook and Schuyler went off in search of game and returned an hour later with a pair of bighorn mountain sheep. No more than a few minutes from camp, Bourke found a snowfield the side of which had been slowly eroded by the wind, exposing the unmelted icy strata to a depth of some sixty feet— snow that he supposed in all likelihood would never melt to flow down to the Bighorn River. Snows that might well have rested there for hundreds of years.

While the sun's light remained in the sky, deerflies, titlarks, and butterflies flitted about through the trees, as well as the ever-present and troublesome mosquitoes. But once the sun disappeared and the air cooled at an amazing pace, no more was man nor beast bothered by buzz or sting.

"I want to return to camp by Tuesday afternoon," Crook announced that night after their supper of mountain mutton and boiled elk heart. "So you may hunt until noon tomorrow—when we'll depart for camp."

"Tuesday—that would be the fourth," Davenport said in sudden realization.

"Yes!" Mills cheered. "The Fourth of July!"

"Bloody good, General!" Royall agreed. "The Centennial Fourth."

"I wouldn't miss that celebration in camp for a go at all the Kid's girls at the Hog Ranch!" Finerty exclaimed.

"Well said, my young correspondent," Crook replied. "There will only be one Centennial Fourth—and we should all spend it with the men of the Big Horn and Yellowstone Expedition."

"Hurrah!" Bourke shouted.

Wasson raised his coffee tin and cried, "Hurrah for the birthday of our Grand Republic!"

True to his word the following day, Crook packed up and departed camp at noon, even though Finerty and Mills had not returned from their morning's hunt.

"Should I stay behind, General?" Bourke asked.

"What purpose would that serve, John?"

Bourke shrugged.

"Exactly," Crook answered. "They'll make it back when they make it back. And when they do, they'll find us gone. They, like any of us would do, will just have to follow our trail back over the crest."

"You're certain, sir? I was just hoping you'd—"

"All right, John. I'll leave one of the packers here to wait for our two tardy boys—if that'll make you feel any better."

By six o'clock the trio of laggards caught up with Crook's party, and the general ordered them all to bivouac in a grassy mountain glen, where, over their cheery supper fires, Finerty and Mills recounted their tale of making it all the way to the western reaches of the Big Horns until they looked down upon the great open expanse of the undulating desert basin.

Throwing back his blankets the next morning, Bourke discovered it had snowed through the night. The bracing cold and surprising return of winter at this altitude seemed to invigorate the men, who had a snowball fight as their breakfast coffee boiled and bacon sizzled in the skillets resting over dancing flames. With a stern reminder from Crook that they needed to be making for Camp Cloud Peak, the party packed up to continue their downhill trek, reaching Goose Creek just past noon that Centennial Fourth.

Come evening as the camp reveled as best it could on coffee, hardtack, beans, and bacon, John Bourke strode over to the Irishman's fire and joined in the salutes and toasts the men were offering one another. "You're as American as any man now, Seamus Donegan!"

"You really think so, do you?"

"Aye," John Finerty agreed. "My blood and yours may come from that blessed Isle of Eire, Seamus—but it's our hearts that make us Americans. Now and forevermore."

"To America—the last great hope of all democracies!" Robert Strahorn cried, raising his cup of steaming coffee as twilight fell.

"To our blessed country," old Dick Closter added his voice.

"And to that beautiful wife of yours, Seamus," Bourke said, suddenly remembering Samantha left safely back at Fort Laramie.

"To the Irishman, our new American!" Wasson said. "And all those little Americans yet to be born in this land of freedom!"

Hoisting his own cup of black coffee, Bourke added, "Long may our beloved Star-Spangled Banner wave!"

*   *   *

He stared out the window of his spacious office at Fort Leavenworth, Kansas, at the massive flagpole planted in the center of the parade. How those Stars and Stripes tossed in the midsummer breeze.

This, the greatest nation on earth.

With her powerful cavalry just been wiped out on the Little Bighorn.

Nelson A. Miles, colonel and commander of the Fifth Infantry, stared at the banner snapping high in the air of the central plains, and thought on Custer.

"Damn, but you were a shooting star, weren't you, Armstrong?"

Turning from the window, Miles settled back against the horsehair-stuffed cushion on his well-used chair. How he wished George Crook had given him the chance Alfred Terry had given Custer. It was too early, far too early, to know just what the hell had happened that made Armstrong get his unit swallowed up by those primitive savages —surely, it must have been some grave tactical error: dividing his forces when confronting an overwhelming enemy; perhaps running out of ammunition at a critical time in the battle only to discover he was too far from his lines of supply; or . . . something, by damned! There had to be a reason why Custer finally went and did it.

"Hell, you were a tragedy waiting to happen," Miles murmured to himself. "It could have happened on the Washita—we both knew that—but you pulled your fat from the fire just in time down there, didn't you?"

For a few minutes more he stared at the yellow telegraph flimsy in his hand, struggling to have the disaster in Montana Territory make sense to him. For so long he and Custer had been, by and large, the friendliest of rivals. Armstrong the darling of the army's cavalry, Miles the finest infantry officer ever to set a marching boot down on the plains. And, Nelson had to admit time and again, both of them exhibited about the same high opinion of himself.

That was, after all, what drove the few, the chosen, the fated to greatness, wasn't it?

"Was it just your moment come, Armstrong? Was it . . . your turn at immortality, goddammit?"

Laying a flat hand over the flimsy, Miles pushed himself up and away from the desk, stepping over to the window again. Outside, the shocking news was already spreading like prairie fire. He could see the knots of officers and enlisted gathering. You didn't keep this sort of thing quiet when it came in on the wire from department headquarters in Omaha, transferred in from Division HQ in Chicago. For the moment Sheridan was off making a nuisance of himself at Fort Laramie, out there somewhere.

The dark and dashingly handsome Miles wondered how the little Irish general was taking it. For so long Custer had been his darling. His protégé. He and Sherman were grooming the dashing cavalry officer for greatness—then Armstrong went and did one foolish, impetuous thing after another. And in the past few months even Sheridan had given up protecting Custer, on ever seeing Custer rise to command his own regiment.

So how was Sheridan taking it? Was he stunned? Was he angry beyond belief? Was he at this very moment throwing everything he had against the hostiles who had killed his very own wunderkind?

When would Sheridan ever learn where he should put his trust?

Miles shook his head. Hell, when would his wife's own uncle, William Tecumseh Sherman, learn?

Just days ago word came that Nelson's most bitter rival, George Crook, had battled Crazy Horse to a standstill before retreating to Goose Creek.

"Son of a bitch is licking his wounds, by God!" Miles grumbled. "And I bet that's where he'll sit until Sheridan sends him enough troops to surround the Black Hills!"

Shit, he thought, curling up the end of his long mustache. Sherman and Sheridan had better give him a chance at Sitting Bull and all those savages that went and chewed up Terry's finest cavalry. At long last they better give Nelson Miles and the Fifth Infantry a chance at closing that bloody chapter on the northern plains.

That is, if Sherman and Sheridan were really serious about ending the Indian problem once and for all.

If the army brass thought they were going to keep Nelson Miles sitting on his thumbs here at Leavenworth while sending Lieutenant Colonel Joseph Whistler to lead Miles's own Fifth Infantry north to whip the Sioux—those fat-bottoms in Washington City had another thing to think over!

In a flurry he whirled from the window and plopped himself back into his chair, taking up a lead pencil. On a single sheet of long paper he began composing the telegram he would send to Sherman. Starting here and now he would badger the brass in the War Department until he secured his field command. By damn, he sure as hell wouldn't let Whistler go marching off with Nelson Miles's Fifth Infantry! Not when there were glories to be won whipping Sitting Bull out there on the Yellowstone and the Tongue and the Powder!

Once they gave Colonel Nelson A. Miles his orders for field command—they'd have this Sioux War all but ended!

Nelson knew there wasn't a thing he could not do: from defeating the hostile Sioux and Cheyenne, to getting himself elected President of the Republic. He had been careful, damned careful, charting every move, every step along the way throughout his career. His education at the Academy, even his marriage to just the right niece—it all laid the foundation for what should have made Nelson Miles the greatest commander in the history of the Army of the West. Right up there in the military texts with Washington, Taylor, and Grant.

"But now you've gone and done this to me, Armstrong," he groaned softly as he flung down the pencil, then rose to stare out the window. Gently laying his forehead against the mullioned windowpane, Miles stared out at the sun-splashed parade where the buzz of tragedy continued unabated.

"Dammit—how am I ever going to compete with the memory of a dead man? How can I, a mere mortal, Armstrong—ever hope to compete with you again—now that you've become a legend on that bloody hillside somewhere in Montana? Now that you've become a symbol of our national honor that must be avenged? Now that you've become a myth? Bigger than you ever were until that day you fell, bigger than you'd ever been in life?"

Chapter 10

6 July 1876

THE LITTLE HORN MASSACRE

Confirmation of the Disaster.

Special Dispatch to the New York Times
CHICAGO, July 6—At the headquarters of Lieut. Gen. Sheridan this morning all was bustle and confusion over the reported massacre of Custer's command. Telegrams were being constantly received, but most of them were of a confidential nature and were withheld from publication.

DETAILS OF THE BATTLE

Graphic description of the fighting—
Major Reno's command under fire
for two days—every man of Custer's
detachment killed except one
scout—affecting scenes when
relief arrived.

Special Dispatch to the New York Times
CHICAGO, July 6—A special to the *Times* to-night

from Bismarck, recounts most graphically the late encounter with the Indians on the Little Big Horn.

"All? All of them?" Samantha asked, her voice barely audible.

Nettie Meinhold gripped the newspaper, her elbows outflung to keep from getting herself crushed by the press of female bodies all wanting to read the story for themselves. The stocky, German workhorse of a woman bellowed above the clamor, "Quiet!"

Some of the women backed away somewhat, and Third Cavalry Captain Charles Meinhold's wife shook the paper indignantly. "This is my newspaper, and I'll read the stories to you again if you'll be kind enough to listen. I'm just as worried as any of you."

"Custer's really dead," murmured a full-bodied woman beside Sam who reminded Samantha of her mother. "Hard to believe."

Nettie Meinhold reminded, "It says so right here."

"But n-not all of them?" Samantha asked again.

"No," one of the other women growled with that aggression born of great fear, her eyes brimming with worry, glistening with tears. Her lower lip trembled as she turned away.

That was just the way Sam felt. Trying to control herself, to keep from crying like all those who had hid their faces at the first reading of the newspaper's banner headlines. Some just weren't able to bear up under the bloody truth.

"Those are savages!" one of them cried out in anguish, sobbing in her hands.

Another groaned, "They say you won't find a better unit in this army than Custer's Seventh!"

"Listen to you!" Emma Van Vliet snapped angrily, her arms flying like a big bird's wings. "Here we are—wives of the Second and the Third—every last one of us . . . and you're knuckling under saying Custer and his Seventh were the best?"

"To fall . . . all of them—"

Someone whined, "It wasn't all of them!"

"Only half the regiment!"

Mrs. Van Vliet growled at them, "They weren't the best. Not to be crushed like they were—"

"Still, dear God! Half a regiment!"

Nettie Meinhold tried calming them a moment. "Listen, Custer and his Seventh couldn't be the best. Look what happened to them. Why, to be defeated by a bunch of godless savages?"

Mrs. Dorothea Andrews inched forward, saying, "Don't you all realize they're the same Indians our men are marching against?"

Somewhere in that knot of fearful wives one of the women went weak-kneed, crying out, "Dear Father in heaven!"

Two others caught the woman as she began to crumple there on the porch to Old Bedlam, and struggled through the crowd with their burden, heading for the door.

Over and over Sam hypnotically rubbed her hand across her belly, feeling faint, hearing the women moaning, wailing, sobbing, and crying for those wives who had lost their men far to the north on a dusty summer hillside. Army wives understood loss.

And the shocking news that was that day careening across the nation like a black cloud of evil portent brought worse than worry to the women waiting at Fort Laramie.

They had husbands with Crook. Men like those who had marched off to war with Custer.

Putting out a hand, Sam kept from falling, light-headed, bracing herself against a pole supporting the porch awning.

Oh, Seamus!

A few women sobbed into their aprons or hands, but a few cursed as saltily as any veteran teamster, reviling against the Indians who had butchered the Seventh. Against the Indians who might be closing in on Crook at that very moment.

Oh, Seamus, my love! God, watch over him!

She leaned her head against the post and closed her eyes, attempting to conjure an image of Seamus . . . so far away.

Will Crook's men be the next to march into the maw of death?

"I suppose you're here to plead your case too, Mr. Donegan," George Crook said with a wry grin inside his strawberry beard tied up with red braid that Thursday morning, 6 July.

"Yes, I am, General." For a moment Seamus flicked his eyes at the newspaperman from Chicago.

"Well—I've just approved of Mr. Finerty here going along with Lieutenant Sibley's escort."

Donegan replied, "He's the sort does like adventure, sir."

With that Finerty snorted. "Adventure's much better than dry-rotting around camp, Seamus."

John Bourke stepped over to slap the newsman on the back, saying cheerfully, "What sort of epitaph do you want me to have put on your gravestone, John?"

Crook nodded, his lips pursing briefly. "I'm not sure Mr. Finerty realizes he may get more adventure than he bargained for. Haven't you told him what happened to you and Frank on your scout north?"

"He told me, General," Finerty answered. "But I've made up my mind that I'm going to get out of camp every chance I can. What better way to inform my readers on just what an army campaign is but by sharing in every facet of an army campaign?"

"All right," Crook replied, turning to the commander of E Company, Second Cavalry. "Captain Wells, you'll see that our correspondent here is provisioned from your stores."

"Very well, General," said Elijah R. Wells, Second Cavalry, turning to his company's lieutenant. "Mr. Sibley—

you'll see that you bring Mr. Finerty a hundred rounds of Troop E ammunition?"

At the same time, Crook turned again to his Irish scout, scratching that red-hued beard flecked with the iron of his many winters, and of all his many campaigns. "Very well, Mr. Donegan. You'll accompany the escort and pack-mules I'm sending with Frank and Big Bat. I have no fear you'll make yourself more than useful."

"Good to have you along, Irishman," Grouard said, stepping forward to stand within that circle. "But I'll say it again, General—I don't need no soldiers along. I'll take the Irishman here—but you can keep your escort. They'll just make for trouble. Me and the other two can move quicker, keep out of sight better than a whole bunch of your soldiers can."

"Request denied, Grouard," Crook responded gruffly. "Lieutenant Sibley and his men will accompany you—and that's the last I want to hear of it. When can you be ready to depart, Lieutenant?"

Sibley stiffened, saying, "We'll pull out at noon, General."

So it was that Seamus volunteered to probe north with two of the army's most experienced scouts, the three of them to be escorted by Lieutenant Frederick W. Sibley, E Troop, Second Cavalry, who went on to handpick twenty-five men and mounts from the regiment for Crook's reconnaissance.

After Grouard and Donegan escaped from the Lakota camps somewhere to the north of Goose Creek and returned from their journey north, the expedition's commander wanted to know not only exactly where that enemy village was but some idea where it might be headed. In addition, Crook was hoping Grouard and Pourier could slip around the Sioux once again to make contact with the Crow and, as the pair of half-breeds had done before the Battle of the Rosebud, convince the tribe to send a good number of their warriors to fight alongside the soldiers when the Big Horn and Yellowstone Expedition resumed its campaign against the Lakota and Cheyenne.

With four days' rations Sibley's patrol got away just past noon, crossing Big Goose Creek to head northwest along the stream's bank for more than a dozen miles before Grouard told the lieutenant they were going into camp.

"Why are we stopping here?" Sibley asked as the scouts slid from their horses, his soldiers obediently remaining in their saddles.

"This is about as far as we're gonna go before dark," Frank explained, tossing up a stirrup so he could loosen the cinch.

"We'll go on after the sun goes down," Big Bat added from the far side of his mount.

Sibley clearly was not understanding. "But the general wants us to push north with all possible speed."

Donegan was slipping the curb bit from his horse's mouth after loosening the cinch. "And we will push on," Seamus confided. "But we won't go anywhere but to hell itself if we get spotted by one of those wandering war parties Bat and Frank saw a couple days back. Better for us to move on after dark."

While the soldiers had celebrated the Centennial Fourth of July, Grouard and Pourier had ventured north on the line of march Crook intended to take when he resumed the campaign. For the better part of two days they had probed north, angling over along the Tongue to the country where the enemy village appeared to be heading that last week in June when Frank and Seamus had made their miraculous escape. In the space of twenty miles the half-breeds had spotted several wandering war parties daringly close to the Goose Creek camp, intent on keeping an eye trained on whatever Three Stars would have up his sleeve.

It didn't take much more convincing than Donegan's reminder of just how the Sioux were running all over the territory for Sibley to grudgingly agree to wait out the sun's falling behind the Big Horns before they pushed on.

After boiling themselves some coffee while they sat out

the coming of darkness, the thirty-one riders were preparing to move out in dusk's dim light when Pourier cried out, "Look, Grouard!"

In the deepening shadows Seamus made out the murky form of a lone horseman lurking at the mouth of a nearby ravine. Without hesitation he and Grouard flung themselves into the saddle and kicked their horses into a furious pursuit. At the same instant the mysterious rider turned tail and disappeared over the crest of a hill. For the better part of a half hour they searched for the horseman without success in the deepening gloom. Back at the mouth of the ravine where the rider was first spotted, Grouard dropped to the ground beside Donegan.

Handing his reins to the half-breed, Seamus pulled a wooden lucifer from his vest pocket. With a scratch of his thumbnail the yellow flame leaped into the darkness with a flash. Kneeling, Donegan spotted what he had suspected. Tracks that confirmed his fear.

"Look's like they're gonna know we're coming."

"Damn," muttered Grouard. He glared across the hillside at the Sibley escort. "Damn them soldiers. Should've been just us three."

"Chances are, that red son of a bitch would have seen just us, Frank. Whether there was three or thirty of us—we would've still been spotted." He wagged the match out as soon as it scorched his fingers. Donegan pulled on his glove again.

"Think we ought to go back?" Grouard asked.

"If it were up to me—I'd say we try," Seamus admitted. "We could turn back now. Or we could turn back tomorrow, or the next day. I'm for making a try of it: seeing what we can find out, for as long as we can."

The half-breed smiled. "But just as long as I don't run us onto that village again, right?" Grouard asked as he rose to his feet with Donegan.

"Damn right. Just as long as you don't go down to talk with any of them red h'athens and tell 'em your bleeming name!"

He wagged his dark head. "No more talking to them Lakota."

"Frank," Seamus said confidentially, grabbing the half-breed's arm, "let's don't tell what we saw here."

"Why?"

He said in hushed tones, "Let's just tell 'em what we saw was an elk."

"Why not level with Sibley?"

"You want to be escorted by a bunch of sojurs any more edgy than that bunch with the lieutenant already is?"

"You got a point, Irishman. All right—a elk it was."

Donegan watched the half-breed raise his left leg painfully, almost like a man suffering an attack of severe rheumatism. "Something wrong, Frank?"

Grouard struggled twice before he got his boot stuffed into the stirrup, then raised himself slowly, settling into his saddle very gently. "Got me the white man's sleeping sickness."

"Sleeping sickness?"

"What a white man gets from sleeping with the wrong woman."

"You mean your pecker's weeping."

"Sore as anything I ever had," Grouard complained. "Can't even walk right . . . and sitting in this saddle's about to kill me."

"Maybe we get back to Crook's camp, you'll get one of those army surgeons to see what he can do for you."

"I know what they can do for me," Grouard grumbled with a shudder as Donegan climbed into the saddle. "They can cut my pecker off here and now. I don't ever plan on using it again."

"Leastways not with one of Kid Slaymaker's girls at the Hog Ranch."

The half-breed wagged his head dolefully. "Way I feel, I ever get well—this is one fella ain't never going in Slaymaker's doorway again."

That night the patrol made another twenty-five miles, marching northwest along the base of the Big Horns, mov-

ing through the tall grass and startling one covey of sage
hens after another into sudden flight.

"We're riding part of the old Fort Smith trail,"
Seamus said to Finerty just past eight o'clock when the
moon rose.

"Fort C. F. Smith? On the Big Horn?"

"That's right."

"How you know about that?"

"I spent a cold winter and a wet spring there—many a
year ago now. Hoping a friend down at Fort Phil Kearny
would join me and we'd make it on to the Montana gold-
fields over to Bannack and Alder Gulch."

"Jesus and Mary, Seamus!" Finerty gushed in the silvery light of that moonrise. "I'll bet you knew some of
them fellas who got trapped in the hayfield that August."

"Knew 'em, Johnny boy? I was with 'em."

"At . . . you were at the Hayfield Fight?"

"I was a civilian hay cutter." He shook his head with
the remembrance. "Aye, that summer's day we cut down a
lot more'n hay, John. Them red h'athens threw the best
they had at us nigh onto that whole day—before they give
up when the sojurs finally come marching out to relieve the
siege."

Sibley's voice came down the column, "Quiet in the
ranks!"

Finerty leaned over to whisper, "You'll tell me more
tomorrow? All about that fight?"

Seamus only nodded as they rode on, the moon continuing its rise behind them, illuminating the ground ahead
of the Sibley patrol. For the next few hours the only sound
was an occasional snort of a horse, the squeak of a McClellan saddle, or the click of iron shoes on streamside pebbles,
heady silence broken only by the occasional whispers of the
half-breed scouts as they conferred on the best trail to take.

Just past three A.M. as the first gray line of the sun's
rising leaked along the horizon to the east, Grouard turned
in his saddle to say, "Lieutenant—we oughtta think about
finding a place to camp."

"Daylight coming. Yes. By all means, Grouard."

"We'll rest here for a few hours before we see about going on," the half-breed said. "Pick some men to watch the horses, and wake us come sunup."

"Where you think we are now, Irishman?" Finerty asked after they had loosened cinches and picketed their animals in a sheltered ravine back among the foothills above the upper waters of the Tongue River.

"Not far from the Greasy Grass . . . the Little Bighorn."

The packer known as "Trailer Jack" Becker slid down into the grass nearby, dusting his britches off.

Donegan asked, "How's your mules, Jack?"

"They'll hold up better'n these'r army horses, that's for certain."

Donegan pulled his hat down over his face and laid his head back into the thick pillow of tall grass. "I don't doubt you're right about that at all."

It seemed as if he had no more than closed his eyes when Grouard was kicking the worn sole of Seamus's boot. He squinted and blinked, rubbing the grit from his eyes as he hacked up some night-gather and spit. The sun was making its daily debut out there on the plains.

"Come with me, Irishman."

They picked up Pourier on their way through the crowded bivouac. All three mounted and led out as the soldiers jostled into a column of twos, coming behind while Sibley himself clung to the scouts. After riding no more than a half mile, they were confronted with a tall, steep-sided bluff squarely on the trail they were taking.

"Lieutenant," Grouard declared, "take Bat and the Irishman with you into that ravine, yonder. I'll go up top on foot and glass what's below."

Sibley nodded and said, "Very well."

Grouard next turned to Bat and Donegan. "If you see me take my hat off, you boys come on up, pronto."

Seamus watched the half-breed move off less than a hundred yards before he dismounted and led his horse into the ravine with the rest of the party. From there he watched Grouard slip down on his belly just shy of the crest of the ridge, pull his field glasses from the pocket of his canvas mackinaw, and peer over. It wasn't but a heartbeat before Grouard tore off his floppy sombrero and waved it.

"C'mon," Pourier grumbled to Donegan as they leaped to the saddle and rode to the tree where Grouard had tied his big black.

"Looks like bad news," Donegan whispered as he slid down onto his belly beside Grouard.

"Here, Bat—take this glass and look and see if those are Injuns or just rocks over on that hill."

"My God—we are gone!" Pourier complained once he had himself a look. "Shit, Frank. The whole damn country's nasty with the red bastards!"

"Of course it is," Grouard replied, then added optimistically, "but—maybe they're Crows."

As quickly, Big Bat grumbled, "Remember last month? I'm the son of a bitch what knows the Crows. And them are Sioux."

"How you know for sure?" Seamus asked.

"When a war party of Crow are on the warpath, no man ever goes ahead of the leader," Bat explained. "But with the Sioux—it don't matter. Look yonder. See? That bunch closest down there ain't riding in no order. That's Sioux, I tell you."

"Lemme have a look," Donegan demanded, reaching for the field glasses.

Indeed, it did appear the whole valley of the Tongue far to the north of their ridge was blanketed with Indians already on the march—heading south toward the main channel of the river. But closer still was that war party of half a hundred, pushing south in advance of the main village.

Donegan gave the field glasses back to Grouard. "You remember the elk we saw last night, Frank?"

The half-breed nodded.

Pourier looked at them both, back and forth, then said, "Wasn't no elk, was it, fellas?"

"We been found out," Donegan said.

"That bunch right down there is heading this way to rub us out right now," Grouard declared.

"They won't find us on the river," Donegan said, his mind working fast. "The way they're headed right now."

"But they're bound to pick up our tracks easy enough," Pourier added.

"You go get those soldiers moving," Grouard said. "I'll stay up here and watch those Injuns—see when they come on our tracks. Take the lieutenant's men up the ravine into the hills."

With Big Bat, Donegan whirled about and slid back down the steep slope to reach their horses. Not long after they returned to Sibley's patrol and got the soldiers started up the narrowing ravine, he saw Grouard wave his hat again.

"I figure that means they've crossed our tracks, Irishman," Pourier grumped.

"Yeah—Frank's beating a retreat now."

Seamus said, "We stand a better chance of getting away in the hills—"

"Or even holding 'em off," Pourier interrupted.

Seamus said, "I'm with you: let's see what we can do to stay out of their way."

By the time they reached the bottom of the trail that the Indians had used for years to go into the Big Horn Mountains to cut lodgepoles,* Grouard was no more than a hundred yards behind them . . . the war party screeching only a half mile behind him. The next time Donegan turned to look down their backtrail, he found the warriors streaming off the trail, along the side of the slope.

"They're going for the head of Twin Creek," Grouard said, the morning's breeze nuzzling his long hair across his eyes.

---

*Just above the present-day town of Dayton, Wyoming.

Seamus asked, "Gonna try to cut us off?"

"Yeah," answered Pourier. "Some of 'em are waiting there on the trail so we don't go back down the mountain."

Sure enough, a dozen or so of the war party had halted and milled about on the soldiers' backtrail.

"You figure they got us shut in, Frank?" inquired Big Bat.

"Good as they can."

Sibley reined about and rode back to join the three scouts, asking, "What chance do we have to outrun them, Grouard?"

"That's our only chance. You keep your men moving as fast as the horses will carry them. Tell your boys not to save anything—those horses have to run and climb faster'n those Injun ponies!"

Putting heels to his mount, Grouard was soon out of sight, headed into the thick timber as Pourier and Donegan urged the soldiers on up the lodgepole gatherers' trail.

After a rugged climb of more than five miles in the space of some two hours atop the wearying horses, Sibley remarked to the scouts, "I haven't seen any Indians for some time now."

"Me neither," Bat admitted.

"Doesn't mean they're not down there," Donegan said.

Sibley sighed, slowing his mount at the top of the low rise, where he peered into a wide, grassy bowl. "We'll halt over there."

"Halt?" Big Bat exclaimed. "For what?"

"We've got to make some coffee for these men— they've had nothing to eat for more than a day and a half. At least a little coffee—"

"I'd advise against it, Lieutenant," Donegan grouched. And as he watched, Sibley and his sergeants slid from their mounts, beginning to unsaddle. "No—don't take them saddles off, fellas!"

"You won't be ready if we get surprised and gotta ride out in a hurry!" Pourier advised.

The savvy advice did not matter. It didn't take long for the soldiers to have their horses unsaddled and coffee fires smoking. Donegan took a few sips of the offered brew, his anxious eyes nonetheless prowling the backtrail where it emerged from the line of timber below them. He expected to hear gunshots at any moment, announcing the arrival of the warriors—perhaps war cries on the slope above them from those who had jumped Grouard at the Twin Creek trailhead. A few minutes later, to Donegan's great relief, the half-breed appeared.

Reining up, with wide eyes, Grouard demanded, "You stopped for coffee?"

Sibley asked, "Care for some?"

"Might as well join us, Frank," Donegan said with a shrug.

As Grouard slid painfully from his saddle, Pourier turned to Finerty, saying, "You came along to have yourself a big adventure, didn't you, John?"

Finerty nodded, peering at the half-breed over the lip of his cup.

Seamus nudged the reporter and declared, "That's what you told us, Johnny boy. Have yourself a big adventure."

Big Bat continued. "You know why we haven't been caught here drinking coffee, don't you, John?"

The newsman's brow crinkled suspiciously. "No—why?"

"Because the Sioux are waiting up there, on up where they got a ambush laid for us."

"An ambush?" Finerty squealed. "God-*damn*! Quit pulling my leg!"

Donegan said, "I figure Bat's probably right, Johnny."

Finerty grew fidgety, his hands flitting, spilling some coffee. "Ambush! This'll bloody well be the last scout I ever come on!"

"Tried to tell you," Grouard said with a nod. "I'm afraid Bat's right: we likely got a warm time coming."

"But don't you worry, Johnny boy," Donegan cheered,

slapping the newsman's knee, "when this is all over—you'll have lots of good stories to send back to your readers in the East."

"If he makes it out alive," Bat added with a grin. "I got a feeling Finerty's big adventure in Injun country is only starting."

Chapter 11

First Week of July
1876

THE LITTLE HORN MASSACRE

THE CAUSES AND CONSEQUENCES

Fruits of the ill-advised Black Hills
Expedition of two years ago—
Ability of the army to renew
operations effectively discussed—
the personnel of the charging
party still undefined.

Special Dispatch to the New York Times

WASHINGTON, July 6—The news of the fatal charge of Gen. Custer and his command against the Sioux Indians has caused great excitement in Washington, particularly among Army people and about the Capitol. The first impulse was to doubt the report, or set it down as some heartless hoax or at least a greatly exaggerated story by some frightened fugitive.

VIEWS AT THE WAR DEPARTMENT

The confirmatory dispatches from
Sheridan's head-quarters in Chicago—
feeling among Custer's friends.

WASHINGTON, July 6—Not until late this afternoon
did the War Department receive confirmatory reports of the news published this morning of the
terrible disaster in Indian country.

MISCELLANEOUS DISPATCHES

A list of officers killed—feeling over
the disaster—a regiment of frontiersmen
offered from Utah.

SALT LAKE, July 6—The citizens here are very much
excited over the Custer Massacre, and several of-
fers have been made to the Secretary of War to
raise a regiment of frontiersmen in ten days for
Indian service.

SAN FRANCISCO, July 6—A dispatch from Virginia
City reports great excitement at Custer's death. A
meeting has been called to organize a company.

TOLEDO, July 6—A special to the *Blade* from
Monroe, Mich., the home of Gen. Custer, says the
startling news of the massacre of the General and
his party by Indians created the most intense feeling of sorrow among all classes . . . The town is
draped in mourning, and a meeting of the Common Council and citizens was held this evening to
take measures for an appropriate tribute to the
gallant dead.

Escorted by Captain James Egan's hard-bitten K Company of the Second Cavalry, Bill Cody had accompanied
the youthful, baby-faced Colonel Wesley Merritt on that
ride north to take over field command of the Fifth Cavalry
on the first day of July. Besides being an act of utter humiliation to Lieutenant Colonel Eugene Carr, Bill figured Mer-

ritt had no business taking over what had long been regarded as "Carr's regiment" in the field.

Why, the "Old War Eagle" had led the Fighting Fifth since sixty-eight, for God's sake!

No two ways about it—Merritt had been in the right place at the right time: already out west as lieutenant colonel of the Ninth Cavalry, and perhaps even more important, in the field acting as inspecting cavalry quartermaster for Sheridan's Division of the Missouri when the lieutenant general decided to use the Fifth to block reinforcements to Sitting Bull's hostiles.

Upon graduation from the U.S. Military Academy in 1860, Merritt was first assigned to the Second Dragoons. But as soon as Fort Sumter was fired upon less than a year later, his career began to parallel Custer's closely: both had become brigadier generals at the same time, just prior to the Battle of Gettysburg, and both had commanded victorious cavalry divisions under Sheridan during the Shenandoah campaign in the final weeks of the Civil War.

Everybody wanted to have a crack at the Indians who had defeated the Seventh Cavalry, Cody figured. Even Wesley Merritt.

When the terrible news from Montana Territory caught up with Sheridan, he was visiting Camp Robinson, planning to do what his department could to stop the flow of warriors off the reservations at Red Cloud and Spotted Tail. Almost immediately the lieutenant general hurried back to Fort Laramie—where for days on end he remained angry, hurt, confused, and stunned as all get-out by the Custer disaster.

Still, Bill had learned one thing was certain about that little Irish general: he wasn't going to sit around licking his wounds. Sheridan was the sort who would strike back—and strike back with everything he had.

"By God—those red sons of bitches will hear a trumpet's clarion call on the land!" Sheridan vowed, slamming a fist down on Major E. F. Townsend's desk at Laramie hard enough to stun every other officer into utter silence. "If it takes every man in my department, Sitting Bull and Crazy Horse will pay dearly—and I'll make sure they keep on paying until I think they've been brought to utter ruin!"

Cody had no doubt that Sheridan would make good on his word.

Accompanying Merritt from Laramie was another correspondent hurried into the field by an editor eager to beat the competition, another reporter chomping at the bit to snatch some new angle on the Sioux War suddenly exploding across the nation's papers with banner headlines: Cuthbert Mills, who was sending copy back east to the New York *Times*.

Cody recognized Mills as a tenderfoot from way off, but he did not join in "laying for" the reporters the way the rest of the entourage did, both soldiers and civilians. Nevertheless, Bill did have himself a few laughs at Mills's expense, what with the way the others "stuffed the greenhorn." What a caution that slicker from the East had turned out to be!

But it was not the prose of those tenderfooted reporters Bill figured he would long remember. Instead, the most lasting impression was made by the verse composed by his friend, the amiable John Wallace Crawford, widely known as the "poet scout" of the prairies. More of a nimble rhymester than a poet in the truest sense of the word, Crawford nonetheless entertained one and all every evening with his offhand recitations and impromptu circumlocutions involving the day's march and the personalities along for the campaign.

Born in 1847 in County Donegal, Ireland, Crawford's parents emigrated to America while Jack was still a boy. Almost immediately the youth went to work in the Pennsylvania coal mines. Bereft of any learning, totally illiterate, Jack was only fifteen when he enlisted in the Forty-eighth Pennsylvania Volunteers with his father. After young Crawford was wounded at the Battle of Spotsylvania, he convalesced at the Saterlee Hospital in West Philadelphia, where he was taught to read and write by a Sister of Charity.

A few years after the end of the war, both his parents died—causing Jack to decide he would start life anew out west. With the discovery of gold by Custer's expedition in 1874, Crawford headed for the Black Hills, then the following year worked a mail contract between Red Cloud and the rail depot at Sidney, Nebraska. As one of the founders of Custer City in the Hills, he was selected to serve as chief of scouts for their volunteers with the outbreak of the Sioux War—a group called the Black Hills Rangers. It was at this time that Crawford acquired the title of "Captain Jack," as well serving as the region's correspondent for the Omaha *Bee.*

Time had come for the Fifth to get over its outward suspicion of its new colonel commanding and get back to business. On the second of July, Merritt marched his troops four miles to the east, so they could bivouac on better grass that much closer to the well-beaten Indian trail Little Bat had discovered. The men remained confident and their mounts well fed—not only on the grasses of those Central Plains, but on seventy-five thousand pounds of grain that had arrived from Laramie nine days earlier.

Then on the morning of 3 July a small war party was sighted by outlying pickets no more than a mile from the regiment's South Cheyenne base camp. Captain Julius W. Mason's veteran K Company was ordered in pursuit as they were beginning their breakfast.

"Saddle up, men! Lively, now!" was the shout from the company's lieutenant, Charles King, as Cody leaped into the saddle with Jack Crawford at his side.

"Lead into line!" King ordered. "Count off by fours!"

"By fours, right!" Mason gave the command while Cody and Crawford galloped away, hoping to eat away at what lead the warriors already had.

The day before, Mason had been informed that he'd been promoted to the rank of major, with a transfer to the Third Cavalry, which was presently serving with Crook's Big Horn and Yellowstone Expedition. Yet Mason had told Colonel Merritt that he intended to stay with the Fifth until such a time as the present campaign was brought to a completion.

Down into the trees at creekside the two scouts led K Troop, through the deep sand, then finally a climb back up onto the grassy hillsides where the race could begin in earnest.

"Here comes Kellogg's I Company, fellers!"

Cody heard a soldier from K make the announcement behind him as they tore after the distant horsemen. Merritt had ordered out a second troop for what was hoped would be the first action of the campaign.

But after a frustrating and circuitous chase of some thirty miles lasting several hours, all of it spent following nothing more tangible than a trail of unshod ponies, and then finding the war party splitting off onto diverse trails, all leading in the general direction of the Powder River country, Mason ordered Lieutenant King to take their company and return to camp at four o'clock, empty-handed. However, because Bill and Jack Crawford, riding far in advance of K Company, had managed to fire some shots at the fleeing horsemen in the early stages of the chase, the affair went down in the official record of the Fifth Cavalry as "the fight near the south branch of the Cheyenne River, Wyo."

If the soldiers hadn't killed any of the enemy or taken any prisoners, at least the Fifth was credited with forcing those fleeing Cheyenne warriors to abandon their slower pack-animals burdened beneath agency supplies plainly being carried to the hostiles in the north.

Still, by the time the troopers returned to Merritt's camp, there were casualties to be tallied from the thirty-mile chase. A dozen horses were so badly used up that Carr decided it best to have them returned to Laramie. Worse yet, the mounts carrying two heavy troopers did not even make it back to camp, having dropped dead under their weighty burdens during the Fifth Cavalry's first pursuit of the enemy that season.

Those two horses would not be the last animals to

drop in their tracks before the summer's Sioux campaign was out.

On the following cloudy, dismal morning, that of the Centennial Fourth, Merritt ordered the regiment to strike camp, begin a countermarch, and scout back to the south, in the direction of Fort Laramie. The colonel realized that the Indians now knew of the presence of his troops and that further patrolling along the Mini Pusa would prove fruitless. Two companies with worn-out horses accompanied Merritt and the supply wagons due south along the valley of the Old Woman's Fork, with the colonel's intentions to rendezvous all battalions forty-eight hours later at the army's stockade erected at the head of Sage Creek. Meanwhile the regiment's commander dispatched Major John J. Upham with three companies to march to the northwest, up the Mini Pusa for one last scout of the Cheyennes' possible crossing. At the same time, Carr was sent off east to the Black Hills with another three companies, again to look for recent signs of activity.

By the sixth of July, the Fifth Cavalry had reassembled, establishing their camp no more than seventy-five miles north of Fort Laramie on Sage Creek at the stockade guarded by a single company of infantry who were assigned to watch over a section of the Cheyenne–Black Hills stage road. Merritt promptly sent a courier south with reports for Sheridan. The rider was back by ten o'clock the next morning while most were having a leisurely breakfast and some officers were enjoying a cool bath in one of the creek's shallow pools.

Cody himself escorted Major Townsend's courier to Merritt's tent, then watched the colonel open the flap on the thin leather dispatch envelope as the scout poured himself another cup of coffee . . . about the time he heard the colonel quietly exclaim, "Good Lord!"

He looked at Merritt's hands shaking, how the officer's youthful face suddenly went gray with age and utter shock, carved with deep concern. It frightened Bill. "Colonel?"

"They . . . the Seventh . . . Custer too . . ."

"What about Custer and the Seventh?"

Merritt wagged his head, choking as if on something sour, unable to speak. All he could manage to do was hand the dispatches over to Cody.

> We have partial confirmation of
> Custer's disaster, which, from
> the papers, appears to have been
> complete. Custer and five
> companies entirely wiped out.

Once he had read them, and reread them a second time, Bill gave the pages back and turned away, pushing himself through a cadre of officers all hurrying like ants atop an anthill to hear for themselves the unbelievable news.

Bill had known Custer. Why, he had even ridden stirrup to stirrup with the golden-haired cavalry officer, hunting buffalo together on the plains of Kansas. Custer was the sort so vital, so alive! Hero in war. Conqueror of Black Kettle's Cheyenne. Custer the Invincible!

Charles King came bounding up, his hair still wet from his morning swim. He stopped Cody. "Bill! Bill—is what I hear true? Dear God—say it isn't true!"

Cody could only nod as more anxious men gathered around them in a knot of fierce disbelief.

Silence fell over that camp beside Sage Creek like a suffocating blanket of doom. This was a gallant, romantic era when the officers of one cavalry unit had friends among other regiments. Most of those men serving with the Fifth lost comrades or classmates, soldiers who fell with the Seventh at the Little Bighorn.

So in the awful stillness of that summer morning, Bill quietly confirmed the worst for those who pressed in close, "Custer and five companies of the Seventh are wiped out of existence. It's no rumor—General Merritt's got the official dispatch."

"Where?"

"North of here—Little Bighorn."

"Official?"

"Sheridan himself."

"Custer? Dead?"

"Confirmed. Twelve days ago. On the twenty-fifth of June."

King grabbed Cody by the arm. "You'll be all right, Bill?"

"Yes," the scout eventually answered, throwing his shoulders back somewhat, his long hair brushing his collar. "There can be no doubt now, Lieutenant, that before a fortnight has passed, we'll march north to reinforce Crook."

"This is going to be bigger than any of us could have imagined," King said. "Sheridan will throw everything he has at them after losing Custer."

"But, you know, Lieutenant—if we are just now finding out about the battle, one thing's for damn sure: the Indians down at Red Cloud and Spotted Tail already know."

King snapped his fingers, saying grimly, "Which means if they weren't preparing to jump the reservation and head north—they'll be doing it damned soon."

With a nod Cody replied, "Hotter'n ever to join up with the war camps that wiped out Custer and half the Seventh Cavalry."

Sheridan himself would have even hotter plans for the Fighting Fifth.

Later that evening Lieutenant William Hall, acting regimental quartermaster for the Fifth Cavalry, rode in from Laramie with fresh dispatches. A gravely disappointed Merritt learned that he was not to take his eight troops of cavalry and push toward the Powder River country to unite with Crook. Instead Sheridan told him he should either march on to the Red Cloud Agency to bolster the army's force at Camp Robinson, or march back to Fort Laramie to await further orders.

Whichever the colonel should decide was best.

*   *   *

That hour's halt for coffee and hardtack proved itself a
deadly delay for Sibley's patrol.

As the soldiers relaxed around their tiny fires there in
that grassy glade, Seamus heard more and more of them
boast that the Indians would not dare follow them into the
mountains. Despite how the scouts appealed, there was
simply no convincing the lieutenant's men that danger lay
ahead.

Grouard had long ago given up in disgust and joined
the soldiers on the ground, dropping on the grass painfully
to curl an arm under his head and close his eyes.

"You gonna be all right, Frank?" Seamus asked.

The half-breed whispered low, his eyes flicking down
to his belly, "Just this damned woman's weeping sickness."

"It's gotta hurt."

He lay on his side, breathing shallow as he made himself more comfortable, knees drawn up. "Worse'n anything
I ever had."

It was early afternoon when Pourier and Donegan decided the soldiers had enjoyed a long enough halt.

Bat went over and nudged Grouard. "Time to go," he
told the other half-breed.

Clearly in pain, Grouard moved stiffly to rise, struggling to climb back onto his horse as the soldiers resaddled.
He walked his horse over by Sibley to say, "You just keep
your men close together behind me," as he rose in the
stirrups to rub his groin with a grimace. "Tell 'em to ride
fast and keep up with me. They gotta keep up and—be
ready to fight."

The patrol moved out behind their scouts in single
file, following Pourier, Donegan, and an ailing Grouard,
pushing up through the forests thick with lodgepole, dotted
with open parks carpeted in tall grass and wildflowers,
winding their way through a tumble of boulders as big as
railroad cars.

They hadn't gone all that far when Pourier signaled a

halt and slid from his horse. In the middle of the trail lay a pair of crossed coup-sticks.

"Bad medicine," Big Bat grumbled, picking one up and cracking it over a knee.

As Pourier tossed the pieces aside, Grouard and Donegan twisted this way and that, the hair on the back of their necks fuzzing like a fighting dog's.

"*Heap* bad medicine," Bat repeated as he snapped the second coup-stick over his thigh and tossed it to the side of the trail.

"Let's get off this road," Donegan suggested. "They know we're coming."

Grouard agreed. "Damn betcha, Irishman."

Seamus wagged his head, eyes searching the shadow and light of the timber ahead. "Now we know for sure they're up there—somewhere."

Grouard led off this time, passing Pourier as Big Bat swung into the saddle. For the next half hour Frank did the best he could to keep them to the right of the well-used trail, hanging as much to the trees as possible. With thickening timber standing to the left and in front, and a jumble of high boulders and trees off to the right, a tangle of deadfall lay directly in their path.

With a jerk Donegan turned in the saddle at the hammer of hooves and the snapping of tree branches on their backtrail.

"The Indians! The Indians!" squawked the packer, "Trailer Jack."

Both Becker and one of the soldiers who had been lagging behind came whipping their mounts into those who formed the end of the file. At that moment the boulders to their right erupted in gunfire. Warriors appeared behind the rocks, beginning to shout while they fired their weapons, closing the trap.

"To the left—by the saints!" Donegan shouted. "Ride to the left!"

In among the trees and some low-lying rocks Sibley's men flooded in a panic, the three scouts closing the file as every last one of them leaped from his horse, scrambling to whatever cover he could find, and turned to fight.

"Finerty?"

Seamus knelt over the newsman lying flat on his back among the legs of his mare that stumbled to the side, out of the way, as Donegan came up. Finerty fluttered his eyes open. While the tree branches above them snapped and rattled with bullets, the air whining with lead, Donegan laid a hand on the fallen man's chest and pleaded, "Say you're not hit, Johnny!"

The reporter slowly propped himself up on an elbow, swiping dust and pine needles from his face and hair. "Son of a bitch! That goddamned bastard threw me!"

"Your horse?"

"Gloree, that hurt!" Finerty exclaimed as he rolled onto his knees.

With his first glance Seamus plainly saw the blood slicking the lathered chest, saw the oozing hole. That next moment the animal crumpled onto its forelegs, settled, then kneeled onto its side, big chest heaving.

Donegan said, "He's done for, Johnny."

"Goddamn good and well too," he grumbled. "Cursed animal—throwing me the way it did."

"You dumb shit!" Seamus growled, shoving Finerty backward into the dirt and needles. "The poor thing threw you when it was hit."

In amazement the reporter just stared at the man standing over him. "I . . . I didn't—"

"He took that bullet for you!" Seamus bellowed, turning on his heel and flinging himself behind a tumble of deadfall. It hurt something deep within him when a big, beautiful animal gave its life for its master.

Other horses whickered and whinnied, crying out in pain as stray bullets connected, falling among the army's frightened mounts and Trailer Jack's braying mules milling behind them in the timber.

"We gotta get back into the woods, Frank!" Pourier hollered.

"You're right, Bat. Get some cover," Grouard replied anxiously, and began waving his pistol. "Lieutenant! Take your men into the timber! Back into the timber!"

"Bat!" Seamus bellowed. "Stay with me here and cover the retreat! We gotta make enough lead fly to force them red h'athens to keep their heads down in them rocks. Just long enough."

For a moment Pourier looked longingly at the retreating soldiers, then flung himself back up the slope to join Grouard and Donegan at a small cluster of boulders.

Seamus slapped the half-breed on the shoulder. "Thanks, Bat. I owe you."

Pourier winked and shoved his cheek onto the stock of his Springfield carbine, looking for a target.

In no time Sibley got his detail up and moving without having to prod a single man. Latching on to their horses, the soldiers zigzagged down to their left with the mounts, Becker bellowing at the mules, all of them racing through a few trees for some thicker stands of pine and fir a few hundred yards farther down the slope. There among some deadfall the men tied off the animals and turned about, flopping onto the ground behind nature's own breastworks.

"Look on up the trail, Frank," Seamus huffed after his run as he finally slid in between Grouard and Pourier near the soldiers, pointing the long, octagonal barrel of his Sharps up the slope where the trail wound itself between two high bluffs.

The half-breeds nodded.

"Yeah," Frank said. "If they got us in there—none of us wouldn't come out with our hair."

Pushing the Sharps lever down, Donegan ejected the empty cartridge, then replanted a live round in the breech. "Seems those warriors dogging our tails was just a little too anxious to close the trap, don't it?"

"Lucky us," grumbled Finerty as he crabbed up to join the three, whining lead following the white men into the timber.

Grouard rolled onto his back and found Sibley, then instructed, "Lieutenant, tell your boys not to fire a shot until they got a good target."

"These men have fought before," Sibley snapped testily.

"Just remind 'em!" Donegan added. "We're going to need every last bullet we have before this day's done. Maybe by the time we try to get back to Crook."

Nodding, a grim Sibley responded, "All right."

"And . . . Lieutenant," Seamus said, causing the officer to halt in a crouch, "tell your men it's a good idea to keep one last round in their pistols for themselves."

Chapter 12

7 July 1876

It wasn't as if Seamus had to tell Sibley's soldiers that they might not make it out of that fix alive. They all knew the odds they were facing.

"Men," the lieutenant raised his strong voice above that clutter of deadfall and low rocks where he had his detail ringed in a ragged crescent, "you can all see that the Indians have discovered us. If we can make an honorable escape from this trap—all together, I might add—we will attempt it. If retreat should prove impossible, let no man among you surrender."

Seamus looked over a few of the grim faces of those soldiers listening while they peered over fallen trees at the enemy's ground upslope. It looked as if the troopers truly understood.

"You must hear me," Sibley continued. "There is no surrender. If we can't escape—we must die in our tracks. Those savages will show us no mercy if we're captured. Make every shot kill, men. Make every shot kill."

Sibley crabbed back toward the scouts and settled in near Seamus.

"You did good, Lieutenant," Donegan said quietly. "If

they know how bad things are and listen to you—we still might have a chance of getting out of this."

His eyes narrowing on the Irishman, Sibley asked, "You really think so, or are we just putting off the inevitable?"

"Man can't ever lose hope," Seamus said. "Man's always gotta try."

" 'Specially when it comes to his own scalp," Pourier added.

Over the following minutes the screech of war cries and death songs grew as the warriors emerged from the boulders and began to work their way down the hillside toward the soldiers, firing as they came through the timber. Working to the left and right through the standing trees to close in on the white men lying among their breastworks, the Indians eased into rifle range, starting to pour a concerted fire upon their enemy.

"See that fancy son of a bitch?" Seamus asked the two half-breeds, indicating a warrior who appeared to be directing the others: a chief dressed in moon-white buckskins and wearing a long, flowing war bonnet. "Either one of you ever see him before?"

When Pourier shrugged, Grouard said, "Reminds me of a fella called White Antelope."

Big Bat squinted, looking closer, then replied, "But he's Shahiyena."

"And a mean one to boot," Grouard added.

"Cheyenne, eh?" Donegan asked. "So they're mixed in with them Lakota what wiped those soldiers out on the Greasy Grass?"

Frank nodded. "Likely are. All blood cousins."

"Blood is right," Seamus murmured.

A soldier yelled off to their left, "Here they come!"

Twisting about behind the bulwark of the deadfall, Seamus saw the big warrior in the white buckskins waving the rest to follow behind him.

"They're charging!" Sibley shouted.

"Make every shot count!" bellowed Sergeant Oscar Cornwall.

Sergeant Charles W. Day reminded them, "Shoot low! Shoot low!"

"Aim for White Antelope!" Grouard instructed his two companions.

"Damn right," Pourier replied. "I'll do everything I can to drop that bastard!"

On came the first concerted charge of the afternoon, led by that war chief in the showy buckskins bright with quillwork sewn down the leggings. Beside White Antelope rode another warrior, bare-chested and wearing a buffalo-fur headdress, one horn protruding from the center of the warrior's forehead.

Seamus held high, leading that horseman beside White Antelope with too much of the big buffalo gun's front blade. The gun shoved backward into his shoulder violently, once again reminding the Irishman of the weapon's great power. Quickly he jerked down on the lever, dropping the rifle's breech as it flung empty brass out of the smoking chamber. Gun smoke curled up in a gray wisp—a reassuring fragrance to a veteran frontiersman, as sweet smelling as would be water to a thirsty mule.

As Donegan stuffed the hot, empty cartridge into his left pocket, the war cries crashed on his ears, louder still in a growing crescendo. The pounding of two hundred or more hooves thundered through the trees, reverberated from the boulders beyond them. From the right pocket of his canvas mackinaw, Seamus pulled another long golden bullet and shoved it into the rifle, ripping back the lever to close the breech, and resighted on the charging warrior.

This time as he laid his finger on the back trigger, he held even higher and did not lead the buffalo-horned horseman as the warrior's pony crossed from left to right along the front of the soldier line. Another inch higher, he calculated, as he set the back trigger. He felt his way to the front trigger with the same finger-pad and held his breath, squeezing.

In the puff of smoke that drifted the way of the soft breeze there in that stand of evergreen, Seamus watched the warrior pitch sideways, his single-horn headdress spilling in the opposite direction.

"Got him!" Pourier hollered at that exact moment.

"*I* dropped White Antelope!" Grouard protested.

"It was my damned bullet!" growled Bat.

"That makes two of 'em—we got more saddles to empty, God-bless-it!" Seamus bellowed at them both.

The soldiers flung their wool coats from their arms, shedding the heavy garments in the shafts of hot sunlight that streamed through the forest canopy overhead with a shimmering radiance. For the better part of a half hour the warriors kept up a hot fire, inching down the slope. Then with some yelling among them, the gunfire slackened. A voice called out from the trees up the hill.

"What's he saying?" Donegan asked.

Pourier wagged his head, his shoulders sagging, then finally replied, "They know I'm here."

"Only a lucky guess," Seamus replied. "What'd he tell you?"

"Said, '*Oh, Bat—come over here. I want to tell you something. Come over!*'"

"They was just guessing you was with the soldiers," Grouard said, shifting uncomfortably on the hard ground, his face a canvas to his pain.

"Maybe they see me," Bat grumbled sadly. "They're calling out for the trader's son."

Donegan asked, "Trader's son?"

"That's me," Pourier responded. "Shahiyena know me. My papa was a trader to the Indians."

"Like Reshaw's?"

Bat nodded. "Yeah, like Louie."

The taunts and luring words that emerged from those midafternoon shadows in the woods continued. A while later Grouard straightened a bit, cocking his head, then declared, "Now they're calling for me."

Pourier grinned haplessly. "Yeah, Irishman. They calling for the Grabber. That means there's Lakota up there too. Next—they gonna holler out for you."

"You stupid idiot," Seamus growled with a wide grin. "Ain't none of them know me."

Scratching a dirty cheek, Bat said, "Maybeso they don't before. But they will now."

As the sun fell on toward the cathedral peaks towering above them, the firing from the warriors rose and fell, fortunately to no effect but to frighten and wound the horses, and to make a lot of noise as the bullets slapped tree trunks and whistled through the snapping branches. At times there was so much lead flying over their heads that it reminded Donegan of hailstones rattling on a clapboard roof that summer he had spent at Fort McPherson, scouting for the Fifth Cavalry—a remembrance that made him think on Cody, made him wonder if Bill really did enjoy that life he had chosen, a career that had taken Donegan's old friend far from the prairie, far from the freedom of a nomadic horseman.

If they made it out of this, Seamus vowed, he'd learn of the showman's whereabouts—perhaps even to take Samantha to see one of his plays back east. Sam deserved to visit the East. To be draped in fancy evening dresses and driven in a fancy carriage to the theater where Cody's play would entertain the crowds of eastern greenhorns clamoring for some of that vicarious adventure on the high plains. Perhaps even to Boston Towne. He hadn't been back since he had gone marching off to war. And that was an eternity ago.

But he vowed Samantha would one day have her fancy gowns and her own goddamned carriage too.

"How far you make us from Goose Creek, Bat?" Sibley asked, interrupting Donegan's dreamy reverie.

"Forty miles."

Grouard shook his head, saying, "Closer to fifty miles."

"No matter," Pourier replied, turning back to the officer. "We sit here much longer, Lieutenant—them Lakota gonna have time to bring enough warriors here to rush in and wipe us out in one big charge."

The green-eyed Sibley chewed on an end of his long mustache. "I take it you're suggesting we try to make a dash for it?"

Donegan shrugged, the first to respond for them all. "We can sit here and wait for them to come in and chew us up. Or—we can do what we can to make a run for it."

Eventually the lieutenant said, "Take our chances, eh?"

"We can take chances here—or on the run," Pourier reminded.

Grouard laughed with a throaty snort.

"What's so funny?" Sibley demanded, bristling.

"Not you, Lieutenant," Frank replied. "Just heard voice of an old friend of mine. Warrior named Standing Bear—hollered for me."

Seamus asked, "What'd he say?"

"He saw me get off my horse, walking sore with my legs far apart."

"That's just the way you been walking," Seamus declared.

With a nod Grouard continued. "Standing Bear said I moved like I had the bad-disease walk the pony soldiers get from lying with the white man's pay-women."

Pourier added, "Then Standing Bear asked Frank, '*Do you think there are no men but yours in this country?*' "

Donegan wagged his head and said, "Goddamned country's full of warriors, that's what."

"Irishman, the bastard asked me if I could fly up into the air, or burrow like the badger into the ground," Grouard replied acidly. "They figure they got us, and there's no way out now except to fly or dig our way out under the mountain. He says they'll have my scalp for Sitting Bull before sundown."

"We wait here much longer, Frank—they might even try to burn us out," Pourier advised.

"Before we burn—I vote for trying to break our way

out," Finerty finally spoke, his eyes darting among them, lit with nervousness.

Donegan turned and said, "Thought you were busy collecting flowers, Johnny."

"Just a few—the ones I could reach—got them pressed between the pages of my book where I was making some notes on our . . . our predicament. Mountain crocus, and a forget-me-not growing within my reach. Somehow the beauty in life seems so, so very sweet this afternoon, Seamus."

"Always does seem all the sweeter when death looms close, my friend." With a wry grin the Irishman turned to Sibley. "You need to get your men ready, Lieutenant."

The officer nodded, saying, "I'll tell them to prepare to mount."

"No," Seamus said, gripping the lieutenant's arm. "Better to leave the horses."

"Leave the horses?" Finerty asked.

"If we leave the animals here," Donegan explained, "we might have enough of a lead to fool the sons of bitches and make it out on foot."

"Abandon our mounts?" the lieutenant asked, his face carved with disbelief.

"Irishman's right," Grouard said. "Only chance is make those warriors believe we're still here because our horses are."

Sibley shook his head emphatically. "I don't like leaving those horses for the enemy to capture. If we abandon them—we must shoot them."

"We go and shoot all those mounts," Donegan explained, "that war party will figure out what we're trying to do. But if we leave the horses standing—that might be our only chance to reach Goose Creek alive."

"Besides," Grouard instructed them, "I'll lay odds them warriors are sitting on all the easy ways out of these hills. Horses wouldn't make it under us where we need to go. Our only chance is to cover some real rugged ground . . . on foot."

"What about sending one of our men?" the lieutenant suggested. "The best rider we have—send him off to get reinforcements from Crook."

"We don't have the time to wait for Crook," Donegan argued.

Pourier agreed. "It'll take the better part of two days for any help to reach us."

"And like Frank said," Donegan added, "the h'athens could fire the forest around us and smoke us out right into their guns. No, we don't have much time left, Lieutenant. If we're gonna do it, we've got to do it now."

"I suppose you're right," the officer relented, finally yielding to the advice of his three scouts. He prepared to crab off on hands and knees, then turned back to say, "It's plain we are looking death in the face here."

John Finerty snorted sourly, "And I can feel the grim reaper's cold breath right here on my forehead, sense his icy grip round my heart."

"Never been in a fix like this before?"

"No, Seamus. But often I have wondered how a man must feel when he was confronted by inevitable doom and there was no escaping it."

"Just remember to keep a bullet for yourself if things don't work out for us," Seamus said softly.

"Don't worry, you bloody Irishman—I'll blow my own goddamned brains out rather than fall alive into the hands of those gore-hungry savages."

"What you worried about, Finerty?" Bat said, his eyes bright with sudden devilment. "Now you're gonna have lots of good stories to send your paper when we get you back to Crook's camp!"

The newsman snarled, "Damn you, Bat—you're always making fun at my expense!"

Valentine Rufus crawled up to Finerty. His weather-beaten face was prickled with stubby gray hair. "Lieutenant says for us to sneak back to the horses. Get all our ammunition from the saddlebags. We're taking all of it we can carry when we leave the horses."

"All right, Private," Finerty said. "But my horse is up the hill, and I ain't going back there to get a damn thing out of those saddlebags."

"You stick with me, then," Rufus said. "We'll share ammunition and see this through together."

"Are you Irish?" Finerty asked.

"No." The old soldier shook his head. "Don't rightly know what I am anymore."

The newsman winked at Donegan as he said to Rufus, "Well, from the sounds of your pluck, Private—you damn well should have been Irish."

"Go on with the private now," Seamus instructed. "Me and Bat are going to make sure they think we're still in here while the rest of you slip away."

Finerty knelt at the Irishman's side to whisper, "What are you going to do?"

"Just keep up some firing, make 'em keep their heads down. Between the two of us you should get a good jump."

Finerty laid his hand on Donegan's shoulder. "And you'll catch up soon?"

"Don't you worry, Johnny boy. I'll be running right up your backside in a damned fine fashion before you know it."

After quickly shaking hands, Seamus watched Finerty follow Private Rufus, both of them crawling off to join those who moved among the eight horses still standing, other soldiers laboring over the saddles of the animals fallen to the warrior fire, every man frantic to retrieve what he could before Sibley ordered his soldiers on into the timber beyond. Swallowed by the shadows.

"Let's go to work," Seamus said grimly, turning his shaggy face up the slope.

Without a word of reply Pourier nodded and rolled onto his belly behind some deadfall to fire his Springfield. Yanking open the trapdoor, the half-breed rammed home another shell and aimed in a different direction. Between the two of them they placed a scattering of shots all round the half crescent where the warriors hollered and kept up a desultory fire on the white men's position.

After a few minutes Seamus turned to Pourier. "Why don't you head on out?"

"You coming?"

"Gimme a minute or two more," Donegan explained. "Wouldn't do for us both to stop firing at the same time."

Bat's face showed how he measured the weight of that. "All right. But I'm going to wait for you a ways down in the timber, just past the horses."

"Go on. I'll be along straightaway."

By the time he fired a half dozen more shots and looked back over his shoulder, Seamus could no longer hear or even see Pourier. The breech on the Sharps hissed and stank when the sweat from his forehead dropped into the action, sizzling, bubbling as it vaporized on the super-heated metal. It had worked, by God. The warriors hadn't tried anything more than shouting and shooting from afar.

Looking left and right, he could see no good route for him to take but straight back. On his belly Seamus slid, pushing himself, dragging the Sharps through the dead needles, clumps of grass and dust that stived into the air, capturing fragments of golden light among the sunbeams streaming through the thick canopy of emerald-green tree branches.

His horse was dead.

Gently he rubbed its muzzle, for a moment remembering the big gray. Remembering how the General had carried him to that sandy island before it fell, more than one bullet in its great and powerful chest.

Fighting back the smarting of tears, he quickly yanked loose the latigo tie lashing the twin bags to the back of the saddle and threw his weight against the dead animal to free the off-side pouch. In the bags were rolled the two long shoulder belts of Sharps ammunition, along with his re-loading tools. As he flopped them over his shoulder, Seamus heard the reassuring clatter of a few boxes of car-tridges for the pair of army .45s he wore belted over his hips. It took but a few seconds more for him to tear loose the rawhide tie holding the coil of rope to the saddle, quickly lashing it round and round his waist above the pistol belts.

Under the weight of it all, Seamus turned downhill at a crouch, racing for the Tongue River somewhere below them a mile or more. But suddenly he stopped and gazed once more at the carcasses of more than twenty-five dead horses, gripped with the remembrance of the animals Forsyth's fifty scouts shot to make bulwarks against Roman Nose's charging, screaming, wailing Cheyenne.

He closed his misting eyes a moment, seeing the laughing face of Liam O'Roarke.

Recalling the pain that sank clear to his marrow, here on this timbered hillside, feeling once again the aching, empty hole that had torn through the middle of him with the dying of a beloved uncle on that sandy island turned bloody in the middle of an unnamed river.

Chapter 13

7–8 July
1876

That Friday afternoon the Sibley patrol was fifty miles from rescue.

Their only hope was to help themselves.

It seemed the soldiers understood that—every last yard they bounded down that hill, across a small, open glade before they entered thicker timber where old, leaning trees interlocked with those younger lodgepole pine still standing and an extensive patch of burned trunks testifying to an ancient forest fire, the whole maze conspiring to slow their flight. From that point on the men began to stumble over deadfall, tripping on rocks hidden in the grass, their soles slipping as they tried to clamber over fallen trees. Yet not a single murmur rose from the lieutenant's soldiers as they scrambled back to their feet and kept on running down, down, on down through the timber. The air filled only with the rasps of their burning, swollen lungs as the Tongue River came in sight below them at last.

Sweating beneath his heavy coat that he had refused to take off, Seamus caught up with Pourier. Beside Bat he kept on pushing to reach the soldiers who were gradually passing Grouard. The half-breed moved in great pain—but he lumbered quickly enough in his wobbling gait, cursing behind teeth he kept gritted all the way down that rugged mile of descent to the river. Racing ahead of Grouard, the first of the soldiers plunged off the bank of the Tongue, into the icy water, without the slightest thought of taking the time to locate a ford.

"Step on the goddamned rocks!" Pourier huffed as he lunged to a halt at the grassy bank. "Can't leave a trail for them to follow!"

Hurrying a few yards downstream, Sibley himself started to cross the river atop a fallen tree while still more of his patrol waded right into the Tongue, not heeding the half-breed scout's warning. Halfway to the far bank the lieutenant's boots slipped on the loose bark of the rotting trunk, and he pitched headlong into the soul-chilling current. Sergeant G. P. Harrington and Corporal Thomas C. Warren leaped in right behind Sibley, pulling the sputtering lieutenant from the swift current and hauling him to the far bank between them as they struggled against the bobbing froth of mountain snow-melt.

"N-never was much of a swimmer," Sibley gasped on the far side.

"The river's running high and wild," Donegan said. "So much runoff at this season. Ain't many a man can swim against that current."

Directly above them stood the foothills, slopes that lay rumpled in one rise and fall after another all the way into the Big Horns themselves. At that moment the forest far above them echoed with a half-dozen volleys of renewed gunfire.

"Won't be long before they find out we're gone," Big Bat moaned as he bent at the waist, catching his breath, his soggy clothes muddying a puddle at his feet.

Seamus gazed back across the Tongue, his eyes searching the far slope they had just scampered down. A sudden, wild cry of half-a-hundred voices raised a furious, shrill call.

He said, "I think they found out, Bat."

A few of the soldiers began to chuckle behind their hands. More of them joined in until the entire bunch was laughing, slapping one another on the back, congratulating themselves on their escape downhill—roaring at the disappointment the warriors must be feeling. It was good to laugh, Seamus decided. A good, long laugh, for they had escaped from one peril, yet still faced another, if not greater, danger. Between them and Crook lay fifty-odd miles of mountainside, granite spire, timber, raging river, and narrow canyon precipice.

At a time like this a man surely deserved to laugh in the face of danger, even spit in death's eye.

"Let's get moving," Sibley ordered, firmly back in control. He pointed at the slope above them. "We're going up, Frank?"

Grouard nodded there in the lengthening shadows of late afternoon. "We got to go where no Indian on horseback can go. Go where even no Indian on foot will want to go. It's going to be tough."

"Only way we're making it out of here and back to Crook," Sibley said with resolve. "Take us back to camp, Grouard."

Into the deepening of dusk and on into the brief alpenglow of twilight descending upon those mountains, the scouts led Lieutenant Frederick W. Sibley and his twenty-five handpicked veterans. Through the rugged breech of granite walls and dizzying mazes of thick timber, where Seamus thought only a mountain goat could find footing and make itself a trail, first Grouard, then Pourier, led the detail upward toward the crest of the divide, ever working south by west as the sun fell and darkness swallowed that high land. The air chilled within moments of the sun's disappearance. Though not one of them complained just then, from time to time Donegan heard the telltale chatter of teeth, like the clatter of dice in a bone cup.

The moon rose and arched overhead in its slow, hour-by-hour spin toward the western horizon beneath some clouds congealing like grease scum atop a meaty stew. With full darkness upon them the sky suddenly opened up with explosive charges that lit the entire span of granite spires above them, hurling shards of icy hail and wind-driven rain down upon the hapless wayfarers, drenching them all for a second time that day.

Yet all the while the two half-breeds pressed on, despite the ferocious wind that toppled over the weaker lodgepole and made the less determined of the soldiers whine and whimper, begging to stop. On Grouard and Pourier doggedly led Sibley's patrol ever toward Camp Cloud Peak. Straight on into the teeth of that mountain hailstorm, bent over as they pushed into the mighty gales until even the strongest among them began to lag, soaked to the marrow, chilled to the core, clinging to his last shred of strength.

From the position of the Big Dipper and the North Star once the heavens began to clear, Seamus judged it to be an hour or so past midnight when Baptiste Pourier stopped at the edge of a small, starlit glade near the skyline.

"I gotta rest," Bat whispered hoarsely, his chest heaving.

"It's all right," Seamus confided, following the others quickly scurrying beneath a generous outcropping of overhanging rock. "We come far enough, Bat. Let's all rest for a while."

Beneath the shelf of granite they would be out of all but the strongest wind. Here, where they collapsed ten thousand feet or more above sea level. Here where the hungry, thirsty, exhausted, and frightened men could curl up, clutching nothing more than their rifles, and try to catch a few minutes of cold, fitful sleep.

Once that day they had walked themselves dry in the clothes each of them had drenched in crossing the Tongue. Shoddy boots had begun to crack and split. Agonizing blisters troubled almost every toe, rubbed raw with the wet stockings and spongy, ill-fitting boots.

Now they were soaked again, the ground around them white with icy hail.

But they were alive. Not one of them lost. They had escaped from sure death through nothing more than pure pluck and gumption. And though their miserable bellies cried out for food, though every man lay there through that cold night shivering until he feared his teeth would rattle right out of his head—they were alive.

Nearby some voices rose quickly and boiled into anger. Almost frozen with weariness, Seamus nonetheless rolled over onto his hands and knees and crawled past most of the others huddled beneath the rocky shelf. At the far end he found Pourier arguing with Sergeant Day.

"Hey—Donegan," the soldier said. "Maybe you can talk some sense into him."

Bat growled, "Tell him to leave me be, Irishman!"

Turning to Donegan for help, Day explained, "I told him we shouldn't kindle a fire."

Seamus strained to make sense out of it in his numbness—weary, hungry as he was. "Why no fires?"

"Lieutenant's orders."

For a moment Donegan stared down at the first feeble flames Pourier had coaxed out of some dry pine needles he found blown back under the rocky outcrop. "He's probably right, Bat. Fire here at night—"

"Go away, Donegan. Just leave me be."

"Injins below can spot the light from a long way off—"

Pourier whirled on Seamus, snarling, "I rather be killed by a Injun's bullet tonight, than I wanna freeze to death. Now you tell this goddamned sergeant to get out of my sight, or I just might gut him myself."

Donegan was relieved when the sergeant began to back away.

Day grumbled, "You ain't gonna listen to me, half-breed—then I'm gonna roust the lieutenant and make my report that you was breaking his orders."

"Go ahead, for all I care!" Pourier snapped. "Don't make no difference, 'cause I'm gonna have my fire."

After watching the sergeant shamble off, Donegan thought about going back where he had been. But he promised himself he would do it later. Right now it seemed that such a crawl would take too much effort.

So he asked Pourier, "Mind if I stay right here with you?"

Bat shook his head. "No problem with sharing my fire with you. Every man in this bunch is against lighting a fire, until he can see just how good the warmth feels."

Turning at the sound of movement nearby, Seamus saw Sibley hobble up on sore feet and sink to the ground.

"Bat—I can't let you have a fire if I've ordered the rest of the men not to start them."

"Keep your boys warm, it would."

"But you ought to know better than any of us how dangerous a fire is up here—"

"No more dangerous than anything we done today. No man can see the fire, not with this rock above us, that timber down there."

"We can be spotted from down there on the side of the mountain—"

"They ain't following us up here, Lieutenant. Besides, the way I built this little fire, no one gonna see the flames. I'm cold—so I'm gonna warm myself. No matter what you say."

Sibley shook his head. "I'll have to put you on report."

"I don't give a damn no more. Report me to Crook. Report me to Crazy Horse too!"

In those few minutes Seamus had watched most of the color return to Sibley's face as he sat so close to the cheery flames.

"All right, Bat—you can keep your fire if you think we're in no danger."

"Nope, none."

The lieutenant seemed to apologize as he shivered uncontrollably a moment. "I am awfully cold myself."

"You sit right here with us," Donegan suggested. Sibley only nodded, spreading his hands over the low flames. "Soak up some warmth while you can. It can make a body feel so much better."

As the minutes crawled by, most of the men inched over to encircle that small fire, drawing not only warmth from it, but what seemed to be hope as well. Just beyond the spill of that dancing light, a soupy mix of snowy rain swirled and jigged in the black and gloomy darkness.

In wide-eyed wonder Sibley watched one of the men in particular as the soldier crawled up to the circle of warmth and comradeship. "Private Hasson—where are your boots?"

Without raising his head to look at the lieutenant, the soldier replied weakly, "Don't know, sir."

"You have them here with you?"

He shrugged. "Said I don't know."

"Hasson—where's your boots?"

Shrugging, he whispered, "Lost 'em sometime through the day, Lieutenant."

"Lost them?"

"Took 'em off to cross one of them creeks," he said, his dark, sunken eyes never leaving the fire, refusing to look at anyone else.

With a simple gesture of his hands, Donegan made it known to Sibley that it would likely be useless to rant and bellow, much less to punish the man for his careless stupidity.

Moving over beside the lieutenant sometime later, Seamus whispered, "There's nothing you could ever do gonna punish him worse'n what he's gonna put himself through tomorrow—being without his boots for all those miles still staring us in the face."

"I think you're right, Irishman," Sibley replied quietly. "I suppose we should all be grateful we escaped with our lives. No matter how little they might be worth at this moment."

One by one the men curled up where they were, or fell

into an exhausted, fitful sleep sitting around Pourier's small fire.

"You're wrong, Lieutenant," Donegan said. "Our lives must be important. Damned important. Seems God Himself has spared us for some reason."

The lieutenant looked over at Seamus, his eyes brimming with gratitude. "Right again, Mr. Donegan. Every one of these men is someone's son. Some woman's husband. Some child's father. Yes. The life of every man here is worth more than that man can ever imagine. And thank God for reminding us of that."

The wind rose and fell, howling off the granite peaks above their pitiful shelter. As the rest began to snore with the deep rhythm of slumber, Donegan felt an immense weariness settle over him. Beyond them in the wilderness awaited the demons of hunger, cold, and sudden, bloody death. But, for this night, those demons were held at bay by the flames of that tiny fire.

Seamus prayed. Thanking God, for now he truly believed he would make it back to Samantha. To be there at her side when the babe chose its time to come.

Thanking God for sparing his life, just one more time.

That night the distant flares of lightning streaked with fingers of green phosphorescent light out over the eastern plains, reminding Seamus of a barrage of distant artillery, softening up the enemy's position before the cavalry was ordered in. He did not want to remember much of what he had seen fighting with the Army of the Potomac, struggled not to recall most of what he experienced riding with Sheridan's Army of the Shenandoah. How they had laid waste to the lives of all, not just the Confederate soldiers.

It was that way against the Indians. Total war, Sherman and Sheridan called it. Deprive the enemy of his food supply. Destroy the enemy's homes. Capture and kill the enemy's families. And ultimately you'll bring your enemy to his knees.

Into the chill gray of that first streak of light smearing

the east, the scouts had Sibley's men up and moving out. For no more than three or four hours those weary soldiers had sparred with sleep, shivering within their wool shirts and britches still damp from the day's exertions and the night's onslaught of rain and hail. From the site of the ambush they had carried only a Springfield carbine and what ammunition they could stuff into their pockets and belt kits.

Some had been so weary that cold dawn that Sibley allowed them to leave behind 10 cartridges each, 250 in all, which the lieutenant buried beneath a rock before he, Donegan, and Pourier started prodding them to their feet.

"You walk," Sibley tried cheering them as he put the soldiers into motion behind Big Bat, "you'll get warm."

"Damn right. Better'n sitting on the cold ground any longer'n I have to," grumbled Private George Rhode.

"We'll be warm already by the time the sun comes up," the lieutenant cheered.

"If we only had something to eat," whimpered Private George Watts. "I'd feel so much better."

Soon, Seamus thought. Soon. "C'mon, Frank," he said, pulling at Grouard's arm.

The half-breed tugged his arm loose. "I think maybe I stay here some more. Don't feel like walking too much today."

"You ain't staying here," Seamus said, looking after the last of the others. A soldier turned around and stared at them dumbly over his shoulder but kept on shuffling down the trail that disappeared into the pines. "No man I know of ever died of what you got."

"I just wanna rest. No more walking—"

"Up you go," Donegan huffed, struggling to pull the half-breed to his feet. "Now, walk."

"Leave me here."

"Walk, goddammit."

Grouard's dark eyes narrowed, and for a moment his hand gripped the pistol he had belted at his waist. Donegan looked at the hand, then at the scout's eyes, then back to the dark hand, tensing and relaxing on the pistol butt.

"I ain't going without you, Frank. So—if you mean to stay and get yourself killed, then it's two of us gonna die here when those Injins find us."

"Damn you, Irishman!" he swore without opening his teeth.

"Go on, curse me—you black-hearted sore-peckered half-breed," Seamus said, shoving Grouard off toward the path the others had taken. "Call me every name you can think of, just as long as you keep walking."

When the bright orb finally did poke its head above the eastern prairie, the sun found them stopped at the edge of a steep precipice, looking down on a southern fork of the Tongue River.

"Ain't none of us gonna make it out of there alive," growled Sergeant Oscar Cornwall.

"Can you find us another way around this canyon?" Sibley asked, turning to Grouard.

The half-breed rubbed at his crotch, then straightened. He appeared somewhat strengthened by the walk. Better moving than soaking the cold out of the wet ground. "That's the way we got to go. South. Ain't no other way."

"I can't ask my men to risk their lives—"

"You don't have to ask them," Grouard spat. "You order them."

"Maybe we can find a way down," Seamus said suddenly, stepping between the two men as Sibley began to lunge forward. "A way that won't be so bloody dangerous."

"All right," Sibley said quietly, taking a step back.

"C'mon, Frank. Let's see what we can scare up."

Within a half hour the pair was back, getting the soldiers on their feet once more, leading the patrol down a little-used game trail they stumbled across. Back and forth it slowly descended through the forest in an undulating switchback that finally reached the left bank of the river far below from the precipice where they started. For the better part of the morning the men had stubbed toes on hidden rocks and stumbled over deadfall, the thin soles of their boots giving little protection from the mountain wilderness. Hour by hour they each grew more tenderfooted until they reached a small meadow on the streambank, where the country opened up to view. Grouard halted, leaning over at the waist, gasping for air in his pain. The rest came down to the meadow one at a time, their chests heaving.

Sibley asked, "How far do we have left to go?"

Peering off to the south, Frank said, "We come halfway."

"Hear that, fellas?" the lieutenant cheered. "We're halfway home."

"And we come through the hardest part," Donegan added. "The rest can't be anywhere as bad as what you come through already."

Downstream the hills rolled gently away toward the eastern plain. To the sore-footed soldiers that direction beckoned like a willing woman with her arms opening to a man.

"We can make good time now that we're out of these hills and timber," Sibley declared.

Grouard shook his head and pointed upstream. "No, we got to go there."

John Finerty stepped forward, asking, "Why, in heaven's name?"

"Out there," Pourier responded, "where the soldiers wanna go is some of the best hunting country there is. That means the chances are good we'll run right into a hunting party."

"Maybe even some of those red bastards ambushed us yesterday," Seamus added his voice to the argument. "No, Lieutenant. We can't dare chance the easy way. If you wanna get back to Crook's camp, we got no choice but to stay with the country too tough for an Indian to follow us on foot."

Chapter 14

8 July 1876

"Let them half-breeds go where they wanna go, Lieutenant."

Grumbled another soldier, "To hell, for all I care—I'm for heading out for the easy country."

All around Donegan the ragged, ravenous troopers mumbled and murmured their protests.

Turning to his dejected patrol, Sibley declared, "You heard the scouts, men. We've no choice but to take their advice and count on them to get us free of this danger." Then he turned to the half-breeds and said, "Let's go."

The lieutenant followed the scouts. Without looking back, the trackers led Sibley's men more than half a mile upstream before they found a place where the cascading Tongue flowed through a widened channel. Here the river did not froth and foam, compressed into a narrow trough, forced to run wild and high. Pourier led the way for them, raising his carbine over his head as he placed one boot carefully in front of the other across the stony streambed, step by step sinking deeper and deeper into the cold current.

Seamus turned to find Private Patrick Hasson limping down to the bank. The soldier stopped thirty feet away from the water, wobbly and unsteady on his bloody feet, his stockings in shreds that exposed the swollen, bruised flesh.

"C'mon, Hasson," Sibley called out from the edge of the water. "We must cross without delay."

Sinking slowly to the ground, Hasson never looked at the lieutenant. "Not going. Can't go on."

Sibley trudged back up the bank and knelt beside the soldier, trying his best to coerce him into moving. Then the lieutenant threatened Hasson with punishment if he didn't get to his feet. And in the end, when he finally took a good, long look at the soldier's battered, swollen feet, Sibley admitted nothing was going to convince Hasson to move.

"You want to stay here?" the lieutenant asked.

"Ain't going on, sir. Not another step."

"You know what might happen to you out here?"

"I got my pistol," Hasson explained wearily. He looked around him a minute. "Figure I'll crawl over there in them bushes and wait."

"We'll send a horse back for you. Be a couple days, way I see it, Private."

"I'll wait."

Sibley nodded. "You want some more cartridges for your revolver?"

"That'd be nice of you. Thanks, Lieutenant. If them red sonsabitches show up, I'll take as many with me as I can before they get to me."

Donegan watched Sibley rise from Hasson's side and move down the bank to stand a moment with the rest before the lieutenant ordered them into the water. The Irishman was followed by Grouard and the packer. But unlike Pourier had done, Seamus and the others plopped to the ground and quickly pulled off boots, socks, britches, and shirt, binding it all together in a bundle they wrapped around their carbines and held high over their heads.

Some of Sibley's men elected to keep their clothing on to make the cold crossing. Others stripped themselves so that they would have warm, dry clothing to pull on once they emerged on the far side of the bone-chilling tumble of snow-melt. One after another they inched down into the stream, with the naked lieutenant bringing up the rear. For the tallest of the men that mountain runoff swirled below their armpits. For the shortest among them, the cold water splashed at their chins.

Then, in the middle of the stream, one of the last handful to brave the deceptively strong current slipped. Flipping backward when his feet lost their purchase on the streambed below, he collided with the man behind him. Beneath the icy flow they both disappeared as those around them all set to bellowing. Sibley pushed forward in the stream, Sergeant Day turned slowly and pressed back toward midstream . . . then the two poked their heads up again, standing a few yards downriver, sputtering and gasping for air.

"I . . . I lost my rifle, Sarge," the first, Private Henry Collins, apologized.

The second wagged his head, shaking it like a wet dog, as he bent over to peer into the frothing surface of the water, shuddering uncontrollably. "D-damn you, P-private!" Sergeant Oscar Cornwall chattered. "Made me lose my carbine too."

"Go on, men," Sibley prodded them now. "Get out of this water."

"Need my rifle," Collins whimpered.

Cornwall turned on the private, his big hands opening and closing in futile anger. "What you need is a good beating for making me lose mine, you horse's ass!"

Seconds later they were all standing on the far bank, heaving with their exertions against the cold, their famished bodies having struggled against the weighty shove of the current, shuddering with cold. Each of those who had left their clothes on sorrily stood dripping, the grass and dirt beneath them grown soggy on the far bank. Sibley emerged from the water, teeth chattering, to plop onto the ground and frantically untie his clothing, yanking it on as quickly as any man could who was convulsively shaking.

Kneeling with Bat, Seamus helped the half-breed

gather some dry grass beneath some willow, knotting it before Pourier set fire to his twist. Over it the two laid larger and larger twigs.

Sibley came over, shoving his foot down into a boot. "Another fire, Bat?"

"I figure your men can use a fire about as much now as they did last night."

"Might make 'em feel some better after that crossing," Donegan explained. "Maybe a wee bit more ready to set off again. How about you letting them take a little rest here for a while?"

"Yes," the lieutenant answered. Already the liver-colored bags beneath his eyes sagged with extreme fatigue. "We all could do with some rest."

A half hour later Pourier stood with the Irishman to kick dirt over the coals. "Time we pushed on," Bat said.

The rest slowly got to their feet, some in their still-soggy uniforms. Warmed by his dry clothing after the cold plunge, Seamus turned to start away again, finding Grouard doubled over at the waist, wobbling, nearly ready to keel over.

"You gonna be all right?" he whispered to the half-breed.

Grouard replied, "The river cold . . . and cold tied my sore belly in knots."

"Can you stand?"

With great discomfort Frank eventually straightened, his breath coming ragged and fast with the pain. "There. Little better."

Pourier came over and stopped. "You want me to lead off?"

"No, Bat. The Irishman showed me this morning: if I keep moving, I'll be all right. Keeps my mind off it."

Seamus watched Grouard set off slowly, lumbering up the right bank that rose to disappear into a seemingly sheer wall. One by one the soldiers followed. Finerty and Becker fell in near the middle where they could. Sibley and Donegan brought up the rear as the two half-breeds led them up a steep trail climbing that rocky canyon wall, climbing ever on toward the sky. For most of the trip upstream they were forced to inch one boot right in front of the other along a narrow trail no more than a foot wide. When there were stunted juniper branches or the exposed roots of pine and cedar the men could cling to, the soldiers moved hand over hand. When there was nothing else but the cracks and protrusions on the rock wall itself, the men slowed to a crawl, inching along some five hundred feet above the frothing waters that poured between huge boulders below them. Above, the top of the canyon was still another two hundred feet away.

Yet they made it. As dangerous as it had been, they all gathered at the top of that rocky shelf and caught their breath with sheer relief. Not one of them was curious enough to peer back over the edge into the canyon they had just scaled. After resting for a few minutes they set off again into the rolling, timbered slopes that led them toward the foothills. Through the next few hours they stopped every mile or so for a rest, using shade when they had it, keeping a close eye on their backtrail as they grew wearier and wearier. Calling a halt more and more often, their meager supply of strength flagged.

By early afternoon the men began to complain of thirst, their tongues swelling, sticking to the roofs of their pasty mouths. With another patch of rugged country behind them, Grouard and Pourier started them down toward the river bottom once more. In pairs and trios the men lumbered to the water's edge, gathering where the Tongue eddied in a shallow pool. They would lean out on their elbows, drinking long and deep of the cold river. With no canteens saved after the ambush, they were able to take none of the icy water with them. Only what a man could drink before pushing on.

Back toward the line of timber on the slopes above, Grouard led them, heading for a point pocked with numerous boulders, Donegan trudging second in file. No more than a quarter mile had they covered when the half-breed suddenly dived onto his belly. He twisted about, signaling frantically for the rest to flatten themselves on the ground. He was holding a finger to his lips as Seamus dragged himself up beside Grouard.

Donegan whispered. "What'd you see?"

Without saying a word Frank pointed back to the north, the direction they had fled earlier in the day. Donegan spotted the two dozen or more warriors, easy enough to make out at this middistance, emerging from the edge of a hillside, on the march east toward the gentle country.

"From here I can't see if they're painted for war or not," Donegan whispered.

"Don't matter," Frank grumbled. "They find us out here, it won't mean nothing that they ain't painted. They'll have our scalps."

The lieutenant slid up behind them, stopping near their boots.

"A war party?"

Grouard only nodded.

Sibley asked, "What you want us to do?"

Quickly Donegan looked this way and that. Above them, in the direction Grouard had been heading, stood a low knoll cluttered with small boulders.

"Up there," Seamus suggested.

Grouard nodded. "Lieutenant, take your men up there to those rocks. Keep 'em low. And quiet. We can make a stand of it there."

Without a complaint Sibley pushed himself backward and went about giving his men their orders. One by one those frightened scarecrows got to their feet and scurried up the slope in a crouch, diving in among those rocks, where they sat heaving loudly. It was the toughest exertion they had endured all day.

"You think they might be that bunch what ambushed us?" Seamus asked.

Grouard shook his head finally. "Don't believe so. See? Don't seem like that bunch is following tracks."

Seamus replied, "They are moseying pretty easy, at that."

"Could be a hunting party."

More horsemen emerged around the edge of the distant hill. Donegan said in a whisper, "Could be they're a big war party."

"Chances are," Grouard said glumly, pushing himself up from the ground slowly, his face showing the measure of his pain.

Pourier watched the pair approach, the last to reach the rocks. He asked, "Are they coming?"

"Likely they are," Grouard said quietly.

Donegan watched the effect of those words on the two dozen men scattered in among the boulders. He heard Sibley sigh, watched the lieutenant get to his feet, standing there as a clear target should the enemy present themselves at that very moment.

"All right, men. We must be ready to sell our lives as dearly as possible."

"Jesus God," John Finerty whispered, wagging his head and making the sign of the cross.

Patting the newsman on the shoulder fraternally, Seamus glanced at Finerty's big shoes, a soldier's brogans clearly too big for the civilian, curved up at the toes the way they were. He grinned, for they reminded him of a leprechaun's green slippers—had they not been constructed of such heavy cowhide, thick-soled and scuffed nearly free of all black dye during the past few weeks of campaigning in the wilderness.

"We're in pretty hard luck of it," Sibley continued, his voice even. "But damn them—we'll show those red scoundrels just how white men can fight and die, if necessary."

"We'll take all we can with us," vowed Corporal Warren.

"That's right," Sibley continued. "We have a good position here among these rocks. Let every shot you make count for an Indian."

Seamus watched the men silently go about the inspection of their weapons and ammunition, reminded how men of a certain kind hunker down and go strangely quiet when confronted with the prospect of certain and sudden death. Reminded how some men grow loudmouthed and boisterous, strutting like fluffed-up cocks, while other men go crazed and cowardly . . . but those who never really think of themselves as particularly courageous just don't say a goddamned thing—because they're dealing with it inside. Men grow quiet, thinking on loved ones left behind at home. Worrying more about those they would be leaving behind than about their own desperate situation.

It always was the quiet ones who struck Seamus as the bravest of all.

Looking around him, he felt sure they could make a stand of it right there in those rocks, even if they were outnumbered, three, maybe even four, to one. On their left, not far off to the north in the direction where they had come that day, there lay a steep precipice that overhung the stream where they had just quenched their thirsts. Off to their front the woods thinned out on the eastern slopes of the knoll. To the south there wasn't much cover at all across the rolling hillsides. Still, to their rear they were well protected by an irregular line of boulders of all sizes. To the south, on their right—that was the only direction the enemy horsemen could make a charge out of it.

For the next hour the scouts, soldiers, and civilians watched the war party cross leisurely from left to right, eventually heading onto the heaving plain cut into turkey tracks by the jagged flow of those many feeders of the Tongue River.

Behind Donegan, Pourier got to his feet in the lengthening shadows of afternoon. "Time we should go, Lieutenant."

Sibley looked over his men one more time. "I think we should rest awhile more."

"Already had a rest," Grouard said, stiffly shifting from one sore buttock to the other.

The lieutenant sighed. "I ought to give the men a little more rest."

Seamus looked them over himself. Their eyes had filled with growing despair, sagging in weariness, the skin on their faces gone haggard with fatigue. Nothing but water for over a day. Finally the Irishman gazed at the sky, calculating the sun's fall. He turned to Grouard, then to Pourier. They both nodded weakly.

"All right, Lieutenant. Suppose we sit tight right here for a while. Maybe till the sun goes down."

"Yes," Sibley replied in a voice that registered no victory, much of the verve gone out of his speech. "Till the sun goes down."

Chapter 15

8–9 July
1876

"Time to get your men up and moving," Seamus said as darkness sank down on the Tongue River. He turned from the lieutenant to watch the men wake one another slowly, most every one of them moving in that painful manner of men gone too long without something in their bellies.

Kneeling by Grouard, the Irishman said, "Let's go, Frank."

"Don't know that I can," the half-breed complained, shifting from one buttock to the other. "Why'n't you just leave me to come along later?"

"C'mon now, I ain't leaving you," Seamus said. Shifting his rifle to the left hand, he reached down to cup his right under Grouard's arm.

"I ain't leaving you neither," Pourier said, although reluctantly. "You got yourself in this fix with your pecker always wanting to bury itself in any woman you can find, Frank. But I s'pose I'll lend a hand getting you out of trouble this one last time."

Grouard twisted, trying to thrust off their hands as they struggled to pull him up. "Just leave me be!"

"You're coming," Seamus said as they yanked Grouard to his feet, and he shrugged them off at last, stepping away from both. "You're coming if I gotta drag you in a litter my own self."

"No man's ever gonna drag me into Crook's camp!" the half-breed spat at Donegan. "If you're so dead set on me going back with you—I damn well gonna go back on my own two feet."

They plodded away like men will who have gone too long without sustenance, men who have continued to demand of themselves the ultimate in sacrifice without replenishing their abused bodies with what was needed to keep them going. With any luck at all, Seamus figured, by this time tomorrow they would be eating their fill of everything Camp Cloud Peak had to offer.

Even half-boiled beans, along with some greasy salt pork and that damned hard bread. Anything, anything at all sounded like a feast fit for royalty right now. He sucked on his tongue, figuring he could try fooling his stomach for one more day. Convince it he was eating something, chewing something, swallowing something. If only his tongue. For just one more bleeming day.

"No, Donegan. W-we can't."

The Irishman turned and stopped, finding the lieutenant halted five yards behind him. Back ahead of Seamus now, Pourier stopped beside Grouard. Arrayed to either side of Sibley in a ragged crescent were his soldiers. Off to one side stood the rail-thin packer and a gaunt, wild-eyed John Finerty.

Seamus wasn't able to figure out what was happening just then. "What'd you say, Lieutenant?"

The officer squinted against that first light of sunset. He looked as if he were fighting to find the words. Just the right ones. "I've got to think of the men, Donegan. You must understand."

He wagged his head. Nothing came clear. "I don't."

"We're not going that way anymore." Sibley pointed
off to the foothills, the way the scouts were taking them.

"Where we going, then, Lieutenant—if not back to
Crook's camp?"

"That way," the officer answered, jabbing a finger at
the air. "Take us where the going is easier."

For a moment Donegan too searched for the right
words, how best to explain it to these men who had just
reached the end of their string. "You said you was thinking
of the men—well, so am I. We head down there where you
want to go, chances are we'll bump right into that war
party we saw moving east onto the plains a while back. If
not them, we'll run into some other hunting or raiding
party. Damn right—I agree—you best think of the men."

Sergeant Charles W. Day stepped forward, leaning on
his short carbine to say, "We ain't none of us going with
you, Irishman. Staying with the lieutenant. He's gonna lead
us back to Crook down that way—where the going's easier."

Seamus looked at the courageous lieutenant, sensing
that Sibley had rallied his men all that he could. The officer
had done everything good order and the honor of his rank
demanded of him. A proud man, he still stood erect, as
straight as he must have on that parade at West Point. His
chin jutted determinedly. Donegan couldn't help admiring
the man. Couldn't help but remembering other lieutenants
who had led his company in mad charges against J.E.B.
Stuart and others. Men who would always do things much
more bravely than they did things smart.

But there would never be any faulting them for their
courage.

"All right, Lieutenant," Donegan said quietly, knowing he had already given in. "Suppose you tell me how you
figure to lead these men back to Crook, when you don't
know the way."

Sibley swallowed, licking his cracked, sunburned lips.
After he stared off into the distance a moment, he said, "I'll
get them there. I'll keep heading south along the foothills.

And I'll get them there." Then for just a moment his eyes softened. They seemed to plead for understanding. "I . . . I've got to try, Donegan. By God, at least I've got to try."

Seamus's eyes stung a moment, sensing the rise of a deep respect, something more like admiration, for the officer at that moment. "What say you let us lead you, Lieutenant?"

"M-my way?"

Seamus nodded.

"You . . . you would?" Sibley said, taking a step forward, as if he really didn't believe.

Seamus turned for a brief moment, his eyes touching the other two scouts. Then he looked back at Sibley. "That's right. All . . . three . . . of . . . us."

So it was that they took that great, unexpected gamble with what they thought was left of their shredded, sore-footed, pinch-bellied lives. And made another long night's march of it into the heart of that Indian hunting ground.

The sky was beginning to gray with the coming of false dawn as they reached the banks of a stream.

Sibley asked, "What is this, Bat?"

Pourier answered, "Big Goose, I say."

Grouard nodded in agreement, standing wide-footed as he could without actually squatting.

"What time do you have, Sergeant Day?" Sibley asked.

"Just after three A.M., Lieutenant."

"Let's keep going," Seamus told them.

"Cross another creek?" came a whimper from the darkness that swallowed the group behind Sibley and his noncoms.

"That's right," replied the lieutenant.

"That water's cold as ice," Valentine Rufus said, stepping forward.

Sibley inquired, "Was it you complained?"

"No. It was me, Lieutenant," and another soldier inched forward.

"Collins. You been holding up till now—"

Henry Collins tried to explain. "I can't face another

crossing. Getting soaked, sir. I'll not make it to the other side."

"I'll help you," Sibley offered.

"No, Lieutenant. Leave me."

"Me too, sir," Sergeant Cornwall added.

The officer tried to coax the pair, cajole them, even threatening them with court-martial if they did not follow.

"You can shoot me now—or I can just wait here for the Injuns to get me, sir," Collins admitted. "But I ain't going another step."

Finally Sibley relented. "If I leave you two here, you must promise to stay right here. Stay back to the brush over there. We'll send horses for you. You won't have to cross another swollen river on foot."

It was just as well, Donegan decided. Let them stay there so the rest could press on while the light was coming on that ninth day of July. Sibley could not risk the lives of the others while he argued with the obstinate pair. Funny, he brooded as they cat-walked down into the cold waters of Big Goose Creek, how men who will resolve to face bullets and war clubs and scalping knives won't dare set foot again into a mountain stream. Courage is not only a fleeting thing for some, he thought, but a fickle mistress as well.

By the time the detail crossed to the south bank and plodded on, Grouard told Sibley he figured they still had a dozen miles left to go. The cold of the stream poured through what was left of the soldiers' battered boots cut and carved by rocks and hard abuse. On they limped into the coming of day, heading for the mouth of Little Goose Creek. Haggard and starving, the men fairly dragged their rifles through the dust and grass, the detail getting strung out for several hundred yards through the tangle of willows and cottonwoods.

Near five o'clock they spotted some warriors moving from south to north, off to the east of them. With little or no cover to speak of, none of the men made any effort to conceal themselves. Instead they watched the distant horsemen move on past.

Seamus said, "If they saw us—"

"They had to see us," Bat interrupted.

Donegan kept his head turned as he walked. "But they ain't coming."

"Figured they didn't see us," Grouard said.

"No way they could miss us," Pourier protested.

"Must think we're from their village."

Sibley grabbed Donegan's arm, clutching it in weary desperation as he pleaded, "You don't think that big village has attacked Crook, do you?"

"Ain't like Injuns to attack an army camp."

"Still, they jumped us at the Rosebud," grumbled Sergeant Day.

"We ain't got far to go now," Seamus gave as his only reply. "Just keep moving: we'll be having breakfast with the rest of Crook's boys."

They grumbled, whispered, murmured among themselves. Yet they kept moving. That was most important. Keep them moving.

"The birds!" Sibley squealed suddenly.

Until that moment Seamus hadn't been aware of them. Those tiny prairie wrens, each no bigger than the palm of his hand. The branches of the trees and willow were thick with them. Chirping and warbling with the coming of day.

"One of 'em ain't much more'n a mouthful," Donegan replied.

"A mouthful?" asked Sergeant Day. "I could do with just a mouthful. What do you say, Lieutenant?"

Sibley asked, "Mr. Donegan—care to go bird hunting with us?"

Some of the men threw down their carbines and tore at the buttons to their cavalry tunics. Bare-chested, they crept as close to the birds as they dared, then flung their shirts over the branches. After a few frantic attempts, met only with a maddening flutter of hundreds of wings, Sibley cried out.

"I got one! Dear God—I got one!"

The lieutenant carefully pulled a hand from beneath the shirt he had used as a net and produced a small sparrow. With a sudden snap of the bird's neck Sibley began yanking clumps of feathers from the creature's tail, back, and breast. Then as Seamus and some of the others watched, the officer sank his teeth into the raw, red, feathered flesh of the small bird.

Donegan asked, "Don't you wanna cook him first, Lieutenant?"

The bird between his teeth, Sibley looked up at the Irishman, his eyes glazed in some primordial ecstasy. He licked his bloody lips as he reluctantly took the bird out of his mouth, sucking so he would not lose a single drop of all those juices. Wagging his head, he replied, "Don't want to take the time to get a fire started." Then he bit down ravenously again on what was left of the tiny breast.

Pourier wagged his head and said to the lieutenant, "That's pretty rough."

"Yes, Bat," Sibley replied, his mouth turned a bright crimson, "but I'm so hungry that I don't know what to do!"

In the following minutes others began to capture their prey, devouring the tiny birds raw, the meat and blood still warm.

Donegan said to Pourier, "Let's see if we can find some of those Injin turnips you told me of."

Leaving the bird hunters behind as the sky lightened, the pair strode through the brush with their knives ready for digging. From time to time Bat would drop to his knees, showing Seamus the leafy top of the wild plant, uprooting it with his knife. Hastily scraping the moist dirt from the plump tuber, one or the other would split his treasure in half and share what he had just unearthed. At first Donegan thought it tasted like licking the bottom of a stable stall and figured the root couldn't give him much animal strength—the way the bird meat would those who were devouring the wrens and sparrows. But the prairie turnips just might give him enough that he could limp on in to Crook's camp.

"Let's show the lieutenant and his men what to look for, Bat."

Back among the soldiers, Pourier held out two of the leafy tufts and instructed Sibley's men on how to find the turnips in the boggy ground. Within minutes the soldiers had scattered to dig up their own.

It wasn't long before the sun rose off the east, red as a buffalo cow's afterbirth strewn upon the new prairie grass. The coming of that ninth day of July found Sibley's shabby, bloodied patrol setting out again. Up each new slope they crawled, more dead than alive, expecting, hoping, praying each in his own way to find on the far side that inviting fringe of cottonwood that would mark their arrival at Little Goose Creek. But disappointment was all they found for the next hour and a half. More and more hills. More valleys. More rugged, rocky ground.

"Look!" Sibley said, loudly.

The party stumbled to a halt, those behind coming along at a clumsy lurch, finally stopping among the rest as they pointed ahead. Two horses grazed near the crest of the next hill.

Seamus warned, "We better wait here, Lieutenant."

"Yes," Sibley agreed, motioning for his anxious men to be patient. "We'll see about things."

As they watched, the horses eventually turned, and even from that distance the men could see that the animals were saddled. The shimmer of reflected metal flashed beneath the sun's new light. The glimmer of carbines in saddle boots.

"Mary, our Mother of God!" Finerty exclaimed, lunging forward.

He was the first of the massed wave that hurried out of hiding from the brushy willow, making for the hillside.

"Careful!" Donegan bellowed, struggling to hurry along himself, afraid of what might be a trap.

On the slope of the far hill a pair of men suddenly

rose from the tall grass, lumbering toward their animals and yanking their carbines out of saddle pockets.

"Don't fire!" hollered someone near the front.

Others pleaded weakly, "Please! Don't shoot!"

"Stand and identify yourselves!"

"Lieu . . . Lieutenant Frederick . . . Frederick Sibley. U.S. S-second Cavalry."

"Shit!" one of the two cried, the butt of his carbine sinking to the grass. "We thought you was dead, sir!"

"We were," Finerty spoke for them all as he came forward, a dozen of the soldiers right behind him. "Believe me—we were surely good as dead."

Sibley himself came forward. The two soldiers snapped salutes as the lieutenant asked, "Are you on picket duty?"

"No, sir," one answered. "We got permission to go hunting this morning. Break up the monotony at camp."

"M-monotony?" Finerty repeated. Then he broke out in a crazy, hysterical laugh.

"Told you while back, newsman," Bat chided. "Said you'd have lots of good stories to tell your readers, you decide to come with us."

"Damn you, Bat!" Finerty roared, whirling on the scout. "Leave me be about it!"

Sibley said to one of the pair, "Private, I want you to ride back to camp. Get some horses from your troop, any troop. And ask Captain Dewees or Rawolle for that matter—" The lieutenant caught himself and remembered his academy courtesy. "With my compliments, of course—ask them to supply an escort to return with those horses."

"Yes, sir," the soldier said, and trotted up the slope to his mount.

Sibley hollered as loud as he could, "Tell them we've left three men behind who can't come in on foot."

The private reached his horse, turning to reply, "I will, Lieutenant."

Seamus came forward to stand beside Sibley. "And, Private?"

"Yeah?" the soldier answered as he rose to his saddle.

"Before you go, empty your saddlebags of everything you have to eat."

He seemed confused. "Everything I have to—"

"You heard the man," Sibley instructed. "These men . . . my men—they haven't had anything to eat . . . to eat in—"

"A long goddamned time!" Finerty roared for them all.

Chapter 16

8–13 July
1876

THE INDIANS

Another Indian Agent Heard From—
A Piteous Appeal

WASHINGTON, July 14—Indian Inspector Van Derveree reports that at a council with the Indians of Red Cloud and Spotted Tail Agencies, June 30, the chiefs and others expressed a willingness to relinquish the Black Hills country on the terms offered by Van Derveree. The chiefs promised to keep their people at home, and to remain about the agencies. They declare, and the evidence here sustains their declaration, that the only Sioux who are absent are the Cheyennes who have committed depredations in the neighborhood and who have gone north to join the hostiles . . .

Appended to the report is the following statement of Bear Stands Up, an Indian of the Spotted Tail agency, who arrived from Sitting Bull's camp June 25th . . . Sitting Bull sends word that he

does not intend to molest any one south of the
Black Hills, but will fight the whites in that country
as long as the question is unsettled and if not settled as long as he lives . . . He does not want to
fight the whites—only steal from them. White men
steal, and Indians won't come to the settlements.
Whites kill themselves and make the Black Hills
stink with so many dead men . . . Sitting Bull
says if troops come out to him he must fight them,
but if they don't come out he intends to visit this
agency and he will counsel his people for peace.

Colonel Wesley Merritt did not choose to march east to
the troubled agencies that eighth day of July.

Nor south to Laramie.

Instead he decided on a third option: to stay put right
there on Sage Creek, where he felt more mobile, closer to
the agencies, and unquestionably closer to the northbound
trail used by any hostiles fleeing the reservations. From that
stockade he could respond quickly to trouble in either direction—Fort Laramie or Red Cloud.

Through the next four days the regiment sat, fighting
the thumb-sized horseflies that tormented man and beast
alike. Scouting parties were sent out, but none returned
having sighted any war parties or any fresh trails. Then on
the evening of 11 July, the night the Fifth drew its first beef
ration of the campaign, more orders arrived.

"We're marching back to Laramie," King explained to
Cody.

On the lieutenant's face it was plain to see the ardent
fervor to get in his licks against the enemy. Ever since learning of the Little Bighorn disaster, that feeling was something tangible and contagious: Bill was himself every bit as
eager to get a crack at those who had wiped George Armstrong Custer and half his regiment from the face of the
earth.

"From there we're going north to Fetterman," King
went on to explain Sheridan's new orders. "Then we can

finally be on our way to reinforce Crook camped somewhere near the Big Horns."

At dawn the next morning, Wednesday, the command
marched away from Sage Creek, heading back to the Cardinal's Chair on the headwaters of the Niobrara River, sixteen
miles closer to Fort Laramie. That evening brought exactly
the sort of furious thunderstorm that midsummer had
made famous on the western plains, complete with deafening thunder and a great display of celestial fireworks, accompanied by a generous, wind-driven mix of rain and hail
that painfully pelted the regiment, soaking every soldier to
the skin.

Beneath overcast skies on the morning of the thirteenth, the Fifth plodded eighteen more miles and went
into camp by another prominent landmark in Wyoming
Territory, Rawhide Butte. Sundown brought with it another
drenching thundershower.

That very night it was whispered that Merritt had relieved Captain Robert A. Wilson from command of his A
Troop under a dark cloud of suspicion. Cody learned from
Lieutenant King that Wilson had long been a shirker who
had conveniently wrangled himself periods of leave during
the regiment's roughest duty in Arizona during the Apache
campaign. But until the long, arduous scouts Merritt had
demanded of his men, as well as the soul-crushing news of
the Custer disaster, no one had wanted to believe the captain was in reality a coward.

"Surgeon Powell told me in confidence that Wilson
gave himself a nosebleed and swallowed the blood," King
declared to the Fifth's scout after dark that night. "Seems
he intended to go on sick call and spit it back up to make
the physicians think he was bleeding from the lung."

"How did the surgeon know Wilson was shamming?"

King whispered, "Powell says blood brought up fresh
from the lungs looks a lot different. So on checking him
over, they found where Wilson had cut the membranes
inside his nose. Found out, he immediately broke down
and admitted the ruse."

No longer considered an officer of the Fifth, Wilson was compelled by Merritt and Carr to resign his commission as soon as the regiment returned to Fort Laramie, one short day's march to the south—or take his chances with a court-martial. Wilson again chose the coward's way out.

But instead of marching for Laramie the morning of the fourteenth, at reveille the colonel called his officers together to inform them of the dispatches he had received late the night before. Cody stood nearby, every bit as expectant as any of those veterans in blue.

"I've received news from the agencies, via Major Townsend at Laramie. He in turn received word from Major Jordan at Camp Robinson—wired on the eleventh—that states the Indians intend to make a mass break for the north in a matter of days."

"That means they could be fleeing north any day now, General," Carr advised.

"Exactly," Merritt replied.

"With the general's permission?" Cody said sourly. "Of course the Injuns are going to jump their reservations—I'll bet they already heard we've abandoned their Powder River trail and left the way wide open for them."

Several of the other officers murmured their agreement with Cody that they should never have marched south, away from the Cheyenne River.

Raising his hand, Merritt quickly quieted them. "I want to break camp on the double this morning. General Carr and I have determined to march southeast rather than directly south toward Laramie."

"What about our orders to march north to reinforce Crook?" asked a clearly disappointed Captain Julius W. Mason.

"May I answer that, General?" Carr inquired, using Merritt's Civil War rank. When the colonel nodded, Carr continued. "We've discussed this and are both of the same mind. It seems our most pressing urgency is to stop the flow of warriors north, to prevent them from reinforcing the hostile camps that crushed Custer's Seventh. To do that, in our opinion, takes higher precedence over reaching Crook for the present time."

"Remember, gentlemen," Merritt drove home his point in the gray light of dawn, "there are between eight hundred and a thousand Cheyenne warriors still on those two agencies. We could have our hands more than full right here, without having to march north to the Big Horns to join up with Crook for a fight. At the moment, those warriors think their highway is open. I intend to take the Fifth and close the trap on them." After a minute's thoughtful pause the colonel concluded, "If there are no further matters to discuss at this time, let's be marching east."

By noon the Fifth came upon the place where the Camp Robinson–Fort Laramie Road crossed Rawhide Creek. Merritt immediately dispatched Major Thaddeus Stanton to press on to Camp Jordan, there to determine the present situation at Red Cloud Agency. Captain Emil Adams's C Troop was to accompany Stanton as far as the trail's crossing at Running Water Creek, a branch of the Niobrara River, at which point the old German's men were to begin patrolling along the Robinson-Laramie Road. While awaiting Stanton's report, the rest of the regiment would remain in bivouac at Rawhide Creek, sixty-five miles southeast of the Red Cloud Agency—ready to ride at a moment's notice.

How long they would have to wait, no one could say. Some men fished, others caught up on sleep, but just about all debated what should be Merritt's next move to stem the outgoing tide of warriors from the reservations.

They wouldn't have to wait long for word that the Cheyenne were coming.

In a matter of hours those troopers of the Fighting Fifth would vault back into their saddles, and they wouldn't climb back out for something on the order of thirty-six hours.

But waiting was about all they did in Crook's camp.

Every interminable hour that dragged by seemed to

bring renewed grumbling from Crook's officer corps that the army ever relinquished its three posts along the Bozeman Trail. If Forts Reno, Phil Kearny, and C. F. Smith were still manned, they argued, chances were Sitting Bull and Crazy Horse would have never gained a foothold in this hunting ground. And even if the Sioux had made just such an attempt despite the presence of the army, then any campaign by Crook or Terry would be able to operate that much closer to supply depots.

Now with this Sioux campaign grinding on much longer than any military man would have thought possible, it was abundantly clear at every campfire discussion that the officers of the Big Horn and Yellowstone Expedition believed the army should immediately set about erecting its three posts in the heart of the hostiles' country: perhaps first to reactivate old Fort Reno or a new post somewhere on the headwaters of the Tongue; another in the Black Hills to protect the miners, settlers, and growing businesses flocking there; and a third somewhere on the lower Yellowstone, ideally at the mouth of the Tongue River.

"If the army did that," Captain Anson Mills told his compatriots that eleventh day of July, "the army would thereby maintain its presence and military influence over the wild tribes so that no hostile elements on the reservations would ever again seek to flee for what the Indians claim as their land, to recapture what they remember of their old life."

"Their old life is over!" John Finerty snarled. "This is beautiful land—and emigrants damn well ought to come in and snatch it up, take it away from these savages."

John Bourke asked the newsman, "You don't think we can live with the red man if the Indian stayed to his agencies?"

"No," Finerty said flatly, plainly still suffering from his harrowing escape. "Better if the whole tribe of Indians, friendly and otherwise, were exterminated."

"Johnny boy," Seamus said at their noon fire, "you're

sounding just like General Sherman—even Phil Sheridan himself!"

"Damn right I agree with them!" Finerty growled. "And a lot of these men do too, Seamus. We all detest the red race! Don't you?"

Donegan's brow knitted as he brooded on that a moment, then pulled the stub of his briar pipe from his lips and said, "It's true that the red man's done his best to raise my hair—that much is for sure, Johnny. But to paint them all with that same black brush—why, I'm not about to do it. I've seen too much good in some Injins, scouts and trackers and others, to condemn the whole of them. I could have stayed back east in Boston, even your Chicago, and not seen a single Indian for all my life. Maybe some white men brought this on themselves—taking what ain't theirs."

"Wait a minute, Irishman," said Frederick Van Vliet of the Third Cavalry. "So what should become of those good, God-fearing folks who want to come out here to settle, raise a family, and make a new life for themselves?"

Seamus wagged his head. "You're asking the wrong man, Captain. I'm for sure no politician, and I don't have any easy answers on the tip of my silver tongue."

"Then perhaps you should think things over," Finerty advised, "until you know what you want to believe in."

"Oh, I know what I believe in, Johnny boy. I damn well know what I believe in," he replied, his bile rising at the challenge. "Seems to me what should happen to folks who come out to settle on land that belongs to other people should be what happens to any folks who steal something that don't belong to 'em."

"What?" Finerty demanded in a shrill voice. "You're saying white folks should pay those black-hearted savages for the land they want to farm?"

"Can't you see, Donegan?" Mills jumped into the argument. "That's exactly what the land commission is doing at this very moment: trying to strike an accord for the purchase of the Black Hills. But the Indians are balking."

Seamus shook his head in disbelief. "So we don't get what we want—we'll take it anyway?"

"I say we were meant to pacify this land from sea to shining sea," Captain Peter D. Vroom said. "To make it fruitful and we to prosper thereby."

"But to do that," Donegan said, "the fighting men on both sides are made victims of the war between the War Department, sent to fight the Indians, and the Interior Department, supposed to watch over the welfare of the Indians."

Finerty cheered, "I say the Grant administration's done the right thing: turning the Indians over to the army. Now it's time to let the army settle this once and for all!"

"Odd, don't you think, Johnny—that the men on both sides of this war are being killed by government bullets?"

With a snap of his fingers the newsman said, "By the saints—I think you've got something there, Seamus. That could well be the germination of a great editorial I could write on the utter insanity of the government giving weapons and bullets to our helpless red wards, who then escape their assigned reservations, using those bullets to kill the soldiers that same government sends to drive the red savages back to their agencies."

With the correspondent's last few words, Donegan began to peer to the south over Finerty's shoulder, his attention drawn to the nearby hills where pickets had been signaling with their semaphores. Suddenly the brow of a distant hill dippled with over two hundred horsemen.

"Johnny boy, looks like you're gonna get another chance to show just how much you hate all red men," Seamus said with a grin, "both friendly and otherwise."

With a start Finerty and some of the others twisted about, stunned to see the tall lances carried by those distant warriors.

"Brazen sons of bitches, ain't they?" John Bourke said. "To dare venture this close to an armed camp."

"Those aren't Sioux, Lieutenant," Donegan said, as Pourier strode up. "Right, Bat?"

The half-breed replied, "Snake."

"The Shoshone?" Finerty said. "They're back?"

"They promised Crook they'd return," Bourke marveled as he turned to leave. "By damn, the general will want to see this!"

Down from the slopes came that colorful procession of fluttering feathers and streaming scalp locks tied to halters, rifle muzzles, and buffalo-hide shields. Bright-red or dark-blue trade-cloth leggings were shown off by some, while most wore only a breechclout and moccasins under the warmth of that summer sun. They carried rifles and old muzzle-loading fusils, a few even proud to brandish a cap-and-ball revolver. Wolf-hide and puma-skin quivers stuffed with iron-tipped arrows and their sinew-backed horn bows hung at every back.

And at the head of them all rode Tom Cosgrove, that veteran of the Confederate cavalry who had made a new life for himself near Camp Brown on the Wind River Reservation after the war, marrying into the tribe and raising a family of his own, then once more answering the patriot's call when what he loved most was threatened by the enemy. With his two closest friends, former rebels Nelson Yarnell and Yancy Eckles, Cosgrove had brought eighty-six Shoshone warriors over the mountains last month to answer Three Stars's plea for scouts and Indian auxiliaries. After the army's stalemate on the Rosebud, the Snake had abandoned Crook to return home.

Now the three were back, this time bringing 220 warriors.

Yet it was an old, stately warrior who caused the greatest stir as the picturesque parade approached camp: a handsome, wrinkled, and gray-haired war chief who sat proudly erect as he led his tribesmen to the camp of the Three Stars.

"Who is that, Bat?" Seamus asked.

"Only can be Washakie."

"The old chief himself," the Irishman replied. "Old

Big Throat himself told me Washakie goes back to the first time white men came to these mountains."

Pourier nodded. "Days of Jim Bridger, Shad Sweete, and Titus Bass—old trappers like them. Why, Washakie's put some seventy-two or -three winters behind him already. And he still looks strong as a bull in spring! Lookee there, he's brought his two sons along with him. Those boys right behind Washakie, riding with Yarnell and Eckles."

"By damn!" Finerty said. "Even back east we've heard that year in and year out Washakie has been one of the most loyal allies the army could ever hope to have."

Donegan turned to the newsman with a grin to ask, "You mean you're gonna get soft on Injins now, John? Figuring maybe the army shouldn't go and kill 'em all?"

"Maybe you just oughtta let me be, Irishman!" Finerty snapped. "Say, Bat—who are them two squaws riding behind the old boy? His wives?"

Pourier shook his head. "I don't figure Washakie to bring his women. They must be the wives of the two Snakes who stayed with us."

Donegan asked, "That pair of warriors what were too badly wounded for the others to take back to Wind River on travois?"

With a nod Pourier replied, "Yeah. Likely those women come to be with their husbands, help put 'em on the mend."

Finerty shook a raised fist in the air and cheered, "Hurrah! Hurrah for Washakie's soldiers! Now Crook can go whip Sitting Bull and Crazy Horse!"

"I don't think we'll be going anytime soon," Anson Mills grumbled. "No matter that the Shoshone have returned, I'll wager Crook will wait some more, at least until the Fifth gets here."

"Why tarry so long—if the enemy is all around us?" Robert Strahorn asked.

"I suppose it's an old military axiom I learned at the

academy," Mills replied. "A commander must never, never underestimate his enemy."

"With this army made to retreat from the Rosebud, followed only days later by Custer's regiment being butchered," said Captain William H. Andrews of the Third Cavalry, "we've twice felt the savage, brutal, and bloody power of our enemy."

"Don't you fear. When we finally do march," Mills told them, "it will be to destroy what bands we don't drive into the agencies. When we march—it will be to end this Sioux War once and for all."

"You looking for someone, Seamus?" Strahorn inquired.

He said, "Yes. Someone . . . one of Washakie's warriors. A fighting man."

"One of the Snakes?"

His eyes misted over and he blinked them unsuccessfully. "Someone I stood back to back with a few weeks ago —not knowing *when* I would die with all those Sioux charging in to overrun us . . . sure only that I was going to die."*

After a moment of reflection Strahorn asked quietly, "Then this should be a joyful reunion for you."

"Goddamn right, Bob!" he said, turning to the newsman with a wide grin creasing his weathered face. "A bloody joyful reunion it will be for two fighting comrades who escaped death by climbing back out of the mouth of hell!"

---

*The Plainsmen Series, Vol. 9, *Reap the Whirlwind.*

Chapter 17

12–16 July 1876

The Utes—Crook

CHEYENNE, July 14—Negotiations have been making for some time through Captain Nickerson, of General Crook's staff, with the Utes, who are all enemies of the Sioux on account of oft-repeated attacks on them, to secure their co-operation in the present movement against northern hostile Sioux . . .

Gen. Merritt's Fifth cavalry arrived at Fort Laramie to-day, and will move north via Fetterman to join Crook, from whom no additional news had been received, although no fears are entertained of the safety of his command.

Custer's late action has had the effect to take courage out of couriers, and none can be had to make the trip.

Sitting Bull Killed

CHICAGO, July 14—The *Tribune* has a special from Fort Lincoln, given further details of the Little Horn fight, and says that Sitting Bull was killed and also a white man named Mulligan, Sitting Bull's chief adviser . . . It is thought that Sitting Bull's band obtained nearly $20,000, the soldiers having just been paid.

John Finerty wasn't going to talk Quartermaster John V. Furey out of a new pair of shoes, much less boots. When the newsman went back to Furey's wagon camp in the morning to beg even a used pair out of supply, the answer was still no.

Dejected, he clomped back to the bivouac he was sharing with the three other reporters, staring down morosely at the upturned toes on his brogans most all the way. What worked well in the city did not work well out here. But then, back in Chicago a man did not willingly walk mile after endless mile through deep and icy snow as he was forced to do on the Powder River campaign back in March; nor did a Chicagoan repeatedly dunk his shoes in bone-chilling mountain streams and allow them to dry right on his feet—something guaranteed to make the toes curl up on the finest Irish footwear cobbled in that windy city by Lake Erie.

Flies buzzed and droned from sunup to sundown, and this morning of 12 July was no different from all the others endured in Camp Cloud Peak in the weeks since Crook's fight on the Rosebud. Except for the Sibley scout, it was *BOREDOM* in a boldface banner headline.

"So you've had your fill of scouting for a while, eh?" Baptiste Pourier had asked Finerty earlier that morning.

"Just stay away from me, Bat!"

The half-breed had chuckled. "When I come over here to ask you to go out with me and Frank—I figured you'd tell me you had lots of stories to write for your paper back east. Stories about the time you almost lost your hair with Lieutenant Sibley!"

John had whirled on the scout, growling, "Told you to stay away from me!"

"Easy, Johnny," Seamus Donegan had cooed. "He's just trying to pull your leg."

"So you're going out to scout again, Seamus?" Finerty had asked his fellow Irishman.

"Sure am. Like Bat told you, the three of us're going to show Washakie and some of his warriors where we got ambushed in the mountains. Last night, soon as Grouard told him about our fight, Washakie wanted us to take him to the place where we killed White Antelope. Sure you don't wanna come along?"

"No, thank you," Finerty had grumbled. "I've got some dispatches to catch up on."

He'd take a little more boredom before he grappled against a wilderness crawling with scalp-hungry hostiles.

Besides bacon, beans, and biscuits, boredom was a commodity in plentiful supply. For literate men like Finerty, the lack of reading matter weighed particularly heavy. Except for two small libraries of paperback books a pair of officers had hauled north in their saddlebags, there was only the dog-eared, grease-stained, three-week-old newspapers that came up from Fetterman with the supply wagons to make the rounds of camp, then make the rounds again and again until the papers fell apart with so much handling. Come night the flies and other winged pests disappeared, but the wolves, coyotes, and now the Shoshone auxiliaries all raised their primal voices to the stars and the moon. Even an inveterate gambler like Finerty found the idea of a game of poker or keno too odious for words.

That Wednesday morning Crook was having his troops prepare to break camp again just as they had been doing every few days, this time for a move to a new streamlet less than two miles to the north. Here the men would try the fishing in some new creekside pools and the horses would luxuriate in new pastures. This periodic changing of camp also accomplished another object lost on most of those soldiers whose task it was to make the moves. While the sergeants did allow the men brief liberty to swim, fish, or hunt, there was no time off that would allow real boredom to set in.

Every other day the tents were struck, to be pitched in a new camp a few miles away. Horses were constantly herded from one patch of grass to another, picketed and hobbled against brazen raids by the enemy. Wagons had to be loaded up for every move, then unloaded when the new site was reached. New sinks near the creeks had to be dug for the mess cooks, and new latrines were a must for an army the size of the Big Horn and Yellowstone Expedition. On those days when camp was not to be moved, the cavalry troops exercised their horses at a walk, trot, and gallop, which kept each man in constant contact with his animal.

This steady rotation of fatigue details made Finerty come to believe that the greenest recruit who had marched north from Fort Fetterman with Crook in May couldn't help but be a hard-muscled, savvy campaign veteran by the end of the summer.

Like the nightly visits of the Sioux come to try running off some of the horses or Tom Moore's cantankerous mules, as well as the warriors' daily attempts to set fire to the grass surrounding the white man's camp, every afternoon saw a thunderstorm roll across the valley with enough fidelity a man could set his watch. Before the onslaught of today's downpour, Finerty figured to enjoy this sunny morning by getting in a little fishing, making only a halfhearted effort and using some of the abundant grasshoppers for bait—more an excuse to doze in the shade of rustling cottonwoods than to catch anything. He was nearly asleep when he heard the first voices of those fishing across the narrow creek.

He sat up at the excitement in their voices, shoving his floppy slouch hat back on his head, blinking his eyes, shading them to peer into the distance where many of the other fishermen were pointing off to the north. Already his heart pounded with the memories of his narrow escape from the Sioux, swallowing hard—afraid they were under attack. With the smoky haze clinging to this high country after the hostiles' last attempt to burn the soldiers out, John couldn't be sure—but it appeared to be only three of them. Likely only scouts for a larger war party.

Quickly glancing over his shoulder, he reassured himself that he wasn't so far from camp that he couldn't make it back on foot, even in those damned worn-out brogans. Headed his way loped Captain Anson Mills, trailed by a hastily assembled squad of troopers from his M Company following him out of camp.

Looking again to the north, he saw the trio of riders ease off the top of that nearby hill, urging their mounts down toward the stream where Finerty stood with other fishermen.

A growing chorus of voices behind him told the newsman that the camp had indeed been alerted. Perhaps it was only some of the men who had gone to the site of the Sibley ambush early that morning with Washakie and his warriors. But as the breeze nudged aside some of the gray haze, Finerty saw that the trio rode army horses, not the smaller Indian ponies. Of the riders two wore dusty blue tunics while the third sported a greasy gingham shirt. Kepis rested on all three heads.

"Them's soldiers!" someone shouted as Mills and his men rattled and jingled past, prodding their horses down into the creek and splashing up the far side without slowing.

"Soldiers?" Finerty said, realizing the trio was just that as he tossed aside his handmade willow fishing pole and stood staring at the water. "Shit. Not again," he grumbled, then lumbered down into cold water, soaking his old shoes one more time.

Wet to the knees, John slogged up the north bank and trotted after Mills and his detail, reaching them about the time the captain halted his M Company and awaited the approach of the trail-ragged trio.

When they halted, all three horsemen saluted wearily. It was a moment before one of the trio licked his lips and asked, "Captain?"

"Mills—M Troop, Third Cavalry."

"This is General Crook's camp?"

"It is," Mills replied. "Who do I have the pleasure of addressing?"

"Benjamin F. Stewart, sir. Private, E Company. Seventh U.S. Infantry."

"Good Lord," Mills murmured almost under his breath. "Are you attached to General Terry's Dakota column?"

One of the others nodded and said, "James Bell, E Company, Captain Mills. Yes, sir. We come from General Terry's camp on the Yellowstone."

"Mouth of the Rosebud, sir," the third gushed. "William Evans, I'm with E Company too."

"The three of you . . . rode down from the Yellowstone?"

"Yes, sir," Stewart answered. "We have dispatches from Terry. We'd appreciate you taking us to see General Crook."

Lieutenant Charles King was one of the first to be electrified by the news from Captain Thaddeus Stanton that reached Colonel Wesley Merritt by courier just past noon, the fifteenth of July.

Camp Robinson
Saturday July 15 1876
General
    A considerable number of Sioux Warriors
left here for north this morning. The Cheyennes
are also going . . . The Indians think you are
still at Sage Creek & along there, and count on
getting by you easily . . . The agent here is
thoroughly stampeded by the threatening bearing
of the Indians since the Custer fight . . . Thinks
there are not troops enough to protect the agency
in case of trouble.

I will wait here until I hear from you. Send a
small escort when you wish me to join you . . .

                                        Stanton

General Merritt
P.S. 12. m. It seems now that the Cheyennes left
last night—all except a few old men & women.
So you will have to hurry up if you catch any of
them. About 100 Indians, wounded in Crook's
fight, are reported to be distributed among their
friends here . . . Indians leaving here will
doubtless scatter in any direction in small parties,
to get by you. Let me know where & when to join
you.

                                        Stanton

The Cheyennes have disposed mostly of their
lodgepoles, and take their families on ponies.

"The Cheyenne are breaking!"
Through their bivouac now the word spread like wild-
fire through the Fifth Cavalry: the colonel had decided to
postpone their march north to reinforce Crook for the
week it would take to countermarch and catch the escaping
Cheyenne in a trap. Surely his superiors would understand
that such an action must take precedence over Sheridan's
orders to join the Big Horn and Yellowstone Expedition.

Two things were clear from Stanton's dispatch: the
agency Cheyenne still believed the Fifth was off to the
northwest, blocking the route they must travel to reach
Sitting Bull's confederation; in addition, the Cheyenne appeared fully confident in their ability to elude the pony
soldiers.

Much shorter but every bit as urgent was Major Jordan's own dispatch to Merritt:

I have the honor to report that I have just received reliable information that about 800 North-

ern Cheyenne / men women and children /
containing about 150 fighting men, and a good
many Sioux all belonging to Red Cloud Agency
are to leave here tomorrow for the north . . . it
is my belief that a good many Indians have been
leaving since the receipt of the news of the disaster of Lieutenant Colonel Custer.

"Now we'll slam the door shut on them," King vowed.
"We better," said Lieutenant Colonel Eugene Carr. "If
we don't get there in time, those Cheyenne will join with
the hostile Sioux who already wiped out half the Seventh.
And once together, no telling what trouble the united tribes
could cause. Why, I can imagine how easily they would roll
right over the settlements in the Black Hills."

Carr had reason to be concerned. Only a few weeks
had passed since Sheridan had appointed him the commander of a new "Black Hills district" carved out of
Crook's Department of the Platte.

"Deadwood, Custer City . . . all the rest," King
agreed, imagining what slaughter there would be should
the warrior bands strike the far-flung settlements and small
pockets of miners and prospectors.

According to Major William H. Jordan, commander at
Camp Robinson, at least eight hundred Cheyenne were
moving north to join Sitting Bull's hostiles. But this would
be something different: this time the regiment was not
chasing the Indians; now their task was instead to cut
across the warriors' trail. Here they were no more than a
day's ride from Fort Laramie at that moment, so it would
take what Merritt called a "lightning march" if there was to
be any hope for the Fifth turning on its heels to be far to
the northeast when the Cheyenne showed up.

"To get there," King said with exasperation as he
looked at the old map Carr had spread across the scarred
top of his field desk, "these eight companies will have to
remain undiscovered while we march across three sides of a
square, riding like the wind itself."

"Yes," Carr agreed, dragging his fingertip across the paper, "while the enemy traverses the fourth side."

"And," King said, looking into the eyes of that veteran campaigner, "when this weary outfit finally gets there—we'll still have to be ready to fight the very devil."

Within an hour of receiving the dispatches from Stanton and Jordan, trumpeters blew "Boots and Saddles" over that camp at Rawhide Creek. In a matter of minutes the regiment was on the march. Merritt had waited long enough. And though they realized they might well be outnumbered at least two to one, his men had nonetheless been itching for this moment.

The Fifth would again prove its mettle.

Merritt was leaving a small guard of the Ninth Infantry to escort his wagon train under the command of the regiment's own Lieutenant William P. Hall, with orders to come on at all possible speed, even to catching up after the rest of the troops had gone into bivouac after dark. At the same time that the column of fours set out for the west, to fool any lurking scouts into believing that they were merely heading for Fort Fetterman country and not backtracking for the Niobrara, the colonel dispatched a courier racing toward Camp Robinson with orders recalling Stanton, and yet another horseman sent galloping south to Laramie to inform Sheridan of Merritt's intentions and reasons for disobeying his commander's orders.

Into the shimmering heat of that afternoon the troopers pushed their animals. The Cheyenne would have no more than a short twenty-eight-mile journey to the northwest to reach the crossing come Monday morning. On the other hand, after a trip of thirty-five miles with what they had left for light that day, the Fifth would still have to endure a forced march of more than fifty miles on Sunday to be there before their quarry had flown.

Fourteen miles later a short halt was called at Rawhide Creek. While the men watered their horses by companies, some of the soldiers waiting their turn filled their bellies with the hardtack they had stuffed into their haversacks from Hall's wagons. In half an hour they were back in the saddle, this time riding north by west. When the sun keeled over toward the far mountains at five P.M., Bill Cody turned their noses square north for the Niobrara, reaching the river by sunset.

Finally at ten P.M. the order was given to halt, picket the horses, and go into bivouac for what they had left of that night's darkness. They unsaddled under the tall, naked buttes at the mouth of the Running Water near the Cardinal's Chair. They had completed their grueling thirty-five-mile march as planned.

After Carr assigned Captain Edward M. Hayes of G Troop to post pickets around the herd and establish a running guard through the night, the rest of Merritt's command lay upon the cold ground and huddled under their blankets. Come morning those four hundred troopers realized they still faced the daunting prospect of putting in a march of more than fifty miles. If in the next few hours their horses could just get enough of the skimpy buffalo grass to eat . . .

"The Fifth's done it before," Eugene Carr reminded the veterans at officers' call that night. "You men who were with us in sixty-nine when we tracked down the Cheyenne that time can tell the new boys. This has always been the sort of outfit that can do the impossible. We've always put in longer marches than any other outfit—and popped up where the enemy didn't expect. And now, men—we're going to do it again. By damn, we're going to do it again!"

Just as King was drifting off to sleep at midnight, Lieutenant Hall rolled in with his train, traces jangling like sleighs, mules snorting with the smell of water in their nostrils, and an entire company of infantrymen bellowing in hunger, rubbing sore rumps as they clambered down from the wagons. The young lieutenant laid his head back down on his arm, filled with a renewed and respectful awe at what those men of Hall's had just accomplished: the way they had kept those vital and cumbersome supply wagons moving across that broken, rugged ground, no more than two hours behind the cavalry.

It wouldn't be the last of William P. Hall's surprises.

Beneath the stars at three o'clock that Sunday morning the men were rousted from their blankets by sergeants growling commands up and down the rows of sleeping troopers. The men awoke to find breakfast waiting for them —although there would be nothing fancier than bacon and bread to wash down with their coffee. What they got was served in the chill predawn darkness with only a few minutes to spare for a man to relieve himself before he had to throw a saddle on the back of his weary horse and slip a bit into a set of reluctant jaws after the animals were fed their own good breakfast of oats from a nose bag, compliments of Hall's supply wagons.

By five o'clock the men were pressing their knees against horses' ribs, following Merritt upon his high-strutting gray, bidding farewell to the valley of the Niobrara, marching north. By midmorning they had crossed the rugged divide between the waters of the Niobrara and the Cheyenne, turning hard on to the east where an hour later, at 10:15 A.M., the head of the column once more hoved into sight of the palisaded walls of the Sage Creek stockade. Lieutenant Taylor of the Twenty-third Infantry and half his H Company came to stand at arms, welcoming back the cavalry. But the Fifth was to enjoy less than an hour out of the saddle while horses were watered and the troopers wolfed down rations from their haversacks.

About the time Hall rumbled in with his train, Carr was already preparing his men to move out. After every company replenished its ammunition supply from the freight wagons—each man ordered to carry every last cartridge he could in his thimble belt and belt kit, as well as filling every spare pocket—the troopers mounted up with three days' rations in their haversacks and marched away east by northeast as Merritt conferred with Hall. They decided to leave the lieutenant's large supply wagons behind at the stockade. After watering the thirsty stock only the smaller company wagons rolled away from Sage Creek, emptied and stripped bare of everything. Within the gunwales of those bumpy, hard-ribbed wagons Merritt crammed two companies of infantry, belonging to the Twenty-third and the Ninth.

By noon Carr slowed the column's pace to four and a half miles per hour along that stretch of the Black Hills Road. Less chance of raising a telltale cloud of dust over the summer prairie that would betray the regiment's approach. At two-thirty the lieutenant colonel again called for a halt beside a dry creekbed. No watering the horses this time. From there they followed Cody and White due east, leaving the well-traveled road for the trackless prairie.

At five P.M. Merritt ordered a halt for watering their trail-weary stock, then pushed on into the lengthening shadows. More torturous miles across the treeless, rolling heave of undulating grassland. Far off to the south stood the tall, austere, striated Pine Ridge that sheltered the reservation from all but the most brutal of cold winter winds. Almost as far away to their left lay the dark, rumpled corduroy of the Black Hills.

Hours later at sundown King spotted a distant line of meandering green, far ahead on the pale prairieland. Cottonwood, willow, and alder, and another of those rare water courses that crisscrossed this arid country. Minutes later Cody and Buffalo Chips loped back to the head of the column, their long hair caught in the wind as they tore their hats from their heads and waved them for all to see.

"Trail's in sight!" Buffalo Bill shouted, bringing the big buckskin around in a tight circle; a cascade of dust sent in a rooster tail made a rosy gold in the sun's dying light.

Merritt stood in his stirrups, gazing into the distance like an old cavalryman. "Any hostiles in sight?"

"Not a goddamned one," Buffalo Chips White replied.

Instantly nettled, Carr demanded, "We haven't missed them, have we? Are we too late?"

Cody wagged his head. "Trail's old. Nothing new's come this way."

Carr and Merritt gazed at one another, their lips thin lines of determination, but their eyes twinkling with intense expectation, glittering with the satisfaction of an impossible task well-done.

Down to the timber the Fifth rode, the end clearly in sight. By nine o'clock and the coming of dark, the troopers had unsaddled and made camp close beneath the bluffs. Here the narrow creek swept around in nearly a complete circle, forming the high ridge that would protect the regiment's cooking fires the men buried deep in pits from discovery.

In thirty-one hours this group of weary animals and trail-hardened men had covered more than eighty-five miles.

"I couldn't be any prouder of you," Merritt told his subordinates that night during officers' call.

"We're in their front," Carr reminded the men. "The enemy will be here in the morning."

"And we'll be ready for them," Merritt vowed.

"General, sir?" King asked.

"Yes, Lieutenant?"

"Do we know the name of this little creek?"

Merritt turned to his scouts with a gesture.

Cody stepped forward, loosening the colorful silk tie knotted around his neck. "It's a tributary of the South Cheyenne, Lieutenant."

King pursued his answer, saying, "Do we have a name for it—for the record, I mean?"

With a nod Cody replied, "Only what the Indians call it."

"What is that, Mr. Cody?" he pressed. "What do the Indians call this creek?"

"Lieutenant King," the famous scout answered in that hush surrounding them all, "it's called the Warbonnet."

Chapter 18

13–17 July
1876

Crook Heard From at Last—Still In
Camp at Cloud Peak—Terry Wants
Him Up North

CHEYENNE, July 15—The following is from Crook's
Camp Cloud Peak, July 12, via Fetterman tonight:
Three soldiers from General Terry's command, at
the mouth of the Big Horn, have just arrived. General
Terry's dispatch to Crook confirms Custer's
fate, and implies very plainly that had Custer
waited one day longer Gibbon would have joined
him. Terry is anxious for Crook to join forces, make
plans and execute them, regardless of rank. The
Indians are still hovering about the Little Big Horn,
one day's march from here. They have fired into
camp every night of late, and tried to burn us out
by setting the grass on fire all around.

On the 6th, Lieutenant Sibley, of the Second cavalry,
with twenty-five men and Frank Gruard and
Babtiste Pouerier as scouts, went on a reconnaissance.
They were discovered and surrounded and

followed into the timber of the Big Horn mountains, where, by hitching their horses to trees and abandoning them, the men were enabled to escape on foot by way of a ravine in the rear. They all got back alive, and probably this diversion saved the company from a grand attempt of stampede or capture.

The Snake Indians, two hundred strong, joined us here yesterday, but unless you come soon no offensive operations will be likely to take place until your arrival.

The Fifth cavalry, from Cheyenne Crossing, and a wagon train and additional infantry are due from Fetterman to-day. The health of the command is good. Gen. Gibbon's reserve forces were met by the victorious Sioux, dressed in Custer's men's clothes and mounted on their horses, firing into the soldiers. The Indian village passed gave evidence of white men's presence, kegs of whiskey, etc., being found. Signal fires supposed to be in reference to the incoming wagon train, are visible to the east of Crook's camp on the extreme south waters of Tongue river.

When none of his civilian scouts would volunteer—no matter how much money was offered—those three hardy privates had stepped forward to carry General Terry's messages away from that camp along the Yellowstone on the morning of the ninth. With separate copies of the dispatches sewn into each man's clothing, the trio left the mouth of the Rosebud at sundown. It had taken them three nights of travel, lying in cover throughout each day, as they threaded their way through a wilderness overrun by the hostiles they knew had already devoured half of Custer's gallant Seventh.

From the Little Bighorn battlefield, the trio simply wandered south in the wake of the fleeing village. When the trail divided for the first time at Lodge Grass Creek, the

soldiers chose the left-hand trail, which led them over to
the upper Rosebud where the Indian trail again divided.
Many travois headed east, toward the Tongue. But a pony
trail continued south, up the Rosebud toward the country
in which, they'd been told, they might locate Crook's camp.

Although ragged and exhausted, Bell, Evans, and
Stewart sat for hours before huge assemblies of Crook's
troops relating horrific stories about the battle scene and
the carnage Terry's men had discovered beside the Little
Bighorn. There wasn't anyone more astonished that the trio
had managed to poke their way through enemy country
than George Crook himself. Off hunting eighteen miles
from camp in the Bighorn Mountains that morning of the
eleventh, he eagerly read Terry's letter in silence as soon as
Mills brought it directly to him. Crook immediately called
in his hunters and escort and hurried back to Goose Creek.

"Gentlemen," the general addressed his subalterns after a bugler summoned them for officers' call, "I think we
can all agree that there are too many in this army who have
underrated the valor and the numbers of our enemy, along
with their willingness to fight."

"All we want is another crack at them, General," Mills
said.

Apparently he spoke for most of them, officers eagerly
nodding their heads in agreement.

"But I want you all to listen to General Terry's letter—
before we go galloping off into God only knows what,"
Crook instructed.

> "The great and to me wholly unexpected
> strength which the Indians have developed seems
> to me to make it important and indeed necessary
> that we should unite, or at least act in close coop-
> eration. In my ignorance of your present posi-
> tion, and of the position of the Indians, I am
> unable to propose a plan for this, but if you will
> devise one and communicate it to me, I will fol-
> low it . . . I hope that it is unnecessary for me

to say that should our forces unite, even in my Department, I shall assume nothing by reason of my seniority, but shall be prepared to cooperate with you in the most cordial and hearty manner, leaving you entirely free to pursue your own course . . ."

Asked Lieutenant Colonel William B. Royall, "Have you decided upon a course of action, General?"

"Only what it has been all along," Crook replied, disappointing many of the most eager to get on with the campaign. "To await the arrival of the Fifth Cavalry before resuming the campaign."

All that night there raged heated debates over what should be Crook's course of action, as well as many murmured complaints about the man more and more of them referred to sneeringly as "Rosebud George." To many of the enlisted and some in the officer corps as well, it was beginning to appear irresponsible, if not downright criminal, to allow the enemy to withdraw from their front without doing a thing to find out when they'd left, and where they were headed.

Yet what was hardest to take was that after three defeats at the Powder, the Rosebud, and on the Little Bighorn in that many months, it appeared the army had lost its will to win the Sioux campaign, if not lost its nerve altogether.

The following day, a Thursday the thirteenth, Major Alexander Chambers returned from Fetterman, bringing a train of supply wagons stuffed to the sidewalls with food, ammunition, and news from home, escorted north to Camp Cloud Peak by seven companies of the Fourth Infantry. Official dispatches from Omaha told the general to expect a detachment of Ute coming up from Colorado Territory, hungry for a chance to get in some blows against their old enemies. Chambers personally handed over private letters to Crook from Sheridan, which informed him that Merritt's Fifth Cavalry was on its way back to Fort

Laramie, from there to Fetterman, with orders to hurry with all dispatch to reinforce Crook's impatient Big Horn and Yellowstone Expedition.

"Seamus!"

Donegan turned at the sound of John Bourke's voice, finding the young lieutenant trotting his way.

Bourke huffed to a halt and held an envelope out at the end of his arm. "Mail call!"

"Truly? For me?"

Slowly the lieutenant dragged the envelope sensuously under his nose, inhaling deeply. "This just came up with Chambers's train from Fetterman. I think this one for you came from someone you know at Laramie."

My dearest Seamus—

How frightened I am for you. I'm frightened for me too. We've just received news of a terrible massacre to some soldiers gone to fight the same Indians you are searching for.

I don't think I've slept much since. When I have, it's only to awaken myself screaming with horrid dreams. I don't know what toll this is taking on the baby, this, my grave worry for you.

I walk twice every day now, of each afternoon and evening. It's so beautiful down by the river, I know you love this sort of quiet. Usually so quiet you can hear the breeze in the cottonwoods. A cool, shady place I go with my blanket. There's a spot I'll show you when you come back to me. A place I go to spread my blanket, sit and read all your letters again and again, mostly so our child can hear the sound of his father's words, if not the sound of your voice.

For those long, hot hours each afternoon, it is a wonderful place to hide, reminding me of a place back in the hardwoods where Rebecca and I used to hide from Mummy when we were girls back home.

I don't know how to tell you this, but I don't feel like I have a home now, Seamus. I used to have one, but that was where I used to live when I was growing up. And then in Texas I vowed to cleave unto you. Ever since, you have been my home. But you are not here. So this is not my home. My home must be far, far away, so heavy is my heart.

Home is where you are, right now, holding this letter, reading my words. I wish I could tell you that everything is fine here, but it is not. Oh, the baby is doing well. And you would not imagine how big I am getting! But, ever since the news about Custer's men, Laramie has become a somber place. Even gloomy. Such sad faces on all the men and especially the women.

Oh, how I wish you were here! You made me laugh so! You could chase away any dark, threatening clouds just by smiling at me with your gray eyes. How I need to see you smile with those eyes once again.

The more I think on it—and I have nothing but time to think—Crook was miraculously lucky to escape from the Sioux like he did on Rosebud Creek. Must have been more than luck, though, for I was praying that God watched over you. He did. And the rest were watched over with you.

What joy you brought me with that little telegram. And a week later came your letter, telling me all about that fight. Dear Lord—how horrible it must have been for that group of Royall's soldiers to find themselves surrounded and cut off from all chance of escape! How brave were that man and the Shoshone scout you spoke of— the two who stood over the bodies of others who had fallen to the enemy's bullets. How selfless and brave!

I'm just so thankful to God that nothing like that happened to you during that fight.

I am sure you have heard all the news of the disaster on the Little Horn. It's all that anyone talks about. It's all I can think about when the baby isn't kicking and I'm not thinking about you. The only other news to tell you is that the Fifth Cavalry came through here recently. General Sheridan has ordered them north to the Black Hills where they will prevent warriors from going to join Sitting Bull and Crazy Horse. Their arrival, then their departure, was the biggest stir we've had here in a long time.

And you'll never guess who I met. I could not really believe it, but it was him. Buffalo Bill Cody. Your old friend. Such a gentleman. We had a lovely talk about all that you have told me again and again, and how you showed me the Elephant Corral in Denver. He has been back east on the stage for a few years now, but told me he had to return west when the Indian war began. He asked all about you, and I told him what I knew—at least all I knew of you since Texas. Oh, you should see him, Seamus. He couldn't be more proud to be scouting again for his old friends in the Fifth Cavalry.

As I looked at him, his long hair and mustaches and that finely tanned buckskin coat of his, I think of you. And in his smile I see you smile, happy to be doing what you love to do. Like Buffalo Bill Cody himself, riding out in front of some great army marching after the blood-thirsty savages who butchered General Custer and all his men. Yes, I studied him as we talked, thinking how alike you both were, the freedom and the wilderness, how in love you both are with your work.

For a short time this place really seemed like

a fort, cavalry soldiers everywhere, going about their business with great urgency. Then it was quiet again, and every woman here had time on her hands again. So much time to think about a husband up there in Indian country with Crook.

When you return *home* to me, I will take you to this place where I write you my letters and read the letters you have sent me. It's here I talk to the baby for hours on end, every afternoon and evening. It's here I think on you.

Dear, I think on you when I wake each morning and when I lie in that bed alone at night. Remembering your touch. Remembering your kiss.

But here in the cool shade of this place, with the river gurgling past my hiding place, with the breeze in the branches overhead, it's here I think most of you and never fail to ask God to keep you in the palm of his hand.

My prayer is to bring you home to us, Seamus. Come home as soon as you can. Come home to us.

Samantha

Magnitude of the Sioux War

CHICAGO, July 15—The Times' Bismarck special says the impression prevails that the military authorities do not realize the work they have to do. The Indians' hostile camps are believed to number at least ten thousand, and while there are many women and children, nearly all of these are effective in a campaign. There are certainly five thousand to seven thousand Indians who can and will fight until subdued; and the fate of Custer should be a warning that they intend to make thorough work, and have confidence in their ability to do it . . .

There are less than three thousand troops all told operating against the Indians, and nearly half of these are used in guarding wagon trains or supply depots, while there seems to be a disposition on the part of each command to win glory for itself without the aid of co-operating forces. Until more effective measures are taken you may look for continued disaster or an abortive campaign.

"You'll see that I'm awakened at three-thirty—so I can awaken the colonel?" asked Lieutenant William C. Forbush, Wesley Merritt's regimental adjutant.

Charles King answered, "Yes. You can count on me."

King watched the young officer turn away, then stood for a moment more with Captain Mason. The pair of weary officers had just unfurled their blankets, preparing to catch a few hours' sleep. But at that very moment up walked Forbush, stumbling in the dark over a fallen tree and creating quite a commotion as he scrambled back to his feet and dusted himself off, coming to deliver Merritt's orders. Mason's Company K was ordered to establish a forward picket post to the southeast, closest to the trail crossing.

"Why did Merritt choose K, Captain?" King whispered when the adjutant was out of earshot.

Mason wagged his head wearily. "I don't know, Mr. King. We pulled picket duty last night, and you were up all night with Captain Hayes. Merritt must think we're the best, even when we're operating without much sleep—or he wouldn't have chosen us."

King wagged his head. "There is some small compensation, Captain."

"What would that be?" Mason asked with a yawn.

"At least I'll be the one to first see the enemy," the lieutenant said. "Permission to select the men for the forward observation post?"

Julius Mason nodded. "Agreed. K will remain on duty to your rear once you have selected your spot."

Choosing Sergeant Edmund Schreiber and Corporal

Thomas W. Wilkinson, King left that reassuring circle of troops and horses behind where they had gone into bivouac beneath some bluffs that rose above the sluggish Warbonnet. Penetrating the inky, starlit darkness on foot, the trio groped their way forward as Mason went about posting his outflung pickets in the hollows and depressions they came across in the rolling landscape. By keeping to the low places those camp guards would be better able to discern objects against the night sky. What there was left of night, anyhow.

"You must exercise the utmost vigilance," Mason told his troopers before scattering them to their posts. "Since this is not the sort of picket duty where you can keep yourself awake by walking, you'll just have to stay alert the best you can. Keep your bunkie awake, whatever you do."

After finding a knoll where he could leave Schreiber and Wilkinson, King rejoined Mason to walk the rounds.

Upon reaching the Warbonnet, Bill Cody had gone alone to the southeast, returning a half hour later at slapdark to report that the hostiles must still be to the southeast. No fresh sign. It was so quiet out there that Charles figured there couldn't be an Indian inside of a hundred miles of their bivouac. But then the hills and ridges surrounding their camp slowly came alive as coyotes set up a disharmonious chorus that rose and fell, rose and fell again. At least, King rebuked himself for hating the noise, *these coyotes might well warn us of the enemy's approach.*

The first hour passed, then the second, and finally at one o'clock Mason and King set out again on their hourly prowl along the outer perimeter of their defenses. They were challenged at every sentry post, and the pair responded with the countersign. But upon nearing a post established down in the willows by the stream, there came no challenge to halt and identify. Creeping closer, they found the young soldier dozing in the shelter of the eroded bank.

King sneaked in behind the picket and wrenched his

carbine out of his hands. Instantly the surprised soldier leaped to his feet, Mason scolding him.

"Soldier—don't you realize the enemy might have forward scouts, feeling their way north?" the captain explained.

"Y-yes, sir."

"You're aware sleeping on duty is a court-martial offense?"

The soldier swallowed with an audible gulp. "S-sir, am I—"

King interrupted, handing the soldier his carbine. "We've got to be ready, all of us. This is your post. It's up to you."

Contrite, he took his rifle, clutching it across his chest. "I promise, sirs. Promise I won't let you down."

Chapter 19

17 July 1876

Dispatch from Crook—What He Will Do When Merritt Comes

WASHINGTON, July 17—General Sheridan has forwarded the following dispatches to Sherman: I had already ordered General Merritt to join General Crook, but he will be delayed a few days, attempting to intercept the Indians who have left Red Cloud Agency. I would suggest to Crook to unite with Terry and attack and chase the Indians, but I am so far away that I will have to leave them as I have done.

CAMP ON GOOSE CREEK, Wyoming, July 13, via Fetterman, July 15.—My last information from Red Cloud Agency was that the Cheyennes had left there to reinforce the enemy in my front. As this takes away all the disturbing element from that section, I have availed myself of the lieutenant general's permission, and ordered eight companies of the Fifth Cavalry, under Col. Merritt, to join me at this point. The best information I can get from the front is that the Sioux have three fighting men to my one. Although I have no doubt of my ability to whip them with my present force, the victory would likely be one barren of results, and so I have thought better to defer the attack until I can get the Fifth here, and then end the campaign with one crushing blow. The hostile Indians are, according to my advices, encamped on the Little Horn, near the base of the mountain, and will probably remain there until my reinforcements come up. I received a dispatch from General Terry this morning asking me to co-operate. I will do so to the best of my ability.

GEORGE CROOK
Brigadier General

At three A.M. that Monday morning King's teeth began to chatter as the coldest hours of the day descended around them. A half hour later the coyotes were still in good voice as the lieutenant picked his way through the bivouac to find Merritt rolled in his blanket beneath a tall cottonwood.

"Colonel?"

The veteran of Beverly Ford and the Rappahannock came awake immediately, sitting up and tapping Forbush beside him. "Thank you, Mr. King. You may now return to your company."

"It's time for me to move to our forward observation post, Colonel."

"Lieutenant London, who I've put in charge of A Troop, is ready for you to relay word to me," Merritt explained. "Send news the moment you see anything. Anything at all."

King would relay word back to a low ridge immediately behind him, where sat Private Christian Madsen, Company A, as his horse cropped grass in a shallow swale below him. Although a recent immigrant from Denmark, Madsen was far from being wet behind the ears, nor was he a young shavetail recruit. Instead this solid, older soldier

Lieutenant Robert London had chosen from his company to carry word to Merritt himself was a cast-iron, double-riveted veteran of both the Danish-Prussian and the Franco-Prussian wars on the European Continent, as well as having served a hitch in Algeria with the French Foreign Legion before coming to America, wandering farther west still to this opening frontier.

After sliding in between Schreiber and Wilkinson atop a commanding knoll, King swept his eyes over the land-scape becoming an ashen gray before him. Some two miles away against the southern sky lay a long ridge that extended around to their left, where it eventually lost itself to the rise and fall of the rolling countryside. Farther yet to the north-east stood the sharp outlines of the Black Hills themselves, at that moment brushed with hues of the faintest pastel-rose. As the minutes continued to grind by, both the Hills and that ridge to the south grew all the more distinct as night seeped from the belly of the sky.

In that predawn light King could now make out the shape of an even better observation post, a taller hill rising another four hundred yards off. "Come with me, fellas."

Minutes later, as all three of them hid just beneath the crest of that small conical mound, the lieutenant found he commanded a full view of everything moving on the land between their post and the distant ridges. Behind them the trees bordering the Warbonnet could be made out in the middistance, the cottonwood and brush laced with a wispy fog rising off the creek as it poured sluggishly toward its meeting with the South Fork of the Cheyenne. Back there waited 330 enlisted men as well as 16 officers, in addition to their surgeon, along with Bill Cody and his 4 other scouts.

Grinding his teeth on nothing for the moment, King thought how just about now the others were pumping life into the small fires they buried in the sand, starting to heat up some coffee. What he'd give for a hot, strong cup of army brew right now. And he brooded that they'd be laying

out slabs of that pungent salt pork in their frying pans as
the coffee water heated to boiling.

As if it had overheard his thoughts, his own stomach
grumbled, protesting. Man just wasn't meant to fight on an
empty stomach.

Due south he could begin to make out the outline of
the fabled Pine Ridge that stretched all the way from western Wyoming Territory, on through Nebraska, then angled
north toward Dakota. Time and again King swept the
whole country with his field glasses, scouring the horizon
from east to west in a 180-degree arc. Off to the west in the
growing light he could begin to see the deeply chewed trail
the Fifth made reaching this point last night. But off to the
east—nothing moved.

By 4:30 A.M. all seven companies had saddled their
horses and were awaiting action in the cold stillness of the
sun's emergence. The chilled air refused to stir. The silence
was almost crushing. Behind the observation knoll, King,
Schreiber, and Wilkinson had left their horses with two
pickets in a shallow depression. At times the lieutenant
could even hear the animals tearing at the abundant prairie
grass. King swore he could even hear the thump-thump of
his own heart beat as he peered into the distance coming
alive with the new day's ever-changing light. For a moment
he studied the faces of the men on either side of him,
finding them drawn and haggard with nonstop fatigue,
their eyes sunken and draped with liver-colored bags.

"Lieutenant!" Wilkinson called out in a harsh
whisper, suddenly coming to life—tapping King on the upper arm.

Immediately he trained his glasses in the direction the
corporal was looking. "You see something?"

"Saw something move."

Schreiber crawled back to the crest of the mound on
his belly, shading his eyes against the brightening sky.

"Look, Lieutenant!" Wilkinson gushed. "There . . .
there are Indians!"

"Where?" Schreiber demanded.

Slowly the corporal rose on his hands and knees, bringing one arm up to point to the southeast. "That ridge . . . can't you see them?"

It took a few moments, maybe as much as a minute, not any more than that—as King strained his eyes, squinted, twirling the adjustment knob this way with painstaking precision, then back the other direction just as slowly.

"I see 'em, Lieutenant!" Schreiber said.

"Yes," King replied, the hair rising at the back of his neck. "There's a second group now."

A third small knot of five or six horsemen appeared on the distant ridge, then dropped back out of sight. For the time being none of those warriors seemed to be in a great hurry to advance, but instead seemed intent solely on something off to the southwest of where King lay observing the entire panorama with the sun's rising. Over the next few minutes he counted a half-dozen small parties popping up to the crest of the distant ridges, then turning about and disappearing from sight.

Finally King turned to Schreiber. "Sergeant—send word back to the signalman from A Troop. He'll alert the command."

"Tell 'em the Injuns are coming?"

"Yes," King replied.

Down the backside of the slope the sergeant slid until out of sight. Then he trotted on down to the horse-holders, gesturing as he whispered his message. One of the troopers flung himself into the saddle and tore off toward the lone trooper from A Company waiting on a knoll halfway back to the Warbonnet bivouac.

"Way they're acting, you think they've seen us?" Wilkinson asked as Schreiber crawled back in beside them.

"Don't think so," King replied. "They keep popping over, watching something. If they knew we were here, they'd be gone already."

"That's right. If they knew we was here," the sergeant agreed, "we'd never knowed they was there."

For the next thirty minutes the trio didn't take their eyes from the southeast as the sun continued its climb. Then King turned at the snort from one of the held horses in the depression below them. Coming up on his resplendent buckskin, Bill Cody led seven soldiers: Merritt and Carr, along with Major John J. Upham and aide-de-camp Lieutenant J. Hayden Pardee of the Twenty-third Infantry as well as three from the colonel's staff. All of them came to a halt and leaped from their saddles, hurrying up the slope at a crouch behind the scout. Without a word the colonel and his lieutenant colonel trained their own glasses on the distance, watching the dark specks appear and disappear in the distance, now narrowed to less than two miles. From the rear hurried three more of Cody's scouts—White, Tait, and Garnier—along with several more curious officers loping in from bivouac to have a look for themselves.

Merritt turned to Forbush, his regimental adjutant, asking, "Have the men had their coffee?"

"Yes, sir."

"Then return to the company commanders with my instructions to mount the regiment and have them formed into line."

"Yes, sir." Forbush slid down the slope and trotted to his horse.

"What do you think they're after?" the colonel asked as he turned around to train his eye on the distance.

"Don't know for sure, General," Cody answered. "But they're sure acting like they're watching something."

The knoll was growing crowded with soldiers and scouts when King asked, "The Black Hills Road?"

"Could be," Merritt replied. "It lies somewhere out there."

"I don't think so," Cody argued, shaking his head. He was dressed in a dashing black outfit, tailored in the lines of a Mexican vaquero's. "The road is off over there—more to the east. And those warriors are watching something coming in from the west."

"Besides, no one would be using the Black Hills Road

now," Carr agreed with his scout. "They've been warned off of it because of the agency scare."

"That can't be the Black Hills Road," King responded. "Off to the west—that's the Sage Creek Road, on our back-trail."

"The way those warriors're keeping themselves hid from the west," Cody explained, "I'll lay a wager they're keeping an eye on something coming from that direction."

Merritt asked, "Then they have no idea we're here?"

"Just look at all of them!" Carr marveled.

It was as if the light suddenly ballooned across the entire horizon at that very moment. Every ridge and hill screened from the west was now alive with warriors, all of them excitedly moving about.

Carr wagged his head, rubbing his gritty eyes with two fingertips as he muttered, "What in thunder are they laying for?"

"By glory—that's it!" Cody bellowed. He pointed west now.

"There! Yes! I see them!" Merritt said.

"Is that—Oh, dear God!" Carr replied. "That's got to be our own supply train."

Better than four miles away the white tops of Lieutenant Hall's company wagons began to pop up on the distant horizon as the light swelled around them. Hurrying his teams as fast as he dared push them, Hall was bringing along those two companies of infantry.

"By doggies!" Cody said, then chuckled. "Those Injuns think they've found 'em some easy pickings."

"All alone on the Sage Creek Road," Charlie White added.

"But those wagons aren't filled with plunder," Carr said with a smile.

Merritt couldn't help himself, clapping in glee. "Great Jupiter—have we got a surprise in store for them when they ride down to jump those wagons!"

White cheered, "They'll roll those covers back and let those red sonsabitches have it!"

"I don't believe this! Hall's made an all-night march of it," Merritt announced.

"I, for one, General," said Carr, "am glad he did."

With a nod Merritt agreed. "I suppose he's made himself the bait in our trap, without even knowing it."

"Nothing those Injuns want better," Garnier observed, "than a supply train loaded with plunder headed to the Black Hills settlements."

"Instead," Cody said, a big smile creasing his face, "those wagons are loaded for bear."

King interrupted their celebration, pointing in another direction as he said, "Will you look at that, sirs?"

Off to the southeast they saw a bright-colored, plumed band of warriors separate from the hundreds and kick their ponies into motion. At a gallop they rode down into the bottoms and at the base of the hills, staying out of sight from the oncoming wagons. Unknowingly, the nine or ten horsemen were closing the gap between them and the soldiers' lookout post.

"They spotted us?"

"Naw," Cody said. "If they knew soldiers were here, there'd be more than just that little bunch coming."

"What do you suppose they're about?" Merritt wondered.

"Them," Cody said gravely.

Every man on that hill now trained his glasses to the southwest. A pair of riders broke into view, riding well ahead of the bow-topped wagons.

"Couriers?" Carr asked.

"I'd bet money on it," Cody said. "General, Colonel . . . appears that Hall is sending you word he's coming in."

"But those two don't realize they're about to get chopped up!" King said. "That band of warriors is going to butcher those couriers before they even know what surprise the rest of the red bastards have in store for the train."

"Dear Lord—those men are riding to their death," Merritt muttered.

"Look, General!" Cody said. "There—see that ravine where that war party is riding?"

"Yes."

"Down there—see—where the ravine's mouth opens onto the road," Cody said confidently. "That's where they'll likely jump those couriers."

"I can't allow that to happen," Merritt grumbled.

Carr wagged his head and said, "But if we fire on them now, we'll scare off the rest of the warriors before we can engage them."

"By Jove, General," Cody cheered as he got to his feet, dusting off the resplendent braided vaquero costume he wore that day. "Now's our chance. We can ride out and cut those red hellions off!"

"Yes!" Merritt rose, gripping Cody's arm. "It's up to you, Cody. Cut them off!"

The scout turned on his heel and sprinted downslope as Merritt whirled on King, gripping the lieutenant's arm. "Stay here, Mr. King. It's your call: watch till that war party is close under you—then give the word! The rest of you come down, every other man of you."

"Yes . . . sir!" King saluted and watched the others start their hurried race down the slope to their mounts.

Again the hair on the back of his sunburned neck prickled with anticipation. Two hundred yards behind him to the north he watched as the first of the six companies of mounted troopers moved into line and halted—brought up by their company commanders as soon as Private Madsen had carried word to camp: Indians had been spotted. Now the Fighting Fifth was fronting out in a thin blue line against the green and brown of those rolling hills, horses colored by troops, carbines glittering with a dull blue sheen in that first light of day.

King's heart was thundering now, and his mouth had gone dry. He tried licking his lips with a pasty tongue as he turned back to the south. In the distance a hundred lances stood out against the summer sky, feathers and scalp locks fluttering on the renewed breeze. The horsemen watched their own ride on down that ravine, ready to cut off the two unsuspecting couriers.

Again Charles glanced over his shoulder. Cody, White, the half-breed Tait, and a half-dozen men from his own Company K waited in the saddle atop anxious animals—tightening gunbelts, straightening clothing, tugging hats down on their brows. All of them with their eyes trained intently on King above them on the hill. Halfway down the slope Merritt, Carr, and their aides waited out of sight.

King was the only man left at the top now that the enemy was drawing dangerously near. Stretched out flat on his belly, he swallowed hard, wishing he had brought his canteen along. Instantly knowing there was no amount of water that would ever wet a man's mouth when it had gone dry with the anticipation of battle.

He could not give the word too soon, or the warriors would escape. And he could not wait too long—the couriers would be swallowed up before rescue could race round the hill.

Now he could hear the hoofbeats. Or was it the pounding of his heart? No, it was the hoofbeats of those war ponies.

No longer did he need his field glasses to watch the oncoming collision. Everything seemed to loom closer and closer, ever closer.

He turned and flung his voice downhill. "All ready, General?"

Merritt answered, "All ready, King. Give the word when you like."

That thunder had to be his heart.

No, it was the hammering of those hooves as the warriors reached the last hundred yards of ravine.

Ten seconds.

God—but they were beautiful men: their dark skin made golden in the coming light.

Eight.

The new light reflected off the bright war paint, brass arm bands and bracelets, the silver gorgets.

Six seconds.

The way the wind whipped their hair, the scalp locks tied to fringed leggings and shields, fluttering beneath the jaws of the onrushing ponies.

Four.

What horsemen these, he marveled as he began to reach for the brim of his slouch hat he had laid on the grass beside him. Never again will there be any the likes of these.

Two seconds left.

In my hand I hold your fate. In my very hand, I hold vengeance for the death of Custer's Seventh!

Then, as the racing warriors burst from the mouth of the ravine, King bolted to his feet, waving his hat and bellowing as Cody exploded away in a blur.

"Now, lads! In with you!"

Chapter 20

Moon of Cherries Blackening

Indians on the Offensive

OMAHA, July 17—Telegrams received here yesterday are to the effect that the Indians are moving on Medicine Bow, a station on the Union Pacific, almost due south of Fort Fetterman, it is supposed for the purpose of capturing or destroying the supplies which have been stored there recently in great quantities by the government, there being 50,000 rounds of ammunition among other things. A small force of Indians could seize and destroy these stores, as Medicine Bow is a small station, and the country round about sparsely settled. Their destruction at this time would seriously impede military operations against the Indians.

His name was Yellow Hair.

Not because yellow was the color of his own. No, Yellow Hair's was as black as any Cheyenne's. His skin as dark as his red earth home.

Hay-o-wei.

Instead, Yellow Hair was named for the scalp he wore. The hair of a white woman he had killed, so went one tale.

But Yellow Hair knew better—it was the scalp of an important man. Hair he had taken seven winters before along the Little Dried River.* Among his people a warrior was known by the coups he counted, by the ponies he stole, by the hair he took and the women left to mourn. Yellow Hair knew there must have been mourning when he took that scalp.

Instead of cutting it up to tie along the sleeves of his war shirt, instead of stringing small pieces of it around the edge of his war shield, Yellow Hair instead stretched the scalp on a small hoop of green willow and to that hoop tied a long thong. This he wore around his neck. It was the biggest victory he had ever won—this fight with the yellow-haired man.

A tough and worthy opponent. So he proudly wore the hair of that enemy around his neck ever since. They had called him other names when he was a child, when he was a brash youngster wandering with Tall Bull's band of Dog Soldiers raiding and stealing from Comanche country on the south, to Lakota country on the north.

Then Tall Bull was killed at the Springs on a hot summer's day, much as this one promised to be. The soldiers attacked without the slightest warning from their herd guard. Yellow Hair and the others stayed behind long enough to protect the children and old ones as they fled into the sandy hills and crossed the river† to safety. The pony soldiers and their scalped-head scouts‡ did not pursue for long. He had learned the scalped heads would not—not when there was plunder among the lodges, not when there was something of a proud people to steal or destroy.

But Tall Bull was dead. And for weeks they had wandered aimlessly while some of the other war chiefs argued

---

*Sand Creek, Colorado Territory.
†The South Platte River.
‡Pawnee Indians.

as to just where they should go. Some families broke off
and went their own way. A few bands even returned to the
south that autumn, to live with relatives down on the
southern agency.* But not the true Dog Soldiers like Yellow
Hair. They continued to raid on into that autumn. And
early that winter he took his scalp down by the Little Dried
River where five winters before the soldiers had attacked
old Black Kettle's village of peace-loving Shahiyena. A lot of
good it did the old chief to tie that white man's star flag
from his highest lodgepole. Four years later Black Kettle
was killed by Custer's men.

Now both Black Kettle and Tall Bull were dead. A man
could die fighting, or he could die doing what the white
man ordered him to do. To Yellow Hair's way of thinking,
the old peace chief was a pitiful man, worthy only of scorn
for his stupidity in believing in the white man's word. Black
Kettle deserved to die for putting his trust not in his own
people, but in what the white man considered truth.

But Tall Bull—it mattered little that he was dead, for
he had died an honored man: a warrior who never shrank
from the task at hand, a man who always thought of his
people first, a fighter who went down defending his people,
his home, and the land where he had buried the bones of
his ancestors. That was the death of a true warrior and
patriot of the People: to die with honor, to lay down his life
fighting off the white man.

That autumn after the defeat of the Dog Soldiers at
the Springs, Yellow Hair rode with three others for many
days to the south, on beyond the Cherry River.† There they
came upon a camp of white buffalo hunters one cold,
frosty evening. Slowly, the four warriors approached the
white man's camp, asking for coffee, even a little tobacco
for their pipes. Instead they were given nothing but the
loud words and the muzzles of the hunters' guns, gestured
away.

*Darlington, Indian Territory.
†The Smoky Hill River.

The next morning they killed the first as he crept into the bushes and settled over an old tree with his britches around his ankles to relieve himself. Then they slit the throat of the one sitting in the predawn darkness, watching over their horses and mules. After they had run these off into the hills, the four warriors waited for the five hunters to come for their animals. They did not have to wait long— for the white man is nothing without his animals. Especially these brave hunters who came to slaughter all the buffalo.

In their ambush all were soon killed except one who used the bodies of his friends to hide behind. It took a long time for the warriors to get close enough to that one whose hair seemed to shine like the white man's crazy metal, so much like the rays of the sun was it. That lone hunter killed two of Yellow Hair's friends that morning before Yellow Hair and the other warrior finally worked in close enough to hear the heavy breathing of the white man.

It had been a long time since the hunter had last fired a shot.

Carefully Yellow Hair crawled on his belly toward the bodies of the white men they had killed. Behind them he heard the quiet murmuring of the brave hunter. At last Yellow Hair raised his head over one of the bodies and was surprised to see the white man lying on his back, a bloody wound along the side of his head, an even bloodier and bubbling wound soaking the front of his greasy shirt. As Yellow Hair rose to his hands and knees, the white hunter looked at him with eyes as hard as river ice, then cursed him, growling something in the white man's language with his bloody tongue, pointing that pistol at the warrior, its hammer cocked.

The hunter pulled the trigger and laughed. Laughed very loud because the weapon he let drop at his side was empty. For a moment Yellow Hair stared at the hunter, not understanding—then decided the white man laughed because he had left himself without any bullets.

Yellow Hair knelt over his victim as the man tried to

push him off, but did not have the strength. Then, taking the white man's own knife from the scabbard on his belt, he took the hunter's hair. While the enemy was still breathing.

When he had finished, Yellow Hair had gotten to his feet, holding his trophy aloft, shaking it in the enemy's face. Then slashed the white man's throat, listening to him bubble and gurgle until he no longer struggled to breathe through the gaping, gushy wound.

"You have done a brave thing!"

Yellow Hair had turned to look behind him. His friend, Rain Maker, stood near, having watched it all.

"You have done a great thing!"

"He was a mighty enemy," Yellow Hair said, holding out the scalp as if to show it off.

Rain Maker yelped, a low cry leaping from far back in his throat. Then he said, "From this day on your people will call you Yellow Hair!"

Ever since he had ridden a rising star among the Shahiyena.

In the late autumns most of the warrior bands wandered back onto one agency or the other, either at Red Cloud or over at Spotted Tail. Through the seasons his people remained closer to the Lakota than they did to their own southern cousins down in Indian Territory. And with the coming of the new grass that fed their ponies and made the animals strong, the warrior bands once more wandered west and north off the reservations.

It had been so this summer. He and the rest of his staunchest holdouts had been out hunting for scalps in the Paha Sapa,* killing those white men who scratched in the ground for the crazy rocks near the sacred Bear Butte. It was there they learned of the rumors that a great fight had taken place far to the west. In the country of the Powder and the Rosebud, on a river where the Lakota traditionally

---

*The Black Hills.

hunted buffalo and antelope—a place called the Greasy Grass.

In that country, the story was told, in the span of no more than eight suns, the warriors of Crazy Horse and Sitting Bull had twice defeated great armies the white man had sent against them.

Now the word was being spread: Bring the people! Come north! Soon the white man will be gone forever!

Like some of his friends, Yellow Hair had family living with Little Wolf's band back there on the agency at Red Cloud. While most of the other warriors in that war party hurriedly rode off to the west to join the great chiefs in their defeat of the white man, Yellow Hair and a handful of his friends raced south to spread the word among their people still remaining on the reservation. Those women and children, the old ones and those too sick to help themselves, they would all need the courage of the warriors to flee from the soldiers of war chief Jordan at Camp Robinson.

So it was that they had finally gathered more than eight-times-ten-times-ten of Little Wolf's people and other stragglers behind the ridges north of the agency three days ago. And yesterday they had started north. The Shahiyena had a wide road to travel, a road wide-open as well! To travel so slowly, to bring their families along, these were warriors who had every reason to feel confident that no white man, no soldier would raise his hand to stop them from joining the Hunkpapa medicine man in the north. He was the one with power now—for hadn't he seen the white man's ruin in his vision?

For those last few days they had waited on the agency, deciding whether to go or not. Scouts brought word that soldiers were prowling the very same country the Shahiyena would have to cross if they hoped to reach the Powder River hunting grounds. Then scouts returned from the Mini Pusa,* bringing news that the soldiers had turned

*The Cheyenne River.

around and were marching back to the south, toward the Buffalo Dung River, and had abandoned that country between the reservation and the Paha Sapa. As if fleeing from the danger in those mighty villages to the north who had just crushed two armies.

The way was clear!

Yesterday Yellow Hair and the warriors had started them out. No soldiers from Camp Robinson came out to try stopping the People. They hadn't even seen a single white man all that day. Then this morning, as camp was coming to life and the women were loading their travois for the day's journey, scouts came in with a report of a train of white-topped wagons that was coming from the west. Coming from the white man's forts and cities, bound for his settlements in the Paha Sapa.

That would mean those wagons were loaded with supplies: boxes and cans of food, bolts of cloth for the women, whiskey for the warriors, brass and iron kettles, tin cups and butcher knives, maybe even bullets and guns. What a gift the Everywhere Spirit had delivered Yellow Hair's people as they began their journey to freedom!

They were fleeing the white man's oppression and the slow starvation of the reservation . . . and this was the Everywhere Spirit's reward—this train filled with supplies to take with them as they moved to the north country, never to be forced into returning to the agency again.

He was sitting behind the hill now, gazing at the small mirror he could hold in the palm of one hand, straightening his face paint, when one of the young scouts came tearing up on his pony.

"There are two of them," the youngster said breathlessly. "They left the wagons and are now hurrying ahead of the rest."

Yellow Hair asked, "Which way are they coming?"

The scout pantomimed, arching his arm west to east.

The war chief's eyes narrowed gravely. "If they move their horses too fast, they will see our warriors behind these hills—and our surprise for the wagon train will be ruined."

"We must kill the two riders," growled Rain Maker.

"Yes," Yellow Hair said to his good friend, the one who had seen him take the brave man's scalp many autumns before. "And we will lead them."

Quickly he pointed to a handful of others who would come—men like Beaver Heart, Buffalo Road, and other old friends. Not a large party, but enough that they could easily swallow up the two riders and kill them behind one of these rolling hills without alerting the others. The wagon men would roll on down the white man's road toward the Paha Sapa, not knowing that death waited for them all this new day as the sun rose in the east.

"Come!" Yellow Hair shouted as he kicked heels into the ribs of his strong pony.

Behind him Rain Maker and the others yelped as they streamed out from the far side of that knoll and followed Yellow Hair into the shallow ravine. The sun was chasing shadows off the land, rising strong and confident this morning. The way his people were once more rising above the land.

This was to be their summer. The time of his people.

On they raced down the bottom of the ravine, listening to the fading shouts of encouragement from the warriors who would lie in waiting, hiding until the signal was given to attack the wagons.

Closer and closer they galloped toward the white man's road at the mouth of this ravine.

In the coldest hour of that morning Bill Cody had awakened himself as he used to do all the time, at least before he had gone east to begin performing on the boards. It was a good life, and it paid him well enough.

But it was nothing like this: rising before the sun and saddling up, walking his mount through row upon row of sleeping soldiers, and finally climbing into the saddle beyond the pickets. To ride alone below the waning stars, just he and these grassy hills, having put Warbonnet Creek at his back so he could look to the south and have his eyes

behold nothing but this great inland sea. Bill had enough
time to circle west, ease on south, then angle over to the
east, where the Cheyenne were sure to be somewhere on
that road.

He wanted to know where they were, so he could tell
Merritt how much time they had before the Cheyenne were
up and moving. Before the Cheyenne bumped head on into
the Fighting Fifth.

Sure enough, Bill found the village in the smudgy gray
light of that dawn. But by the time he had wandered back
to the west so he would not be discovered by any wandering scouts, and returned to the regiment's bivouac, Bill
found the soldiers already up, finishing breakfast, some
having saddled their mounts while others were busy oiling
the trapdoors of the Springfields, packing themselves down
with ammunition.

He caught up with Merritt as the colonel was climbing
into the saddle.

"I just received good news, Bill," Merritt said in that
Gatling-gun, rapid-fire speech of his when he grew excited.
"Messenger came in with word from our forward post.
They've spotted Indians."

"Probably the advance party of the village I found
waking up this morning, General."

"I'm going to see this for myself," the colonel said
with a smile.

They had gone to the high ground, waited—and were
rewarded quickly enough. The Cheyenne thought they were
about to swallow up those two couriers, then ambush a
wagon train. Were they going to be surprised!

And now he sat atop his buckskin, his hat tugged
down on his long brown curls, pulling down the bottom of
that short-waisted Mexican coat of black velvet drenched
with a blood-hued scarlet braid, resplendent with silver
conchos and white lace adorning the cuffs. None of the
oncoming warriors he would meet in a matter of minutes
could outshine him. Too bad these dowdy, dusty, frumpy
soldiers knew nothing of the importance of such things. A

man must look his best, wear his finest, when he rode into battle. Perhaps only a true warrior like himself understood these Cheyenne they would strike in a few heartbeats. A man always wore his finest when going against the enemy.

"All ready, General?" King asked above him at the top of the hill.

Merritt rose slightly in a crouch just down the slope from the lieutenant, gazing over Cody and the rest, then peering back to the line of troopers gathered in the middistance. "All ready, King. Give the word when you like."

No matter what Bill did to prepare his weapons, to straighten his clothing in these anxious minutes, he never took his eyes off that lieutenant up there. A good soldier, King was going to give them the signal so he and the rest could get the jump on those warriors riding down to ambush the two couriers.

The hardest part was this waiting.

As it had been all these years. The hardest thing he had ever done—making a new life for Lulu and the children. Doing that for them, when all he really wanted was to be right here, right now. Waiting to lead the Fifth into battle. Suffering that exquisite burn of hot adrenaline pumping into his blood—there was nothing finer.

God, but life was sweet!

As much as he loved Lulu, as much as he loved the children and the applause and the hundreds of women swarming and swooning around him . . . it was here that he knew his heart was at rest. Here where there was still adventure enough for any man. Even a man who loved danger as much as William F. Cody.

King was turning . . . by God—he was turning!

Bill looped up another six inches of rein. The buckskin beneath him sensed it, sidestepped suddenly before Cody brought the big horse under control.

"Easy. Easy boy."

The lieutenant was reaching to the side where he had laid his hat. Reaching for it at the same time he was starting to turn at the top of that knoll above Cody.

Sliding his tall boots back into the stirrups a wee bit, pressing down with the balls of his feet . . .

Then the lieutenant swept his hat off the ground, waving it as he clambered to his feet, his mouth opening in the new day's light, hollering with a roar.

"*Now*, lads—in with you!"

Bill Cody didn't need to be told twice.

Chapter 21

17 July 1876

Right from the first jump Bill was ten lengths ahead of the rest. And the way his long-legged horse was eating up the ground as it charged around the foot of the hill, there was no way any of them were going to catch him.

Cody pulled the pistol from his belt and thumbed the hammer back.

By Jove! He was going to be the first there to surprise the enemy. The first to wade into them. How he prayed he would be the first to raise a scalp. Yes, by glory: to take a scalp . . . a scalp for Custer!

"This is for you, Armstrong," he whispered into that summer wind whipping at his eyes as he laid low along the neck of the big buckskin surging forward with dilated nostrils. "May you rest in peace after this day—avenged at last!"

No theater had ever offered him a finer stage than this. Bill could never remember playing before such an enthusiastic audience as the soldiers he knew were now watching him at this moment. If the fates did indeed deem that a man's life must—in the great totality of all things—be summed up in one supremely delicious moment . . . then this was his. To win or lose in the coming combat mattered not. Only the game of it all. To playact before the perfumed and starched set back east, that simply was not living.

Laying one's last breath on the line, pitting his life against these foes—gambling it all in the adventure and lust of the chase . . . now this was living. This was his moment!

In the far distance the sharp-edged, grassy southern ridges boiled with movement as two hundred warriors bolted from hiding, hungry for taking Hall's wagon train at last. They hadn't yet seen Cody and his rescue party.

Those Cheyenne have no idea the Fifth lies in wait to ambush them!

But what was the prettiest of all was how that small war party suddenly turned atop their racing ponies as they burst out of the ravine onto the Black Hills Road, the wind whipping their hair, surprised to find Cody and that handful of soldiers hot on the braid-bound tails of those war ponies.

Cody aimed—fired his pistol at their wide, glistening backs.

Suddenly like a boulder parting a mountain stream, the warriors reined left and right in a savage maneuver, most of the them slipping to the sides of their animals as the hooves kicked up great, glimmering, golden cascades of dust into the new sunlight. Stunned with surprise, they nonetheless turned to confront their attackers.

Two of the war party fired off shots at the hilltop behind the onrushing Cody, one shooting from under the neck of his pony.

In an instant Bill looked them over, deciding on the one he wanted more than the rest: he rode a gorgeous gray horse, larger than the smaller ponies. Wearing that splendid feathered bonnet, he must surely be a chief—and if not a chief, then at least a mighty warrior. A worthy opponent.

With the gunfire the Cheyenne ponics pranced and reared, frightened as the white men closed on them. Under the necks of their animals the warriors fired a volley. Most had only a foot locked over a rear flank, only a hand visible clasped into a braided loop of mane. Bill heard a bullet whine past. Another so close he made out the snarling hiss. Surely close enough now—he pulled back on the hammer again, deciding to try a shot at that warrior in the magnificent headdress, the warrior who was shouting, the breeze whipping the long tail of his warbonnet.

At the very moment he leveled the pistol over his buckskin's head and squeezed off the shot, the war chief's pony reared in fright, its eyes grown as big and white as Lulu's china saucers, its nostrils flaring. Cody was close enough that he saw the lathered moistness gathered at the crude, rawhide hackamore the warrior used for a rein.

When the big gray animal came down on its forelegs, it stumbled to the side, careening crazily away from Cody's rush. The war chief doubled over at the waist, grasping his thigh and losing his hold on the pony as it keeled over, spilling its rider. Into the grass the warrior tumbled, rolling in a heap as the pony crashed to the dust, legs kicking wildly, head thrashing, fighting to rise. Closing the last few yards, Bill watched his fallen enemy shove his warbonnet back from his brow as he picked himself out of the dirt, struggling onto one knee, his other legging bloodied.

In that next breath the buckskin collided with the fallen pony, legs a'jumble, spilling in a blur.

Spinning tortuously, Cody felt himself hurled into the air. Flung to the ground with enough force that it knocked the breath from his lungs, he rolled and rolled through the grass, clutching the pistol that dug into his ribs with each tumble. Dazed for a moment as his body skidded to a stop, he spat dirt from his mouth, swiped it from his eyes. Blinking, he found his enemy rising with a struggle twenty paces away, no more . . . and bringing up his pistol.

Jerking his thumb down, he found the hammer still cocked as he wobbled to his feet, unsteady, light-headed. Turning to the left so that he presented as little a target as possible, he coolly extended the right arm to its full length and brought the front blade down on his enemy. There on the warrior's chest, that amulet, that fetish—that gorget of yellow hair. That savage totem taken from one of the warrior's victims.

Barking, the Cheyenne's pistol spat fire.

With a jerk Cody knelt to make himself smaller at the Cheyenne's shot. Then not really aiming—Cody snapped off his shot a heartbeat later—without thought, hesitation, or aiming.

Sensing it, by instinct. If a man had to think about making such a shot, he would most times think of nothing more as a dead man.

Pitching backward, the warrior crumpled into the grass as Cody heard the thunder of hooves. How his ears rang from the fall. He shook his head violently to clear it, but still the thunder drew ever closer. A few feet away the war chief's legs kicked just as the dying pony's had thrashed. Bill dashed toward him, his thumb drawing back the pistol's hammer once more, arm held out from him, muzzle pointing at the magnificent, near-naked body he approached.

Standing over the warrior, Cody looked first at the hole opened in the middle of the Cheyenne's chest. Then his gaze crawled across the Indian's face, watching the open eyes glaze. It seemed all breath suddenly went out of the warrior as he stared up at his enemy; his body seized with one last, great convulsion, then went limp.

With shrill war cries three of the other six Cheyenne immediately kicked their ponies into motion, dashing up the shallow slope for Cody. Screaming, brandishing their lances and war clubs, light reflected from one rifle barrel. A hundred yards behind them came at least half a hundred more, intent on rescuing the body of their fallen chief. Breaking the ridge behind them, fully two hundred more horsemen raced for the spoils in those wagons of the white men.

Then as suddenly as they had put themselves in motion, the three naked riders reined up, wheeled hard about, and tore off in the opposite direction. Spurring down the

slope and up the far side, they mingled among the rest
starting to turn on their heels, beginning to retreat.

Whirling about at a crouch, Bill found Mason's K
Company thundering up, that guidon snapping in the
breeze above them. It was for this moment he had returned
home to the west, here to his plains. On impulse he yanked
the butcher knife from his belt scabbard, then bent over the
fallen warrior, slashing the narrow thong that tied the bonnet beneath the dark chin. Rolling the body over onto one
shoulder, Cody dragged the feathered headdress free with
his left hand, then turned just as Captain Mason and his
men were almost upon him.

Holding the fluttering, feathered trophy high at the
end of his extended arm, Cody stood in triumph over his
vanquished enemy, bellowing at the top of his lungs as the
captain and the first row of troopers shot past.

"First scalp for Custer!"

In a rumble they swept past, a blinding blue blur of
dust and eager, frightened faces—hollering out their cheer
at him as wave upon wave of fighting men chased the rest
of the war party that had turned and fled as soon as their
leader was spilled.

"First scalp for Custer!"

Over and over he yelled his valiant oath at the passing
horde of cheering horsemen, Cody standing there above his
enemy as the stinging yellow dust swirled about him, bellowing until his throat grew as raw as grated flesh. Shaking
the bonnet in the air, in victory, in revenge.

"First scalp for Custer!"

King was bounding side to side in sheer exuberance by the
time Merritt and Wilkinson raced the rest of the way up the
slope as Cody bolted around the base of the hill.

For a moment the war party disappeared from view
behind a low ridge in that broken country. They emerged,
suddenly to wheel about just as Cody and the others were
swallowed up by the landscape. Surprised and confused,
the Cheyenne milled for a moment, some of their ponies

rearing. The last of the seven horsemen to emerge from the ravine reined up in the confusion, fighting to bring his animal under control halfway between Cody and the knoll, where King stood watching in stunned, openmouthed silence.

Flinging his lance aside, that warrior yanked a rifle to his shoulder and fired a shot.

With a shrill whistle the bullet sailed past the hilltop.

Merritt growled, "By Jupiter—that red bastard's firing at us!"

Immediately Corporal Wilkinson asked, "Permission to fire at that son of a bitch, General?"

"Granted!"

The soldier slapped his Springfield carbine to his shoulder and snapped off a shot at the moment the warrior slipped behind his pony.

King thought he saw the Cheyenne's shadowy form peek beneath the animal's neck—then a second shot whined right past Merritt.

"Get that son of a bitch!" shouted the colonel.

As Wilkinson yanked up on the trapdoor and ejected the hot copper cartridge, King gazed into the middistance. "Look to the front, General. Look! Look! Here they come! By the dozens!"

The nearby ridge bristled with horsemen tearing on a collision course for Cody and his party, making for the hill where the lieutenant stood taking in the whole panorama.

Merritt whirled about and shouted down the slope, "Send up the first company!"

In the next moment the colonel sprinted off, joining Forbush below, where both leaped into the saddle. King watched them wheel left to the east around the base of the hill, spurring at an angle to catch up with the first company Lieutenant Colonel Carr had put in motion. Deciding it was time for him to leap into the action, King darted down the hill for the horse-holders. He was surprised to find Donnybrook frightened, the horse shying from him, jerking wild-eyed to break free as the lieutenant freed the throatlatch and snagged hold of the reins. The horse reared once, yanking cruelly against that crippled right arm wounded by the Apache in Arizona Territory. Rearing a second time, Donnybrook pulled King off the ground, making him wince with gut-felt pain in that arm as he gritted, short-reining the animal as he struggled to stuff his boot into the hooded stirrup while the fractious horse continued to prance around in a tight circle.

With Carr's order to charge the enemy, Captain Mason had taken his K Company across that last two hundred yards of flat ground south of the creek, speeding on toward the base of the hill where King now spurred his mount to overtake his platoon as the entire company slowed. Ahead of them lay open ground, with mounted Cheyenne bristling from every hilltop across a mile-wide front.

"Drive them, Mason!" Carr shouted as he pulled his horse out of that formation moving forward at a walk. "But look out for that main ridge!"

Julius Mason wasn't long in bawling, "Front into line!"

Left and right the blue-clad horsemen of K peeled off at a walk into a broad phalanx for the charge.

"Bugler!" Mason bellowed.

Those most stirring, brassy notes rose to the summer sky as the horses of K Company burst out of their walk, rolled into a lope, then surged into an uneven gallop. Beneath him, all around him, King heard the heaving chests of the mounts as the animals carried their wiry riders down the slope and across the Black Hills Road, on up the side of a ravine and into that open country scarred by coulees and the erosion of a million springtimes.

On they tore, on past Cody, who stood there in his dusty black theater outfit above a single fallen warrior, holding aloft a feathered warbonnet, shouting out to Mason's troops as they galloped past.

"First scalp for Custer!"

K closed on half a mile before the enemy finally realized what they were facing. At a quarter of a mile some of

the Cheyenne fired their rifles and pistols at the charging
blue phalanx. It took a few moments for the painted, feathered horsemen to spread themselves as if to receive the
charge, ponies racing both east and west to flank the oncoming pony soldiers.

"They get behind us—we'll have our hands full!" Mason growled.

Looking over his shoulder, King saw that Carr had
ordered another company into the pursuit. The stunning
bandbox grays of Robert H. Montgomery's B Troop were
breaking to the rear and right around Mason's K. Just sixty
yards behind them Sanford C. Kellogg's I Company came
front into line and immediately spurred their mounts into
the charge. Now 150 men rode straight for the enemy that,
for the moment, still had those three companies easily outnumbered two to one.

Looking back at the Cheyenne who a moment before
had been closing in around his company, King found the
warriors reining up, shouting excitedly at one another, firing random and wild shots. Almost immediately the retreat
began: first as a trickle, then a swelling tide as the surprised
warriors clearly recognized they were about to be overwhelmed. In panic they whirled about and kicked their
ponies into a furious rush toward the south.

Their wild and frantic scattering reminded King of
chaff flung carelessly across a floor.

At the summit of the next ridge Mason halted his
company after a chase of more than three miles. Their excited horses jostled and bumped one another as the soldiers
swallowed down the surges of their own adrenaline, watching their foes disappear into the ebb and flow, rise and fall
of that rolling, grassy landscape, escaping farther and farther with every breath the troopers and horses gulped hun-
grily. The ground all around them had been littered with
reservation blankets and agency provisions, anything of any
weight the warriors could discard in their flight.

Suddenly a loud, booming volley of gunfire rumbled
off the western hills. Followed by a second rattling volley.

Squinting, with his back to the early light, King found them. No more than a half mile off to the west Lieutenant William Hall had hurriedly halted and corralled his wagons. Those concealed infantrymen had scrambled from beneath the dirty oiled canvas and were already deployed in platoons by their sergeants, admirably accounting for themselves with their Long Tom Springfields, helping to send the Cheyenne on their way.

"That bunch gets back to the reservation," Captain Mason groaned, "we can't touch 'em."

"Sure as sin," King agreed. "Those Cheyenne get back across that line, they'll belong to the Indian Bureau again."

Clattering to a halt on K's right and left flanks, the other companies came up noisily, men hollering, horses neighing.

"Permission to pursue the enemy?" Montgomery shouted above the angry murmurs and curses of his men as they watched the enemy disappearing through the hills and coulees like ants scurrying over a picnic blanket.

"Yes!" Kellogg bellowed his assent as he stood in the stirrups, joining the other officers in looking for their regimental commander. "I still want a piece of those red bastards my own self!"

"We ought to try catching them before they're the agent's good Indians again!" Corporal Wilkinson grumbled.

"You just gimme a chance, and I'll make them all *good* Injuns!" Sergeant Schreiber bellowed. "Just like Phil Sheridan wants to make all Injuns good Injuns!"

Far, far in the distance the soldiers could see the Cheyenne village of travois clutter and pony herds turning about and beginning to scatter into the morning's haze that lay against the stark emerald beauty of the Pine Ridge. Little Wolf's people had heard the distant gunfire and, seeing the first of the retreat heading back their way at a gallop, were fleeing in a panic.

"Run, you cowards!" King shouted, his voice joining

the rest as they flung their curses at the backs of the retreating Cheyenne. "Run, you beggarly, treacherous rascals!"

Corporal Wilkinson hollered, "You tell 'em, Lieutenant!"

Charles King did feel up to venting his spleen: "For years you have eaten our bread, lived on our bounty. You're well fed, well cared for. You, your papooses and ponies are fat and independent—but you have heard of the grand revel in blood, scalps, and trophies of your brethren, the Sioux," he hollered at the dust the Cheyenne left behind. "And now that you have stuffed your packs with the Great Father's rations, stuffed your pouches with heavy loads of his best metallic cartridges, you hurry north. But run, you cowards! Go—for this is no fight of yours!"

Chapter 22

17–22 July
1876

Details of Merritt's March

CHICAGO, July 19—The following official report of Colonel Merritt was received at military headquarters to-day:

RED CLOUD AGENCY, July 18, via Fort Laramie, July 19—As indicated in my last dispatch I moved by forced marches to the main northwest trail on Indian creek, and in thirty-five hours my command made about seventy-five miles, reaching the trail Sunday evening about 9 o'clock. The trail showed that no large parties had passed north.

At daylight yesterday morning I saddled up to move on toward the agency and at the same time a party of seven Indians were discerned near the company, moving with the intention of shooting and cutting off two couriers who were approaching Sage creek. A party was sent out to cut these off, killing one of them. The command then moved out at once after the other Indians in this direction and pursued them, but they escaped, leaving four lodges and several hundred pounds of provisions behind.

After scouring the country thoroughly in our vicinity, we moved at once towards the agency. At a distance of twenty-five miles to the northwest of the agency the Indians broke camp and fled so that we did not succeed in catching any of them. The trail was much worn, and the indications were that hundreds of Indians were driven in by our movement. From the repeated reports which I can't give in this dispatch, I was certain of striking the Cheyennes, and to accomplish this marched hard to get on the trail, taking infantry along to guard the wagons and to fight if necessary . . . I am certain that not a hundred Indians—or rather ponies —all told, have gone north on the main trails, in the last ten days.

The Cheyennes whom we drove in yesterday, took refuge on the reservation toward Spotted Tail . . . Our appearance on Indian and Hat Creeks was a complete surprise to the Indians in that vicinity, but those farther in were informed by runners so that they got out of the way.

I have just received your dispatches of the 15th. I will move without delay to Fort Laramie and as soon as possible move to join Crook. My men and horses are very tired, but a few days reasonable marching with full forage will make them all right.

Mason, Montgomery, and Kellogg held their three companies at the top of that ridge, waiting for Merritt and Carr to come up with the rest of the regiment after it had secured enough rations from Hall's wagons to provision the men for two more days.

"It's going to be a stern chase," Merritt told his company commanders in those minutes before they set off on the trail of the fleeing Cheyenne. "And I don't really know just when we'll see our wagons again."

Some six miles south of the Warbonnet the Fifth Cavalry marched through the site where Little Wolf's people had been camped the night before. Besides a dozen lame ponies the soldiers found nearby, the escaping Cheyenne left four lodges standing among the jumble of lodgepoles and burned smudges of their fire rings. Scattered for hundreds of yards in all directions lay burlap sacks, canvas pouches, grease-stained blankets, and the heaviest of cast-iron cookware: all of it discarded in the haste of their flight.

Neither did Merritt's troopers tarry long.

For another two dozen miles of rolling, nearly treeless, grassy plain they pursued the enemy. Then only four miles short of the northern boundary to the Red Cloud Agency, the Cheyenne trail turned abruptly east.

"They're skedaddling for Spotted Tail, General," Cody told Merritt and the rest of those at the head of the column when he rode back up with scouts White and Tait.

"We might still catch them, sir!" Lieutenant King said optimistically.

For several long moments Merritt stared east into the afternoon shadows along that hoof-chewed, travois-scarred trail. Then the colonel turned to his staff.

"No, Mr. King. We likely won't catch them now." There arose some quiet grumbling from those in the ranks within earshot near the head of the column. "These men are weary. We pushed hard to reach the Warbonnet on time, and we got there, by damned."

"Yes, we did that, General," Carr agreed.

"Besides, the fact is that by now those Indians are already within the control of the Indian Bureau. So—after punishing these men and horses with hard chases for three solid days—I'm taking this regiment south to Red Cloud."

"Then what, sir?" Lieutenant Forbush asked.

Taking his hat from his head and swiping a gloved finger inside the brow band, Merritt replied, "Why, then we join up with Crook to go whip the Sioux."

"At least we won't have to face those Cheyenne warriors," King said.

"Damn right," Cody added, pointing off to the southeast. "Yonder goes a few hundred Cheyenne who won't be joining up with Crazy Horse and ol' Sitting Bull!"

"I think it's a job well-done, gentlemen," Merritt exclaimed, clearly proud of himself. "We can feel good not only that we've prevented the Cheyenne from going north, but that now the word will spread: the Sioux will learn that it isn't wise to break from their reservations. All in all, it was a good day."

Carr snorted caustically. "But we killed only one of the enemy."

"Nonetheless it was a successful battle," Merritt argued.

Eugene Carr shook his head. "With your permission, General—it wasn't a battle. More of a minor skirmish."

For a moment Merritt appeared shocked by the stinging criticism. Finally he said with even iciness, "I will extend you the courtesy of reading my report before I submit it. Be that as it may, you can write your own subreport exactly as you see it, General Carr."

The lieutenant colonel replied with a forced, stony civility, "Thank you. I will."

After the troopers made camp that night, several brazen Cheyenne warriors cautiously visited the fringes of the Fifth Cavalry bivouac, contrite and far from belligerent while they actively sought out the tall scout dressed in the black velvet costume decked with scarlet braid—that warrior with the long brown curls who had conquered their war chief called Yellow Hair.

While the fight was still fresh in every man's mind that Monday evening and on into the morning of the eighteenth, Merritt set his officers to penning their separate reports. That duty done, many of the company commanders, as well as the enlisted personnel, took this first opportunity in many days to write home—telling loved ones and friends of their grueling forced march, of the

daring surprise they laid for the fleeing Cheyenne, and of
Cody's shoot-out with the warrior whose name Little Bat
incorrectly translated as "Yellow Hand." With every new
rendition told around their mess fires or expanded in writing home, the skirmish became a battle, and Cody's fight
with Yellow Hair became Buffalo Bill's glorious and deadly
duel with Yellow Hand, the most fearsome Cheyenne chief
on the plains.

On Tuesday morning Merritt marched his column on
to Camp Robinson, where he and the rest of his command
expected to enjoy as much as two days of layover while they
waited for their wagon train to catch up before having to
resume their journey to Fort Laramie. Captain Emil Adams's Company C rejoined the regiment at Red Cloud
Agency after Merritt had detached them on 14 July to
watch over the crossing of the Running Water. The colonel
used his time that night of the eighteenth to compose a
report of the fight of the Warbonnet he would telegraph the
following morning to Major Townsend, commander at Laramie. From there Townsend wired the news to headquarters in Omaha, the report flying on to Chicago and points
east where everyone waited impatiently for any crumb of
news about a victory—no matter how small—something
good to come from all the disappointment and disaster that
so far had greeted the nation that Centennial summer.

It was there at Red Cloud that the Fifth's famed scout
penned his own letter to wife Louisa, back at home with
their children in Rochester, New York.

> We have come in here for rations. We have
> had a fight. I killed Yellow Hand a Cheyenne
> Chief in a single-handed fight. You will no doubt
> hear of it through the paper. I am going as soon
> as I can reach Fort Laramie the place we are
> headed for now. Sent the war bonnet, bridle,
> whip, arms and his scalp to Kernwood to put up
> in his window.

. . . We are now ordered to join Gen. Crook and will be there in two weeks.

Merritt was indeed still under Sheridan's explicit orders to reinforce Crook's expedition languishing in the lee of the Big Horn Mountains. Every one of those troopers figured the wait at Camp Robinson for their supply wagons would give the regiment a welcome chance to recoup themselves. Instead, the surprising Lieutenant Hall hoved into sight at noon that Tuesday, leading his short column of his white-topped company wagons, a scant few hours behind the hard-marching cavalry.

Their reports complete, Merritt gave his company commanders no more than two hours to reoutfit, draw rations and ammunition from Hall's train, then at two-thirty P.M. put the Fifth back on the trail to Fort Laramie. After a march of ten miles on the eighteenth, making another twenty-five miles on the nineteenth, they pushed a tiresome twenty-eight miles on the twentieth. Putting the last thirty miles behind them, the regiment marched into Fort Laramie just after three o'clock on the afternoon of the twenty-first.

That Friday evening Bill Cody found King at his mess fire, enjoying a cup of coffee and relishing some of the sutler's tobacco in his battered pipe.

"Ho, Bill!" King called out cheerily. "Come join us!"

"You're just the man I was hoping to find," Cody replied, settling on a cottonwood stump at the fire.

The lieutenant said, "The fellas here would like you to tell us again of your fight with Yellow Hand."

Cody leaned back, rubbing his palms across his thighs, and nodded. "All right—but with one guarantee from you, Lieutenant."

"What's that?" King asked.

"You write down what I tell you—since it happened to me and I'm the one ought to know."

"Write it down?" the lieutenant inquired.

"Yes. That's why I came to find you: wanted to ask you if you'd write a newspaper story."

"A newspaper story?"

Cody nodded, again rubbing his hands expectantly on his buckskin britches. "There's others—these correspondents and such—they're going to write their own stories their own versions of what happened . . . but I want to be sure there's one story written just the way it really happened, Lieutenant."

"Why, sure!" King answered enthusiastically. "I can do that, Bill. I'd be *honored* to do that for you, in fact. Have you got a paper in mind you want me to see gets your own story?"

"The *Herald*."

"New York?"

"That's right."

King got to his feet, anxious. "I'll get some paper from my tent and be right back."

After that first night the lieutenant, that famed scout, and the Fifth Cavalry did not have long to tarry at Fort Laramie. Sheridan was ordering up the rest of the regiment to join in the march to reinforce Crook. Dispatches awaiting Merritt with post commander Townsend stated that Captain George F. Price's E Company was already on its way from Fort Hays by rail. F Company under Captain J. Scott Payne was to join Price along the Smoky Hill line so that both companies would ride to Cheyenne together.

But after Sheridan had Company H coming from Fort Wallace, Kansas, and L Troop on its way from Fort Lyon in Colorado, the lieutenant general changed his mind. Instead of sending them on north with Merritt to reinforce Crook, Sheridan decided that once they arrived at Laramie, both companies were ordered east to bolster the defenses at Camp Robinson in the wake of the Cheyenne's attempt to flee the reservation.

After resting no more than twelve hours at Fort Laramie, Merritt and Carr had the men up at first light on the twenty-second, intending to use only one day to take on supplies from the post quartermaster for Hall's wagon train, as well as force the fort's and regimental blacksmiths to work overtime at their fires, anvils, and hammers, reshoeing every animal that needed work before heading north to the Big Horn country.

Before the Fighting Fifth would again march into harm's way.

This time against Crazy Horse and that Hunkpapa visionary known as Sitting Bull.

It wasn't women.

But the supply train those seven companies of Chambers's infantry escorted up to Camp Cloud Peak from Fort Fetterman had brought with it the most seductive lure just shy of rounded breasts and full thighs.

Whiskey.

A civilian peddler had lived up to his reputation and become a bummer, talking Major Alexander Chambers into allowing him to bring his own wagon and two teamsters along for the trip north with the army's supply wagons. Having learned that Major Arthur, the district's temporary paymaster, would accompany Chambers north to pay Crook's men in the field, this wily civilian realized he'd have a captive market all to himself: soldiers with nowhere to spend what little money they might have in their pockets after seeing to it some of their pay was sent back east, home to loved ones. No matter what army scrip those soldiers would have left, that whiskey trader was bound and determined to relieve them of every last farthing.

And for his special customers—those who had a bit more money jangling down in the pockets of their wool britches—the peddler even let the grapevine know that he had a couple of women who wouldn't mind servicing the inhabitants of Crook's cavalry camp—for a small fee, of course.

That pair who came all the way north from Fetterman disguised as teamsters went right to work lying down on the job to earn their wages the very next day, the fourteenth of July. Problem was, there didn't seem to be that many soldiers who could afford the trader's pricey whiskey, much less his more seductive wares.

At Camp Cloud Peak was one soldier who did have just enough money to get himself into a fine mess—Captain Alexander Sutorious.

A good man he was, Seamus believed, thinking back now to that Monday, the seventeenth, when Crook finally discovered what had been going on behind his back all the while the general was coming and going, in and out of camp on his hunting trips into the hills. When Crook got wind of the shenanigans—his pale, mottled face turned a pure crimson.

Having ordered the peddler arrested, as well as seizing the civilian's whiskey barrels and taking the two working girls into custody, Crook had no more than settled down to a cup of coffee that afternoon when Lieutenant Bourke had shown up with news of the most unsettling kind.

Faced with the undeniable evidence, the general had no other choice but to place Captain Sutorious under arrest —charged with being drunk on duty. He had failed to place his pickets correctly for that evening's watch. The following day court was held, and Sutorious was found guilty in the field and relieved of his command. The captain, as well as the three civilians, would remain with the expedition until he could be sent south to Fetterman, then on to Fort Laramie for incarceration until Sutorious would be separated from the service.

"I think the sentence was too damned severe," John Finerty complained to Donegan that night after the trial.

Seamus wagged his head. "Can't agree with you more, Johnny. But that was the decision of the man's fellow officers."

"But if they thought they could get away with getting drunk and poking one of those ugly wenches—the rest of 'em would've done the same damned thing!"

Donegan had to agree. Sutorious was just the unlucky one to get caught. Or the one who suffered a lapse in good

sense that compelled him to drink just before he had to go
on picket duty.

"I just don't understand those officers punishing one
of their own that way," Seamus continued. "The captain's
sergeants ain't no shavetails. So what's the rub when
Sutorious got a little too much barleycorn under the gills?
His sergeants know how to post and rotate the guard."

"Seeing what damage that whiskey peddler's caused,"
Finerty replied, "I wish the field court had the jurisdiction
over that civilian."

Seamus asked, "If it did—what do you think should
happen?"

"Understand that I really liked Sutorious," the newsman answered. "I think he's a damned fine soldier. So I'd
like to see the son of a bitch flogged before the whole camp,
whipped within an inch of his goddamned life!"

After the disgraced Sutorious was shipped south with
the next escort and Crook impounded the whiskey, putting
it under the control of the surgeons for the rest of the
campaign, the momentary excitement was over, and things
settled back into the same dull routine.

Waiting for the Fifth Cavalry to arrive. Fishing. And
waiting. Hunting. And more waiting. Reading again and
again the old newspapers that told them that five commissioners had been appointed to negotiate with the Sioux for
the Black Hills; news that Rutherford B. Hayes, who had
commanded a brigade under Crook in West Virginia during the Civil War, had been nominated by the Republicans
for President.

And still more waiting.

On the nineteenth four Crow warriors rode into camp
with dispatches for Crook from the Limping Chief—Colonel John Gibbon—on the Yellowstone. However, there
proved to be nothing new in those messages: after waiting
for many days for the return of the three white couriers
General Terry had sent south, Gibbon had feared the worst
and merely copied Terry's letter to Crook before sending it
off with a quartet of his own Montana-column scouts.

The success of those Crow couriers encouraged Crook to urge civilian packer Richard Kelly to give it one more try pushing north with letters destined for Terry. In just the past week Kelly had made two attempts, so just before dawn on the twentieth, the mule skinner slipped out of camp, hoping this third journey would be the charm.

That day, as they did early every morning, Washakie dispatched his warriors into the surrounding hills to gather what information they could on the movements of the Sioux. It wasn't long before the savvy old chief was able to advise Three Stars that his soldiers were facing as many as three Lakota warriors to every one of Crook's men. And to add the insult of salt rubbed in Crook's brooding wound, nearly every night brought another of those frightening, lightning-fast, but ineffective raids on the herds that succeeded in accomplishing nothing but raising the gorge of every man who wanted to be done with the endless waiting so they could march north to find Sitting Bull and his savages.

With every raid one thing was becoming abundantly clear: the enemy sure wasn't abandoning the country, and they sure weren't acting at all intimidated by Crook's army.

One scouting party led by Washakie's son discovered that the great camp was breaking up slowly—many of the smaller bands moseying unhurried and unpressed to the northeast, in the direction of the Powder. But, reported another party of the Shoshone who had just returned from the headwaters of the Little Bighorn, perhaps the Sioux camps were breaking up because they were apparently growing hungry. In one abandoned village Washakie's scouts found hundreds of dog and pony bones.

Before this campaign was out, the Indians wouldn't be the only ones to survive by eating their animals.

"Washakie says that time will take its toll on the Lakota," John Bourke explained one evening at a fire.

"Yeah, time will have to!" Finerty grumbled. "This army's growing fat and lazy with nothing to do."

"I remember when Crook had this bunch lean and

trail hardened," Seamus agreed. "Back in March, and again when we headed for the Rosebud too."

"You fellas have to look at things the way the general is," Bourke said. "The commander who finally goes into battle against Crazy Horse and Sitting Bull and all their hellions will be studied in the decades to come at the Academy. And greater still, the nation will grant that general every reward, even the presidency."

"Like Washington?" Finerty replied. "Like Jackson and Taylor and Sam Grant himself?"

"Exactly," Bourke said. "Because the spoils are so rich this summer—it seems to me that it's now every general for himself."

Finerty asked, "So why is Crook relying so much on that Washakie?"

"Hold on there, John. Don't you think we should give that Shoshone chief credit?" Bourke responded. "He's recommending that the general just sit tight until all the problems of quarrels between petty chiefs, of feeding so many people, of grazing so many ponies—all those problems will mean the breakup of that huge village Custer's regiment bumped into."

Unbeknownst to Crook, his soldiers, and his Shoshone scouts, that village had already fragmented and the splinters were wandering off to the four winds. Only the summer roamers, those warriors who fled the reservations each spring and hurried back to the agencies every autumn, remained behind to harass the soldier camp every night and set new fires in the grass each day.

The toughest of their lot, the hostile winter roamers under such chiefs as Crazy Horse, Crow King, Sitting Bull, and Gall, had abandoned the Tongue River country not long after the Sibley skirmish. Already they were heading toward the hunting grounds around the Owl River, what the white man called the Moreau. From there they would wander over to the Thick Timber River, shown on the army's maps as the Little Missouri—there to spend the rest of the long, lazy summer days hunting buffalo in peace.

Twice they had defeated the soldiers sent against them. Again and again they had stymied the soldiers sitting on their thumbs beside the Elk River.* And they had realized that Three Stars Crook was clearly in no rush to leave the security of his camp in the shadows of the Big Horn Mountains.

"It will be a good summer," the Sioux were likely telling one another.

They had yet to hear Little Phil Sheridan's trumpet on the land.

---

*General Alfred Terry's Montana and Dakota columns at the Rosebud Landing on the Yellowstone River.

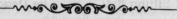

Chapter 23

23 July–2 August 1876

Another Courier Gobbled Up—The Utes on the War Path

Omaha, July 20—A message received this morning from the commanding officer at Fort Fetterman, says a private courier has just arrived from the command on the field, who left the night of the 17th. The day previous a courier was started with the mail and official matter, but has not yet arrived. All quiet and well in camp.

Captain Nickerson, aid de camp to General Crook, returned last evening from Rawlins, Wyoming, whither he went on business connected with securing the Ute Indians of the White river and Bear river regions in Colorado, to unite with General Crook in his campaign against the Sioux. Although there was a delay of about twenty days, occasioned by the obstinacy of the employed scout or agent, the Utes will nevertheless be able to reach General Crook in a few days, to take a hand in the war against the Sioux, who are their inveterate enemies, and who have fought and plundered them for years at every available chance.

Sitting Bull Said to be Dead, Sure Enough

St. Paul, July 20—A *Pioneer Press* and *Tribune* special from Bismarck says the statement that Sitting Bull was killed in the fight with Custer is confirmed from Indian sources. Crazy Horse and Black Moon were also killed. The statement that Sitting Bull's band of Uncpapas lost one hundred and sixty killed, and that the total loss of Indians will reach nearly four hundred, is renewed.

"You can entrust your letter with me, Mrs. Donegan."
     Just then the shrill notes of "Boots and Saddles" floated over the Fort Laramie parade in the chill air of dawn.

Sam looked up into the face of the tall plainsman, his dark-brown hair spilling over his collar in curls, just the way Seamus's did. She realized again that her husband had spent nights and days, miles and seasons, boredom and terror, with this famous man. Shivering with dawn's chill, she slid the folded pages she had sealed with wax into his open hand and pulled her heavy shawl more tightly around her shoulders.

Cody asked, "Is there anything special you want me to tell him when I see him, before I hand him your letter, or after? Anything I can tell him for you in person?"

Before she could stop herself, the words tumbled out, "Tell him to hurry home." Then her gaze fell to the ground, sorry she had said it. When she finally looked back up, she found Cody grinning softly at her.

He looked down at the folded, sealed pages in his hand. "There is no doubt in my mind, Samantha—that you are in all ways a woman who could surely bring a man home from a distant war."

She watched the tall man stuff her letter inside his shirt before pulling his fringed gauntlets over the cuffs of his buckskin coat. Everything about him was fringed now. Gone was that theater costume of black velvet he had worn into Laramie two days before. Fort sutler Collins had provided Cody with a box in which the scout packed the scarlet-trimmed outfit before he had Collins tie it up in yellow twine and post it back to Rochester, New York.

"It's where my wife waits for me," Cody had explained yesterday to Samantha, that one long and intensely busy day Colonel Wesley Merritt allowed his Fifth Cavalry to prepare before embarking for Fetterman, and on to the Big Horns. "So, you see? I am no greenhorn to this matter of men going off to war."

"That . . . New York seems so far away," Samantha said.

He nodded, lips pursed beneath that brush-straw mustache. "Yes, but even when Lulu waited back at Mc-Pherson for me—it was all the same to me. A mile or ten thousand. A day or a whole campaign. When a war comes between a man and his woman, it matters not how far they are apart, nor does it matter for how long, Samantha. What remains important is that those two people keep one another in their hearts."

"Yes," she said, suddenly deciding. "You can remind him of that, Mr. Cody."

"Bill, please."

"Bill, yes. Remind Seamus of what I've told him and written him so many times: that there are times that I think of him, almost feel him draw near just through the power of what I feel in my heart—and that makes this lonely ache a little more bearable."

Cody slipped the wide-brimmed sombrero from his head and held it over his own heart as he took up the reins to the big buckskin. Beyond them the bugles were blaring the notes that formed up the ranks. Then with the rattling noise of a child's wind-up wooden toy clattering across an uneven floor, the sergeants in every one of those cavalry companies yelled and shouted and bawled and hollered out their one-word order.

"Mount!"

Cody leaned close for a moment. "To feel him near you with the power of your love for him—ah, that will make a man like Seamus more happy than you could ever know, Samantha. I am dead certain that your words will drive all the lonely ache from his heart, believe me!"

He planted the hat back atop his long curls, then slipped one tall, knee-high boot into a stirrup.

"Tell him . . ." Then she suddenly felt shy as Cody turned there in midmounting, waiting for her to continue. She held her fingertips against her lips as she whispered, "Tell Seamus that I love him."

He nodded and rose to the saddle, bowing slightly at the waist when he said, "By all means, Samantha. To Seamus that will mean the most."

She came forward a step, her fingers lacing around the reins just short of the buckskin's bit. Important that here in these last few moments she could stand close to a man who would soon be standing this close to Seamus—she wanted to say so much but could not think of where to begin, how to get it all out.

"Mr. Cody—"

"Bill. I asked you please, Samantha."

With one hand holding the shawl around her, she now took her other hand from the buckskin's reins and placed it softly on her swollen belly, rubbing it slightly the way she liked to sense the contact on her taut skin below the layers of clothing, the way she knew the child must like to feel her touching, caressing.

"Yes, Bill. And tell him . . . tell Seamus that *we* both love him."

Cody smiled with his lips pursed for a moment, then blinked his eyes, moving his lips before any words came out. He turned away briefly, swiping his eyes clear. When he turned back to look down at her, the plainsman had to

clear his throat before he could say, "That, Samantha . . .
that will mean *everything* to him."

She watched him tap the brim of his hat as he
squeezed his knees against the buckskin's ribs and the horse
moved off.

"Column of fours!" bawled a loud voice that carried
over the entire width and breadth of the grassy parade. "By
the right—turn!"

Easing quickly into a lope, the plainsman reined away
toward the head of the column that was making its turn
four by four by four, the blue-starred and red-striped guidons barely troubled in the still, cold air of that dawn this
twenty-third day of July.

Then the infantry band started up. Oh, how she had
come to hate the song.

> The hour was sad I left the maid,
> A ling'ring farewell taking;
> Her sighs and tears my steps delay'd—
> I thought her heart was breaking.

Something gripped her chest more every time she
heard it. Forced to watch more and more men marching off
to this God-blessed war against the Indians.

> In hurried words her name I bless'd;
> I breathed the vows that bind me,
> And to my heart in anguish press'd
> The girl I left behind me!

How she hated hearing the brass horns, rattling
drums, and reedy clarinets pitch into the notes of that
mournful song.

> Full many a name our banners bore
> Of former deeds of daring,
> But they were of the days of yore
> In which we had no sharing.

Hated even more how some of the women sang the words aloud as they waved their hankies and trotted along beside the departing column, blowing kisses at the mounted soldiers, hated how the little ones clutched their mothers' breasts, hated how the toddlers stumbled through the grass and gravel beside the prancing horses, hated how some of the older ones beat on toy drums or only a tin pie plate held before them by a loop of yellow twine around their necks . . . all of them saying good-bye to the husbands of other wives, to the fathers of other children, that cheering, banging, singing crowd saying good-bye to those men who had no wives and children to bid them farewell, to wish those soldiers all Godspeed.

Good Lord—she bit her lower lip as the tears came down—how she hated this song!

But now our laurels freshly won
With the old ones shall entwin'd be;
Still worthy of our sires each son,
Sweet girl I left behind me!

Notes from Northern Forts

CHEYENNE, July 21—The courier who left General Crook's camp on the eve of the 16th inst. has not reached Fort Fetterman. As in former instances, his horse may have given out. Seven companies of General Merritt's Fifth cavalry arrived at Fort Laramie to day, and will leave for Fetterman tomorrow or the day following, together with three additional companies of the same regiment, ten in all.

Missing Courier Arrived—News from Crook's Command

CHEYENNE, July 22—The courier who left Goose Creek on the 16th arrived at Fort Fetterman to night. His delay was caused by having met at

Powder river a body of 200 Indians, from whom he escaped, hiding himself in the timber for twenty-six hours. One Indian followed his trail 9 miles. He says they were evidently waiting for him and fears that the couriers who were sent from Fetterman on the 16th instant with despatches for Crook have been interrupted, as he saw their trail this side of the river, but not beyond. His delay ran him out of rations, compelling him to fast two days.

He left all quiet in camp. The hostile Sioux are believed to be north of Goose creek, about forty miles, and not far from the scene of the late massacre on the Little Big Horn. They have not fired into camp lately nor attempted to burn it out, although the parched condition of the grass rendered this somewhat easy . . .

The command moved seven miles north on the day of the courier's departure, to another branch of the Tongue river, near the Big Horn mountains, where they will camp until the 5th cavalry—which will leave Fort Laramie on Monday—reaches it, about the 5th of August. Gen. Crook will make no aggressive movement until this event, and when— if the couriers he dispatched to Terry advising him to join him reach that command—he will have made a junction with Terry, and the next action will prove a decisive one.

Sun and sweat, dust and mud, mosquitoes and flies, rain and heat. And waiting.

Seamus had read those three letters Samantha wrote him, brought up with the rest of the mail and newspapers in an irregular schedule of couriers and supply trains. Life was going on in the world around them. Hell, chances were that even the Sioux campaign was going on without them!

The general chafed more than normal at the wait he himself had imposed on the command. Word was that Merritt should have arrived by now. Where was he? Crook asked, plainly restless, even to the point of anxiety. Sheridan's messages told Crook that he had ordered the Fifth Cavalry north to reinforce the expedition. So what was taking them so long to get here?

There was no action taking place south of Camp Cloud Peak, that much was for sure. It was all to the north, between them and the Yellowstone where the Montana and Dakota columns waited out reinforcements as well. Somewhere in between them were the Sioux. What Seamus feared most, however, was that while the generals were playing mumblety-peg over what to do with their armies, the enemy was slipping away to the east, right out of their grip.

Back and forth Crook and Terry were dispatching couriers, holding a regular correspondence between Camp Goose Creek and the Rosebud Landing on the Yellowstone. Debating just what to do, and when to do it. To combine their commands? If so, where? What was heard of the hostiles? Was it better to chase with a smaller, more mobile column? Or merely to follow with thousands of men and simply herd the Indians back to their agencies?

Crook wrote to Sheridan:

> On Powder, Tongue, and Rosebud rivers the whole country is on fire and filled with smoke. I am in constant dread of attack . . . I am at a loss what to do . . . All indications are that the Sioux are in the Big Horn mountains, from which they can see clear to the Yellowstone and discern the approach of Terry's column . . . I don't think they will fight us combined, but will scatter . . . Should the Indians scatter unhurt, they would have greatly the advantage over us, as we would be obliged to divide accordingly, while their thorough knowledge of the country and rapidity of movement would enable them to concentrate on and destroy our small parties.

One way or the other, Crook soon determined that he would once again strike out with his mule train, abandoning tents and all extra comforts. It was the only way to track the Indians, to move as fast as the Sioux, to be as mobile as his enemy.

And now that Sheridan had concurred with Crook that the Big Horn and Yellowstone Expedition should wait until Merritt brought up his Fifth Cavalry, Seamus would be sitting right here on his saddle galls with the rest of them.

The Fifth! And Colonel Carr—the fighting turk of the Summit Springs campaign!

At times he squeezed his memory really hard and could remember some of the faces, a few of the names, and even the dim recollection of a woman's face—the one captive they did get out of Tall Bull's village alive there at Summit Springs seven summers before.

Eight days back, on the twenty-fifth, Crook ordered out his first formal scouting party of Shoshone. The warriors made it only some four or five miles to the South Fork of the Tongue when they ran into a roaming war party of Sioux and both sides exchanged insults before the Snake returned to camp.

Two days later Crook had camp moved again, five more miles to the northwest, locating some grass that had been too green for the Sioux to burn.

The next afternoon, the twenty-eighth, dispatches arrived from Sheridan, telling Crook that the Fifth was on the road and could be expected by the first of August. Back in Chicago, Sheridan prodded Crook into resuming full-scale scouting operations, urging him to have his camp ready to resume the campaign at the very moment Merritt's column arrived. As well, the division commander informed the leader of the Wyoming column that Colonel Ranald S. Mackenzie and six full companies of his Fourth Cavalry had been ordered up from Fort Sill in Indian Territory to plug the void left at Camp Robinson and the Red Cloud

Agency when Merritt's troops departed to reinforce the Big Horn and Yellowstone Expedition.

The afternoon of the thirtieth Crook finally got his Ute scouts. For better than two weeks they had been held up at their agency in Colorado Territory because the bureau agent would not allow them to answer Washakie's plea for assistance against their mutual enemy. But then Sherman finally saw to it that some substantial evidence of bribery and fraud against the agent was made available to his superiors in the Indian Bureau. It wasn't many days before the War Department was given control of all western agencies, whereby Sheridan promptly removed the agent and placed him under arrest, freeing the thirty-five Ute to hurry north.

Upon reaching the Wind River Reservation, however, they discovered Washakie had grown impatient waiting on them and gone ahead. The Ute crossed the Big Horns and rode into Camp Cloud Peak without Crook's usual pomp and fanfare, due to the fact that at that time most soldiers and Shoshone alike were fighting a grass fire whipped out of control by the wind muscling right through Washakie's camp of willow-and-blanket wickiups.

Soldier and Shoshone alike used blankets, blouses, and branches to slap at the spreading flames until the meandering wall of fire reached a war lodge where the auxiliaries stored their ammunition. As bullets began whining and whistling through camp, everyone dived for cover until the cartridges had all exploded and they could get back to the dirty job at hand. After a fight of over three hours a change in the wind finally saved the day, as well as saving the rest of camp plainly in danger if nature had enforced its will that day.

On Monday morning, the thirty-first, Louie Reshaw took a dozen Shoshone on his climb over the Big Horns to investigate an Indian rumor that the Sioux had crossed over the mountains and were firmly planted in the Big Horn Basin. The half-breed returned the next afternoon after suffering through a severe snowstorm among the high sum-

mits, reporting to Crook that they had found no evidence
of the hostiles in the mountains, much less in the western
basin, except for small parties gone to hunt for game or
lodgepoles.

"They didn't see no buffalo either," Baptiste Pourier
explained to the rest what he had heard when Reshaw reported to Crook.

"Bad sign, Bat," Grouard grumbled.

Seamus nodded in agreement. "Plain as the nose on
your face that the Sioux won't be hanging around here—
not if the buffalo have wandered to the east."

"That's where the Sioux went," Grouard said. "Follow
the buffalo east."

Minutes later Tom Cosgrove came to fetch Grouard,
saying, "Crook wants you to guide for me and some of the
Snakes."

"Where we going?"

"Northwest along the base of the foothills."

Grouard slowly got to his feet and stretched, the days
of cramping and pain in his groin over with, by and large.
"He want us to look for anything special?"

"Just the usual."

Tapping the brim of his hat, the half-breed grinned
and said, "Suppose a ride with Cosgrove is better than sitting here being bored by you, Irishman."

Seamus blew the half-breed a kiss. "I love you too,
Frank."

This wasn't a snappy army bivouac any longer. All a
man had to do to realize that was look around that Tuesday
morning, the first day of August. In the weeks since they
had marched away from Fetterman to bump into the Sioux
at the Rosebud, through all those endless days of waiting
here on Goose Creek, this had become a camp of squatters:
the very best of them unkempt, wearing only pieces of uniform, their boots gone from shiny black to a dull coffee
color, every man of them ragged and shaggy and not giving
a good goddamn about it, either.

Why should they? Seamus asked himself. Wasn't going

to make a hill of beans if they sat out the rest of the campaign right here, waiting for autumn and winter to shut everything down like closing the lid on a pauper's coffin. Nail it shut.

The bugle blew again. Another officers' call.

Their days were ruled by the bugle: from reveille at sunup through fatigue and stable duty, noon mess and evening retreat, finally ending in "Tattoo" late each summer night. It seemed that if the boredom didn't kill them, then the rock-solid regularity of the trumpet calls would surely make a man wish he were dead.

So he read her letters over and over until he was afraid the ink would fade and the paper would crumble in his hands. Where once he could smell the scent of her lavender or gardenia perfume she dolloped at the corner of every sheet, now there was only the smell of dust and sweat, only the smear of his dirty, greasy fingerprints at the edges of each page.

He cradled them all in his lap, rereading his favorite lines. Nearby the officers of the infantry were playing the cavalry officers in a well-matched game of base-ball. Ringing the field was a crowd not only of enthusiastic enlisted men, but also curious Indians downright stupefied to watch this peculiar pastime of the white man.

"The Fifth is coming!"

At the call Seamus looked up to find Finerty lumbering his way in those clumsy brogans of his, shouting it again.

Grumbling, Donegan said, "I know. We're all waiting for the Fifth."

"No," Finerty said breathlessly as he skidded to a stop. "I mean, a courier just came in from Merritt."

"A courier?"

"Fella named White. Civilian scout. Carried word from Merritt telling Crook his ten full companies of cavalry are less than a day away."

His heart pounded. "Gonna be here tomorrow?"

Finerty slapped his thigh. "Damn right they are!"

"Blessed Mither of God—that is good news!" Seamus replied thoughtfully. "Now we can be about getting this goddamned campaign over so I can get back to Samantha."

"You ought to come meet the guy who carried in the messages for Crook."

"Why?"

"He's over at Tom Moore's camp now, with soldiers and mule skinners hanging on him like flies on a carcass because he's telling 'em the whole story of how on the way here the Fifth ambushed eight hundred Cheyenne over on a creek called the Warbonnet and drove 'em all right back to the Red Cloud Agency."

"The Fifth had 'em a fight of it, you say?"

"And you've got to hear this Charlie White tell the story of the first scalp for Custer."

Seamus's brow knitted quizzically. "The first scalp . . . for Custer?"

"The one took by Buffalo Bill."

"B-buffalo Bill?"

"Damn right!" Finerty cheered. "Can you believe it? We're going to get to meet the famous frontier scout and master showman of the eastern theater, ourselves! Right here!"

"Bill Cody?"

"None other! Won't it be something for me to tell all my readers about, Seamus—this meeting such a famous man?"

He grinned slightly. "Sure will be, Johnny boy."

"Won't you want to meet the famous Buffalo Bill yourself now, Seamus?"

"Oh," Donegan replied, that impish grin growing into a wisp of a warm smile, "for sure and certain I do want to shake hands with Buffalo Bill Cody!"

Chapter 24

3 August 1876

Crook's Plan of Operations

WASHINGTON, July 24—The following dispatch has been received by General Sherman: "The following dispatch from Gen. Crook is transmitted for your information. Gen. Merritt will reach Gen. Crook's camp on August 1, with ten companies instead of eight as at first contemplated. Gen. Terry has moved his depot from north of Powder river to Big Horn, on the Rosebud, and has notified me of his intention to form a junction with Crook.

P. H. SHERIDAN
Lieut. General.

HEADQUARTERS, BIG HORN AND YELLOWSTONE EXPEDITION, CAMP ON GOOSE CREEK, WYOMING, July 18, via Fort Fetterman—To General Sheridan, Chicago: I send in a courier to-day to carry in duplicates of my dispatch to Gen. Merritt, for fear the originals may not have reached their destinations. I send a courier to General Terry to-night to inform him that I will cooperate with him, and where to find me; also, giving him what information I have in regard

to the Indians. It is my intention to move out after
the hostile tribes as soon as Merritt gets here with
the Fifth. I shall not probably send in another courier until something special shall require me to do
so. I am getting anxious about Merritt's not reaching here, and the grass is getting very dry . . .

> GEO. CROOK
> Brigadier General

The plan of the campaign is to make a combined
movement of three columns with Fort Ellis as a
base. Two of the columns will move directly
against the Indians, and one against their villages. General Sheridan will, according to the
present plan, establish his headquarters in the
field at some advantageous point on Goose creek,
about forty miles northwest of Fort Phil Kearny,
and near the scene of Crook's battle on Rosebud.
The force of these three columns will amount in
the aggregate to between 4,000 and 5,000.

Two days after marching away from Laramie and crossing
the North Platte River on the army's new iron span, Bill
Cody led the Fifth Cavalry to the mouth of LaPrele Creek,
the site of Fort Fetterman, on the afternoon of 25 July.

Waiting there for Merritt was a mixture of strays and
civilians, along with a handful of unattached officers who
had been on leave or assigned duty at other posts when the
news of the Custer disaster reached the outside world. Now
they had raced to Wyoming Territory, eager to attach their
fates with Crook's column. Even a naval officer, Lieutenant
William C. Hunter, presented himself to Colonel Merritt
and, like the others, was allowed to accompany the Fifth
Cavalry as a "volunteer."

To Lieutenant Colonel Carr's disgust, the regiment
found a few newspapermen hanging about the post, waiting to march off to the Sioux War. A New York *Times*
reporter named Talbot, along with an unlikely looking

stringer for the Associated Press, and Barbour Lathrop writing for the San Francisco *Evening Bulletin*, all had been waiting at Fetterman for Merritt's reinforcements to arrive so they could complete their trip to join Crook's Wyoming column.

Immediately crossing the Platte below the fort, Merritt and Carr established bivouac on the north side of the river, checked the post commander for any last-minute dispatches from Chicago, Omaha, or Laramie, then went about drawing any last-minute supplies depleted since leaving Fort Laramie two days before.

At eight o'clock the next morning, a Wednesday, those eight companies of the Fighting Fifth were pushing past Kid Slaymaker's Hog Ranch, marching into the badlands of central Wyoming Territory, a country ablaze with sunlit clouds of alkali dust and sagebrush flats.

It was well past midnight two days later when Cody had the regiment camped and asleep in the rainy darkness beneath the bluffs along the North Fork of the Cheyenne. As if it were a dream, he thought he heard a distant bugle calling out of the cold, drizzling mist.

"Charlie!"

White strode over as Cody put the pistol he had been oiling back in its holster. "What you need, Bill?"

"Listen."

For a few seconds they both strained to hear beyond the noise of camp, the whickering of their nearby mounts cropping at the good grass.

White asked, "That a bugle, Bill?"

"What I thought," Cody replied. "Best you go alert Merritt."

The colonel promptly had one of the company buglers go with Lieutenant Charles King and Cody to the high ground above the riverside camp, with orders to begin playing "Officers' Call," then wait a minute or two for a response, then play it again, repeatedly in that fashion until Cody could determine if it was an Indian ruse or not.

Even as he, White, the lieutenant, and the trumpeter

were reaching the top of the bluff . . . there, faintly in the distance, Cody heard it again.

"Blow your horn," he quietly ordered, his soft words adding all the more drama to the ominous moment.

A few heartbeats after the bugler's last note had drifted out into the rainy darkness, Bill again made cut the dim, sodden call from afar.

King said, "Sounds like it's coming from the south."

"It sure does. Give 'em another blow on that horn."

Back and forth the trumpeters played the song that would summon all cavalry officers, while closer and closer that other horn came—until Cody thought he could just make out the dull glimmer of brass and bit and carbine below him in the rain-soaked darkness. He lumbered down the gummy slope to the sodden prairie below, stopping a few yards away from a group of officers at the head of a column of weary, wet troops.

"Is that you, Buffalo Bill?"

"It is!" he cheered back, relieved to hear a voice of someone who evidently knew who he was. "Who goes there?"

"By Jehovah—don't you remember me, Bill? It's George Price."

"Captain Price? That really you?" Bill asked as he strode out of the gloom and right up to the men gathered beneath their rain-drenched guidon. "Damn, but it's good to see you, Captain. Who the hell you got with you?"

"A battalion: my own E Troop, and I brought along Captain Payne's F Company with me. Both of us racing all the way up from Cheyenne in a lightning march."

"Seven days' worth of march!" J. Scott Payne added.

"Whooo! That's getting high-behind, fellas. We was hoping you'd reach us by Laramie. Then Merritt hoped you'd come in by the time we reached Fetterman."

"Hell, Bill," Payne replied, "the way you've had the boys covering ground, we're lucky we caught up with you before you went and captured Sitting Bull!"

Price agreed, saying, "We've been pushing these men

and horses pretty hard for a solid week just to get here—forced marches and all."

"Merritt's gonna be plumb happy to see you both, fellas!" Cody cheered. "C'mon—let's get your men into camp where they can gather round a fire and get a hot cup of coffee down 'em."

Two days and two long marches later the Fifth camped near the ruins of old Fort Reno on the Powder River. In the heat of the following day the snowcaps on those distant mountain peaks proved to be a seductive lure for the men. That first day of August, Cody led the ten companies of the Fifth Cavalry across Crazy Woman's Fork and was closing on the Clear Fork just past one P.M. In the distance he sighted a few small herds of dark, shaggy buffalo, plain as paint against the verdant green of the nearby hills. Along with a small cadre of eager officers, Bill secured Merritt's permission to make meat for the hungry column. As the buffalo were shot, skinned, and butchered by a detail of men selected from each company, the main body of the command marched on past the mirrored surface of Lake DeSmet, which lay in the midst of a basin of near-naked hills. That night in their bivouac made just south of the ruins of old Fort Phil Kearny, the men ate better than they had in weeks, and their stock had one of its last opportunities to take advantage of unequaled grazing.

"We ought to be getting near Crook's camp, aren't we, Bill?" Merritt asked after they had stuffed themselves on buffalo tenderloin.

"Real close, General. I could take a ride out tomorrow and likely reach the forks of Goose Creek by afternoon."

Merritt shook his head. "I want to keep you with me, so we'll choose someone else." He looked over at White. "How about him, Bill?"

"Chips?" and he grinned. "Sure. He'll find Crook's camp with no problem."

White stood, eager to please. "You want me to carry a message, maybeso a dispatch to Crook, General?"

"Yes. I'll write it first thing in the morning and send it

with you right after you've had breakfast. We're going to let General Crook know to expect the Fifth for supper day after tomorrow."

The general had been so excited when White had delivered Merritt's note, absolutely buoyant to learn that the Fifth was only hours away, that on the following morning of August 3 he had his Big Horn and Yellowstone Expedition strike camp and countermarch eighteen miles to the south along the foothills of the Big Horns so that they might unite with Merritt's 535 officers and men that much sooner.

So it was that something on the order of a mile off Cody spotted horsemen, perhaps a dozen, no more. They weren't Indians, that much was for sure, not the way they rode in a column of twos, with a couple of spare fellows off to the side. Scouts, he thought to himself. Behind them, as far as the eye could see, the horizon lay smudged with smoke. At times the smudge to the air was enough to sting the back of his tongue.

Halting at the top of the next rise, Bill turned in the saddle and took his hat from his head to wave to Merritt and Carr still a quarter mile behind him at the head of the column. Then he sat and waited. This would be as good a place as any, he decided. He stretched his back, pulling at some stiff muscles, and watched the riders move out of a walk into a ragged lope. They had spotted him. Some pointed in his direction.

God, is this ever pretty country, he thought to himself. Look at them peaks up there. Bet they never lose their snow, either. He felt thirsty immediately, hungering for a cup of that water straight out of those glacier fields, water so cold he remembered how it could set his teeth on edge.

Looking back at the riders, he could make out Charlie White now, riding off to the left of that bunch of soldiers with another civilian. A big man. A fella who rode his horse damned fine. One of Crook's half-breeds, no doubt. Most white men simply couldn't ride a horse that good. A few Bill had known in the past could, men like himself, born to the saddle. Friends like White and Texas Jack, like Bill Hickok and that Irishman he and Wild Bill had scouted with for Carr back in the winter of sixty-eight and sixty-nine.

The remembrance made him think of Samantha and her letter, then made him squint his eyes and study the distant figures. Maybeso.

The officer up front tore the hat from his head and waved it at Cody. It was Royall. By damn, that was Royall! Smiling, Bill sat up straighter in the saddle. The major who had been with the Fifth when it defeated Tall Bull at Summit Springs was now a lieutenant colonel with the Third. How grand it would be to see him again in a few more minutes.

One last time he turned in the saddle and saw the headquarters group coming on at a gallop, Merritt and Carr beneath the snapping of their regimental standard and the general's own flag. They had seen the riders coming out to greet them.

By the time Cody turned back around, he saw the two civilians suddenly kick their horses in the flanks, watched as White put his quirt to work front and back to squeeze more speed out of his dapple. Both of the horsemen leaned forward like men accustomed to wrenching every last drop of effort out of those magnificent animals.

Yes, that man racing White up the slope was one of a kind. The tall boots and loose, grimy, collarless shirt, with long hair spilling over his shoulders, hair streaming out with the wind beneath his wide-brimmed hat. White's was blond, every bit as light as Custer's before he lost his on the Little Bighorn. But that stranger's—now that was brown, pretty much like Cody's. But the way it caught the light, maybeso it had some blond in it. That, or the man was starting to gray.

From here he simply couldn't tell for sure, not the way the two riders sprinted up that last long grassy slope toward him, closing on the last fifty yards. Not the way the horsemen laid so low along the lunging necks of their animals, hunkered down on the withers and whipping manes.

They both shot past Cody, swooping by on either side of him with a rush of wind and hammer of hooves, yelling out to him, to one another, to their horses, laughing as they sawed their mounts around in that belly-high grass. In that grand circle the stranger whipped his hat off his head and slapped White on the back with it.

"By the blood of the Virgin Mary!" the big man bellowed with a voice that made Cody's heart seize in his throat. "It sure is good to see you've fared well, *Buffalo Bill!*"

"Seamus," he whispered, able to get nothing more past his tongue for the moment.

Then Cody kicked his right leg over his saddle and dropped to the ground, bolting off at a dead run to meet the tall gray-eyed Irishman there on that hilltop as the sun began its fall toward the purple bulk of the Big Horns.

"Seamus Donegan! Damn, it is you!"

He dropped to the ground, yelling, "Come here and give your old partner a big hug, Bill Cody!"

They embraced and jumped, slapped and cried, then hugged some more, both of them babbling like schoolgirls on the annual spring picnic.

"Charlie, you know that Buffalo Bill here," Seamus said, his arm looped over Cody's shoulders as he turned to speak to White, who held the reins to their three horses, "he saved my life once."

"In a goddamned shitter, it was!" Cody choked, laughing so hard.

"In a sh-shitter?" White asked, wagging his head in disbelief.

"Damn right," Donegan said, nearly lifting Cody off the ground with that arm he had locked around Bill's shoulder like a singletree.

Cody gazed at his old friend, saying, "Never have I regretted a minute of the time we had together, Seamus."

"Listen," Donegan said to White, his voice thick with

emotion, "we'll have to tell Chips here about the time we tracked some horse thieves all the way to the Elephant Corral in Denver City for Major Carr."

"Major Carr?" Cody snorted. "I'll have you know he's our lieutenant colonel now!"

Donegan turned to face Cody, securing Bill's shoulders in both his hands. "And just look at you, Bill—damn, but there's nothing like seeing old friends again."

The Irishman drew him into a sudden and fierce embrace that Bill was sure was going to crush his ribs, and when Donegan let him go, he remembered.

"Damn you! Don't go and squash my surprise! Here I brought something for you all the way from Laramie—"

"Laramie?"

"—carrying it careful as a fudge pie so I could hand it over to you just like it was handed to me," Bill said, reaching inside the flap of his shirt, where he had carried that perfumed letter between it and his longhandle underwear for the last dozen days.

"For me?" Donegan asked in a whisper as Cody brought out the folded pages.

"You know someone at Fort Laramie, don't you?"

"Sam? Samantha?"

Bill nodded as White leaned forward to get a look for himself. Cody handed the letter over to the misty-eyed Irishman.

"You met . . . Sam?"

"Ah, a lovely one you've got there, Seamus! And she's carrying your first, she tells me."

He watched Donegan swallow hard and swipe at a tear that just began to track down his dusty cheek. "Yes," he said so quietly Bill knew it was really a sob. "Our f-firstborn."

"She says it's going to be a boy, Seamus."

Donegan nodded. "Sam told me the same thing."

Bill leaned in as if confiding a secret. "Listen, I've had experience with these things, you know—what with Lulu and me having three of our own . . . and, well—you just better learn to trust them women when it comes to such things."

"Ah, damn!" Donegan said after dragging the letter under his nose. "I was hoping she had perfumed it with some of that lilac water she uses."

Confused, Bill's brow crinkled. "She did. Don't it smell like her good perfume now?"

"The bloody hell it doesn't!" Donegan roared. "Smells just like Bill Cody smeared his mule sweat all over my wife's love letter to me!"

Chapter 25

4–5 August
1876

"So I take it that you've made a life for yourself in the army over the past seven years since we saw you last," declared Lieutenant Colonel Eugene Carr.

Seamus snorted. "Not by my own hand, I haven't, General!"

Cody pounded Donegan on the shoulder, saying, "Seems more times than not he finds himself in the wrong place at the wrong time, General."

"No matter that it was the wrong place and damn sure the wrong morning," William B. Royall added, "I couldn't have been happier to have any one man with me at the Rosebud than I was to have this irreverent, shaggy-haired Irishman!"

They were having a time of it that evening after supper around their fire, these old comrades in arms. Royall had long served in the Fifth before coming to a field command in the Third, so tonight he and Seamus made welcome their old friends from that cold, empty-handed campaign of the winter of sixty-eight, those battle-tested veterans of the Cheyenne summer of eighteen and sixty-nine. In addition, many of these reunited officers of both the Third and the Fifth had served under Crook during the Apache campaign in Arizona.

Here and there in that circle of laughter, warmth, and camaraderie sat the newsmen hungry for any kernel of a story, along with John Bourke and those officers new to the West eager to hear a retelling of the war stories by Cody and the officers. Eager to hear Buffalo Bill's own gut-grabbing rendition of his hilarious robbery of a beer wagon, aided and abetted by fellow scouts Wild Bill Hickok and Seamus Donegan in the panhandle country of west Texas that terrible winter campaign when they had served as beaters to drive the hostile Cheyenne toward Custer's Seventh Cavalry, which ended up catching Black Kettle's village on the Washita.

What a joyful, heart-brimming reunion this was, Seamus thought as he gazed round at those faces illuminated with the flicker of the fire's merry light while the stars came out over that Big Horn country. This was one of the few rewards a fighting man could claim after years of service to his country, after one campaign and battle and fight after another—to gather with old friends and swap stories and yarns, tell windies and lies and poke fun at one another here in these last few hours before they once more picked up the yoke and stepped back into harness, getting on with the deadly business of this frontier army and what every last one of them prayed would be the final war with the Sioux.

Before supper that evening Merritt and Carr had joined Crook in the tent the general had turned into a war room. No one else had been allowed into their discussions, not even aides and adjutants. Just the three old warhorses, intent on deciding just what to do and where to go now. Surely they talked about Terry's two columns sitting things out up there at the Rosebud Landing on the Yellowstone.

Upon finding Carr still leading the Fifth, Seamus once again allowed himself to feel eager instead of anxious. If anyone knew how to chase and fight these wandering nomadic warrior bands, it was the "war eagle," Eugene A. Carr. Time and again the old soldier had proved that he understood how to take the starch right out of such guerrilla forces. So at that meeting, Donegan felt assured, Carr must certainly have convinced his superiors that the only way to catch up to, much less capture and defeat, the fleeing Sioux and Cheyenne, was to break the cavalry off into smaller, highly mobile battalions, ration those strike forces for many days, and send them off to take up the trail of the slower-moving villages. Surely Carr had argued that in keeping together these two thousand men of the Big Horn and Yellowstone Expedition, even if Crook abandoned his wagons and relied on his mule train, they could never hope to find anything more in their hunt than track soup.

So the very next morning Seamus was just as shocked as most of the line officers to hear Crook explain their plans.

"With General Merritt's wise counsel, I have decided to organize the expedition as a united column," the bearded general told that great assembly of subalterns gathered beneath the rattling leaves of the cottonwoods beside upper Goose Creek.* "From Chief Washakie's scouts, as well as from Grouard's forays and Reshaw's trip into the mountains, all the best intelligence I have tells me the enemy village is but two days' march north of here—still massed in strength."

Donegan leaned to the side and whispered to Cody, "Shit. The Lakota have skedaddled, heading north by east. They've burned the grass on their backtrail."

As Crook droned on, Bill wagged his head, telling the Irishman, "The way we turned those Cheyenne back at Warbonnet, and the way things looked here when we come in—why, I was feeling damned good about this campaign. But this morning I'm not so sure about things anymore."

"Something in the pit of my belly tells me this army ain't ready to catch the Sioux, not just yet, it ain't," Done-

---

*Site of present-day Sheridan, Wyoming.

gan replied. "Crook and Terry and all the rest may talk a good game, but it seems to me they're not ready to do what it takes to beat the Sioux at their own game, Bill."

"If they want to find the Indians," Cody said under his breath, "let them send a battalion, which I'm willing to guide myself. I'll wager any man we'll have our fill of fighting before we strike the Little Missouri. Crook ain't going to find any hostiles by hauling this big army about the countryside. No, Irishman, unless they break these units up," Cody advised, "all Crook will succeed in doing is wearing out his men and breaking down his horses."

That fourth day of August, Seamus had no way of knowing just how the events of the next five weeks were to prove Bill Cody right.

Crook went on to explain that he was organizing the cavalry as a brigade, under Merritt's command. Under that umbrella Carr would maintain command of the two battalions of the Fifth itself, with Royall at the head of the three battalions of the Third, as well as the one battalion of the Second.

Seamus looked over to watch the expression on Carr's face, then whispered to Cody, "There, you see how the old eagle can't hide his disappointment at that?"

"Sure," Bill replied. "What do you expect? It wasn't that long ago that Carr was Royall's superior. And now Crook's gone and put Royall over four battalions to Carr's two."

Detachments from the three infantry regiments were consolidated into a battalion under the command of Major Alexander Chambers. Medical director for the campaign was to be Dr. Bennett A. Chambers, newly arrived with the Fifth Cavalry. Crook extended Major John V. Furey's assignment as expedition quartermaster.

"And now for a small change in regard to my scouts," Crook said, instantly snagging Donegan's attention. "General Carr's battalion of the Fifth will maintain the trackers and guides it brought up—with one exception. I am reassigning William F. Cody to headquarters, designating him as chief of scouts for the BH and Y."

Seamus watched Cody nod to Crook, but over Bill's shoulder the Irishman saw the uncomfortable disappointment on Eugene Carr's face turn to an unmasked glower.

"The rest of Frank Grouard's scouts will remain in their present assignments with the Second and Third, along with the rest of the irregulars, all under the nominal command of Major Stanton. Serving him will be Chief Washakie and Captain Cosgrove in direct command of our Indian auxiliaries, with Captain Randall acting as my liaison with our allies."

Crook took two more steps forward, so that he stood at the center of that ring of officers. "Gentlemen, it is my intent to capture the Sioux between us and the forces of the Montana and Dakota columns now on the Yellowstone, some one hundred twenty-five miles north of where we are standing. We'll march north, as I understand Terry is marching south, and together we can crack Sitting Bull's confederation like a walnut in the jaws of a nutcracker."

Turning slightly, Crook motioned for his adjutant to step forward. "I'll have Lieutenant Schuyler read the orders of the march."

Walter Schuyler, on detached service to Crook from the Fifth Cavalry, held out his sheaf of pages and began to speak. "The command will march at seven A.M., five August, eighteen and seventy-six, 'prepared for action.' Each man, officer, and enlisted, packer and civilian volunteer included, is to take along what is on his back and no more. He is allowed one overcoat and one blanket, along with an India-rubber poncho or one half of his shelter tent. No tents will be allowed but one, that provided for the surgeons in their care for what wounded the columns might suffer. Travois poles have been cut and will be brought along for use as litters in transporting our casualties. Four extra horses, not to be packed, will be led by each company. Currycombs and brushes will be left with the wagons."

Schuyler stopped for a brief moment, his eyes flicking

to the general, who only nodded slightly before the young
lieutenant continued. "The command will be rationed
from this point for fifteen days: half rations of bacon,
sugar, coffee, and salt. Full days' rations of hard bread.
There will be no rations of vinegar, soap, pepper, etcetera.
Four days' rations will be carried on each mount, the remaining supplies to be distributed among the pack-mules.
Only pint cups are to be carried by each man. Each mess is
to provide one frying pan, one carving knife and fork, one
large coffeepot, one large tin platter, one large and two
small tin ladles, one sheet-iron mess pan, and all the necessary bags for transporting the sugar, coffee, bacon, and
hard bread."

The lieutenant raised his eyes and cleared his throat.
During that pause Crook overheard the murmuring. Holding a hand in the air, the general quieted the grumbling
assembly and Schuyler resumed his reading.

"Two hundred fifty rounds of ammunition is to be
assigned to every man. One hundred of that will be carried
on his person, and the rest distributed among the pack-
mules. Lieutenant John W. Bubb will act as chief of com-
missariat, to work in conjunction with Mr. Moore, who is
in command of our train of three hundred ninety-nine
mules, which the packers will break down into five divisions, each led by a bell mare. Cavalry commanders are to
see that each man in their units is equipped with lariat,
sideline, and picket pin."

With a hacking cough the lieutenant cleared his throat
and continued. "In conclusion, each company is to turn
over all surplus to Quartermaster Furey, who will be in
charge of our train of one hundred sixty wagons and who is
under orders once again to fort up his train in this vicinity,
to here await our return."

Schuyler shuffled to the last page and read on.
"Reveille will sound at four A.M. At five o'clock the trumpeters will sound 'The General,' to strike tents. *Special instructions for action:* all officers and noncommissioned
officers to take constant pains to prevent wastage of ammu-

nition. Signed, George C. Crook, Brigadier General, Commanding, Big Horn and Yellowstone Expedition, Camp Cloud Peak, Forks of Goose Creek, Wyoming Territory."

"Thank you, Lieutenant," Crook said as he again stepped forward and Schuyler backed away into the large ring of officers. "Are there any questions?"

Captain Julius Mason raised his hand.

Crook pointed, saying, "Major Mason?"

"What do we plan to do for rations after the fourteen days is up, General?"

Crook slapped a twig against the side of his leg, then replied, "By that time we should reach the other commands on the Yellowstone. They're supplied by steamer traffic. We'll eat off General Terry's Dakota column."

There was some stifled laughter before Crook asked, "Is there any other concern?"

Waiting while the men jostled uneasily, looked around the ring at one another, some shuffling their feet anxiously, the general finally concluded, "All right, gentlemen. We are all more than eager to get under way. Use the rest of the day in making your preparations for the march. We'll be under way at first light."

Gale-force winds roared off the Big Horns through the expedition's last night under canvas, leveling most of the tents. Weary men were jolted awake in the maelstrom, clambering to their feet, rubbing their eyes as they stood shivering beneath the force of the wind, struck silent by an awe-inspiring sight. In the foothills west of camp an eerie crimson glow lit the starry postmidnight sky. Stretching for more than a five-mile front along the hills, the leaping flames of fires started by a war party licked like gold tongues against the dark horizon.

"Sonsabitches!" Charlie White spat sourly, pulling his thin army blanket around his shoulders, the gale whipping at the brim of his hat.

"This wind's gonna do a lot of their work for 'em tonight," Seamus added, his eyes already smarting with the smoke easily carried aloft miles from the fires.

Here where the scouts had pitched their camp on the northern edge of the army's bivouac, Donegan listened to the growing rush of wild things scurrying, leaping, lunging out of the darkness, racing through the camp and on to the safety of the prairie beyond. Every little creature seeking safety.

Few men got back to sleep before dawn's bugle call.

A miserable portent of things yet to come.

More Troops Coming

CHICAGO, July 25—Gen. McKenzie, with six companies of United States troops, has been ordered from the Indian territory to Red Cloud agency and vicinity, via Cheyenne and Laramie, to take the place of Gen. Merritt, who goes with the Fifth cavalry to join Crook.

Nearly 2,300 men marched away from Camp Cloud Peak that sunny Saturday morning: 1,500 cavalry, 450 infantry, in addition to Tom Moore's packers and that Falstaffian assortment of white and Indian scouts.

Once again Crook was cutting himself loose from his supply line. They were leaving Major Furey's train behind, where more than two hundred discharged soldiers waiting for escort south to Fetterman, along with teamsters and other unattached civilians, all well armed, would chain the wagon wheels together into a corral, putting the creek at their backs, then dig rifle pits inside their bulwarks and sit out the wait, keeping a watchful eye over more than a thousand horses and mules remaining under their care. With so many capable men left in Furey's command, Crook did not need to deplete his strike force by leaving an escort behind when he marched the Big Horn and Yellowstone Expedition away toward the Tongue River.

"Lead into line!" came the command, echoed again and again as the dismounted troopers walked their horses into company formation for inspection.

Then the Fifth's commander ordered, "Bugler—sound the *mount!*"

As the stirring notes floated over Goose Creek there at the peep of day, 20 officers and 515 soldiers swung into their saddles with a rattle and squeak of arms and bridle.

"Column of fours!" was the next call. "By the right— fooor-rad! March!"

Setting out in the rear of all the rest with Carr's headquarters group, King, as regimental adjutant, raised himself in the stirrups to look ahead at the three columns already wending their way along Goose Creek. Troop by troop of the cavalry fell into line in the wake of those fourteen companies of seasoned infantry that had departed three hours earlier, just past four o'clock. Lieutenant Colonel Carr commanded ten troops of the Fifth, with Captain Henry E. Noyes leading five companies of the Second, and Major Andrew W. Evans riding at the head of ten troops of the Third. The ranks of both the Second and the Third contained some new men, seventy-six in all, troopers Merritt had picked up at either Laramie or Fetterman, bound for Crook's camp to replace soldiers ending their terms of duty.

On the right flank rode the thirty-five Ute and two Bannock, with Captain George M. "Black Jack" Randall in the lead. Serving as the advance guard were Washakie's two hundred. The handful of Crow that Gibbon had dispatched from the Yellowstone weeks before rode as a rear guard, covering the exposed flank of the Fifth Cavalry. All the allies wore white strips torn from Quartermaster Furey's empty flour sacks. Having learned firsthand from the deadly confusion the Indian allies had caused his nervous troops at the Battle of the Rosebud, Crook ordered his brown-skinned auxiliaries to wear the long white flags tied above their scalp locks or in their warbonnets—somewhere easily visible by anxious soldiers in the heat and terror of battle.

Looking over the scorched countryside they entered that August morning as the column followed Prairie Dog

Creek down to its junction with the Tongue, King worried over Crook's decision not to increase the size of his pack-train, using extra animals to haul forage for the horses. As far as the eye could see to the north and east, the blackened, sooty land lay devastated by prairie fire. Truth was, in order to pack even those fifteen days of rations, the command was required to strip itself down to the lightest of marching order.

If they made good time, and the fates were with them, Charles tried to cheer himself as the sun grew hot and the sooty cinders rose in dark clouds under every scuffling foot and plodding hoof—then Crook's men would be eating from Terry's stores at the Rosebud depot. But that hope meant Crook was clearly relying on the other columns having enough in their larder to share with the Wyoming expedition.

No two ways about it, the young lieutenant decided, the general was gambling against the house on this one: entrusting the lives of twenty-three hundred men and nearly three thousand animals to no more than their prayers for good weather, good grass, and just plain good luck.

Chapter 26

8–10 August
1876

Gen. Miles to the Front—Strength and
Purpose of the Hostiles

BISMARCK, D.T., July 25—The six companies of infantry under Gen. Miles arrived yesterday, and left for the Yellowstone this morning, taking on board here one hundred and sixty recruits, two three-inch Rodman guns, forces and supplies. Army officers generally blame Crook for a failure to co-operate with Terry, believing that he was anxious to win laurels without assistance or interference. One gentleman, but little inferior in rank, insists that Crook knows little of the plans of the enemy, and lacks the experience desireable in one commanding an army operating against a wily and savage foe. All agree that one of the greatest mistakes in the campaign is the under estimate of the number of the Sioux, and of their disposition to fight. General Miles says he is satisfied that nearly all the fighting men from Standing Rock are out. He stopped there long enough to look the

ground over; and the agent at Lower Brule adds
that his Indians are all out, and those from the
Cheyenne agency, not to speak of Spotted Tail and
Red Cloud are certainly with them. The hostiles
have been largely reinforced since the battle . . .
A Sioux scout in the employ of the government at
Fort Rice, after the recent battle said he always
knew the Sioux outnumbered the whites, and that
he believed they would conquer in the end. The
idea prevails to a great extent among the warriors
who go into the campaign, that they are better
armed than the whites, with a knowledge of every
ravine in the country, and almost every tree from
behind which an Indian can shoot a cavalry man
and they are confident that they will win. Well informed river and frontiers-men insist that the Indians have an effective fighting force of at least
10,000 well armed and abundantly supplied.

With Nelson A. Miles in the lead and the regimental
band playing the rousing, patriotic air "Sherman's
March to the Sea," six companies of the Fifth Infantry had
boarded sixteen stuffy Missouri Pacific freight cars at Leavenworth, Kansas, early on the evening of 12 July and rumbled north by rail through towns heavily draped in black
bunting to mourn the Little Bighorn dead. All the way to
Yankton, South Dakota, they rode, where to the cheers of
an immense throng of well-wishers at the dock the colonel's foot soldiers marched two by two up the gangplank
and crowded onto the decks of the *E. H. Durfee*, a steam-
powered stern-wheeler that would take them up the Missouri to Fort Buford at the mouth of the Yellowstone, then
to the Rosebud Landing where, early on the afternoon of 2
August, nearly four hundred men of the Fifth marched
down the gangplank onto the soil of Montana Territory,
reinforcing General Alfred Terry's battered, butchered, and
demoralized command.

On their crawl north against the Missouri's current,

Miles had been overjoyed to see the citizens of those riverside communities turn out to wave handkerchiefs, hold up banners of good wishes, and raise their voices as the steamer chugged its way into Dakota Territory. But upon passing the Standing Rock Agency, the colonel grew angry when he learned that the agent there had recently delivered nearly one hundred thousand rounds of ammunition to nonagency Indians.

Possessors of a proud and honored tradition of battle readiness that dated back to the earliest days of the Republic, the Fifth Infantry had been organized in 1798. Over the next fourteen years the regiment was periodically disbanded, reactivated, then ultimately consolidated with other units during the War of 1812. From that point on, however, the Fifth stood proud and alone through the Black Hawk war of 1841–42, then marched courageously across the border to fight the Mexican War of 1845–48. No less a hero than the redoubtable Major General Zachary Taylor had commanded the Fifth at the battles of Resaca de la Palma and on to Monterrey. Later placed under the leadership of Major General Winfield Scott, the regiment distinguished itself at Churubusco and Molino del Rey, as well as when storming the walls of the palace at Chapultepec, which finally brought about the surrender of Mexico City.

For the next few years the Fifth was posted in Indian Territory, then briefly used in fifty-seven to quell a Seminole uprising in Florida. Before long the regiment proudly marched beneath its banners back to the opening frontier, part of the government's war against the uprising of Brigham Young's Mormons in Utah Territory. During the long and bloody conflict of the Civil War back east, the Fifth remained in New Mexico Territory, capably holding the thin blue line against Confederate incursions from Texas, principally at Peralta and Apache Canyon.

In the days of the army's reorganization following the treaty at Appomattox, the Fifth was included in the Department of the Missouri, assigned to garrison the Kansas Forts Riley, Hays, and Wallace, as well as Fort Lyon in Colorado

Territory. After seeing extensive service during the Cheyenne outbreak in sixty-eight, the regiment was consolidated
with the old Thirty-seventh Infantry when it acquired a
new commander, Nelson A. Miles.

Through his leadership the colonel had proudly seen
the Fifth become one of the finest Indian-fighting outfits
on the plains—tested by the Kiowa, Southern Cheyenne,
and the powerful Comanche in the Red River War of 1874–
75. So grew his reputation as a hard-bitten, no-nonsense
officer, yet a soldier at times unashamedly sentimental, as
when his men rescued two young white girls, the German
sisters, held captive by the Cheyenne.*

Standing now on the deck of the *Far West,* at the door
to the room General Terry was using as his office, Nelson
remembered that Sunday morning of the twenty-third of
July when the *E. H. Durfee* reached the landing across the
river from Bismarck, Dakota Territory. He had quickly dis-
embarked ahead of his troops and hurried up the slope to
Fort Abraham Lincoln to pay his respects to Custer's
widow. How he had struggled to find words to express
himself, looking into Libbie's face, reading the anguish in
those red-rimmed eyes . . . and scolding himself for
thinking almost exclusively of his own wife, Mary. Would
she survive so great a tragedy? he asked himself again.

"You have no idea of the gloom that overhangs that
post with twenty-seven widows," he had written home to
Leavenworth, trying to explain to Mary the air he sensed
about Fort Lincoln, perhaps even trying to sort it out for
himself. "I never saw anything like it. Mrs. Custer is not
strong, and I would not be surprised if she did not im-
prove. She seemed so depressed and in such despair."

And now he was here, a matter of miles from the
dusty hillside where Custer had fallen. Only a hard two
day's ride from where the real Autie had died, where the
mythic and immortal George Armstrong had been given
birth at the hand of the vengeful Lakota.

*The Plainsmen Series, Vol. 7, *Dying Thunder.*

God, how he resented Custer for the way he had died! How he hated the man's memory more than he had ever loved the man himself.

Even though Nelson had decided he would find the Seventh Cavalry demoralized from its devastating loss, he hadn't been ready for the shock he received upon arriving at the Terry-Gibbon camp that second day of August.

"I never saw a command so completely stampeded as this, either in the volunteer or regular service, and I believe entirely without reason," he had confided in a letter to Mary. "Terry does not seem very enthusiastic or to have much heart in the enterprise."

To Miles's way of thinking, General Terry clearly had been bested by events, if not by the likes of Crazy Horse and Sitting Bull. And Colonel John Gibbon—why, he was slow and plodding at best, overly cautious and downright scared at worst. Someone needed to seize affairs in Montana Territory, with a firm grip. But Terry and Gibbon refused to move in those first weeks after the disaster on the Little Horn, waiting for more than merely reinforcements and supplies, perhaps waiting on the indecisive Crook somewhere in the shadow of the Big Horns, three days' ride to the south. As much as he might rail about his superiors here on the frontier, Miles found much to complain about when it came to the eastern brass as well: he despised Sheridan for his excessive reliance on cavalry and even criticized his wife's uncle, William Tecumseh Sherman, for his lack of attention to organizational matters.

"The more I see of movements here," the energetic and outspoken Miles wrote his wife from the mouth of the Rosebud, "the more admiration I have for Custer, and I am satisfied his like will not be found very soon again."

Then after five windy, rainy days of indecision, vacillation, and heated argument in that camp Terry's soldiers had disparagingly named "Fort Beans," a delay during which Nelson wrote home that "the campaign thus far would not have been creditable to a militia organization," Terry was finally moved to put his command on the march,

planning to head south so they could effect a union with
Crook's command known to be somewhere beyond both
the headwaters of the Rosebud and the Chetish Mountains.
Even though they were about to go into action, Miles nonetheless remained disgusted: the enemy plainly was no
longer to the south. The Sioux were fleeing to the east.

The following morning at three A.M., 8 August, bugles
blew reveille, and at five the combined Dakota and Montana columns, some 1,700 strong in horse and foot, along
with 75 white, Arikara, and Crow scouts, all marched away
from the mouth of Rosebud Creek. Terry was bringing
along 240 heavily laden freight wagons, stuffed to the gunwales with forage and rations to last thirty-five days, leaving behind 120 dismounted cavalry troops and Company G
under Captain Louis H. Sanger of the Seventeenth Infantry
to post a guard around the supply depot. Gibbon, a former
artillery instructor at the U.S. Military Academy who was
known to the Indians as the "Limping Soldier," commanded a brigade composed of four infantry battalions
from not only Miles's Fifth, but the Sixth, Seventh, and
Twenty-second regiments. Major James S. "Grasshopper
Jim" Brisbin was given leadership of both his own four
troops of the Second Cavalry out of Forts Ellis and Shaw in
Montana Territory, as well as command over Major Marcus
Reno's remnants of the Seventh Cavalry, a regiment reorga-
nized in recent weeks into eight troops.

For two days that column of infantry, cavalry, wagons,
ambulances, and beef herd crawled beneath a torrid, cloudless sky at something worse than a snail's pace, suffering
galling temperatures that reached 105 degrees. The anxious
Terry and the nervous Gibbon put their Crow scouts out
far ahead and flung wide on both flanks. It wasn't lost on
Nelson Miles that Reno's Seventh was retracing the steps it
had taken marching to the regiment's destiny at the Little
Bighorn. Gloom and fear hung like a murky pall over the
column as Miles grew all the more impatient.

At two o'clock that first afternoon some of the far-
ranging Crow scouts returned to the column with a report

of sighting the Sioux about forty miles ahead. About five P.M. another band of Crow who had gone to make contact with Crook's column rode in to tell of sighting a large body of Sioux making for the Rosebud from the Tongue River. After covering only eleven miles in a twelve-hour march, a halt was ordered in a wooded area that in June had served as a campsite for the enemy village that destroyed Custer's five companies. In the misty twilight Terry's Arikara and Crow scouts discovered the tree burial of an infant.

It revolted Nelson's stomach to see the trackers drag the little body out of its resting place, hack it to pieces, and defile the scaffold.

Now more than ever he felt convinced he had to find some way to shed himself of Terry and Gibbon, just the way Custer had detached himself. Through that chilly and drizzly Wednesday evening of the ninth, Miles brooded on the trap that snared him, brooded on how to extricate the Fifth Infantry. He needed a miracle and he needed it now.

This plodding behemoth of a column would never catch the Sioux, much less bring the warriors to a decisive battle. And if Terry should ever succeed in uniting with Crook's column—why, this nightmare campaign would be as good as over. They'd both suck each other dry as they lumbered along the enemy's old trails, wearing out men and breaking down the horses.

And in the end neither column would have a single warrior, much less a decisive battle, to show for it when the season closed down the high plains for the coming of winter.

"It looks like an organization for a walk-around," he wrote Mary by firelight that evening. "If this kind of campaigning is continual, it will last a year or two without much credit to the army."

Setting his pencil aside, Miles snorted. "A stern chase," he muttered to himself sourly, recalling Phil Sheridan's words in prodding both Terry and Crook to get up off their numbing rumps and go after the enemy that had murdered Sheridan's fair-haired boy. Nelson wagged his head, muttering, "A stern chase, my ass."

The very next afternoon Nelson Miles stared south into the distance—watching as his worst fears took shape out of the shimmering, heat-baked plain of southern Montana Territory.

Prospect of an Early Fight

CHEYENNE, July 26—Advised from General Crook's command in camp on South Fork of Tongue river, July 23, via Fort Fetterman, July 26, are of importance. The main body of Sioux are believed to have taken to the Big Horn mountains where game is more plenty and grass fresher. The Indian efforts to burn the grass of the valley make it almost imperative on Crook to follow them up at once. His force musters about 1,200 regular soldiers and citizen volunteers, besides 200 Snake allies, and he feels he can at least hold his own on any ground that emergency may select. It is expected that the wagons will be parted with on the main Tongue river, near the mountains, and with a pack-train loaded with from fifteen to twenty days rations, a vigorous but careful advance will immediately follow. It is not deemed advisable for Crook's force and Terry's force to join previous to a move under one or other of the commanders. It is thought that the Indians would make a stand against one of the columns, and that by engaging them and having the other column reserved to either fight or follow up with, something decisive may be expected during the summer campaign. The enemy is believed to be on the headwaters of Ash creek and Little Big Horn, not far from the Montana and Wyoming line, and from thirty to forty miles from Crook's present camp. General Merritt left Fetterman this morning with eight companies of the Fifth cavalry. Two more on the way to Fetterman will take a hundred and fifty recruits and follow in a few days.

On the seventh of August, Crook's Wyoming column crossed from the Tongue westward to the Rosebud on a wearying march of twenty-two miles over rough and broken country, every yard of it beneath a merciless sun. In that valley the Shoshone scouts came upon an immense trail, the earth scarred by thousands of unshod pony hooves and hundreds upon hundreds of travois poles.

That day Seamus saw the first of the scaffolds bearing the Sioux dead killed in the Rosebud or Little Bighorn fights. It brought the Ute and Snake guides no end of delight to haul down the burial platforms, tear open the buffalo robes and blankets, robbing the graves of their bows and quivers, even a nickel-plated revolver or perhaps a Winchester "Yellow-Boy." But the superstitious allies gave wide berth to one particular scaffold, believing it was surrounded by "bad medicine." Only Ute John, one of the so-called Montana Volunteers, was brave enough to profane the platform in hopes of a splendid reward—finding it of such a vintage that instead of riches upon slashing open the burial robes, he was greeted with a nest of field mice.

The Shoshone also delighted in halting wherever they found a rattler along the column's march. Several of the allies would dismount and tease the snake into coiling, hollering the only English they had picked up from the troops: "Got tamme you! Got tamme you!"

After having enough of this sport a warrior chosen from among their number would lance the snake before they remounted and continued down the Rosebud.

Sunset found the column a few miles downstream from where Crook fought his frustrating duel with Crazy Horse eight days before Custer was destroyed. Just below the site of their bivouac that seventh day of August, Grouard and the Crow discovered where the enemy had recently encamped, tepee rings covering a mile-wide strip of bottomland that stretched for more than four miles along the Rosebud. Grouard reported that the Crow allies judged the site to be no more than ten or twelve days old. Although that estimate of age was grossly mistaken, this discovery of the seven massive camp circles convinced every one of the command's officers that the extensive site had indeed been the camp of the great village they had fought that long, bloody day seven weeks before.

Instead of having been the place where Sitting Bull's village stood when the Sioux fought Three Stars on the seventeenth of June, it was in fact where the hostiles had camped on the tenth of July as they were turning back around, meandering to the north and east at a leisurely pace. A succession of war parties that had been harassing Crook's Goose Creek camps, and setting the rear-guard grass fires, had crossed over that trail, making it all but impossible for any of the Shoshone, Ute, or Crow trackers to judge accurately the age of the site.

Little grass remained to feed the column's animals after the enemy's twenty thousand ponies cropped the valley bare. Two days into Crook's chase of the Sioux, the slow and gradual destruction of the cavalry command had begun to tell already. While the enemy did not stand and fight the soldiers who followed them, the Sioux nonetheless had already begun to strike at Crook's vulnerable Achilles' heel: horses gone more than two months without their accustomed forage, now forced to subsist on that scorched prairie, could not possibly do what the Big Horn and Yellowstone Expedition would soon require of them.

Mile by mile the toll would add up, and fifty days from now the destruction would be all but complete.

The sun rose sluggishly on the morning of the eighth, emerging an opaque orange behind murky skies smudged with the thick haze of nearby prairie fires that choked man and animal alike. After crawling at a snail's pace for some five miles, Crook called a halt for his column and ordered his scouts to probe the ground ahead while his troops took advantage of some patches of grass the enemy had failed to burn off. During their wait the bony horses and mules were put out to graze. With the sun high in that endless blue dome, scout Jack Crawford rode in from the south with another civilian. Widely known on the frontier as the "poet scout," John Wallace Crawford had set out from Fetterman on the twenty-eighth of July with his dispatches for Crook. He had reached Furey's wagon train four days later, only to learn that the expedition was somewhere to the north.

The general glowered as he read a letter of rebuke from Sheridan.

> If you do not feel strong enough to attack and defeat the Indians, it is best for you to form a junction with Terry at once. I have sent to you and General Terry every available man that can be spared in the Division, and if it has not made the column strong enough, Terry and you should unite your forces.

"I brought something of interest for you too, Buffalo Bill," Crawford declared as he turned to his erstwhile theatrical partner and reached into a saddlebag to pull forth a bundle wrapped in wide-wale corduroy. Peeling back the cloth, he brought forth a bottle of amber liquid to the envious gasps of those nearby.

Cody took the bottle from Crawford, and Donegan hovered at his shoulder to get a read on the label.

Bill asked, "Who's this from?"

"Colonel Jones."

"Proprietor of the Jones House?" Cody asked.

Crawford nodded. "None other."

"You mean to tell me you brought this all the way up from Cheyenne for me?"

"He give it to me a while back, weeks as a matter of fact. Said to run you down when I had a chance."

Donegan wagged his head in amazement and asked, "And you haven't thought once in all those weeks, all those long, thirsty days and cold nights riding north to Sioux country, not once did you consider pulling that cork and having yourself a taste of that beautiful whiskey?"

Cody turned to Seamus with a look of amused consternation on his face and pointed the neck of the bottle at Crawford, saying, "You're a dense one, Irishman. This here Captain Crawford is about the only scout who could pull off that journey without draining the bottle Colonel Jones sent for me."

"Hard to believe, it is, it is," Seamus said wistfully, staring at the lovely hue of that whiskey.

"Not hard to believe at all, Irishman," Cody replied. "You see, Crawford's just the man for such a job—he's got to be the only teetotaling scout I ever met!"

Late that afternoon the Shoshone returned with news of more Sioux trails coming in from the west to join the main route. Crook had the command remount at six and during that night's march many of the cavalrymen sang Negro melodies learned during the recent war, as well as some popular Irish songs. They did not camp at the bend of the Rosebud until long after the moon had set at 2 A.M. and the wind had quartered around, heaving right out of the north.

On the following day's cold march into the teeth of a wind-driven drizzle that steadily became a slashing, gale-driven rain by midmorning, the column passed several old camps littered with the bones of dogs and ponies: more ample evidence that the warrior bands clearly were no longer living off the fat of the land as they moseyed toward the northeast. Throughout the twenty miles made that morning and into the afternoon, the age of the trail freshened. What had at first been a trail some two weeks old became ten days old, then shortened to a week, and by the time the column made bivouac on the Rosebud below Lame Deer Creek, it was believed they had compressed the enemy's lead to no more than four days.

"The goddamned heat and dust and breathing all that ash was bad enough," Donegan grumbled at the smoky little fire he and some of the other scouts somehow kept burning in the fury of the storm that visited itself upon them that night. "But rain and mud and wet wool blankets can take the starch right out of a strong man."

With only one thin gray army blanket in addition to his saddle blanket, Seamus shuddered with the cold that pierced a man to his marrow. He was not alone, for that August night in the valley of the Rosebud, Surgeon Bennett's thermometer fell far below freezing by dawn on the tenth.

Captain Emil Adams strode through the bivouac of his C Troop, Fifth Cavalry, rousting his men from the hard, cold ground by telling them exactly what they did not want to hear in that thick Prussian accent of his.

"Vake up, boys! Surgeon tol't me his termometer says it was *zero* few minutes ago."

"What thermometer?" asked Second Lieutenant Edward L. Keyes.

For no more than a moment that question confounded the old German. Then he smiled wryly and replied in that colicky bullfrog accent of his, "Vell—any tammed termometer t'at vas tammed fool to get here! Und'stan't?"

The laughter that greeted Adams's declaration served to warm many of the men as they rolled from their frost-covered blankets and stomped about on frozen limbs to greet the sunrise and to water their horses at the banks of the Rosebud, where they discovered a thick rime of ice crusted along the creek.

After marching a few miles north that Thursday morning beneath a most welcome sun, with all those hooves and boots kicking up great columns of dust and stifling ash, Washakie's scouts discovered a recent campsite, its sun-dance lodge as well as some buffalo-hide lodges still standing. Now at last they were getting close enough that the scent of their prey was strong in their nostrils.

At noon Crook ordered a brief halt at the mouth of Greenleaf Creek, right where Grouard's detail of scouts found the hostiles' trail turning due east—headed for the Tongue. The half-breed stood with Donegan, Cody, and many of the others while Crook, Merritt, and Carr debated their next move. A murmur of no little excitement came rippling through their midday bivouac from the north.

"Indians!"

"By the devil!" Crook growled, slapping his gauntlet against his leg, whirling on his battalion commanders. "Form up! Form up!"

No one really needed to shout orders—the infantry was already coming into line and the cavalry were already catching up their horses. Panic and fear, the jingle of harness, and the slap of carbine against McClellan thundered through that valley as noncoms barked and screamed and formed up the commands, making them ready to receive the enemy's charge.

Behind that racket rose the screeches and war cries, the drone of war songs and the beating of hand-held drums, as the allies quickly made their medicine before they would ride off to fight their ancient enemies. Washakie's scouts and the Ute were leaping atop their ponies, whipping the animals in a merciless gallop to the north hoping to catch a glimpse of the Sioux who had stymied the Three Stars Crook, then killed the Long Hair named Custer.

Bile clogged the back of Donegan's throat. God-and-bloody-damn, he thought. This was just as things had been that morning Crook's command had made their halt along the banks of the Rosebud back on the seventeenth of June.

Here we are again: not just caught flat-footed with our pants down again—but caught completely napping!

Chapter 27

10 August 1876

Later from Crazy Horse

CHEYENNE, July 29—Previous reports via the Missouri River agencies are in part confirmed by news received at Fort Laramie from Red Cloud today. Runners have arrived at that agency, said to have come from Crazy Horse's band of Menneconjous, and stating that that chief, with a portion of his band, had left Sitting Bull's domain and are en route to the agencies avowedly to treat for peace. The turning over of the agencies at Red Cloud and Spotted Tail has not been without difficulty. While a majority of the Indians are disposed to submit gracefully there is quite a number who express dissatisfaction at having soldiers placed over them, and a final council is being held at Red Cloud today.

Some dissatisfaction is felt by the Indians at the meager supply of food, which consists entirely of corn, flour and beef. They insist on sugar, coffee, and tobacco, in fulfillment of stipulations, and further attributing the departure from the agencies of those who have joined the hostiles to this fact rather than a desire for war.

If Crook had put Eugene Carr in charge of this column with himself as scout, brooded an unhappy Bill Cody, why—they'd likely be about the business of catching the fleeing Sioux by now. But, he considered with a sigh, even though he and the Fifth's lieutenant colonel shared the same mind in that respect, and even though Crook had him assigned as chief of scouts, no one had thought to ask Cody for anything more than the most minimal advice.

Thank God for the sun that had warmed the air by midmorning.

On either side of Cody the valley began to widen, the scorched hills rolling away toward the striated bluffs that rose like yellow-and-red walls on the east and west. Far to the north, perhaps as much as ten miles or more, Bill spotted the wisps of a distant dust column. He would keep his eye on it as he probed far ahead of the marching infantry, Merritt's cavalry bringing up the rear behind them. Keep his eyes moving across the slopes of the timbered hills dotted with pine and juniper and stunted cedar. Once again the breeze came in company with the dawn that morning to clear the air of the ash and smoke. How good it was to breathe this elixir of the high plains.

Just before beginning their march earlier that morning, Carr himself had commented, "The grandest country in the world for Indian and buffalo now. Two years hence it will be the grandest place for cattle."

After covering some twelve miles since leaving last night's bivouac, Cody began to feel suspicious about that column of dust rising from the northern horizon. After loping the buckskin back so that he could quietly report his discovery to the general, Crook ordered him ahead to determine what the expedition's column might be facing.

Atop the next rise Bill halted, pulled out his field glasses, and trained them on the distance. Sure enough, whatever moved beneath that thick cloud of dust and ash was slowly covering ground. He waited a few minutes, watching the cloud, unable to see anything but the dust column for the intervening hills.

Hearing the yips and hammer of hoofbeats behind him, Bill turned to find some oncoming Shoshone. They too had spotted the strangers in the distance and come racing forward. Behind them charged the handful of Crow. Farther back more of the Shoshone, the Bannock, and a dozen or more of the Ute. On either side of Cody they came to a halt and fell silent. For a long, eerie moment, they regarded that cloud now rising no more than six miles in the distance. Then with a sudden, concerted explosion, the entire group yelped and savagely wrenched their ponies about-face, kicking moccasins into the animals' flanks and sprinting back toward the head of the column. There Bill figured the allies would hurriedly make their medicine: painting, taking covers off shields, checking weapons, and singing their medicine as they prepared to ride into battle.

As he again brought the field glasses to his eyes, Cody made a little sense out of the distant, antlike figures, figuring them to be feathered and fringed horsemen charging about. Behind them came many, many more—some moving left, others speeding to the right, those in the center circling up, all clearly in preparation for battle. But as those feathered horsemen out in front were joined by units forming up row by row by row, it gradually dawned on Cody that they might in fact be Terry's command.

For several more minutes he continued to watch in that warmth of the morning's sun, studying the middistance through his field glasses until at last he saw the wheeled caissons of the Gatlings and the Rodmans brought up to center, their gun crews deployed in readiness. On the rise and fall of the gusty wind Bill caught faint snatches of blaring bugles about the time he saw far to the rear of the artillery those dirty canvas bows of white-topped wagons hurrying into a defensive corral.

"I'll be go to hell right here!" he exclaimed. Then

turned with a start as the hammer of hooves interrupted his muses.

Coming up strong behind him were at least three dozen of the allies, by this time fully painted and decked in their finest battle array. In a clatter of noise and billowing cloud of ash, they skidded to a halt around the renowned Buffalo Bill.

"Not the Sioux," he announced with an impish smile on his face.

But when they returned only quizzical looks of total disbelief, he realized none of them understood. Stuffing the field glasses back into a saddlebag, Bill put his hands to work with sign talk for the allies.

"Not Sioux. Soldiers. Walk-a-heaps. Pony soldiers. Their scouts—Sparrowhawk and Corn Indian scouts."

For a moment they seemed dubious of his assertion. Then suddenly one of the Shoshone laughed and nodded, saying something to the others as his hands signed.

"Good joke the white soldiers do on us! This good joke for us to make war on soldiers—and not on Lakota!"

When the rest of them all had their laugh, cheering behind them at new arrivals reaching the scene, Cody told them, "You stay. I go. I go talk to their soldier chief."

"We come with you," signed the big Shoshone.

"No," and Bill shook his head too. "The soldier scouts think we are Lakota. I want no shooting."

The Snake grinned hugely and bobbed his head. "Yes —they think we are Lakota. We think they are Lakota, and we ready to fight. Good joke the white man do on us!"

Leaving the allied scouts on the crest of that hill, Cody put spurs to the big buckskin and loped north toward the distant figures. As he drew nearer, he clearly made out the Indian trackers riding back and forth, back and forth in the vanguard, giving their little ponies their second wind. Immediately behind them he saw the guidons snapping on the sharp breeze. Company by company, ten in all.

Second Cavalry to the right. Those would be Brisbin's men. And covering most of the ground on the left, brought front into line for battle, were the remnants of Reno's Seventh.

How they must be smarting, Bill brooded as he closed on a mile of the distant horsemen. *They were butchered, they lost half of their officer corps—and when they saw us, they figured they were finally going to get their revenge. How disappointed they must be seeing me instead of Crazy Horse making for their lines. All those men mauled by the Lakota—chomping at the bit to get in their licks.*

Three quarters of a mile out he saw the wide front of cavalry bring their carbines forward on the black leather slings. Fragments of distant orders bawled over the cavalry units floated his way on the warming winds. In throbbing cadence with the buckskin loping beneath him, Bill rose in the stirrups, tore the wide-brimmed, cream-colored hat from his curls, and began to wave it at the end of his arm like a semaphore.

In a matter of heartbeats a half-dozen riders broke away from the cavalry front and headed in his direction under a single headquarters flag. Bill slapped the hat back on his head and put the spurs to the buckskin. The horse leaped away, racing into a ground-dizzying gallop. In moments he reined up, raising dust and ash, as the officer in the lead signaled a halt.

"Who do I have the pleasure of addressing?" Cody asked, looking over the men for any familiar face.

"Captain Thomas B. Weir, Seventh U.S. Cavalry," the dark-eyed man replied with a snap. "Just who the hell are you?"

Bill swept the hat from his head once more and made a graceful showman's bow of it. "William F. Cody, Captain. At your service. I bring General Crook's compliments."

"Buffalo Bill Cody?" asked the standard-bearer in a gush.

Weir silenced the soldier with an obsidian glare and immediately demanded, "What are you doing out here?"

"Guiding Crook's column, Captain."

Weir attempted to peer over Cody's shoulder. "General Crook? That's his column coming along behind you?"

"So it was the Wyoming column raising the dust yonder," a second officer said. He nudged his horse forward and held out his hand. "Lieutenant Edward S. Godfrey. Seventh Cavalry."

"Thank you for your courtesy, Lieutenant," Cody said as he shook the offered hand. "Sorry to hear how the Sioux butchered your regiment on the Little Bighorn."

"We'll have our revenge," Godfrey swore.

"Only a matter of time, ain't it?" Bill sat back in the saddle. "Looks like you fellas were ready for battle."

"Our scouts reported seeing what they took to be the enemy south of us—marching our way," Weir explained.

With a grin Bill replied, "And we saw what we first took to be the Sioux north of us, heading straight for our line of march. So that leaves one big question unanswered, fellas: just where in bloody hell did the Sioux go?"

Troops Coming Forward

New York, July 29—Three hundred soldiers for the Sioux country will leave tomorrow morning.

Washington, July 29—One hundred and twenty-one recruits are to be forwarded to regiments in Dakota and Colorado, and 44 to General Terry's command.

The Secretary of War has sent to the House a dispatch of General Sheridan, recommending the increase of companies of Second, Third, Fourth, Fifth, and Seventh Cavalry to one hundred men each, as was done for two regiments on the Rio Grande.

Gen. Sheridan estimates that the number required to fill the regiments of cavalry on the frontier and in Texas to the maximum of 100 men to each company will raise 2,500 men, at the expense

of $1,534,800. Gen. Sherman prefers the regular en-
listments to volunteers.

"General—Terry's got wagons enough to move at least a
corps," Cody growled as he eased out of the saddle near
Crook's waiting command.

"What do you mean?" John Bourke asked, watching
the showman and scout wag his head.

"Were they really gonna try to catch the Sioux hauling
around lumber like that?"

Cody put into words a lot of the sentiment felt among
the Big Horn and Yellowstone Expedition when the two
columns finally joined there in the valley of the Rosebud
where the Indian trail turned sharply to the east at the
mouth of Greenleaf Creek. The enemy had squirted out
between the jaws of Sheridan's nutcracker. The Sioux and
Cheyenne were running free.

Angry to discover that his prey had escaped, perhaps
even more nettled that he had been captured by General
Alfred Terry, Crook ordered his command into bivouac
and sat down to await Terry's arrival. Bourke agreed—let
Terry come to Crook.

"This command is now too large," the general grumbled as he sat in the shade to wait. "We won't find any
Indians while a force like this sticks together."

Within the hour a headquarters contingent from the
Dakota and Montana command rode into camp under
their guidons and regimental banners. Crook's personal
cook, Private Phillips, gathered up what eating utensils he
could beg off the officers and, upon a strip of canvas spread
upon the ground, served Terry's staff a lunch of the best
Crook could offer—hard bread and salt pork—as the two
field commanders talked of what they must now do. That
evening Terry returned the favor and played host, spreading
before Crook's staff a banquet feast, complete with a variety
of meats as well as canned vegetables.

When the frank discussions began in earnest after supper, Terry pointedly asked, "General, why didn't you in-

form me that you were changing your plan of action, going to sit out a wait for reinforcements?"

To which Crook replied by asking his own question, "General—how have you remained totally unaware that the hostiles have all fled, and into your department to boot?"

"Listen, George," Terry said, his eyes softening, "I want to make it clear right from the start that I'm not going to pull rank here as the senior officer."

"Agreed," Crook replied with a sigh. "We have bigger fish to fry than deciding who commands what."

With their points made in the first moments of that tense conference, the two then got down to determining how best to give chase. While both steadfastly refused to accept that they were weeks behind the hostiles, Terry and Crook knew only one thing for certain: the enemy had turned east and was heading either northeast for the Yellowstone or would continue straight for the valley of the Little Missouri.

But in the event that Sitting Bull's people were in the process of heading north . . . Terry called in Colonel Nelson A. Miles.

"I'm detaching you, Colonel," the general told the commander of the Fifth Infantry. "Take your companies on our backtrail in escort with our wagon train and return to the Rosebud depot. There you are to load your men aboard the *Far West* and establish outposts at every possible crossing of the Yellowstone between the mouth of the Rosebud and the mouth of the Tongue."

Wearing a look of great satisfaction, Miles asked, "On the north bank of the river, General?"

"Yes. You will also establish a depot at the mouth of the Powder so that our two columns can draw upon those supplies of rations and ammunition when needed as we march east."

"When may I depart, General?"

"As soon as your men and the wagons are ready, Miles."

Terry then turned to Crook. "Before the colonel departs, I will restore your column to a full fifteen days' rations. I'll be stripping my command down to light marching order as you have your command, General."

"I'm to understand that you're firm in your decision that we should unite in our pursuit?" Crook questioned.

"Yes," Terry answered.

"But don't you see—as commander of the Department of the Platte, my concern is following Crazy Horse and the southern Sioux who range over hunting grounds south of the Yellowstone. My fear is that now, with the bands moving off to the east, they're about to threaten the settlements in the Black Hills."

"And as commander of the Department of Dakota," said Terry, "I'm primarily concerned with Sitting Bull's bands of northern hostiles who usually range north of the Yellowstone, in fact all the way into Canada. My gravest worry is that the Sioux will cross the river, for at that point they have an open field all the way to the border. I won't be able to pursue them once they've crossed into Canada."

Bourke could read the despair creeping into Crook's eyes, the undercurrent of self-directed anger he must harbor for stumbling into the other column: now he would have to assume a subordinate role. For a man used to wielding the power of field command, for a fighting man suddenly to have to answer to a desk-wielding bureaucrat —this had to be about the toughest thing George Crook had ever swallowed in his army career.

Crook pursed his lips as his eyes narrowed, staring at the stained and dog-eared maps that lay on the field desk between the two generals. As distasteful as the admission was, he finally said, "Alfred—you are in command."

Throughout their long discussions that evening, John Bourke continued to draw decided conclusions from his observations of both column commanders. While Terry was attired in a handsome uniform befitting his rank, complete with shoulder boards and straps, Crook looked more the part of an old frontiersman or campaigner in rough canvas clothing. Among all of Crook's staff, there wasn't a

complete uniform to be found. In fact, in some of the
cavalry companies that had been campaigning since spring,
it had become next to impossible to tell the officers from
the enlisted.

Late that evening after tattoo, Bourke went on to write
in his journal:

> General Terry's manners are most charming
> and affable; he had the look of a scholar as well as
> a soldier . . . He won his way to our hearts by
> his unaffectedness and affability. He is the antith-
> esis of Crook in his manner. Crook is simple and
> unaffected also, but is reticent and taciturn to the
> extreme of sadness, brusk to the point of severity.
> Of the two, Terry would be the more pleasing
> companion, Crook the stauncher friend. In
> Terry's face I thought I detected faint traces of
> indecision and weakness; but in Crook's counte-
> nance there is not the slightest trace of anything
> but *stubbornness, stolidity, rugged resolution, and
> bull-dog tenacity*.

Events would not be long in proving Bourke entirely
correct in his assessment of his commander.

It wasn't just the dissimilarity between the two commanders, though. From the moment they encamped next
to one another, the differences between the two columns
were about as plain as the noses on a two-headed calf:
Crook's men shambled about in shabby uniforms, dusty
and faded, their slouch hats all but shapeless on their
heads, while Terry's men and animals looked better fed
from their wagon train, the enlisted more rested from having spent their nights under canvas. In fact, most of the
men out of Montana and Dakota looked as if they were
preparing to drill on the parade of some post back east.
With the possible exception of the Seventh Cavalry—
Reno's men looking haggard and disgusted as well as just
plain trail worn—the northern jaw of Sheridan's pincers

appeared to be a well-outfitted army recently arrived in the field.

On the other hand, the Big Horn and Yellowstone Expedition had all the makings of little more than a ragtag band of motley brigands, horse thieves, and highwaymen.

So it didn't surprise Bourke that the men raised no cheers when the two commands met. What was there, after all, to celebrate when you saw just how good the other fellows had it? Nonetheless, the allied scouts attached to both columns raised enough of a howl for all. Shoshone, Crow, Bannock, Ute, and Arikara united in both backslapping and the white man's customary shaking of hands all around as they shouted out their excited greetings right in the midst of the indifferent soldiers.

Bourke couldn't help but be envious of the luxury enjoyed by Terry's men. Reno even spread out a Brussels carpet on the floor in his tent, and one of Terry's staff had a rocking chair in his—now, that was the way to campaign! In turn Terry's officers clearly were appalled at the Spartan conditions suffered by the Wyoming column, for each night the Dakota column slept in large wall tents complete with portable beds and even sheet-iron stoves to ward off the cold. Hospital tents served as dining rooms for the officers.

Crook's command slept under the stars, wrapped only in their saddle blankets, and had a solitary tin cup and a sharpened stick to broil their bacon come suppertime.

Even Bill Cody was quick to see the real difference between the two commands. Later that evening the chief of scouts walked up to Bourke's fire beside Seamus Donegan and declared, "Fellas, between them two generals, it's clear to me who's the real Indian fighter out here in Sioux country."

"Damn right, Johnny," the Irishman added. "It's plain to see who means business."

"I think you've both just discovered that our column has something that runs even deeper than all the tents and crisp uniforms and fancy carpets could provide," Bourke agreed. "Something I don't think Terry's men share: an esprit de corps."

Donegan nodded. "In the weeks to come, when this outfit runs out of hard bread and bacon, when we run low on ammunition and our horses become nothing but bone-racks . . . that feeling of esprit de corps, that camaraderie between fighting men, will be what separates the men from the boys. It will be the only thing that keeps some men going when others fall down on their faces and want to die right where they lay."

Chapter 28

11–15 August
1876

Crazy Horse Wants to Come in
and Make a Treaty.

OMAHA, July 29—An official telegram from Fort
Laramie says a courier has just arrived from Red
Cloud who says that Red Cloud told him that
Crazy Horse was coming into the agency very
soon; that his band was on the way there, and
twenty lodges had already arrived. Crazy Horse
has sent word to Captain Egan that he will see
him, shake hands and make a treaty. The friendly
Indians lately arrived won't talk about the fight,
and pretend to know nothing of it. A council was
held at the Cheyenne camp while the courier was
detained there to talk over the change from the
civil to military authorities. Many opposed it, but
Red Cloud has expressed satisfaction at the
change. Fears are apprehended that any attempts
to deprive the Indians of ponies and arms will be
met with resistance, as they can muster a large
force well armed, while the number of troops at

the post is very small. It is thought they will allow themselves to be numbered without opposition.

During that evening of the tenth, for no apparent reason, the horses of three companies of the Fifth Cavalry snapped their sidelines like twine, tore their picket pins from the flaky soil, and stampeded for the hills.

With that commotion the entire command believed themselves under threat of attack for a few tense minutes until Lieutenant Colonel Carr organized a detail of experienced wranglers to pursue the horses of Troops A, B, and M. Late that night the horse soldiers returned with their catch, and the encampment settled down for what was left of the night.

Early on the morning of 11 August, Nelson Miles and his Fifth Infantry marched away to the north, accompanied by Terry's wagons filled not only with provisions for the Yellowstone River outposts, but also with what sick and disabled the combined columns would need to move downriver by steamboat. Yet it wasn't until eleven o'clock that Crook and Terry finally took up the trail Crook had been following as it turned sharply to the east at the mouth of Greenleaf Creek, leading toward the divide that separated the Rosebud from the valley of the Tongue.

Colonel John Gibbon, who had been in command of soldiers sent into the field as far back as March, looked over the condition of Crook's and Chambers's infantry as it moved at the vanguard of the march, declaring, "Why, soldiers—you're even dirtier than my men!"

And the men of James Brisbin's Second Cavalry made a widely circulated joke of the dilapidated, threadbare condition of the rear of the britches worn by Crook's horse soldiers, nicknaming the troopers "the ragged-ass patrol."

This immense command encompassing some four thousand men assigned to thirty-six troops of cavalry and twenty-five companies of infantry, not to mention all the attendant civilians, scouts, and Indian allies, lumbered along in the dusty wake of the fleeing hostiles. It wasn't long before the men of the Wyoming column had themselves a good belly laugh at the expense of Terry's pack-train. The Montana and Dakota soldiers had attempted to take horses and mules used to pulling wagons in harness and convert them into something that resembled Tom Moore's unequaled pack-train. Hour by hour Terry's train dropped, lost, or ruined more supplies than the whole of Crook's command had spoiled since the end of May when the Wyoming troops marched north from Fort Fetterman.

It didn't take long for Washakie's warriors to recognize the difference between the two columns. By the end of that first day the Shoshone were already growing disgusted with the pace and ineptness of what they called the "Yellowstone soldiers."

The sun rose high and hot that afternoon as the column toiled nine dusty miles up the divide and down again into the scorched valley of the Tongue, stifling ash rising from every boot, every iron-shod hoof.

Along the timbered riverbank the scouts came across the site of a huge village. It was there that the Indian trail split, one branch heading upstream, the other down. Nearby the scouts found the skeleton of a solitary miner who had been killed a few months before, then left to predators. Around the body lay many empty cartridges, attesting to the lone man's last great fight. Close by lay the carcass of his dead horse, also ravaged by beasts of the prairie. Some of Major Stanton's Montana Volunteers saw to it the prospector's bones were given a decent burial before the men rejoined the march.

Up and down the west bank of the river stood old cottonwood trees from which the hostiles had peeled the bark, the better to paint on the exposed grain as if it were a pale-colored canvas: hieroglyphic figures shown carrying off captured women, hunting buffalo from horseback, and scalping soldiers.

Worrying most that Sitting Bull's hostiles might reach the Yellowstone ahead of his column, Terry vetoed Crook's suggestion and ordered that the entire command wheel left into line and march four more miles downstream through the blackened river valley, where they went into bivouac at the mouth of Beaver Creek under darkening skies and stiffening winds. Threatening storm clouds massed overhead as the cavalrymen picketed their horses on what patches of unburned grass each company could locate against the hills. Coffeepots had barely begun to warm over mess fires when the sky opened up with a chilling deluge.

In the wind-driven torrents the men did what they could: platoons combined blankets and gum ponchos, which they threw over quickly improvised wickiups lashed from willow saplings. But with the way the rain was flung horizontally at a man, nothing kept out the storm. In less than an hour every soldier sat morosely in the spongy mud, huddled close around his struggling fire, teeth chattering, cold to the marrow and filled with despair.

Seamus sat in the midst of a puddle of cold water, his one blanket draped over his shoulders and head, already soaked and unable to turn any more of the torrent. To Cody he grumbled, "This goddamned rain is gonna wipe out a lot of our sign."

"Don't much matter now, does it, Irishman?"

For a moment he watched Cody staring into the sputtering flames of their fire feebly fighting nature's onslaught of wind and water. "Sure it does, Bill. S'pose you tell me what's eating you."

With a shrug Cody eventually replied, "I just been figuring on packing up and riding back to Laramie."

"Head home?"

He nodded. "This bunch isn't going to find any Indians, Seamus. You know that well as me."

"So—just like that? You figure on heading back?"

Cody readjusted his blanket. "I got contracts. Business commitments."

"Your theater show?"

"Yeah. Me and Texas Jack ought to make another go of it," he replied. As he tossed another wet limb onto the fire, Cody said, "Now, if Crook and Terry would turn this campaign over to Carr and Royall—then I'd stay on. Make no mistake of that, Seamus."

For his part the Irishman was without much to say in the way of something that would change Cody's mind. All he could do was stare at the flames, each tobacco-wad-sized glob of high prairie rain smacking the limbs with a hiss. "Wish you'd stay. If only for me."

Dawn finally came Saturday morning, with no real letup in the downpour. While Crook and Terry waited in that soggy bivouac with their combined columns, they ordered their scouts to take to the field in hopes of determining which of the trails might prove to be the main route of the escaping hostiles.

"These are old trails, General," Cody advised Crook just past noon when the guides and trackers returned.

"My Crow scouts tell me they might be as recent as three days," Terry countered.

"No. Cody's right," Donegan said. "At least three weeks old."

Crook turned to Grouard. "What do you say, Frank?"

For a moment those obsidian eyes looked at Cody and Donegan. "Old trails, General."

Terry wheeled on Crook. "If that trail is as old as your scouts are saying it is—then one thing is certain, General: you weren't correct in your beliefs as to when the hostiles took flight in your front."

Crook immediately bristled, as did some of his staff standing nearby in the cold chill of early afternoon. "General Terry—I stand by my assertions, and my actions. Do you have a complaint to lodge against me, sir?"

The affable Terry, suddenly confronted by the bulldog Crook, waved a hand and his blue eyes softened. "No, General. No complaint against you. Forget it."

"With the general's permission," Gibbon spoke up, "if General Crook's column had only informed us of the hostiles' flight, we could have put ourselves across their trail and caught them."

Lieutenant Colonel Royall harrumphed, "I seriously

doubt that your force would have been of sufficient numbers or experience to capture that village."

At that moment more of the subalterns from both
camps weighed in, sniping at the other column now that
the long march, the cold, the rain, all of it was plainly
showing in the raw edge that was every man's nerves.

"Are our scouts in agreement on anything?" Terry inquired.

"Yes, General," Crook answered. "Seems most of them
say the biggest trail is heading downstream."

"Toward the Yellowstone?" Terry replied, worry in his
voice. When Crook nodded, Terry added, "Let's get these
men moving down the Tongue."

At a snail's pace the united columns dragged themselves through the mud and rain for all of a torturous thirteen miles before making camp at twilight on the twelfth.
When they could, the men chose a slope for a place to settle
and curl up. That way the water could not gather in depressions around them as they sat out the storm beneath their
soaked blankets, eating soggy hardtack and chewing on
their raw bacon. The storm lessened near dark, but within
an hour it roared back over them with renewed fury. There
was little sleep in that bivouac for those four thousand men
for a second night in a row.

Dawn of the thirteenth came gray and colder yet to
those soldiers whose clothing and blankets hadn't dried for
more than two days. Men stamped about, blue-lipped, with
their teeth chattering like boxes of dominoes, until afternoon when the rain tapered off to a misty drizzle. That day
Merritt's cavalry shot the first of its played-out, ill-fed
horses. Those cavalrymen who could not bear to kill their
mounts simply abandoned the animals right where the
bony beasts had crumpled into the mud and refused to go
on.

By the time the command went into bivouac another
twenty-four grueling miles down the Tongue, it was becoming ever clearer to even the dullest recruit that they
weren't going to catch the Sioux. But maybe the horses

would begin to fare better, for by now much of the grass remained unburned, and there was more of it.

If anyone had taken notice, that grass was one more solid argument that proved the hostile village was scattering to the winds.

Tom Cosgrove showed up at Donegan's fire that Sunday night, in search of more than coffee or tobacco for his pipe. "I remember you telling me you fought for the Army of the Potomac. And with Sheridan in the Shenandoah."

With a nod Seamus replied, "You figure we ever looked across a battlefield at one another?"

Cosgrove shrugged, grinning a little, then sighed and went somber. "This fight's already over."

"Naw. We haven't begun to look, Tom."

Wagging his head, the old Confederate said, "Crook might keep looking, but he's not going to find them. And he sure won't be finding the Sioux with the Shoshone along."

"Why? Washakie thinking of rolling his blankets and heading home?"

"Yeah. And I can't blame 'em none, neither. The Snake never been this far north—this far away from home."

"You leaving tomorrow?"

"I don't rightly know right now. Only sure thing is it's just a matter of time before we pull out."

Daybreak on the fourteenth brought with it more gray, sodden skies and no letup in the rain. At seven the columns got under way: Terry's led by the Seventh Cavalry, Crook's by the Fifth. Against the stronger, grain-fed mounts of the Seventh, Carr's gaunt horses looked ready for the boneyard. That morning the wind hurried the rain before it once more as the men were forced to cross and recross the Tongue thirteen times in less than ten miles before the Indian trail turned away again to the east, following the narrow banks of Pumpkin Creek.

Many a man gazed downstream wistfully. Barely fifteen miles away flowed the Yellowstone itself, with its sup-

ply depots and rations and tents and dry, warm blankets—
all of it a most inviting proposition to the men ordered to
keep up, back in ranks, don't straggle—keep up!

After a climb of more than six miles out of the valley
of the Tongue, the order was given to halt and go into camp
just past noon. Here the cavalry unsaddled and put the
stock out to graze in the slashing torrents of bone-chilling
rain while the infantry simply sat down and curled up right
where they had stopped.

Minutes later Lieutenant Colonel Royall galloped his
horse down past Chambers's foot soldiers to the bank of
the Pumpkin and halted in front of Major Andrew Evans's
still-mounted battalion of the Third Cavalry.

Royall, a hard-bitten veteran of Summit Springs and
the Battle of the Rosebud, growled, "Didn't I order you to
put your battalion in camp along the river, facing east?"

Evans, widely known as a man who could split a hair
as fine as fuzz on a hog, immediately came to attention and
retorted, "Yes, sir. You did. But this ain't a river. It's only a
creek."

For a moment Royall's cold face flushed as he seethed
in anger, then shouted, "*Creek* be damned! It's a river—a
river from this time forth, *by my order,* sir! Now damned
well do as I order you!"

"Yes, sir!" Evans answered, and hurried off to get his
companies into bivouac across the Tongue.

For the rest of that rainy day and on into a stormy
night, the command lay in along the bank of Pumpkin
Creek, where the best that could be said of the land was
that the enemy hadn't put it to the torch. Here the animals
grazed on what skimpy grass grew in that naked country.

"Muggins Taylor rode in with messages for Terry,"
Frank Grouard said as he came up to Donegan picketing
his big horse on a patch of old grass.

"What's the news?"

"Miles been up and down the river on the steamboat.
He reports no sign of Sitting Bull's people crossing the
Yellowstone."

"That means they've got to still be east of us."

Grouard nodded and did not say anything more for the longest time until he commented, "Two-day grass."

"This? Why you call it that?"

"We camped in this country many times, when I lived with Sitting Bull's Hunkpapa. Lakota say a bellyful of this grass will do a pony good for a two-day ride."

Seamus stroked the withers of his exhausted, played-out animal. "Frank, right now I'll settle for just one day's ride on a bellyful."

On the morning of the fifteenth the bone-weary command followed the Indian trail of pony hooves and travois poles scouring the ground as the fleeing hostiles headed eastward up the bank of the Pumpkin.

A small puppy was found by one of the first infantrymen passing through an abandoned campsite. He knelt, finding the dog as eager for companionship as he was when it raced over and leaped into his arms. Unbuttoning his tunic, the foot soldier carried his new friend along as they got acquainted.

At the top of the divide the trail left the creek and entered the badlands, which filled the men not only with more despair, but also with an overwhelming sense of lonely desolation. For as far as they could see to the north and east that fifteenth day of August . . . nothing moved but the heavy, sodden gray clouds scudding low over their heads. As ugly as was that scorched valley of the Tongue they had left behind, it was beautiful compared to the country they now faced.

That morning more than a dozen of Terry's infantry could not go on and were placed by stewards in horse-drawn travois that bobbed, bounced, and jostled across the broken, muddy ground. Mile by mile the route had begun to tell on the animals. Here and there the first of the Second, Third, and Fifth cavalries' horses were either abandoned by their riders, who switched saddle, blanket, and poncho to one of the led horses when they left a mount behind, or the worn-down horse was simply shot where it had dropped, unable to limp on behind its pleading master.

By noon that Tuesday the sun broke through the clouds and the humid air grew stifling as the scouts gazed down into the widening valley of the Powder River, called Chakadee Wakpa by the Sioux. The Crow and Arikara guided the columns down Four Horn Creek* to its mouth, making a ford where the clear and swift-running creek joined the Powder from the southwest to mingle its waters with the milky, muddy, alkaline river. On the column continued its numbing march down the east bank of the Powder. It wasn't long before the last of the barebacked horses led by each company had been put in service, replacing those that had played out in the climb up from the Pumpkin. Those soldiers who were thereafter forced to abandon their animals simply left everything behind: saddle and blanket, bit and bags. A trooper put afoot carried away only what he could on his back, trudging along beside the faltering column of horses.

Yet even the infantry did not have an easy go of it that fifteenth of August. One can imagine how it must have conspired to ruin a foot soldier's healthy state of mind as hour by hour he watched powerful, gracefully strong animals giving up and going down: tramping endlessly through brutal country, mud sucking at one's heavy and unforgiving brogans, their leather already cracked and split from days and nights of incessant rain—feet become two bloody stumps of raw and blistered flesh, ankles and calves swollen from the cold and the exertion and the stream crossings.

When they had no more travois for the sick and lame, the officers begged the Indian allies to double up and carry those soldiers who could not go on by their own steam. Yet there was one who was left, unnoticed, as he scrambled up beneath some concealing brush along the bank of the Powder and hid himself as the rest of the column lumbered

---

*Present-day Mizpah Creek.

past. There that Ninth Infantry cook named Eshleman intended to die by the hand of a hostile warrior or give himself to a predator of the high plains—anything but press on with the rest.

Just before dawn that terrible gray day, Seamus had in fact discovered that his horse's shoulder was a mass of oozing wounds. The animal actually shuddered as Donegan chewed a sliver of tobacco and rubbed pieces of the moist wad into the open wounds before he lay the saddle blanket back over the lesions. And throughout that long and terrible day the Irishman would lean forward against the great beast's shoulder, whispering again what he had whispered that dawn before setting out with the other scouts.

"I'll strike a bargain with you," and he stroked its powerful neck. "You will carry me and I will keep you from going down. Just remember that if you go down, I am simply too weary to get you back up again. And I'll have to leave you, or . . . or worse. And—I don't even want to think of that happening."

Hour by hour man and beast both held up their end of the pact. When it seemed the horse was close to collapse, Seamus dismounted and led the animal, off and on, for what seemed like half the day.

Early that afternoon the Shoshone found the trail dividing once more, with the deepest and widest road that remained after the pounding rains still pointing eastward toward the Little Missouri River.

As some of the Indian allies halted at that fork in the trail, Donegan came to a stop beside the dark-skinned half-breed who had once roamed this land as an adopted Hunkpapa. For a moment Seamus wiggled a loose back tooth with his tongue, realizing that was a first sign of scurvy—one of the most dangerous afflictions of an army on the march.

"How far east you think they'll run?" Seamus asked his old companion.

Frank Grouard shrugged his shoulders, gazing off into the distance where the trails scattered like a covey of quail busted out of the brush, only to disappear. "Don't know for sure, Irishman. What I do know is the Little Missouri is good wintering ground. Sitting Bull's Hunkpapa use it year after year."

"Wintering ground? This early?"

"No, they won't winter up this early—but they're for sure headed for the Little Missouri."

After slogging more than thirty miles through the bone-chilling mud of that morning followed by the blazing sun appearing in a clearing sky that afternoon, Chambers's infantry were the first to go into camp. To everyone's amazement the major's command hadn't suffered a single man to drop out through the day-long ordeal. In fact, Crook's foot soldiers were the first to reach camp that night, arriving long before the cavalry trudged in, half of the horse soldiers dragging their led mounts behind them.

That night another storm moved in, and the heavens opened up again for the fifth night of cold misery in a row.

Chapter 29

16–18 August
1876

Graphic Account of Custer's Fight
From the Hostile Band.

CHICAGO, August 1—Capt. Holland, of the Sixth Infantry, commanding the station at Standing Rock Agency, writes to General Ruggles that seven Sioux Indians who were in the battle of June 25th have arrived at Standing Rock and give the following account of the battle: The hostiles were celebrating the sun dance when runners brought news of the approach of the cavalry. The dance was suspended, and a general rush followed for the horses, equipments and arms. Major Reno first attacked the village at the south end, across the Little Big Horn.

Their narrative of Reno's operations coincides with the published account, how he was quickly confronted and surrounded, how he dismounted, ran in the timber, remounted and cut his way back over the ford and up the bluffs with considerable loss, and the continuation of the fight for a little

time when runners arrived from the north end of
the village or camp with the news that the cavalry
had attacked the north end, some three or four
miles distant. A force large enough to prevent
Reno from assuming the offensive was left, and
the surplus available force followed to the other
end of the camp, where, finding the Indians successfully driving Custer before them, instead of
uniting with them, they separated into two parties
and moved around the flanks of his cavalry. They
report that a small body of cavalry broke through
the line of Indians in their rear and escaped, but
were overtaken within a distance of five or six
miles and all killed.

After the battle the squaws entered the field to
plunder and mutilate the dead bodies. General re-
joicing was indulged in, and a distribution of arms
and ammunition was hurriedly made. . . .

Sitting Bull was neither killed nor personally engaged in the fight. He remained in the council tent,
directing operations. Crazy Horse, Large Band,
and Black Moon were the principal leaders . . .
The fight continued till the third day, when runners, kept purposely on the lookout, hurried into
camp and reported a great body of troops, General
Terry's command, advancing up the river. The
lodges having been previously prepared for a
move, a retreat in a southerly direction followed,
towards and along the Rosebud mountains. They
marched about fifty miles, went into camp, and
held a consultation, when it was determined to
send into all the agencies reports of their success,
and call on them to come out and share the glories
that they were expected to reap in the future.

. . . They report for the especial benefit of their
relatives here that in the three fights they had with
the whites, they have captured over one hundred
stand of arms, carbines and rifles (revolvers not

counted), ammunition without end, and some sugar, coffee, bacon and hard bread. They claim to have captured from the whites this summer over 900 horses and mules. I suppose this includes their operations against the soldiers, Crow Indians, and Black Hills miners.

. . . I have since writing the above heard from the returned hostiles, which they communicated as a secret to their friends here, information that a large party of Sioux and Cheyennes were to leave Rosebud mountain, the site of the hostile camp, for this agency, to intimidate and compel the Indians here to join Sitting Bull. If these refuse, they are ordered to beat them and steal their ponies.

By that Wednesday morning of the sixteenth, finding and catching the fleeing hostiles had become secondary.

For Terry's men as much as for Crook's command, with the Sioux plainly two weeks ahead of them, it had now become a matter of survival. Simply to find food and blankets, someplace where they could recoup and sort out what to do next.

General Alfred Terry convinced a dejected George Crook that their combined columns should limp on downstream the twenty-four miles it would take them to reach the mouth of the Powder River at the Yellowstone. While the Montana and Dakota columns set up their tents and cots, Brussels carpets, and rocking chairs on the west bank of the Powder, the Big Horn and Yellowstone Expedition made their miserable camp in the mud on the east bank with nothing more than what they had with them the day they marched away from Camp Cloud Peak. While Terry's men eagerly cut open tins of meats, vegetables, and canned peaches, Crook's impoverished soldiers had to relish the same old fare of salt pork, hard bread, and coffee. Why, Terry's men even shaved at marble-topped washstands with mirrors!

With no tents to shelter them, the Wyoming column

could only build bonfires around which they dried their
stinking blankets and campaign coats like bands of ragged,
wretched thieves. For the horses of the Second, Third, and
Fifth cavalries, however, their lot had improved. Not only
did the animals now feed on some sixty thousand pounds
of grain, but in addition the horses and mules reveled in
the abundant and luxurious buffalo grass found at the
mouth of the Powder. The hostiles hadn't been there to
torch their backtrail.

Several hours after they had reached the Yellowstone,
Bill Cody and Seamus Donegan watched a rescue party of
Crow scouts return from upstream. Alfred Terry had been
late in learning that Private Eshleman, an officer's cook
with the Ninth Infantry, had thrown in the towel and given
himself up for dead.

"I may be forced to abandon or shoot some horses,"
Terry grumbled. "But I won't allow myself to lose one more
man if I can help it."

As soon as he became aware of Eshleman's plight, the
general had dispatched a half dozen of Gibbon's Crow to
backtrack up the Powder and find the lost soldier. Eshleman was nearly crazed when the Indians brought him in,
trussed up hand and foot like a Christmas turkey and
lashed atop one of the barebacked ponies.

"As mad as a March hare," was how Seamus Donegan
put it when together they watched the surgeon's stewards
pull the raving soldier down from that pony, screaming
and snapping at his handlers.

"He might well be one of the fortunate ones," Cody
groaned, seeing how they lashed the soldier down to a hospital cot to keep him from injuring himself in all his
thrashing.

"I'll never understand the workings of humankind,"
Donegan said quietly. "Either him or you: for saying a
madman may well be more fortunate than those of us who
made it here whole."

Bill turned to the Irishman. "Are we really whole,

Seamus? Oh, we may appear to be, despite our ordeal. But are we really whole?"

In addition to the deranged cook, a few of the officers and more than a handful of soldiers had been so incapacitated by the grueling march, their constitutions weakened beyond repair by diarrhea, acute dysentery, and inflammatory rheumatism, that the surgeons ordered those cases put aboard the *Far West* as soon as it arrived, to be transported on the steamer's next scheduled run downriver to Fort Buford at the mouth of the Yellowstone. In addition, there were others who were going to leave of their own volition—some of the newspapermen who had decided days back that there simply wasn't going to be a Sioux campaign that year, and to trudge overland with Terry or Crook in a fruitless and exhaustive search for the hostiles would be nothing short of sheer lunacy.

The noisy appearance of the *Far West* at five o'clock that afternoon of the seventeenth brought out every one of Washakie's warriors. Wide-eyed, some with their hands clamped over their mouths, they stared and gaped as the stern-wheeler heaved around the far bend in the river and chugged toward the mouth of the Powder, putting in against the north bank of the Yellowstone. This had to be the most wondrous sight to the Shoshone, who had never before seen a river steamer in their part of the west. That day and for many days to come, the mighty "smoking house that walked on water" would be the sole topic of discussion in the Snake's camp, and upon their return to the Wind River Reservation.

The Shoshone were not the only warriors excited to see the steamer. Nearly four thousand soldiers crowded the banks to view this singular reminder of civilization brought here to the wilderness. Captain Grant Marsh's cabin girl, a Negress named Dinah, had modestly covered her eyes or diverted them as the steamer drew in sight of the camp, what with so many naked soldiers frolicking in the sunlit river after all those days of rain and gloom.

Even Lieutenant Adolphus H. Von Luettwitz, E Troop, Third Cavalry, was caught unawares of the power of the stern-wheeler as he was laundering some of his clothing at the edge of the water. The steamer's powerful wakes tumbled one right after the other against the bank and caused the lieutenant to topple into the river, shouting his untranslatable German oaths as he sputtered up from the choppy Yellowstone, having lost half his uniform to the mighty river's current.

That following morning, Friday, the eighteenth of August, the sky dawned clear and mercifully blue as Crook's men went aboard the *Far West* to unload two days of forage and very little rations for two large armies. It wasn't long before the men began to spread the rumor that they might well be resuming their chase of the hostiles at any moment —rumors seemingly given official credence in dispatches brought up from Fort Buford. General Sheridan was instructing his two field commanders to construct stockades in the heart of the hostiles' hunting ground.

Sheridan wrote:

> The [congressional] bill for increasing the company strength of [regiments of] cavalry in the field passed Congress . . .
>
> I will give orders to General Terry today to establish a cantonment for the winter at Tongue River and will send supplies there for 1500 men, cavalry and infantry. I think also of establishing a cantonment for the winter at Goose Creek, or some other point on your line, for a force of 1000 men. I will send you 100 of the best Pawnee scouts under Major [Frank] North, regularly enlisted, as Congress has increased the number to one thousand.
>
> We must hold the country you and Terry have been operating in this winter, or else every Indian at the agencies will go out as soon as we

commence   dismounting   and   disarming
them . . .

"At first light Terry's Rees come back from scouting
those trails scattering to the east of the Rosebud and found
the grass burned off," Donegan told Bill that Friday afternoon. "Only thing that means is the hostiles moved
through this country at least a week ago."

Nodding, Cody replied, "Right. Shows the Sioux
crossed over that ground before these heavy rains started."

"So tell me what Crook and Terry hope to learn by
sending you down the Yellowstone on that riverboat."

"Crook doesn't want any part of this," Cody stated,
blowing on his tin of coffee. "He only wants that boat to go
up to the Rosebud and get his supplies."

"But Terry has the rank," Seamus said. "And even
more important: it's Terry's boat, and Terry's supplies—so
Crook's got to go along with everything Terry wants."

"Including Terry's idea to send me and Louie Reshaw
down to the mouth of Glendive Creek to see if we can
figure out what the hostiles are planning to do."

"Mr. Cody!"

They both turned to find one of Terry's staff hailing
them, hurrying their way. Bill flung the lukewarm dregs of
his coffee at the fire. "Looks like they're ready to give me a
ride on that goddamned boat."

"Watch out, Bill. See for yourself all the bullet scars in
that iron they riveted up around the pilothouse."

Cody held out his hand and shook the Irishman's. "I
didn't come back out here to scout for the army just to be
killed while taking a lark of a ride on some goddamned
riverboat. I intend to make it back home to Lulu and the
children."

"Sounds like you've made up your mind to cash in
your chips and go back east."

Pulling on his fringed gloves, Cody said, "Just as soon
as this ride on the river is damned well over."

Sioux Attacking Steamboats—Terry
Falling Back

ST. PAUL, August 7—A Bismarck special to-day to
the *Pioneer Press* and *Tribune*, says the steamer
Carroll arrived this morning from General Terry's
camp, having on board General Forsythe and
twenty sick and wounded soldiers. The *Carroll* on
her way up, when near the mouth of the Powder
river, found the Indians on both sides of the river,
and for two and a half hours they kept up a running fire upon the boat, only wounding one soldier
slightly. The steamer *Far West*, after leaving Fort
Buford for Terry's camp found her load too heavy
and discharged part of her cargo, principally
grain. At this same point the Indians attacked the
Far West . . . The Indians stood on both banks of
the river and with oaths dared Col. Moore with his
troops to leave the boat and land. A few shells
were fired from a twelve-pounder which scattered
the Indians and they disappeared from the south
bank.

Dave Campbell, pilot of the *Far West* with two
Ree scouts, then landed and went out to reconnoiter, but finding the Indians were endeavoring to
cut them off, they turned and started as fast as
was possible for the boat. Seven Sioux had circled
as to intercept them, and it became a race for life.
The horse of one of the scouts began to fall behind
and was soon shot, when the rider started on foot,
but it was no use. The same Sioux who had killed
the horse soon reached him and put a bullet
through his lungs. Dave Campbell heard the shot.
Looking behind and seeing the wounded scout
laying on the ground, he said to the other scout,
"We must go back and get that man."

Although it was as much as their lives were
worth, they turned, and as they did so they saw the

Sioux dismounted from his pony, fired, and the Indian fell with his scalping knife in his hand. Dave and the Ree then scalped the Sioux and started with the wounded man for the steamer. During this time Col. Moore, although with three companies, sent no one to the relief of these three men. Finally Grant Marsh, captain of the *Far West*, called for one hundred volunteers, and fifteen soldiers immediately offered their services, but Col. Moore ordered them not to leave the boat. However, eight of them, contrary to orders, went with Capt. Marsh and brought in Campbell and the two scouts. Colonel Moore threatened to court-martial these eight men then and there, and the steamboat men don't hesitate to pronounce Col. Moore's conduct cowardly in the extreme.

Terry has fallen back eighty miles from his camp on the Big Horn, and is now camped near the mouth of Rosebud. A scout from Gen. Crook reached Gen. Terry July 22, barefooted and almost destitute of clothing. Crook was but seventy-five miles from General Terry's command and trying to reach him. The Indians, however, kept picking off his men, driving in his scouts, and stealing his stock, so that his advance was very much retarded, only being about six miles a day. The men in both commands are reported very much disheartened.

On the afternoon of the eighteenth Seamus sat on the south bank of the Yellowstone and watched as a Bozeman City trader floated downriver in his Mackinaw boat, hailing the soldiers.

"Homemade ale and dry goods!" the peddler bellowed as he rose to his knees in his rickety craft. "Come and get what's left of my homemade ale!"

As he came in sight of the army's encampment, the civilian proclaimed that he had sold half his wares to the

soldiers left to garrison the depot at the mouth of the Rosebud and wished to sell the rest of his heady beer and dry
goods before pushing back upriver for home.

Like a flock of goslings swarming around a farmwife's
ankles as she scatters corn, officers and enlisted alike nearly
swamped the poor man's little boat as they rushed into the
water to be the first to have call on his ale, as well as his
other goods.

"Yeah, I've got a frying pan," he answered one officer's
request.

"How about a coffeepot?"

"Yes, one of them too."

"You have any canned fruit?"

"A little. Got more of tinned vegetables."

"Shirts? You got any?"

"A few hickory shirts left. And some canvas britches
too."

"Give me one of each!"

"Save a pair of them pants for me!"

The bearded, sunburned men huddled round that
trader's boat, exchanging what little money they had for
what the Bozeman merchant sold at exorbitant prices, men
forced to buy with their own funds clothing that the army
hadn't seen fit to provide its ragged, nearly naked soldiers.

While they waited for Cody and the *Far West* to return
from his scout downriver to the mouth of Glendive Creek,
Crook and Terry held a curious correspondence, discussing
just how ready Crook really was to resume his chase, since
he steadfastly repeated that he still required a full fifteen
days of rations and forage. The latter was proving to be the
most crucial—plainly there wasn't enough grain to recruit
Crook's broken-down horses.

Early on the evening of the eighteenth, Terry wrote to
Crook, saying:

> Since I saw you, I have found that our sup-
> plies of subsistence are larger than I supposed
> . . . your commissary still needs 200 boxes of

hard bread. Of these, I can furnish 100 boxes
. . . The difference between this amount and the
15 days' rations, of which you spoke, is so slight
that I think it ought not to detain us. But perhaps
your animals are in such a state that a further
supply of forage and a longer rest would be
desireable for them. If such be your wish, I am
certainly willing to wait until the forage can be
obtained.
P.S. Col. Chambers mentioned to me today that
his men need shoes badly. If the steamer goes to
the Rosebud, I can give him the shoes which he
needs.

This correspondence presented a most unusual cir-
cumstance—to find the cautious Terry suddenly impatient
to be at the chase once more; and to discover that the
tenacious Crook had begun to find excuses to delay.

But as far as Seamus Donegan was concerned, the wily
George Crook was merely maneuvering so that once he had
what he considered enough supplies, he was going to break
free of his superior, Alfred Terry.

Exactly as the survivors of the Seventh Cavalry said
Custer had talked of doing before they left Gibbon and
Terry behind at the mouth of the Rosebud and marched
south for their rendezvous with destiny.

That was enough to give a brave man pause.

Donegan prayed Crook was not about to march his
Big Horn and Yellowstone Expedition into the very same
maw of hell that had devoured Custer and five companies
of cavalry beside the Little Bighorn.

Chapter 30

19–26 August
1876

Work Suspended

St. Paul, August 7—In consequence of low water in the Yellowstone and the inability of troops at this time to afford protection to building parties, the order for the construction of new forts on the Yellowstone has been countermanded.

Terry About Ready to Move

New York, August 7—A correspondent telegraphs that Gen. Terry hopes to be able to begin his march by the 9th inst. Under date of July 31st, the correspondent says: "We have just met the Steamer *Far West*, on her way down to bring the supplies left at Powder river, which we found in possession of the Indians. Capt. Thompson, of the Second cavalry, committed suicide just before the troops left the Big Horn river."

Late in the morning of the nineteenth, Bill Cody surprised everyone by riding in alone on his buckskin instead of returning on the *Far West,* having made the dangerous trip upriver on horseback so that he could more closely study any sign he might come across along the south bank of the Yellowstone.

After receiving the scout's unproductive report, Terry sought out Crook, finding the general seated on a rock at the edge of the river, scrubbing his only pair of longhandles in the muddy water.

"I've decided to send the boat upriver to fetch forage and supplies for you at the Rosebud," Terry told him. "And the shoes Chambers requested."

"Once I'm reprovisioned, I'll set out at once," Crook vowed.

A few hours later the *Far West* reappeared, chugging beneath afternoon skies to tie up against the north bank. Even from the vantage point of the steamer's wheelhouse, Louie Reshaw hadn't spotted any sign that the hostiles had crossed the Yellowstone. Terry ordered Captain Grant Marsh and pilot Dave Campbell to leave at once for the mouth of the Rosebud, where they were to take on all the supplies previously left in depot there before returning to the Powder. That evening many of the newspapermen went along to enjoy the moonlit trip upriver.

"It was beautiful," John Finerty gushed as he strode up to Lieutenant Bourke's fire at Crook's headquarters the next morning. "Nearly a full moon—"

"I don't have time to listen to stories about your riverboat ride right now," Bourke interrupted snappishly, watching how his words brought the newsman up short.

"What—"

"Things aren't good right now: Washakie just told Crook that he's leaving."

"All of them?" Finerty turned this way and that, saying, "The Shoshone? They're leaving?"

"Back to their reservation at Wind River."

"Whatever for?"

John shrugged. "Shit, my only guess is they really don't want to fight the Sioux as bad as Crook does."

"No, John. There's something more to it than that," Finerty pressed, grabbing hold of Bourke's arm. "Tell me what Washakie said to the general when he broke the news."

Bourke didn't want to tell him, didn't want any newsman to know, really. But with the way the general was going to be butchered by Davenport when the correspondent reported this setback, John felt there should be at least one other newsman who could put enough slant on things to counterbalance Davenport's nasty, anti-Crook point of view. It could only be Finerty.

John sighed and looked at the correspondent. "The Shoshone don't think we're going to catch the Sioux."

"Hell! Truth is, I don't think we're going to, either! So what else did he tell Crook?"

"They didn't like Tom Moore's slow-moving mule train."

"Those can't be the only reasons. Why, most of Washakie's warriors rode with that 'slow-moving mule train' all the way to the Rosebud earlier this summer!"

"All I can say is they don't like it now, Finerty. Besides, like Crook says—there just seems to be no stopping them because it's getting close to annuity time."

"Annuity?"

Bourke answered, "The provisions they get from the government agent there at Wind River. Washakie wants to be there when his people come in to receive their goods."

"Well, we've still got Cody and Grouard and the rest."

The lieutenant shook his head. "That's some more bad news: Cody resigned this morning. I just heard about it myself. I haven't even told the general yet because he's been in a dither about the Snakes . . . and now Cody's calling it quits."

"Cody? Why, in God's name?"

"He told General Terry about the same thing Washakie did: that it appeared the soldiers did not want to fight, that he had worn himself out chasing Indians who had cleared out of the country a long time ago. He really let Terry have it, telling the general all about his scouting ability, how he took that Cheyenne's scalp at the Warbonnet—but that Crook and Terry didn't want to listen to him when he pointed out fresh trails that needed to be followed."

Finerty shook his head with confusion and asked, "W-wait. You said Cody found some fresh trails?"

Bourke sought to wave it off. "That's just what I've heard—he probably didn't. But he complained that the generals were relying too much on their Indian scouts and not enough on fellas like him and Grouard, Donegan, and Buffalo Chips."

"So he's leaving for sure? No one able to talk him into staying on?"

"Yeah, the Irishman is down in Terry's camp right now, trying to convince Cody to stay on for a few more weeks at least. But Cody says he's convinced the army doesn't want to find any Indians."

"John," Finerty replied, "you know, Cody might just be right. I myself thought of joining some of the fellows cashing it in."

"You, John? Why—you've been with us since the winter campaign!"

"And you don't think a man gets tired of all this Injun hunting?"

"But you're a veteran campaigner now," Bourke protested.

"Frankly, I see little prospect for catching the enemy now. Nothing to be gained by my remaining out here but more mud, more misery, and a lot more miles crawling through rough country."

"One good battle, that's all Crook needs—"

Finerty interrupted. "One good battle and things would suit me, John. But I fear the last shot of the campaign has already been fired."

"We're going to take on supplies and resume the march—"

"No," Finerty interrupted again, shaking his head. "Supplies aren't what we need. We need to leave the green infantry behind so they won't slow us up. Just the hardened foot soldiers who can keep up with the cavalry. Beyond that, what we need most from the army is horses for the cavalry that aren't ready for the glue factory!"

Bourke bristled visibly as he said, "The mark of a good soldier is always doing the best he can do with what he's been given."

Finerty tried out a weak grin. "Listen, John—don't take my criticism personally. I just think the circumstances have turned this expedition into nothing but a theatrical campaign."

"Theatrical?"

"Exactly—just like a Chinese stage battle I once saw in Chicago: the combatants constantly rushing about in an excited manner, chasing after unseen enemies they can't ever catch. What was amusing, though—the enemies seem to find and harass their pursuers."

"Chinese stage play, eh?" Bourke grumbled. "That's what you think of Crook's summer campaign?"

"Perhaps—"

"Sounds as if you've been listening to the likes of Reuben Davenport and his cowards' school of back stabbing!"

"Back stabbing? Who?"

"You, and that Davenport. Why, we even found out Davenport offered a hundred dollars to a courier Crook hired to carry his dispatches, if the courier would deliver Davenport's stories first and delay Crook's dispatches by at least twelve hours!"

"I'd never do a thing like that, John!"

"Nonetheless, it sure sounds like you have worn out your welcome, John Finerty," Bourke snapped with a flourish of indignation. "Perhaps you'll be better served by returning to Chicago. Good day!"

He whirled away from the newsman without allowing Finerty another word to his face.

"John! Come back!"

Bourke kept on walking, shouting back at the reporter, "Perhaps you would be more comfortable in one of the cushy bunks on the steamboat—or eating in the dining room of some hotel back in Chicago rather than sleeping in the cold mud and eating raw bacon with the rest of us!"

"I'm not leaving!" Finerty yelled at the lieutenant's back. "Don't think you're going to get rid of me this easily, John Bourke. Anything you soldiers can take—John Finerty can take!"

Indian Rumors of an Engagement— Terry Victorious.

CHICAGO, August 10—The *Times'* Fort D. Sully special says: Indians from hostile camp have arrived with the report that Terry's command had encountered the hostiles, and the latter had been flanked by Gen. Gibbon and badly beaten. The Indians acknowledged one hundred wounded, and said that Sitting Bull had been shot through both thighs. They are quiet on the subject of the number killed. An Indian can travel by a direct route from Sitting Bull to the agencies sooner by several days than a courier could reach Bismarck from Terry. The report is generally believed here.

"You promise me you'll write. Tell me when the baby comes," Bill Cody asked in dawn's chill light as a mist hung over the mouth of the Powder River.

After a dry Sunday and Monday, during which time Lieutenant Colonel Carr drilled his cavalry, Tuesday saw a renewal of wind-driven rain. And there had been no letup on Wednesday. But this morning the wind refused to put in an appearance as the skies continued to drizzle morosely.

"Promise me," Cody repeated, squeezing harder.

Seamus felt Bill's hand tighten on his, refusing to let go for the longest time. "Yes."

"You have the address in Rochester I gave you?"

The Irishman could only nod. All he thought of was that farewell he had bid Cody back in November of sixty-nine—after Bill had saved his life, shooting the huge mulatto who was about to slit open Donegan's throat.*

"No matter where the troupe is appearing, I'll always get your letters through Lulu. Just be sure you write—or have Samantha write if you want."

"Yes. Samantha."

Cody pulled Donegan close, and they embraced there in the damp and the cold, pounding one another on the back again, this time in sadness at their parting. As he held the Irishman against him, Cody whispered in Donegan's ear, "Be sure you let me know if it's a boy or not."

"Sam says it will be."

"Write me."

Donegan backed away, holding Cody at arm's length. "I don't know if we'll ever see each other again, Bill."

Cody blinked and tried out that grand smile of his. "We damn well will, Irishman! You can count on that! And if ever you decide you want to come east—I'll find work for you."

"I already told you I couldn't live back—"

"But you haven't given it enough thought, or talked it over with Samantha. Remember, there'll always be a place for you at my table, Seamus Donegan. A place for you and yours."

Dragging his hand under his nose, Seamus tried to smile bravely. This was the second time he was saying farewell to a good, good friend. And—dammit—it just never got any easier.

Reluctantly Cody turned to go and moved off through a throng of well-wishers toward the gangplank that would lead him up to the lower deck of the *Carroll* where the captain waited, his lantern-jawed pilot leaning out from the window on the wheelhouse above. That Thursday daybreak a thousand soldiers tore off their hats, cheering, those gath-

---

*The Plainsmen Series, Vol. 4, *Black Sun*.

ered on the fringe of the gauntlet slapping Cody on the back if they could reach him as he walked through their midst. Already Buffalo Chips had Bill's big buckskin lashed in among some bales of hay on deck. White stopped, shook hands; then the two scouts hugged before Bill shooed his friend down the steamer's gangplank.

The pilot yanked hard at the whistle cord, giving it three short, steamy squeals over that Powder River depot. Soldiers on shore began releasing the thick hawser ropes, heaving them toward a trio of civilian stevedores at the deck rail. Bill leaped up the steps to the wheelhouse, where he leaned from the window and removed his big sombrero, waving it to the wildly whistling, stamping mob on shore as the pilot worked his wheel hard to port preparing to back into the shallow rapids of the Powder River to make his turn, yelling down the pipe to the engine room, bellowing at his boilermen to stoke the fire to her.

Donegan stood on the bank that morning of the twenty-fourth day of August, trying to blink away the sting of tears as he watched Cody look directly at him, his mouth moving. For all the clamor and cheering, the belching of those greasy stacks and the throbbing hammer of the steam pistons—Seamus could not be sure. Again he carefully watched as Cody said something from up there in the wheelhouse as the *Carroll* lurched out into the current, ready to put about at the mouth of the Powder.

"Take care of your family, Seamus!"

Donegan smiled and nodded. Then he yelled back, "By God—I will always do that!" Then he joined the rest in giving the famous scout and showman a rousing send-off.

"With God's help," Seamus quietly repeated minutes later as he watched the black smoke belching from the twin stacks disappearing around the far sandstone bluff, "I will always take care of my family."

He didn't know how long he stood there as the soldiers drifted away, looking downriver. Long after smoke from the steamer's twin stacks faded from the sky beyond the river bluffs.

Now Cody was gone. Along with the Shoshone and Ute and Bannock as well. What few Crow remained behind were divided between the two columns. The surgeons had loaded eighty-four sick and disabled aboard the *Carroll*, soldiers on their way back to the East, returning home to loved ones. Along with most of the correspondents.

All that remained were the men who would see things through to the bitter end.

At seven that morning bugles blew above Crook's camp at the mouth of the Powder River, calling out the clear, clarion notes of "Boots and Saddles." Minutes later "The General" was sounded. There were no tents to come down—only blankets to be rolled up as the last boxes of rations and ammunition were lashed onto the sawbucks cinched to the hardy backs of Tom Moore's trail-hardened mules. Forage-poor horses whinnied and the mules hawed in protest, not at all ready to plunge back into that wilderness scorched by the enemy. Perhaps those weary, rib-gaunt beasts foresaw the ruin yet to come.

"You going with us?"

Donegan turned to find Frank Grouard looking down at him from horseback. The half-breed handed Seamus the reins to the Irishman's horse.

"Thanks, Frank."

"Glad you're staying on, Donegan. Hope I got everything of yours packed."

Looking over his bedroll and lariat, quickly glancing in the two small saddlebags, Seamus looked up and said, "Ain't much for a man to look after, is it?"

"If you don't have it, I figure you can't loose it," Grouard said, reining his horse around. "C'mon. Crook wants to cover ground today."

Swinging into the saddle, Donegan said, "I don't blame him—what with having us lollygag around here for five days."

Into the hills the first of Chambers's infantry followed the headquarters flag recently fashioned for Crook by Captain George M. Randall and Lieutenant Walter S. Schuyler. Although primitively constructed under the crudest of field conditions, it was nonetheless impressive as the Big Horn and Yellowstone Expedition got about its stern chase of the hostiles: in the general shape of a large guidon, equally divided between a white band on top—a towel contributed by Major Thaddeus Stanton—and a red band below—a gift of Schuyler's own red underwear—with a large blue star affixed in the center—cut from Randall's old, faded army blouse. With a drawknife, pack-chief Moore had one of his litter poles carved down to the diameter of a flagpole, and ferrules were made from a pair of copper Springfield .45/70 cases.

That flag was to lead them east, on the trail of the warriors who had slaughtered Custer's men.

After fleeing Terry for eleven miles up the Powder River, Crook finally dispatched a courier with a note to explain that he had left, intent on pursuing the hostiles who likewise were making their escape. It wasn't long after that courier had left with the general's belated farewell that scout Muggins Taylor rode into that muddy midday bivouac with a letter from Terry.

> I came up on the boat to see you, but found you had gone. The boat brought up your additional rations, but of course will not land them. I can send your supplies, forage, and subsistence to the mouth of the Powder River, if you wish it; but if you could send your pack train to the landing, it would be better, for the boat is very busy.

A few hours later a second courier from Terry caught up with the escaping leader of the Wyoming column, marching farther up the Powder.

> Your note crossed one from me to you. I sent Lt. Schofield out to find you, supposing you were within four or five miles, and intended to go

out and meet you if you were near. My note has
explained fully all that I wished to say.

I still intend to leave at six in the morning. I
hope your march will not be so long as to prevent
my overtaking you.

In no way did George Crook want Alfred Terry to
overtake him.

After suffering terribly through another night of incessant drizzle, Crook had his command up at dawn, huddling
close around smoky fires to chew on bacon and hard bread,
drinking steamy coffee to drive away the damp chill that
pierced a man to his core. Through mud and the sort of
sticky gumbo that balled up on the horses' hooves, the
column crossed and recrossed the Powder throughout a
tiring thirteen-mile march and made camp at the mouth of
Locate Creek beneath sullen clouds that evening. It wasn't
long before the wind came up and the rain boiled out of
the heavens with a vengeance.

All day Donegan had been brooding on the expedition's plight, unable to shake off his misgivings and his
confusion that for some unexplained reason Crook had relented and allowed his expedition to lie in at the Powder
River depot for five days, awaiting supplies. Then suddenly,
before they had taken on their full fifteen days' compliment
of rations and forage, the general ordered his men to strike
camp and depart without giving Terry any word that he
was departing.

There could be one and only one reason for this precipitous and unwise act: Crook wanted to shed himself of
Terry more than anything. Even more, perhaps, than assur-
ing that his expedition had its full allowance of supplies.

In the days and weeks yet to come the Big Horn and
Yellowstone Expedition would pay for that thoughtless act.
And pay dearly.

Donegan and Grouard drove a picket pin into the
flaky soil, tying the other end at an angle to a nearby tree.
Over this they hung their two blankets, then drove hastily

carved stakes through the edges of the wool blankets that continued to whip and flap beneath the rise and fall of the hellish wind. It wasn't long before those blankets could turn no more water, and the mist began to spray down upon the two scouts.

Despite the crash of thunder accompanying the bright flares of ground lightning, the Irishman had just made himself warm enough in a corner of their crude shelter when the hail began to batter against the taut, soggy blankets, rattling with a racket that reminded Seamus of the grapeshot falling among the leafy branches surrounding those farm fields at Gettysburg.

It wasn't until long past midnight that the last rumble of thunder passed over them, its echo swallowed off to the east. One by one Crook's men crawled from beneath their blankets and ponchos, out from under the brush where they cowered, and with trembling fingers tried to light the damp kindling. By dawn's cold light there were hundreds of pitiful, smoky fires where Crook's stalwart gathered.

Later that cold morning, Seamus shuffled over to Lieutenant John W. Bubb's commissary to request some tobacco, even purchase some if he had to part with what little he had left in the way of money.

"This is all?" Donegan asked as Bubb laid the small block of pressed tobacco in the Irishman's palm. Seamus stuffed his other into the pocket of his britches. "I'll buy some—pay good money, Lieutenant—just lemme have more."

"Can't," Bubb replied. "Every man's rationed to that, or less."

"Rationed, on tobacco?"

"Back at the Yellowstone all I could get my hands on was eleven pounds."

"You mean this is it for me?"

Bubb nodded. "Likely will be—until we see either one of the Yellowstone River depots again . . . or Fort Fetterman."

He watched the lieutenant turn away, going about his other business.

"God bless us," Seamus muttered sourly as he trudged off into the cold and rain. "And I pray thee—watch over us all."

Chapter 31

25–26 August
1876

Courier Headed Off

OMAHA, August 10—The courier sent to Red Cloud agency from Fort Laramie, Monday last, returned there last night, and says that when near Running creek he was met by six Indians, who shot at him and wounded his horse. He hid among the sand hills and escaped.

What General Sheridan Says

WASHINGTON, August 11—Following is General Sheridan's letter to General Sherman, transmitted by the president to congress to-day, with his message, asking for more cavalry or volunteers:

CHICAGO, August 5, 1876—*General W. T. Sherman:* —I have not yet been able to reinforce the garrisons at Red Cloud, at Spotted Tail or at Standing Rock, strong enough to count the Indians or to arrest and disarm those coming in. I beg you to see the military committee of the house and urge on it the necessity of increasing the cavalry regiments to one hundred men to each company. Gen. Crook's total strength is 1,774 and Terry's 1,873, and to give this force to them I have stripped every post from the line of Manitoba to Texas. We want more mounted men. We have not exceeded the law in enlisted Indian scouts; in fact we have not as many as the law allows, as the whole number in this division is only 114. The Indians with Gen. Crook are not enlisted or even paid. They are not worth paying. They are with him only to gratify their desire for a fight and their thirst of revenge on the Sioux.

P. H. SHERIDAN, Lieut-Gen.

In the forenoon of 25 August the *Carroll* put off from the north bank of the Yellowstone River where the captain, crew, and passengers had spent an uneventful night, though they took the precaution of keeping armed pickets on shore to alert the steamer should hostiles put in an appearance.

This second day of their trip downriver Bill Cody found himself even more anxious to return to his loved ones, perhaps even more so than any of the others onboard —the sick and disabled, as well as the correspondents who were fleeing back to hearth and home. If to others it seemed he had chosen to rake in his chips and call it a night, so be it. Bill wanted to be as far east as possible, as fast as possible—with not a single reminder of what he might be leaving behind out here in the wilderness he loved with all his heart.

Throughout yesterday's leg of the journey Cody had paced the upper deck until the reporters cornered him in the afternoon to seek his opinion on every facet of the summer campaign. Just so he wouldn't have to tell them what he really thought of the army's hunt for the hostiles, Bill hid the rest of the afternoon and into the evening. Not until this morning had he ventured out from the crew's tiny bunk room, to settle on a bench in the pilot's wheel-house as the *Carroll* sped on down the Yellowstone for Fort Buford, on to Fort Lincoln and beyond—taking him into the rest of his life.

"Smoke," called the pilot, pointing, then hit the stained outer lip of a brass cuspidor with a flying gob of tobacco juice.

Bill stood, peering downriver, out past the tall cap-stans, where he saw black columns smudging the sky. "A steamer?"

"Yup. Likely looks to be two of 'em."

Within minutes the captain had ordered his pilot to put in along the north bank just above the mouth of O'Fallon's Creek, where they watched the progress of the two steamers churning up the Yellowstone. With their shrill, steamy greetings the *Josephine* and the *Yellowstone* whistled and put in near the *Carroll* as the passengers— civilians and soldiers alike—hollered out greetings, lumber-ing down gangplanks to go swapping stories.

Two days before, the *Yellowstone* had been fired upon by hostiles some thirty miles below the mouth of Glendive Creek. One soldier was killed. The next morning during their stop at Lieutenant Rice's Glendive stockade, the pas-sengers aboard the two steamers learned that war parties had been a constant source of nuisance, attempting to run off the herd and destroy the outfit's supplies. Perhaps be-cause of those reports of enemy activity farther down the river, instead of continuing his journey out of hostile coun-try, the *Carroll*'s nervous captain chose to put about and follow the other steamers upriver.

Bill had no sooner begun to register his colorful com-plaint than a familiar voice called out his name.

"Buffalo Bill!"

Turning, Cody found the face of an old friend and business associate. "Texas Jack!"

Jack Omohundro, a longtime friend on the plains as well as Bill's recent partner in their stage productions back east, raced up the gangplank just as the *Carroll*'s crew hoisted it out of the way and put off from the bank.

They shook and pounded one another on the shoulder until Bill asked, "Where the hell did you come from?"

"Coming upriver on the *Josephine*!" Omohundro replied. "After you run off last spring, I figured I could sit on my ass back east, or I could come out here and get some action for myself. Hell—it's all over the press back there how you took that Cheyenne's scalp!"

"What're you going to do here?"

"I'm scouting—for the Fifth Infantry."

"Nelson Miles?"

"Well, not rightly. Not just yet anyway," Omohundro equivocated. "As soon as I run onto Miles, I'm sure I can land me a position. I came upriver with Lieutenant Colonel J.N.G. Whistler, who's bringing with him two more companies of the Fifth Infantry to join Miles and General Terry."

"Jack?"

Bill and Omohundro both turned to find a slim, weasel-faced officer climbing the ladder to the upper deck. Jack leaned and whispered from the side of his mouth, "That's Whistler."

"Jack!" the officer exclaimed. "I was hoping I'd track you down. I can't find anyone onboard any of the steamers who will act as courier for me."

Omohundro explained to Cody. "Colonel Whistler here has been begging for a rider to take messages ahead to General Terry."

"Important?" Cody asked.

"Yes, sir." Then Whistler peered at the long-haired stranger. "Do I know you?"

Bill took off his hat and performed a little bow from the waist. "William F. Cody, at your service."

"Colonel Cody?"

"Yes."

Whistler presented his hand while tearing his hat from his head. "A pleasure to meet a true American hero, sir!

Why, the story of you and that war party that had you surrounded at Warbonnet Creek—and how you handily did in their chief . . . why, it's an inspiration to us all!"

Cody cleared his throat, nervous at so much effusive praise. "These messages—you say you can't find anyone to carry them?"

"Why, no, Colonel Cody."

With a shrug Bill offered, "I will."

Omohundro immediately turned and seized Cody's arm. "Are you sure about this, Bill? No reason you should take such a dangerous chance."

Cody did not even look at Jack, preferring instead to say to the officer, "I have my horse onboard. When can you have the dispatches ready?"

"Why . . . they're ready right now. But I must insist that you take advantage of my own horse."

"Yours?" Cody asked.

"Yes. A blooded thoroughbred. Onboard the *Josephine*."

Bill pulled on his gloves and gestured to the door of the wheelhouse. "Splendid! I suggest you present yourself to the pilot and have him put us in at the next clear channel along the south bank."

The officer bobbed his head happily, replying, "Of . . . of course!"

Cody watched Whistler turn on his heel and barge right on through the wheelhouse door.

Omohundro asked quietly, "Just where were you going when we bumped into you, Bill?"

"Home, Jack."

"Christ, Cody—I was coming out here to grab some of the adventure and fun for myself, and here you're booking it in."

Bill smiled. "Doesn't appear I'm done for . . . not just yet."

"That's got to be a dangerous route—right through the country Sitting Bull's warriors are swarming over. If you already decided to head back home—why would you want to take this chance?"

"Jack," Cody said quietly, slapping an arm over Omohundro's shoulder, "if you're giving me the choice of riding back upriver on a slow-moving steamboat, or forked in the saddle carrying dispatches and having myself an adventure of it . . . now, just what the hell did you think I was going to choose?"

Those reports of the raids on the Glendive stockade and war parties firing on the steamboats, news that Cody carried to Terry, was exactly the sort of intelligence calculated to arouse the general's worst fears that Sitting Bull's minions were indeed preparing to flood across the Yellowstone.

As soon as Cody reached the mouth of the Powder with his dispatches, an anxious Terry decided he must first consult with Crook. Taking Cody as a guide for his small escort of staff and leaving the rest of his command to come on as quickly as they could, the general hurried up the Powder until they ran onto Crook's miserable camp late on the rainy afternoon of 25 August.

"Excuse me, General Crook," Cody said as the two commanders were about to duck under a canvas awning to begin their conference. "Could you tell me where I could find one of your civilian scouts—Donegan?"

"The Irishman? Why, last I knew he rode on ahead with Grouard and White to scout the countryside and see how the trails were scattering. Why?"

"Just wanted to say good-bye to him. For a second time. That's all."

Unable to talk with Donegan or White, either of his old friends, Cody settled nearby as the two generals had their courteous, if strained, consultation. Now firmly convinced that all recent evidence pointed to the hostiles converging and massing on the Yellowstone prior to making their race for Canada, Terry suggested a twist on Sheridan's joint maneuver to capture the hostiles between them: his Dakota and Montana columns to work along the north bank of the Yellowstone while Crook's men would come up from the south—hammering the Sioux against Terry's anvil.

Despite Terry's enthusiasm, Crook steadfastly refused to believe that the Crazy Horse Sioux would turn toward the Yellowstone, much less cross to the north.

"If they turn in any direction now," Crook argued, "they'll go south—right for the settlements I'm sworn to protect."

In his conference with Terry, Crook learned that sufficient rations and ammunition lay in storage at Fort Abraham Lincoln on the Missouri River, should the trail of the wandering hostiles extend that far to the east. Assured of that northeastern supply line, Crook stated that the following morning he planned to dispatch a courier to Major Furey in command of his wagons on Goose Creek, with orders to proceed by prudent marches for Custer City in the southern Black Hills, where the supply train was to await Crook's arrival with the rest of the expedition in the weeks to come.

Not once in their discussions, apparently, did Terry confront Crook with the fact that he had up and left without letting his superior know. Never did Terry press his position as senior officer in the campaign, but instead decided to let Crook pursue the trail of the fleeing Sioux they had run across while marching down the Powder a week before.

In all likelihood Terry understood Crook was not about to be moved to pursue a course other than the one he had already selected for himself. While at the Yellowstone Crook had received a telegram from Major Jordan at Camp Robinson that stated eight warriors had come in to surrender at Red Cloud Agency, reporting to the agent that the main body of hostiles was about to turn south.

Not north to the Yellowstone, and on to Canada, where Terry feared Sitting Bull's people would then be free to raid into the Montana settlements.

Instead—here was proof enough that the Sioux were

about to heel south for the Black Hills. Straight for Crook's own department.

Terry bid Crook farewell and good luck, having decided he would go back to his column's camp on the Powder that night. On the morning of the twenty-sixth he planned to turn his Montana and Dakota troops around and point them north, back to the Yellowstone—giving George Crook free rein to follow the hostiles' road.

In the end the two hammered out a compromise of sorts. Terry would keep his men active on the river, as well as moving supplies to the Glendive stockade for Crook's use, should the fleeing Sioux lead Crook in that direction. Meanwhile, Crook remained free to follow the hostiles' trail, wherever it might take his Big Horn and Yellowstone Expedition.

"Bill, I know this is asking a lot, but I need you to make another ride for me," Terry said late that evening of the twenty-fifth following his conference with Crook, and long after his command went into bivouac just below Crook's camp on the muddy banks of the Powder.

Cody settled atop one of the canvas stools under the canvas fly outside Terry's spacious tent. "Where to now, General?"

"Back to Whistler," the officer explained as the sky went on drizzling and the wind came up. "Tell him not to let the steamers go downriver. He must retain them all for my use to patrol the Yellowstone. And I want clarification on the reports of Indian activity along the river as well. But probably most important—I want Whistler to take his two companies back to the mouth of the Tongue, where he can commence building huts for the winter."

Captain Edward W. Smith, Terry's adjutant, graciously offered, "Mr. Cody, you can have my horse for the return trip down the Yellowstone. Appears you might have used up Colonel Whistler's thoroughbred in bringing those messages to the general."

"Why, thank you, Captain," Cody replied, turning to

study Smith's horse. "Looks like a sturdy animal. Yes—I'll take you up on that offer."

It wasn't until sometime after midnight that Bill made out the dim glow of the lamps on the bow and stern of the three steamboats, each one gently bobbing atop the Yellowstone's current in the patter of unending drizzle. Finding a suitable place to make a crossing, Bill presented himself to Whistler and handed over Terry's messages.

The lieutenant colonel read over the dispatches written by Captain Smith, then looked up at the civilian with worry lining his face. "Terry wants clarification that the Sioux are making a show of it along the river? Why, the hostiles have been a damned nuisance ever since you left, and it's been getting worse. I'm afraid things are about to fall out of the frying pan and into the fire."

"Seems like I missed all the fun you fellas been having."

"Cody," Whistler continued, his brow furrowed in worry, "I've got to send information to the general concerning the Indians who have been skirmishing around here all day. All evening long I've been trying to induce someone to carry my dispatches to Terry, but no one seems willing to undertake the trip. So I must fall back on you. It is asking a great deal, I know, as you've just covered over eighty miles on horseback; but it is a case of extreme necessity. And if you go, Cody—I'll see that you are well paid for it."

"Naw. Never mind about the extra pay, Colonel," Bill said, taking his wet buckskin coat from the back of the chair and shaking more moisture from it. "But get your dispatches ready. I'll start as soon as I swap my saddle over to my own horse."

"Won't you at least have another cup of coffee?" Omohundro suggested, stepping forward to hand his friend the steaming tin.

"All right, I will, Jack. While the colonel here gets his dispatches ready and you go saddle the buckskin."

Even though he had just come in from a long day's

journey; even though the hostiles had been skirmishing
with the soldiers on the steamers from first light until dusk;
even though he was about to ride his own favorite horse on
that perilous return trip—Bill Cody tucked those letters
inside his shirt and dashed down the gangplank to take up
the reins from Omohundro and leap once more into the
saddle.

As the steamer's crew was swinging in the gangplank,
Omohundro called out from the rail, "You watch your hair,
Buffalo Bill!"

"I sure as hell will, Texas Jack—at least until Lulu can
run her fingers through it!"

As Cody had left to ride back to Whistler through the badlands in the rain and the darkness of that night before, an
anxious Terry wrote Crook an afterthought, seeking to per-
suade Crook one last time to join him in his concentration
of troops along the Yellowstone.

> There is one thing which I forgot to say and
> that is that it appears to me that the band which
> has gone north, if any have gone there, is the
> heart and soul of the Indian mutiny. It is the
> nucleus around which the whole body of disaf-
> fected Indians gathers. If it were destroyed, this
> thing would be over, and it is for that reason that
> I so strongly feel that even if a larger trail is
> found leading south, we should make a united
> effort to settle these particular people.

Crook would not be deterred. He would not be
turned. He would have his victory. And he was determined
to share it with no one.

Six hours after leaving Whistler on the *Josephine,* Cody
reached the muddy outskirts of Terry's camp along the
Powder, just as the column was about to undertake its
march back to the Yellowstone. Bill had just covered over

120 miles in less than twenty-two hours, pushing through some of the roughest country on the high plains, across badlands clearly infested with warriors still bristling and brazen following their victory over Custer's Seventh.

That dawn Terry cheered, "Never thought I'd see you back here so soon, Mr. Cody!"

"Didn't really count on it myself, General. Whistler needed a courier—and it appears I was the only one who wanted a breath of fresh air!"

Chapter 32

26–29 August
1876

What Forsythe Says.

St. Paul, August 10—General Forsythe, of General Sheridan's staff, passed through the city yesterday, having left Terry's camp at South Rosebud a week ago last Tuesday. In conversation with army officers while here General Forsyth corrected many erroneous statements recently telegraphed from Bismarck . . . It was stated that General Terry had fallen back eighty miles, which is mere nonsense, and gives a false impression to the public . . . The evening before General Forsythe left General Terry, a scout from General Crook's command had reached General Terry. General Crook was then somewhere near the head waters of the Rosebud river, or between that and Tongue river. Now, at this time General Terry was at the mouth of the Big Horn river, and in order to make communication between himself and General Crook easier, he dropped down the river to the mouth of the Rosebud . . .

The scout alluded to furnished the news that Indian trails had been found leading to the east between Gen. Crook and the Yellowstone. A junction of Gens. Terry and Crook at a point further east than the Big Horn was likely to prevent the escape of the Indians to the east and north of the present scene of operations. Another misstatement is to the effect that the troops under General Terry are disheartened at the prospect before them . . . On the contrary, Gen. Terry and his men are in the best possible spirits, and are only too anxious to meet the horde of savages in a square fight. There is no fear as to the result.

The Indians, he learned, were still supposed to be massed somewhere between the Rosebud river and the Big Horn. The impression prevailed that one of two alternatives was left them—either to scatter to the eastward and toward British America, or southward to the Big Horn mountains. Though they were in front or in close proximity to Gen. Crook's command, it is not believed that they would show fight or allow Gen. Crook or Gen. Terry to get a chance at them in a body.

In a predawn mist that twenty-sixth day of August, with Terry's latest appeal in hand, George Crook once more sought to make his point as diplomatically as possible, without expressing that he did not want to chase Terry's Sioux. He wanted to chase his own. Taking pen in hand, he wrote:

> My understanding has always been that Crazy Horse, who is an Oglala and represents the disaffected people belonging to the Southern Agencies, is about equal in strength to Sitting Bull, who similarly represents the Northern Sioux; besides, it is known that at least 1500 additional warriors left Red Cloud Agency and joined

Crazy Horse this spring and summer and are supposed to be with him here.

Should any considerable part of the main trail lead in the direction of the Southern Agencies, I take it for granted that it must be his, which will not only increase the embarrassment of protecting the settlements in my department, but will make me apprehensive for the safety of my wagon train.

Should I not find any decided trail going southward, but on the contrary find it scattering in this country, or crossing to the north of the Yellowstone, you can calculate on my remaining with you until the unpleasantness ends, or we are ordered to the contrary.

We march this morning. Good bye.

As the infantry slogged into the lead through the mud, sergeants bawled orders for the cavalry to form up for inspection. Chewing on a little of that tobacco he could beg off Lieutenant Bubb's commissary, Seamus Donegan sat with half-breed Frank Grouard, both of them sullenly waiting, watching Terry's far-off column inch its own way toward the Yellowstone.

One trooper nearby began to grump, "I'll sooner desert than come on another one of Crook's Injun campaigns!"

"Och!" swore his Irish companion. "It was the devil's own whiskey that brought me to ruin—with no place to go but enlist!"

"Whiskey!" hollered a third. "Ah, sweet whiskey! Now, George—wouldn't you just wish you had a little drop of whiskey to mix with all this water here'bouts?"

"Mix?" the second soldier replied with a snort of objection. "No fear of you mixing any water with your whiskey, Tim! You always take it straight!"

Tim spat in disgust, saying, "Bad luck to the ship that brought me over, then. If I had taken my old mother's advice and remained in Cashel, it isn't a drowned rat I'd be this morning."

"Och! Be-jaysus!" grouched George. "If this isn't the most god-damnblest outfit I ever struck in my twenty-five years of sarvice!"

"Aye," agreed Tim as the sergeants ordered the units into a column of fours. "Devil shoot the generals and the shoulder straps all around! Sure and they have no more compassion on a poor crayture of a soldier than a hungry wolf has on a helpless little lamb!"

The horse soldier behind Tim hollered out, "A tough old lamb you'd be, Timmy! A wolf would have to hold his head a long way from the wall afore he could eat you."

"No coffee till night," Tim continued to complain. "And we'll likely eat our bacon raw again come supper— for the sagebrush won't burn worth a lick, even if the rain would let up!"

The Big Horn and Yellowstone Expedition put its nose down to the trail, on the hunt once more.

But while Crook, Bourke, Finerty, and many of the other soldiers and civilians who would chronicle this leg of the expedition all wrote that they took up the "Indian trail" that dreary, sodden morning of 26 August—the column was instead following the heavy wagon trail that General Terry's engineers had graded and bridged on their westbound march back in May.

Grouard, Donegan, and Charlie White all had their own suspicions early on, but it was a pair of Ree Terry had loaned the expedition who weren't long in confirming Crook's mistake. After all, those Arikara trackers should know: they had been part of that great forty-plus force who had marched out of Fort Abraham Lincoln with a hopeful Terry and an ebullient Custer on the seventeenth of May.

Later that Saturday morning the Ree came to Grouard, plainly confused, wondering why Three Stars was merely backtracking a soldier road instead of pursuing the Sioux trail.

"Sweet Mither of God! If this isn't a glorious start,"

Donegan grumbled. "We're told we're giving stern chase to the enemy, when all we're about is going on a grand fishing trip!"

"Ain't you ever fished for Sioux?" Grouard asked, looking disgusted. "Terry and Gibbon done a lot of it lately. The secret is, you just don't ever bait your hook."

With a nod Seamus replied, "Yeah—so you don't ever have to worry about catching something."

Stripped to the bone, packing along two days' less rations than that pitiful fifteen days' supplies would have allowed them, and without bringing along a single nose bag of grain for their gaunt, worn-out animals, they pointed their column to the northeast. Crook had his men marching into fire-blackened prairie, a country cut with a hundred muddy, alkaline creeks, making for the Little Missouri badlands.

That afternoon about four o'clock the command settled into the adhesive mud along the West Fork of O'Fallon's Creek after marching more than twenty miles, a camp made all the more miserable by a wind-driven rain. At sundown many of the command saw signs of abundant game, but the general had issued strict orders against firing any weapon. Even the company trumpeters had been instructed to pack away their bugles. The enemy was out there, came the explanation.

Just where, it was any man's guess.

North by east the infantry led them out at seven A.M. the following Sunday, the twenty-seventh, marching into a rolling country that showed no evidence of timber. Near noon they reached the main branch of O'Fallon's Creek, where the packers had a problem forcing some of their mules across. In two more hours Crook had them in bivouac on the East Fork of O'Fallon's, a small blessing for those older veterans who were already showing signs of approaching sickness: rheumatism and neuralgia.

Late that afternoon eight Arikara scouts rode in from Terry's command with his instructions to the Ree that they were to serve the Wyoming column, as well as carry a letter for Crook.

> I have had a reply to my dispatch to Whistler. Rice was not attacked, but the steamer *Yellowstone* was. I shall return, cross over, march enough north to determine, if possible, whether the Indians have made for Dry Fork, and if they have not, or if I believe there is still a considerable body of them on the river, I shall turn to the right. I shall cover the country west of Glendive Creek and be at the Creek in five days, unless I go north.
>
> I shall send a steamer to Buford with orders to take on supplies and come up to Glendive and await orders. She will supply you.

Beginning to worry about the prospect of scurvy running rampant through the command, Crook met with his officers and instructed them to have the men eat the cactus and Indian turnips found in abundance along the line of march. That night a few soldiers pulled the spines from some prickly pear and tried frying it in their skillets over greasewood fires sputtering in the incessant drizzle. Most tried a single bite, then turned away to spit out what they had in their mouths.

"I'll chance the scurvy," one old file growled after hacking up the slimy pulp.

The sun put in an appearance at dawn on the twenty-eighth, lifting the men's spirits. Throughout the day the air stayed cool and the column covered a good piece of ground, finally going into camp on high ground that overlooked the valley of Beaver Creek still off to the east, and the sun-scoured badlands of southern Montana, with Cabin Creek just below them.

Grouard and Donegan took the eight Arikara scouts to look over the country around the Little Missouri still in their front. They hadn't gone far when they began to run across recent sign. The farther they pushed to the east, the more nervous grew the half-breed and the Ree. Smoke was seen off in the distance behind the rise and fall of the land, great, smudgy columns spiraling into the sodden air.

"These Corn Indians seen with their own eyes what the Sioux did to Custer's men," Grouard said, trying to explain why he was choosing to return to Crook's camp.

"You're 'bout as jumpy as they are, Frank."

He pressed his thick lips together and nodded, turning his horse about. He pointed, saying, "I'm laying there's more'n three hundred lodges down there. Over there and there too. All together, that makes more warriors than you and me wanna tangle with. You remember that graveyard beside the Little Horn, don't you?"

Seamus nodded. "I remember."

Many of the officers refused to believe Grouard's report that night when the scouts wandered in close to dark, just as the rain blotted out the first stars. But it wasn't just the rain that soaked them all again that night of the twenty-eighth. A prairie hailstorm, with stones half the size of a hen's egg, hammered man and beast, chilled the air more than twenty degrees, and left every last one of them frozen to the gills.

With the advent of a fierce lightning show, followed by the frightening hail, a few of the Fifth Cavalry's horses broke free of their picket pins and started their run. Most of them floundered in the creek. Some died, others had to be shot after breaking their legs in that mad dash to freedom.

As far as Seamus Donegan was concerned, the only good thing to be said about that night was that the storm hadn't succeeded in stampeding all their stock. Instead of breaking free, most of the horses and mules huddled in packs, frightened, making the most pitiful of humanlike noises throughout that long, miserable night.

It was already becoming clear to any horseman in that command that most of their animals simply didn't have enough strength to stampede. All those horsemen could do was pray the stock would have enough strength to last out Crook's chase.

Later the Irishman learned that the lightning had struck the prairie not far from their southernmost pickets, starting a grass fire that was whipped along in savage style by the wind but was as quickly extinguished as soon as the hailstorm blew in and the rains arrived.

On Tuesday, the twenty-ninth, the column awoke to another beautiful dawn coming in the wake of another terrible night. As the sun came up, it found most in the command using their folding knives to peel the thick gumbo from their shoes and boots.

"Can hell be much worse than this?" asked Lieutenant Frederick Schwatka of the Third Cavalry, his teeth chattering, as Donegan walked his weary mount out of camp.

"No, not at all. Hell would be a lot warmer, Lieutenant."

"Good point, Irishman! A grand point! Warmer indeed!"

Off the infantry plodded, with the cavalry bringing up the rear behind Tom Moore's pack-train. This day Seamus rode the right flank, ranging far ahead, allowing the horse to have its head as much as he dared. This act was a little kindness that made his heart feel better, what with the way he had stared at the horse's ribby sides that morning, stared at the bony flanks as he flung the saddle blanket over its galled spine.

"You remember that deal we struck back on the Powder a couple weeks back," he whispered to the animal now, though there was not another human ear within miles of him. "You just remember that now." He patted the horse's neck. "Just stay under me and don't go down . . . and I promise I won't let you fall."

Reining up atop a ridge to let the horse blow, Seamus watched the winding progress of the infantry far off to his left. "Soon enough, ol' boy—there'll be plenty of your kind falling what won't get back up. But you just remember our bargain."

His eye drawn by a glimmer of distant movement, Donegan turned to the east, finding Grouard and three of the Ree miles off in the van but loping back toward the head of the column. In the middistance, scout Jack Crawford reined up, waiting. Grouard's group halted momentarily where Charlie White sat atop his horse; then together the five kicked their mounts into a lope for Crawford.

"Looks like they found something," Seamus mumbled to the animal below him as he nudged the reluctant horse down the easy slope toward the valley below. "Bringing in all the scouts now."

On the far side some of the Fifth Cavalry, riding in the vanguard of the column, were dismounting among the tumble of deadfall at the bottom of a five-hundred-foot bluff. Each soldier was laying claim to a log. While some tied their lariats around the largest trunks and had their mounts begin dragging them up the rugged slope, most simply hoisted the unwieldy logs onto the backs of their horses.

"Look at them crazy sojurs, will you?"

From the left Wesley Merritt came tearing up at a hard lope with two of his aides and a color-bearer beneath the regiment's standard. The headquarters flag snapped and fluttered in the chill east wind as Merritt halted at the bottom of the bluff. Far off, Seamus saw the normally unflappable cavalry commander gesturing like a madman, but could hear only scattered fragments of his angry voice float across the narrow valley on the simpering rise and fall of the wind.

". . . violation of the first principle—"

Almost to a man the troopers dropped their logs together, the rest of the timber spilling to the ground as the lassos came free.

"—of a cavalryman: to care better for his horse than he does anything else!"

The colonel continued to berate his men, forming

them up and getting the troopers back in column for the climb up the far ridge as Grouard reached headquarters and halted among Crook's officers. The Ree pointed back to the east, then a little south of east. Grouard gestured too. Then Crook pointed to the top of the ridge the infantry was ascending.

It was there the command finally halted for the night, the cavalry dismounting and the foot soldiers breaking out of formation to settle wearily to the ground on this picturesque divide between Beaver and Cabin creeks.

"What's Crook got on his mind?" Seamus asked as he rode up to Grouard and Crawford more than a half hour later.

"Irishman—I was wondering if you'd wandered off!" Crawford called with his usual cheerfulness.

"Just taking it easy on the horse," Donegan explained.

The half-breed said, "General's going to camp here for the night."

After glancing at the position of the sun in the sky, Seamus asked, "Why so soon?"

"Crook's sending all of us out to cover a big piece of ground," Crawford explained, "while he keeps his troops here."

Turning to Grouard, Donegan asked, "Saw you head back—sounds like you and the Ree found something ahead."

Morosely, the half-breed shook his head. "That's just what's real strange about it, Irishman—we didn't see a damn thing. Rode more'n ten miles out and didn't find any sign of the trail."

Seamus asked, "You think Crook finally understands what he's been following is a wagon trail and not an Injin trail?"

"Looks like he does now," Crawford replied.

"C'mon, Irishman," Grouard said as he tugged on his reins and turned his tired horse about to lead him through the bivouac. "We're all going out for a little ride."

Patting the neck of the weary animal beneath him, Seamus asked, "How little a ride you got in mind?"

Frank looked back over his shoulder at Donegan, his eyes as dark as they'd ever been as he said, "We're going to stay out until we find a trail Crook can follow. A trail that will lead him right to the Sioux."

Chapter 33

29 August–3 September 1876

Crook and the Indians.

WASHINGTON, August 15—General Sheridan states that he has received a similar report from another direction to that published yesterday, stating that a terrible battle had taken place between Crook and the Sioux and that the latter had been almost annihilated. It was thought to be true at Red Cloud agency, and sent to him from Laramie. Therefore, he says, there seems to be more substance in the squaw's story than was at first considered probable.

From Crook Direct.

CHICAGO, August 15—The *Inter-Ocean's* special correspondent with General Crook, under date of August 4th, sends news later than any received from that command. He gives the following as the strength of Crook's force including that of Merritt: Second cavalry, five companies; third cavalry, ten companies; fifth cavalry, ten companies; fourth infantry, three companies; ninth infantry, three companies; fourteenth infantry, four companies.

The cavalry average about forty-five men to a company, and the infantry forty, or a sum total for the present campaign of 1,400 cavalry, 400 infantry, and 250 Indian scouts—total 2,050. Buffalo Bill comes with the Fifth cavalry as a scout and guide.

"Blessed Mither of God—kill that fire!" Seamus snarled as he dived toward the coals.

It had rained earlier in the morning that Tuesday before Crook halted his column and sent out the scouts, so it wasn't all that easy for the three scouts to find some loose dirt to cover the glowing embers. On either side of the Irishman, Crawford and Grouard were instantly aware of just where the danger lay, all three of them landing on their bellies, guns ready as they peered against the horizon where the night sky would silhouette the intruders Donegan had heard approaching.

High clouds had rolled in at dusk, blotting out most of the stars, and the moon had not yet put in its appearance.

Donegan's chest heaved with apprehension as the first two riders broke the crest of the hill no more than a hundred yards away. A moment later the night sky behind them dippled with another pair. Then four—no, five more. He found himself counting them again, and a third time to be sure. Left to right and right to left. Wondering as he did why the hell they were just sitting there. He couldn't hear them talking, but he was sure that was just what they were doing.

Indians just didn't sit there like that and stare off across the night landscape, not without talking things over.

They began to peel off the horizon slowly, disappearing from the crest of the hill. Coming their way. He could hear the soft clop of their ponies' hooves on the sodden ground and rain-soaked grass. Horsemen moving cautiously now . . . halfway to the scouts, still some fifty yards off . . . when they suddenly drew up. Startled snatches of guttural language reached Donegan's ears.

Four or five of them immediately kicked their ponies into a lope, moving directly for the scouts and the coals of their tiny cookfire. One of the horsemen began hollering out in his tongue.

"By the saints—they've seen our fire, Grouard!"

"Shoot 'em!" Grouard bellowed as he got to his knees, bringing up the Springfield carbine with him, slamming it into his shoulder. "Shoot 'em all!"

Donegan pitched the big Sharps to his left hand and with his right pulled one of the pistols from its holster. To his far side and off to the rear Crawford was already firing his two belt revolvers in succession with a steady hammer as he fell back toward their horses. Those orange-and-yellow muzzle flashes flared into the darkness, hurting Donegan's eyes, blinding him in those frantic moments that the three of them went about their ambush of the enemy.

From the warriors came cries of surprise and pain as the bullets whined among them, accompanied by the slap of lead connecting with flesh and bone, the grunt or whimper of wounded men, and the wolf cry of those who smelled this utter closeness of their white enemies. In seconds bullets began to whistle into the timber behind the scouts. Still he fired, hearing some of the trio's shots thud with the smack of wet putty among the horsemen.

It had taken no more than a minute of their skirmishing before the war party whipped about and beat it for the crest, where Donegan watched the warriors flit over the horizon, retreating out of sight on the far side of the hill.

"We gotta ride," Grouard whispered as he moved past Donegan at a crouch.

Seamus snorted. "So you think we've worn out our welcome, eh?"

"Where's Crawford?" Frank asked suddenly.

Donegan peered into the darkness, trying to make his eyes discern something out of the night after the flare of those muzzle blasts. "Last I saw of him he was off to my left, moving back—like he was making for the horses."

"C'mon—he's probably gone down there ahead of us already."

Sprinting into the timber-covered ravine where the trio had tied their mounts before building their cookfire—the first time they had dared stop all that day—Donegan called out in a loud whisper.

"Crawford!"

Grouard lumbered to a halt beside the Irishman among the horses. Both listened to the silence of the night.

The half-breed called, "Crawford—c'mon out!"

"We gotta ride," Seamus called, watching that hill-crest.

Grouard grumbled, "Yeah. Let's go."

"But we can't leave him here."

The half-breed turned on Donegan, saying, "We got no idea what happened to him. Maybe he run off."

"Or maybe he's shot."

"If he was shot," Frank argued, "we'd found him on our way, wouldn't we?"

"Maybeso," Donegan agreed. "All right—let's give a look for him. Then we can go."

Grouard mounted up and took the lead, easing his horse on up the bottom of the coulee and calling out in his loud whisper.

"Shit!" Grouard suddenly hollered as he yanked back on his reins.

There in the middle of the coulee stood Crawford, suddenly appearing out of the brush and the darkness like a specter.

"You scared the piss out of me!" the half-breed snarled.

"Where'd you go?" Donegan asked as Crawford lunged past them to reach his own horse.

"Come down here to hide," the poet scout replied. "Thought you boys would too. Looked like we was outnumbered. Figured this'd be a good place for us to make a stand against all of them."

"Follow me," Grouard directed as he put his horse in motion following the upper coulee out of the creek valley and onto the prairie. "We got to find out where those warriors come from so we can take the general some good news."

While the Big Horn and Yellowstone Expedition had waited out what remained of the twenty-ninth and through all of the thirtieth in bivouac above the headwaters of Beaver Creek, Grouard and what few scouts Crook had along pushed far to the east. Because of Crook's fear that the hostiles would soon be angling toward the Black Hills settlements, the general had sent the Ree to work their way south of east while Grouard's group eased down the Beaver for some forty miles before angling up toward the Little Missouri River, which would skirt around the east side of Lookout Butte.*

Nearing the river that afternoon of the thirtieth, Grouard had stumbled across a good-sized Indian trail that split itself on the west bank—half crossing over, clearly headed north by east for the headwaters of the Heart River.

"That could be Sitting Bull's bunch," Grouard had said as the three scouts had walked over the ground on the east bank of the Little Missouri.

"You're likely right," Donegan had agreed. "Heading around Terry and making for Canada, aren't they?"

"So where's this other bunch going?" Crawford had asked, pointing off south of east. "This trail that breaks off yonder?"

Donegan had gazed into the distance that dusk and said, "South, Jack. Headed right where Crook feared they would."

At that point it had become abundantly clear they had discovered just what the general needed to know so he could plan the next leg of his chase. Turning about and

---

*Present-day Sentinel Butte.

pointing their noses back toward Beaver Creek, they had finally decided it safe enough to chance cooking some of the bacon from their skimpy rations, maybe even boiling some coffee in their tin cups before pushing on. After tying off their horses in the brush of a wide coulee, the trio had found a place where they figured they could build a tiny fire at the bottom of a pit they dug from the moist soil with their belt knives.

The three had no sooner wolfed down their half-fried salt pork and gulped at the muddy-tasting, alkaline-laced coffee than they were surprised by the war party's approach.

Now as they retreated back across the rolling prairie, it wasn't until the trio had gone more than three miles that Donegan discovered he had left his tin cup behind. Patting his saddlebag to be certain, he suffered his loss in silence. That pint cup was all Crook had allowed an individual for a mess kit. It served many purposes—and now he was without one. The Irishman hoped Quartermaster Bubb had a better supply of tinware than he did of tobacco.

Throughout that cold night they rode with the west wind hard in their faces, not approaching the headwaters of the Beaver until the light of predawn had grayed the horizon behind them. The sun itself was just about to emerge from the bowels of the earth as the trio reached Crook's bivouac and wearily dismounted near the headquarters flag.

"The Rees came in last night at dark," Crook declared as the trio was handed steaming cups of thick, sour-tasting coffee.

"They find anything south?" Grouard asked.

"No," the general answered. "But for what you've told me, it looks like I'll send them out this morning to work south of east."

"Where we come from?" Crawford asked.

Crook wagged his head as he peered over a rumpled map. "No. I want them to work the country on south of the Heart. Toward the headwaters of the streams feeding the Cannonball. Those Rees are fresher, and their ponies should have been recruited overnight. We sat things out yesterday, but we'll move on this morning. I'll have you fellas stay with the column today."

Donegan asked, "You going to march, General?"

"Yes, we will, Irishman. To the south I know we can find provisions."

Lieutenant Colonel Carr asked, "In the Black Hills, General?"

"Yes. Either from Furey's train—if he reaches the Hills in time—or from the settlements themselves. I'm sure of having a place to draw rations."

Captain Anson Mills spoke up. "But what of Fort Lincoln, General? Wouldn't we be closer to Lincoln than we are to the Black Hills?"

Crook stared at the ground for a long moment. "Gentlemen, I figure I've lost the better part of two days already waiting to find out that the hostiles have split in two. When we left the Powder, we were already sure they were east of us. Now we know Terry will have his share of them coming his way, and we're pretty sure the rest are heading south by east. That's the bunch I want to catch before they get to the Hills."

"Perhaps we can herd them in to the agencies, General," Colonel Merritt suggested.

Crook considered that momentarily, then said, "Likely not this bunch, General. I think sooner or later we'll have to fight them rather than follow them."

Donegan knew Crook meant what he said. In all likelihood he wasn't even going to consider heading northeast to reoutfit at Fort Abraham Lincoln: that would put him once more in Terry's department.

No matter where he headed, no matter how many or how few hostiles he chased or caught, George Crook was not about to put himself at the mercy of Alfred H. Terry ever again.

Crook at Last Heard From.

CHICAGO, August 16—Adjutant General Drum has just received a dispatch from Fort Brown, Wyoming, stating that a Shoshone Indian has just come in who left Gen. Crook on the 10th inst., well down on Tongue river. He thought Crook would strike the Indians on the 20th.

Pawnee Scouts.

WASHINGTON, August 18—The commissioner of Indian affairs has given permission to General Sheridan to raise a thousand Pawnee scouts for the Sioux war.

Now they had themselves a trail . . . a trail not all that old, either.

After crossing the Beaver, the Big Horn and Yellowstone Expedition marched east through the badlands for the Little Missouri and the headwaters of the Heart River. With five of the Ree sent to the left of the column's advance, Crook had Grouard and the rest of his white and Indian scouts moving far afield—acting as his eyes and ears to avoid bumping into the enemy as he had back in June. Marching a little east of north down the valley of Beaver Creek, the soldiers were greeted with glimpses of the famous Sentinel Butte off to their right in the distance. Word was passing around, however, that the scouts had discovered their big trail was scattering again, the bands separating to find game where they could until winter forced them back onto the agencies.

Still, there were rare moments of relief, if not moments of small joy. In addition to clearing weather, the general had approved of hunting details to be allowed to work the forward flanks of the column as it continued its march, to bring in deer and antelope and even curious jackrabbits that haunted the countryside—a change of diet the surgeons begged for as they saw a swelling number of patients at sick call every morning. Not just the usual aches and pains, the blisters and the twisted ankles. Now it seemed the cold had begun its sinister ravaging of the command through more and more cases of rheumatism, various neuralgic complaints, and the more serious malarial fevers, not to mention the explosion in cases of scurvy and a debilitating diarrhea, which the whole command suffered, caused by the poor, mineral-laden water.

Even Charles King hadn't been immune to bouts with despair as he hung his cold rump over the damp sagebrush and cursed these streams laced with the foulest salts imaginable. But upon reaching the clear, cold water of the Beaver, all but about fifty cases of diarrhea disappeared during their wait for the return of Grouard's scouts.

Then on the last night of August the playful, capricious weather turned downright cruel. Shifting itself out of the north, the wind gusted through their bivouac as the soldiers tried to hunker down in the coulees and gulches beneath what poor shelter they could find, even if it was their sole blanket, every single blanket beaten to a sodden mess by the wailing storm. Few men slept that night, and everyone moved about stiffly on the first day of September as sergeants passed among the outfits issuing a verbal reveille in the cold coming of dawn.

All the command had left them in their haversacks and saddlebags that morning was four days' rations.

Late in the afternoon, while going into camp along the Beaver, one of Chambers's infantrymen was pulling up sagebrush to make himself a field mattress when he cried out and leaped back, shaking one of his hands as if he were beating a snare drum to a marching tune. Dangling at the end of his thumb clung a young rattlesnake.

A throng of soldiers immediately descended on the hapless victim, some wrestling him down into the sage, others yanking at the snake that had its jaws savagely locked around the end of the man's thumb. With his folding knife one soldier slashed the body from its head and flung it writhing to the ground, then went on to use the blade to pry open the clamped jaws.

Screaming in pain through it all, swearing he was sure to die, the victim was carried between four of his companions across the sage, making for the surgeons' camp. Among the limbs of the fire Julius H. Patzki had just kindled to heat himself some coffee, the doctor laid the blade to his own belt knife, deciding to use the superheated metal to cauterize the puncture wounds. As others held up the unconscious victim, Patzki administered ammonia to rouse the soldier, then held a stiff draught of whiskey beneath his nose. The soldier drank, then drank a second dose of that universal medication for snakebite.

"Whiskey," King groaned at his mess fire that evening. "What I wouldn't give to have the whiskey that man got for his bite."

Eugene Carr snorted, pounding the young lieutenant on the back. "Just as long as you could have your whiskey without having the snakebite to earn it, eh?"

"General," King said, suddenly going serious in that gathering of officers around Carr, "if only you would take the Fifth and go on our own march, we would find and whip the Indians."

"Hear! Hear!" cheered many of the others.

The lieutenant colonel wagged his head dolefully. "To the heart of the truth you've gone, Lieutenant. I'm afraid it's going to be as hard for Crook to find the enemy as it is for Mr. King here to find his whiskey!"

Two days later Grouard brought in four Indian ponies, telling Crook they must have been abandoned by the fleeing camp the general could now be certain knew of the column's presence.

"The closer we come on their backtrail," the scout advised during officers' meeting that evening of 3 September, "we can figure on finding lodgepoles and all kinds of abandoned truck. Like them ponies they left behind."

"And," the Irishman named Donegan added, "when we get close enough—we'll know all of that for certain."

"Would you care to explain, Mr. Donegan?" asked George Crook.

"We'll know because we can figure on having ourselves a little fight with their rear guard as they hurry the women and children off."

Crook grinned, stroking at half of that braided beard of his, his eyes twinkling as he looked about that assembly of officers. "Indeed, nothing would please me more, gentlemen—than to get close enough to have a little scrap of it."

Chapter 34

3–7 September
1876

News From the Front—Crook and
Terry Together and Advancing.

Sᴛ. Pᴀᴜʟ, August 18—Captain Collins, of the Seventeenth infantry, arrived at Bismarck from Fort Buford last night. He fails to confirm the squaw reports of a recent battle between the Indians and Terry's force. Scouts from Terry's column, two days out, arrived at Buford on Monday evening. A courier who arrived at the supply depot at the mouth of the Rosebud on the 11th inst., report that Terry's command met the head of General Crook's command early on the 10th.

Crook's men were following a large Indian trail in the direction of the Powder river. On a short consultation of Generals Terry and Crook, the commands were united and proceeded on the trail Crook was following. The Fifth Infantry was detached from Terry's column and ordered back to the stockade . . . In the meantime Terry will come down upon them with the combined commands, and force a battle. It is not positively known whether the Indians are on Tongue river or Powder river.

True to his word, Crook swung the column directly to the east on the third of September after spending the night in bivouac directly opposite Sentinel Buttes.

Some of the Ree had come in at dusk the night before to report finding a sizable trail heading south from the Yellowstone, which showed the hostiles angling off to the east, all the more proof to convince Crook that his quarry wasn't running north for Canada. But what was most important was the trackers' news that the big trail was splitting again. This time the freshest sign in the country showed that the enemy was heading east.

On that very trail Grouard kept the column marching throughout the third, a Sunday. Later that morning the soldiers passed two burning coal ledges, in all probability ignited by the recent lightning storms. Officers kept their commands moving along quickly through those rugged uplands as Crook grew anxious to reach the Little Missouri, where he was certain the hostiles were heading. Late in the afternoon the general ordered a halt along the clear and narrow Andrews Creek.

Near dusk a handful of the Ree scouts who had been perusing the next day's trail halted two miles from the column to have their supper. They had no sooner started to eat when a dozen horsemen appeared on a nearby ridge and hailed them—asking if they were Sioux. The Ree answered with their army-issue rifles, driving off the war party.

Later that evening, long after moonset, the pickets on the east side of camp fired at a handful of warriors spying on the soldiers, but there was no general alarm. The Sioux had not attempted to run off the hobbled and sidelined stock. Instead of rolling out at the first shots, most of the men stayed huddled beneath their wool coats and thin blankets on the cold ground right on through the rest of that miserable night.

In the morning they awoke to find a thick layer of frost covering those blankets, the sage, and the ground.

At two o'clock on that afternoon of the fourth the column entered a region where the hills continued to rise higher on either side of them until the men eventually emerged from a long and tortuous canyon to reach the Little Missouri, a sullen and muddy river like its larger namesake, near the point Terry and Custer had encamped in May on their way west to the Yellowstone. The grain Terry's soldiers spilled while feeding their horses had already taken volunteer root in the damp soil and, nourished by the constant rains, the cornstalks had grown some ten to twelve feet high, each with four or five ears still in the milk. Since Crook already had the men on half rations, the crop was quickly harvested, the off-yellow ears distributed among the men as far as it would stretch, adding a brief taste of something different to their dwindling food supply.

On that riverbank the infantry once again stripped off everything below their belts, lashing it up in their blankets, which they carried over their shoulders, and marched by units across the ford Grouard's scouts had located for a crossing. On the far side Chambers's shivering foot soldiers needed no urging to fall out and scamper back into their warm clothing.

Once everyone was across and into the timber on the east side, Crook called a halt, allowing the men a chance to pick some of the profusion of bright-red buffalo berries, ripening plums, and crimson-tinged wild cherries that grew up and down both sides of the river. Even the fruit of the ever-present cactus was tried, requiring a man to burn off the spines before peeling back the thick skin so that he could roast the inner pulp. Compared to the berries and half-ripe plums, the men found the cactus fruit tasted like a slimy glue. In the midst of all that eating and celebration, simple joys for a soldier, it began to rain again just before the column resumed its march.

Later that afternoon Donegan heard sporadic gunfire coming from the south of east. It lasted for less than ten minutes. A half hour later the Ree rode in to inform Crook they had themselves a long-range duel with a Sioux war party, claiming they had wounded one warrior and un-horsed another by killing his pony before the enemy scattered.

"The next time I come with Crook," John Finerty complained that evening in camp as he held his cracked brogans near the flames dancing in a chill north wind, "I'll know better to bring along more soap and a couple extra pair of stockings. The general would do well to allow the same for his men."

That night the wind brought on its back another spate of sleet to pelt Crook's encampment. The men sat beneath what brush they could find along the banks of the Little Missouri, huddled out of the storm doing its best to rip their blankets from them. Despite the discovery of the corn and the wild fruit earlier in the afternoon, gloom once more descended over the command. They found themselves with less than two days' rations in the middle of a virtual desert. No one, not even the officers, knew for certain just where they were heading, because Crook kept to his own counsel.

On the following frosty, drizzly morning of the fifth, to the maddening confusion and utter bewilderment of his men, Crook had the scouts take them east from the Little Missouri along Terry's road, away from the Indian trail that pointed south. Out of the canyon they climbed along Davis Creek to reach the divide that led them toward the headwaters of the Heart River, where, after passing between Rosebud Butte and the Camel's Hump, they went into bivouac for the night.

It was dusk when Baptiste Pourier and some of Major Thaddeus Stanton's Ree came in from a day of riding along the column's right flank with a report that they had bumped into a southbound war party and had had themselves a short running fight of it. When Big Bat's horse had given out during their retreat, he'd dismounted and prepared to sell his life dearly. Discovering that Pourier was not among their retreat, Baptiste Garnier had wheeled around with a white scout, "Buckskin Jack" Russell, and both had galloped back to make a stand with Pourier. In a brief but hot skirmish Big Bat spilled one of the Sioux, whose body was plucked from the prairie by his companions before they all disappeared into the thickening fog as the sun fell.

About that same time the fleeing Stanton had decided to turn about and find out for himself where the three scouts had disappeared. Upon reaching the trio, he ordered that the whole group pursue the retreating war party.

"If you wanna go," Big Bat had snarled, "go ahead. I'm not."

When his scouts eventually reached camp that evening, a sour-faced Stanton reported the incident to Crook, ridiculing Pourier for what he claimed was cowardice.

Crook asked, "What have you got to say about it, Bat?"

"That son of a bitch over there deserted me," Big Bat snarled, pointing at Stanton. "My horse was down and done for. And I was all but done for. I rode in here this evening on the back of Russell's horse. So if anyone's the coward—it's that lying bastard there!"

The general turned to the officer, asking, "Major—did you leave Big Bat behind?"

"I didn't know he was in trouble," Stanton replied with a shrug.

"You knew he was soon as I did, because I told you myself," Garnier protested. "You knew when I told you me and Russell was heading back to help him."

Crook glared at Stanton. "Major?"

Stanton could only say, "Yes, sir. I'll grant you that it looks that way—"

"Very well, then," Crook interrupted. "We'll hear no more about Bat's cowardice, Major—unless we want to have fingers pointed all around. What I'm most angry about is that I wasn't immediately informed of the presence of a body of hostiles."

"They slipped off in the fog," Stanton explained.

"Yes, well," Crook said, stroking one tail of his braided beard, "from now on I want to know immediately when any of my command makes any contact with the enemy."

Twilight came, and without the cheery warmth of fires the men gathered in angry knots to argue their wretched lot. Only those officers and enlisted alike who hadn't served very long with Crook expressed some self-satisfied wagering that come morning the command would be turning about and making for the Missouri River posts.

"No," with conviction said those who had fought under Crook in Arizona or Sioux country. "The general won't cash it in until he's made a fight out of this. Not yet he won't turn tail."

Even those old veterans who were the sort to grumble and complain in times of peace and boredom, were now the ones who remained steadfast in the worst of times.

"We oughtn't to give up yet," they reminded those younger, those weaker, those whose mettle had not yet been thrust into the crucible. "None of us can give up on account of a little roughing it, boys. After all, the general's sure as hell not the man to give up himself."

That night at a brief officers' meeting Crook finally did admit that the great enemy gathering had in all likelihood already broken up. And—as if expressing his greatest suspicion and long-held fear—he was certain the Sioux were already making for the Black Hills. Because of that, he told them, they would not be heading for Fort Abraham Lincoln, no more than a hundred miles away and his closest source of supply—a march that would take four days, five at the most.

Nor would he be pointing them north to the Glendive depot Terry had promised to provision on the Yellowstone, a little over a hundred miles off.

"We would lose two weeks' time in both maneuvers," he explained. "A week getting there, and a week getting back to where we are standing right here. Between getting there and coming back, I fear we would lose half our horses."

Instead Crook informed that silent throng they would be turning south for Deadwood—nothing less than seven days and 180 miles away across a piece of ground totally unknown to any of the scouts still with the expedition.

After all, he told them, the fact remained that the freshest Indian trails pointed south.

As Seamus stood at the fringe of those sullen, hungry, and cold men gathered in a steady downpour, he couldn't help but wonder if Crook would get his Big Horn and Yellowstone Expedition out of the wilderness this time. And if he did, at what cost?

If Crook had intended all along to march so far, why had he begun with only fifteen days' rations? Why had he allowed his column to move so slowly? And why had Crook allowed his men so many long halts, which did nothing but whittle away at what dwindling supplies they did have left?

And then it came down to asking the most painful questions of all for a man who had served George Crook since the bloody Sioux campaign begun back in the March snows of the sore-eye moon: Did the general know what he was doing? Did he have a plan? Or was he only floundering, thrashing about—hoping Lady Luck would smile on him?

That Tuesday night Crook wrote Sheridan his first report in a full month, summarizing the expedition's movements to date. Once again the general wrote things as he saw them, or at least as he wanted Sheridan to see them—claiming he had been hot on the trail of the hostile village that had remained intact until very recently:

Camp at head of Heart River, Dak., Ty.,
September 5, 1876

Lieutenant General Sheridan, Chicago, Ill.
. . . My Column followed the trail down
Beaver Creek . . . where the Indians scattered
. . . the separation taking place apparently
about twelve days ago.

I have every reason to believe that all the
hostile Indians left the Big Horn, Tongue, and
Powder River country in the village, the trail of
which we followed . . . With the exception of a
few lodges that had stolen off toward the agencies, there was no change in the size or arrange-
ment of the village until it disintegrated. All
indications show that the hostile Indians were
much straitened for food and that they are now
traveling in small bands, scouring the country for
small game.

In concluding his message Crook asked Sheridan to
speed to Custer City twenty days' rations for his men and
two hundred thousand pounds of grain for his stock, stating he intended to use the settlement as the seat of his
winter operations.

After midnight early on the sixth the Ree scouts rode
out under cover of darkness from that miserable, muddy
bivouac, heading east for Fort Lincoln with their dispatches. Once again Crook was left without Indian guides.
He would have to rely on half-breeds Grouard, Pourier, and
Garnier, along with the white scouts still among them.

Just past six A.M. the infantry sergeants had their men
formed up and shambling off, marching due south for the
nearby Heart River after a breakfast at half rations. No
sugar and salt were left—every last vestige of them had
been washed from the packsaddles by the relentless rains.
Only two days of the sodden hard bread and bacon was left
them. Four days remained of their coffee supply. And that

morning the surgeons put in their plea with the scouts to shoot what game they could for the sake of the sick being hauled along on the bouncing travois in the midst of Moore's mule train. Just as Moore was about to move out his packers, Lieutenant Bubb led some of his men over to Dr. Bennett A. Clements with the last of the quartermaster's luxuries.

"What have you here?" the surgeon asked.

"The last of what I have to offer for your casualties," Bubb explained heroically. "Two cans of jelly, seventy pounds of these white beans, and a half-dozen tins of vegetables."

First thing that morning the men had to cross the rain-swollen Heart River, forced to construct a bridge using the wooden boxes of their ammunition taken from the back of their pack-animals. A torrent of thunderstorm runoff rushed down every wide coulee and narrow ravine as the prairie soil, already soaked from recent days of nonstop rain, flooded beneath them. Even the bright, cheering orb of the sun itself was soon lost behind a thick bank of clouds gathering in that gray, overcast sky. Yet there was enough light that many of the weary men noticed the flashes of signal mirrors from nearby ridges and hilltops. However slow the column moved, however painful their progress, the enemy was watching the soldiers.

Horses plodded, some weaving out of column, refusing or unable to obey their riders any longer. Infantry soldiers dropped out constantly as the screws that attached the soles of their brogans wore into the mushy inner layers and gashed the bottoms of their miserably cold feet. Throughout that long, terrible day the men began to straggle farther and farther out on both flanks, some lagging far to the rear in despair and exhaustion. More than a few horses gave out that Wednesday, and most of the laggards butchered strips of lean red meat from the flanks of the bony animals that had fallen and could not be made to get back onto their legs. For the first time at the rear of that march, men began to chew on the tough, stringy, raw meat, sucking out what nourishment they could. Occasionally a man might dig up a wild onion or an Indian turnip, perhaps even find a few miserable berries clinging to the patchy brush that hugged the narrow water courses. But it made little difference now. The horse-meat march had begun.

After trudging thirty miles over that sodden country in a cold, rainy fog so thick it was difficult to maintain the column's bearing, after crossing both branches of the Cannonball River and stumbling across a cactus-infested desert terrain, the men limped into bivouac at a cluster of small alkaline water holes some six miles south of Rainy Buttes, where they could find no wood to boil their coffee. Those who could get some of the damp grass ignited held twists of it under their tun cups, though most of the soldiers choked down their miserable ration of bacon and hardtack that night with only the milky water in their canteens.

Any man who had been lucky enough to shoot one of the prairie dogs in the many villages the column marched through that day ravenously tore the raw flesh from the tiny bones. Two of Tom Moore's packers had brought down a hawk that afternoon and attempted to cook the meat they hacked from its breast in a tin cup, but the damp grass only smoldered and smoked and turned the water so black they abandoned the soggy meat altogether. Whenever an unlucky jackrabbit wandered close to the bivouac, the soldiers descended on it with lariats, nose bags, and saddle blankets, chasing the creature from all sides until it was run to death.

In the end as twilight fell, every man huddled beneath his thin blanket and turned to cutting the thick gumbo from his boots or shoes with his folding knife, helplessly shuddering in the rain as the wind came up.

As the sun fell out of the low-hanging clouds, creating those few intoxicating moments of light before the orb was lost behind the western horizon, the scouts returned to report having a short skirmish with the Sioux, who apparently were still moving south just ahead of the soldiers.

Near dark Quartermaster Bubb's men issued rations

for the next day. With no bacon left, it was a quarter ration
of coffee and bread. Barely enough to cover the palm of a
soldier's hand, much less fill his belly.

"I just hope we overtake the hostiles in the next day or
so," John Bourke opined in the darkness and misery of that
night. "Have ourselves a fight that would partially compen-
sate us for our privations and sufferings."

"It's the poor creatures of burden that I'm worried
most about, Johnny," Donegan replied. "Gone weeks without good feed, forced to scrounge for grass where the Sioux
haven't burned it off—these animals are starving to death.
One by one, by one."

For the past few days Seamus had remained committed to his horse, although more and more of the men knew
they would likely all be reduced to eating horse meat just to
survive. Like Tom Moore's packers, the Irishman religiously
rubbed bacon grease on the horse's open sores and
wounds, situating the saddle blanket just so in hopes it
would not aggravate the oozy wounds suffered by the bone-
bare creature.

At reveille the next morning word came down from
command headquarters: abandoned horses were to be shot
and butchered for food.

This was nothing short of unthinkable for a horse soldier!

Beneath clearing skies the column stumbled out that
seventh day of September, and in less than an hour all but a
dozen of the cavalrymen had dismounted and were pulling
their reluctant horses along, cajoling, begging, pleading
with the animals to keep moving—just so the troopers
would not find themselves forced to shoot their animals,
the companions they had relied upon for many months.

By afternoon many of the men were collapsing with
the animals beside the trail as rain clouds rumbled back
over the land and released their torrent. At one point the
expedition was stretched out for more than twenty miles.
Every now and then Seamus heard the sodden report of
some soldier's weapon.

He flinched with every gunshot, turning every time to look over his shoulder at the horse plodding on his heels, its hooves caked with gumbo plastered clear to its hocks. On and on Seamus trudged, every fifth step forced to yank on the reins to keep his horse stumbling behind him. Each one of those echoing gunshots killed a little piece of the horse soldier that was Donegan, each bullet ripping through the heart of a horseman.

Along both sides of that march the skeletal soldiers jumped on the animals just shot, skinning back the hide and carving away the warm, juicy meat even before the heart of horse or mule had ceased its beating.

Here and there every few yards sat another man, trooper or foot soldier, his rifle lying in the mud beside him, his head slung disconsolately between his hunched soldiers as the heavens rained down upon them all. Some of the men openly cried as they rolled over onto their sides and curled up into fetal balls, giving in until others, those a bit stronger, came along and hauled their weaker comrades out of the mud. Once pulled up, the most weary and desperate among them dragged their feet through the endless mud, often supported between a pair of comrades, unable to go on without help.

Late that afternoon an Arikara courier rode in to give Crook a dispatch from Terry, reporting that supplies awaited the Big Horn and Yellowstone Expedition at the Glendive cantonment.

The news was too late to do them any good. They had long ago passed the point of no return.

As the head of the column went into camp that afternoon of the seventh, Crook stood guard over a half-dozen wild rosebushes, the hips of which he would allow only Surgeon Clements's sick to use. Lieutenant Bubb had several of the hard-bread boxes broken up and the thin wood distributed through the command to start their pitiful fires.

Yet by some miracle, or by the grace of God Himself, they had slogged through another thirty miles that day. Still, with the coming of dark that Thursday night, the disembodied whispers and grumbling swelled to epidemic proportions. More and more of the men voiced their undeniable despair in the anonymity of that dark night. No longer were they merely questioning their commander. Now they were demanding his head.

"Crook ought to be hanged!" was the call raised in the rainy gloom.

Seamus knew these men were the sort who could stare adversity in the eye, even smile in the face of sudden death if told the reason why. No, it was not the hardship, starvation, and endless toil that brought the expedition to the brink of mutiny—it was the general's tight-lipped silence. Surely, his soldiers told one another, Crook has no idea what he is doing, no idea what to do to save them.

They had reached the bitter end . . . and the general's only choice was to provision his men from the Black Hills settlements.

As night squeezed down on the land and the stragglers continued to lumber in from the miles upon miles of barren landscape littered with the carcasses of dead horses and mules, George Crook sent John Bourke to fetch Captain Anson Mills.

Seamus had a good idea what was afoot.

He prayed he would be allowed to go.

Chapter 35

7 September 1876

Wyoming
Indian Campaign Over.

CHEYENNE, August 26—From all indications on the movements of the hostiles it appears Generals Crook and Terry will be unsuccessful and the troops will probably return to the mouth of the Tongue river on the 25th inst. The command will then refit for another dash, which it is hoped will be more successful . . .

Thus the campaign will be extended late in the season, and if necessary resumed early in the spring. It is thought sufficient supplies can be forwarded for the troops before winter sets in. The fall campaign will be full of hardships, but not so dangerous as another season's murderous work . . .

A still later dispatch, dated August 23, says Crook and Terry, after following the trail discovered on the 12th, moved thirty-six miles down the Rosebud. The northern trail was abandoned on the 14th, and the command pursued the southern trail, crossed Tongue river to Goose creek, thence returned to Powder river and followed it to its mouth, which they reached on the night of the 18th, where they went into camp and will remain until the 24th. The wagon train and all the supplies at the mouth of the Tongue river are being shipped to the mouth of Powder river . . .

The Indian trail diverged from the east bank of Powder river about twenty miles from its mouth south toward the Little Missouri, whence the command will follow speedily. The entire command is short of supplies, and unless otherwise ordered Terry will march such as are not needed to Fort Lincoln. Crook's command will scout toward the Black Hills and via Fetterman. Crook and Terry both think it is too late for extending field operations. The Indians on the southern trail are believed to be moving toward the agencies . . . The campaign is therefore practically closed, unless further instructions come from the lieutenant general.

After delivering General Alfred Terry's messages to Lieutenant Colonel Whistler of the Fifth Infantry, Bill Cody waited with the steamers *Josephine* and *Carroll* on the Yellowstone. In leaving Crook's column behind farther up the Powder on the twenty-sixth, Terry's men reached the Yellowstone the following day, then used the two steamboats to transfer all personnel and equipage to the north bank.

That evening the general asked Cody to guide a selected force on a scout to the north. The following morning of the twenty-eighth they set out for the Big Dry Fork of the Missouri and in the next two days began to run across fresh sign that the Indians had been hunting buffalo north of the Yellowstone. Always the cautious one, Terry determined that Miles or First Lieutenant Edmund Rice at the Glendive cantonment, eighty miles away, should be alerted to the discovery. Cody volunteered to make the ride, start-

ing at ten o'clock on the soupy night of the thirtieth,
plunging through the dark across a piece of country he had
never crossed before.

At daybreak, after putting only thirty-five of the eighty
miles behind him, Cody decided to wait out the day in
hiding because of the wide stretches of open prairie that lay
before him. Tying his horse in the brush of a steep-walled
ravine, he curled up on his arm and went to sleep.

The sun was high when he was suddenly awakened by
the thundering of the ground beneath him. Crawling to the
mouth of the ravine, he saw a herd of buffalo charging past
on the prairie just beyond where he lay, the lumbering
animals raising clods from the wet prairie—pursued by at
least thirty warriors armed with rifles.

Quickly he turned back into the ravine and hurried to
his horse, throwing blanket and saddle onto its back, prepared to take flight should he be discovered—but as luck
would have it, the hunters were too involved with their
buffalo and hadn't paid any notice to Cody's trail crossing
the prairie. In less than ten minutes they circled back, dismounting not far from the mouth of the coulee where he
sat in hiding to claim their animals and begin butchering
for meat, tongues, and hides. With these loaded onto some
extra horses Bill swore had to be cavalry mounts, the Sioux
rode off to the southeast.

Damn. Just the direction he had been taking to reach
the mouth of Glendive Creek.

With the coming of that night, and not having seen
another sign of the hunters, Bill felt secure enough to slip
out of the ravine. This night he pushed due east, making
as wide a detour as he felt he could to avoid a brush with
the warriors or their village, wherever it might be to the
southeast. The sun was coming up as Cody rode up to
the stockade and hollered out that he had dispatches for
Rice.

Over a cup of coffee and some fried beef, Bill told the
soldiers all about the happenings upriver. Then Rice told
Cody he wanted to get a message to Terry as well—to in-

form the general that his stockade was suffering daily attacks and harassment from the Sioux in the immediate area. On his third cup of coffee Cody volunteered to follow his backtrail to Terry's command, which he expected to have returned to the Yellowstone from its foray to the north.

Without incident Bill headed west, running into the column east of the Powder, when he turned around to guide Terry's entire command back to Glendive. Three days later a steamboat put in at the stockade. Cody realized it was high time to go.

"One hundred eighty . . . and two hundred dollars," said Captain H. J. Nowlan of the Seventh Cavalry, acting assistant quartermaster for General Terry. "That should be all your pay, Mr. Cody."

"Thank you, Captain."

The officer saluted, then held out his hand. "Believe me, the pleasure is all mine, Colonel Cody! General Terry is awaiting you at the gangplank."

Sure enough, Terry stood waiting with most of his staff and that gaggle of reporters in the midst of a great crowd of onlookers as Cody prepared to shove off downriver, this time for good.

After a round of shaking hands and good wishes, Bill finally climbed the cleated gangplank to the lower deck of the *Far West* and shook hands with Captain Grant Marsh. Overhead pilot Dave Campbell hung from the window of his wheelhouse surrounded by iron plate and hollered down.

"Good to have you aboard again, Mr. Cody!"

"Good to be onboard, Mr. Campbell!" Bill replied, taking his hat from his head and waving it at the pilot. "How 'bout this time we really do get me down the Yellowstone?"

"Let's cast off!" Campbell roared, pulling on his steam whistle three times.

The stevedores on deck hollered at the soldiers on

shore to heave them the weighty hawsers while the pilot hollered down the pipe to his engine room, then stuck his head out the window once again.

"You're headed home now, Mr. Cody! Ain't a thing going to turn us around again!"

Along the bank that sixth day of September the soldiers whipped themselves into a frenzy, bidding the scout and showman farewell from the Indian wars.

For the last two weeks serving with General Terry's command, Bill had earned two hundred dollars—the most he had ever been paid for scouting. Not that he didn't deserve it, mind you. Why, he had been in the saddle almost constantly, pushing through foreign country filled with hostiles day in and day out. But as good as it was, it still wasn't the sort of pay he figured he could make once he got back east again.

Cody watched the bluffs of the Yellowstone fall away behind him. Ahead lay Lulu and the children. And a future of his own making.

William F. Cody had made his last ride as an army scout.

Indian Matters.

CHEYENNE, August 31—A courier who left the camp of Crook and Terry on the 20th, at the mouth of Powder river, arrived at Fort Fetterman to-night. The command was then on the trail which was estimated at 10,000 ponies. The camp fires indicate seven distinct bands. There is reason to believe that the Indians are almost destitute of food, and traces left in the deserted camps indicate that they are reduced to the extremity of using raw hides for food. All the Snake allies have gone home, the Crows remaining. General Crook fully expects to strike Sitting Bull in a few days.

*   *   *

Despite the condition of his horse, Donegan knew he had to go with Mills. He had to do something more than march along in that column of half-dead men and all-but-dead animals another day.

Late in the afternoon of the seventh of September, Crook had halted them on the banks of the Palanata Wakpa, the white man's Grand River. At dusk the general called an officers' meeting and told the men what he had decided.

In the hearing of all, Lieutenant John Bourke read the general's concise orders to the Third Cavalry's Anson Mills: "The brigadier general commanding directs you to proceed without delay to Deadwood City and such other points in the Black Hills as may be necessary and purchase such supplies as may be needed for the use of this command, paying for the same at the lowest market rates. You are also authorized to purchase two ounces of quinine, for use of the sick."

"I discussed my plan with General Merritt and Colonel Royall before calling Colonel Mills in to inform him," Crook explained. "Immediately following this conference Mills will come among the commands and select the fifteen healthiest men from each of the ten troops of the Third Cavalry. Every company commander is to make available to the colonel his fifteen strongest horses as well. Make no mistake on this, gentlemen. Mills's relief column must be mounted on the best we have left us."

"What's to be done with the rest of us, General?" arose a question.

"We will remain in bivouac tomorrow, and the following day we will take the command on Mills's trail as he hurries south with Quartermaster Bubb."

A captain asked, "We're going to continue marching after only one day of rest, General?"

And a lieutenant chimed in, "Why not sit it out until Mills returns, sir?"

"We could do that: just sit down here and wait,"

Crook replied. "But if we keep moving south, our men will be that much closer to relief when Mills brings supplies back from the Deadwood merchants."

"How's Mr. Bubb going to bring the provisions back?"

"Good question," Crook answered. "I've already told Tom Moore he's to select fifty of what he has left of his mules, along with fifteen packers, to accompany Colonel Mills to the south."

Crook went on to explain the command structure of the relief expedition: with scouts Grouard, Crawford, and Donegan he was sending along Lieutenant Frederick Schwatka, who would act as Mills's adjutant, as well as Lieutenants George F. Chase, Emmet Crawford, and Adolphus H. Von Leuttwitz, with assistant surgeon Charles R. Stephens. In addition, both Robert Strahorn and Reuben Davenport volunteered to go along. Mills's relief patrol was to depart that evening as soon as the men and horses were selected.

As far as Seamus Donegan was concerned, Crook had to be given credit. Unlike most of those armchair generals who had commanded the Union's armies during the early years of the war, George C. Crook had always suffered no less than the greenest recruit in his command.

As much as other, lesser men might snipe and find fault in the general's decisions, for the most part the Irishman believed Crook had done what he thought best. The general had marched and countermarched his expeditionary force on just about every trail he came across after the fleeing hostiles.

He had put his men on half rations, then reluctantly approved of butchering the horses.

And without fail Crook had always deployed his scouts to prowl in all directions to scare up a fresh trail for his men to pursue.

But now, to look at the man, Seamus knew even Crook was close to the end of his string. This was no longer an army campaign. This was no longer a matter of catching the enemy and driving them back to the agencies.

This had become nothing less than pure survival.

Another Trail Discovered.

ST. PAUL, September 4—A special dated bank of the Yellowstone, August 27, via Bismarck, 4th inst., says: The latest intelligence received concerning the movements of the Indians lead to the belief that Sitting Bull's band of Unkpapas are trying to cross the Yellowstone and reach their proper hunting ground on the dry fork of the Missouri. Acting upon this belief General Terry directed General Crook, with his column, to move eastward to the Little Missouri, following the trail leading from the Rosebud, while General Terry with the Dakota column has crossed the Yellowstone and marched north and east to cut off any parties moving toward Fort Peck. You will hear no end of extravagant stories about the attack on the steamer *Yellowstone* on her late trip up the river. She was fired on by a few Indians, and one man was killed, but beyond this no harm was done, and the affair is quite destitute of significance.

Just past nine o'clock that night of September 7, Crook emerged from the dark to grip the bridle to Anson Mills's horse as the captain rose to the saddle. For a moment the general peered into the rain, then turned back to the captain, saying, "Should you encounter a village, Colonel— you are to attack and hold it. But if you can successfully cut around their village, do so—for you must remember your primary mission is to secure supplies for this column."

Atop his saddle, Mills saluted. "Very good, General."

Crook replied, "We'll be watching for your guidon, Colonel Mills. Praying. Until then."

Donegan watched the old man back away, his shoulders rounded almost like a man who had been beaten, a man close to his last wick. Then the general slowly raised those shoulders, straightened his back, and squared the shapeless hat on his head before touching the fingers of his right hand to his brow.

"I know you'll do us proud, men," Crook told those 150 gathered behind Mills and his scouts. "We're counting on you."

The captain saluted, then tugged down the brim of his hat, cocking his head to the side to ward off the drizzle as he raised an arm in signal.

"At a walk!" Schwatka gave the order. "For-rad!"

Tom Moore's packers ended up whipping sixty-one mules out of that misery-ridden bivouac on a small, northern branch of the North Fork of the Grand River. Desiring his party to travel in the lightest of marching orders, Mills had commanded his men to strip even more—they were to carry no more than fifty cartridges each for their Springfield carbines—half of what they had been carrying a month ago when they had marched out of Camp Cloud Peak on Goose Creek. Seamus worried: with all they had seen over the past few days, the chances were good the captain's outfit would run into a sizable war party. That very afternoon, in fact, they had stumbled across the wide trail of a big village moving south for the Black Hills.

So if the soldiers did have a scrap of it, would they have enough ammunition? Crook had made it clear that he intended to lay over a day right where the column was. Scary thing was that should Mills run into the enemy, the general's decision to give the column a day's rest meant the captain could expect neither reinforcements nor resupply of ammunition in time to do any real good.

As Donegan rode to the front with Frank Grouard to pierce the utter gloom and darkness of that muddy wilderness, leading Mills and 150 troopers into the unknown, the Irishman felt all but crushed by the sudden realization.

From here on out, they were on their own.

Chapter 36

8–9 September
1876

The *Inter-Ocean* Special.

CHICAGO, September 4—The *Inter-Ocean's* Bismarck special says the latest by couriers arriving to-day from the expedition is as follows: the general feeling among both officers and men is that the campaign has been and is likely to prove an immense wild goose chase. No Indians have been seen of late, with the exception of occasional small bands making their appearance for the purpose of stealing or harassing small parties engaged in the movement of supplies on the Yellowstone. The main column has not succeeded in overtaking slippery Sitting Bull, and is not likely to this season . . .

August 27 the Seventh cavalry were on Ofalens creek, and Crook had started the day before with his command for Glendive creek . . . Crook strikes down the south bank, and by this continued movement they expect to bring about a colli-

sion with the Indians who are along the banks of
the river.

The dark and the rain were as suffocating as being inside
a pair of these leather gloves he wore.

Like the lid to a well-scorched cast-iron Dutch oven,
the sky seemed to hang above them, right overhead, all but
a few inches beyond a man's reach.

This endless wilderness swallowed every fragment of
sound but his own. The jingle of the big curb bit. The
squishy squeak of the saddle beneath him, the bobbing,
plodding heave of the horse as it struggled on step by step
with the rest that followed, and that peculiar sucking, wet-
putty pop each time the animal pulled a hoof out of the
muddy gumbo and plopped it down onto the prairie again,
and again. And again over the next three hours.

Off to their left a little, the prairie sounds changed
near midnight. If a man listened just right, he could tell
that something out there was different. Not the same monotonous rhythm of the rain hammering the sodden prairie. Frank had Donegan signal back to Mills, stopping the
long column. Then Grouard slipped down into the mud
and knelt. A moment later a bright corona around the half-
breed flared with sudden light as the head scout struck a
match, holding it cupped in both hands.

In the halo of that light glittered the reflection of a
large pond of water. It was the patter of the heavy rain
striking its surface that had been just that much different
from the sound of rain hammering the prairie's sodden
surface. Frank crabbed left, then right, until he flicked the
burned match into the pond and the whole world was dark
once more.

"You saw something," Donegan said as Grouard
emerged from the drizzle.

Climbing into the saddle, Frank said, "Tracks, Irishman. Lots of tracks."

"What's that you say, Grouard?"

They turned back to find Mills inching forward. The

half-breed said, "Tracks, Colonel. Travois. Ponies. Lots of fresh tracks." He pointed. "Going south."

"Won't be good to bump right into them in this dark. Damnable rain," Mills grumped.

"No good, we go and do that," Frank replied.

"Grouard—I want you to ride farther ahead of us. I need you to give us plenty of time to react if you bump into anything. Put Crawford and Donegan out a little wider on both flanks."

Donegan said, "Hard for us to see the column, Colonel."

"You'll just have to do the best you can," Mills argued. "I don't want to be surprised by a bloody thing."

Grouard watched Crawford and Donegan move off into the gloom, then turned about to take up the front of the march. "Wait five minutes, then lead them out, Colonel."

"Very well," Mills replied.

Grouard disappeared into the midnight rain and darkness.

For another two hours they probed ahead. And for all their trouble the rain only fell harder and the night grew darker. After eighteen grueling miles feeling their way to the south along the Indian trail, Mills called a halt at the edge of a shallow ravine.

"Stay with your mounts," was the order passed back through the command. "Sleep if you can on your lariats—until daylight."

The sergeants nudged them awake at four A.M. on the eighth, rousting them from the cold, muddy ground, driving the men from their soggy blankets. After tightening cinches, shoving the huge curb bits back into the horses' jaws, and pulling up the picket pins to be stowed in a saddlebag with the lariat, Mills had his patrol on the march again—without a thing to put in their bellies.

No matter, there wasn't that much to eat, anyway.

On they tramped into the gray coming of that overcast morning as the rain slackened, then drifted off to the east.

The sky was gray and black above them. The prairie beneath the bellies of their horses was pretty much the same color, and what small pools of water had collected here and there reflected the monotonous color of the dreary sky overhead.

From the horizon far beyond them emerged some high ground, pale in color, easily visible from a distance. Those buttes were like a beacon in what dim light the jealous clouds permitted the sun to cast upon this rolling land.

It wasn't long before the fog rolled in, first forming in the low places, down in the coulees. Then like a growing thing it crawled up to take over the prairie itself. Becoming thicker all the time, like Mother Donegan's blood soup coming to a boil on the trivet she would swing over the hearth in their tiny stone house back on that miserable and humble plot of ground where his father had died trying to grow enough to feed a family.

By seven o'clock Grouard had the soldiers skirting to the east of the northern end of a long and narrow landform that would one day soon be known as Slim Buttes. When he found a brushy ravine filled with plum trees, their branches heavy with fruit, the half-breed suggested a halt. Eagerly the men attacked the brush, stuffing the shiny, rain-washed plums into their mouths with one hand as the other hand pulled more off the branches.

An hour later Mills had them back in the saddle and inching off again through the soupy fog. Uneasily they probed south until noon, when the captain called another halt. This time Grouard brought them into the lee of a low bluff, protected from view to the east, from the prairie. On some good grass the horses were allowed to graze at the end of their picket pins and lassos. Then Mills allowed the men to gather some wood, dig fire pits, and boil some coffee in their tin cups. By one o'clock they were back in the saddle, Lieutenant Emmet Crawford's battalion taking the lead, something warm now in all their bellies to go with the wild plums they had enjoyed for breakfast earlier.

Having had nothing to eat since leaving Crook's column, the men knew the plums and coffee were better than nothing at all. Fear is always a poor feast for an empty stomach.

Just past three o'clock, not long after the thickest of the fog lifted, Seamus watched Frank Grouard reappear at the top of a rise more than a mile ahead of the column. Expecting Frank once more to do as he had been doing most of the day, checking on the column's advance as he kept far in the lead, turning around after a moment to disappear again over the hilltop, Donegan was surprised this time when the half-breed rode back toward the column, at a gallop.

Off on the far left flank Jack Crawford had seen Grouard too and was loping back toward the van of Mills's column.

"C'mon, ol' boy. Time to find out what's got Frank so spooked he's willing to kill his horse to tell about it."

The half-breed was already telling his story to Mills and his officers by the time Donegan got near enough to hear snatches of the tale.

". . . ridge yonder . . . some three miles."

Grouard was pointing. Time and again he turned in the saddle, pointing toward the Buttes that they had been skirting to the east ever since morning.

"Herd of ponies. Forty. Maybe a few more."

"Sioux?"

By now Seamus picked up all of Frank's answer. "Chances are good, Colonel. That's who we been following, ain't we?"

"You see anything of a village?"

Donegan came to a halt in that knot of horsemen as Grouard replied, "A small one. Down in a little bowl made by a ravine that cuts down from the bluffs. Think the Sioux call it Rabbit Lip Creek."

Glancing at the western sky and the aging of the day, the captain asked his head scout, "Can we take them at dawn?"

Grouard nodded. "Only time to do it. I saw hunters

south of their camp. Coming in with game. Might be other camps nearby."

The captain licked his lips, then grumbled, "Don't doubt they've found game. Red bastards been running off everything in this country." Then Mills stood in the stirrups, peering off to the east. "Crawford," he said, flinging his voice to the scout, "did you pass anything back on your side of the column what might conceal the command for a few hours?"

"Yes, sir, Colonel," Jack Crawford answered. "I can show you a place where we can lay in for a while."

"Lead us there," and Mills turned to his lieutenants. "Gentlemen, have the command follow that scout into hiding. We'll discuss our options once we're sure we haven't been discovered."

"Options?" Lieutenant Schwatka asked.

"Yes," Mills replied. "Whether or not to attack."

"I thought our primary mission was to secure food for the column, Colonel," said George F. Chase.

Mills's brow knitted in consternation and he said, "Just take your men into hiding, Lieutenant."

Behind a low ridge northeast of the enemy village, with his troops concealed and pickets posted to guard against their discovery, Mills put the question up for discussion. About half of the officers and noncoms urged caution, voicing concern for attacking an enemy village of unknown strength, while the other half cheered for an immediate attack.

"It's time we finally got in our licks," added Adolphus Von Leuttwitz.

"But do we know just what we're charging into?" asked Emmet Crawford.

"Sure as hell Custer didn't," Chase groaned.

Bubb said, "Colonel Mills, as your second in command, I suggest we send word back to General Crook immediately, before we pitch into anything."

"Request denied, Lieutenant," Mills snapped, clearly tiring of the debate. "I'm sure you will all remember certain Academy courses in military strategy—even in philosophy—that teach just how often success, even victory, rests upon a man making his own luck, taking what advantages there are and striking quickly."

"Besides," Von Leuttwitz said, "we all know the Indians won't stand and fight. They'll scatter before a vigorous cavalry charge."

Then Mills added, "I want you all to remember that we might do what some of you suggest and make a wide detour of that village—only to find that tomorrow some hunting party discovers our tracks and sets out in pursuit of our tired horses. No, I say—this is our chance to seize the advantage."

After a spirited argument of it, Mills finally called an end to the discussion and told his officers he had decided they would retire a safe distance, and there the command would wait out Grouard's scout of the village.

"And if it will make you all feel better, I'll go with Grouard myself to determine the makeup of the village," Mills explained, quieting the murmured clamor. "How many lodges and wickiups, how many warriors might be in there." He looked at the half-breed. "We'll find out what we're facing."

He then ordered Crawford and Donegan to lead the soldiers to the rear and hide themselves in a brushy ravine 150 feet deep with a narrow stream running through the bottom.

At twilight Donegan settled into the soggy mud beside Mills. "Colonel, you figure we ought to send a rider back to alert Crook that you've run onto a village?"

Mills turned as if smarting at the question. "I'll know that answer as soon as I return from making a reconnaissance with Grouard, Mr. Donegan."

"Didn't mean to rile you, Colonel. But the both of us can remember what we pitched into over on the Powder River last winter, remember how we expected reinforcements to show up from the rear—"

"My memory isn't faulty, Mr. Donegan," Mills

snapped, getting to his feet. "This, I assure you, is nothing like that. Our situation is that Crook remains far behind, and unavailable for support."

"But if we give him a chance to know what we're pitching into, maybe we could hold off till he could get here."

"I'll trust you to keep your nervous worries to yourself, Mr. Donegan—and leave the military planning to me. Your anxiety has already infected Lieutenant Bubb. Now, if you'll excuse me, I figure it's dark enough to reconnoiter the enemy's stronghold."

Seamus watched the captain move off through the soldiers, who dozed or talked in small groups, smoking their pipes and boiling their coffee over small fires ignited at the bottom of pits. A crumb of hard bread and a scrap of bacon broiled on a stick would have to do while some of the packers boiled down a soup of pork grease and a few handfuls of flour.

Seamus decided he would save what little he had left—certain there would be wounded. At times like this—with the waiting and the unknown and the dread—if a man only thought of someone else, he could feel the presence of something bigger than himself.

Refusing to listen to the growl of his aching stomach, he tried to sleep but only dozed, part of him painfully aware of every new sound in the misty night. Sometime later he made out Grouard's voice. Donegan went over to hear the half-breed's report on the layout of the village.

"You went in by yourself and just walked back out with them two ponies?" Seamus asked after Mills had turned aside to organize his lieutenants for the attack. Grouard held the leads to a pair of Indian horses—one a beautiful pinto, the other a sleek black stallion.

"I told the colonel the village might be too big for us. Then he said he didn't take me for a coward."

Donegan asked, "Too big—how many lodges?"

Looking away, Grouard answered, "Maybe forty, forty-five lodges."

Seamus studied the half-breed. "We can take 'em, can't we, Frank?"

"I went in there, didn't I?"

"That should prove to Mills you aren't a coward."

"Told him the both of us couldn't go no closer together. He smells like a white man. And the dogs was likely to start barking."

"But you didn't answer me straight, Frank: we gonna be able to take that village?"

When the scout did not reply as he continued to stroke the muzzle of the black pony, Seamus said, "How'd you get your spoils of battle?"

Grouard shrugged. "I lived with the Lakota before. I can look Injun."

"Good for you, Frank. Besides, the warrior those ponies belonged to won't be needing them pretty soon anyway, right?"

"Injuns don't need good horses like these—right."

"But you're a damn fool to take that chance of getting caught, and getting these sojurs killed with you."

Grouard glared at Donegan. "Didn't ever know you to get so worried about a little danger before, Irishman."

"Maybe you're right—just say I'm getting nervous in my old age," Seamus replied. "This a bunch you know?"

Now he wagged his head. "Didn't see a thing I recognized. Maybeso they're Sans Arc. Maybe Miniconjou or Burnt Thigh—the Brule. Nobody I know in there."

Donegan said, "You be sure to come get me when Mills is ready to go in."

Grouard nodded and moved off with his two new Sioux ponies.

Trudging back to his clump of buffalo-berry brush he shared with Crawford, Donegan glanced at the clouds suspended low overhead. They seemed to hang just beyond the reach of his fingertips. Even in their grayness the clouds reflected the orange dance of the crimson-titted fires buried in their tiny pits. For a moment he stopped and peered off to the southwest, in the direction of that long ridge of buttes, wondering if the hostiles were paying attention to the night sky, hoping they would not notice the far-off glow reflected from so many soldier fires.

Then he tugged his hat brim down and set off again through the rain, hoping the foul weather would keep the Indians in their lodges. Praying.

When he reached the brush, Seamus pulled his collar up around his neck and sank back to the ground, leaning against the wet saddle and closing his eyes, tried for some sleep. Instead of peace he dreamed fitfully on Samantha. Finding her calling him out there in the fog, her voice edged with worry. He could not find her, no matter how hard he tried—going this way, then that, as he plunged madly through the soupy fog and driving rain.

She kept calling to him, never coming any closer. He suddenly shuddered in the cold, awakening himself.

In the darkness he crossed himself, thinking on these starving, worn-out men and animals. Their horses were covered with oozing sores, and what the men had left of their uniforms was now little more than wet rags that clung to their skeletal frames as they shivered in the cold. Some wiped their gun barrels to kill time, or polished their meager supply of cartridges to make the sleepless hours pass.

Sometime before midnight some of Moore's mules tried to stampede but were kept from escaping by the horse guard. A while later at a clap of nearby thunder some of the cavalry mounts did make a break for freedom, but the troopers rounded them up and brought the horses back, once more driving the picket pins into the soggy ground that simply had no hope of holding those iron stakes secure.

They were a good bunch, Seamus decided. When these men should have been filled with nothing greater than fear at their own survival, nothing greater than despair—most had rallied at the prospect of getting in their blows, their spirits raised at this chance to even the score for the frustrating stalemate on the Rosebud, for Custer's disaster on the Little Bighorn.

With nothing in their bellies they would be going into battle.

So it was the Irishman crossed himself and started mouthing the words that came back to him despite all the intervening years. Words taught him long, long ago by that village priest back in County Kilkenny. The sort of catechism one never forgot. Here on the brink of battle asking God to watch over and protect, to hold him in the Almighty's hand.

After all these years wherein he had never darkened the door of a church—to discover that he was still steeped in that faith a fighting man never really lost.

Chapter 37

8–9 September
1876

I f John Bourke had learned anything at all during his years
with George Crook, it was that the general could surprise
his men with a sudden change of his mind.

And he did just that at dawn on the morning of the
eighth.

It was raining again, raining still. With every man in
that bivouac expecting that they would be laying over for
the day, just as Crook had promised, no one saw much
sense in getting up and moving about. The news shot
through their forlorn camp like a galvanic shock wave.

"Boots and saddles, boys!" the old sergeants bellowed.

One of those most surprised growled, "What the hell
for?"

"What for, you ask?" sneered an old file. "Why, the
general's issued marching orders, me fine young fellers. So
you'll be dancing a merry tune soon enough, you will."

Crook did indeed have them up and out of the mud,
and marching off that Friday morning—the general's very
own forty-eighth birthday. It hadn't taken long for the men
to finish what crumbs of hard bread they could scrape from

the bottom of their packs and haversacks, richer yet if they still possessed a sliver of the rancid bacon tucked away in one of their pockets. All most could do for themselves was to carve a stringy steak from one of the nearby carcasses. And if a half dozen of them could scrape together enough for a shared cup of coffee, they felt all the more royal for it —even close to human as the infantry set out on the flanks of the plodding cavalry, moving across that inland sea of mud and fog, wispy sheets of rain driven on the back of a biting wind.

No matter what was on the menu that morning, it had been more of the milky, bitter water for all, and a matter of tightening one's belt another notch.

After no more than an hour the gaunt animals again began to falter, and the troopers went afoot. On either side of the straggling cavalry, foot soldiers plodded by in their gummy brogans, as cheerful as any man could be, calling out to their comrades in the cavalry.

"Say, yez boys! You want us give you a tow!"

"Yeah," cried another footslogger, "for a small fee, why—we'll be happy to tow you and your bag-of-bones horse there all the way to the Black Hills!"

For most of that morning the horse soldiers struggled to keep their animals going. But by noon the shooting began once more, and soon the backtrail was littered with carcasses, the bony dead over which the men clustered like predatory scarecrows, like flocks of robber jays, each with his own knife, hacking free a choice flank steak he would suck and chew on as he trudged forward in the wake of George Crook, doggedly making for the Black Hills.

They put twenty-four miles behind them that day, through the fog, across the muddy wilderness, dragging their weapons and what horses did not fall, what carcasses were not left behind to mark the passing of the Big Horn and Yellowstone Expedition. That day at least the wind pummeled them from behind—not straight into their faces.

When the advance reached a tributary of the South

Fork of the Grand River, they went into camp. It was a blessing to find that here there was wood, albeit wet wood. But the first firewood they had run across in something on the order of ninety miles. In no time hundreds of smoky fires smudged the twilit sky as the commissary officers selected the three poorest animals from each company to be shot, butchered, and fed to the men. For tonight Crook's soldiers would not have to haunt the backtrail like thieves and shammers, butchering the fallen horses for the best steaks after the column had marched on.

Horse tenderloin wasn't on the menu for Surgeon Clements's sick cases that evening. At sundown the scouts brought in five antelope. There were plenty of plums as well as bullberries to be found with a little hunting along the banks.

Once some of the deadfall in that riverside camp began to dry out near the fires despite the continuing rains, and once the men started cooking their stringy meat on the end of sharpened tree limbs, John Bourke saw the spirits of most lift a few notches. He had never thought he would see morale sink as low as it had the past two days. What more they would have to face before Mills got back from Deadwood, he dared not consider.

For most it was impossible to sleep again that night, forced to hunker close to the fires they would keep feeding with damp, smoky wood until dawn. Amazing, John thought sometime after ten o'clock that night, how a little warmth could give a man a bit of pluck.

"Happy birthday, General!"

Coming up out of the dark was Wesley Merritt, along with Eugene Carr and William Royall, Alexander Chambers and ten more battalion officers.

"Gentlemen," Crook called out. "Come in out of the rain."

Bourke and the general scooted shoulder to shoulder to allow the others room under the overhanging shelf of rock they had located along the riverbank.

"No birthday feast tonight, General?" Carr asked with a great smile.

"No, but a man won't have a problem quenching his thirst!" Crook roared.

"I'm a hippophagist at last!" Carr said, then rocked with laughter.

"What's that, sir?" Bourke asked. "I've never heard the term."

"It means he eats horses," Merritt answered grimly.

Carr nodded and said, "I've become a real connoisseur."

"I expect we won't have to eat our horses too much longer," Crook explained. "If our scouts are correct in the distance remaining to Deadwood City, we should expect to meet Bubb's pack-train coming back sometime on the eleventh."

Royall said, "Tonight let's just be thankful we found some wood for the men."

"That truly is a blessing," Crook replied as he stuffed a hand inside his worn wool coat to pull out a sixteen-ounce German silver flask.

"Is . . . is that what I think it is, General?" Carr asked, flushed with anticipation.

Twisting loose the cap, Crook held it beneath his nose, then said, "Yes, gentlemen. A man's due on his birthday, don't you think? Especially when he's celebrated as many birthdays as I have."

"I'm afraid I forgot my cup," Royall whined.

"No matter," Crook cheered. "We'll pass the flask until it's empty!"

"Hear, hear!" some of them cried as Crook put the flask to his lips and drank.

"A happy birthday to you again, General!" Merritt added when he was handed the flask.

"And a joyful round of thanks for sharing your liquor with us!" Carr said. "You've been keeping this quite a secret, eh?"

"I knew there'd come a day to celebrate," Crook replied. "If I hadn't caught the Sioux by the time my birthday rolled around, then I figured I'd have myself one happy little celebration anyway."

Sitting there that night in the glow of the firelight reflected from the rock shelf, watching the warmth flickering on those beaming faces, John again marveled at George Crook. He willingly suffered everything the most common soldier suffered. He ate no better, slept no warmer. Perhaps because he had never considered himself above the privations he asked of his men, General Crook never failed to silence most all the criticism leveled at him for making just this sort of rugged, grueling march.

Once more Bourke felt proud to be part of the general's staff, prouder still that Crook had asked him to "club it" together—to share their blankets for shelter, share their blankets for warmth.

Late that night after the others had gone and the rain beat down on the rock shelf above them, John tried to sleep, his back against Crook's.

"General?"

"Yes, John."

"You think those Sioux ahead of us are as hungry as we are?"

Crook didn't answer right off. When he did, he said, "We've seen evidence that they've been eating their own dogs, their ponies, John. But it really doesn't matter how hungry they are now. Only thing that matters is how hungry they're going to be after we destroy their villages and drive them off with nothing else but the clothes on their backs."

Near one A.M. that Saturday morning, 9 September, the sergeants passed among Mills's command, giving the order to resaddle and mount up in the cold and darkness. With chilled, trembling hands the troops completed the tasks and formed up, finally moving out close to two-thirty. A thick fog roiled along the damp ground as the men inched ahead through a swirling, misting rain.

Grouard halted Mills a mile out from the village, where the captain explained their organization for the dawn attack, then deployed the troops.

Emmet Crawford was to lead fifty-six dismounted troopers to the right flank, while Adolphus H. Von Luettwitz would take another fifty-two dismounted men to the left flank, both wings to spread out with skirmishing intervals between each soldier.

With the village thus securely "surrounded" from the north, Frederick Schwatka would move forward with his twenty-five mounted troopers, accompanied by reporter Robert Strahorn, and once it was light enough to see the front sights of their carbines, they were to charge with their pistols drawn—straight through the heart of the enemy camp, stampeding the enemy's ponies as they went, planning to re-form on the far side.

John Bubb and the remaining twenty-five soldiers acting as horse-holders would remain in the rear with Tom Moore and his fifteen packers, along with newsman Reuben Davenport—all with orders to dash forward at the first sound of gunfire to close the noose around the village.

If their surprise attack was a success, they would drive off most of the warriors and capture some of the hostiles, and they could start plundering the village for its food supply to be used by Crook's column before putting the rest of the Sioux property to the torch. As those men sat in the rainy darkness waiting for dawn, each one knew this could well be the first victory over the enemy for the U.S. Army in the Sioux campaign, a war begun back in March along the ice-clogged Powder River.

"But should the enemy prove too strong for us," Mills said before he deployed his officers, "you are to unite and take a high piece of ground, somewhere that we might put up a strong defense until relieved."

"Relieved by Crook, Colonel?" asked Schwatka.

"Yes, Lieutenant."

The prospect made Donegan shudder, recalling that bare ridge, the high ground above the Little Bighorn where

he and Frank Grouard had stumbled across the carcasses of
more than a hundred horses, where they had had to thread
their way through that graveyard of a butchered battalion
of fighting men.

"Take the high ground and hold it," was how the captain repeated his order.

And with that Mills moved his three wings into the
dark.

Canapegi Wi. The Moon When Leaves Turn Brown.

A season when the buffalo berries were ripe and the
women gathered them to begin making pemmican for
those winter months when the hunting would be hard and
the bellies empty.

Their bellies were already very empty, brooded American Horse. The more they wandered this direction and that
to stay out of the way of the two soldier armies, the less
game they found. Already the men had to kill most of the
dogs, and a few of the poorer ponies. Just so that the little
ones would have something to eat.

More and more there was talk about going south, all
the way back to Red Cloud's agency. There, more argued
every day, the old and the sick and the very young could
find something to eat. The white man's flour and his pig
meat. No real choice to a Lakota warrior.

Still, with each new day American Horse found himself thinking more on it, for the sake of these people.

Such a thing was all but laughable to a warrior. To run
before the soldiers now was all but unthinkable. To retreat
back to the agencies?

The soldiers had come probing into Lakota hunting
ground from two directions. But his people had stopped
the soldiers of Three Stars on the Rosebud. Then they had
defeated Limping Soldier's army on the Greasy Grass. Yet
the white man did not leave them alone.

Even now the army marched on the backtrail of this
little village, harrying his people the way buffalo wolves will
follow along in the wake of a herd, waiting for a calf to be

abandoned by its cow, waiting for an old bull to fall, unable to rise.

Although the seven great circles had begun slowly to separate days after defeating the soldiers along the Greasy Grass, nonetheless most of the clans and warrior bands had migrated in the same general direction. First to the south toward the mountains, then veering off east toward the Tongue, and finally setting a course for the north once more. After crossing Pumpkin Creek the bands had splintered, by and large, for the first time along the Powder near the mouth of Blue Stone Creek. Here the Shahiyena of the North broke off and continued for the White Mountains* under their chief Dull Knife.

Hunting as they continued east, the Lakota warriors set fires in that country they were abandoning not so much to deprive the soldier horses of something to eat but more because it helped the new grass grow early the following spring. Every summer they had done the same, for as long as American Horse could remember. It always meant good grass next year for their strong little ponies as well as for the buffalo, who would migrate to this country once more on the winds. Most of the Lakota bands wandered on east, fording Beaver Creek and on to the Thick Timber River† as they slowly ambled toward the various agencies close by the Great Muddy River itself.

Sitting Bull's Hunkpapa, Crazy Horse's Hunkpatila, the Sans Arc under Spotted Eagle, even American Horse's own Miniconjou—other chiefs too—like Black Moon, Four Horns, and No Neck—all the bands had maintained contact throughout the last two moons of migration. In the nearby country even now those other bands remained ready to lend assistance in the event of an emergency, though they must travel and hunt separately. Better to break into small camps for hunting now that game was becoming scarce.

*The Big Horn Mountains.
†The Little Missouri River.

There was still a long way to go before his people would reach Red Cloud's agency.

Before then perhaps they could force the white man to give up the chase, to clear out of Lakota country for good. Without a fight—this would be all anyone could ask!

After two long, hard fights on the Rosebud and the Greasy Grass they did not have that many bullets left. Even with the number of weapons and bullets taken from the soldier bodies—the Lakota did not have enough to make another big fight of it against the white man. Better to stay out of his way if they could.

But while they avoided the soldiers, it made sense to remain ready and watchful. And arm themselves for that day they might use up all their bullets. So it was that many of the older warriors taught the young men how to cut iron arrow points from old frying pans and iron kettles.

A good fighting season this had been—driving off Three Star's soldiers from the Rosebud, crushing the rest who came to fulfill Sitting Bull's great vision. Among all the bands the Lakota had lost fewer than ten-times-ten warriors altogether in both great battles! So even though the lonely women had mourned, the camps had much more to celebrate.

Those had been good days to die! The very best his people had ever known.

Now roaming scouts kept the camps informed of where the two armies were marching. They knew each time the two armies were reinforced by more soldiers. And they knew when the two joined into one. It wasn't long, however, that reports came saying that half of the soldiers were staying along the Elk River.* And the others were coming east, heading for the Owl River,† led by the traders' sons‡ who were scouting for the soldiers. Traitors such as they would likely follow any trail they could find.

---

*The Yellowstone River.
†The Moreau River.
‡Baptiste Garnier, Frank Grouard, and Baptiste Pourier.

It was not a hard thing to find a trail, American Horse scoffed. After all, all the big clans were here. Crazy Horse's people were but a few miles away to the south. Even Sitting Bull had come down from Killdeer Mountain in the north with his Hunkpapa faithful, camped close by to the east a ways, where the old medicine man mourned the death of a son who never recovered after he was kicked in the head by a pony during the waning of the last moon.

In his Miniconjou camp of more than twenty-six-times-ten, the chief even included a handful of Shahiyena who had splintered off from Dull Knife, a few Oglalla under war chief Roman Nose, and even some Brule lodges—all drifting south for Bear Butte in the Paha Sapa.* Among these other bands he was known as Iron Plume, sometimes called Iron Shield or Black Shield. But among his people, his own familial clan, he had long been known as American Horse. While his mother had been Miniconjou, his father, Smoke, had been Oglalla. Long ago in the dawn of the white man's Holy Road far to the south, Smoke had been one of the first Lakota met by Francis Parkman. After his father's death American Horse had remained with his mother, living with her people.

Not long ago at twilight he had gone out to look over the village, to look beyond the hide lodges and brush wicki-ups at the knotting of the ponies here and there on the surrounding hillsides. American Horse liked this time of day best, when the lodges lit up from inside, beckoning a man into their warmth—like a woman raising the buffalo robe to show her naked body to her man. Three-times-ten, plus seven more . . . those buffalo-hide lodges stood close together in a narrow, three-pronged depression of coulees running toward the Rabbit Lip Creek, all of it sheltered from the cold north winds by a grassy ridge. Across the timbered stream to the south another grassy embankment rose into the broken countryside at the base of steep clay and limestone buttes. For the most part the lodges them-

---

*The Black Hills.

selves would stand concealed from soldier eyes, hidden by the chalk-colored ridges that rose on the north, west, and south of their camp. Those bluffs* lay in a near perfect north-to-south line for some twenty miles, and spreading anywhere from two to six miles in width, all of them covered for nearly half their height with an emerald cap of pine and cedar. Here in the bottom his people camped out of the wind, with good timber for their fires, plenty of grass for their horses, and cold, clear water flowing down from the high places.

In this camp on the Mashtincha Putin† lived warriors who like hundreds of others had made one by one the hundreds of the soldiers of Sitting Bull's vision fall on that sunny ridge back in the Moon of Fat Horses. Here lived Miniconjou war chiefs named Red Horse, Dog Necklace, and Iron Thunder. Men who in these greatest days of their people were at the peak of their power.

But why was it that American Horse saw little future in fleeing to the reservations for the harsh winter and escaping to the free prairie come spring? How long could they go on like this? The great herds were shrinking, just as the clear, pure water holes in the last hot breathless days of summer shrank to muddy wallows.

American Horse shuddered with the chill gust of wind here on this high ground where he looked down upon the lamplike lodges, beckoning him with their warmth. The cold and the wet had driven his people south toward the agencies earlier than usual this hunting season. Unrelenting storms and drenching rain had convinced them they should make for Bear Butte, from there an easy journey on to Red Cloud's and Spotted Tail's agencies to make ready for winter.

To go in and beg the white man for flour and pig meat for their families . . . what utter humiliation that was for

---

*Slim Buttes
†Rabbit Lip or Hairy Lip Creek, present-day Gap Creek, a tributary of Rabbit Creek, itself a tributary of the nearby Moreau River

warriors whose eyes had witnessed such greatness in turning back Three Stars on the Rosebud, such victory in crushing the nameless soldier chief who brought his white men prancing down on their great village beside the Greasy Grass.

With the rise of the wind American Horse pulled the heavy buffalo robe about his shoulders, enjoying the sensuous feel of its hairy warmth on his cheeks. Into his lungs he drew the fragrance on the wind, smelled the smoke from those many fires below him, kettles on the boil, supper warming.

Up from the creek bottom floated the agonized cry of Little Eagle's daughter.

Her time had come. Her child ready to be born. What pain he heard in her cries drifting all the way up here, where they reverberated from the chalky walls. This was the only crying he wanted to hear from the lips of his people: the birth of their children into freedom. No more did American Horse want to hear the wails of women in mourning, the whimper of little children so hungry and cold that their eyes sank into their sockets. No more did he want to hear the cries of the old ones unable to keep up on their bloodied feet as the villages fled from the marching soldiers.

Never before had they so soundly defeated the white man. Perhaps it was true that these were their *finest* days. But, he thought, if this was indeed their finest season, then it could mean only one thing: that from here on life would only get worse for the Lakota.

The wind shifted again, a strange sound carried on it.

American Horse looked back to the north, smelling that wind a moment, wondering. Then peered to the west. No, not from the west. Only from the north. If they ever came at all, he convinced himself, they would come out of the north.

Then he pulled the buffalo fur over his ears and

trudged down the sodden hillside to that small gathering of lodges. Thinking, hoping, and praying to the Great Mystery that His people had not yet seen their zenith.

Knowing in the pit of him that perhaps they had already visited the last of those finest days.

Chapter 38

9 September 1876

His nose felt like it was as big as his boot.

Dribbling, Seamus wiped it on the sleeve of his canvas mackinaw.

God, did that hurt!

Raw and angry, sore beyond belief. His nose itself was as red as these buffalo berries clinging to the nearby bushes.

But at least he wasn't so sick that he couldn't climb into the saddle. Not so immobilized with pain that the only way he could move was to lie on a travois pulled along by one of Tom Moore's mules.

"Ready, boys!" whispered Lieutenant Schwatka as he rode along their front.

Atop a sloping ridge formed by two shallow coulees that eventually united at the north edge of the village, the cavalry horses pawed the earth. Weary, all but done in—the animals wanted to move, or get the damned weight off their backs. One or the other. The animals had waited out most of the night grazing. They should have enough bottom in them to make this short charge through the village.

"Coming light, Lieutenant!" some trooper said down to Donegan's right.

"Steady now! Steady!"

He watched Schwatka look to the east. Von Leuttwitz was in position somewhere over there, somewhere still out of sight in the murky light. Over where the dawn was just beginning to balloon around them. Then the lieutenant glanced to the west, as if he expected to catch a glimpse of Crawford's men.

Minutes ago all three units of Mills's attack had come to a halt after using up more than an hour to grope their way out of the deep ravine and quietly inch forward together across the sticky, muddy prairie beginning at the foot of Slim Buttes, a long, craggy ridge that dominated and towered over the entire landscape. Frank Grouard led them through the frosty darkness toward the village he had scouted, where he had stolen two ponies. When the half-breed had Lieutenant Schwatka halt his twenty-five, the scout disappeared for a few minutes before he reappeared with another half-dozen Sioux ponies.

"More of 'em up there," Frank said in a low hush as he drove the six ponies to the rear right through the midst of Schwatka's mounted troopers. "You go on, Lieutenant. I'll be back soon as I hide these away in a coulee for safe-keeping."

With the coming light Seamus recognized the outlines of more ponies grazing here and there in their front. Still some distance off, the bulk of the herd cropped the wet grass, completely indifferent to the soldiers. Raising his face into the cold breeze that tortured his nose, he found the wind was still in their favor.

They moved up a bit more, halted again, nearing the fringe of the herd now. Beyond, farther still, rose the tops of the first lodges. Silent. Hulking. Only the barest wisps of firesmoke stealing from the upper swirl of lodgepoles. Schwatka deployed his twenty-five about the time Grouard reappeared. He rode up and stopped somewhere on the far left flank. From where Donegan sat atop his horse at the right end of the formation, he wasn't sure he could pick out the half-breed in the dim light.

Up ahead, no more than a matter of yards, really, a horse snorted. One of the Sioux ponies.

Then another one whickered, and one of the cavalry horses answered with a whinny of its own.

"Dear Mither of God," Seamus swore under his breath, "get your hands on his nostrils." He prayed the other outfits were in position.

Of a sudden the grassy rise before them erupted in a swirling movement and deafening noise: the cries of ponies, the surprising hammer of more than fifteen hundred hooves. Just as they would if a bolt of lightning had cracked its fiery tongue into their midst, the pony herd exploded into action.

"Stampede!"

At Donegan's shrill warning, Schwatka yanked his horse about and stood in the stirrups.

Another soldier hollered, "G'won, Lieutenant! Give the order!"

"Charge!" Schwatka yelled, his mouth a black hole within his neatly trimmed mustache and pointed goatee, waving the pistol in his hand as he kicked heels into his horse, which bolted off beneath him with a shocking burst of energy.

Raggedly the twenty-five tore themselves from motionlessness to a furious gallop in the space of two heartbeats, strung out as they were across some sixty yards. Over the unknown ground they raced, sweeping the frantic herd before them across the brow of the hill and down into the narrow, three-fingered depression.

Out of the gray light of false dawn loomed the hide lodges.

With a shudder Donegan remembered their attack on Powder River. Many of these men had been there. He wondered if they remembered, as he remembered it.

He saw the first lodge as he shot past it —the door flap securely lashed down against the wind and rain. At the rear a long gash suddenly erupted in the wet hide. From it bubbled three children, then a woman with a babe in her arms. She stopped, looked at him as he rode past.

Then Seamus was among the rest of the village.

All around him the Sioux were hacking their way out of their lodges. Warriors fell to one knee, firing rifles and pistols, then rose to run again, stopping after a few yards to fire another round. On either side of the Irishman the troopers' pistols popped in a steady rattle. All about him the bullets slapped against the taut, wet buffalo hides, sounding like the arrhythmic fall of icy hailstones. The air stung his cold cheeks, and he knew his nose must be dribbling in his mustache again. Swiping at it with his left arm as he sighted a warrior, Seamus immediately wished he hadn't touched the nose. The tender tissues screamed in pain.

Angry at himself, he brought the pistol out at the end of his arm and snapped off the shot by instinct, without really aiming. The warrior pitched backward, arms and legs akimbo, falling behind a lodge.

Within seconds the Sioux were streaming from the village, the first of them beginning to reach the pony herd. Children screeched and women cried out, hurrying the little ones along. At the rear tottered the old and the lame, the sick and the wounded lumbering behind in their midst. On the far side of the village stood a line of low bluffs. Racing across the creek to the southwest, most of the Sioux were escaping around the end of those bluffs, fleeing onto the rolling prairie. The rest of those in the village splashed across the narrow creek, up the south bank, and turned right at the ridgeline, scurrying like quail into the darkness and brush.

He knew there would be coulees and ravines up there, scars upon the face of this land where rain and snow had scratched their fingers of erosion over the millennia as the waters tumbled off the prairie to the creek. Creek flowing on to the stream. And stream into the river. Just the way the Indians flowed right and left at the base of the low bluff. Like a boulder parting the waters.

Suddenly he was alone. Reining up, Seamus watched another handful of the Sioux flit past him in the gray light, disappearing upstream in the brush along the creek pouring out of those chalk-colored buttes that stood immediately above them in the coming light of day.

With all the echo reverberating from those heights, it seemed the whole prairie was alive with a steady rattle of gunfire.

Seamus wheeled his horse about, and the animal fought the bit for a moment as he patted its wet hide along the big neck, straining his eyes into the dim gray light of dawn to find something familiar—anything—out there through the fog and mist dancing among the lodges. Schwatka had his mounted troopers turning just then, there at the end of that bluff across the creek from the village. They had done what Mills had ordered, but they hadn't stopped the escape. The pony stampede had seen to that, flushing the quarry ahead of the charging soldiers. Now instead of closing the door on the south end of the village, Schwatka's men could only watch in frustration as the Sioux scampered across the hills, scattering like hulls of grain flung across a hardwood floor.

Where was Crawford's detachment? They should have been down to the creek by now—

Then Donegan saw them. Clear across the village on the far hillside, already united with Von Leuttwitz's men. Instead of pushing east from their right flank to prevent most of the escape toward the buttes, Crawford had led his men right into the northern end of the village to quickly join the other dismounted skirmishers fighting under Von Leuttwitz's command. Together those hundred-plus men worked in concert, pushing west into the village.

As Donegan rode slowly along the edge of the low bluff, his pistol sweeping over the brush in the event he scared up anything on two legs, he noticed Schwatka's men corralling more than two hundred ponies at the bottom of a wide, grassy swale. Most of the animals quieted and went back to a restless grazing, while a few continued to leap and dart along the circumference of the circle.

Now he peered north into the growing light, wondering why Lieutenant Bubb's men hadn't shown up on schedule either.

As Donegan rode up and halted near Mills, the dismounted captain snagged a soldier's bridle, yelled something up at the man above the din of gunfire, then quickly stepped back to slap the horse on the flank. The private shot away, lying low in the saddle, racing north.

The captain whirled, seeing Donegan. "I was looking for you, Irishman! Could have used you as a courier. I've just sent orders to Bubb to get his ass up here, and now! I don't have any idea what's keeping him," Mills snapped angrily. "I want him to send a courier to Crook—tell him what we've pitched into—send us reinforcements. Grouard says there's other villages within a few miles of us."

Seamus felt uneasy about it, saying, "We can expect company real soon."

"We'll need Crook here fast."

Seamus said, "He's two days behind us—"

"Don't tell me the obvious, Mr. Donegan! Tell me something that will help us hold on until Crook gets here!"

"What happened to Von Leuttwitz's men? Wasn't he supposed to get his sojurs in position southeast of the village to shut the village's escape hatch?"

"I was up there with Von Leuttwitz—and from what I can figure out, the ponies stampeded before anyone could get into position." Mills's eyes narrowed on Donegan. "A soldier like me will take what he can get, Mr. Donegan—and do the best he can with it!"

His harsh words fell like Gatling-gun fire; then the captain suddenly turned left, and right, dashing off into the melee without taking his leave.

The rifle fire began to dwindle, weak pockets of sound rising against that hollow to the southwest of the village only when some of the warriors attempted to make a dash at the captured ponies. Soldiers swarmed among the lodges, kicking their way through the door flaps, cutting long slashes in the wet hides. Here and there the ravenous troopers emerged from the lodges with a pistol in one hand, booty in the other.

Just seeing them eating, hollering at one another, laughing and stuffing more food into their already full mouths was enough to make Donegan's own mouth water and his stomach grumble in complaint.

"There more in there?" he asked a soldier squatting outside a lodge, his carbine laid across the tops of his thighs as he used both hands to tear loose, bite-sized chunks from a thin strip of dried meat.

"All you can eat, my friend!"

Inside he took a moment to let his eyes grow accustomed to the dim light, all that was given off by the embers of the occupants' night fire, and what little of sunrise could penetrate the thick hide walls. He sniffed, not so much to snort the dribble hung pendant at the end of his raw nose as to see if he could smell anything remotely like food. Down to his knees he went beside the fire pit, where lay an assortment of kettles and a frying pan. In a kettle some cold soup. He ripped off his glove and tested the thick, cold liquid with a finger. Licking it, Seamus smiled. Fishing out a chunk of cold meat, he thought of warming it over the warm coals—then stuffed it into his mouth and tore off a hunk. Suddenly he stopped chewing, his eyes locked on the large ornament hung from the dew-cloth rope at the back of the lodge, suspended over the Indian bed, a thick pad of blankets and buffalo robes.

Half-red, half-white. Company I. Seventh U.S. Cavalry.

A goddamn guidon from one of the outfits destroyed with Custer!

Outside he heard a loud voice hollering for a surgeon. The way things had happened, Donegan hadn't expected there to be any casualties. Plunging his bare hand down into the cold stew, he fished out several large portions before he ducked out of the slash hacked in the side of the lodge, his hand dripping on his canvas britches and boots.

A soldier dashed up to Crawford, strain present in his voice. "Von Leuttwitz is hurt bad, Lieutenant!"

Crawford asked, "Von Leuttwitz? Where's Mills?"

"The colonel's with Von Leuttwitz—he was right beside him when he was shot. Lieutenant was just standing there: giving orders, rallying the boys when he got hit."

Turning, Crawford hollered out above the withering gunfire. "Get me Surgeon Stephens!"

All about them officers and sergeants were barking their orders, passing down commands from Mills, who remained on the east side of the village, orders to establish a skirmish line at the southern and western edges of the village. It was there the warriors had re-formed and were just then beginning to snipe at the soldiers who now had full possession of their lodges.

Assistant Surgeon Charles R. Stephens trotted past, swinging an overstuffed haversack in each hand, right behind a pair of soldiers who were hurrying him to a hillside on the east side of camp.

"—in the leg," one of the troopers said in a fragment Seamus overheard. "The knee."

"Dammit," Mills growled as he emerged from the fog. He turned to a knot of soldiers down on their knees, carbines at the ready. The captain tapped one of them on the shoulder. "Trooper, I want you to carry my orders to the officers you can find—tell them we don't have time now to commence the destruction of the village. They must forget it for now. Instead I'm ordering every unit to set up a defensive perimeter. Skirmishers out—and hold, by God! You understand my orders?"

The soldier's head bobbed, almost as hard as his Adam's apple did. "Yessircolonel."

"Just hold the line! Got that?" He nudged the soldier away. "Now, go!"

Mills turned around, finding Donegan. "Son of a bitch," he muttered with a shake of his head. "We need reinforcements. We need more ammunition. We need to hold the line until Crook can get up here with the rest. Jesus," he sighed, ripping his hat from his head and shaking the rain from it before he planted it back atop his greasy hair.

"We got our hands full—that's for sure," Donegan replied. "Holding that herd Schwatka captured. Keeping the warriors out of this village."

Mills nodded, his grim face creased with a look of determination. "Just holding on . . . like Powder River, isn't it, Mr. Donegan?"

"Yes," Seamus replied. "And we will hold on—just like we done at the Powder."

"Colonel Mills!"

They both turned to find a soldier hurrying up, a guidon flapping in his hand.

"What you have there?" Mills demanded.

"Private William J. McClinton, C Troop, sir," the soldier huffed. "Found this in a lodge while I was . . . was—"

"Finding yourself something to eat, Private?" Seamus asked in interruption.

McClinton eyed the Irishman sheepishly. "Some meat, yeah. Then this caught my eye."

"Mine too," Donegan said, taking hold of the edge of the guidon, turning to Mills. "From Custer's bunch at the Little Bighorn."

Grabbing the guidon, Mills said, "Bloody damn! It confirms this bunch helped destroy the Seventh."

"I'd be proud to give you it, Colonel," McClinton said effusively.

"You're sure, Private?"

"Absolutely, sir."

"Thank you! Thank you, soldier," Mills responded. "Go finish getting yourself something to eat, then get back on the skirmish line. That's where I need every last man."

"I'll do just that," the private said. "We're having a hot time of it, ain't we, Colonel?"

*   *   *

"What do you make of that, Mr. Bourke?"

"Don't know, General."

John squinted into the misty distance while he reached back for his saddlebag and pulled out the field glasses. Training them on the distant objects that bobbed and swam like dark insects behind sheets of hard rain, he slowly spun the adjustment wheel.

Crook waited patiently beside him as the others came to a halt behind them. "More hunters?"

"I can't be sure," Bourke began. "But—it doesn't appear to be warriors. No feathers."

"Let me have a look," George Crook said.

That morning at breakfast there wasn't enough grease to fry their ration of horse meat, so the lieutenant had broiled both his and the general's at the end of a stick held over the fire. No coffee left them to wash it down. Only gritty water the color of buttermilk.

In a cold downpour that began at dawn, the company commanders had inspected their men, cavalry captains counting what half-dead horses still remained in service. These were formed up, and what troopers had been put afoot fell in behind their scarecrow comrades mounted on the bony animals. It didn't take long for the column to string itself across the hills. Lieutenant Colonel Eugene Carr's Fifth Cavalry was assigned that day to close the file and bring up the stragglers. Because of the plodding pace of the rest of the command, the Fifth hadn't yet been given orders to mount up, much less to move out. They were still in camp almost an hour after Crook and his headquarters staff had set off.

After making no more than five miles Crook and Bourke had halted briefly at a creek they were attempting to identify from their obscure maps.

Perhaps the South Fork of the Grand, suggested one of the staff.

No, said another. Must be the North Fork of the Owl or Moreau River.

That's when Bourke and the rest caught sight of the two riders.

"They've seen us!" Walter Schuyler shouted.

"And they're coming in," John added, watching the pair through the field glasses as the two horsemen put their animals into an uneven, labored gallop. "They're white men, General."

Crook mused, "Couriers from Mills?"

"Could he have run across something, General?" Wesley Merritt asked.

"Let's go find out," George Crook said, putting heels to his horse's flanks.

For the better part of the next ten minutes they moved ahead, watching the approach of the pair, one a packer, the other a ragged soldier.

"General Crook! General Crook!" the civilian hollered, repeating it several times as he drew close enough for the soldiers to hear his words.

"George Herman, General!" he rasped when he came to a halt.

Crook asked, "You're one of Tom Moore's men, aren't you?"

"Served you since Arizona, sir." And he took a big gulp of air.

Bourke watched the soldier at Herman's side, tight-lipped, his eyes filled with dread. "Are you coming from Mills?"

The packer nodded. "Lieutenant Bubb asked that scout Jack Crawford to carry this, but he refused to come. So Bubb give us the best two horses he had," and Herman stuffed a hand inside both his coat and shirt to pull out a crumpled piece of folded paper he presented to the general. "But we was both ready to come on foot if these here horses give out, General."

"This is from Mills?"

"Bubb, General." As Crook tore the paper open and read, the civilian continued, explaining to the other officers, "Colonel's gone and captured a village of Sioux. He ordered Lieutenant Bubb to send you the word that he's took the village but he ain't sure he can hold on to it."

"Can't hold on to it?" Crook snarled as his head snapped up. "What's he gotten himself into, Mr. Herman?"

"Forty-one lodges they counted," Herman answered. "Got a pony herd surrounded, and they're holding off the warriors best they can, General. Red devils acting like they want the village back real bad, and they got our boys surrounded pretty good. But we're putting up a hot fight of it."

"Where exactly?"

Twisting atop the bare back of his played-out horse, the packer pointed. "South of here along the buttes. Maybe eighteen, no more'n twenty miles."

Now for the first time the soldier spoke up, his eyes animated. "Damn, but we figured we'd have to ride all day before we come on you, General. Lieutenant Bubb reminded us you said you was keeping the whole column in bivouac."

"Thank God I didn't!" Crook grumped as he raised his eyes from the hurriedly written dispatch in his hands. "Says here that Grouard states it's a village commanded by Roman Nose—a Brule. Says the place is filled with supplies."

"That's damned good news, sir!" Merritt cheered. "These men could use a change of diet."

The soldier courier pressed, "Colonel requests you hurry reinforcements, General."

Schuyler asked, "Has Mills taken any casualties?"

Nodding, the trooper responded, "Lieutenant Von Leuttwitz, and another, I think a corporal."

Royall shrieked, "Von Leuttwitz—killed?"

"Wounded, sir," the courier answered. "Pretty bad, though. But the corporal's dead."

"Damn," Crook muttered, folding the paper up and stuffing it inside his wool coat. "Mills doesn't have near the ammunition he'll need to hold on to that village if the enemy makes it hard on his men."

"I pray we can get there in time with these played-out horses," Merritt complained.

Crook stared into the distance a moment longer, then turned to his officers. "We won't get there in a hurry like this, gentlemen. We must send only our best—push ahead as fast as they can march."

"Our best?" Royall inquired.

"I want each of your battalions to strip itself for a forced march," Crook ordered. "Only those horses and men capable of making the race to save Mills."

"General! Looks as if there's another rider coming in!" Schuyler called out.

They all twisted in their saddles, watching the distant speck galloping their way.

"Let's just pray this isn't news that Mills has been overrun," Merritt murmured almost under his breath.

"Yes, General," Crook agreed. "Let's pray your reinforcements can get there in time to save those men."

Chapter 39

9 September 1876

"Mills has his back to the wall," Lieutenant Colonel Eugene Carr told the officers of the Fifth Cavalry in the hearing of his troopers, who pressed close when he returned from the head of the column. "And Crook's ordered us to save him."

He then went on to inform his men that a third courier had reached headquarters with a second dispatch for the general. "At the time the rider left, Mills already had one dead, and six wounded. He's called for more surgeons, as well as reinforcements and ammunition."

Ordering his company commanders to break out all those men incapable of making the race, leaving behind every horse unable to carry its rider at a trot, the officers were told to stand what was left by companies and prepare for inspection. As the word spread through them like Sioux prairie fire, those once dejected, disgusted, and demoralized men within moments became alert and eager, rejuvenated and ready for whatever toil might be asked of them.

Even the lieutenant, whose old Arizona arrow wound was daily growing more aggravated by the continuing cold and dampness.

After their long and fruitless chase Charles King could

understand that radical change of spirit overcoming every man as the lieutenant began working down the line of what troopers still had horses. It was going to be damned disappointing for a man to learn he was being left behind, King brooded. Hell, it hurt him when he ended up having to tell the lightest man in the whole regiment that he wasn't going to make that ride.

"But, Lieutenant King—"

"No more complaints, Lieutenant London," King snapped, moving down the line.

The next trooper and horse were no better a pair, except that soldier weighed twice what wiry Second Lieutenant Robert London weighed.

"Sorry, Mullins. You're staying back. Fall out."

"Lieutenant!" cried London, leaping to King's side. ".Lemme ride Mullins's horse."

King shook his head, saying, "I just said he wasn't going."

"Look," London pleaded, "I can't make my own horse carry me any ten miles, sir. But I can ride Mullins's horse: he'll carry my weight there, every inch of the way."

"Take him, Lieutenant London," Mullins said, handing the small man his reins.

The wiry trooper asked, "It's all right, Lieutenant?"

"If Mullins doesn't mind—you can ride in with us."

"Hurrah!" London cheered as King stepped away, on down that pitiful front of scarecrow soldiers and their bone-rack horses.

One by one the officer inspected the readiness of Carr's men and horses, ordering more than a third to fall out and come along with the infantry. By the time he was done, King turned and looked over those who would be making the dash, what men and mounts Carr would lead in that race south to rescue Mills. For a moment doubt gripped his heart. Maybe it was the sight of those bony horses. Perhaps it was those scarecrowlike soldiers. King wasn't sure . . . but then, all around the lieutenant, up and down the entire column, men began to cheer and spirits rose higher than they had been in many a week.

"We'll get in our licks now!"

"Hope Mills saves some action for us!"

"I'll take a scalp of my own!"

"I'll take Crazy Horse's hair myself!"

In less than fifteen minutes Merritt had 17 officers and 250 men selected from the three regimental battalions, in addition to a pair of doctors—Medical Director Bennett Clements and Assistant Surgeon Valentine McGillycuddy—who would accompany the relief column with their trio of pack-mules laden with medical supplies.

Just past seven o'clock that dreary, cheerless morning, the rescue began.

"Column of twos!" rang the command that bounced back from the nearby hills. "At a trot! Forward!"

Into the teeth of a cold rain they set out on that desperate charge at double time, loping across the gumbo-laced landscape, those starving troopers clinging to the McClellan saddles cinched around the ribs of pitiful, played-out horses. But for the moment, for the next few hours, for the rest of this glorious day—these men had something other to think about than their aching bellies.

It wasn't long before those cavalry officers who were left behind organized their remaining men and animals, then marched out on foot with Major Chambers's infantry, dogging the backtrail of Merritt's rescue command. How little it mattered that earlier that morning they all had awakened hungry, wet and cold, utterly weary, discouraged, and disheartened.

All that was suddenly forgotten now that their privations had served a purpose. The enemy was but a few miles ahead.

At long last they would get in their licks.

"Here, Irishman—take part of what I found," one of M Company's troopers said as he handed a chunk of the agency tobacco to the civilian.

Seamus answered, "Thanks. I'll keep it for later." He slipped it down into a pocket of his rain-soaked mackinaw.

Besides some meat, in those first few minutes that the soldiers claimed possession of the village, they also found a good supply of reservation tobacco—the worst grade of the product there ever could be—but it was tobacco nonetheless, and the soldiers had been without for far too long. Most of the men stuffed a chunk inside their cheek before the officers got them hurrying off to the skirmish lines Mills was establishing around the captured lodges.

Grouard said, "One of the soldiers rooting through the lodges come up with some money."

"Money?"

"Army scrip—pay bills," Grouard replied.

"A lot?"

The half-breed grinned. "Fella told me he counted more'n eleven thousand."

"Dollars?" Seamus exclaimed. "Sweet Mither of Heaven!"

"Custer's money."

Donegan nodded, remembering. "Took off all them dead we run onto."

"And another bunch of soldiers just come across a little girl," Grouard went on to explain. "They was digging through the lodges looking for army ammunition, and when they pulled back a big stack of robes and blankets, up jumps this little girl—no more'n eight or nine winters old —crying and screaming so hard she flushed all them soldiers right out of the lodge!"

"Why the hell did the troopers get scared off by a little girl?"

"I suppose they figured she was screaming so hard there had to be bigger Injuns in the lodge—so she could warn others she was found."

"What'd the sojurs do with her?"

Grouard answered, "Mills come over and took her back by the hospital tent, where he gave her something to eat, make friendly with her. Says he's gonna adopt her."

At the moment Lieutenant Von Leuttwitz had fallen beside Mills, scout Jack Crawford had rushed up and torn off his colorful bandanna, quickly tying it above the right knee to act as a tourniquet. Then the biggest man in the village, Sergeant John A. Kirkwood, gamely looped the semiconscious Von Leuttwitz's arms around his own shoulders, and righted himself with the lieutenant on his back for a clumsy, lumbering ride into camp to find Dr. Clements.

For a precious few minutes the firing died off. And the men felt cocky enough to believe they had control of the village, believing they had driven off the Sioux they hadn't been able to capture. The quiet wasn't to last very long.

It didn't take the warriors more than a few minutes to get their families out of danger before they turned back to snipe at the soldiers, harassing the white men not only from the rocky walls west of the village, but from just about any point of ground high enough where they could take a shot or two at the white men busy among the lodges. It wasn't long before the Sioux marksmen were even walking bullets in close to the surgeons' hospital. Mills wasted no time before he called off the looting of the lodges, deciding it could wait until the rest of the command came up.

For now they had only to keep the warriors back, to hold on to the village. For a day and a half at least.

Maybe by tomorrow morning at the earliest, help would arrive.

Crook was at least twenty-five miles behind them. It would take the rest of that day for Bubb's courier to reach the general—if the trooper wasn't picked off by a hunting party wandering out of the other camps in the area. By the time Crook could get a relief force saddled up and ready on what second-class horses they had left, then punished those animals to hurry here to the village—why, it would be morning at the earliest. If all went well.

Hell, Seamus brooded gloomily—if all went well, there might even be some of them still here to rescue when Crook's relief rolled in.

A few minutes after the Sioux warriors began to heat things up once again, Mills ordered both Bubb and Crawford to take platoons of men to the south and west of camp, with instructions to prepare rifle pits where pickets could keep some of the pressure off the village itself. Just before he took his detail to the skirmish line, Bubb ordered one of his hardy veterans to a high and rocky butte less than a mile away to the north of the hostile camp, where the soldier was to watch for Crook's relief party and signal when the reinforcements came in sight.

From his pack-mules Bubb handed out a dozen folding spades, really nothing more than collapsible entrenchment tools, to his fatigue detail. Across the creek to the southeast they found four or five shallow buffalo wallows the men immediately went to work on deepening. One wallow in particular faced the brush-covered mouth of a narrow ravine southwest of the village. There the soldiers could see glimpses of a hole the camp's children had dug in the bank of the coulee, enough to excavate a shallow cave of sorts. To that cave burrowed back in the ravine, a group of warriors, women, and children had fled in the first minutes of the attack and were now beginning to take shots at Bubb's riflemen as they dug themselves in.

"We can flush 'em, Sergeant!" declared Private John Wenzel, A Troop, Third Cavalry. "All we gotta do is make things a little hot on 'em with some lead flying in there, and they'll come running out, begging for their lives."

"We've got 'em trapped like rats," agreed M Troop's blacksmith, Albert Glavinski, "with nowhere to run."

"Are you game, Sergeant Kirkwood?" asked E Troop's sergeant, Edward Glass.

"I suppose we can't go wrong if we rush 'em together," replied M Troop's John A. Kirkwood.

Yet as soon as the four crawled over the lip of their rifle pit, Private Wenzel was driven backward against Kirkwood with a sickening crunch of bone as a bullet from the ravine smashed into his head. Before they could react from the surprise, more lead whined among the soldiers.

A bullet entered Sergeant Glass's right wrist, tearing out his elbow, shattering the arm and making it useless.

Nearby Kirkwood whirled, sensing the heat of a bullet's path along his back. He spilled down the side of the pit and lay gasping at the bottom. Bringing his bloody hand away from the wound, he asked Glavinski, "How . . . how is it?"

The blacksmith shook his head in disbelief and replied, "Just a flesh wound, Sarge. Only grazed you. But another inch, and it'd cut your backbone in two."

"Damn," Kirkwood growled, peering at the pulpy mass at the back of Private Wenzel's head. "Shame about him. He knew more about a horse than any other man of us."

Within heartbeats Anson Mills dashed up to the pit as other soldiers pulled the casualties back among the lodges toward the surgeon's hospital. "How many are in there?"

No one seemed to have an answer.

It was then and there the captain determined to send that third courier to press his point, to tell Crook that he was already taking casualties and running low on ammunition. Praying that Bubb's couriers or that third rider—one of them—would get through and bring on their rescue.

"Forget the ravine for now," Mills wisely told his men. "We'll wait until the column gets here to smoke them out."

At nearly the same time, Crawford's detail began having a hot session of it driving a fiery knot of warriors from some of the lowest rungs of the nearby bluffs. For those few minutes while the Sioux moved higher up the ridges, Crawford's soldiers began to dig in for the long haul. From those and Bubb's improvised pits, the cavalrymen could now hold the sniping warriors a bit more at bay, pushed back from the camp itself where the Sioux had been making things tough on the wounded and the horse-holders. Each time the warriors made an abortive attempt to charge the two hundred ponies that soldiers were guarding, Crawford's men turned them back with cool and deliberate fire.

Most of the rest of his men Mills positioned on the

low bluffs directly to the north and east of the camp, where they could command a good view of those warriors who had secured themselves on the rocky shelves that ascended the buttes from the prairie floor.

Not long after Mills had secured the village and drove the Sioux fleeing from the perimeter, Dr. Clements had requested that a lodge at the center of camp be saved for the hospital. In it he and Assistant Surgeon Stephens already had Von Leuttwitz and another seriously wounded soldier, Private Orlando H. Duren of E Troop, Third Cavalry, stretched out on the buffalo-hide bedding as the minor skirmishing continued unabated.

As soon as Sioux marksmen set up shop on the rocky terraces above the village and began to rain rifle fire down on the lodges, Clements asked Mills to help with moving his hospital. Dragging the agonized Von Leuttwitz, Duren, Kirkwood, and Glass from the lodge into the open on buffalo robes, a half-dozen soldiers then quickly dismantled the lodge and moved the poles to the gentle slope of a hillside north of the Indian camp. There the troopers did their best to rewrap the poles with the heavy, sodden buffalo-hide cover before Clements and Stephens helped their stewards drag the wounded back inside.

Before long the coming day's light was brightly reflected from the chalk-colored buttes north and west of camp, helping to dissipate the wispy fog from all but the lowest places in that first half hour of fighting. Behind gaps in those castle-rampart-like ridges, Mills and the others had watched mounted warriors parading back and forth for some time.

"They've sent runners to the other villages," was the rumor that too quickly became anxiety as morning began to grow around them with the sun's rising. "They're coming back with more warriors'n you can shake a stick at."

Nothing Donegan could think of would counter the truth in that. Fact was, they knew there were other villages in the area. They had failed to surround the camp and seal up its occupants before nearly all the Sioux escaped.

Chances were damned good that warriors from this camp were already speeding to other hostile bands in the area, spreading the alarm.

"Shoot only when you've got yourself a clear target!" A sergeant nearby passed on the order that was rapidly becoming general throughout the skirmish lines.

"Murph's right," another veteran sergeant agreed. "We gotta save every bullet and make it count."

This was perhaps the greatest danger: Mills's attack force being put under siege while they slowly ran out of ammunition, and in the end were overrun by reinforcements coming in from other camps because they simply had no more bullets left and Crook was still miles away.

Maybe they were all fools to believe the column could get there in time. Perhaps it would be better, Seamus considered, for them to take care of themselves here and now.

"If we found the guidon, Colonel," Donegan explained, "that means this bunch fought at the Little Bighorn."

"We know that," Mills replied, worry in his voice.

"And if this bunch fought the soldiers there, they likely picked up some of the weapons and some of the ammunition off Custer's dead, stole out of the saddle pockets of the Seventh's horses."

"What are you driving at?" Mills growled. "Trying to cheer me up, Irishman?"

Seamus wagged his head. "No. Don't you understand? That means we might find some cartridges—"

"Among the plunder from the lodges!" Mills exclaimed. "Brilliant!"

The captain immediately sent a dozen men to quickly scour through the lodges again—but not for food this time. For ammunition.

Nearby a soldier came out of a lodge jingling a small leather pouch filled with copper cartridges. With his other hand he greedily ate some cold meat. Not far off three women prisoners and an old man began to laugh, pointing at the soldier.

Seamus said, "Frank—ask them why they're laughing at that soldier."

After a few moments of talk back and forth, Grouard turned and said, "They asked me if I knew what kind of meat they had in their lodges. Said I figured it was buffalo, maybe antelope. So they laughed at me and said the soldiers ain't give 'em enough time to be hunting buffalo, and the antelope hunting has been poor."

His eyes narrowing, Donegan asked, "So what kind of meat is it?"

"Nothing we ain't been used to lately," Grouard answered with a wry grin. "Seems everybody in this country took to eating horse and pony."

"What the hell you think Captain Jack's up to?" Grouard asked a minute later.

Not far away the white scout Crawford hurried down the slope of a hill standing to the north of the village, pulling one of the packers' mules behind him. At Crawford's shoulder ran newsman Robert Strahorn. They stopped at the first crude rack of poles erected outside a lodge and began to tear the strips of drying meat from the rack, stuffing them into the canvas panniers lashed to either side of the mule's sawbuck. In a momentary lull of fighting a shot suddenly echoed in that creek bottom. The mule sank on its forelegs, rolling onto its side as Crawford and Strahorn dived for cover behind a lodge.

"Hey, Lieutenant!" the poet scout hollered out.

On a nearby hill Frederick Schwatka answered, "What can I do for you, Crawford?"

"We got us a sniper out there."

"Shit, we have us a whole passel of snipers!" the lieutenant bellowed.

"How 'bout seeing if you can catch sight of any smoke over yonder that will tell us where that sniper's laying in."

"Can't see any gun smoke, Crawford!"

"You just watch with them glasses of yours now," Crawford hollered. "He'll be sure to make a try for me when I come out!"

Up bolted the white guide, jumping from cover and sprinting to the far edge of the creekbed some fifty feet away, where he turned in the slippery mud, then raced back as another shot rang out just as he reached his hiding place.

"The sniper ought to be over there," Crawford instructed, huffing and breathless. "Try your glasses over by that big tree."

Sure enough, Schwatka wasn't long in declaring, "I got him in sight, Jack."

Crawford asked, "Send some of your boys over to root him out, will you?"

After a squad of the lieutenant's men made short work of the sniper, Strahorn and the scout went back to the dead mule and succeeded in pulling free one of the canvas panniers, filling it with the stringy pony meat they took to share between the hospital and those officers overseeing the fight from the nearby hilltop north of the village.

"What they yelling about now, Frank?" Donegan asked minutes later when some warriors among the rocky ledges across the creek began to holler again.

"They say Crazy Horse is coming."

"Crazy Horse," Seamus repeated. "His own self, eh?"

"They say there's a lot of camps in the area—just what I told Mills before he got us in this fix."

"So Crazy Horse is gonna come rescue the Sioux before Crook can come rescue us—that it?"

Grouard nodded. "Something like that, yeah."

"Hey, cheer up, you damned half-breed," Donegan said. "Just remember that Crazy Horse doesn't know what we know."

"What do we know he don't?"

"That Crook's coming."

Frank wagged his head. "Yeah. He's coming. But he might just get here too late to help us."

Donegan looked around at the village, letting Grouard wallow in his despair. They had flushed the enemy from their homes and driven them into the hills, driven them up the bluffs that commanded a view of the camp. True, Mills did control the village and half of the hostiles' pony herd—but the captain hadn't been able to capitalize on his victory. A fierce and determined counterattack by the Sioux had forced the soldiers to dig in and establish a defensive perimeter, fighting with what they had left of their meager and dwindling ammunition.

"No matter what," Seamus finally remarked as he watched the movement of warriors on the distant shelves along the face of the bluffs, "at least Crook's got him his first victory of this goddamned Sioux war."

"Forty lodges," Grouard replied. "It ain't much, is it?"

"After months of frustration, trailing the hostiles all over the territory—I'll bet the army will take what victory they can get after disappointments at the Powder River and the Rosebud, after Custer was butchered at the Little Bighorn."

Grouard grinned. "Any little win better than nothing, eh?"

"I guess we'll just have to wait till Crook gets here," Seamus said morosely a while later.

"Yes, Irishman. Crook or Crazy Horse," Grouard replied. "We just have to see who gets to us first."

Chapter 40

Moon When Leaves Turn Brown

American Horse thought they would be safe camped beside Rabbit Lip Creek at the foot of the cliffs that nearly enclosed their village on three sides. These bluffs had been carved over time by rain and melting snow, cut by smaller ravines and larger canyons running jaggedly to the valley floor, sculpted by the ever-present wind that blew along their heights to form every terrace, every one of the shelves that made climbing easy for the children who came here to play.

As protected as this place was, still the soldiers had found them.

Long time back scouts said the soldiers divided. Some staying on the Yellowstone while another army marched east, then turned south on the trail of American Horse's own Miniconjou and the other villages camped in the area. But, those scouts reported, the soldiers were running out of time: their horses were failing them, and more than half of the white men were already afoot.

Most of the old men agreed that the soldiers were not a threat. The army could not travel fast enough to catch up to American Horse's people before the Miniconjou reached Bear Butte.

But now he peered through the leafy bullberry and other brush at the mouth of the ravine where he and some of his people had fled with the opening shots—as the ponies thundered through camp and the soldier bullets fell on the taut lodge skins soaked by days of rain like the falling of hailstones.

Out there on the muddy side of the creek bottom lay Little Eagle's granddaughter, only minutes old when the soldiers attacked. The young mother had no husband, for he was one of those killed in their great victory over the soldiers on the Greasy Grass. A glorious death!

But now Little Eagle's daughter was alone. Without a husband she lived again with her parents while her time drew close. She carried a warrior's child in her belly.

With the first hoofbeats, warning shouts, and gunfire, she had stumbled from her birthing bed with the newborn infant wrapped beneath her blanket, frightened and screaming while Little Eagle slashed a hole in the side of the lodge and her mother shoved her into the cold wind and rain. Around them madness swirled as ponies and people stampeded out of camp, away from the hairy-mouths and their angry guns.

Running for the creek bottom, the woman had been struck by a bullet. As the mother fell, the newborn pitched from her arms into the brush. The soldier's bullet had passed through the mother's shoulder and smashed into the infant's head the instant before the woman stumbled and fell.

Forced to leave everything behind but what they had on their backs, American Horse and his woman came across the young mother moments later in their own escape, finding her blood seeping into the puddle of mud below her. They bent to lift her, raising her between them, and quickly hurried on, dragging the young mother into the ravine with them. Already there were some hiding back in the shallow cave. No matter that there was little room in that cave—the tangled brush and a few short trees hid them all, and the soldiers could not see into the ravine.

At the same time, American Horse and the others could watch everything happening on this west side of the village without being discovered. At least not until the soldiers dug a rifle pit and one soldier started to approach the ravine.

Moments ago he and the other warriors had decided they would give up their lives at a terrible price—killing as many of the white men as they could until they were rushed. Still, American Horse kept praying to the Great Mystery that help would come from the other villages.

Sitting Bull and his warriors. Crazy Horse's fighting men.

Maybe they would not have to wait long until someone came to rescue them. But until rescue came, American Horse and the other men would guard the ravine the way a sow grizzly defended her cubs.

If necessary, they would give up their lives to save their families.

Knowing that Crazy Horse or Sitting Bull would soon be here to avenge their deaths.

Fifteen more horses gave out in Crook's push to rescue Mills. Fifteen more troopers put afoot to follow along the best they could.

After punishing their mounts through the mud and the mist, through the gumbo and sheets of driving rain at a trot for some four and a half hours, the cavalry came into earshot of the village. Charles King could hear sporadic gunfire echo from the chalky bluffs that hulked beneath the low-hung clouds.

Some two dozen warriors surprised some of the rescuers when they swept over the brow of a hill at the rear of the column's march, waving blankets and snapping pieces of rawhide, shouting and blowing on whistles to frighten off what they could of the trail-hammered horses stumbling along on the tail end of things. As soon as some of

Captain Henry E. Noyes's battalion of the Second Cavalry halted and fired a volley in their direction, the hostiles withdrew out of carbine range.

"This is part of the bunch that butchered Custer!" hollered one of Mills's men who rushed up on foot, waving some object as the men of King's K Troop drew up.

"Dismount!"

More than two hundred dropped to the ground raggedly, their worn-out horses shuddering, troopers flinging rain off their coats and gum ponchos.

King called out to the Third Cavalry soldier, "Let me see what you have there!"

He trotted over, shaking a cream-colored, blood-splattered glove for all to see. "Just take yourself a lookee here, Lieutenant. These here was Captain Keogh's gauntlets—read for yerself. Got his own name right inside!"

"And the red devils got their goods off them goddamned agencies!" attested another soldier trotting up to the crowd knotted around King, holding up a half-filled flour sack emblazoned with the stamp of the Indian Bureau.

Glancing around at the dead ponies sprawled in the mud, the lieutenant quickly assessed the scene and handed the gauntlet back, saying, "Looks like you fellas have hung on by the skin of your teeth."

"Yes, sir," the trooper with the bloody gauntlets replied. "Colonel Mills was never a man to let go once he's sunk in his teeth."

"Yup. Just like a bulldog," the second soldier responded. "Once he's got a village in his jaws, Mills won't let go."

"Good for him!" King cheered, then turned to give his squads their skirmish orders, sensing the hot flare of pain shoot through that old Apache arrow wound. The continued cold did this, every time. He swallowed down the bile that threatened to come up. No matter. There wasn't much of anything in his stomach to begin with.

"General Carr!" Anson Mills shouted, jogging up. "Good to see you!"

"What's your situation?" Carr inquired as he swung down from the saddle of his weary horse.

"We're holding," Mills replied, recapturing his breath. "We've got possession of the village, but the hostiles have the heights above us. Lieutenants Bubb and Crawford have skirmishers dug in and holding the perimeter from lunettes and rifle pits. There is one troublesome bunch of holdouts. Down there, sir."

"In the creek bottom?" Carr inquired.

"Against the south bank," Mills explained. "We've got some of them trapped in there. They're socked in there real good. So good they've already killed one of my men and wounded at least three others."

"Perhaps we should avoid that ravine for now, Colonel."

"As you wish, General."

"We'll let Crook decide what he wants to do with that bunch when he comes in."

Mills asked, "Is the general coming with the rest of the column?"

"No, he came with us," Carr answered, looking behind them. "Should be here any minute."

"Grouard informs me that he fears some of the escapees have gone to alert the other villages in the area."

Carr appeared grave. "Other villages, eh?"

"Yes, sir," Mills said, his eyes alive with something more than worry now. "So I've got most of my men holding a picket line to the south. Watchful for any hostile reinforcements."

Carr turned to some of his officers and sent them off with orders to bolster Mills's skimpy defenses.

"Damn, sir—but it's good to see your men show up so quickly," Mills said effusively. "With as much ground as the couriers had to cover, I was fearful it wouldn't be until tomorrow morning at the earliest until—"

"Crook was lucky this time, Colonel," Carr interrupted. "Instead of laying over in camp as he had planned, we pushed on. It likely saved us a day in getting to you."

"And in all probability it saved my command, General."

"But you've held on, Colonel Mills. Job well-done!"

"Thank you, General! I'm damned proud of my men: called on to move through the darkness and pitch into a village of unknown strength raised here in the heart of an unknown wilderness on the heels of the Custer disaster. You can bet I'm proud of these soldiers!"

Crook came into camp near the tail end of the rescue column, hearing the warnings of Mills and the rest concerning snipers. Instead of taking cover where he could direct the fight from a position of safety, he chose to wade right into the action himself. The general had Bourke and Schuyler plant his personal flag on the highest knoll northeast of the village proper. At the same time, Carr established his regiment's headquarters a little to the west of the village. And when Merritt rolled in, he chose to raise his flag a ways to the north of Carr, on the hillside where Schwatka had begun his charge.

There was little need to picket or sideline the horses. Most of the outfits decided there simply wasn't enough strength left in any of the animals that would allow the warriors to run them off. Instead the companies sent their horse-holders back a few hundred yards to the north and well behind the skirmish lines, taking the horses to the narrow feeder creeks, where they could be watered and allowed to graze after their punishing race.

Taking K Troop to the picket line, Lieutenant King glanced over the village, counting thirty-seven lodges, along with four more sets of lodgepoles standing on the periphery without any hide covers.

As King squatted down in a muddy buffalo wallow, joining the weary troopers already there, an old sergeant in the Third Cavalry growled, "These sonsabitches been sucking at the government teat, they have, Lieutenant."

"Sort of like the rest of us, eh?" the officer replied.

"I'm serious, Lieutenant," the soldier said with a sharp wag of his head, his bushy eyebrows narrowing so that it appeared the two had become one. Tobacco juice dribbled from his lower lip, darkening the crease that ran from the corner of his mouth into the yellow-stained bristle of white chin whiskers. "In them lodges back there we found us some reservation tobacco, 'long with agency cloth and corn. A goodly bunch of flour sacks too."

King shuddered. "Hell—if you're half-right, Sergeant —sounds like the government's been feeding these Indians better than it has us!"

With the way Crook's rescue column got itself strung out in that four-and-a-half-hour trot, the head of Chambers's infantry was right on the heels of Merritt's straggling cavalry riding to the rescue by the time those last horse soldiers came in sight of the village.

Except for that time back in seventy-two when he had expected Captain Jack's Modoc to kill him in the Oregon Lava Beds,* Seamus couldn't remember when he had been so glad to see the homely faces of so many soldiers. God, was it good to have the company!

As soon as Crook assessed the scene and put plenty of men out on the picket lines, he gave Mills's attack force first crack at any and all souvenirs they could pull from the lodges before he ordered details to go in search of everything edible in the camp. Only then, he said, would he get serious about the destruction of the Sioux village.

"I'll wager he remembers how stupid Reynolds was on the Powder," Donegan told Grouard.

"Damn right," Frank replied. "All that food and them buffalo robes Reynolds had his soldiers burn. Could've filled our bellies and kept us warm, they would."

What a horn of plenty the Sioux lodges proved to be: besides flour, corn, beans, and tins of jellied fruit, the men found haunches of freshly killed game as well as over two

---

*The Plainsmen Series, Vol. 5, *Devil's Backbone*.

tons of dried meat. Little matter that it might be pony meat. No one with a hungry belly complained.

In addition to the food, soldiers dragged out all sorts of saddles and harness, bolts of calico, cloth dresses and shirts, iron cookware and kettles, along with some tinware —including plates, knives, and spoons. As well, they counted more than two thousand raw buffalo, elk, deer, and antelope hides the women had yet to flesh and tan. And the soldiers found more than a hundred blankets inked with the stenciled letters: *USID.**

Still, one pile drew the greatest attention as more and more plunder was laid atop the growing mound where Crook himself stood in silence, watching as cases of ammunition, cartons of percussion caps, revolvers, old muzzle-loading fusils, and modern repeating carbines were all thrown into the heap. And a man had only to watch the general's face to read the simmering anger written there as soldiers discovered more and more souvenirs taken from the Little Bighorn in those lodges destined for destruction.

Besides the I Company guidon and Captain Myles Keogh's buckskin gauntlets, the troopers found more than a dozen McClellan saddles. Among the pony herd Lieutenant Schwatka's men reported counting at least three bearing the Seventh Cavalry brand. From here and there soldiers brought up a handful of orderly books in which some of the Indians had begun to draw their pictographs; more cash and army scrip; an officer's blouse; a great many letters written to and by members of Custer's ill-fated five companies, some sealed and ready for posting home to families and loved ones at the time those companies marched down into the valley of the Little Bighorn.

"Give them all to Lieutenant Schuyler," a stoic Crook instructed as the process continued. "We'll see they are posted as soon as we reach Camp Robinson."

For Donegan, just looking at those letters was like catching glimpses of anonymous ghosts.

---

*United States Indian Department

Seamus put his hand inside his own wet coat, his fingers brushing the small bundle of letters he kept tied with one of Samantha's hair ribbons, stuffed deep in an inside pocket next to his heart. Here remembering the one who awaited his return, he found his heart heavy as a stone, saddened to think how these letters written by Custer's fallen troopers would one day soon arrive at their destinations back east, reaching fathers and mothers, wives and children and young sweethearts—seeming so much like haunting voices from the dead.

As much as he thought those grim souvenirs might blacken the angry hearts of Crook's fighting men, what angered some the most was the discovery of several "good conduct" certificates among the plunder pulled from the lodges. One had been issued the previous January just before the deadline when Sherman and Sheridan had given Crook a free hand to march after the winter roamers.

> Spotted Tail Agency, Jan. 14, 1876
> The bearer of this, Stabber, belonging to this agency, will travel north to visit his people. He will return to this agency within 90 days, without disturbing any white man. If he needs any little thing you will not lose by giving it to him. This is true.
>
> F. C. Boucher

And another, written a month later, read:

> Whitestone Agency, D.T., Feb., 1876
> *To any United States Indian Agent:*
> This is to certify that Charging Crow, an Indian belonging to Santee's band, is a true man to terms of the treaty, and uses all his influence with his people to do right. I cheerfully recommend him to favorable considerations of all.
>
> Yours, respectfully,
> E. A. Howard, United States Indian Agent

The more plunder the soldiers pulled from the lodges, the more rage there must have been among the warriors on the nearby hillsides who were forced to watch this looting of their camp. From time to time they were able to walk some of their bullets in among the troops at the skirmish line.

Nonetheless it was still an unknown number of Sioux who had taken refuge in that brushy ravine who were proving to be the most bothersome to Crook's men working among the lodges. Near the outskirts of camp, the concealed snipers kept the soldiers ducking and diving for cover until Crook decided he had no choice but to clean out the ravine.

The winding coulee meandered back from the creekbank for more than two hundred yards into the side of a jagged spur of ridge jutting off the face of the chalky butte itself. Eroded to a depth of nearly twenty feet along its steep sides, its bottom extended in width from some fifteen feet to as narrow as six feet, all of it a tangle of brush. None of the soldiers could get a clear shot at the hostiles who had taken refuge in the ravine because of that matted snarl of thorns and buffalo berry—unless a man dared to get right up on the opening of the ravine.

One soldier lay dead already for trying.

With Crook's arrival some of Tom Moore's packers had chided the soldiers for their slowness to rush the enemy trapped in the ravine. But when the mule skinners and a few foolhardy troopers made their own rush, they were immediately repelled by an onslaught of rifle fire from the hidden marksmen.

In the face of such stubborn resistance, the general had no choice but to deploy troops to advance on the mouth of the ravine. They set up a constant, withering fire, shooting into the brush in an attempt to drive the occupants out while more and more soldiers gathered on the slopes of the hills north of the action to watch the show. Hidden in the brushy ravine, unseen women wailed and children cried out pitifully. Above the curious soldiers, warriors gathering along the ridge shelves shouted encouragement to those who were trapped. On the hillsides across the creek bottom from the ravine's mouth stood several hundred troopers and foot soldiers, all soundly cursing the Indians cowering in their cave, venting their spleens at their cornered quarry.

Crook, Bourke, Schuyler, and the rest of the general's staff took up position west of the ravine. Just to the east of them and closest to the mouth hunkered some of Crook's scouts: Big Bat and Little Bat, with Buffalo Chips Charlie stretched out between the half-breeds, given the general's orders to talk to the Indians in their own tongue and convince them to surrender.

As Seamus and Grouard watched, they could hear only bits of the scouts' talk to those in the ravine, what with the clamor and gunfire and hellish din of soldiers and warriors all yelling themselves insensible, as well as the screaming and wails of those squaws and children snared in what surely must be a death trap.

"General," scout White called out to Crook, "Big Bat tells me these Sioux are saying there's more hostiles coming to jump us. Says Crazy Horse is camped nearby."

"I couldn't ask for a better birthday present," Crook replied. "No matter that he's a day late!"

Turning back to the half-breed scouts, White grumbled loudly as he crawled closer to the edge of the ravine, saying, "If you boys don't have the nerve—I'll show you a good shot myself!"

Once, then twice, the two half-breeds pulled at White's legs, yanking him back from the exposed lip right below some thick brush.

"Leave me be, boys!" White hollered, trying to kick his legs free of the two scouts lying farther down the steep slope. "I can see one of the redskins in there, and I can put a bead on him in a heartbeat."

One last time Big Bat reached out to get a new purchase on his fellow scout, but that third time White snapped his legs out of reach and rose slightly on his knees to quickly bring his carbine to his shoulder.

A bullet slammed him backward at the very instant that single gunshot thundered out of the ravine and rolled across the narrow creek bottom.

"Oh, God!" White groaned as he was flung down the embankment, his rifle tumbling out of his hand. "My God! I'm done for this time, boys!"

Garnier and Pourier scrambled down the muddy slope and were at his side in an instant. But it was plain to see by the bright, glistening stain on White's chest that he was shot right through the heart. With his eyes fluttering, Charlie's legs twitched convulsively for a moment more; then he went limp as his bowels voided.

"Lieutenant Clark!" Crook bellowed.

"Yes, General?" answered William Philo Clark, detached from the Second Cavalry to serve as one of Crook's staff. Having come upriver by steamboat to join the expedition on the Yellowstone, he came bounding up to the general in a pair of fringed buckskin britches and a buckskin jacket, buttoned clear up to his throat, all of his clothes properly baptized with Dakota mud.

"Get those bastards!" Crook yelled as Clark loped up. "Call for volunteers, Mr. Clark! Twenty men—take them down there and clean out that nest of vipers!"

Clark saluted. "Very good, sir!"

Following the lieutenant, those men who had volunteered to flush the hostiles crouched forward more in a flurry of bravery and energy than in any good sense. Another barrage of shots from the ravine tore through the soldiers' ranks. Private Edward Kennedy of C Troop, Fifth Cavalry, bellowed like a gutted hog as he went down, hit in both legs, most of one calf blown away and spurting blood in gouts. Nearby Private John M. Stevenson of Company I, Second Cavalry, dropped his carbine and wrapped both hands around his left ankle, blood oozing between his fingers as he pitched to the stream bottom, groaning in pain.

Along the side of the ridge at the top of the ravine

some of the spectators pitched some burning brands into the brushy depths, but the torches had no effect on the hostiles, landing instead on damp ground where they were soon to snuff themselves out with no dry tinder to catch and hold the flames.

When more of the curious and angry onlookers edged forward, Crook ordered them back while Lieutenant Clark re-formed his men and prepared for a second rush of the ravine. From a protected lip near the mouth of the coulee, Clark had his volunteers fire three point-blank volleys into the brush. Each round of shots was followed by a renewed wail from the women and even more pitiful screams from the children.

"Call your men back, Lieutenant!" Crook finally ordered, his face showing the strain of frustration.

Clark's volunteers gladly withdrew from their suicidal mission.

As the soldiers backed away from harm's way, the general hollered at Grouard. "Frank—how many women and children do you suppose are in there?"

"No way I can say, General."

At that moment close to a hundred soldiers swarmed off the slopes and into the creek bottom, rushing the mouth of the ravine, seething with their own anger. Lieutenant Clark was forced to stand, exposing himself to a bullet in the back from the hostiles in the coulee as he railed at the enraged soldiers, attempting to physically restrain some of those at the head of the mob.

On the nearby hillside Crook cried out like a scalded cat, ordering every last one of his officers to regain control of their men.

Lieutenant John Bourke and Captain Samuel Munson of the Ninth Infantry joined in, putting their bodies between the soldiers and the enemy. For fevered minutes it became a free-for-all there on the edge of the coulee, as much a wrestling match as a shouting and cursing fest. For all their stouthearted courage Bourke and Munson were overwhelmed and knocked off their feet, sent sailing into the depths of the ravine, where they landed among some women and children splattered with plenty of mud and blood, all of them screaming like banshees rising right out of the maw of hell at the sudden appearance of the soldiers in their midst.

Surprised and caught off guard, the warriors didn't have time to turn from where they had been intently watching the mouth of the ravine in time to see the two white men before the pair of officers scrambled up the soft, giving side of the ravine, shrieking for help and hands to pull them to safety.

"Bejaysus, Johnny!" Donegan grumbled as he hauled back, yanking Bourke up the muddy, sodden side of the ravine.

The lieutenant landed squarely on Seamus as the screams of the women and children died behind them.

"Thanks, Irishman," Bourke huffed breathlessly, his face smeared with mud as he crawled off Donegan. "I owe you for that."

"Aye, Johnny—you do owe me," Seamus said, grinning. "Once we ride back to Fetterman, I'll expect your gratitude in a whiskey glass."

Chapter 41

9 September 1876

The lieutenant called Bourke was more than muddy from his spill into the ravine; from what Baptiste Pourier could see, the soldier was shaking like a wet dog when the Irishman pulled him out of danger. As far as Bat knew, the wide-eyed, frightened young officer had never been that close to the enemy before—ever. Not even when the Sioux nearly surrounded and captured him on horseback during Crook's battle on the Rosebud.

As he crouched there beside Frank Grouard waiting to see just what the soldiers and their officers would do next, Pourier heard Crook suspend the assault on the ravine. Then Crook called for Bat and Grouard. The half-breeds crawled back from the mouth of the ravine, turned, and headed over to see what the general had on his mind.

"Talk to them," Crook said, a little desperation creeping into his voice. "See if you can get them to understand I don't want to have to kill every last one of them."

"It ain't gonna do no good," Grouard grumbled. "Them are Sioux in there."

"Frank's probably right," Pourier agreed. Everything he knew of the Lakota told him they wouldn't give up. "They sooner die than come out."

"I asked you to give it a try," Crook repeated, this time glaring at the two scouts. "Do I make myself understood?"

"Pretty plain to me, General," Grouard replied before he turned away with Big Bat.

Pourier said nothing as he slid back down the creek bank and returned to the mouth of the ravine.

Frank called to the Sioux in their own tongue, "You will not be killed if you come out now."

"Why don't you come in and get us, Grabber!" was the bold reply. "Come in and get us with your soldiers!"

"Seems they know your voice good, Frank," Pourier said, poking an elbow in Grouard's rib.

Against Crook's orders some soldiers answered the courageous Sioux taunt with rifle fire directed into the ravine. It took some perilous minutes before officers silenced those guns and ordered their men back so the negotiations could continue.

"You think maybe these soldiers kill us by mistake?" Pourier wondered. "Maybe they shoot us in the back—they want those Sioux so bad, eh?"

Ignoring Bat, Grouard again pressed his offer.

"This is how you tell us to surrender?" came the loud voice from the ravine.

"It was a mistake!" Bat hollered in Lakota.

"Is that the other trader's son out there?" demanded the angry voice in the ravine. "The one who came with Grabber bringing soldiers to destroy our camps, to kill our women and children?"

Grouard told them, "The soldier chief wants to let your women and children come out before they are killed."

The warrior replied, "But you send bullets to prove the lie in your words."

"No—the soldier guns are quiet now," Grouard answered.

"We do not worry about the soldier guns, Grabber. Very soon Crazy Horse will be here to take every one of those guns from your soldiers!"

Grouard turned and slid back down the slope with Pourier. At the bottom he signaled Crook with a shrug. The frustrated general waved his arms, shouting his command. In turn his officers ordered their men to resume their bombardment of the ravine.

"By Jupiter," Crook grumbled to his staff, "when will those Sioux see just what will happen if they don't surrender?"

Bat hunkered low on the cold ground with Grouard while the renewed barrage continued, wishing he had a cup of hot coffee. After more than an hour the general again called a stop to the noisy siege. As the gunfire died off, Crook asked his half-breed scouts to take up negotiations once more. While Grouard started talking to the hostiles again, Pourier crept up the slope, inching along the edge of the ravine on his belly beneath the thick brush, hoping to get himself a look at its occupants.

Suddenly, to his surprise, right below Bat huddled a woman who muttered as if she was talking to herself.

Leaping down the side of the coulee, Pourier found her very frightened, shivering with cold and painted with sticky mud. Although she immediately lunged away from him, Bat spoke softly to her.

"Come with me. Meet the soldier chief. See that he will not harm you if you surrender now."

For a moment more her wild, wide eyes held abject fear. But when she began to babble, pleading for her life, tears streaming from her eyes, Bat knew he had convinced her. If he could get one of the Sioux out safely, the rest would come as well.

Slowly he reached for her muddy hand when the brush behind her parted. Through the branches appeared a warrior with a pistol in his hand, pointed at Pourier. Between the two of them huddled the squaw.

Bat grabbed the woman's hand, whirling her around, shoving her in a heap toward the warrior. As he dived to get out of the woman's way, the warrior yelped in anger, finding himself suddenly without his pistol. Pourier had ripped it from his enemy. Now Bat had them both covered. The woman argued with the man, but he said nothing. Only his hate-filled eyes spoke volumes.

While the half-breed debated with himself how he was to get his two prisoners out of the ravine without the soldiers shooting them all, a very old woman appeared from the brush. Under her arm was a young girl he supposed could be no more than nine or ten summers. Grandmother and granddaughter were both splattered with mud and blood and gore.

Pourier quickly motioned with a pistol barrel, pointing to the mouth of the ravine. "Go. We show you now the soldier chief is a man of his word. Honor. He will not kill those who surrender."

Near the brushy mouth of the coulee Pourier ordered his captives to halt. Then he hollered so the soldiers could hear. "Get me General Crook!"

"Who the hell is that in there?"

"Pourier!"

"The scout?"

"Yes—get me General Crook!"

"How the hell did you get in there with the god-damned hostiles?"

"It don't matter—just get me Crook. I come out if I talk to him!"

"C'mon out, Bat!"

Relief flooded over him. It was the general's voice. "I got some prisoners for you, General. Some of those what wanna give up."

Cautiously he pushed through the brush into the open, his chest hammering like a steam piston as he looked at all the muzzles of those rifles and pistols pointed his way. But Crook was there, extending his hand. Urging him on.

Turning slightly, Bat reached back into the brush and took the hand of the old woman. Even though her face registered her immense fear, she was the first to walk toward Pourier. Then the young girl, and at last the young woman came forward at a crouch, as terrified as a snow-shoe hare surrounded by prairie wolves.

"This cannot be Three Stars," the old woman said to the half-breed. "The soldier chief?"

For a moment Pourier looked at Crook, then understood the woman's confusion. The general wore no finery. In fact he had nothing on to indicate any rank at all. His boots were as muddy as any soldier's, his long caped wool coat as ragged as those worn by the Montana Volunteers, and his nondescript hat was shabby protection from the rain that dribbled through his beard.

Pointing at Crook, he told her, "Yes, this is Three Stars."

Almost immediately the old woman's face drained of fear, and her expression reverted to one of relief when she realized she was under the care of the soldier chief. When she lunged forward to grasp Crook's hand in a flurry, nearby soldiers jumped in, seizing her, scared for the general's safety. But the old squaw only petted Three Stars's hand, gripping it for her life, murmuring quietly at the soldier chief's side.

When Crook motioned his soldiers back, Bat said, "She says they are from Spotted Tail, General."

"The agency?"

"Yes. Says they was going in to get food."

Crook blinked a moment, then asked, "I suppose we're all hungry, aren't we?"

Assured of safety now, the young woman went to stand on the other side of the general. From the folds of her blanket she took an infant whom she had hidden through the entire tense ordeal with Baptiste at the bottom of the ravine. Hardly half a year old, the baby's face was a picture of pain—yet the stoic child, surrounded by so many hairy faces, did not cry as its mother brought it into the light and the cold. She gripped one of the child's ankles in a crimson-drenched hand, attempting to stop the flow of blood. There was no foot below that hand: shot off by one of the soldier bullets.

"How many more are in there?" Crook asked in a quiet voice, his eyes registering his own pain as he looked over his four new captives.

Bat wagged his head. "Don't know for sure."

"Then tell the others, talk to them in their language—and convince them that these will be cared for. Convince them that all will be safe if they just surrender now."

Singly and in pairs nine more women and four more children soon emerged, seeing for themselves that the soldiers did not immediately shoot their prisoners as they had expected. In all, seventeen surrendered, crowding in a circle about the red-bearded soldier chief. One of the young women, shot through the hand and bleeding on the muddy ground, paid no attention to her wound, but instead huddled close so she could understand all Bat's assurances—when three shots cracked the discussion, bullets whining overhead. The soldiers and Sioux captives all scurried for cover like an overturned nest of field crickets.

"Looks like the rest ain't gonna give up," Pourier declared to the general.

"Then I'll just have to convince them that they have to surrender," Crook said, "or die."

After his prisoners were taken back to safety into the village, Crook ordered his officers to bring a concentration of fire from both his infantry and cavalry on the mouth of the ravine. For close to an hour Bat watched the soldiers pour more than three thousand rounds into the brush. As clouds of gunsmoke hung above the whole scene in the sodden air, the general called again for the assault to stop.

"Tell them again that I will grant them my mercy," Crook told Baptiste. "But they must come out now."

Once more Pourier crawled to the mouth of the coulee with Grouard, and they called out to the Sioux warriors. For close to an hour they appealed to the warriors, and just when it seemed all efforts were about to fail, one of the squaws rejoined Crook on the hillside, asking for the chance to talk to the warriors. In moments she joined the half-breeds at the ravine opening, calling out to the men barricaded within. It wasn't very long before one young warrior came out, holding a carbine across his chest.

"This one, her husband," Bat explained.

Crook accepted the man's rifle and took his hand, shaking it before he directed the warrior to stand beside him and call out to the others. A strong voice answered from the ravine.

"They will come out," Baptiste translated, "if their lives will be spared."

The general asked, "Who is that in there?"

"The chief—one what wants to come out," Grouard explained.

"Tell him I want no more killing today," Crook replied.

Cautiously, Pourier and Grouard crept farther into the ravine and waited. Then waited some more, listening as muffled voices argued. More long, interminable minutes. At last a tall warrior inched forward stoically, one arm clutched at his middle, a bloody sash tied around his lower belly, and his other arm slung over the shoulders of a younger warrior.

Bat exclaimed, "You are wounded."

The tall one pulled part of the damp sash from his belly, showing the half-breeds his terrible wound. He had been shot in the abdomen, and part of his intestine was already protruding from the gaping wound.

As the older one replaced the sash around his wound, the young warrior looked at the two scouts and asked, "You are the traders' sons?"

"Yes," Pourier replied. "What is your name?"

"I am Charging Bear."

Unable to take his eyes off the older man for long, Big Bat turned back to the tall warrior, marveling at his immense courage. "Are the others coming?" he asked in Lakota.

"Only two," Charging Bear responded.

Again Pourier looked into the older man's eyes, the warrior's face ashen with agony—with each flush of pain, grinding down on that small stick shoved between his teeth. "And you—your name—who are you?"

Slowly the handsome warrior dragged the stick from his mouth and drew himself up proudly. "I am American Horse. Chief of the Miniconjou."

As Seamus watched, American Horse gave his rifle to the soldier chief with solemn dignity. Through the half-breed interpreters the Sioux leader told Crook he would surrender if the lives of the last two warriors in the ravine would be spared.

Amid angry shouts of "No quarter!" from the soldiers looking on, Crook gave his guarantee, and American Horse called to the holdouts. When the younger warrior attending the chief was turned over to Colonel Chambers's guard detail, Surgeon Clements and his stewards took charge of the wounded American Horse.

Slowly the doctor pulled back the bloody sash from the sticky wound. More of the intestine escaped the hole. Gritting on the stick between his teeth, the chief immediately poked and shoved the best he could, pushing the bowel back into the ragged hole in his belly. But it was no use.

"I'm sorry, General," Clements told Crook. "The wound is mortal."

Crook turned to Grouard and said, "Tell the chief he will die before morning."

American Horse made no reply when told. His face registered nothing more than the pain already visited upon him. Clements led the chief away, hobbling slowly toward the small fire nearby, where the rest of the captives warmed their cold hands and feet. The chief settled among the women and children, his teeth still clamped on the stick. The surgeon left to return to his hospital tent, explaining that there was nothing else he could do for one so seriously wounded. It was but a matter of time.

Charging Bear stayed with Crook for a few minutes,

talking to the soldier chief through the half-breed interpreters.

"Very soon Crazy Horse will come to free our village," the warrior warned the general. He went on to express convincingly his belief that word of the attack had already reached the other villages in the surrounding countryside, and a great fighting force was then on its way, likely to arrive before nightfall.

Crook said, "You tell this man that's just what I've hoped. I've prayed for nothing less than a good fight with Crazy Horse for a long, long time." Then he had the infantry guards take Charging Bear away.

It did not take long before the last two warriors appeared from the tangle of brush farther up the ravine. One of them wore a corporal's tunic, taken from Custer's own L Company. He was eager to shake hands all around with the scouts and the officers—in fact, with any soldier who would shake hands as he grinned, relief washing over his face.

With the surrender of those last two warriors, Frank Grouard counted what the holdouts had left in ammunition. Six cartridges each. When the prisoners were escorted from the scene, Sergeant Von Moll of the Third Cavalry brought in a squad of his soldiers from Private Wenzel's own A company to claim the body, the rifle still gripped in the dead man's cold hands. Two empty cartridges lay near his right side, a live round still in his carbine, cocked and ready to fire.

As the angry troopers carried away their comrade, Donegan followed the half-breed scouts into the ravine. They found the walls of the coulee riddled, tracked, and scarred with the paths of thousands of bullets. Twisting, brushy yards from the entrance they discovered five bodies: three women, a warrior shot in the head, and an infant.

Bullets had repeatedly found one woman's body, what was left of her clothing crusted over with muddy slime and coagulated blood. Her neck was nearly severed by one shot, three more had torn open her chest and shoulder. Two more grisly holes in each arm and leg. The bodies of the other two women had suffered nearly as many wounds— one with her head blown completely in half, clear down to the upper palate. From what Seamus could see, it appeared the warriors had used the bodies of their dead to hide behind during the onslaught of soldier lead.

Curious himself, Captain Anson Mills entered the ravine behind the three scouts, accompanied by the young girl who had been discovered in a lodge hiding beneath a pile of robes and who had attached herself to the officer. At the sight of one of the dead women, the girl rushed forward to fall upon the body, crying pitifully. She hugged the body, brushed the matted hair from the bloody face, her little tears falling upon the cold cheeks as she wailed.

"Her mother," Pourier whispered to Mills and Donegan.

The captain wagged his head. "Why . . . why the women?"

Crook had his men drag the battered bodies from the coulee, where they lay for close to an hour while soldiers looked over the enemy dead. It struck Donegan as a pagan ritual, this satisfying the curiosity of the soldiers who had lost their own comrades in battle. While most only stared at the bodies before moving on, some chose to spit on the corpses.

Yet no soldier defiled the dead like Ute John, also known among the column as "Captain Jack."

Chattering in his garbled pidgin English, the civilian member of Stanton's Montana Volunteers made quite a show of it for a crowd of curious soldiers as he knelt over each of the squaws and scalped them with elaborate ceremony, demonstrating to the white men just how it was done.

"Injun style," he explained, his mouth half-filled with rotted teeth.

Having joined the troops in May when a band of miners had affixed themselves to Crook's column, John was in reality only half-Northern or Weber Ute, the other half

Shoshone. Called Nicaagat by his own people on the Wind River Reservation in Wyoming Territory, he had acquired a desperate thirst for the white man's whiskey. That thirst took him to Salt Lake City for a six-month sojourn, during which time he claimed he'd been Christianized by Brigham Young's Mormons.

"Ute John's a Klischun," he proudly reminded the onlookers, perhaps to convince them that what he was doing to the dead was not so barbaric an act as it might appear. "A Mo'mon Klischun."

A loving Mormon family had given him shelter and taught him the rudiments of the English language. He had been "heap washed" of his sins, as many as three times in one year, and got a "heap b'iled shirt" of his very own to wear when he attended Sunday meetings to hear Prophet Brigham preach for hours on end.

While most of the soldiers turned away from the grisly spectacle, a few clamored to have a try at the scalping themselves. Donegan grumbled and started to turn aside, disgusted that none of the officers attempted to stop this savage depravity of tearing the hair from women's skulls.

"What's the matter with you, Irishman?" one of the old files asked Donegan. "You seen a lot worse before, I'd care to wager."

"I have," Seamus replied bitterly.

"So where the hell you get off being so goddamned righteous about it?" the veteran snarled. "Them prisoners the general took sure as hell getting treated good, ain't they? Just think how things'd be for a bunch of us white men if we was took prisoner by a village of these sonsabitches. What fun they'd have killing us off real slow! So you just think about that, Irishman—before you go off being so goddamned high and mighty and looking down your nose at the likes of us gonna take a little revenge for what we seen done to our friends in the last ten years."

Looking over that sullen group of angry soldiers who had turned to glare at him, Donegan finally said, "When I rode for the Army of the Potomac, and served Sheridan's

Army of the Shenandoah—I never once killed a woman or a child. And I'll be damned if I've got to stand here and watch a coward take his revenge on women."

"Just shut your mouth and go 'way," Ute John grumbled, wagging his knife where he knelt on the ground to slice apart one of the women's scalps so that each of the sympathetic soldiers could have a small lock.

"You best go, Irishman," the old veteran suggested caustically. "Since you can't seem to remember that these Injun bitches fight just as hard as the bucks."

"Goddamned right," one of the other soldiers chimed in.

The veteran continued sourly. "I seen enough of my friends cut down by red bitches—it don't make me no never mind to kill all the squaws I can."

Another soldier cried out, "Just means there's fewer wombs for these red devils to make papooses!"

Seamus straightened, the words smacking him like grapeshot. Back there at Laramie, his woman carried his child in her womb.

Looking squarely in the old Apache-fighter's eye, he quietly said, "An old file like you what seen so much killing during the war, so much killing since—never took you to be a man what fancied butchering children and babes."

For a moment the veteran stood there in utter silence, haughtily glaring back at the Irishman. Then Donegan thought he saw an almost imperceptible quake shoot through the man, a quiver crossing his big shoulders that visibly shook the two small and faded chevrons sewn on his muddy sleeves. When he finally spoke, his mighty jaw trembled, but his gaze was steady.

"I had me a family once. So don't you ever again say O'Reilly's not a man to protect the little ones what can't protect themselves."

The old soldier turned on his heel and crossed the five yards to where Ute John was holding court, shoving his way into the midst of those reveling soldiers, and picked up the body of the dead infant off the soggy ground, all to the stunned silence of everyone, even Seamus Donegan. Like a great white oak sheltering a tiny seedling, the veteran cradled the dead infant within his arms as he elbowed his way from the angry, cursing mob and strode past Donegan, his eyes brimming with tears.

"Cawpril," Seamus said quietly just as the man passed him.

The soldier stopped. His shoulders heaving once, he finally turned round as Donegan walked up and touched the man's arm. "This morning when we was going through the lodges, I remember seeing a small piece of blanket what might work nicely."

With a nod the soldier followed Seamus to a lodge where they found not only a blanket to wrap around the infant's bloody body, but a basket large enough to serve as a coffin. Only then did the two take the child across the hillside to that small fire where the prisoners sat within a ring of guards. The old soldier laid the basket at the feet of the young women. No one moved. Not American Horse, not Charging Bear, not any of the women. They only stared at the two white men, perhaps unable to comprehend this surprising act of kindness in the midst of the cruelty, barbarity, the utter savagery of both sides of this great Sioux War.

It wasn't long afterward that Seamus and the corporal went to sit on a grassy hillside above the ravine, there to talk about wives and children and all that the loss of family could destroy in a man—when the attack the captives had promised came to pass.

Chapter 42

9 September 1876

Just past four o'clock surgeons Bennett Clements and Valentine McGillycuddy ordered a quartet of troopers to lock down the limbs of a heavily sedated Lieutenant Adolphus Von Leuttwitz. Because the bullet was still lodged in the bone, this grisly, open-air amputation could be put off no longer.

It amazed those who watched just how much fight was still left in the officer, rambling with fever and groggy by virtue of heavy doses of morphine administered throughout the afternoon, as the huge, serrated knife began to bite into that torn flesh above the wounded right knee. Completely around the limb Clements drew his knife in a long circular motion, the blade sinking through the thick muscles, where it scraped along the femur. Then at just the moment the knife was withdrawn from that deep incision, McGillycuddy was already pushing his handsaw's blade through the bloody gash, working feverishly to hack through that largest bone in the human body.

Unlike those Civil War surgeons who after a short time became so proficient in amputations that they could remove an arm in eight seconds, a leg in no more than eleven, these two had approached their surgery as a last resort—praying that by sacrificing the limb, they could save their patient's life.

In moments Clements yelled for the infantry bayonet he had buried in the coals of a nearby fire. With it the surgeon cauterized the severed stump as a steward dragged away the useless limb and wrapped it in a small piece of greasy blanket taken from one of the captured lodges about to undergo destruction. As the lieutenant thrashed and fought, both surgeons sealed off the bleeding vessels and daubed the great open wound with iodine, wrapping it in clean surgical dressings before moving on to perform the same task on Private Edward Kennedy, who had been wounded in both legs during the siege at the ravine.

About the same time, just minutes past four P.M., Sergeant Von Moll's men from A Troop were turning the damp sod with Lieutenant Bubb's spades, carving out two graves west of the ravine for scout White and Private Wenzel—when the sudden war cries and the gunfire reverberated from the bluffs to signal the attack.

"Injuns firing into the herds on the front of the Third Cavalry!" came the alarm.

That moment found many of the cavalrymen who had been put afoot during the march taking part in the auction Mills's men were holding just north of the Third Cavalry camp at the northwest corner of the village. One by one they were selling off the ponies Crook had awarded them for attacking the enemy village. It had become a rowdy and raucous affair, with a lot of good-natured disputes as to the value of various animals from the other regiments, as well as arguments concerning just how the troopers from the Fifth and Second could be trusted to pay their debt when the expedition finally reached their duty stations.

But all that was forgotten when the Sioux rode down on Rabbit Lip Creek to continue the Battle of Slim Buttes.

"This has to be them three hundred lodges of Oglalla the prisoners told us about!" Baptiste Pourier huffed as he rushed up, joining Donegan.

They dashed past Captain William H. Powell and his

G Company, Fourth Infantry, under Crook's orders to begin the burning of the lodges, and of everything else not already salvaged for food or souvenirs. In the midst of the growing battle, towers of oily black smoke began to rise into the leaden, heavy air.

"This bunch won't have no problem turning back a few warriors," Seamus replied in the noisy clamor of dogs barking, men shouting orders, the keening of women prisoners mingled with the cries of their children.

All around them men scampered up from their blankets where they had been napping, or snatched up their weapons as they leaped to their feet beside cookfires where they had been feasting on the spoils of the captured village. At long last Chambers's infantry and the rest of Merritt's cavalry would get a crack at the enemy. For the moment all hunger and fatigue were forgotten. This was, after all, exactly what they had marched and starved and frozen for.

"Them prisoners said there was other camps nearby too," Bat added. "Not just the camps of Crazy Horse, He Dog, and Kicking Bear."

Above them mirrors flashed in the hills that surrounded the natural amphitheater. To the south some among the milling horsemen signaled their answer. In a matter of minutes the entire southern perimeter seemed to crawl with hostiles as the warriors swarmed over the rolling hillside, intent on retaking the village in one fell swoop. Just beyond the soldier lines atop a trio of low ridges that stood southwest of the camp, many warriors dismounted and began a long-range duel with soldiers of the Ninth and Fourth infantries.

Crook's first orders to his battalion commanders was to protect their stock. For days they had abandoned or shot their horses, forced to go afoot. There wasn't a cavalryman on the battle lines now who wanted to give up what ponies they had just captured, much less lose any more of their own horses and mules to the screaming horsemen pressing in from nearly all points of the compass.

"Sound to arms, Bradley!" Lieutenant Colonel Eugene

Carr bellowed to his chief trumpeter. "I won't let the red bastards have a one of my animals!"

But just as some of Carr's troopers reached what was left of their herd, a half-dozen Sioux horsemen on fresh, well-fed ponies rushed through their midst, stampeding more than half of the big, bone-lean, and leg-weary American horses. Reacting quickly, Corporal J. S. Clanton of Captain Montgomery's B Troop snagged a halter and flung himself bareback aboard one of the grays, kicking furiously to catch up to the lead horse as a half-dozen other men followed in the corporal's wake to lend a hand.

When almost among the screeching, painted enemy, Clanton drew beside the first escaping mount, leaning over to latch on to the horse's dangling halter. He succeeded in turning it and the rest who followed just short of some thirty onrushing Sioux, making a wide five-hundred-yard circle as Lieutenant Colonel Carr watched the rescue in awestruck admiration. Returning with all of Montgomery's grays, the men and officers of the Fifth Cavalry raised their cheers and gave Clanton a stirring round of applause.

But off to the southeast on the other side of camp, about ten Sioux horsemen had better luck, managing to break through the infantry's lines to spook a few cavalry mounts being held in the creek bottom near the heart of the captured village.

Now in control of most of his stock, Crook ordered Major Chambers to have his infantry retake the high ground just seized by the enemy southwest of the village. Chambers directed Captain Andrew Burt to take two companies of the Fourth, along with one of the Ninth and one of the Fourteenth regiments, to move out on the double from their bivouac at the north side of the camp, rushing straight through the smoking village and across the stream to climb the cutbank, where they began to push back the sudden and fierce attack.

On the nearby slopes the Sioux taunted, yelled insults, exposed themselves, and patted their rumps to show their contempt for their enemy.

"Steady, men!" shouted the officers scampering up and down that line of infantry. "Keep your proper intervals!"

"Don't fire until you get in range!" ordered a sergeant to his platoon as they crossed the creek to join in the fray. "C'mon, now. Forward at double time!"

After a volley the sergeant growled, "Dammit, Sparks, are you firing at the Black Hills? Never waste a shot, boys!"

Throwing the heat of his very own H Company of the Ninth under Lieutenants Charles M. Rockefeller and Edgar B. Robertson, along with Captain Gerhard L. Luhn's F Company of the Fourth and the Fourteenth's C under the command of Captain Daniel W. Burke, Captain Burt temporarily held Lieutenant Henry Seton's D Company of the Fourth in reserve. At the same time Burt called up three additional companies to hold the cutbank itself, then leapfrogged ahead, pushing his battalion forward, attempting to wrench the momentum away from the enemy. There on the slopes of those southwestern hills most of this second fight in the Battle of Slim Buttes was to rage until nightfall.

It did not take long for more of the Sioux to realize where the soldiers had herded most of the cavalry horses. Rushing in a wide arc around the eastern perimeter of the village, the warriors put great pressure on what few troops Merritt had left behind to watch over the herds. As soon as he saw the sweeping blur of the enemy rushing past him, Major Alexander Chambers, recognizing the move for what it was, ordered two companies of the Ninth Infantry to move out at double time north of the village site, charged with holding the ridges against the threat to flank the soldiers.

At the same time that Merritt was ordering Lieutenant Frederick Sibley's E Company to station themselves as a rear guard to drive in all stragglers and used-up horses still coming in, he also ordered Major Henry E. Noyes forward with a mounted I Troop of the Second Cavalry to set up a skirmish line east of the village. They were the only troopers to fight on horseback. The rest of the horse soldiers from the Second, Third, and Fifth regiments inched forward on foot, making dismounted foragers' charges in conjunction with the infantry.

Throughout the late-afternoon battle Crook's destruction of the camp continued uninterrupted.

Moving from hilltop to hilltop above the jagged soldier skirmish lines rode a war chief atop a white horse. He first appeared near the bottom southeast of camp, then he was seen leading warriors to attempt to capture some horses, then minutes later he was spotted rallying warriors on the three hills southwest of the dismounted cavalry. Because of what American Horse and the other prisoners had warned the soldiers, Crook's men believed this warrior was Crazy Horse.

However, old Sioux veterans of the battle would one day attest to the fact that it was instead Sitting Bull who made himself the most visible and taunting target of the afternoon.

Right in the heart of the fray stood Captain Julius Mason's battalion of Fifth Cavalry, where the Sioux hurled their first massed charge, screaming down the slopes, against the soldier lines. Yard by yard as the troopers pushed back against the horsemen, Sergeant Edmund Schreiber of Charles King's own K Company fell. Less than a minute later a bullet tumbled Private August Dorn of D Troop.

While Major John J. Upham's battalion of the Fifth surged forward to take some of the pressure off the left flank of Mason's line, it was William B. Royall and his scarred Third Cavalry veterans of the Rosebud fight who flushed the Sioux from the rugged heights both northwest and immediately west of the village. How many of those men who followed the lieutenant colonel into that skirmish rallied their comrades-in-arms by asking them to remember the nightmare of their fight beside the Rosebud, history did not record.

After waiting nearly three months to avenge that day, the Third did not just hold the line—they pushed back, and pushed hard, driving the flood of retreating warriors down the slopes onto the backs of Eugene Carr's surprised battalion of Fifth Cavalry, who had just begun to attack those Sioux sniping from the crests of the southwestern hills.

For a half hour, frightening confusion rumbled over the heights and spilled down through the ravines and coulees as the warriors poured around the ranks of Carr's dismounted skirmishers like a foaming cascade bypassing a floodgate. Through it all, in the midst of that snarling hail of bullets whining through the trees and slapping against the rocks, Lieutenant Colonel Carr sat astride his gray stallion, buoying his Fifth.

"See there, men! They can't even hit me—what damned wretched shots they are!"

Meanwhile to the east the action began to drag out for much of the next hour as Burt's infantry inched forward, pushing the enemy back, back, back through each narrow draw and tangle of brush—the deep, reverberating booms of their Long Toms contrasting with the sharper cracks of the cavalry carbines. In a whirl of color the retreating warriors regathered and concentrated, firing back on infantry without inflicting any damage, then scurried off a few more yards before turning to fire on the soldiers once again, seeking all the time to find some point of weakness in the soldier lines. Always the Sioux kept at least five to eight hundred yards between their position and Burt's oncoming footmen.

Just behind the infantry scampered newsman John Finerty, straggling along in his big, clumsy brogans—writing down bits of action, the names of soldiers, and snippets of orders. In these final minutes of the afternoon's battle, another soldier suffered a minor wound, and the officers watched a warrior topple from a horse, his body quickly scooped up by his companions and raced to the rear.

"Look at that, will you?" hollered one old Irish soldier near Finerty. "I sure softened the wax in that boy's ears!"

Seeking to put an end to that long-range skirmishing,

Major Upham's battalion of the Fifth succeeded in driving the Sioux from the three low hills southwest of the village by sweeping in on the enemy's right flank—scattering the warriors in confusion and fear as other units pressed in from behind to reinforce Upham's troops. Most of the fleeing Sioux escaped to the west, scaling the rugged chalky ridges and terraces where they could hide among the dark pines, there to overlook the campsite from afar. It had been that way for almost an hour: the Sioux driven from one place, dashing away to pop up attacking another spot along the soldiers' skirmish line.

Despite Upham's success, Crook was not content merely to flush the enemy from the hills. He hungered to make them stand and fight. As the sun began its final fall, he therefore ordered his dismounted cavalry to attack the western bluffs themselves. As a cloudy dusk began to swallow the land, the troops pushed into the hills at the base of the bluffs. Below them in the sodden air hung the thick, moist smudges of gray gun smoke and oily black columns rising above each one of the burning lodges, all of it tumbling together to create a fog clinging to every nearby ravine.

Pushed north along the jagged shelves of those gray heights, the warriors suddenly swept down, attempting to rout some units of the Third Cavalry situated northwest of the village. But in a steady rattle of gunfire the dismounted troopers held their ground and within fifteen harrowing minutes were pushing the enemy back, the muzzle flashes of the guns on both sides lighting up the pale hue of the buttes.

Dusk soon gave way to darkness, and with the arrival of night's secure cloak away slipped the warriors, leaving the soldiers in control of the bluffs, the hills, and the full perimeter of the village itself. It was a clear victory for Crook. Although he likely outgunned the warriors, estimated by his officers to number between six and eight hundred, he could claim, nonetheless, a victory. Sitting Bull had attacked a Three Stars twice stronger than Crook had been on the Rosebud, leading his warriors into battle this day against a soldier force three times stronger than that of Custer's five companies destroyed along the Little Bighorn.

In the first confusing moments of attack the warriors had captured the high ground—but with able officers and diligent soldiers, the Big Horn and Yellowstone Expedition had regained the battle's momentum, retaken the heights, and eventually driven off the enemy as night fell.

John Bourke took a quick tally early that evening, reporting to the general that the units counted a total of eight soldiers wounded. For most of the battle the warriors had been firing down upon the soldiers, and that "factor of terrain" had caused most of the Sioux bullets to sail harmlessly over the heads of the white men. As was normally the case, enemy casualties were entirely unknown, but Carr estimated that they had killed or wounded as many as seven or eight of the Sioux. Another officer reported off the record that fourteen warrior bodies were found on the battlefield, while another four had been carried off—nothing more than an educated guess made from an examination of the pools of blood found on many of the rocky ledges where the Sioux had made their stand.

"That Reuben Davenport needs someone to take him down a notch or two," Crook's young adjutant complained as he came up to kneel at the captives' campfire beside Donegan.

"What's that pain-in-the-ass reporter saying now?"

"The wag is saying Crook's soldiers missed a grand opportunity by not following up and capturing the warriors."

"With this bunch of worn-out men and what we've got left of horses?" Seamus asked, incredulous. He snorted a sour laugh. "You're serious? He wanted us to traipse after them Sioux and squash 'em, eh?"

"I bet ol' Crazy Horse figured he would find just Mills's men here," the lieutenant said.

"He and the rest got themselves a good surprise, then, didn't they?" Seamus replied.

"Those Sioux were wise to retreat when they did after running into more soldiers than they counted on."

"Wasn't but an hour's scrap, was it?" Donegan asked, trying to coax a young child to his knee with the offer of a hard cracker.

"She's a tough one, Irishman," Bourke replied. "A real screamer. You get anywhere close to her, she'll shriek your ears off."

"You wanna try?" Donegan asked, holding the cracker to the lieutenant.

"Maybe I have something that'll help." Bourke pulled his field haversack off his shoulder and fished around inside until he pulled out the small tin of fruit preserves. "Lemme see your belt knife."

With Donegan's knife the lieutenant spread the wild-currant jam atop the hardtack, then held it out for the young girl, who could be no more than five years old.

"Take it, it's *washtay. Wauwataycha*," Bourke told the youngster in her own tongue.

No matter—at first she refused even to consider the offered treat, but eventually crept forward, snatched the cracker out of the soldier's hand, then darted back to her place among the other captives. There she squatted in the smoke of the fire and took her first bite of the sweet. Her eyes lit up, and her tongue swirled across her lips so that she wouldn't miss a morsel. Seamus chuckled at just how fast the youngster devoured that cracker.

As she stuffed the last crumbs into her mouth, the girl crawled right over to Bourke's knee and squatted as if completely unafraid, looking up at the lieutenant with imploring eyes, her hand held out.

"Looks like you've made you a friend at last, Johnny!"

"It does, at that," Bourke replied. "Have you any more tacks?"

"This is my last," Donegan replied, pulling the cracker from his mackinaw pocket.

"We don't have to take your last."

"Go ahead. I'll rustle up some more of that pony meat

for supper tonight. Hate to admit it, but I'm beginning to grow quite fond of four-legged riding stock."

Fitting that a crimson sunset flared for but an astonishingly beautiful moment over those pale-gray buttes dotted with emerald evergreens: an appropriate requiem, perhaps, for a people who had already witnessed the zenith of their greatness.

Below the chalky terraces glowed the remains of some three dozen bonfires, each one what had once been a Sioux lodge. Across the hillsides flickered much smaller dots of reddish embers where gathered the battle-weary soldiers once more wolfing down the dried meat and berries they had captured and held on to as victors. On the heights as well as down across the eastern flats Crook posted a strong line of pickets while silence crept in once more to rule this wilderness. As a soft rain returned to patter on blankets, coats, and gum ponchos, some of the camp guards heard strange noises and cried out their challenges, only to find they had captured a riderless enemy pony abandoned in the Sioux retreat and now wandering in to the sound of humans.

Unlike the miserable bivouacs of the last two weeks, tonight one heard songs, jokes, and laughter. Once more men were eager about their prospects. Many of those who days before had been grumbling that the general ought to be hanged were this night heard to boast, "Crook was right, after all!"

They ate their fill in the rain, gathered at their hissing fires, caring not about the morrow.

"C'mere and try some of this, Seamus," John Finerty called out.

"What's on the menu there, newsman?" Donegan asked.

"Pony."

"Had me some already," and he squatted near the reporter.

"Not cooked fresh you haven't," Finerty replied. "See?

I've become quite a connoisseur, Seamus. Cavalry meat, played out, sore-backed, and fried without salt is stringy. Leathery, and tasting just like a wet wool saddle blanket too. Downright nauseating."

"I've tasted my fill of that too, thank you."

Again Finerty offered the Irishman a piece, saying, "Now, a full-grown Indian pony has the flavor and appearance of the flesh of elk."

"And you're an expert on elk, are you, now?"

"I've been hunting many a time with Crook, haven't I?" Finerty protested. "But perhaps best of all—a young Indian colt tastes like antelope, Seamus. Or mountain sheep."

"So what of mule meat?" asked Robert Strahorn from across the fire with a full mouth.

The reporter from Chicago shuddered. "Mule, eh? Fat and rank, perhaps best described as a combination of all the foregoing—with a wee taste of pork thrown in."

"There's some that think a mule loin is just about the best thing in the way of prairie victuals," Seamus told them, "second only to buffalo."

Finerty sneered, "And what sort of dunderhead would that be?"

"They're called Kwahadi Comanche, Johnny boy," Donegan replied, standing to stretch out his cold, cramping muscles. "And pray you don't ever have to campaign down on the Staked Plain of west Texas against those devils incarnate."

Chapter 43

9–10 September
1876

Not long after the last echoes of gunfire faded from the nearby bluffs, a pair of sore-footed troopers from the Fifth Cavalry limped out of the darkness, hailing the pickets surrounding infantry camp. They had been some of the first forced to abandon their played-out horses that morning when the entire column followed in the wake of Crook's rescue, which placed the pair as the last stragglers on the trail.

As they approached the northern end of Slim Buttes, the weariness of the muddy trail overwhelmed them, and they decided to lie down and nap among the shelter of some rocks they found in a ravine. At the moment the Sioux chose to launch their attack, the two hapless soldiers were awakened rudely. It didn't take them long to figure out they would be a lot safer staying right where they were than attempting to thread their way through the hostile horsemen in hopes of reaching the army's lines. They hadn't dared to raise their heads from their ravine until long after dark.

The steady, eerie throb of death chants and wails of

mourning women floated down from the shelter half where the surgeons had done what they could to make American Horse comfortable. Out there in the night, evil spirits lurked, ruling that dominion just beyond the fire's light.

Seamus shuddered and crossed himself superstitiously, sitting at a fire with John Finerty, Lieutenant Bourke, and others, staring mesmerized at the sputtering flames—then turned suddenly, tearing his revolver from its holster as a dark figure crouched from a gash in a nearby lodge.

With the audible double click of so many pistol hammers, the ghostly form stopped immediately, one leg in, one leg out of that slash in the buffalo hides, slowly standing erect in his long calf-length blanket coat of many colors, staring at the three barrels glinting with a dull light beneath the fire's dancing aura.

A pair of black eyes twinkled as the dark-skinned Indian tried out a lame smile, lifting his hands into the air and stammering, "T-there ain't a thing w-worth having in the hull damned outfit."

"Who in the thunder are you?" Donegan demanded.

"Ute John," he answered sheepishly as he inched into the light, his hands shaking as the Irishman advanced on him. "Some call me Cap'n Jack."

"Bejesus—you gave me a start!" Finerty exclaimed.

Donegan got close enough to press the revolver's muzzle against the tracker's head. With his empty hand he grabbed the Indian's chin and turned the brown face from side to side in the firelight. "Damn—it is you. The squaw scalper. Should've killed you right off." In disgust he turned away, stuffing his pistol into the holster on his hip.

"What are you doing there?" Bourke asked.

The Indian replied, "Looking for plunder."

"You're lucky to have a few lodges still standing, you sick bastard," Seamus added. "Cap'n Powell's gonna finish putting 'em all to the torch come morning."

Ute John's head bobbed, and he said, "I see what I find before the fires."

"G'won!" Bourke demanded. "Get out of here before I have you put under guard myself."

Early that rainy evening the general ordered that the four corpses Ute John had scalped and mutilated be given to the captives so they could perform a proper burial. With Grouard and Pourier, Crook then wrung what information he could from his reticent prisoners. From them the general learned that not only was Crazy Horse in the neighborhood, but Sitting Bull was as well—with plans to take his Hunkpapa north to the Antelope Buttes to trade. What came as the most discouraging news, however, was hearing that the bands had indeed split and scattered, most making for the reservations, and already far ahead of his column.

"Charging Bear keeps saying this bunch wasn't on the Greasy Grass, General," Big Bat reported. "Says they didn't fight the soldiers on the Little Bighorn."

"Then ask him why we found in their lodges the gloves of one of Custer's men, why we found their horses among these ponies, why we recaptured the pony soldiers' flag in this camp," Crook snarled.

To Three Stars, Charging Bear repeated the assertion that visiting Oglalla of the Crazy Horse Hunkpatila band brought those spoils from the Greasy Grass fight into camp.

In the end Crook used his interpreters to drive home his point that the army intended to punish all who remained off their agencies, then concluded by telling the prisoners he would release them the following morning. They would be allowed to remain there in the midst of their destroyed village, where they could bury their dead in the manner of their people.

Late that night six more stragglers showed up. The soldiers had left Crook's bivouac to hunt early that morning, before word had arrived of Mills's attack and everyone had set out on the rescue. They had returned later that day to find nothing but the column's tracks. Now the six greedily chewed on the dried meat offered them at the cheery fires as sheets of mist hissed around them, and told of being attacked by a dozen or more warriors who had held them under siege for some four hours before withdrawing. Nonetheless, they had waited until dark before pushing on in hopes of finding what had become of Crook's command.

During the night the surgeons kept their stewards busy constructing additional litters from lodgepoles, to which they lashed shelter halves or pieces of captured blankets for the morning's journey, when Crook would lead them south once more. Only three days before, the general had ordered Mills and Bubb to secure rations among the Black Hills settlements. But at that moment the Big Horn and Yellowstone Expedition was no closer to relief as the rain and gloom settled down on Slim Buttes.

With their amputations on Von Leuttwitz and Kennedy complete, Doctors Clements and McGillycuddy turned their attention to American Horse. As the surgeons knelt beside their patient, some of the friends of Private Wenzel nearby grumbled profanely.

"Why don't you just put a knife through that son of a bitch, Doc?" suggested one of the dead private's comrades.

"Yeah," agreed a second bitter friend. "I'll be happy to finish off that red bastard my own self."

"You bastards!" another old file shouted. "Why, I ain't got no use for a doctor that'd do anything for a goddamn Injun!"

Valentine McGillycuddy whirled on the troopers clustered nearby. "The next one of you who says a damned thing will answer personally to me! Are you men no better than animals? As for myself, I've taken an oath to relieve suffering—and I won't see a man in pain without giving aid. No matter the color of his skin!"

Despite his great pain and the many appeals from the half-breed interpreters, the chief steadfastly refused any of the white man's "powerful medicine" when the surgeons offered a hypodermic of morphine or an inhalation of chloroform. Instead American Horse had one of his wives cut a new bullberry branch to clamp between his teeth as he suffered his new agony in silence. While the doctors inspected and cleaned the terrible wound, removing part of the ruptured bowel, then closing the site with crude sutures, American Horse clenched both his eyes and teeth shut, nearly chewing through the stick before he passed out. Finally McGillycuddy had some soldiers hold the chief down so that he could administer an injection of morphine that would allow the chief to rest peacefully while death approached.

Fever's sweat beaded the patient's brow when he awoke later, as the painkiller seeping through his veins began to wear off. Through interpreters Clements explained that there was little else they could do in what time the chief had left. At his side remained his two wives and three of his children throughout that night, all of them chanting a mournful death dirge as a soaking rain steadily drummed on the canvas tent fly stretched above the dying warrior. Into each face he gazed as the hours passed his last night, each tear-tracked cheek he touched with trembling fingertips, removing the battered stick from his bloody lips to murmur soft words of endearment to those loved ones. Perhaps to tell them that with his death he had secured their freedom come the morrow.

In the cold darkness beyond that pitiful scene flickered the hundreds of tiny watch fires where huddled the weary soldiers who had eaten in one evening enough rations to feed them for three days. They curled up on the muddy ground beneath their sole blanket and gum poncho to reap the slumber of the victorious, their bellies stuffed with buffalo tongue and dried pony meat, along with the fruit of buffalo berries, wild plum, and chokecherry. Above them on the hilltops and chalky buttes the pines soughed a mournful song beneath the rush of a plaintive wind that from time to time drove the rain before it in sheets.

To the north along the army's backtrail Seamus heard the call of the song-dogs as coyotes discovered another of the bony horse carcasses and called in the prairie wolves. There is no other sound on earth quite like that, Donegan decided as he tossed another limb on that fire long after midnight, unable to sleep, and thinking on loved ones far away.

It was long after the last shots had faded from the hills when Sergeant Von Moll's men from A Troop finished their graves. By that time Von Moll found Lieutenant Joseph Lawson fast asleep, unable to read from his Common Book of Prayer over the departed. In the light of burning brands taken from the nearby fires and held high overhead, the spades had scraped the last bit of earth from the graves. With Private Wenzel's body wrapped in his ragged blue overcoat, and Charlie White tied within a funeral shroud of thick gray army blanket, the soldiers slowly lowered each into their last resting places. In the absence of that devout lieutenant's Irish Presbyterian reading of the burial service, Von Moll improvised and repeated what verse he could remember from childhood over those dark holes.

Beside White's grave Seamus had crossed himself and murmured a prayer remembered from his early catechism, thinking of the young man's friend, Bill Cody. And of the last time the friends had been together.

Nearby John Finerty repeated lines from an old poem.

No useless coffin enclosed his breast,
    Not in sheet or in shroud they wound him;
But he lay like a warrior taking his rest;
    With his martial cloak around him.

Later when the burial detail sat huddled around a fire listening to the rain hiss as it fell into the flames, their damp blankets steaming in the chilled air, a figure approached out of the darkness.

"We'll need another grave, Sergeant."

Von Moll and the rest turned to find a somber Surgeon Clements halt inside the warm corona of firelight.

Anxiously, Finerty asked, "Von Leuttwitz, Doctor?"

"No. Private Kennedy. He didn't survive the amputation," Clements answered, gesturing into the darkness. "I waited to tell you until you were finished with the others."

Into a third grave Von Moll's men consigned the soldier's body along with his severed limb, then scooped out a shallow hole in which to bury Von Leuttwitz's leg. The soldiers were just beginning to turn spades of the damp soil into the graves when the eerie darkness erupted with wails.

A cold dash of ice water spilled down Donegan's spine as he turned to gaze up the hill, looking through the sheets of rain at the dim, flickering firelight near the tent fly, where the women who were gathered at the side of American Horse keened and screeched and tore at their hair in bitter remorse. Nearby the children began their own high-pitched cry.

"What do you suppose that's all about?" Finerty asked.

"The chief just died," Donegan replied, quickly crossing himself again. "His spirit is free at last."

The newsman shuddered, wagging his head. "Damn— I wish I had some whiskey right about now."

With a nod Seamus said, "First Wenzel and White, then Kennedy. And now American Horse. All of 'em killed at the ravine. Fitting it is that their souls take flight together."

At first light the Sioux had Crook's men up and out of their frosty, wet blankets. The warriors pressed in on the outlying pickets as soon as there was enough light to pick out targets in the roiling fog that clung to the low places that Sunday morning.

"Roll out! Roll out!" came the order as the third fight of Slim Buttes got under way.

Every man who bellied up to the picket lines peered into the shifting mists for the enemy's charge as the fog began to burn off, but there was no concerted assault made against those four companies of infantry who were ordered up to hold the line. Nonetheless, here and there the warriors made it a warm skirmish in trying to break through the soldier positions while Major Upham's battalion of the Fifth Cavalry continued to carry out Merritt's order to destroy any remaining enemy property: guns were shattered, then tossed into the flames of what lodges Captain Powell hadn't put to the torch the previous afternoon. In a matter of minutes, with the echo of gunfire rattling all about that camp in the chill gray light, leaping bonfires illuminated the dark underbellies of the clouds suspended right over their heads. Meanwhile, the men destroyed iron kettles and tinware by chopping them into fragments, or crushing them under the hooves of their horses.

Shivering in the cold drizzle, Charles King fought the fevered stiffness in that old Apache wound as he rolled up his blanket. He brooded on the way the cold from a night on the ground had seeped right into that shoulder, then stomped over to the mess fire, where he chewed on the enemy's dried meat and gulped at a cup of hot coffee made from beans found in the captured lodges. He didn't have a chance to finish his breakfast before K Company was ordered out to replace the infantry Crook had taken off the line and put into column, forming up for their day's march.

At the same time, the general ordered Lieutenant Colonel Eugene Carr to bring the prisoners to him.

Through Grouard he told the Sioux, "We are not making war on women and children such as you. Those of you who so desire are free to stay and rejoin your people—but you must caution all your friends that the American government will continue to peck away at all hostiles until the last one is killed or made a prisoner. The red man will be wise to surrender and return to his agency instead of pursuing this hopeless war. It's shameful of any man to expose his wife and children to the very great possibility of death."

"General," Frank Grouard said after Crook's interview had reached its conclusion, "Charging Bear wants to go with us."

"Go with us?"

"To stay with you. Says he wants to scout with me."

Crook's eyes narrowed. "To scout against his own people?"

Nodding, the half-breed said, "Figures it's better that his people make peace, he says."

Then with some random fire coming from warriors sniping on the bluffs and hills to the southwest, the general and Merritt assigned both Mason's and Upham's battalions of the Fifth Cavalry to act as the rear guard while the rest of the column pulled out.

Just past eight o'clock the first units of infantry pushed south in a column of twos, crossing a rain-swollen Rabbit Lip Creek with orders to protect both flanks of the twelve two-horse litters and travois drags loaded with the wounded, who were commencing their jolting march of agony, placed in the immediate care of Dr. Albert Hartsuff for the journey. During the long, damp night, a handful of troopers had been employed in constructing and strengthening those three litters and nine travois. Crook made it clear to Dr. Clements he did not intend to be hampered by his wounded for long. Besides the amputee lieutenant and seven wounded soldiers, as well as Lieutenant Alfred B. Bache's severe case of debilitating rheumatism that left him unable to move, Surgeon Hartsuff transported a lone civilian, packer James B. Glover, who, like Von Leuttwitz and Kennedy, was also shot in the leg.

As soon as Crook and the main command began to disappear beyond the nearby hills, the Sioux swept down on the Fighting Fifth, pressing in from all sides as the troopers completed their final destruction of the village. King realized there was nothing like the sight of retreating soldiers to give warriors courage and make them bold. In the stinging stench of that smoke-filled air some of the prisoners bolted into the brushy ravines to rejoin their people as the troopers knelt by platoon and attempted to hold the enemy at bay while the horse-holders moved up with their mounts.

The Sioux, laying down a harassing fire, turned their attention to the end of that long file of infantry. As a consequence, Merritt directed Carr to bring up on the right Mason's entire battalion, consisting of Captain Samuel S.

Sumner's and Captain Robert H. Montgomery's men, to drive off those warriors who were making things hot for the infantry skirmishers as they retired behind Surgeon Hartsuff's wounded. At the same time, Carr ordered Upham's battalion to take up positions along the ridge directly south of camp and there hold back the growing pressure from the Sioux.

"Stand to horse!" came the order above Mason's battalion, every man eager to pull out. "Mount!"

Scarcely had that long-awaited word echoed off the bluffs than the enemy began a determined attack. On all sides rose screaming, screeching warriors who had sneaked into every one of the hundreds of ravines under cover of darkness in the predawn hours.

"Dismount!"

Sending his mount with the rest of their horses and holders south to catch up with the rear of the retreating column, King watched his beloved Donnybrook retreat beyond the hills. No matter all his efforts to save Van, his other blooded thoroughbred. Days ago the animal had finally collapsed, unable to rise and move on. Now as he watched his last hardy mount disappear, the lieutenant prayed he would not have to leave a second horse behind, knowing how troopers who came along after him would butcher his beloved animal.

"Form them up by platoons, Mr. King!" bellowed Major Upham.

The cavalry commanders were now putting their dismounted troopers to the test. Up one hillside and down the next they made a gradual and orderly retreat, covering Crook's rear flank while the Sioux turned up the heat. As the cavalrymen reached a new hilltop, the order rang out.

"Halt!" the lieutenants who had remained on horseback bellowed above the footmen. "Face about! And—*fire!*"

With each new crest gained, brown-skinned horsemen swarmed over the hill the soldiers had just abandoned: screaming, charging, shooting—keeping up every bit of pressure they possibly could as the troopers attempted to hold them off, if not scatter them like chaff.

"Make your shots count, boys!" a stalwart, bearded sergeant hollered above his platoon as the rattle of gunfire reverberated from the buttes like hail off a snare drum. He was outlined against the sky by the black smudges of smoke drifting up from what was left of American Horse's village. "Don't throw your lead away without making them red bastards pay!"

It was one thing for a soldier to stand and hold off the enemy. Altogether different was it for a soldier to be asked to do the same while falling back.

Atop a grassy rise a lieutenant abruptly reined up his horse beside that old Irish sergeant conspicuously moving up and down his line of kneeling men, exhorting his platoon as they held off the screaming onslaught, gun smoke thick as thunderclouds about their heads. "Sergeant!"

"Yessirlieutenant!"

"How many goddamned times have I got to tell you to keep down?"

"Sir, I—"

"Now, by God!" the lieutenant interrupted. "I want you to keep your head down. So do it—now!"

"B-but, sir—"

"Sarge," the officer said, his tone a bit softer as he leaned forward to confide, "if I lose you—I just might lose this whole damned outfit. Now, just do as I ask and keep your blessed head down."

By and large the cavalrymen on that last line remained quiet in that cold morning's fight, perhaps only speaking low to the bunkie beside them, sharing a handshake and a quick, guttural cheer when one of their number spilled a warrior from his pony, maybe even issuing a yelp of pain or a call for aid when a Sioux bullet found its mark and the soldier crumpled into the mud and grass, clutching a leg or arm or belly while his fellows rushed to carry him along in their ordered retreat.

"What . . . what day is it, sir?" a wounded man asked of the officer bending over him.

"Sunday," Charles King answered as two soldiers came up to lift their wounded comrade between them.

"Sunday," the soldier repeated with a pained grimace as he was raised. "I imagine back home it's about time Ma is leaving for church."

For a moment King just stared at the wounded trooper's back, forced to think on Sunday and church and home. Forced to recall what had happened to Custer and his men on a bloody Sunday not long ago.

Had it not been for Carr's skillful battlefield maneuvers and his ability to hold his men under what might have otherwise been overwhelming pressure during one attempt to outflank his command, the troopers of the Fifth Cavalry might have suffered a rout. But the lieutenant colonel spun Kellogg's I Company on the right so they were there waiting when the galloping horsemen came over the rise—straight into the teeth of more than fifty Springfield carbines.

What really took most of the starch out of the warrior charges, however, was Carr's order for each unit to leave a half dozen of its best shots lying concealed just behind the brow of the next hill while the rest of the companies continued in retreat, acting as bait to pull the Sioux into a headlong rush. On the horsemen charged; then with a single word from the lieutenant colonel, two dozen marksmen rose from the mud and onto their knees, slamming rifles into their shoulders and aiming point-blank at the mounted, painted, feathered, and screaming enemy within spitting distance. Ponies reared in the face of those exploding muzzles, men cried out in pain, others dashed in to pull bodies from the no-man's-land as soldiers flipped up the trapdoors and slammed in another copper case while the angry screams haunted that thin line and the eagle wingbone whistles keened like a banshee's wail off the pale buttes above them.

When the Sioux retreated, the fight was all but over.

In this hot, grimy, hour-long skirmish—that fourth of the Battle of Slim Buttes—Carr's dismounted Fifth cavalrymen turned back every one of the Sioux charges, knocking down five of the enemy while the soldiers themselves suffered three wounded before the warriors were eventually turned back into the pine-covered hillsides. From the flanks of the troopers' slow, foot-by-foot withdrawal, the hostiles had kept up a withering fire for the better part of an hour as the troops retreated up and down for more than two miles.

It was proof enough for even the hardiest veteran that they had failed to dampen the Sioux's fighting spirit.

It was only then that Sitting Bull's warriors drifted away and let off their attack. At long last Mason's battalion was freed to step out in a lively effort to catch up to the retreating column and their led horses, now long out of sight.

But if the Sioux had shown they were still full of fight, so had Carr's Fifth Cavalry.

Yet now it appeared Crook was hardly interested in consolidating his minor victory, not the least bit in bringing the enemy to a full-scale fight.

The general may have believed he was marching his expedition south.

To the Sioux, Three Stars was retreating.

Chapter 44

10–11 September 1876

Camp Owl River, Dakota
September 10, 1876

General Sheridan, Chicago.

Marched from Heart River passing a great many trails of Indians going down all of the different streams we crossed between Heart River and this point . . . Although some of the trails seemed fresh our animals were not in condition to pursue them.

From the North Fork of the Grand River, I sent Captain Mills of the Third Cavalry, with 150 men mounted on our strongest horses, to go in advance to Deadwood and procure supplies of provisions.

On the evening of the 8th he discovered near the Slim Buttes a village of thirty odd lodges and lay there that night and attacked them by surprise yesterday morning, capturing the village, some prisoners and a number of ponies and killing some Indians. Among the Indians was chief

American Horse, who died of his wounds after surrendering to us . . .

In the village were found, besides great quantities of dried meat and ammunition, an army guidon, portions of officers uniforms and other indications that the Indians of the village had participated in the Custer massacre.

Our main column got up about noon that day and was shortly after attacked by a considerable body of Indians, who, the prisoners said belonged to the village of Crazy Horse . . . The attack was undoubtedly made under the supposition that Captain Mills's command had received no reinforcements.

The prisoners further stated that most of the hostile Indians were now going into the agencies, with the exception of Crazy Horse and Sitting Bull with their immediate followers. Crazy Horse intended to remain near the headwaters of the Little Missouri and about one half of Sitting Bull's band . . . had gone north of the Yellowstone . . . with some Sans Arcs, Minneconjous and Incappas had gone to the vicinity of Antelope Buttes, there to fatten their ponies and trade with the Rees and others . . .

We had a very severe march here from Heart River. For eighty consecutive miles we did not have a particle of wood; nothing but a little dried grass . . . During the greater portion of the time were drenched by cold rains which made traveling very heavy. A great many of the animals gave out and had to be abandoned. The others are now in such a weak condition that the greater number of them will not be able to resume the campaign until after a reasonable rest.

I should like to have about five hundred horses, preferably the half breed horses raised on

the Laramie plains or in the vicinity of Denver
and already acclimated to this country.

    I intend to carry out the programme men-
tioned in my last dispatch . . . and shall remain
in the vicinity of Deadwood until the arrival of
my wagon train.

George Crook
Brigadier General

With every painful southbound step of that Sunday's
march John Finerty wished with all his soul that he
was back among the prostitutes and whiskey mills of old
Chicago.

    It mattered little to any of them anymore that the
hostiles' trails all appeared to be headed south, gradually
inching off to the east in order to skirt around the Black
Hills settlements, still seventy miles or more to the south,
making for the agencies now that the weather had turned
colder, gloomier, wetter. Crook's infantry staggered along
both flanks, and the horses plodded in loose formation all
morning, pairs of men talking over the fight and dreaming
back to that feast they had enjoyed. None of them sure just
where they would find their next meal. Knowing only that
what dried meat was left after the troops had gorged themselves had been packed on Tom Moore's mules and ruled
off limits.

    "They're keeping it safe for the wounded," Bourke
explained once the Fifty Cavalry caught up with the rear
end of the march.

    "And the rest of us?" Finerty asked.

    "Why, Johnny," Donegan cheered, his face grimed
with gunpowder from that morning's rear guard clash,
"we'll be dining on horse again tonight!"

    The prospect failed to make the newsman's mouth
water.

    For the better part of the forenoon more than fifty
warriors dogged the retreat of the Fifth Cavalry, then
harassed the rear of the column's line of march, hoping to

pick off stragglers and capture any horses the white men might abandon. But in the end even they turned back, and the hillsides eventually grew quiet.

Crook had his prize: a village captured and destroyed, as well as driving off repeated counterattacks. He had as spoils some two hundred ponies, representing half of the hostiles' herd. What animals he hadn't put into service for his cavalry he had his men kill. Of the seven captives three chose to march with the soldiers, saying they would remain with Three Stars until the soldier chief reached the agencies. With very little left of what was originally estimated as more than three tons of dried meat Mills had discovered in the enemy camp, the general had no other choice but to push on for the settlements. That, and brood on what he might do now to make his slim victory count for something.

It mattered nothing that Crook had his men build fires over the graves they left behind, then marched a thousand horses across that hallowed ground in an attempt to obliterate all trace of the burials. An empty effort, because the prisoners he set free and those warriors watching from the hills knew where the enemies' bodies had been buried. Once the soldiers were gone from sight, the digging began.

In the continuing rain American Horse's women cut down saplings with which to build their burial scaffold.

Shortly after noon the head of the army's column discovered that the high, chalky ridge at the foot of which they'd been marching made a sharp angle to the east. About two P.M. Crook called a halt after making only fifteen miles. For much of the morning the surgeons repeatedly protested to the general how the march was taking a terrible toll on the wounded. Neither blanket nor gum poncho could turn the wind-driven rain that pelted those least able to protect themselves.

While most of the casualties were carried on travois pulled behind a single horse, the most seriously wounded were placed on litters. Constructed from a pair of lodgepoles lashed fore and aft by surcingles between a pair of Moore's mules, the amputees were laid upon a piece of canvas or blanket tied around the poles to form a crude stretcher. For a man who had lost the greater portion of one of his legs, it was no cushioned ride in a royal coach.

"Goddamighty—goddamighty!" cried Adolphus Von Leuttwitz repeatedly in his excruciating pain. "Gimme a pistol, please, somebotty gimme a pistol!"

For most of the morning he had been begging, cajoling, even ordering soldiers to hand over their service revolvers to him so he could put himself out of his misery.

"Jus' shtop and leaf me right here!" he would order in his thick accent once he realized no one had turned over their revolver to him. "Leaf me und go on so I can die on dis spot!"

As the column went into camp that afternoon, the surgeons tied an awning between some trees so they could begin to devote their attentions to changing dressings and checking for infection. As the canvas was going up, four packers volunteered to help unhitch the mule-borne litters and lower the patients to the ground. When one of the civilians walked past Von Leuttwitz's stretcher, the lieutenant lunged for the packer's pistol, managing to wrench it from the holster and get the muzzle pressed against his head before the civilian gripped the officer's hand and wrist. The struggle was on. Only by jamming the meat of his thumb beneath the hammer did the packer keep the gun from going off before two other men rushed over to wrestle the pistol away from the distraught officer.

Whimpering in his defeat, Von Leuttwitz flung an arm over his face and groaned, "V'at diff'rence it make to you, dommit! I no longer vant to live if I cannot be a fighting man. Not a soldier—life is not vorth living!"

It wasn't only the condition of Crook's wounded that caused the general to halt early in the day. Perhaps every bit as much was not knowing what lay on the other side of the ridge standing immediately in front of him. This seemed like a good place to make bivouac, so the battalions put out a strong guard, expecting the Sioux to put in another show.

Carr's Fifth Cavalry rear guard straggled in as camp was being made beside a narrow, clear-running stream flowing northward out of the towering bluffs. Here at least there were good water and ample grass for their horses. Still, many of the men could think only that twenty-four hours before they had been dining on buffalo and wild fruits, while here they sat beneath a driving rain, once again supping on broiled pony steaks and their private miseries.

"It's better than a broken-down cavalry nag," Donegan observed as he chewed another mouthful of the tender and juicy red meat. "Far, far better than the best cut a man can butcher from one of Tom Moore's wormy mules."

"Horse," John Finerty said with a shudder. "I don't think I'll ever climb into a hack, take myself a winter's sleigh ride, much less sit on a saddle quite the same again." Before his eyes he held a chunk of the roasted meat on the end of his knife blade and considered it. "Ah, such equestrian delight." Then plopped it into his mouth with the relish of a starving man.

As the sun fell out of midsky, inching for the western horizon, a dozen men from Captain William H. Andrews's I Troop of the Third Cavalry finished raising the sole buffalo-hide lodge Crook had not destroyed. In it Medical Director Clements and his surgeons could retreat from the rain with their wounded.

Here and there troopers moved through camp carrying on their shoulders great quarters of the butchered ponies like beef loins. It was a grim feast they had that night as every man filled his belly, not really caring so much what the morning would bring.

"You figure we can keep going much longer eating such meat?" Finerty asked a while later.

"Pray we don't have to find out, Johnny." Donegan wiped a sleeve across his mouth and beard, then held his hands over the fire, warming them as he said, "Not enough fat on a dozen of those Sioux ponies to season the gruel for a sick grasshopper."

With their midday meal out of the way and enough wood laid in for the coming night, many of the soldiers used the rest of the afternoon to fashion crude leggings and moccasins from the tanned hides they had discovered in the Sioux village and saved from Powell's destruction. Seamus cut thin slices from a piece of brain-tanned buckskin he had rescued and stuffed inside his shirt during Mills's attack. Then he used his knife to hack off the stiff, hardened pieces of raw horsehide he had knotted around his boots many days back, when they had begun to fall apart with wear and the constant rain. Wrapping new strips of flexible buckskin around and around his lower foot and instep before knotting the ends, he could crudely hold the flapping sole to the upper part of his boot.

At their fire the Chicago newsman asked, "You hear that Jack Crawford ended up with the rifle American Horse handed Crook?"

"The one the chief surrendered to the general?" Seamus asked.

"Yeah."

"How'd the poet end up with it?"

"Don't really know for sure," Finerty replied. "But I figure he talked Crook out of it with one of his silver-tongued rhymes, eh?"

"It would have to be a mighty pretty poem to be worth the value of that rifle, Johnny."

"Seems Crawford's got him an eye for collectibles too," Finerty went on. "From the camp's spoils the poet ended up with another rifle—a Spencer repeater—and a Colt revolver."

"Likely one what belonged to Custer's dead," Donegan replied sourly.

Meanwhile Crook composed his dispatch to Lieutenant General Philip Sheridan back at Chicago headquarters.

There wasn't much to gloat about—but it was a victory. After Powder River, Rosebud Creek, and the disaster at the Little Bighorn . . . after traipsing around for more than a month looking for a fresh trail, any trail . . . why, surely Sheridan would have reason to celebrate now.

Surely Little Phil's trumpet had been heard upon the land.

Slim Buttes was the first victory of what had turned out to be a very long and costly Sioux war.

WYOMING
From the Black Hills.

CHEYENNE, September 11—Advices from the telegraph camp near Hat creek, this morning, say that the Indians drove back a government courier who left Fort Laramie with dispatches for General Crook. He was to make another start from Hat creek this morning.

From Red Cloud.

RED CLOUD AGENCY, NEB., September 11—This morning a supply train of about thirty wagons left this agency escorted by three companies of the Fourth artillery, equipped as infantry, for Custer City. The supplies are for Crook's command which it is reported is to be there the 14th.

The night before, when General Crook had asked Frank Grouard to carry his report on to Fort Laramie or to the nearest point where a telegraph key might be found, the half-breed had refused—then refused again, even when Lieutenant Bubb volunteered to go with him through that unknown and dangerous country to the south.

But when Crook asked him to guide a second relief column under Captain Anson Mills, Grouard agreed. This time the general's order was not only more specific, it was explicit.

"You have one mission and one mission only," Crook explained. "To return from the Black Hills settlements with provisions."

It would mean no less than saving the lives of the Big Horn and Yellowstone Expedition.

"And if you can," the general added, "find out what threat the hostiles have presented to Deadwood and the other mining communities."

This time the general was hurrying forward a special detail that would not be big enough to strike the enemy. Instead Mills's force—comprising the best of his very own M Company, Third Cavalry, as well as fifty handpicked troopers from Carr's Fifth Cavalry—was half the size of that detail he had led away from Crook's column on the seventh. And again the general chose Lieutenant John W. Bubb as commissary officer charged with the purchase of the needed supplies. Along with Second Lieutenant George F. Chase acting as subaltern, Mills would be joined by reporters Reuben Davenport and Robert Strahorn. Frank Grouard, bearing Crook's report for General Sheridan, would accompany the detail at least as far as the Black Hills on the first leg of his journey to Fort Laramie. Upon reaching the mining settlements, Jack Crawford, who was the one scout most familiar with the Black Hills and was carrying reporters' dispatches, and Seamus Donegan would both serve as guides to bring the wagons back to the general's desperate men.

None of Tom Moore's mules were taken south when those seventy-five men pulled out just before dawn that Monday morning, the eleventh of September. Instead of the broken-down army horses, each man rode one of the captive Sioux ponies.

After so many days of rain without letup, no one much noticed that the sun did not put in an appearance that morning as the men and ponies snorted frostily in their climb up the slopes of the terraced buttes. Again the clouds hovered close, fog shrouded the land for as far as a man could see with field glasses, and it began to rain.

Seamus pulled the big collar on his canvas mackinaw up around his neck and prayed the little grass-fed Indian pony beneath him had the bottom to carry him all the way to Deadwood.

Chapter 45

11 September 1876

Crook Heard From.

CHEYENNE, September 11—General Crook has been heard from under date of the 2nd. He has followed the trail to the Little Missouri without finding any Indians. The trail was found to split in several directions. Crook thinks the southern band may have moved backward toward the mountains, and he is somewhat apprehensive for his wagon train. It is expected that he will move in that direction.

When Baptiste Pourier led Crook and the rest of the column away from that miserable bivouac on the morning of the eleventh, John Finerty climbed stiffly into the saddle and shivered almost uncontrollably, not knowing if he could ever again count on being warm and dry.

In the early light of dawn Lieutenant Von Leuttwitz had awakened from a feverish nightmare that convinced him his leg had been exhumed from its grave by the hostiles, who desecrated it. Crook dispatched Captain Julius

Mason with a small battalion of Carr's Fifth Cavalry to take their backtrail to the destroyed village.

As the rest of the command began to climb south by west up the muddy slopes, the cavalrymen mounted on their horses began to press at the rear of the infantry, where a good-natured banter began to fly back and forth between the men.

Upon passing some of the foot soldiers, a trooper turned and leaned down from his saddle, asking one of the infantrymen, "Casey, old man! How are your corns this fine morning? Tell me, now—is it fine walking? Wouldn't you rather be riding a fine horse like this one?"

With a snort of derision the old soldier answered in his peatiest brogue, "To hell wid your harse, I say! And g'won wid you too, you weak-brained idjit! Why, we're gonna walk your harse off his four legs and then we'll eat him!"

Above them that dawn the very heights of the chalk-colored buttes blocking their path remained shrouded in a thick fog that rained a cold and constant drizzle down on the men and animals. Up, up they climbed, most of the cavalry forced to dismount and drag their horses behind them, inching back and forth to switchback their way upward into the numbing mist, strung out in a long single column snaking its way into the clouds across the face of the pine-dotted escarpment.

Finally at midmorning they stood on the southern edge of the jagged cliffs and looked down upon the great endless prairie as barren as the surface of the moon. Finerty could see nothing on the foggy horizon that would inspire hope. Nothing like the dark and jagged outline of the Black Hills. Down, down Big Bat led them, Crook's men dropping once more into the muddy wilderness. Their only choice was to push on, or lie down and die right there.

By noon the drizzle had ballooned into sheets of rain as the head of the column reached a formation called Clay Ridge. Again there was no way to detour east or west. As they climbed into the badlands and skirted what they could of the narrow ravines and coulees cut by centuries of erosion, the horses and mules slipped and stumbled crossing the naked, muddy slopes with men on their backs. And when the soldiers climbed down from the saddles, they found their boots sinking in the sticky gumbo that refused to release them, tiring out the weary men as they continued to plod forward lugging up more than a pound of prairie with every step—climbing and descending, climbing and descending all the more, marching ever southward, following what had to be an old Indian trail, if nothing more than a game trail.

Just when Finerty felt his lungs could take no more, just when he was certain the burning muscles in his legs would not last another step, those foot soldiers marching in the vanguard of the cavalry reached a sheer ledge. By the time the newsman got to the ledge, he looked out and feared for the worst—unable to see a thing. Peering into the mists and dancing sheets of rain that obscured the prairie below them, it appeared the whole world had been swallowed up by the sky. Then John caught a glimpse of the faint blue column a hundred yards below and to the left. The infantry at the head of the column was descending slowly, disappearing into the maw of a gray cloud bank.

All around them on those bluffs rose rocky spires that resembled the sharp pinnacles on houses of worship as they scraped the underbellies of the gray clouds that continued to rain down on them, a geographical formation that prompted Finerty to propose they should rechristen the place Church Spire Range. But such sacred thoughts did not last, pushed aside by the temporal, earthly necessity of putting one foot in front of the other.

Throughout that day more of the army's mounts gave out, pushed just about as far as they could go without forage. While some of the horses and mules were abandoned, most were shot. At one difficult ravine Finerty watched a trooper ahead of him pull and drag his horse as far as it would go. It shuddered at last and sank to its knees, head lolling to the side as it rolled, its ribby sides heaving.

The grim-faced soldier removed the saddle, then knelt be-side his mount, yanking up the mule ear on his holster as he patted the horse's foam-flecked muzzle. After a few mo-ments he finally worked up the courage to fire a single bullet into his old companion's brain.

Rising from the mud, the trooper gathered kindling and struck a fire before returning to his horse, this time to kneel beside the rear flank, where he cut out a tender steak he then began to roast over the yellow flames in that cold and dreary mist. In the space of a half hour the soldier got to his feet once more, shouldering his carbine to march on, joining the other stragglers at the rear of the column.

It wasn't long before Crook ordered a short halt, tell-ing Tom Moore to lighten the loads on his pack-mules by burying hundreds of pounds of heavy ammunition. After that they struggled on in desperation across that rugged ground, the wounded in their litters and travois suffering more than any others. All through the day Von Leuttwitz had grumbled in pain, begging his stewards to stop, again pleading with those men from Captain Williams H. An-drews's I Troop of the Third Cavalry for a pistol he could use to shoot himself. And at every crossing of a tiny stream, at every jolting descent over a narrow ravine, the lieutenant cursed the mules, cursed the nearby troops, cursed the skies and all of creation in two languages.

At midafternoon Baptiste Pourier crossed a fresh and sizable trail of lodgepoles and unshod pony hooves point-ing south for the agencies.

"They might be some of them what come back to help American Horse's people by attacking us," Bat declared. "Looks like we're moving them and other camps in for the winter. You wanna follow, General?"

Crook wagged his head, as weary and worn down as any one of his soldiers. "No. We're going where I can feed these men, where I can recruit more horses—and only then can I continue this campaign."

As the day wore on, the watchfulness of the rear guard and the flankers on both sides of the column waned, and those weary, starving men lost all fear of attack. It was nothing more than an ordeal, a crucible of survival.

Major Alexander Chambers's infantry continued to set the pace, and it wasn't long before they were again out-doing the cavalry that struggled to keep up with their failing mounts. Farther and farther behind, the stragglers strung out in the rear. More and more often one would hear the pop of pistols as the troopers put their horses out of their misery. Then in the midst of all the grumbling and the complaints, Finerty heard a bit of rousing belly laughter erupt among the last of the foot soldiers slogging just ahead of him. He lumbered up to find out what could be so amusing.

"Oh, and for sure," replied one of the Irish among those infantrymen to Finerty's inquiry, "we were just laughing at a new joke making its way back along the column."

John sighed. "Good. I'd be willing to hear anything that could give me a smile right about now."

The soldier grinned and replied, "This evening we're going to tell all those big, strong cav'rymen with their big, strong mounts that if Gen'ral Crook marches this expedition long enough and far enough, why—the infantry will eat all their damned harses!"

Farther and farther the column stretched itself out as more and more animals gave out and weary men collapsed by the side of the trail, gasping and begging for a chance to rest. Ahead of them lay a seemingly limitless stretch of wasteland that made the strongest man among them groan with despair. In his mind Finerty fought to describe the scene, to arrange his adjectives just so for his eastern readers. "A ghastly compound of spongy ashes, yielding sand, and soilless, soulless earth, on which even greasewood cannot grow, and sagebrush sickens and dies," he composed. "The meanest country under the sun."

But, he laughed to himself—there simply wasn't any sun.

Late in the afternoon the fog thinned as they reached

the southern edge of the buttes, and as the mist lifted, there lay the dark-blue wall far to their front. Through the mud and the fog and the mist and the misery, they had struggled another twenty-one miles that day.

"Bear Butte," Pourier said, pointing to the singular prominence off to the southeast. "Where the Lakota and Shahiyena go to seek their visions and pray."

As the half-breed described it, Finerty stood hunched over his small tablet, shielding it from the drops spilling from the brim of his hat as he scribbled down notes with a lead pencil.

"And there," Bat said, indicating the lofty peak rising to the southwest, "that is the peak the Lakota call Inyan Kara."

At long last. The Black Hills. Relief. Food. Four walls and a roof, a place where Finerty could get out of the rain and the cold. Many times had he enjoyed the best nightlife Chicago had to offer—all the whiskey and willing women a young man about town could ever desire.

But as they went into bivouac that night, John wasn't sure he had seen anything that looked any better, anything that had stirred his heart more than the sight of those blessed blue-tinged hills rising right out of the wilderness.

Beckoning him home.

With General George Crook in the lead, continuing to push his men painfully that day of the eleventh. Slower and slower the column plodded south by southwest, moving past the east slope of Deer's Ears Buttes, those twin conical heights rising abruptly from the prairie floor. Because they could be seen for many miles in all directions, they had long been known to frontiersman and Indian alike.

Near Owl Creek, the Heecha Wakpa of the Sioux, along the South Fork of the Moreau, itself a tributary of the Missouri River, John Bourke rode back with the order to halt and go into camp. At least here they had plenty of wood.

After building huge bonfires the men gathered in the

great circle of warmth to dry their steamy wool clothing, turning first one side, then the other to the flames where they roasted their horse-meat steaks. Washing his supper down with water from the nearby creek, the lieutenant was beginning to doubt he had ever really eaten such delicacies as ham and eggs, even a rare porterhouse steak. Perhaps it was only a dream. It had been so long ago.

Mason's battalion of the Fifth Cavalry reached the bivouac that evening after dark, picking up and dragging with them most of the stragglers along the way. Grimly the major reported that upon returning to the village site, they had found that the Sioux had indeed dug up the graves and desecrated the bodies. And Von Leuttwitz's greatest fear and worst nightmare was realized—the hostiles had butchered his severed leg.

For Surgeon Clements's train of litters and travois, it was travel fast, or travel gently through the rugged badlands. Hampered by the frequent stream crossings and the coulees, hampered by the rains and by so many stops to tighten surcingles, the hospital limped into camp well after dark as the wind picked up and brought with it an icy, pelting rain. For the wounded there was no longer any hard bread nor bacon, no longer even any salt to season the pony meat and that one haunch of antelope an officer had donated to the surgeon's mess. Rummaging through their haversacks, other officers found a little salt, a half pound of sugar, and two quarts of flour they were able to shake loose from the bottom of their packs. And in the end Valentine McGillycuddy's thick and nourishing antelope stew was augmented by a dessert of a few tins of preserves an infantry officer had guarded with his life for weeks.

Out of the rain and the wind, once more beneath the buffalo hides of that captured lodge, with warm and delicious food in their bellies, Bourke found flagging spirits begin to brighten among Clements's wounded. Even in grumpy Lieutenant Von Leuttwitz himself.

That afternoon John had begged himself some of the liver from an antelope killed along the trail. The meat would not stretch far; nonetheless, the lieutenant carried his treasure into camp in his nose bag as if it were a kingly ransom. For long and glorious minutes he suspended it on a green limb, broiling the liver over some pulsating coals, preparing supper for himself and the general. They had no more than halved their modest portion when a loud ruckus erupted at the commissary headquarters nearby.

In Lieutenant Bubb's absence the chief butcher and his men had to answer the demands of almost two thousand ravenous soldiers and civilians, expertly dividing what they were given each night in the way of ponies to be slaughtered for supper. This night the butcher stood there in his blood-crusted woolens, shaking his gleaming knife at a dark-skinned Mexican prospector up from the southern border of Texas, one of Major Stanton's Montana Volunteers. In a spicy blend of two languages the Mexican threatened the butcher for killing a Sioux pony the volunteer had had his eye on and was anxious to save for his very own use once the expedition broke up back at Fort Laramie.

Back and forth they argued, the chief butcher brandishing his big and very lethal knife, the Mexican pounding his chest with one hand and provocatively wagging his gun in the other until Lieutenant Colonel Carr stepped in and broke it up. Scattering the curious spectators, Carr turned on the volunteer.

"Go on now. Get back to your camp and cause no more problems tonight, or I'll see you put under arrest and thrown in irons at the first military reservation we come to!"

With menace in his dark eyes, the sullen Mexican turned about, intending to take up the reins to the Indian pony he had ridden up to the commissary, the same Sioux pony he had been riding since the capture of the enemy's herd.

"*Dios!*" he exclaimed, shoving his shapeless hat back on his brow. "*Dónde* . . . where is my horse?"

Up stepped four of the butcher's assistants. The first flung down a frayed bridle at the civilian's feet. The second dropped an old and tattered saddle blanket into the mud. Then the grinning third dropped a scarred and much-used saddle atop the filthy blanket. And the final butcher's assistant stopped in front of the Mexican to hold out a long, thick strip of red meat on the end of his huge butcher knife.

"Your pony?" the assistant asked. "Why, mister—General Merritt told us we needed just one more horse to make enough provisions for tonight's mess. Saw yours standing right there. Closest to commissary . . . so we knew you wouldn't mind."

The volunteer began to sputter in that heated blend of English and Mexican, mad enough to spit nails when Carr once more stepped between him and the butchers.

The lieutenant colonel tore the lean meat off the butcher's knife and slapped it into the Mexican's hands. "Looks like this is your ration for the night. I'd suggest you go cook that steak before it goes bad on you."

Chapter 46

12 September 1876

The worst was yet to come.

When the men rose stiffly that Tuesday morning, no one had any idea what awaited them as they morosely stood around the smoky fires in that darkness before dawn and tried to warm themselves in what soul-robbing fog and mist clung to the banks of Owl Creek.

This was to be the day strong men reached the end of their ropes and lay down to die in the mud beside that endless trail crossing an unforgiving wilderness.

No sooner had Crook given his command for the column to form up than the rain moved in, starting gently at first but within an hour falling in such solid sheets that a man had to hunch his shoulders up and turn sideways against the force of the storm, just the way horses and mules would turn their rumps against a howling norther. Lumbering into the gales, the infantry led out at four A.M., Clements's train of wounded in their midst, each one grumbling in his own private misery beneath the onslaught of Mother Nature's worst. An hour behind them the cavalry set out. Nearly two of every three troopers were already afoot, stumbling along through the thickening quagmire beside those in their company still mounted on the bony horses.

Under Crook's orders Major John J. Upham selected 150 men from the Fifth Cavalry, all mounted on the best of the captured ponies, to follow up that lodgepole trail they had crossed the day before. Given the limited rations the commissary could provide from its dwindling supplies—two ounces of dried buffalo meat per man, a few coffee beans, and what pony meat each soldier had managed to save from last night's supper—Upham's troopers disappeared into the mist, heading south by east down Avol Creek toward Bear Butte.

With the old arrow wound stiffening his shoulder in a hot pain, Charles King watched his friends leave, gratified that his horse, Donnybrook, wasn't deemed strong enough to go with Upham's patrol. Nonetheless, he was still very much perplexed and confused by Crook's decision to send out that scouting party.

When the general had been confronted with a force of attacking Sioux the morning of the tenth, Crook had marched the column away. Then, upon finding a fresh but small trail, the general had waited more than twelve hours before deciding to send some of his cavalry in pursuit. Those very inconsistencies had begun to cause cracks in the confidence King held for the general. What Charles feared most was that the tenacious bulldog Crook wasn't all that sure himself of just what he should do anymore.

So the lieutenant took his hat off and waved at some of those Fifth Cavalry friends who turned and bid a half-hearted farewell to those they were leaving behind that cold and gloomy morning. In minutes Upham's patrol was swallowed by the land and the incessant rain.

Because Major Mason's battalion was that day assigned to bring up the rear of the march, ordered to sweep along with them any and all stragglers, Charles King did not leave Owl Creek until just past seven A.M. The wind came up, inching down the temperature, seeping into the marrow of every one of those once-hardy fighting men until all a man could think of was just taking the next step. Wondering when he would lose the willpower, the guts just to keep moving. Already the neuralgia in that old Apache war wound made King grit his teeth with each flush of sudden, hot pain.

It wasn't much past nine when the first horses started to play out. Along the left and right flanks rang the pistol shots as more and more of the troopers went afoot, caching their saddles and bridles in growing piles left upon the barren prairie. Heaving their soggy saddle blankets to their shoulders, the unhorsed soldiers set off on foot. At the rear the dismounted horse soldiers began to straggle farther and farther behind in a weaving, wobbly, unsteady column snaking south by southwest toward the prominence of In-yan Kara.

Twice that morning when Clements's own stock failed and gave out, the surgeon had to beg ponies off those officers who rode the Sioux horses. One time he went from man to man, pleading, until he reached Charles King, who reluctantly slid from his saddle and handed over the reins, barely able to rotate that shoulder wounded years before in Arizona.

"God bless you, Lieutenant," Clements said before turning away into the spinning curtains of rain, dragging the pony behind him through the deepening gumbo.

Men stumbled past King as he stood there, settling up to his ankles in the pasty mud, and swiped his glove across his face. It did not help. With the swirling sheets of rain, his face was wet a moment later. He looked south, finding he could not see the head of the column where Crook rode. Too far away in the roiling mist.

King turned and squinted into the north, holding down his hat's flapping brim against the rising gusts of wind, wondering just how far back they were strung out. One by one the men of his own Fifth Cavalry trudged past, planting one boot on the slippery, adhesive prairie, leaning forward to yank the other foot out of the gumbo, then drag it forward, a most conscious act by men whose will to live diminished perceptibly with every single one of those tortured steps.

"Goddamn. Goddamn. Goddamn. Goddamn. Goddamn," one of them muttered quietly as he heaved himself past, issuing his oath with each lunging step.

Others plodded past without raising their heads to look at King, murmuring only to themselves, their lungs heaving with weary fatigue, vowing death at the end of a rope to Crook and all his officers, cursing the Sioux and their army as a whole.

Charles felt the sob begin to flutter in his own chest and fought it down, swallowing hard. Turning, blinking into the dancing swirl of sheeting rain, King found an infantryman collapsing to his knees into the mud some yards off to the right.

Slowly the soldier crumpled forward, crying out to God. "Take mercy on us, Lord! Deliver us from hell!"

"C'mon," King said quietly as he bent over the soldier. Helping the man struggle to his feet, the lieutenant found he was able to stifle his own growing despair and hopelessness. "Let's walk together awhile, you and me."

With an arm around one another they lumbered forward unevenly, the ground sucking at their feet so that they careened first this way, then that.

And the rain continued to fall.

More and more horses gave out.

One by one the men collapsed by the side of the trail among the cactus and the stunted grass throughout that long, terrible day in the history of the Army of the West.

Yet they somehow struggled on.

At the crossing of the next swollen stream the mules carrying Von Leuttwitz's litter floundered, stumbled, and pitched their sputtering passenger into the muddy, foaming water. The lieutenant struggled to keep his head above the surging current as three of Captain Andrews's men reached him and pulled him out, lifting the man gently into their arms and carrying him up the slippery bank on the far side. While they wiped what they could of the mud from the

lieutenant's face, others hurried to repair the loosened sur-
cingle. Then as Von Leuttwitz continued cursing the troopers as if they were his torturers, the soldiers gently laid him
into his litter once more and moved on.

Into the rain.

Through the mud.

Past the men who crumpled to their knees and beat
the soggy ground with their fists in utter despair. Whimpering like children.

This hunger. This utter bone-weary fatigue. This cold
with no hope of warmth. This twelfth day of nonstop rain,
without prayer of deliverance.

These were enemies even the strongest among them
simply could not defeat.

Give them a band of warriors. Show them an enemy
village. Ask them to stand and face charge after charge after
charge of screeching, wild-eyed red horsemen. They could
do that. After all, they were soldiers.

But this! No man, no matter how strong of body, no
matter how unshakable of will, no . . . no man was prepared for something like this. If endurance, if life itself,
were a candle that glowed inside each and every one of
those soldiers—then the wick was all but gone, and the
weakened flame flickered, sputtering, just short of snuffing
itself out.

A few of those who would somehow be strong enough
this day would eventually pay in the years to come from the
deprivation. A few became crazed even that day, were
bound and tied by their friends, carried along by their
bunkies—raving, wild-eyed, foaming, lunatic men whose
crippled minds were never to recover.

Not long after noon King trudged up to a pair of men
hunkered in the sticky mud among the cactus. One of them
proved to be the surgeon McGillycuddy, who more than
two hours before had stopped at that spot to help a young
soldier.

"Huntington, Henry Dustan, sir," the officer identified himself to the lieutenant as King squatted to his side. "Second Lieutenant, sir."

Dr. Valentine McGillycuddy explained, "I came upon Mr. Huntington here some time back. Found him doubled up with cramps."

In sympathy King looked down at the officer hunched in a fetal position, his legs crimped against his belly. "Have you given him anything for the pain?"

"Very first thing," McGillycuddy replied, "I administered some quinine to relieve the severe cramping. But his pain only worsened as time wore on. I've now resorted to an injection of morphine, afraid it might be a bowel obstruction of some sort."

For a moment King glanced up at the two horses standing nearby, then asked, "Is he ready to mount up?"

"Oh, God . . . dear God, no!" Huntington groaned, his eyes clenched with a rising spasm of pain, his legs trembling.

"Hundreds of men have passed by me," the doctor declared, "but no one has been able to help."

"We're the last," King explained. "You've got to come in with me."

Huntington bellowed, "I can't ride!"

"I simply can't make the man suffer," McGillycuddy explained. "Even the two of us won't be able to get him into the saddle."

"We've got to move out," Charles told the two. "See? There goes the last of the file. And there's a damned good chance a war party could be along anytime to sweep down on defenseless stragglers just like you."

"If you've got an idea," McGillycuddy said, "now's the time to tell us."

"Both of you," Huntington gasped in the middle of a wave of pain, "both . . . just go. Leave me. Don't sacrifice your own . . . own lives."

"Be quiet," the doctor ordered. "I won't be able to sleep tonight knowing I left you out here."

"Me neither," King agreed.

The ill soldier grumbled, "No sense the red bastards getting all of us. G'won and leave me."

"No." Rising from the gummy mud, King stared southwest, south, then southeast across the grassland dotted with spiny cactus. "Maybe there."

"What? Where?" the surgeon asked.

"We can make him a travois. Stay with him, Doctor. I'll be back soon."

Lumbering off toward a wide vee in the low, rolling hills, King made for the dark vegetation that promised what he needed most. With his belt knife the lieutenant cut down some thick saplings, then turned and dragged them back to McGillycuddy. Next he slogged north on their backtrail more than half a mile until he found several of the abandoned saddles and gathered four of the lariats the troopers had left behind. With the ropes King and the surgeon quickly fashioned a crude travois after knocking the branches from the young saplings. With more of the rope they wove a bed, and across that net of ropes the two men laid their blankets.

At first Huntington's thoroughbred objected to having the travois lashed to its saddle. McGillycuddy had to steady the animal while King completed the harnessing, then together they gently lifted Huntington into place. With the young second lieutenant's own gum poncho thrown over him, McGillycuddy held out his hand to Charles.

"Thank you, Lieutenant. I don't believe I caught your name."

"King. Charles King." He glanced into the roiling gray of the western sky. "Now, it's best you get that horse moving with your patient, Doctor. Night's gonna come all too quick."

Twilight was advancing, far faster than any of them cared to realize.

All day long the infantry at the head of the march had been on the alert for one of two things: either the Belle Fourche River, or some game for their supper fires. As the hours crawled by, it seemed neither would come to pass.

No river, and not one wild animal had been seen. Late in the afternoon one of the men on the left flank suddenly yelled.

"Antelope!"

Soldiers along that side of the ragged column turned dully, their reaction time retarded, and stared off into the low hills as if it might be nothing more than a delusion brought on by their hunger, their weakness, and the cold. But no, there in the rain stood four of the white-rumped animals. A buck and his small harem.

They did not wait for permission to fire. Instead the whole left flank began to pop at the quartet of targets, and quickly all four lay in the short, muddy grass. Over the cactus and through the gumbo the ecstatic soldiers bounded with sudden rejuvenation, pouncing on the warm animals, a dozen or more men working their slashing knives on each small carcass, slicing warm strips from the hindquarters, claiming parts of the liver or heart, chewing on sections of the rich, fatty gut while stuffing choice morsels inside the pockets of their mud-crusted tunics and blouses, tender portions saved for a distant supper to be cooked at some unknown, distant bivouac.

Throughout the long, desperate afternoon and into that momentary brilliant flare of sunset the officers were forced to call brief halts with growing frequency. But as Lieutenant Frederick Schwatka said to King during one, "A halt like this is nothing more than suffering at a standstill."

Finally just past dusk Crook and the head of the command spotted a fringe of cottonwood rising among some willow and alder. There they went into bivouac on Willow Creek after thirty-five grueling miles of wilderness. They had been struggling long past the point on their maps where they believed they should have reached the Bell Fourche, which wrapped itself closely along the northern edge of the Black Hills. But their maps were wrong. What they had expected that morning, upon leaving Owl Creek, to be a march of only twenty miles to reach the foothills was instead twice that far.

As darkness settled over the land, the Big Horn and Yellowstone Expedition was still six miles from the Belle Fourche. And Crook's pitiful column was at that moment strung out for more than ten miles to the rear.

Stragglers limped and crawled in throughout the evening. It was nine-thirty before Captain Andrews's men stumbled to the bank of Willow Creek, escorting the surgeons and their train of wounded. After their exhausting ordeal dragging the litters and travois across every ravine, creek, stream, and piece of broken ground, most of Andrews's troopers could not be induced to help with the wounded by unloading the litters or erecting the captured buffalo-hide lodge. At last a few foot soldiers trudged over to volunteer their help. Eventually the wounded were out of the rain and served a steaming cup from the last of Clements's secret cache of coffee.

Some of those stronger men cheered up their wounded, sick, and worn-out fellows, saying, "We're only five or six miles from the Belle Fourche, the scouts tell us. And that means we can't be far from civilization!"

Smoky, muddy, raucous, and profane mining camps —to these ragged men clinging to hope and life itself, the Black Hills settlements had suddenly, somehow, become "civilization."

So it was that the last of the exhausted infantry showed up at half-past ten o'clock while the first of the dismounted cavalry did not begin to limp in until long after midnight. Worse yet, it would not be until the first light of false dawn etched the eastern horizon in gray that the last of those troopers who were put afoot the day before finally stumbled in.

Through the night the hardiest of those skeletal, despairing soldiers realized the rest would rely on someone else to keep them alive. So the few trudged off to scare up enough wood along the banks of the Willow to start their roaring bonfires at the foot of a low ridge in hopes that the lights dancing through the sheets of never-ending rain might serve as beacons to those still lost in the jaws of that terrifying wilderness. Beckoning them onward. Giving the faintest of them hope.

Throughout that long, terrible night many of those men straggling in had plainly used up the last shred of their strength, collapsing within sight of the bivouac's bonfires, unable to make another step, and fell into an exhausted sleep right there in the mud, not even taking the trouble to unroll their wet and crusted blankets before they closed their eyes and began to snore.

Those who still had the strength were asked to report to the commissary, where they helped butcher what few ponies they had left to cook for the rest who kept straggling in all night long.

Additionally Crook had his commanders ask for volunteers, men who would willingly return to the dark and the mud, to venture back into the maze of prairie, where they called out and searched the backtrail for anyone who no longer had the will to keep coming on his own.

That black day had been nothing more than raw survival—grown uglier as each succeeding hour continued to strip Crook's men of their last vestige of humanity.

As Dr. Clements said that night, "These men have reached the limit of human endurance."

It was long past midnight when King himself saw the first flickers of that long line of bonfires shimmering and dancing behind the curtains of hard rain. His shoulder hurt so much, he could think of little else. It helped when the arm did not swing, so some time ago he had stuffed his left hand inside his belt as a crude sling. And on he marched, stumbling forward, faster and faster now with the line of beacon fires drawing him nearer and nearer. Ahead there were voices, and he heard the snorts of horses.

Dear God! he prayed. Let it be camp!

As he plunged onward through the sheets of swirling mist, he made out not that far ahead the form of a half-dozen soldiers and a single horse they surrounded, moving in the same direction—toward the beacon fires. All five or six of the men clung to the animal that occasionally heaved to one side or the other. And then Charles made out the travois lashed to the animal, the crude poles bumping over the stubby cactus that with each jolt caused its passenger to groan.

"Dr. McGillycuddy?"

The horse careened to a stop, and the human forms turned slowly. One of them came back a few steps and stopped, wearily weaving, almost dead on his feet.

"I'm . . . Surgeon McGillycuddy."

"Lieutenant King."

"Lieutenant," the surgeon exclaimed, beckoning the officer on. "Join us—we're almost there." He turned, his arm expressive. "See? The fires."

"Who goes there?" came the demand from out of the darkness, and a dozen to fifteen men appeared a heartbeat later, backlit with the distant bonfires.

King tried to find his voice, but all that came up was the sob he had struggled to hold down throughout that long, terrible day in hell. It was McGillycuddy who finally replied, the only one among them not so weary that he could not speak.

The doctor's voice audibly cracked as he hollered out to the darkness. "The w-wounded t-train."

"Good God, Doctor!" an officer exclaimed as his wet, shiny face came close, looking over them all.

"Lieutenant Rawolle?" King asked, his voice harsh as it emerged from a raw throat.

"Charles King?" Rawolle lunged closer, his teeth bright in the dark shagginess of his mustache and beard. "It is you! Why, we'd all but given up every last one of you for dead."

Chapter 47

11–12 September
1876

To the Irishman those jagged peaks on the near horizon were like a lodestone, mysteriously pulling Mills's men ever toward them like iron filings.

Magnetically.

Irresistibly.

They had reached the Black Hills.

But it hadn't been all that easy.

After leaving the main column behind on Owl Creek that Monday morning of the eleventh, Captain Anson Mills had insisted that the scouts follow the dictates of his compass as they headed a little west of south. From time to time as the fog and mist lifted, they were able to spot Inyan Kara Mountain rising in the distance, its summit and most of its slopes shrouded in a tumble of gray thunderheads. After no more than a few moments the mountain disappeared once more, and they were again swallowed by the vastness of that monotonous, monochrome inland sea.

Just before nine, Frank Grouard signaled a halt and dropped off his horse to examine the fresh trail they had crossed. Then he squinted into the sky, as if he were trying to get his bearings. Turning now to his right, he asked Mills, "What direction is that?"

Seeing where the half-breed pointed, the officer consulted the compass he held in his rain-soaked glove and pronounced, "South. It's south, where we're headed."

Grouard shook his head and turned back to stand beside the captain's mount. "No. It's north. You've got us marching north."

"What the devil are you talking about?" Mills screeched.

"I got a bad feeling Frank's right," Donegan agreed.

The captain glared at Seamus. "One of your gut hunches again, Irishman?"

"Might say."

Mills whirled back to stare at Grouard. "Just what makes you so certain that my compass is wrong?"

"This trail," and Frank pointed down at the muddy tracks. "That ain't no Injun trail. It's ours."

"W-why . . . in heaven's name it can't be *our* trail," Mills exclaimed, his eyes darkening with suspicion.

"It is. I'm certain. I just spotted the tracks of that cow-hocked pony Lieutenant Bubb there is riding."

With his compass held out before him in a trembling hand, Mills declared, "There's no way this compass can be wrong. Without landmarks to go by in this nasty weather, Grouard—I think you're proving yourself of little use. So this command will stick by the compass. It will take us to Crook City and Deadwood." Turning to Lieutenant George F. Chase, Mills ordered, "Let's move them out."

Wagging his head, Grouard mounted up and eased his pony to the side so that he rode by Donegan at the end of the column. This was something new for the two of them. Usually they were in the front, far in the lead. But now Mills had his compass doing the scouting, doing the guiding for them all.

Both of them shook their heads as the compass took them circling back to the north a second time.

It was nigh onto midmorning when Grouard wanted

to stop again. "Colonel!" he shouted, halting and dropping onto the flooded prairie. "You better come take a look at this."

"Halt!" Mills growled as his patrol stopped and he wrenched his horse around savagely to approach the half-breed and Irishman. "What is it now, Grouard!"

Lieutenant Chase took out his big turnip watch and held it out of the rain as he opened it. "Colonel—it's ten-thirty. If we're going to cover more than forty miles today, we can't keep stopping."

Mills rose in his stirrups, glaring at the two scouts. "Why have you stopped us this time?"

"We just crossed our trail again, Colonel," Donegan said, his arm pointing off to the southeast.

"Dammit! Are you and Grouard here disputing this compass again?"

With a nod Seamus said, "I suppose that's it."

Now Jack Crawford spoke up. "We should have crossed Willow creek by now, Cap'n. I know the country where we're heading, but this ground just don't feel right."

"It's merely the weather," the captain argued impatiently, "and none of you can pick out the normal landmarks. That's why it pays to rely on a compass."

Dropping into the mud, Seamus slogged off about twenty feet while the soldiers grumbled behind him. At a small outcropping of red-hued rock, he kicked again and again with the heel of his battered boot, careful not to tear the buckskin he had used in a field repair to lash the sole to the upper vamp. Eventually he knocked loose a chunk of the blood-tinged stone and slogged back to Mills.

"Hold your compass out, Colonel," Seamus demanded.

"Why, what for?"

"Just hold it out, and I'll prove something to all of you."

Bewildered, Mills held out the compass in the palm of his wet gauntlet as the rain continued to patter on its glassy face.

"Now," Donegan instructed, "watch what happens."

As Seamus slowly moved the red stone around the compass in a clockwise motion, the needle followed as obediently as a child's pull toy on a string.

"In heaven's name!" gasped Lieutenant Chase.

Incredulous, Mills asked, "W-what does this mean, Irishman?"

Seamus lowered his stone. "It means Frank and me been right all along. We ain't been headed where we need to go. South ain't there," and he pointed. "Crook City and Deadwood and all the rest of them settlements are over that way."

As a whole those seventy-odd men turned in their saddles.

"Behind us?" Mills asked, still not believing.

"Absolutely right, Colonel," Crawford exclaimed.

"How?" Mills demanded testily.

"These rocks, Colonel," Seamus explained. "This ground's filthy with 'em. They been pulling your compass off all morning. Making us go in circles."

"Two big circles already," Grouard repeated.

"That's right," Donegan added. "Just what I suspected: we've gone and crossed our own trail for a second time."

Mills could only stare at his compass, slowly wagging his head. "I don't believe it. Why, we'll be lost without this compass."

Donegan stepped right up to the officer's horse. "Colonel, we've damn well been lost by using it! Now, why don't you just put that compass back in your saddlebags and let this patrol get on down the trail to the settlements?"

Disgustedly, the captain yanked up on the flap behind his McClellan saddle and dropped the brass compass into its depths. "Lead on, gentlemen. Now it's your turn to show us how you're better than a compass."

As Donegan swung into the saddle atop that buckskin pony, he reminded the officer, "Colonel Mills, don't you remember who led our attack column through the dark and a howling blizzard one miserable cold night last winter? Don't you remember who was it led us to a spot right over that enemy village on the Powder River, just before daylight—doing all of his guiding in the slap-dark of a snowstorm?"*

For a moment Mills looked at the half-breed, then nodded as he turned to Lieutenant Chase. "It was Grouard here. Very well, Mr. Donegan. You've made your point. Mr. Chase, lead the men out."

It was pushing noon when Frank, Donegan, and Crawford stopped the patrol again and dropped to the ground. Leading their horses off to the left about twenty yards, they knelt. Seamus stuffed his right hand into his left armpit to tear off his leather glove. With his bare hand he picked up the pony dung.

"Still warm and steamy, Frank."

They arose together as Seamus wiped the hand off on his wet britches and jammed it back into the glove.

"Can't be ahead," Grouard explained to Captain Mills moments later.

"Headed east?" he asked.

"More a little east of south," Donegan replied. "Almost the same direction we're aiming to go."

"Damn," Mills growled. He sighed, looked back over his short column of twos, then waved Chase close. "Lieutenant—you're to divide off half of the men."

"Separate sir?"

"Yes, I believe it's best that we split up here. Take Crawford with you. He says he knows the Hills."

Mills then went on to explain that if they should encounter a sizable war party, he wanted one group or the other to be sure to reach the settlements and secure aid for Crook's ailing column.

Minutes later Donegan watched the lieutenant lead some thirty men away, pointing their noses for Bear Butte

*The Plainsmen Series, Vol. 8, *Blood Song*.

as the wind came up and the rain washed over them in gusting sheets.

"Pay heed where you see them going," Mills instructed Seamus.

He turned to the officer to ask, "Why, Colonel?"

"There may come a time when I will need to have Chase rejoin us. And I'll need one of my scouts to have a damned good idea where he can find them."

Through the afternoon and into the murky light of dusk, Mills pushed them relentlessly as the ground below them slowly changed from grass and cactus to grass and sage, becoming grass and cedar just before hillsides loomed out of the fog before them, gentle slopes carpeted with the dark, verdant stands of pine and fir.

They had crossed the wide, clear waters of the Belle Fourche.

Was it only his imagination? Seamus wondered as he shivered with cold, with excitement, with anticipation. Or had they really reached the Black Hills? Drawn by some unseen force, were they really there? How he wanted to believe they had been plucked out of the wilderness perhaps by nothing less than the hand of God itself.

"That's the Whitewood!" Grouard cheered to the soldiers as he halted them at the northern bank of a narrow creek.

"Where will it take us?" Mills asked.

The half-breed turned on the captain, grinning, "Why —to Crook City. Crawford said once we get here, it can't be more'n a handful of miles now. And Deadwood's only ten miles beyond it."

A couple of hours after dark they reached Crook City, a ragged column of miserable men on captured Sioux ponies. Except for the disciplined order Mills kept in his ranks as they plodded slowly down the center of that stinking, mud-daubed mining settlement, the patrol would have looked like any band of brigands, freebooters, or borderland raiders. One by one and in small knots, miners and bummers pressed against the grimy windowpanes to peer at the column passing by, or poured from the doorways of saloons and watering holes, from the clapboard and false-fronted shops and hotels, pushing aside tent flaps and stepping out into the rainy night to take themselves a good, long gander at what had just marched out of the Dakota wilderness.

"Who the hell are you fellas?" someone asked from a shadow as the captain halted his rough lot of men in a cordon on both sides of the rutted thoroughfare and prepared to dismount.

"Colonel Anson Mills, Third U.S. Cavalry. Attached to the Big Horn and Yellowstone Expedition under Brigadier General George C. Crook. I've brought the general's commissary officer with me to secure provisions for his troops."

Another voice from the far side of the street demanded, "Where's Crook?"

"Yeah," someone said, stepping into dim lamplight. "Crook hisself with ya?"

"No. Forty miles, maybe less behind us now," Mills replied, exhaustion written on every word. "Two thousand men with him. We've been eating horse and mule for two weeks now."

"Well, now," a new voice called out, and a large, rotund man stepped out of the shadows of an awning and clomped through the mud to reach the captain's side. "I figure you've come to the right place, Colonel Mills. This here town is named after the general. And we're pleased as hell to have the army's protection, we are."

Then the first one of them bellowed out a cheer. And suddenly from both sides of the street the civilians pressed in, tearing their hats from their heads, throwing them into the air, shouting, screaming, whistling, and hooting in sheer joy. The Indian ponies fought their bits, and some attempted to rear, but the crowds latched on to them and held them in the center of that muddy, rutted street while everyone shook hands and laughed, and many of the soldiers couldn't help but cry.

Finally Seamus thought to ask those who stood as close to him as ticks on a buffalo's hide, "Does any man here know where I might get myself a good beefsteak? And a baked potato? And a bottle of whiskey what won't soap my tonsils when I pour it down?"

The Irishman was finishing his fifth cup of steaming coffee and was just about ready to pour his first double shot of whiskey when Anson Mills came up and settled in the rickety chair at Donegan's table in a saloon still fragrant with freshly-sawed lumber. The captain put his hand over the top of the shot glass.

"I'll leave you to have off at one drink, Irishman."

"Why, Colonel—I've waited a long time to drink my fill. Ever since Fetterman, it's been."

"I know you have. But you've filled your belly with just what it should have for the work at hand: warm food, good food, and strong, rich coffee too. So, now, before you drink any more than that one glass I'll leave you have—I want you to remember I've still got men out there. Soldiers in that wilderness."

"Lieutenant Chase," Donegan replied, suddenly realizing as he stared at the whiskey in the glass held underneath the captain's open palm.

"I fear they might have been chewed up by some war party, Irishman."

Donegan nodded, then licked his lips and let his eyes climb up to the officer's face. "My one drink of this blessed piss-hole whiskey, Captain?"

Reluctantly, Mills removed his hand, gently pushing the glass toward the scout. "Surely. If that's what you choose to do is drink the rest of the night while I and Lieutenant Bubb procure Crook's supplies—I can't stop you. We've all been under extreme privation . . . so I will try to understand."

Sweeping the two sides of his unkempt, bushy mustache aside with a grimy finger, Donegan licked his lips, staring at the delicate amber color in the smoky glass. Then as he closed his eyes, he gently poured the whiskey on his tongue and slowly tilted his head back, savoring the sweet sting it brought to his throat as the whiskey coursed its warm track all the way down his gullet.

Then he lowered his chin and opened his eyes, licking the last drops of whiskey from his lips and mustache. Rising from the table, he swept his shapeless sombrero from the empty chair beside him and planted it on his head, snugging up the wind-string below his beard.

Gazing down at the captain, Seamus pulled on his heavy coat, still damp. "You wouldn't happen to have a cigar, would you, Colonel?"

"Why . . . no, I wouldn't."

"Here, mister," said a civilian who rushed forward with a half dozen clutched in his hand. "Take what you want and I'll put it on your tab."

Seizing the long, fragrant, rum-soaked cheroots, each one as thick as his own thumb, Donegan replied, "Thank you, sir. You do that."

Gently inserting the precious smokes within the security of an inside pocket, Donegan dragged his leather gloves from the coat's pockets and turned back to Mills, saying, "If you'll be good enough to pay the six bits I owe the proprietor here, Colonel—and whatever else he's gonna charge for these cigars, I'd be grateful, I surely would. You see"—he leaned forward and whispered then—"I'm a little short for the moment."

"S-short?"

Grinning, he pulled on his gloves and said, "It's been some months since the army's paid me, which means I ain't had me any army scrip in my pocket for quite some time. So, Colonel—I'll let you pay for the meal, my cigars, and that one drink of whiskey. It appears I've still got some more scouting to do for you tonight."

Long after Robert Strahorn left with Mills that morning, the fog remained so thick the captain repeatedly put his compass to use, keeping Grouard leading them a little west of south.

Near late morning they stumbled across a trail of lodgepoles and pony tracks in the mud so fresh that Donegan and the half-breed found horse droppings still steaming in the frosty air. At once Mills grew alarmed.

"Lieutenant Chase," the captain called. "You're to divide off half the men."

"Separate, sir?"

"Yes," Mills replied, looking off into the murky distance where the enemy's muddy trail led. "I want to be sure some of us reach the mining towns—someone brings supplies back to the column."

Chase straightened in the saddle. "Where do you want me to go, Colonel?"

"You're going to be my ace in the hole, Mr. Chase. I want you to take half of the men with you and ride south by east, ready to keep on moving around the foot of the Black Hills if I'm attacked and can't complete my mission."

"East of the Black Hills," Chase repeated. "And then where?"

"On to Camp Robinson. Get word there that . . . that the rest of us have been overwhelmed by the Sioux."

In minutes Mills had his men split in half and Chase was on his way, accompanied by scout Jack Crawford and Denver's Rocky Mountain *News* correspondent. Reuben Davenport would remain with Mills and Lieutenant Bubb, their patrol led by Grouard and Donegan.

Chase led them away from Mills late that morning, and by dark his patrol had nowhere better than the lee of some rocks to take shelter in for the long, miserable night.

The following morning they were up and moving before dawn, crossing many small trails of bands headed in to the agencies. That second afternoon dragged on as the compass led Chase and thirty men through the rainy mist that lifted only when dusk began to settle upon the endless prairie. A quarter mile behind them a suckling colt gamely followed a brood mare one of the troopers was riding. Even when darkness fell quickly, the lieutenant refused to give up the march until the night became so black that they could no longer use the compass and landmarks, much less any stars in the overcast sky above. Finally running across a secluded stand of trees nestled at the base of a hill, with a nearby patch of grass, where they picketed their horses to graze, Chase relented to the complaints of his shivering and hungry men—allowing them to build a small fire they kindled at the bottom of a shallow pit.

As the soldiers chewed on a few scanty strips of dried pony meat they had packed along in their saddlebags since morning, the lieutenant and Crawford discussed what they would do if a wandering war party should discover and attack their patrol. Each of the troopers was to have a specific place to go in order for the outfit to make its best defense. Then out of the darkness appeared the suckling colt, which scared the devil out of the men, and elicited a maternal nicker from the mare.

An old sergeant said, "Cap'n, I sure do think that colt'd taste a lot better'n this here cold jerky."

Chase shook his head. "No. I want you all to understand I'm against killing the animal—better for us to let him tag along in case we need him for a real emergency."

Back and forth they debated it while chewing on their dried meat until the idea became a bit more reasonable to the lieutenant, and he relented to having their fresh meat then and there. No sooner had Chase agreed when a tall, strapping soldier leaped to his feet, seized the young colt around the neck, and slashed its throat in that ring of firelight.

A quarter of an hour later the men were roasting thin slivers of the meat and wolfing it down all but raw.

Supper was gone when they heard a horse coming through the trees and nearby brush.

"God-*damn*," one of them rasped in a whisper as they all rushed for their chosen positions.

On his belly Crawford quickly scooped some muddy soil into the pit, extinguishing their fire. Nearby Strahorn's heart pounded just the way it had last winter when they had found themselves pinned down in that Powder River village. Once more he had thrown in with men ready to sell their lives at a great cost that cold night.

"You boys aren't going to shoot a white man, now, will you?"

Strahorn's ears pricked. Rising to one knee, he hollered out to the darkness, "That you, Irishman?"

"Bob Strahorn? You bet it's me, Seamus!" the voice called back from the gloom. "Call off the guards and ease them hammers back down."

In less than two minutes Donegan was dismounted and stood in their midst, telling them, "Mills sent me to fetch you and your men, Lieutenant."

Chase asked anxiously, "Where is he now, Irishman?"

"Why, just past seven this evening—we rode into Crook City."

Strahorn leaned in close to the scout's face and sniffed for himself. He was smiling when he leaned back. "Is that what I think it is on your breath, Irishman?"

"If you mean whiskey—by the saints it sure as hell is!"

Bob almost wanted to cry as he wrapped his arms around the tall Irishman and hugged. Then he drew back and looked into Donegan's merry eyes.

"All right, you big goddamned leprechaun—how 'bout you taking me to the closest place you know where I can buy you a drink!"

Chapter 48

13 September 1876

It came as a real blessing when Crook didn't prod them out of their blankets early that Wednesday morning. In fact, they languished in camp until noon as those bone-weary men who had any strength left helped the engineering officers corduroy the north and south banks of Willow Creek in preparation of fording the stream.

But while the soldiers labored, even as those who had collapsed up and down the creekbank finally straggled in to join the others around the smoky fires—every man kept his eager, expectant, hopeful eyes trained on that country to the south.

"I will look unto the hills," Charles King murmured as he waded in the chilling, waist-deep water of the creek and dropped another log near those soldiers who were filling in the corduroy of steps. "Yes, I will look unto the hills from whence my help comes."

He closed his eyes and blinked away the tears, remembering that little church back home, and how he and the rest of the children had sat on the floor around one of the lay people each Sunday morning and learned scripture by rote. Psalm by psalm. Hope by hope. Prayer by prayer.

How many times had he asked God to end the rain?

And still it fell. Even until this morning. If the Lord kept this up, Crook's army would have to be about building an ark instead of laying down a corduroy to cross swollen streams.

Merritt himself had asked King to take charge of the work. "Go down to the creek and put the ford into shape," the colonel had requested. "You will find some fifty infantrymen reporting for duty."

The men were there—all fifty of them—but no more than a dozen of them were fit to do anything other than sit on the banks of that muddy stream. Those who did have any strength left would have to complete their job without tools. They had been hewing down the saplings and trimming branches with their belt knives. Each man lugged armloads of these into the rushing current, then plunged them under the water, attempting to anchor them any way they could to the shifting stream bottom.

Finally at noon King reported to Merritt and Crook. "I've done my best, General. *We've* done our best."

Merritt nodded. "I'm sure you have. All of you."

Crook stood to bellow at his officers. "Let's get this column across the creek!"

The general was the very first to try the ford. Twice his weary horse slipped, almost spilling Crook into the water. But in a moment more the old soldier was across the stream and on the south bank, waving the rest on as his mount stood there shivering, dripping, head hung in exhaustion.

It took more than two hours for the expedition to clamber across that shifting ford—down one corduroy, into the deep water, then up the far bank. First infantry, followed by the travois and litters, with several handlers posted on either side of every wounded man. Then came the dismounted troopers, and finally what was left of Crook's cavalry brought up the rear. Just past two P.M. they marched away from the Willow, making for the Belle Fourche little more than a handful of miles away.

Nonetheless, it took them another two hours to reach

that wide, clear-running stream fed by the snows of the nearby Black Hills. Although the banks were muddy, they weren't steep, and the bottom appeared rocky and solid. No engineering required here. Crook waved his hat to spur them on and was the first into the Belle Fourche. Again the infantry formed an escort for Clements's wounded in crossing the rapid stream. Then the dismounted cavalry clustered around their own mounted companies, moving into the water clinging to a horse's tail or latching on to a comrade's stirrup as the animals pulled them to the south bank.

And when they reached the far shore, emerging from the icy cold, the saddles were taken off and the horses picketed on the lush green grass of these prairie highlands. Great fires were started. As some men stood warming themselves right there in their steamy clothing, others stripped off everything and rubbed their purple flesh until it turned rosy.

They had reached the Belle Fourche. Here, if not before, Mills was to meet them. Just gazing at that southern bank of the river made King proud: these two thousand ragged men who appeared to be more a great motley band of ruffians and unkempt scoundrels than what had once been the greatest army ever to take the field on the frontier —they had torn horse meat raw from the bone, and every one of them had a mouthful of teeth loosened with scurvy —they hadn't shaved or bathed in weeks—and not one of them had enjoyed a change of clothing in months. What they had on their bony frames hung in faded tatters. While their faces might be liver-colored with weeks of unending fatigue, their eyes nonetheless glowed with hope.

As if in answer to that hope, a lone trooper rode in from the south not much more than an hour after their arrival on the Belle Fourche—carrying word from Mills that he and Bubb were on their way back! With a herd of beef and thirteen wagons!

For the ancient Hebrews crossing the wilderness who

had their prayers answered when the stones turned to
manna—it could be no greater an expectation than this!

So it was that many of the soldiers moved up the
slopes of the surrounding hills, where they would keep
watch to the south and speculate on what Lieutenant Bubb
might bring them to break their horse-meat fast.

"There!"

A hundred men turned, followed in an instant by five
hundred more leaping to their feet along the riverbank below. Then another thousand. Those who could wearily
trudged up the slopes as fast as their played-out legs could
carry them, their sunken, skeletal eyes wide with expectation as they strained to peer into the distance.

Yes! There! Coming out of the mouth of that canyon!

Cattle?

Dear God! Fifty head of them!

Lumbering down the slopes of the grassy hills, urged
on by Mills's wranglers. Charles could almost hear those
far-off cavalrymen whistle and shout as they drove the
beeves down to that camp beside the Belle Fourche.

And—look there! What's that coming no more than a
mile behind them?

Wagons!

Clean white canvas stretched taut over the swell of
those wrought-iron bows.

Merciful Lord in heaven—wagons!

"Rations coming!" someone shouted.

Then they were all shouting, throwing their hats into
the air with abandon. Embracing and dancing, around and
around and around, arm in arm. Hugging and crying,
laughing and pounding one another on the back like
schoolboys at Mayday recess.

Charles rubbed that old Arizona arrow wound, wondering if Bubb might just have some horse liniment or a
drawing salve. Knowing once more the power of prayer.
Sensing again the presence of his God.

A God who hadn't lifted him from the jaws of death in

Apache country only to let him die in the rain, and the cold, and the mud of this Sioux wilderness.

Then, as if to give a benediction to all their most fervent prayers, patches of blue suddenly appeared overhead as the rain clouds rumbled on past, leaving the sun behind to shine for those last two hours of a grand, grand day.

They had been delivered.

Since leaving Camp Cloud Peak on Goose Creek, Crook's army had suffered twenty-two days of rain, storms of great severity. In the three weeks since leaving General Alfred Terry on the Yellowstone, they had suffered seven days of a "horse-meat march."

But now Seamus was riding down that last long, grassy slope toward the Belle Fourche beside the lead wagon. Twelve more followed, all double-teamed because of the immense weight Lieutenant Bubb had packed in each one, provisions piled right up past the sidewalls, straining against the tailgates.

He had never seen anything like it: the way these men rushed up the slopes toward the beef herd, scattering the cattle. Every trooper yanked out his pistol, every foot soldier pulled free his belt knife, ready to do in those fifty frightened cows right there and then. For a moment Donegan thought a half-dozen soldiers were going to tackle one of the beeves, hamstring the animal, and butcher it right there on the hillside what with the way they all clung to its horns and back and tail, dragging it on down, as it snorted and protested, toward the flashing blue waters of that pretty, pretty river while the sun fell out of the clouds at long, long last.

"Hurrah for old Crook!" they raised the cheer.

Days before—even as little as hours, so it seemed—these soldiers had been clamoring to hang the general. A mutinous rabble ready to string up the man who had brought them such ruin.

But now these same men exalted some two thousand strong as they poured out of that bivouac like a mighty throng, suddenly rejuvenated—willing once more to follow their leader into the jaws of hell.

Seamus couldn't have scraped the grin off his face if he'd wanted to. Especially when the soldiers clambered onto the first wagon even before it could come to a halt. Then the second and all the rest, men leaping beneath the canvas covers, cheering and drowning out the shouts of warning and orders from their officers. Against the sturdy sidewalls of all thirteen of those wagons the men shoved and jostled, nearly tipping over a few of the freighters in the melee while those soldiers inside began tossing out crates of hard bread, cookies and crackers, chests of salt pork along with tins of vegetables and fruits the men stabbed open with their field knives, drinking the juices before bending back the metal lids to spear out the precious fruit or sweet tomatoes.

"Huzzah for Colonel Mills! Huzzah! Huzzah!"

But Captain Anson Mills wasn't there to take his bow.

Instead of returning with the wagons, he had elected to stay behind in Crook City, begging off from making the return trip due to his severe fatigue and the privations suffered in one long battle with the Sioux, and in both punishing journeys to the Black Hills settlements. This afternoon Lieutenant Bubb led the rescue back from Deadwood.

From wagon to wagon the quartermaster pushed his weary horse through the shoving, elbowing, senseless crowd, hollering out his orders on how he wanted the food dispersed. Seamus had to laugh—for not one of them was listening to any courteous order from their commissary officer now. No longer were they forced to take only what he dispersed among them in the way of the butchered horses, mules, or ponies.

Now they were only eating. Eating everything in sight.

Near the tailgate of the third wagon he saw Charles King shoved side to side in the melee as soldiers hurled boxes and cases and tins of food high into the air, where the crowd lunged and scrambled for it all. Fistfights broke out as men struggled over every morsel.

Then suddenly King dropped into the mud, and when Seamus saw him come up, the lieutenant had three muddy ginger snaps he hurriedly brushed off with his dirty hands, then stuffed right into his mouth. He chewed that dirty treat with no less relish than James Gordon Bennett of the New York *Herald* would in dining on fine caviar at Delmonico's.

Every last one of those men were eating as if there were no tomorrow, as if they might not see another meal. After what they had been through, Seamus thought, who could blame them for not giving a damn about that next meal, that next day, that next march and campaign!

"Tobacco!" a soldier announced from a wagon back down the line.

For a moment it appeared all two thousand of the men were going to swamp that single freighter.

"Lordee! We got tobacco at last!"

Already half of the beeves were down in the grass, their throats slit, the precious, thick crimson pouring out in glistening puddles over that lush carpet of green as the men put their knives to work in quickly butchering before they would waddle over to the roaring bonfires laden with great gobs of warm meat spilling across their bloody arms.

Damn, even the worst cut of beefsteak had to taste better than the very best scab-backed, worn-down, bone-rack, and worm-bait horse!

Within minutes some of the men who had snatched eighty-pound sacks of flour had begun mixing up sugar and eggs into batter when they realized they had no skillets. In a heartbeat an enterprising soldier cried out that they could melt the solder joints securing the two halves of their canteens and use them both for small skillets. It was quickly done by hundreds, and soon they brought their roasting pans to a sizzle and were turning flapjacks to a golden brown as men crowded and shoved, snatching the fluffy cakes from the iron spatulas as soon as they were pulled from the coals.

At every fire sat a ring of huge gallon coffeepots, and

around them sat an ever bigger ring of expectant men, soldiers and civilians alike waiting for their first cup of real coffee in more long, cold days and nights than any man should have to remember.

Only the surgeons ate sparingly, advising all within hearing distance to do the same—but no one listened. So Clements and Patzki and McGillycuddy just shook their heads, knowing that come morning they would be crushed beneath the weight of a thousand gastric complaints.

And when the hundreds had eaten their fill and were drinking what had to be the best cup of coffee in their lives, the pipes were lit and cigarettes rolled, maybe even an extra quid or two stuffed back into their cheeks, once more given the luxury of wrapping themselves in warm *dry* blankets for the first time in more than a week while the sun settled beyond the far side of Inyan Kara Mountain.

In a matter of minutes these pitiful, starving wretches reduced to the utter brink of savagery, these crude, uncivilized captives of the wilderness, were soldiers once more. No longer did they stand teetering at the threshold of death's door. Once again these were men who joked, and laughed, and talked at long last of the future.

For now there was a future.

"Seamus."

Donegan turned to find Lieutenant Bourke at his shoulder. Taking the beef rib from his greasy lips, he said, "Johnny! Come—share some of our feast with us!"

Patting his stomach, Bourke smiled and replied, "Thanks, but no. I've had quite enough for now. I'm come to fetch you. The general would like to talk with you."

He rose while sucking the juices from his fingers, then licked the ends of his mustache with a flick of his tongue. "What's Crook want with me now?"

"Now that Grouard and Crawford are both gone on south carrying dispatches and reporters' stories, you're the only one he can ask."

Suspicious, Seamus came to an abrupt halt. "I don't

like the sound of this, Johnny boy. Give me the whole of it, and now."

"Crook is frightened about all that ammunition we had to abandon off the mules and horses."

"Yes?"

"He's sending back a detail of the Fifth Cavalry to retrieve it."

He nodded warily. "So he figures to send a scout with those troops, eh?"

Crook had devised his plan: Seamus, an officer, and thirty picked troopers on the regiment's strongest horses. A journey of more than seventy miles in all, round trip. Sure as hell didn't sound like a Sunday walk in the park—what with the certain likelihood of hundreds of warriors still dogging the army's backtrail, hoping to pick up all the horses and plunder Three Stars's soldiers had abandoned.

"When does the old boy want us to leave?" Donegan asked.

"The general inquires to see if you could be ready to go inside an hour."

Chapter 49

13–15 September
1876

THE INDIANS

End of the Sioux Campaign.

CHICAGO, September 15—The Times' special correspondent with Terry telegraphs under date of Fort Buford, mouth of the Yellowstone, the 8th, via Bismarck, the 14th, that the final breaking up of Terry's command occurred yesterday morning, and all the troops are now en route home, with the exception of two regiments of infantry, which will winter at the mouth of Tongue river . . . By the 15th all the troops will have been withdrawn from the northern country except the Fifth and Twenty-second infantry, containing 400 men. A dispatch just received from Gen. Sheridan countermands the order to winter a regiment of cavalry on the Yellowstone, which renders winter campaigning impossible, and indefinitely postpones the subjection of the Sioux.

Terry leaves the field, having accomplished no

purpose of the expedition, and with one-quarter of his troops killed by bullets or exposure.

As the clouds finally abandoned the sky above the banks of the Belle Fourche that night of the thirteenth, a nearly full moon rose in the southeast beyond Bear Butte.

For the longest time Seamus stood watching it ease itself up off the horizon, yellow as the cream that rose to the surface of buttermilk, and he thought on that most sacred place the hostiles wanted to protect from the white man. How the Lakota and Cheyenne wanted nothing more than to drive these miners and merchants and settlers entirely from the Black Hills.

At headquarters was gathered a happy congregation of citizens—shop owners and merchants of all strata, politicians and the power hungry of every stripe—every last one of them eager to shake hands with General George Crook and those officers who had rescued them from the recent terror and likely annihilation by the Sioux and Cheyenne.

"Four hundred of our citizens have been murdered by the savages since June," one local wag declared at Crook's fire that evening. "And at last the government has made up its mind to protect its citizens!"

Around the group of officers they distributed those luxuries they had carted out from Whitewood, Crook City, and Deadwood in their wagons and buggies: canned meats and candied fruits, fish eggs and cheeses, wines and a better age of whiskey, along with molasses-cured cigars as big around as a cane fishing pole.

For the rest of camp it was a merry night, filled with song and dance and laughter. Warm food and rich coffee, tobacco for a farmboy to chew, for a German to stuff into his briars or an Irishman into the unbroken stump of his clay pipe, then gaze overhead at the stars.

After so, so many nights, just to see the stars again in this sky! So sing they did, every last song they knew, sang with lusty joy.

Down to the bivouac of Carr's Fighting Fifth Cavalry,

Seamus led his Indian pony, figuring he might just as well sleep there among those troopers until dawn arrived and the handpicked detail would march north to retrieve those boxes of abandoned ammunition. It was as merry a camp as he could ever remember being in since that April night back in sixty-five, there in the leafy coolness of the Appomattox Woods surrounding the McLean farmhouse where the Virginia gentleman Lee had just surrendered to old Sam Grant. Yes, indeed—Sheridan's cavalry had done all that had been asked of it, so those gallant horse soldiers had good cause to celebrate the end of a long, bloody, terrible war.

And again tonight the soldiers who had marched this time with George Crook celebrated the fact that Phil Sheridan's mighty trumpet had been heard upon the land. It was plain that they were driving the hostiles back to their agencies. The soldiers had survived their wilderness ordeal.

So it came as no surprise to the Irishman to find that the regiment's prodigious rhymesters were already at work composing new verses for the popular song of the era, "The Regular Army O."

We were sent to Arizona,
For to fight the Indians there;
We were almost snatched bald-headed,
But they didn't get our hair.
We lay among the canyons and the dirty yellow mud,
But we seldom saw an onion, or a turnip, or a spud.
Till we were taken prisoners
And brought forninst the chief;
Says he, "We'll have an Irish stew"—
The dirty Indian thief!
On Price's telegraphic wire we slid to Mexico,
And we blessed the day we skipped away
From the Regular Army O!

Every officer in the army knew George Crook had received his promotion to brigadier due to his leadership during the Apache campaign down in Arizona. In fact, the Fifth Cavalry had long boasted that they themselves had won that star for him. So it was with fond affection that the regiment gave a new nickname to the general following his fight with Crazy Horse in Montana Territory—"Rosebud George" he was called. And during their escape from General Terry and the ordeal of their horse-meat march, it was common knowledge that Tom Moore's packers somehow always seemed to have better food to eat, and more of it, while Carr's horse soldiers grew hungrier with each new day.

So went another new verse to the old song:

But t'was out upon the Yellowstone
We had the damndest time.
Faith! We made the trip with Rosebud George,
Six months without a dime!
Some eighteen hundred miles we went
Through hunger, mud, and rain,
Wid backs all bare, and rations rare,
No chance for grass or grain;
Wid bunkies shtarving by our side,
No rations was the rule;
Sure t'was, "Eat your boots and saddles, you brutes,
But feed the packer and mule!"
But you know full well that in your fights
No soldier lad was slow.
But it wasn't the packer that won you a star
In the Regular Army O!

A rousing night for men drunk not on beer or liquor but on relief, giddy with a full belly of something far more filling than broken-down horseflesh. They had emerged from the wilderness alive but not unscathed. Every last one of them not quite whole. Their terrible ordeal had indelibly scarred them. They would never quite be the same men any of them had been when they had marched north at the

beginning of that hopeful summer, which was to be the last
of freedom for the nomadic Sioux.

"Look! Look there!" Charles King shouted above some
of the singing and laughter and pandemonium.

As more and more of the other officers and soldiers
turned to look where the lieutenant was pointing at the top
of a hill, the singing grew hushed and a prayerful murmur
began.

In the shelter of a rocky promontory Colonel Wesley
Merritt and his staff had pitched their bivouac of blankets
and tent halves just below the crest among a sparse clump
of stunted pine and cedar. Extending from that collection
of crude shelters all the way down the slope to the banks of
the Belle Fourche was a sight that made even the most
hardened and skeptical of them all feel suddenly touched
by the hand of God in their deliverance.

With its rising in those clearing skies that evening, the
moon had projected its shimmering, silvery light behind a
narrow cleft in those boulders above the regiment's camp
—enlarging to heroic size a wind-bared, leafless branch no
taller than two feet in height, crossed at a perfect angle by a
somewhat smaller twig.

As the moon inched from the horizon, the image
slowly crawled across that bivouac of the Fighting Fifth—
until the banks of the Belle Fourche were touched by that
mystical symbol of death and rebirth.

From the midst of those stunned hundreds burst one
doubting Thomas, a young infantryman who had been
celebrating with his friends among the cavalry regiment.
Up the side of the hill he bounded until reaching the crest,
where he discovered the tiny natural cross thus created by
the rising of that full moon. In the splendid brilliance of
that evening he turned around at the crest and with outflung arms shouted his declaration that what they all were
witnessing was no divine manifestation.

But an old soldier—one of those scarred in a long,
bloody war against the south, a trooper who had followed
Eugene Carr's Fifth across the arid plains of western Ne-

braska until they had caught Tall Bull at Summit Springs, one who had stood with Royall to fight the Apache down among the blisteringly cruel mountains of Arizona, one who had cajoled and cheered and herded before him stragglers all along the muddy route of that terrible horse-meat march—now that old file finally spoke to the Irishman beside him.

"I damn well don't need no green shavetail telling me what is or ain't a sign from God." He raised his gray-bristled face to the starry sky. "A man only has to stand here now, and remember what we come through, to know for certain that God Himself put that cross there for us to see—just like it was God Himself what brung us out of the desert."

"Amen," Donegan said quietly as he stared at the moonlit phenomenon, then crossed himself again. "Thy will be done."

Once more he felt in the presence of something much greater than he, something much greater than all of them, white and red. And though Seamus could not bring himself to say that his God was the same as the Indians' God—he knew he would never again believe that his God was any better than the Great Mystery or Everywhere Spirit worshiped by the hostiles he had tracked and fought and killed for more than a decade now.

This year as the powerful in Washington City sent their emissaries west to sweet-talk and bully the tribes into selling their beloved Black Hills, it was enough to give him pause as he stood within the heart of those hills, knowing the hostiles wanted only to drive off from this most mystical of places all white men, to expel every last one of those restless spirits who had been drawn to these streams from all corners of the earth and in the end stayed on for the very same reasons the Indian came here to pray.

The inevitability of the nation's course would eventually crush all resistance, of that he had no doubt. But for the moment Seamus knew that all who came to realize just what treasure was at stake shared in common something quite holy, be they white or red.

Humbled in the magnificent beauty of this place, realizing that every last one of them had been given life when once so close to death—this heavenly light, this cross, this presence of something so great it was beyond understanding—was at this moment enough to bring tears to a big man's eyes, able to utter only one word.

"Amen."

By the morning of the fourteenth a plague of diarrhea struck the camp. Men gone so long on nothing but lean and stringy horse meat had suddenly gorged themselves with all sorts of vegetables and fruits, beef and pork, as well as all varieties of breads. Some men grumbled in spite as they hurried into the brush, but for most their affliction was a small price to pay for deliverance.

Besides, the sun actually came up at down. Without a cloud in the sky.

To lead the patrol Crook sent back to retrieve the abandoned ammunition, the rotation of duty among the subalterns in the Fifth Cavalry fell to young Lieutenant Edward L. Keyes, C Troop. Following Donegan that dawn were some thirty-five men, hardly enough to hold off any united force of warriors seeking to harass, kill, and scalp any stragglers not already come to the army's camp on the Belle Fourche.

But in that Thursday's march, and the anxious return trip of the fifteenth, none of them saw a single feather, not one hostile horseman, as they hurried south again along their backtrail.

Besides the fourteen pitiful abandoned horses they were able to drive south with them, on the backs of a dozen of Tom Moore's pack-mules Keyes's men lashed every last box of ammunition the column had cached during its ordeal. Not one cartridge was lost.

When Seamus led the lieutenant's patrol back to Crook's camp, which had been moved in those last two days from the Belle Fourche up Whitewood Creek, John Finerty trotted up in those deformed brogans of his and, before Donegan could even climb out of the saddle, declared, "Upham's patrol came in without finding a single Injun."

"Same was it with us: we saw trails, but no warriors," Seamus replied.

"But that doesn't mean the Sioux didn't see Upham's men," Finerty said gravely.

"What do you mean?"

"Upham had a private named Milner, Company A—riding out ahead of the rest, maybe no more than a half mile. They said he was following an antelope."

"And the Sioux jumped him?"

"Right. The rest came on his body five minutes after those red bastards did their craftiest work. Found Milner stripped, his whole scalp gone, throat slit from ear to ear, and his chest slashed with two large *X*'s. What would such a thing mean, Seamus?"

"Those two *X*'s mean the Indians found the soldier was a brave man."

"I should say," Finerty agreed. "Upham's men found a lot of cartridge cases around the body. Stone dead—but his flesh still warm as could be."

"Those h'athens can work fast. Believe me, I've seen it with my own eyes," Donegan said.

"Sergeant Major Humme was damned mad. Still mad enough to chew on nails when he came riding in here not long after the Sioux killed his man that he went storming right up to Crook, frothing at the bit and demanding a chance to even the score by killing one of the captives, that Charging Bear fella, with his own hands. Crook sent him away, with a warning that he'd put Humme under arrest if he caused any more trouble."

Seamus said, "Things quieted down after that?"

With a nod Finerty replied, "At night they have—but during the day there's a photographer come up from Deadwood. Rolled in with his wagon yesterday. Ever since, he's been posing the soldiers for photographs."

"I'll bet he's making the money," Donegan grumbled.

"Oh, he's not making cabinet photos for the soldiers to send back to their families," the newsman corrected. "He heard all about the hardships the men suffered on the march—eating the horse meat, slogging through the mud, and all the rest—that he's been posing the soldiers in what I'd call little scenes or vignettes."

"What's his name?"

"Stanley J. Morrow. Told me he had posed the soldiers fighting over horse meat, posed them pretending they're cutting steaks from the flanks of a dead horse, had some of the mules and horses with soldiers in their litters and on their travois—saying he was going to let the folks back east know just how cruel this campaign and the Sioux War really was. Morrow's not a bad fellow, Seamus. He's doing all this at his own expense."

"Then God bless 'im: someone needs to record for history what we all went through on Crook's march."

"Won't be long until we're no longer forced to live off the white scalpers."

"White scalpers?" Seamus asked.

"Those drummers and merchants who ride out here with their wagons loaded with goods priced four, five times the going rate on the frontier," the newsman continued.

"Army's getting provisions sent in here?"

"Damn right they are. Second night after we arrived, a courier came in carrying an envelope filled with six dispatches from Sheridan telling Crook that he should leave his sick and wounded at Custer City, down in the southern end of the Hills—where Sheridan's sent supplies."

"More bacon and hard bread," Donegan said sourly. "Still, there was a time I'd given my left arm for a taste of salt pork, even a mouthful of some moldy tack."

"From what I can tell, things sounded like Sheridan wasn't happy when he learned that Crook was heading south toward the Black Hills instead of chasing the Sioux."

Donegan wagged his head. "I fought for Sheridan in the Shenandoah—so I'd tell that little son of a bitch to his face that he has no room to talk. By God, he wasn't here on that march with us!"

"From the tone of his messages Sheridan's angry with Crook. Wants the general to clear out of the Black Hills and get on with establishing a cantonment on the Powder River in Indian country."

"Sheridan's right on target there. Forget Fetterman, or those Montana posts. Too far south and north. The army's got to put a fort right in the heart of the Sioux hunting ground and hold on to it. Not like they gave up Reno, Phil Kearny, and C. F. Smith back to sixty-eight."

"You won't believe what news came in the last dispatch the courier brought in for the general," Finerty announced, "Sheridan's called Crook back to Laramie!"

That one word had a magical, powerful, potent, and magnetic ring to it: *Laramie.*

In stunned disbelief the Irishman stammered, "F-fort Laramie? Great Mither of God—why'd you wait so long to tell me Crook's heading back to Laramie?"

"I'm going with him, Seamus. General's moving out in the morning—on the double."

"There is a God, Johnny boy!" Seamus cheered. "Never should you doubt—there is a God!"

"I might be more of a believer if we had a dram of whiskey to pour in my coffee. Care to go with me to scare up a steaming cup of something warm, Seamus?"

Donegan immediately stuffed the pony's reins into the newsman's hand and replied, "Perhaps later. Right now I've got to speak to the general!"

He presented himself before General Crook, ready to plead his case, prepared to fall to his knees and beg if he had to. This month was already halfway gone to October. And if Sam's count was right, then with the last days of October would come her time. While he had no reason to believe a woman could be wrong about so important a thing—mind-boggling mystery that it could be to a man—

Seamus nonetheless decided he must not take a chance that Crook's Big Horn and Yellowstone Expedition would mosey back to Fort Laramie so slowly that he would show up late for the birth of his child.

Most of the top officers of every one of the regiments, both foot and horse, encircled that great fire as he approached, each of them gripping a pint tin cup in which the general had splashed some champagne given him by the grateful citizens of the mining towns, some of whom stood here and there among that joyous circle celebrating both the expedition's success at Slim Buttes and the rescue of the Black Hills settlements.

"Yes, I received the lieutenant general's orders late this afternoon," Crook explained.

He stood near the tent half stretched overhead like an awning, boxes of provisions stacked to construct a crude field desk where papers and maps were strewn, held down beneath a pistol, a large brass-cased compass, and his own writing kit composed of an ink bottle wrapped in thick leather and topped with a brass cap to prevent it from breaking in a saddlebag, as well as a series of lead pencils and hefty wooden pens, each one crowned by a metal nib.

One of the Black Hills officials asked, "So you are hurrying back to Fort Laramie, General?"

"I'm to turn the command over to General Merritt in the morning immediately after breakfast. We'll be disbanding the expedition in a few weeks because Sheridan is coming out from Chicago himself, wanting to meet with me and General Mackenzie to plan a fall and winter campaign."

Donegan gulped. "Mackenzie? Of the Fourth Cavalry?"

Crook turned at the sound of the Irishman's voice, his eyes narrowing. "Yes. You know of him?"

"A little, sir. Some. Down in Texas—against Quanah Parker's Comanche."

With a sigh the general said, "I see. Texas. You certainly have made the rounds, haven't you, Irishman? Well

—I have an idea I will be using Mackenzie as the lance of our coming campaign—putting him in the field with his veterans as my strike force. While these men with the Second and the Third have served me faithfully since last winter, it's plain to see that they're simply worn out. The Fourth Cavalry will not only be eager, but more than ready to strike the hostiles."

One of the local citizens asked, "Then it is true you're going to continue the campaign, General?"

Gazing up into the Irishman's eyes, Crook answered, "This war with the Sioux is far from over, I'm compelled to admit. No matter what the eastern press might say about us, we've accomplished too much to stop now simply because of the onset of winter."

Taking one step closer to Crook, Seamus inquired, "So, General—would you be good enough to consider me riding back with your escort when you leave in the morning?"

Crook smiled genuinely and nodded. "I'll see that Major Stanton gets you paid off with a voucher you can use to draw on when you reach Laramie with us."

"W-with you, General? With *you*?"

Crook held out his hand to Donegan. "Why, certainly you can ride along with my party. I see no reason for you to lollygag around here with the expedition as the men rest and recruit themselves. Now, tell me: what's this news I hear from John Bourke that your wife is due to have a child?"

Chapter 50

16–20 September
1876

They might not even call such a collection of crude clapboard buildings and canvas-topped shanties a "town,"
but to the eyes and ears and nose of John Finerty, Deadwood exuded the sweet sensation of civilization!

With Crook's announcement that the Big Horn and
Yellowstone Expedition was soon to be disbanded and that
Sheridan had called him to Fort Laramie, all four of the
correspondents applied to the general for permission to
accompany his party south via Camp Robinson. The likable
Joe Wasson, the much-despised Reuben Davenport, as well
as the affable and eminently sociable Robert Strahorn all
joined Finerty in saddling up that Saturday morning before
reporting to the general's headquarters promptly after
breakfast. Besides the Irishman Donegan, Captain Andrew
S. Burt had requested and secured leave, heading back to
rejoin wife Elizabeth and children at Laramie.

Crook had also given permission to several officers to
accompany him: his aide-de-camp, John Bourke; Major Alexander Chambers; Captain William H. Powell; and Captain Thaddeus Stanton, the Omaha paymaster; along with

adjutant Schuyler, Captain George M. "Black Jack" Randall, and Assistant Surgeon Albert Hartsuff, all had asked to go on that dash south from the Black Hills. In addition, Lieutenant Frederick Sibley led an escort of twenty troopers from the Second Cavalry, along with a complement of a half-dozen mules to carry some medical supplies, ammunition, and an abundant supply of Bubb's food.

All the way south to the settlements along the road that snaked beside Whitewood Creek they passed civilians in wagons, civilians leading pack-animals behind them, civilians alone on horseback—all headed north to that army camp with everything they hoped to sell to the soldiers: canned goods and candles, onions and cabbages, turnips and potatoes, and all manner of vegetables grown locally in the Hills. Here and there the party rode past small herds of cattle grazing on the grassy hillsides, each one of those highly valued herds guarded by a well-armed band of wranglers.

After a short ride of sixteen miles they reached the wooded ravine on the northern outskirts of Crook City, finding it a thriving, smoky community of more than 250 structures erected on either side of the steep slopes rising up from the Whitewood. No sooner had the general's escort appeared at the edge of town than a loud explosion rocked the narrow valley. Finerty pulled his head into his shoulders like a turtle.

"Cannon fire," Donegan explained.

"Cannon?"

"I suppose it's to welcome the town's namesake, General Crook himself."

Indeed, the citizens of the Black Hills settlement were firing off cannons, plus blowing all manner of steam whistles, in addition to loading their anvils with gunpowder to send them cartwheeling into the air with a deafening concussion.

Hundreds of men and some two dozen of the ugliest, most hard-featured, dog-faced women Finerty could ever admit to seeing, every one of them in some state of undress, appeared on the streets, crowded the boardwalks, or leaned from open windows on the second stories of those greater buildings in town. In less than two hundred yards, the street was all but blocked as men fired their revolvers in the air, shouted out their oaths and vows to scalp Crazy Horse themselves, and strained through the throng to shake the hands of those soldiers slowly threading through their midst.

"General! You must come have dinner with us!" roared one local dignitary, gesturing toward his two-story saloon and pleasure palace.

Glancing a moment at the sun, Crook replied, "I suppose we could stop briefly for a meal."

"Very good! Very good!" the entrepreneur said, clapping his hands ecstatically. "We'll see that your horses are grained while we dine."

In moments the entire group was seated at tables, which big-breasted chippies and gap-toothed soiled doves wiped clean, smiling winsomely at each of the celebrated guests. Bottles and glasses and cigars all appeared as if by magic.

"It's our very best, General Crook," the businessman swore. "Nothing but the best for you and your men."

What was in those bottles proved to be some of the strongest whiskey Finerty had ever tasted, even stronger than what had made him sputter when he had first come to Wyoming Territory and Kid Slaymaker's saloon near Fort Fetterman.

"Good God! Is this what they call *forty-rod*?" the newsman asked, wheezing and wiping his watery eyes.

"Indeed it is," Donegan said, pouring Finerty another drink. "If Sitting Bull or Crazy Horse knew how to make this stuff and sell it to the white man, why—the Sioux could whip the whole frontier army in less than a week!"

Once the party emerged from the saloon back onto the street to find their horses watered and well fed, the wild cheering erupted again. But when they left Crook City behind, they could plainly see the town had already enjoyed its short-lived glory. Founded in May, it was already suffering a long downhill slide as the richest gulch had quickly played out and every day more and more miners headed for other nearby strikes or to build their sluices farther upstream.

Quartz and timber were both in abundance—that much was apparent from their ride up the graded wagon road that would take them another ten miles to Deadwood. Every mile saw more teamsters and packers, as well as assorted horsemen, each one of them sporting a pair of spurs with rowels as big as tea saucers, jingling like hawk's bells as they bounced along. A few miles out from Deadwood they came upon a handful of riders who wore the finest in bowlers and claw-hammer coats, brocade vests and fine silk ties —the sort of haberdashery that made Crook's seedy, tattered, unkempt bunch look all the more like a wandering band of Nordic raiders.

"General Crook, I presume?" one of the citizens asked, removing his hat.

"I am George Crook, yes."

"Good day, sir!" The speaker smiled, as well as all those with him. "My name's E. B. Farnum, Deadwood's first mayor. Welcome, may I say. Welcome, indeed, to a grateful town!"

After shaking hands all round with the mayor's aldermen, Farnum reined about and led the party on through Montana City, Elizabeth Town, China Town, then Lower Deadwood, and finally in to Deadwood itself, where the whole town had turned out, waiting expectantly for the general's arrival. No sooner had Crook reached the edge of what was then the business district than thirteen small field pieces erupted in a grand martial salute. Smoke hung lazily over the street as a wonderful breeze teased the red, white, and blue bunting strung from awnings and porches and second-story balconies in a festive salute to the man the town regarded as their savior. Cheering, dancing, shooting handguns—the noise was deafening.

Finerty smiled, watching the general tip his ragged,

weather-beaten chapeau, bowing left, then right, then left again, shaking hands as they inched slowly along, waving to those on porches and balconies, throwing a kiss here and there to the second-story working girls of that mining town —all in the manner of a man running for political office.

"Crook could be elected mayor of Deadwood if he wanted," Finerty had to yell above the pandemonium to the Irishman riding beside him.

Donegan nodded, saying, "Hell—he could damn well be elected governor of the whole bleeming Dakota Territory!"

Drawing up in front of the Grand Central Hotel and gesturing across the street, Mayor Farnum politely offered, "General, should your men wish to make use of our public bathhouse over there, you will find it at your disposal—free of cost."

It had been the first hot water Finerty sank into since that tiny galvanized tub in a whore's crib at Kid Slaymaker's clear back in May. Going four months between good soakings had become too onerous a habit. After he was done, Donegan stood naked and anxiously ready while the bath attendants dumped Finerty's water.

"Look at that, will you now?" the Irishman exclaimed, pointing at the newsman's bathwater being poured into a wooden sluice that went through a hole in the wall, where it spilled into the creek. "I ain't seen the likes of such filthy, scummy water since we camped beside the Powder River!"

In less than an hour the entire detail had bathed and felt better for it, despite the fact they were forced to climb back into the same mud-crusted clothing the attendants had at least brushed and shaken. Out onto the street, as the sun began to set, they again poked their heads, and at once the town again erupted. Both sides of the long main thoroughfare were lined with saloons and drinking houses, restaurants and hotels, mercantiles and those parlors where the soft flesh of women was daily bartered, all of it closely hemmed in by the timbered hills that looked down on the merry celebrants.

At dusk, after the general's staff had ceremoniously panned for gold along the banks of Whitewood Creek, the town's leaders prevailed upon a reluctant Crook to give a short speech from a balcony of one of the hotels. Lacing his talk with a few jokes, most of them at the expense of Sitting Bull and Crazy Horse and their Sioux, the general was even more popular when he walked down to supper than he had been when first stepping onto that balcony.

Again the town fathers stuffed their visitors to the gills, then escorted them over to the Langrishe Theater, where Mayor Farnum and his aldermen presided over a spate of formal speeches. When the officials presented the general with a petition signed by Black Hills citizens urging construction of a military post in their country, the general politely declined.

He went on to explain. "The Black Hills are not in my department. General Terry commands here. Your petition should be presented to the secretary of war. Not to me. But I will be honored to carry your petition to Fort Laramie with me and deliver it there to General Sheridan."

After receiving the crowd's warm appreciation, the general concluded, "When the rank and file pass through here in the days ahead, show that you appreciate their admirable fortitude in bearing the sufferings of a terrible march almost without a murmur, and show them that they are not fighting for thirteen dollars per month, but for the cause—the proper development of our gold and other resources, and of humanity. Let the private soldier feel that he is remembered by our people as the real defender of his country."

When the crowd clamored and hooted for more from Crook, he instead prevailed upon Captain Burt, who excited the packed house by delivering his impromptu tale of their horrid march. Nonetheless, at every turn he extolled his own personal satisfaction serving under a general "who gets things done." Burt went on to tell the miners and merchants just how much he "enjoyed the satisfaction of standing in a Sioux village and watching it burn." Amid the raucous cheers and thunderous applause in response to those stirring comments, Crook's men were officially handed their "keys" to the city.

One of the crowd hollered out, "You better turn over to us those Sioux prisoners you left back on the White-wood! If you take them on back to the agency, Uncle Sam will feed them until they want to take the war path again!"

Burt replied, "No, we can't turn them over to you. We won't give you those Indians to kill, and we won't kill them ourselves—provided they show us where there are more to kill."

By the time Finerty pressed his way out of the theater and onto the street once more with the rest of the general's entourage, he was sure his arm had all but been pumped out of its socket with so much hand shaking.

Taking Donegan by the arm, the pair of jubilant Patlanders strolled down the south side of Main Street until they happened before a likely looking saloon. Inside Johnny Manning's Gambling Hall they were told to put their money back in their pockets.

"Why, hell, fellas," Finerty bellowed. "We haven't any money anyway!"

It made no matter to the miners, who all were anxious to put up for a round or two, treating those who had helped Crook whip the Sioux at Slim Buttes. For some time they drank and watched the gaming tables, where Finerty was surprised to find that more than half the dealers were women—older, hard-faced women who clearly showed the effects of years at a hard life. They nimbly dealt not just poker, but faro and keno and monte too. Beneath the smoky lamplight, cards and whiskey, colorful chips and coins and gold dust, lay spread across the emerald felt stretched over every table. Scales lined the bar, where for every ounce of dust a man could earn himself twenty dollars' worth of credit at the tables, or right then and there with a miner's choice of whiskey, rye, or gin with bitters.

Then it was out the open doorway and down the boardwalk until they found a second likely saloon, and in they went for another series of toasts at Al Swerington's. On and on the evening went in just that way until they both staggered, shoulder to shoulder, down the street reaching China Town, where they crossed to the north side of Main, ducking into Billy Knuckle's Belle Union, then next door to drink at the Big French Hook. Finally they stood on the muddy boardwalk before a sixth watering hole.

Back Donegan rocked on his heels unsteadily, squinting, peering intently at the sign above their heads. "Number . . . Ten? That what it says?"

"Yep—says so right there in plain English, you idjit Irishman!" Finerty burbled.

Wagging his head, Seamus replied, "Who the hell would name a saloon after a god-bleeming-blamed number?"

"C'mon," Finerty said, grabbing hold of Donegan's arm as the big Irishman suddenly froze. The newsman tugged, saying, "Just one more for a nightcap." Then he looked up at the scout's face, gone as white as a ghost, and Finerty's belly went cold as January ice.

Turning slowly, the reporter saw what had stopped Donegan dead in his tracks there before the Number Ten Saloon. A big freshly painted sign nailed beside the open doors, announcing to one and all:

NUMBER 10 SALOON
Where Wild Bill Hickok
was murdered by
Jack McCall
on
August 2, 1876

"Will you look at that?" John exclaimed with an excited gush. "Wild Bill, the famous *pistolero,* was killed right here! And just a few weeks ago! My, my—wait till I write about this!"

Like a statue there beside Finerty, Donegan crossed

himself with a trembling gun hand. Eyes welling, he murmured, "B-blessed Mary, Mither of God!"

"What the hell's wrong with you, Irishman?" Finerty asked, sensing the first quiver of fright at the way Donegan stood transfixed, as if he'd just seen a ghost. "Don't tell me you'd be superstitious having us a drink in there now. Just think what you can tell your children—that you drank whiskey in the same saloon where the famous Wild Bill Hickok was gunned down."

"Murdered."

"Yeah, that's what I said, Seamus. Wild Bill was gunned down right inside there."

Donegan shook his head, clenching his eyes, some tears creeping out at their corners. "No—there wasn't a man what could've gunned Bill Hickok down. Just like the sign says: he was *murdered*."

Inching in front of the big scout, Finerty stared into Donegan's eyes. "You—you knew him . . . knew Wild Bill Hickok?"

Nodding once, he sniffed. "Back to sixty-seven. We scouted a short time together. Me and Cody both."

"That's right," Finerty said, remembering. "The winter you fellas hijacked that load of Mexican beer and made a tidy profit selling it to Carr's soldiers. Well. I'll be damned, Irishman. I hadn't put it all together until now. I see. Well. Under the circumstances I can understand why you might not be thirsty no more. Maybe we have had us enough and should find a place to sleep off the rest of the night."

Eventually the Irishman nodded, quietly saying, "Yeah. Someplace else to go but here."

"My God! Listen to this, Seamus!"

Donegan really wasn't at all interested in what the Chicago newsman found interesting in that copy of *The Black Hills Pioneer*.

Ever since he had stared at that sign nailed to the front of Mann's Number 10 Saloon last night, the Irishman had thought of nothing else but Bill Hickok, fondly remembering their scouting days together, learning of the gunman's meteoric rise to fame as a Kansas cow-town lawman.

Annoyed at the interruption, he dragged his eyes away from gazing out the restaurant window and looked into the face of the reporter seated across the table from him, who was reading a copy of the local newspaper.

Donegan asked, "Does it say anything about Crook's visit?"

"Yes—they've got a really good piece on our campaign and some nice writing on the general's oratorical efforts last night," Finerty answered that morning of the seventeenth. "But it's this editorial you've got to hear: 'Some pap-sucking Quaker representative of an Indian doxology mill, writes in *Harper* for April about settling the Indian troubles by establishing more Sunday Schools and Missions among them.'"

"Just what the Sioux and Cheyenne need," Donegan grumbled. He took another sip of his steamy coffee, then went back to staring out the window.

"There's more here," Finerty continued. "'It is enough to make a western man sick to read such stuff.'"

Without looking at the correspondent, Seamus said, "I never was much of one to read newspapers, anyway. Though I personally have nothing against newspaper*men*."

"Now, listen, Seamus—this here is the clencher! 'You might as well try to raise a turkey from a snake egg as to raise a good citizen from a papoose. Indians can be made good in only one way, and that is to make angels of them.'"

Finally he looked into Finerty's eyes. "By that account, seems Crook's and Terry's armies haven't made too many Indians good, have we?"

For most of the previous night and into the morning, Lieutenants William P. Clark and Frederick W. Sibley had busied themselves pulling all of Deadwood's blacksmiths out of bed and the saloons to work at reshoeing the patrol's horses and unshod Indian ponies. Finally at eight A.M., after a big breakfast and lots of coffee for those who had unwisely celebrated most of the night, Crook had them climbing back into the saddle for their ride south to Camp Robinson.

On the road to Custer City they passed a growing number of wagons: empty freighters rumbling south to the Union Pacific rail line at Sidney, Nebraska, returning north with those precious goods bound for the Black Hills mining camps. In the early afternoon the general's party met three companies of the Fourth Artillery escorting a wagon train ordered north with supplies for Crook's expedition. For more than an hour the groups stopped there beside Box Elder Creek to exchange news of the world for news from the front.

In their travels the following day they passed by the new community of Castleton on the Black Hills route that led them along Castle Creek and on through the shadow of Harney's Peak. Already the new community was home to more than two hundred hopeful miners and merchants. On the outskirts of town, fields had been plowed and a few small cattle herds grazed in the tall grasses. By noon they had reached a plateau, where they looked down upon Hill City, abandoned save for one hardy hermit.

"Why did everyone go?" Donegan asked the old man.

Came the simple answer, "Indian scare . . . and no gold dust."

The sun was settling into the western clouds, igniting them with radiant fire, when Crook's party reached Custer City, aptly named for that one soldier who brought his Seventh Cavalry to explore the Black Hills back in seventy-four, then promptly informed the world of the prospects for finding gold in that land ceded to the Sioux. Here Crook called a halt for the night, and the party reined up outside a likely looking hotel.

"Donegan? Is that really you?"

Seamus turned slowly at the call of his name, unable to recognize the voice. His hand slid closer to the butt of a pistol. He looked at the clean-shaven soldier bounding off the boardwalk toward him, not able to place the man.

"Seamus Donegan! By the saints—it is you!"

"Egan? Don't tell me!"

The captain stopped and spread his arms widely in a grand gesture, cocking his head to the side slyly. "Teddy Egan, his own self!"

They laughed and hugged and pounded one another on the back as John Finerty came over.

"Still tagging along with this worthless bit of army flotsam, I see, John," Egan said after shaking hands with the newsman.

"Ever since the three of us went marching with Reynolds down on that Powder River village," Finerty responded.

James "Teddy" Egan's famous troop of grays, K Troop, Second Cavalry, the same men who had led the charge on the village nestled beside the frozen Powder River which Frank Grouard swore was Crazy Horse's camp back on St. Patrick's Day,* had ever since that winter campaign been assigned to protect emigrant and freight travel along the Black Hills Road between Fort Laramie and Custer City.

A courier from Laramie reached the general just after supper, bearing a message from Sheridan requesting that Crook hurry on and reach the fort within forty-eight hours. That was all but impossible given the condition of their weary mounts and captured Indian ponies. Yet the general would try to press on with all possible speed. To do so, he would require new mounts, immediately requesting Captain Egan to lend fifteen of his sturdy, sleek horses then and there in Custer City on the following morning of the nineteenth. Leaving behind his escort under Lieutenant Sibley to accompany the pack-train under Major Randall, the rest of the officers climbed atop those strong grays of Teddy Egan's and set out at sunrise on a forced march.

---

*The Plainsmen Series, Vol. 8, *Blood Song*.

They had over a hundred miles to go just to reach Camp Robinson.

Glory! But it was good to have a good horse under him once again, Donegan thought. For so many weeks his horse had slowly played out before he finally turned it over to Dr. Clements back at the Sioux village and taken for his own one of the Sioux ponies. But now this was so much better. A fine army mount, surging along with the others on that trail behind Crook, who kept them at a gallop for most of the day. The general shot a deer for their dinner that noon; then they pushed on, reaching some marshy land at the southern end of the Hills by dusk.

Not more than a quarter of a mile ahead lay the waters of the South Cheyenne River. As the sun set far to the west, they struck the wagon road blazed from Buffalo Gap in the Black Hills down to the Red Cloud Agency. Pushing the horses back into a lope, Crook soon had them at a gallop once more.

By ten P.M. they reached a branch of Warbonnet Creek, where they watered the stock and talked of Bill Cody's first scalp for Custer. Crook then asked if the others would agree to press on, and the entire party went back into the saddle for another four hours, when they finally stopped to picket their horses and lie down in their blankets on the frosty ground to enjoy a few hours of sleep.

Seamus told himself he must be getting old. He simply couldn't remember a piece of cold ground ever feeling that good.

Chapter 51

20–24 September
1876

The general had them up at four A.M., resaddled, and back on the road within a half hour, without breakfast or coffee.

Pointing to a ridge still at least twenty miles away to the south, Crook later halted the group as the sun was emerging in the east. "Would anyone care to hazard a guess what that is?" the general inquired.

"Those box-shaped buildings on the top of that high ground?" Finerty asked.

"Yes."

"Could it be Camp Robinson?" asked Robert Strahorn.

"Exactly," Crook replied. "Let's push on, gentlemen!"

That last stretch of country before reaching Red Cloud's reservation took the horsemen through some barren badlands. For the first time in weeks dust rose from the hammering hooves beneath them, covering them all with a fine layer of yellowed talc by the time that dirty detail rode in among the agency buildings. Near the sawmill a fatigue detail was hard at work and turned to watch the band of riders pass by.

One of the soldiers called out to the dust-caked horsemen, "Where the devil have you fellas been?"

"In Hades, of course!" sang out Thaddeus Stanton.

Suddenly a second infantryman slapped the first on the shoulder, exclaiming, "Jesus! They're soldiers!"

"N-not just soldiers—officers!"

With a flurry of salutes to the mud-covered band of officers, the soldiers sheepishly turned back to their work in a great hurry.

It didn't take long for more of an audience to gather on the road easing through the agency buildings. At least a thousand Sioux crowded to take a look at Three Stars himself—the soldier chief who had fought Crazy Horse several suns before the Hunkpatila war chief had defeated the Long Hair beside the Greasy Grass. These men with Three Stars must be some of the same soldiers who had attacked the village of American Horse.

As they moved slowly through the throng of dark-eyed visages, Finerty leaned in his saddle toward Donegan and said, "I wonder if any of these are the warriors we fought at Slim Buttes right before they hurried off to get here ahead of us."

Seamus nodded. "I have no doubt, Johnny. You can feel it in the way they look at us. Makes my marrow go cold."

By pushing Egan's horses so hard, Crook had used them up and was forced to remain at Camp Robinson for the rest of the day and into the next until Randall and Sibley showed up late on the afternoon of the twenty-first. That Thursday evening after supper, Major Jordan and his officers gave Crook's officers a crowded but grand reception held around the stoves in the sutler's store. For many it was a delightful reunion of old warriors, and though they had only coffee and a dram of brandy to share, there was much to toast and celebrate.

Together again the entire party prepared to set out

behind an anxious Crook early on the morning of the twenty-second. They were leaving behind one of the correspondents, Robert Strahorn of the Rocky Mountain *News*, who would be going south to Sidney, Nebraska, alone, where he could board a train east.

"How long's it been, Bob?" Seamus asked as he dropped the stirrup down, finished tightening the cinch.

"Since last February when I came north to Cheyenne, Laramie, and on to Fetterman, hoping to investigate the rumors we'd heard that the army was taking the field for a winter campaign," he replied as the rest of Crook's party milled about, completing the last of their preparations before putting Camp Robinson behind them.

"I don't think I'll ever forget that day beside the Powder River," Seamus said.

"I won't ever forget charging in with Teddy Egan's boys and John Bourke at my side!" Strahorn replied.

"You sure you won't come on to Laramie with us?"

"No, I'm sure," the reporter said. "I've been wanting to see the Centennial Exposition back in Philadelphia, maybe write a story or two about it for the paper. They've got a presidential campaign going on right now too. Good chance for a reporter, you know. Been thinking about both of those things more and more ever since last winter. All through the blasted summer too."

"Just make sure you don't ask for any horse-meat steaks while you're back there!" Donegan cheered, holding out his hand.

Strahorn took the Irishman's in his, and they squeezed more than shook. Then, more quietly than he had been speaking before, the newsman said, "You'll take care of yourself, won't you? I mean, now that I'm not going to be around, Seamus?"

"You watch yourself back *there*, Bob," Seamus said, sensing the sting at his eyes. "I'm afraid you won't quite know how to act with all those civilized folk."

Strahorn smiled and clapped a hand on the tall man's shoulder. "Likely I have picked up some damned crude manners, indeed—what with spending the last half a year with you, Irishman!"

Pushing their jaded horses and captured ponies as fast as they dared, the general and his men rode long into the evening before halting to graze the horses and grab a little sleep.

They were back in the saddle before sunrise on 23 September, reaching the camp of Ranald S. Mackenzie's escort from the Fourth Cavalry that Saturday night. Having left most of his troops behind at Camp Robinson until Wesley Merritt could bring down the Fifth Cavalry to take over the task of disarming the Sioux at Red Cloud, the colonel was already on his way to Fort Laramie, called there to meet with Sheridan and Crook.

Together, the three of them would plan the prosecution of the Sioux War into that fall, even unto the winter if necessary, hoping to bring a resolution to the thorny "Indian problem."

Some time after supper that evening, Donegan made his way to the leadership fire. In that ring of cheery light he recognized a few familiar faces, then carefully measured the back of a tall officer who was talking and laughing with Captain Randall.

Seamus stepped up and said, "General Mackenzie?"

The handsome soldier turned. "Yes?"

Holding out his hand, Donegan pressed on. "You probably don't remember me, but—"

"Irishman!" Mackenzie bellowed, grabbing Donegan's hand and pumping it vigorously with his own right hand that was missing some fingers. "By glory—I sure as hell do remember you!"

Proud and startled at the same time, Seamus said, "I wasn't sure you would, General."

The colonel put his hand to his cheek. "You don't look quite the same as you did."

Touching his own cheek, Seamus said, "Oh, this? With winter coming it won't be long and I'll have that full beard back what I wore that campaign down on the Staked Plain."

"You might look a bit older—but we all do! I can't believe you'd think for one minute I wouldn't remember *you* and that time we pitched down the sheer cliff into the Palo Duro to catch the Kwahadi napping."*

Crook got to his feet and came to stand at the taller Mackenzie's shoulder. "You mean this reprobate really was with you when you flushed Quanah Parker's Comanche into that miserable winter?"

"When we butchered more than fourteen hundred of their ponies," the colonel replied.

"Settlers down that way in the Panhandle talked about that for a long time after," Donegan said as the four correspondents crowded up to listen in.

Mackenzie asked, "So what are you doing here? When did you show up?"

"This evening, with General Crook, sir."

Mackenzie glanced at his superior. "Do you have Donegan serving you as a scout?"

With a nod the general answered, "From time to time he's made himself quite valuable. Quite valuable—all the way back to the mess Reynolds made of things on the Powder River last March. Yes, this Irishman's served me admirably."

"I should say, General," Mackenzie replied, gazing at the Irishman. "You sure have covered some ground, Donegan."

"I have at that, and haven't seen my wife since May."

"A wife, is it?" Mackenzie roared. "Well, now—when did you decide to settle down?"

"Not long after you convinced Parker to come in, General," Seamus answered. "In many ways, though, it seems like it's been ages. Feels even longer since I've seen her."

*The Plainsmen Series, Vol. 7, *Dying Thunder*.

Mackenzie said, "And where is she while you're out scouting for General Crook here?"

"Waiting for me at Laramie."

"By glory! You're no more than a good day's ride from her now, Irishman. I envy you, I do. Getting to see her by tomorrow."

Donegan nodded eagerly. "I can't wait to see how she's . . . well, how big she's grown. She's carrying . . . er, *we're* expecting our first child, General."

"What, ho! Not only do I learn that you've married and settled down—but you're going to be a family man now!" Mackenzie turned to one of his staff officers. "Lieutenant Otis! Bring me that flask of mine. This truly is a cause for celebration and at least one stout toast all around to this father-to-be!"

Then Ranald Mackenzie turned back to slap a hand on Donegan's shoulder in that frosty air beside a merry fire. "Who would have thought—Irishman! That I'd go and find one of the finest white scouts ever there was who led my Fourth into battle."

H. G. Otis came back and handed the colonel his flask of German silver. Taking loose the cap, Mackenzie promptly began to pour a dribble into every one of those cups that suddenly made their clattering appearance out of nowhere.

"Hear, hear, gentlemen!" Mackenzie roared. "To Seamus Donegan! Let's drink to the Irishman! By Neptune's beard, let's all drink to one of the finest scouts it's been my pleasure to follow into battle!"

Samantha saw Martha Luhn dashing across the parade with a bundle of newspapers under her arm, waving one of them as she shouted, disturbing the peaceful quiet of that Sunday morning right as most of the officers' wives were gathering on the front porch of Old Bedlam. It was warm and sunny there, a pretty place to wait until the time came when they all walked over for church together.

In an instant women pressed against the whitewashed

porch banister, crowded on the steps, every one of them listening as Lieutenant Gerhard Luhn's wife hurried their way chattering nonstop, her skirts and petticoats billowing about her ankles like a rush of foam.

"It's true! It's true!" she shouted as she burst past the flagpole.

Now Samantha could make out Mrs. Luhn's words.

"They did capture a village!"

"I told you," Elizabeth Burt declared self-assuredly, moving down to the first step. "When that rumor first got here to us—I told you there was truth to it!"

As Margaret Luhn reached the bottom of the porch steps, a crowd swallowed her, flying hands and arms reaching for the stack of newspapers she held out for the others. This latest edition of the Rocky Mountain *News* had reached Fort Laramie just last night, and Mrs. Luhn had always been the first to stand in line at sutler Collins's trading post, where she commandeered what copies she could for the other wives.

Hugging Elizabeth Burt's elbow, Sam stared at the banner headlines. The bold letters printed in black ink across the newsprint all but leaped off the front page.

New York *Times,* dated 16 September
headlines read:

ATTACK UPON A CAMP OF SIOUX

COMPLETE VICTORY FOR THE TROOPS

How quickly her eyes flew from that brave announcement to the smaller type running completely down the three columns against the far left-hand side of the page.

Crook Stumbles Upon and Surprises
an Indian Village.
CHEYENNE, September 16—A courier who
left General Crook's command September 9,
brings the following news: Since General Crook's

column turned south toward the Black Hills on
the 5th inst. there has been considerable hardship
through wet weather and living on bacon and
hard bread, and a good deal of grumbling. On
the 7th it was decided to send a portion of the
pack train ahead under escort of Colonel Mills,
with fifteen men on the best horses of each company of the Third cavalry, making 150 in all.
Lieutenants Von Lutwitz, Schulle and Crawford
composed the subordinate officers, with Lieutenant Babb, Fourth infantry, chief commissary;
Tom Moore, chief packer; and F. Gruard, Crook's
chief scout. The latter was to serve both as guide
and scout, and on yesterday evening he discovered through the rain and fog, without being
himself observed, a hostile Sioux village, consisting of forty-one large lodges and a band of several hundred ponies and a few American horses.

Mills concluded to attempt an attack with
his 150 men without waiting to send word to
Crook for reinforcements. He fell back a few
miles, hid his command in a ravine, and at two
o'clock this morning marched for the village,
which was situated on a little creek, a tributary of
Grand or Owl creek. He formed on the north
side before daylight and ordered Lieutenant
Schwatta, of Company M, to charge through the
village while the rest of the force, dismounted,
were to form skirmish lines on either side and
pick off the Indians as they came out.

The latter were completely surprised, and
scattered out pell-mell, half-naked, returning the
fire to some extent. Their ponies were effectually
stampeded, but, owing to Mills' small force he
only succeeded in securing the lodges and property therein and about 140 ponies. There was an
immense quantity of dried meat, berries, etc., all
that Crook's whole pack train could carry, and

sufficient to postpone the proposed purchase of supplies. There were wagon loads of robes and savage spoils of all kinds, including some of the equipments and arms of the Seventh cavalry which Custer used in the Big Horn massacre, and various articles of wearing apparel worn on that occasion was also captured . . . Von Lutwig was seriously wounded in the knee, and privates Milbury and Charles Foster, of Company B, Augustus Dorm, of Company D, and Sergeant Glass, company E, were wounded, and private Wensall, of company A was killed in the action.

As soon as she could grab a copy for herself, Sam lumbered up the narrow steps to her tiny room and fell upon the bed, where she continued to read the story, regarding each word just as carefully, every bit as slowly as she had been poring over each one of the newspaper stories the women at Fort Laramie always received days, sometimes as much as a week, after the Rocky Mountain *News* was printed in Denver.

In the morning about 7 o'clock, word reached Crook fifteen miles back, with the main column, and he came forward with two sections of cavalry, reaching Mills at 11 o'clock. The latter had kept up a good picket fight during the forenoon, but Crook was very much disappointed because Mills didn't report his discovery last night, as there was plenty of time to have got the entire command there and so effectually surrounded the village that nothing would have escaped; but the General is also pleased, all things considered.

About 100 yards from the village is a little ravine, in which a band of seven warriors and fifteen women and children were safely lodged in cavernous rocks, and it was in trying to dislodge them that Mills lost his killed and most of his wounded. General Crook desired to save the women and children and, by means of Gruard's interpreting, a parley ensued, and three warriors came out, one chief named American Horse being mortally wounded. Before this parley was effected, however, Frank White, a citizen, was shot through the heart, and privates Kennedy and McKenan of company F, 6th Cavalry, wounded. About twenty minutes past four o'clock this afternoon sudden picket firing sprung up, beginning on Colonel Mason's front, resulting in the wounding of Sergeant Schruber, company K, and private Dorm, company F, Fifth cavalry. It proved to be the result of reinforcements received from Crazy Horse's band and a running attack began all around the circle, but troops were quickly thrown out and the enemy driven off in every direction. The latter got about a dozen horses too poor to get in to camp back a mile on the line of march.

The village was thoroughly ransacked and the spoils divided around. Colonel Mills and his men got the ponies . . . Much ammunition and many guns were found in the lodges, and all evidence is to the effect that the Indians were prepared for the winter . . . It is regretted that other of the villages near by were not surprised and destroyed, but this affair demonstrated the good policy of a stern chase after Indians, even with foot soldiers, who come in here to the relief of the cavalry, as their part in the play gives them renewed vigor and esprit.

No, his name wasn't there. Not printed among the others as she reread the list of the dead. Not even among the wounded. Reassured, her heart hammering as it hadn't in so long, Sam continued down the page.

LATER—September 10th—There was a little picket firing throughout last night, and this morning after the command was on march a number of Indians came down on the rear of the column, but were met with a warm reception by Captain Sumner's battalion of Fifth cavalry, who covered the enemy in the ravines, killed several and disabled others. Privates Foster, company F, privates Wadden, Company M, and Geo. Clantier, company D, were wounded. The command marched fifteen miles to-day toward the Hills, bringing all the sick and wounded on twelve litters. Medical director Clements amputated the right leg of lieutenant Van Letwitz last evening and private Kennedy died of his wounds. No other amputations or deaths are likely to occur. American Horse died last night. Most of the captives are brought along, a few squaws being left back by the General to advise the hostile bands to go into the agency and behave themselves and all will be well with them. Colonel Mills, Lieutenant Cubbard and Frank Gruard go through to the hills to-morrow with a view to secure future supplies.

Lying on her back, holding the paper right above her face, Sam licked her lips thoughtfully, her eyes searching for some word of him. Maybe she had been wrong all along thinking he had gone with the column. Maybe he had stayed behind with the wagons up north at that camp General Crook established before he fought the Sioux on Rosebud Creek. No, Sam decided. Seamus would have come back here with one of the supply trains if he wasn't going to stay on to fight with the rest of Crook's troops.

So again she read the casualties. Despite the fact that she could not find his name anywhere, Sam could not rid herself of that lump in her throat, that cold hole in her chest. She tried to convince herself that there was no way to

know for sure—maybe the correspondent who wrote that
story simply could not list every one of the civilians who
were wounded. Scouts were civilians, after all.

And maybe that's why Seamus's name wasn't printed.
He could have been wounded! He could be on one of those
twelve litters. Bleeding and in pain. But being a civilian—

"Samantha!"

At that first shriek of her name she rolled onto her
side and struggled to sit up. She heard steps, loud footsteps
clattering on the stairs.

"Samantha!" It was Elizabeth Burt's voice. "Look out
your window!"

Suddenly the woman stood framed in the narrow,
open doorway, having flung open the door, the knob still
clenched in her hand. She pointed to the solitary window.
"Samantha Donegan—do as I say! Go look out that window!"

Dread gripped Sam as surely as had the morning sickness that plagued her the first three months of this pregnancy. She fought for air as Mrs. Burt helped drag her from
the side of the narrow bed, across the carpet Samantha had
sewn from discarded burlap bags, right to the window.

"There! Look! Can't you see, dear?"

Elizabeth was tapping on the windowpane with her
knuckle, then pointing with the same finger at the horsemen entering the far corner of the parade. From the northeast. They were ragged. Their horses dusty. Everything
about them frightened her. But she was immediately relieved to find that none of those weary, played-out horses
dragged a litter behind it.

"It's Crook!" Mrs. Burt declared. "He's got his staff
with him!"

She turned to Elizabeth, filled once more with hope as
she asked, "He'll have word from the rest, won't he?"

"Word about Seamus? Is that what you mean,
dear?"

Her head bobbed eagerly, sensing the cold knot in her

chest. She simply had to know. One way or the other, she had to be told.

"Look, Samantha," Elizabeth said reassuringly, patting Sam's shoulder. "You don't have to ask General Crook about your husband. If you look real closely—you'll see one of those riders is Seamus Donegan himself!"

Epilogue

Early October
1876

How he reveled in the feel of her arm curled in his. So simple a joy this was, her walking at his side as they strolled each evening since his return—twelve of them now —both of them bundled against the chill, bracing air that brought a rose to Samantha's cheeks as dusk fell and twilight slipped down upon Fort Laramie.

That first night back, well—it was the sort of night that lived on and on in a man's soul, chiseled deep within the marrow of him. How he had held her and loved her and kissed her and cried with her too; how they laughed now, as they remembered that ache of not seeing one another in four long months.

Right about the time Samantha had reached the landing at the top of the last flight of those narrow stairs, right where she could look down and see Old Bedlam's front door flung open in one grand sweep, in he burst. And there Seamus had stopped, gazing up at her as she gripped the banister for all the support it could give her. His eyes marveling at the sheer size of her.

So, so different from the woman he had left behind in

May. Yet in every way but one—Seamus knew she was still the same.

"Come down," he had said to her softly as more than a dozen of the officers' wives filled in the doorway and the landing behind him, most all of them beckoning her. "Feels like an eternity that I've been waiting to hold you."

Glancing at the happy faces of those who stared up at her, Sam could not find a single dry eye among them. Some blubbered unabashedly. But most dabbed their tears away with the corner of an apron or a handkerchief pulled from a cuff or simply whatever it was they could find.

He wagged his head as she began to descend once more, step by step. "You're simply the most beautiful creature on God's earth."

Her eyes had been wet, her cheeks tracked as she reached the bottom step, where he started to enfold her in his arms, then bent to kiss her lips. She had drawn back, her eyes blinking.

"I won't break, Seamus!" she scolded, taking his big arms still inside that dirty, muddy mackinaw coat of his and looping them around her. "I'm only pregnant. Not made of glass!"

It was then that he did embrace her, sensing the bulk of her against him, the firmness of her swelling breasts. Feeling that arousal he had for so long fought down out there in that wilderness separating him from his mate. Never before had he held a woman who carried a child. Yet here she was, grown in size, brought to full bloom in the time they had been apart.

Late that first night as she had snored on his shoulder, Seamus ran his fingers softly over the changes in her, the heaviness to the breasts to be sure, but more so the taut roundness to her stomach. The way her belly button was stretched so much it even protruded. For now this was the greatest marvel to a simple man—becoming a father for the first time!

The days to follow had simply flowed one into the next with her. Just to enjoy the smell of her, the feel and shape and texture of her, the very nearness of her. To take the cascade of her curls in his hand and smell them, brush them along his cheek, across the lids of his eyes. To experience her in every way he had been deprived of her.

No, he wasn't going back out there, Seamus vowed. Not now that he had learned just how much she meant to his soul.

So every evening they spent this time together. The air so cold of each twilight come to these high plains that he was certain the next day was sure to bring snow. But instead the leaves began slowly to turn, and frost gathered once more on the inside of that single tiny windowpane beside the bed where they held one another throughout the long nights.

Minutes ago they had left Major Townsend's quarters, where Colonel Ranald Mackenzie had invited Seamus and Sam to have supper with him and General Crook. A real sit-down meal, the finest a frontier fort could offer. So now after that sumptuous dinner and paying their respects, they strolled on into the coming of twilight as the wind died.

He looked down at her while they walked along, crossing the center of the parade, heading for the big cottonwoods that lined the banks of the river. Sam's cheeks glowed rosier than ever before, at least what he could remember. It must not all be the cold wind, he thought. Some of it had to do with her condition.

His wife's hunger had surprised him that first night. And every one of the twelve nights since. Just as he had been a bit afraid to hug her so fiercely in those first moments at the bottom of the stairs, so he was frightened of what might happen if he penetrated her warm moistness— what he had dreamed of night after night for those long months of their separation.

"The other women have told me there is no danger, Seamus," Sam had whispered in the darkness of their room that night as she had stroked her fingers up and down the hot, hardened length of him.

"You're sure?" Oh, how he wanted her to be sure!

She giggled, like the flutter of a small bird, and said, "They've all had children, Seamus Donegan. I think they ought to know firsthand, don't you?"

"Just as long as I don't . . . you don't . . . you're so big."

Nudging him over onto his back, Samantha quickly straddled him, almost as nimble as ever despite the size of her. He gasped when she took his flesh into her hand and aimed it true, slowly settling her weight upon his hips.

"I'll make you a promise, Seamus Donegan," she said huskily, her eyes half closing as she began to rock upon him in a slow dance. "If it makes you feel any better, I promise I'll let you know if you hurt me."

"M-me? F-feel any better?" he stammered. "What could possibly feel any better than this?"

Every night since, they had worked their immense passion around the full bulk of her belly. Right now he remembered again how it felt to kneel behind her, to reach around her widened hips, to stroke his hands across the heaviness of her—as if he were caressing the very womb where she carried their child.

Seamus looked down at her in the silver light of that half-moon just then climbing over the tops of the cotton-woods, stripped daily of their autumn-kissed leaves by strong, gusty, tormenting winds.

How he wanted her again, to feel the great warmth of her, to savor the love he felt when he was in her arms. Just walking beside her as he was now, he knew it wasn't enough. He had to have more. Never would he get enough of her.

"Oh!" she squealed in a high pitch.

As soon as she stopped, he stopped. Clutching her arm, he asked fearfully, "What is it? What's wrong?"

For a moment she rubbed her wool mitten across the round expanse of her greatcoat. Her eyes widened in surprise, lips pursed in a little fear. "Oh, oh, oh!"

Her each new utterance of the word alarmed him. As did the way she gripped at his arms, clamped on to them, her fingers like claws. Then it was past. Whatever it was, he could see it disappear, leave her face—tangibly. The way something visible might release her, replaced by the relief that showed there on that rosy face.

Her eyes smiled first.

"Good," he sighed. "I was afraid something we had for dinner had given your stomach a twist."

Now her whole face smiled, and she licked her lips in the dry autumn-night air. Looking up at him from the corners of her eyes as she had that very first night they had met back in the Panhandle of west Texas, Samantha straightened.

"I'm all right," she said. "Let's finish our walk."

Minutes later she snuggled even closer to his side as they moved along, both her arms encircling one of his. Sam asked, "Are you going to take Colonel Mackenzie up on his offer and go with him, Seamus?"

"I'm not even going to consider it. Not with the baby due next month. It has been eight months, hasn't it?"

"Near as I could count, Seamus," she said with that giggle. "I never was much good at arithmetic."

"It doesn't matter. I want to be here when the babe comes. I'll stay here and Mackenzie can march without me."

"But—he asked you himself to go along. There at dinner tonight. Seamus, how can you turn him down, with all that you were through together in Texas? After all, he's the colonel of the Fourth Cavalry, for God's sake! Asking you to scout for him."

"I scouted for him one winter already," Donegan replied with a single wag of his head. "That was enough. So I've got a far better plan for this coming winter: to stay close to the home fires when the winter winds come howling off those mountains north of here."

It took her several moments; then she finally said the words as if she had been rehearsing them: "Seamus, long ago I realized what you were—the sort of man you are. I think I knew what you were before you ever asked me to be your wife. I knew what you had to be before I loved you, what you were when you rode off to fight for Ranald Mackenzie two winters ago."

"But don't you see—it took that winter campaign for me to find out just how much I loved you, Sam."

"And you came back to me, didn't you, Seamus?"

He looked at her a moment while she stopped and turned into him. "Yes," he replied a bit quizzically. "I came back to you."

"And you came back to me twelve days ago. Which just goes to prove that you will always return, because you love me."

He bent slightly and kissed her. "Never any doubt of that in my mind."

"And now I've come to realize it too, Seamus. No matter that you went away last winter. No matter that you've been gone since spring."

"All that is in the past because I'm going to stay with you now. This babe will know it has a father. I want to be there when your time comes. No, Sam. Mackenzie can go find the hostiles without me. It will be a cold day in hell before I go marching off to fight again."

A sudden look of something like pinched confusion crossed her face; then Sam squinted her eyes and murmured under her breath an oath against the pain while she slowly bent at the waist, doubling over. He held on to her the best he could, afraid she was going to crumple then and there in the dried and brittle grasses at the outskirts of Fort Laramie, there at the edge of the timeless, leafless trees.

All he could do was grow more frightened as he steadied her. Breathing in shallow puffs, Sam panted rapidly, like a dog come in from chasing hares across a meadow. This business of women and babes was something he did not understand. Something he doubted men would ever understand.

"Oh-oh-oh-oh!" she grumbled, weaving her body side to side slowly as she groaned, rubbing at her belly.

In moments her breath grew deeper. No longer as fast as it had been. And slowly she straightened.

"I wish I could take the pain from you myself," he told her.

She glanced up at him as she began to rise, her eyes glistening. "Pain is just part of all the joy this child will bring us."

"There was times I hurt just like that," Seamus explained, not knowing what else he could say to make her realize he was trying to understand, "—after eating horse meat day after day. We had us nothing else. Believe me: I know just how bad a bellyache can hurt."

When she finally straightened and drew back her shoulders, Sam put her two mittens along Seamus's cheeks and sighed, "Silly man—how I love you so. But I don't think it's anything I ate."

"You had me scared there for a minute. Are you feeling good enough to finish our walk?"

She pulled his face down with her mittens to kiss his lips. Smiling, Samantha gazed into his eyes, saying, "I'm afraid I'm going to ask you to take me back to our room early tonight."

"Tired, Sam?" Then he shook his head, feeling like a fool. "Of course you are. A woman this close to having a baby is bound to get tired easy enough."

"No," she explained softly, letting his cheeks go and taking a secure hold on his left arm. "At least your son waited until his father returned before he made his debut."

"W-what?"

"You silly, silly goose," she said, patting his arm. "You better get me back to our room now, so you can go fetch Martha Luhn or Elizabeth Burt."

She started out again, but he was rooted to the spot. This was confusing him—scaring him really—making him stammer like a schoolboy presenting a handmade valentine to a freckle-faced girl with braids and ribbons and rosy cheeks. "F-fetch them . . . why?"

"Yes, Seamus—I'm going to need someone there who knows about this sort of thing."

"S-sort of thing?"

"Don't you see, Seamus?" she replied as she tugged that tall plainsman back toward the buildings, the parade, and their room beyond. "I think your son is coming to-night."

Afterword

What began with such bright hope and almost cocky optimism in the winter campaign quickly deteriorated into a disappointing spring after the Powder River debacle, then nearly fell completely apart in the first days of what would turn out to be a disastrous summer.

Back in the fall of seventy-five Sherman and Sheridan had hatched a brilliant plan to take President Grant off the horns of his thorny dilemma: in order to wrest the Black Hills from the Sioux and Cheyenne, the government had to find a way that would compel the tribes to break the law. Then Washington City could send in the army to settle the matter quickly, efficiently. All those who would not obediently return to their agencies would be deemed hostile and subject to annihilation.

That plan was succeeding beautifully in all respects, except one. Instead of convincing the winter roamers—those true, free-roaming warrior bands—to give up their old way of life and return to the reservations, the warrior bands had gone and whipped the army. Yet despite losing so many of its battles, the army was eventually to win the war.

For the better part of seven years following the Fort Laramie Treaty of 1868, Congress had steadfastly refused to entertain any idea of taking back the territory it had granted the tribes in that historic agreement—despite the growing clamor from various and powerful economic and political constituencies back east who were coming to agree that the Black Hills, rich in gold that could be found at the grass roots, should be settled and mined. In a turn of the biblical phrase: it was the duty of white Christians to subdue that portion of the earth and make it fruitful.

It simply would not do to leave so fruitful a region in the hands of savages who were doing nothing to reap the harvest from that land.

But now that Reynolds had been driven off the Powder, now that Crook had been forced back to Goose Creek to lick his wounds, now that half of Custer's Seventh Cavalry had been rubbed out, forcing General Alfred Terry back to tend to his own psychic wounds on the Yellowstone —now that the army had suffered so many setbacks, Congress was suddenly of a new mind. Washington's conscience was a'changing.

Yet it wasn't just the nation's representatives who clamored for results. Reeling from the startling banner headlines that second week of July in their very own Centennial summer, the body politic, the public itself, raised a strident demand for action. Raised their own call to arms!

As John S. Gray puts it:

> The Secretary [of War J. D. Cameron] solemnly proclaimed that the terms of the Sioux treaty had been "literally performed on the part of the United States." (By sending thousands to invade the reservation?) Even most of the Sioux had likewise honored the treaty, but some "have always treated it with contempt," by continuing "to rove at pleasure." (A practice legalized by the treaty!) They had even gone so far as to "attack settlements, steal horses, and murder peaceful inhabitants." (These victims were white violators of the treaty who dealt the Indians worse than they received!)

Cameron's report went on to read like nothing more than perfect bureaucratic doublespeak:

> No part of these operations is on or near the Sioux reservation. The accidental discovery of gold on the western border of the Sioux reservation, and the intrusion of our people thereon, have not caused this war . . .

Citizens back east knew their government had been feeding, clothing, educating the Sioux and Cheyenne at their agencies. And now those ungrateful Indians had bitten the hand that fed them! Shocked and dismayed, the public cried out that simple justice required stern punishment.

So Sherman and Sheridan wouldn't find it at all hard to get what they wanted by midsummer, within days of the disastrous news from the Little Bighorn reaching the East. Suddenly after three years of balking at General Sheridan's request for money to build two forts in the heart of Sioux country, Congress promptly appropriated the funds to begin construction at a pair of sites on the Yellowstone: one at the mouth of the Big Horn and the other at the mouth of the Tongue.

A few weeks later—after a delay caused only by some heated, vitriolic debate over the relative merits of Volunteers versus Regulars—Congress additionally raised the ceiling on army strength, a move that allowed recruiting another twenty-five hundred privates for a sorely tried U.S. cavalry. By railcar and riverboat steamer, these new privates were uniformed and outfitted and were being rushed to the land of the Sioux by late summer.

On the last day of July, Congress authorized the President to take all necessary steps to prevent metallic cartridges from reaching Sioux country. Two weeks later Grant signed into law a bill that raised the strength of Enlisted Indian Scouts to one thousand. And only three days later he put his name on a bill raising the manpower strength of all cavalry companies to one hundred men for each company.

Sherman and Sheridan now had their "total war," just the same sort of scorched-earth warfare they had waged so successfully through Georgia and the Shenandoah. In their minds there were no noncombatants. Any woman or child, any Indian sick or old, was deemed the enemy by virtue of not huddling close to the agencies. As far as General Sheridan was concerned, it wasn't just a matter of using his troops to drive the roamers back to their reservations. This was a war of vengeance against an enemy who had embarrassed, even humiliated, his army.

The last, but by no means the least, of the pieces to their plan, was that Sheridan was finally to get what he had wanted ever since he had come west at the end of the Civil War.

With war fever infecting Washington by the end of that July, Secretary of the Interior Chandler turned over to the army "control over all the agencies in the Sioux country." Both the agents at Red Cloud and Spotted Tail were to be removed without cause and their duties assumed by the commanders of the nearby Camp Robinson (at Red Cloud) and Camp Sheridan (at Spotted Tail). The army would soon begin to demand the "unconditional surrender" of every Indian who returned to the reservations in the wake of the army's big push. No matter that they might be coming in from a hunt, all Indians on the agencies had to surrender their weapons and ponies. They were considered prisoners of war.

So what of those who had remained on the reservations?

It made no difference to the army now in control of the agencies. Not a single penny of their appropriations, not one mouthful of flour or rancid ounce of bacon would be given out until the Sioux had first relinquished all claim to their unceded lands.

"Give back the Black Hills or starve!"

Only 40 of the 2,267 adult males required by the Fort

Laramie Treaty of 1868 to sell their Paha Sapa eventually signed the agreement the government commissioners foisted upon them.

But by then the Battle of Slim Buttes had already taken place. And Slim Buttes was clearly the beginning of the end.

The Sioux and Cheyenne had already ridden the meteor's tail to the zenith of their success at Rosebud Creek and the Greasy Grass. Yet within eleven weeks of their stunning victories, their demise and ultimate defeat were already sealed at what was an otherwise inconsequential fight at Slim Buttes. In a matter of months Crazy Horse would surrender in the south, and Sitting Bull would limp across the Medicine Line into the Land of the Grandmother with the last of his holdouts.

Both of them giving up the good fight.

To learn more about what took place during that dramatic summer among both the warrior villages and the army camps in the territory surrounding the Little Bighorn River country, I offer the following suggested titles I have used to write my story of this Summer of the Sioux:

Across the Continent with the Fifth Cavalry, by George F. Price

Battles and Skirmishes of the Great Sioux War, 1876–1877, the Military View, edited by Jerome A. Greene

Blood on the Moon: Valentine McGillycuddy and the Sioux, by Julia B. McGillycuddy

Campaigning with Crook, by Captain Charles King, U.S.A.

Campaigning with King: Charles King, Chronicler of the Old Army, edited by Paul L. Hedren

Centennial Campaign: The Sioux War of 1876, by John S. Gray

The Chronicles of the Yellowstone, by E. S. Topping

Crazy Horse and Custer: The Parallel Lives of Two American Warriors, by Stephen E. Ambrose

Crazy Horse: The Strange Man of the Oglalas, by Mari Sandoz

Death on the Prairie: The Thirty Years' Struggle for the Western Plains, by Paul I. Wellman

First Scalp for Custer: The Skirmish at Warbonnet Creek, by Paul L. Hedren

Following the Indian Wars: The Story of Newspaper Correspondents among the Indian Campaigners, by Oliver Knight

Forty Miles a Day on Beans and Hay: The Enlisted Soldier Fighting the Indian Wars, by Don Rickey, Jr.

Frank Grouard, Army Scout, edited by Margaret Brock Hanson

Frontier Regulars: The United States Army and the Indian, 1866–1891, by Robert M. Utley

General George Crook: His Autobiography, edited by Martin F. Schmitt

The Great Sioux War, 1876–77, edited by Paul L. Hedren

"I Am Looking to the North for My Life": Sitting Bull, 1876–1881, by Joseph Manzione

Indian Fights and Fighters, by Cyrus Townsend Brady

Indian Fights: New Facts on Seven Encounters, by J. W. Vaughn

Indians, Infants and Infantry: Andrew and Elizabeth Burt on the Frontier, by Merrill J. Mattes

The Lance and the Shield: The Life and Times of Sitting Bull, by Robert M. Utley

Life and Adventures of Frank Grouard, by Joe DeBarthe

The Lives and Legends of Buffalo Bill, by Don Russell

My Sixty Years on the Plains, by W. T. Hamilton

My Story, by Anson Mills

Nelson A. Miles: A Documentary Biography of His Military Career, 1861–1903, edited by Brian C. Pohanka

On the Border with Crook, by John G. Bourke

Paper Medicine Man: John Gregory Bourke and His American West, by Joseph C. Porter

Personal Recollections and Observations, by General Nelson A. Miles

The Plainsmen of the Yellowstone, by Mark H. Brown

Rekindling Campfires, edited by Lewis F. Crawford

The Shoshonis: Sentinels of the Rockies, by Virginia Cole Trenholm and Maurine Carley

Sitting Bull: Champion of the Sioux, by Stanley Vestal

The Slim Buttes Battle: September 9 and 10, 1876, by Fred H. Werner

Slim Buttes, 1876: An Episode of the Great Sioux War, by Jerome A. Greene

War Cries on Horseback: The Story of the Indian Wars of the Great Plains, by Stephen Longstreet

War Eagle: A Life of General Eugene A. Carr, by James T. King

Warpath: A True Story of the Fighting Sioux, by Stanley Vestal

War-Path and Bivouac: The Bighorn and Yellowstone Expedition, by John F. Finerty

Warpath and Council Fire: The Plains Indians' Struggle for Survival in War and in Diplomacy, 1851–1891, by Stanley Vestal

Washakie: An Account of Indian Resistance, by Grace Raymond Hebard

Wooden Leg: A Warrior Who Fought Custer, interpreted by Thomas B. Marquis

Yellowstone Command: Colonel Nelson A. Miles and the Great Sioux War, 1876–1877, by Jerome A. Greene

There are some who place no confidence whatsoever in Frank Grouard's recollections when he told Joe DeBarthe years later that he scouted north from Crook's camp and ran across that piece of ground just east of the Little Bighorn that would come to be known as Massacre Ridge. But by carefully studying the maps of the terrain between Goose Creek and the Greasy Grass, by considering how fast (or how slow) a man on horseback might travel in hostile country after dark, and finally, by adjusting what the half-breed scout recounted by as little as one day—I was able to see just how feasible it would have been for Grouard and his skittish horse to have found themselves among those naked, mutilated, bloated bodies of the Custer dead.

So it seems to me more than reasonable to expect that Grouard could get his facts skewed by a day or so—seeing as how he dictated his life story decades after the fact.

Yet when I'm given an opportunity to read an account fresher than Grouard's, something written closer to the event—I'll go with it every time.

For example, there isn't all that much written on the harrowing adventures of those men who went for that scout with Lieutenant Frederick Sibley. And what is available often varies in the details. Here I have relied on four sources: Sibley's own account, Frank Grouard's recollections, those of John Finerty, and the dictated recollections of Baptiste "Big Bat" Pourier. Since Grouard, Pourier, and Sibley all related their stories many years later, for this novel I have primarily embraced the Chicago newsman's version (with few, minor exceptions)—since I could draw what I believed was a fresher tale from the reporter's dispatches written immediately after his return to Camp Cloud Peak.

I would imagine that for most readers of western history the Sibley scout comes as something new, perhaps just as new as the skirmish on the Warbonnet. While that military success was small (only one Indian killed), the impact of what Merritt's Fifth Cavalry did would long reverberate across the northern plains. Perhaps as many as eight hundred Cheyenne were turned back to their agency, unable to bolster the numbers of those warrior bands recently victorious over Crook and Custer. Yet it was something far more intangible that made the Warbonnet significant that summer of Sheridan's trumpet on the land.

No matter how small it was—it was the army's first victory.

Except for a few tandem-wired telephone poles, that peaceful, rolling prairie grassland near present-day Montrose, Nebraska, seems unchanged in the last hundred-plus years. The place where Cody had his celebrated duel with a Cheyenne war chief was at the time called Indian Creek in regimental returns of the day, then War Bonnet Creek in later military records, but is today called Hat Creek.

There might well be a lot of confusion for those of you who go looking in the northwest corner of Nebraska for the site of that famous skirmish, simply because all three of those names appear for three separate creeks in that immediate area. While "Hat" and "War Bonnet" are two differing translations for the same Lakota term, the name of a tributary of the Cheyenne River (Mini Pusa to the Sioux), the creek called the War Bonnet on today's maps is some forty miles south of what is today called Hat Creek, where the Fifth Cavalry successfully ambushed Little Wolf's Cheyenne.

The creek still rises with spring runoff and falls with autumnal drought, just as it has every year as white homesteaders and cattlemen moved in and pacified the land. For more than half a century no one knew for sure where the site was, nor did anyone seem to care.

By the mid-1880s the nearby town of Montrose had grown to boast a population of sixty-five! When the Sioux began to dance back the ghosts in the summer of 1890, the frightened citizenry constructed a stockade on the highest hill in the event the ghost dancers spilled off their reservation and came looking for white scalps—the very same hill used as a lookout post by King that morning of July 17, 1876.

It would take another thirty years before anyone got interested in marking the spot, and it was a group of Wyoming citizens who ended up doing it.

In 1929, while marking Wyoming's historic sites, the Wyoming Landmark Commission discovered that the Warbonnet skirmish might well have taken place in their state. Four men promptly formed "The Amalgamated Association of Hunters of the Spot Where Buffalo Bill Killed Yellow Hand." Attempting to use Charles King's book, *Campaigning with Crook,* the association found itself empty-handed that first summer, having been sidetracked mostly by confusing geographical names. No success, until they finally followed still-visible wagon tracks of Lieutenant Hall's supply train. Only then did the searchers discover that the site rested less than a quarter of a mile from the buildings of Montrose.

Still the commissioners felt they needed complete verification. In October of that year the four succeeded in convincing an aging Charles King to visit the site. Eighty-four at the time and in failing health, the retired general was unable to identify the battle site.

The "trees were too big," King said.

In July of the following year King returned west to visit the four Wyoming residents, this time joined by Chris Madsen, the Fifth Cavalry signalman who had been near the site of Cody's duel, an emigrant soldier who would later became a famous lawman in Oklahoma Territory and charge to the top of San Juan Hill with Teddy Roosevelt's

"Rough Riders." Madsen had none of King's doubts. Here and there the old cavalryman led the researchers across the site, relating who did what and where. King concurred.

This event led to the efforts made by Mrs. Johnny Baker, wife of Bill Cody's foster son, to erect a monument on the site to commemorate Buffalo Bill's defeat of Yellow Hair. At the same time Madsen led his own subscription effort to erect a second monument, this one to the Fifth Cavalry. Both were dedicated in September 1934. While King and Baker had passed on by that time, an erect and attentive Chris Madsen listened to the glowing speeches given that warm, early-autumn day—then rose to the rostrum in that dry prairie breeze, took off his hat, and wiped a dark bandanna across his forehead, then told that crowd in the simple language of a plainsman what the Fighting Fifth Cavalry had accomplished that morning fifty-eight years before.

Both those monuments can still be seen by the rare visitor who crosses that ground today. On a towering stone and cement spire, a plaque reads:

SITE
Where
Seven Troops of the Fifth
U.S. Cavalry
Under
Col. WESLEY MERRITT
Intercepted 800 Cheyenne
and Sioux, Enroute to Join
The Hostiles in the North.
July 17, 1876
The Indians Were Driven Back to the
Red Cloud and Spotted Tail Reservations.

Nearby, a short, squat stone-and-cement monument stands just about where Madsen stated the war chief fell. It reads:

On This Spot
W. F. Cody
BUFFALO BILL
Killed
YELLOW HAIR (OR HAND)
The Cheyenne Leader Who, With
A Party of Warriors, Dashed
Down This Ravine To Waylay
Two Soldier Couriers Coming
From the West
July 17, 1876

For many years Cody's participation in that dramatic "duel" was doubted in many circles, just as Frank and Luther North had done all they could to cast doubt on Buffalo Bill's being the one who had actually killed Dog Soldier Chief Tall Bull at Summit Springs on July 11, 1869. But none of the assertions from others who claimed to have killed Yellow Hair have withstood close scrutiny. All those boasts are, as are the claims of the North brothers regarding Summit Springs, dispelled by Don Russell in his compelling book on Cody.

Still, a sergeant with the Fifth Cavalry can take credit for providing the best confirmation that it was indeed Cody who met and killed the Cheyenne. John Powers, stationed that summer at Fort Hays in Kansas, was what we now call a "stringer," paid to send back reports on the campaign trail to his hometown newspaper, the Ellis *County Star.*

Powers's account, composed in the days immediately following the dramatic skirmish, confirms the account of Charles King, written four years later in *Campaigning with Crook:* the approach of Hall's wagon train, its guard of infantry companies, Cody's leading the soldiers to ambush the ambushers intent on butchering the two couriers, Cody's firing of the first shot (which killed the Cheyenne's war pony), his firing a second shot that felled the war chief himself, and the charge of the Fifth Cavalry past the scout who stood over Yellow Hair's body.

   That scene brings to mind a minor controversy in the
three accounts used to write the one you have just read.
While one of those contemporary reports (each of them
written by witnesses of the skirmish) states that Cody shot
Yellow Hair *in the chest,* two of them state unequivocally
that Buffalo Bill shot the Cheyenne *in the head.* When one
studies Cody's abilities with firearms exhibited throughout
his life, it isn't at all hard to believe he was in fact capable
of shooting Yellow Hair in the head. Nonetheless, I'm still
uncertain that a hardened plainsman like Cody would
chance taking a shot at his enemy's head, when he had a far
bigger target in the Cheyenne's broad chest.

   While no testimony specifically reports that Yellow
Hair wore his prize scalp around his neck, I have taken that
poetic license with the tale, making the trophy torn from
the head of a white enemy just the target Bill uses when he
takes deadly aim at the war chief.

   And that brings up another interesting question I
haven't been able to answer to my own satisfaction: how
the name Yellow Hair, over time, eventually became Yellow
Hand. Was it primarily Cody's mistake when he sent the
scalp and warbonnet on to his friend in Rochester, New
York? Or was it Baptiste "Little Bat" Garnier who made the
error when he translated the war chief's name for those
right there at the Warbonnet skirmish that hot July morning? Or was it some unnamed historian's attempt to distinguish between this minor Cheyenne war chief and the term
the Southern Cheyenne used when referring to George
Armstrong Custer (Hiestzi, or "Yellow Hair")?

   All we know for certain is that the warrior's name was
indeed Yellow Hair because, it is believed, he proudly wore
the blond scalp of a white man (or woman—accounts dif-
fer on the sex of the person who once wore that yellow
hair). Despite the fact that the sign reads "Yellow Hand,"
any visitor to the Buffalo Bill Museum in Cody, Wyoming,
will see for himself not only this most famous scalp of the
Sioux War, but Yellow Hair's feathered bonnet and trailer,

his pistol and shield, his knife and blanket, along with the dead Cheyenne's bridle and quirt.

It is beyond me how anyone can claim Cody ended up with these spoils if he wasn't the one who stood over the war chief's body, and if he himself didn't remove them from Yellow Hair as the Fifth Cavalry began its chase of Little Wolf's band!

By that time, exactly a month after Crook's stalemate on the Rosebud, the press had already begun its assault on the general and his handling of the campaign to that point. It was the contention of editors both east and west that Terry and Crook would never find the hostiles, that there was little hope of success. While most of the nation's papers clamored for results in the Sioux War, the New York *Tribune* went so far as to blame the government's policy in the Black Hills for the army's lack of success, also claiming that Sitting Bull had made it clear his Sioux would not return to their reservations until the army drove the white men out of their sacred Paha Sapa.

By early August several Montana newspapers were reporting that the hostile Sioux had offered Canadian tribes an alliance against the whites on both sides of the Medicine Line. While the Canadian Cree, Blackfoot, and Assiniboine refused, the citizens of Montana Territory nonetheless fretted. Reminding his Montana readers that across the border lived more than twelve thousand warriors, the editor of the Deer Lodge *New North-West* wrote, "If they were to join the tribes now fighting the United States, nothing on this side of the line could prevent them."

At the same time, the Fort Benton *Record* received a report from Fort Walsh just across the border in Canada that Yankton Sioux were camped close by and "making mischief." Clearly the cry was going out: the public wanted something done, and now.

Fearing most that Sitting Bull would cross the Yellowstone and reach Canada, General Alfred Terry had eventually given up all thought of working in concert with the loner Crook. For a week he worked Bill Cody and his forces north but found nothing of the wild bands. On September 3 Terry received word from Crook, then on Beaver Creek, an affluent of the Little Missouri, that the Indian trail he had been following had petered out. To Terry there was little more his men could accomplish without using up the supplies Colonel Nelson Miles's men would need for the coming winter as they manned the Tongue River Cantonment from which they were to patrol the lower Yellowstone.

On September 5 Terry disbanded his expedition, sent Gibbon's infantry and Brisbin's Second Cavalry back west to Fort Ellis and Fort Shaw, then went with the Seventh Cavalry itself as it limped home to a somber Fort Abraham Lincoln draped in mourning.

If anything was to be done now, it would be up to George Crook and his Big Horn and Yellowstone Expedition to do it. But first they had to find the Sioux.

As the soldiers came trudging along through the mud, weeks behind them, the warrior bands had already reached the traditional camping grounds they had been visiting for generations. Here beside the Mashtincha Putin (what they called Rabbit Lip Creek), they raised their lodges at the foot of those long gray bluffs dappled with jackpine. The Sioux term for the geographic feature, Paha Zizipela, translates to "thin (or "horizontal") butte"—as a snake is thin and moves horizontally, in the sense of the buttes running north-south. These buttes are indeed long (fifty miles) and very thin (less than four miles in width).

The exact number of Miniconjou in that village has long remained a source of controversy. At the time of the battles Frank Grouard told Mills and Crook the village contained two hundred occupants. Anson Mills later stated that he learned from the captives that the village comprised "two hundred souls, one hundred of whom were warriors." Yet this ratio of warriors to other occupants seems unusually high.

However, when we apply the 1855 Thomas Twiss method of counting (whereby it was determined there were two men of fighting age for every lodge—"fighting age" determined as men from their midteens to their late thirties), we find a much more likely figure of seventy-four warriors in that camp that Mills attacked at dawn.

Still, that figure might seem a little high to those knowledgeable in the Plains Indian culture. By applying Harry H. Anderson's computations (7 Indians per normal-sized lodge, of which 1.29 are warriors), we come up with a village population of some 260 Miniconjou and 48 warriors. When you add to those 48 any boys eager to defend their families, as well as older men and a few women who would stay behind to fight—one can see how Captain Mills just might arrive at an estimate of 100 combatants he faced on the morning of September 9.

While we can verify that Crook's combined forces numbered just shy of 2,000 men, historians have disagreed as to the number of warriors Sitting Bull led against what the Sioux believed would be only 150 pony soldiers—those who attacked at dawn with Anson Mills. Estimates range anywhere between 600 to 800, although a few winters later Sitting Bull himself would say that he had led a thousand warriors back to attack Three Stars. No matter if he did have that many—the Sioux were still up against two-to-one odds when they tried to make it tough on Crook's retreating army.

Rumors had long existed that the soldiers had killed their warrior captives before pulling away from the village. Four years after the battle Charles King himself made note of those rumors in his *Campaigning with Crook*, as did Don Rickey, Jr., in *Forty Miles a Day on Beans and Hay*. But National Park Service research historian Jerome A. Greene maintains that, "There is no substantiating evidence for the charge made fifty-nine years later by a deserter from Crook's expedition that the captured warriors were shot to death by the troops before the command left the battlefield."

After interviewing Sioux participants in the Battle of Slim Buttes, as well as some of their relatives, author Stan-

ley Vestal reported that the Miniconjou losses were ten
killed and two wounded. According to the Ricker Papers,
Red Horse claimed seven were killed and four wounded,
while a third Sioux reported the dead as three men, four
women, and one infant—eight total.

What we can be even more certain of is the fact that
the Sioux were fired up, furious beyond words when they
returned to the site of their decimated, burned-out village
after driving off the stragglers at the tail end of Crook's
column retreating to the south. Aware that the warriors in
the hills—as well as Crook's prisoners later to be released—
had watched the soldiers bury their dead, we can have little
doubt that the Sioux did in fact dig up the graves of White,
Wenzel, and Kennedy, and so too the hole where the surgeons had buried Von Leuttwitz's leg. The warriors and
squaws in mourning would almost certainly have taken out
their rage and grief not only on those dead bodies, but on
that amputated limb.

Of great interest to me was the discovery of all that
money and those articles taken from Custer's dead at the
Little Bighorn fight. In his reminiscences Frank Grouard
declared that soldiers combing through the lodges prior to
their destruction found more than eleven thousand dollars.
This, most would agree, is simply too grand a figure. John
Finerty reported to his readers that Crook's troops recovered nine hundred dollars. The real amount is likely to be
somewhere in between, a figure closer to that given by the
Chicago newsman. Allowing for a bit of pilfering here and
there, one might believe there was easily twelve hundred
dollars or more to be recovered in that village.

But more so even than that cash, what piqued my
interest was the discovery of those ghostly relics. Just as one
writer of that time stated, to come across the letters written
to and by the Custer dead must have been like hearing
faint, eerie voices whispering from their shallow graves beside the Greasy Grass. A matter of weeks later Sergeant
Jefferson Spooner recalled that when he had been going
through the lodges, he came across several noteworthy arti-

cles: a locket, a small cabinet photo of Captain Myles Keogh, two gold-mounted ivory-handled revolvers, and a Spencer sporting rifle. The cavalry sergeant went on to state, "The picture and locket I gave to an officer of the 3rd Cav., who claimed them as a relative of the officer killed with Custer, and a revolver I gave to Capt. Rodgers of 'A' Co. 5th Cav. The rifle *I sold some days later for two loaves of bread.*"

The emphasis there is all mine! Only to remind you that in less than a week of that victory over a village filled with dried meat, Crook's troops were on the Belle Fourche and then the Whitewood, trading what little they had with the greedy merchants who came out from the Black Hills towns to charge the soldiers five, six, even seven times the going rate (already inflated due to transportation costs to the mining settlements) for the most basic of foodstuffs!

It seems from the discovery of the Keogh photograph and that locket, from the captain's leather gauntlets, and especially from the "Wild I" company guidon, that whoever secured those souvenirs was among those who overwhelmed that tough band of cavalrymen who attempted to hold the east side of Massacre Ridge. One report states that the swallowtail flag was tied outside the lodge of American Horse, likely attached to the smoke-flap ropes. But Anson Mills states that it was discovered "in good condition, folded up in an Indian reticule with a pair of Colonel Keogh's gauntlets marked with his name."

Yet Mills wasn't the one who discovered that guidon. Charging the Sioux village, Private W. J. McClinton sprinted in with his C Troop from the Third Cavalry, and that very day presented the flag to Captain Mills. Years later when McClinton received his discharge papers from the army, he found the face of the document emblazoned in bold red ink with a testament to the fact that he had captured the guidon. Upon his discharge McClinton remained in the West, soon to become a resident of Sheridan, Wyoming, where he enjoyed a long and successful business career. More than a decade later John Bourke wrote,

"[McClinton] never tires of singing the praises of General Crook and the brave men who opened up the rich valleys of the Tongue and Goose Creek [near present-day Sheridan] to settlement."

But while that guidon went to Mills's care, the story is yet incomplete. Not long after the arduous campaigns of the great Sioux War, Anson Mills loaned the relic, among other "trophies," to the Museum of the Military Service Institution on Governor's Island, New York. Years later upon its return he was dismayed at how the museum curators had allowed moths to have their way with the flag. He promptly had it encased in glass, and after the old soldier's death, the Mills family donated it to the Custer Battlefield National Monument (now renamed the Little Bighorn Battlefield). There visitors can see that very same guidon that flew over the heads of Myles W. Keogh's I Company as they stood their ground along Massacre Ridge, then fell into the dust when the standard-bearer died on that hillside, and finally traveled with the victorious Sioux to Dakota Territory—there to be recaptured by the U.S. Cavalry.

There is still something of a controversy regarding these relics. Are they, in fact, a "smoking gun" proving that this band of Miniconjou were indeed at the Little Bighorn battle? Years afterward Indians on the Standing Rock Reservation claimed that Iron Plume (as American Horse was better known among his people) had not been at the Greasy Grass fight at all. They testified that the Seventh Cavalry relics were instead brought into American Horse's camp by visiting Oglalla in those eleven weeks after the soldiers were wiped out.

Nonetheless, Jerome Greene has stated there is sufficient evidence to believe that some of the warriors who were in that camp on the morning of 9 September had also been camped beside the Little Bighorn on the afternoon of 25 June. Perhaps most compelling are the words of Miniconjou Red Horse given to Judge Eli Ricker in his statement testifying that he was at both fights.

It seems conceivable to me that both sides in this controversy are correct. It is not hard at all to believe that in American Horse's village that September morning there were both those who had fought the Seventh Cavalry on that hot summer day eleven weeks before, and those who had joined up with Sitting Bull and Crazy Horse only in the days immediately following their great victory. The Indian populations of various warrior bands and clan groupings underwent growth and shrinkage throughout that spring, summer, and into the fall, with much coming and going as the seven great circles finally merged in the days before crushing Custer, then almost immediately began to slowly disperse and mosey off to the four winds as Crook and Terry sat on their thumbs—not knowing what to do.

Despite their hunger for a victory of some kind over the Sioux who had defeated the Seventh Cavalry, there was considerable disagreement, and outright argument, over Captain Mills's attacking a village of unknown strength without first alerting Crook. The general himself criticized Mills for not having sent a courier back during the long night of the eighth, upon Grouard's discovering the enemy camp. This, Crook attested, would have given him time to bring up the whole column, surrounding the camp and preventing the escape of all those "two hundred" Sioux into the nearby hills and bluffs.

Another source of heated discussion among Crook's officers was the fact that Mills had opened up the battle with a dangerously limited supply of ammunition. All this criticism quickly made its way into the press of the day. Robert Strahorn wrote in his dispatches to the Rocky Mountain *News:*

> Crook was very much disappointed because Mills didn't report his discovery last night, and there was plenty of time to have got the entire command there and so effectually surrounded the village that nothing would have escaped; but the General is also pleased, all things considered.

Reuben Davenport of the New York *Herald,* never a fan of Crook, nonetheless took this opportunity to rebuke Mills:

> All the circumstances lead to the inevitable conclusion that had Col. [Mills] reported the discovery to headquarters, instead of attempting to steal a march on the camp himself, the whole column could easily have reached and effectually surrounded the entire village before daylight . . . instead of this village of over 250 to 300 hostile savages getting off with whole skins, they could easily have been swooped down upon and annihilated.

How unfortunate that none of those contemporaries of Captain Anson Mills appear to have asked one simple question: what was the best information Mills operated with at the time of his discovery of the village? When he departed from the main column, pushing on with Lieutenant Bubb to secure provisions from the Black Hills settlements, Crook informed Mills and his lieutenants that he would be remaining in bivouac that next day and not moving south on Mills's trail until the morning of the ninth.

So when Grouard discovered the hunters, then the pony herd, and finally the village late on that rainy afternoon of the eighth—Anson Mills had nothing to indicate that George Crook and the rest of the Big Horn and Yellowstone Expedition were anywhere but a minimum of thirty-five miles or more to their rear, right back where his battalion had left them. To send a courier on that backtrail wouldn't have made much sense, at least to me—because given the condition of Crook's men and animals, no courier could have conceivably crossed thirty-five miles of that treacherous, muddy country to reach Crook, and no column could have then marched another thirty-five miles across the same gumbo prairie, in time to launch a concerted attack at dawn!

Everything considered—the distant position of reinforcements from Crook's column, and Mills's dangerously low supply of ammunition—I believe the captain made the only decision he could, and all arguments then and now are nothing more than niggling, meaningless carping.

Still, it isn't hard for me to understand the conditions that would make such heated debates arise: great, passionate welling of sentiment from those who continued to suffer the terrible privations of that campaign, two harrowing days of battle, and the additional horrors of their horsemeat march between Owl and Willow creeks. Simply put, we must remember that those soldiers had been in the wilderness for four and a half months without leave or relief.

In the Huntington Library collections we find the papers of Lieutenant Walter S. Schuyler, who wrote to his father upon Crook's return to Fort Laramie:

> It has been a march through the heart of the enemy's country, almost wholly unexplored by white men, and thoroughly misunderstood by them, a march which has tried men's souls as well as their constitutions, a march which will live in our history as the hardest ever undertaken by our army, and on which the privation and hardship were equaled only by the astonishing health of the command while accomplishing it.

Years after that grueling march of survival and sheer willpower, Lieutenant John Bourke found his own health failing. In writing his book, *On the Border With Crook,* he asked his public to study the roster of those soldiers who had suffered terribly through twenty-two days of constant hunger, cold, and rain.

> If any of my readers imagines that the march from the head of Heart River down to the Belle Fourche was a picnic, let him examine the roster

of the command and tell of the scores and scores
of men, then hearty and rugged, who now fill
premature graves or drag out an existence with
constitutions wrecked and enfeebled by such
privations and vicissitudes.

Fourteen years later in his short story about the campaign, which he titled "Van," Charles King wrote:

> We set out with ten days' rations on a chase
> that lasted ten weeks . . . We wore out some In-
> dians, a good many soldiers, and a great many
> horses. We sometimes caught the Indians, and
> sometimes they caught us. It was hot, dry sum-
> mer weather when we left our wagons, tents, and
> extra clothing; it was sharp and freezing before
> we saw them again.

In an attempt to capture some of that grueling privation, as depicted in a closing scene of this novel, a photographer rode out from Deadwood with his cameras and his
portable, wagon-borne darkroom to record for history
through staged photographs some of what Crook's troops
managed to live through. For this alone we are indebted to
photographer Stanley J. Morrow. With the assistance of
Bantam Books and through the courtesy of folks at the
Little Bighorn National Battlefield who searched through
their photographic archives, we have in this book repro-
duced a few of Morrow's momentous photos.

Perhaps the most evocative picture for me is the one
showing the famous hide lodge salvaged from the captured
village and used as Dr. Clements's "hospital" for the next
several days. The photo, taken after the column had
reached the Black Hills, also shows the captured I Troop
guidon on display. Standing left to right are scout Frank
Grouard, Private W. J. McClinton (who captured the flag),
and Lieutenant Frederick Schwatka. Seated left to right are
Lieutenant Colonel William B. Royall (who commanded a

battalion at the Battle of the Rosebud), Captain William H. Andrews (prominent for his gallantry on Royall's flank during the Rosebud fight), Captain Anson Mills, and Lieutenant Joseph Lawson.

This last officer was generally known as a "character" among his comrades in the Third Cavalry. A native of Seamus Donegan's Ireland, Lawson emigrated to the Ohio River country of Kentucky, where he ran a grocery store, married, and fathered five children before joining the Union Army with the outbreak of the Civil War—at the age of forty! In his remarkable career during the Indian wars, this unassuming soldier never asked any handicap of troopers half his age, being able to stay in the saddle and outride all but a handful of younger men in the Third Cavalry. Six feet tall and thin as a rail, with tobacco juice perpetually staining his scraggly red beard, Lawson had remained behind with Crook and the pack-train at the time of Reynolds's Powder River fight, March 17, 1876. Three months later, after having displayed conspicuous courage during the Rosebud battle, the lieutenant was finally promoted to captain while Crook's column was still recouping in the Black Hills, September 25, 1876. He would go on to distinguish himself at the Thornburg fight against Ute warriors on Colorado's Milk River in 1879 . . . but there will be more on that to come in a future volume of this long-running series.

This buffalo-hide lodge was to remain the personal property of Captain Mills. Knowing that the captain did not return to the Belle Fourche with Lieutenant Bubb and the wagons loaded with supplies, choosing instead to remain behind for a day or so to recoup his strength, we can therefore determine with some accuracy that Morrow took this photo sometime after Mills rejoined the column at one of its Whitewood Creek camps.

By that time Crook and his entourage of officers and reporters were speeding back to Fort Laramie. Yet correspondent Reuben Davenport had already offered five hundred dollars to scout Jack Crawford to break away from

Frank Grouard and Captain Anson Mills—and race to the closest telegraph key. At the same time, Grouard carried dispatches for the three other reporters. In our next volume, *A Cold Day in Hell,* you will be treated to the amusing adventures of that cross-country race between the two army scouts.

After reaching Laramie, correspondent Davenport limped on to Cheyenne, where he finally collapsed as a result of his exertions following the Big Horn and Yellowstone Expedition. On his sickbed the newsman completed a fifteen-thousand-word story that was promptly printed in its entirety by the New York *Herald*—an article in which Davenport declared that Crook should be court-martialed for his conduct on the trail. He believed the campaign from thereon out would be remembered with the same historical disgust as was Napoleon's retreat from Moscow during a cruel Russian winter, despite the fact that "a freak of fortune" had allowed the discovery of a small village and its "inglorious" capture.

About a week after reaching Fort Laramie, John Finerty returned to Chicago, reporting to his editor, Clint Snowden, and the paper's owner, Wilbur Storey. After a series of in-depth articles on Crook's campaign, Finerty's final article appeared on October 6 in the Chicago *Times:*

> Since my return I have had to endure the usual boredom shoved upon an ephemeral human curiosity . . . The constitutional, inevitable, universal "damphool" has asked me a dozen times: "You weren't in earnest when you said you lived on horse meat? Didn't you make that up?" This species of biped jackass flourishes in every community, and can hardly be expected to be absent from Chicago.

On the second of December, 1876, the U.S. Army awarded the medal of honor to those three couriers who courageously carried General Terry's letter south through territory believed to be teeming with hostiles, destined for Crook at his Camp Cloud Peak: Privates William Evans, Benjamin F. Stewart, and James Bell—all of E Company, Seventh U.S. Infantry.

Anson Mills would eventually secure another brevet rank of colonel for his meritorious service in launching the charge on the village at Slim Buttes. Then forty-five years later in 1921, some twenty-four years after he had retired from the army with the rank of brigadier general, and thirty-one years after Crook died, Mills applied through former commanding general of the army General Nelson A. Miles for a Medal of Honor. Those fellow officers who joined Miles in supporting the award read like a Who's Who of officers who served with Crook's Big Horn and Yellowstone Expedition in that terrible march: Major General Samuel S. Sumner, Brigadier General Charles King, Brigadier General William P. Hall, Brigadier General Peter D. Vroom.

But, sadly, Mills had applied too long after the fact, according to the army's regulations. Some historians believe he waited so long because his application would have been denied by Crook, who might still voice his criticism of Mills's "precipitous" attack. If this appraisal is correct, then why did Mills wait a full thirty-one years after his old antagonist's death?

Most confusing are two minor inconsistencies found in otherwise scholarly books. Jerome Greene puts Finerty with Davenport as the two reporters who departed with Mills on the night of 7 September. But one has only to read John Finerty's book to learn that he stayed behind and was with Crook when George Herman, Mills's courier, showed up to announce the taking of the village. We know there were two reporters along from their subsequent accounts of the morning battle. So from my own research poring over the microfilm copies of old issues of the Rocky Mountain News, in which "Alter Ego's" stories of Captain Mills's morning "fight" would later appear, I believe I can trust

John S. Gray's account that it was indeed Robert Strahorn who was there at dawn.

In yet a second discrepancy Greene appears to be the correct party. Whereas Oliver Knight gives "Alfred Milner" as the name of the soldier killed by Sioux along the Belle Fourche during the return of Major Upham's battalion from its fruitless patrol, Greene accurately reports the name from duty rosters in the military archives as Cyrus B. Milner of Company A.

Still, it is the confusion surrounding the identity of "Buffalo Chips" White that most befuddles me. Charles King states that the scout's name was *James* White. John Finerty records him as *"Charley,* alias *Frank* White." Then we find his gravestone at the Slim Buttes battle site is inscribed with the name *Jonathan* White. James and Jonathan, maybe—a discrepancy caused by the slightest error in someone's memory—but where did Finerty ever come up with Frank?

It was likely easier for historians to locate and identify the Slim Buttes site than it was to determine the scout's real first name!

Like so many other dramatic chapters of the Indian wars, the fight at Slim Buttes quickly faded from memory, thrust back into the shadows behind the more startling but no more consequential Little Bighorn battle. Thirty-one years would pass before amateur Indian wars' historian Walter M. Camp, then editor for the "Railway Review," would interview old Miniconjou warriors on the Standing Rock Reservation, thus learning of Crook's attack on their village.

It took another seven years, in 1914, for Camp to convince two veterans of Crook's campaign, Anson Mills and Charles Morton, to accompany him to South Dakota. In Belle Fourche they rented a car and drove north, but after spending several days searching along the eastern face of the buttes, neither could confirm the site of the Miniconjou village. The three returned east empty-handed.

But Camp would not be deterred. Undaunted, he pursued his quest for another three years, and finally, in June of 1917, with the help of a map drawn by Charles King as well as hours of research by Bill Rumbaugh, a ranch hand working for a local cattleman in South Dakota, Camp finally determined the battlefield site.

While working cattle across that ground year after year, Rumbaugh had discovered pieces of shattered iron cookware destroyed by Crook's troops, spent .45/70 cases in the still-visible rifle pits, along with burned lodgepoles and the presence of human skeletal remains. Accompanied by Rumbaugh, in addition to six other local ranchers, an overjoyed Camp finally walked over that hallowed ground and verified the battle site located in the extreme northwestern corner of South Dakota. In his subsequent searches he found a variety of artifacts, including iron tea kettles, galvanized water buckets, broken butcher knives, iron hooks and handles, tin pans, basins, cups and cans, broken and melted glass bottles, broken earthware dishes, coffeepots, clothes buttons, and a stone pestle.

Still, it was the discovery of human skeletal remains that caused Camp the most excitement and speculation. One of the local ranchers took the researcher to the top of a little knoll less than a quarter of a mile from the south side of the creek. There Camp was shown a skeleton, complete but for the skull. Beneath the remains lay a burned and bent carbine barrel, as well as three spent cartridge cases.

On a knoll directly west of this first site, Camp later discovered a second skeleton in much the same condition. Not knowing at the time that Sitting Bull's warriors had boasted of digging up the white man's graves near the village, Camp nevertheless came to that exact conclusion years ahead of the publication of Stanley Vestal's book.

In his own words Camp tells what he discovered:

I proposed that we look for evidence of opened graves, and this we soon found near the west edge of the village site on a low bench from the creek bottom, under a clump of buck brush that had grown up on the two mounds of earth that had been thrown out with the excavations. These two holes in the ground were three feet apart . . . The dirt thrown out had been weather-beaten down into flattened heaps, and enough of it had been washed back into the two trench-like openings to fill them within two feet of the general ground surface.

From subsequent inquiries of survivors of the battle I have learned that the location of these excavations is about at the place where were buried the bodies of the two soldiers (John Wenzel and Edward Kennedy) and of the scout (Charles White) killed in the fight . . . I am, from the evidence, led to inquire whether the Indians, who returned to the village to look for their own dead, might not have dug up these bodies, dragged them up to the two little hills, and had dances around them . . . Can it be, therefore, that the bones of the killed on the victorious side have been bleaching in the sunlight all these years?

Today a visitor can drive east from the small town of Buffalo for twenty-one miles, crossing over the Slim Buttes themselves. Approximately two miles west of the hamlet of Reva on the south side of the highway you will find a bronze-plaque roadside marker and the eight-foot-tall shaft of a stone monument erected on a small patch of state ground a half mile from the actual site of the village. Beyond the nearby fence the rest of the site is land owned by the family of George Lermeny, whom I've had the pleasure of speaking with on the phone but whom I have not had the honor of meeting in person. Lermeny's grandfather came from Canada to settle on that ground in late 1886.

Former Sergeant John A. Kirkwood helped place the stone pylon monument that was financed by Anson Mills after Walter M. Camp confirmed the site. But, despite Camp's protests, Mills elected to place the tall spire a half mile from the village site and close beside the highway, where the old general wanted it to be seen by the cars that passed by on that narrow east-west route. In August of 1920, three years after the ground had been identified, the markers were dedicated, complete with three separate headstones commemorating those white men who fell at Slim Buttes, all enclosed inside a tall wrought-iron fence.

Those two markers are as close as you will get to the battlefield. The passerby, tourist, amateur historian, and researcher are not allowed onto Lermeny's property, where a third marker stands at the mouth of the ravine, indicating where Wenzel and White were killed. Erected in 1956 by the South Dakota State Historical Society, it reads:

> Siege of the Ravine
> American Horse, family
> and six warriors ran here
> at dawn attack. By noon
> four warriors were dead.
> American Horse, fatally
> wounded, surrendered with
> those left. Here Jonathan
> White, "Chips," civilian
> scout, was killed.

In my phone conversations with George Lermeny, the rancher remained adamant that he wanted no further attention given to the site. "It's been too much trouble for us already," he said to me, then went on to tell how in recent years several researchers had come to him seeking permission to go over the village site and the surrounding hillsides with their metal detectors, and to complete analytical terrain surveys. Because those researchers subsequently wrote books on the Slim Buttes battle, Lermeny feels there's been too much of a rising tide of publicity surrounding his family's home.

The Reva, South Dakota, rancher told me, "We've had too much attention given us. I'm hoping things'll eventually quiet down and we can go back to making a living here. This is our family business. Six generations have worked this ground. We just want to be left alone now."

In fact, the home George Lermeny shares with his wife rests in the draw where on that rainy night of September 8, 1876, Anson Mills waited for the gray light of dawn with 150 troopers, located to the northeast (and across the present highway) from the Sioux village.

As much as I was personally disappointed in not getting a chance to meet George Lermeny and to walk that creek bottom, climb those knolls and hills south and west of the village site, look myself for the rifle pits used by Chambers's infantry on the afternoon of September 9, then follow the path of the Fifth Cavalry's retreat on the morning of the tenth—I can nonetheless understand his possessiveness of that beautiful piece of ground.

I can sympathize with it entirely in light of what I see done by visitors at Yellowstone and Glacier national parks, visitors to the battlefields that dot the western plains.

Shamefully, all too few American citizens are truly respectful of our past or do they truly honor the historical and spiritual significance of that sacred ground. As much as I am sorry that this is one piece of hallowed soil I did not get to walk across, much less have the opportunity to sit and listen to the ghosts whisper through the branches of the buffalo-berry bushes heavy with their bright-red fruit— I find myself in total sympathy with George Lermeny.

At the time of Crook's Big Horn and Yellowstone Expedition, Lieutenant Charles Morton served as regimental adjutant to Lieutenant Colonel William B. Royall, Third Cavalry. By 1914, when he was frequently corresponding with researcher Walter M. Camp, Morton had risen to the rank of brigadier general. In a letter the old soldier wrote to Camp on August 19, 1914, Morton included a poem composed shortly after the Battle of Slim Buttes which he credited to an unidentified officer of the Fifth Cavalry, a bit of rhyme that shows how some of Crook's soldiers steadfastly despised their general, no matter the march of time.

At Slim Buttes, neath the noon-day sun,
After the "Third" the fight had won,
Came Crook and pack-train on the run,
    To jump the captured property.

. . . .

Then rose a wild and piercing yell
That rent the air like sounds from hell.
And shots mid herds and pickets fell,
    Stampeding Crook's sagacity.

The skirmish thickens, "Fight, men, fight!"
One buck has fallen on the right.
Wave, George, thy flag in wild delight,
    And snort with mule stupidity.

'Tis done. The ration fight is o'er.
Two hundred purps lie sick and sore.
And ponies' flanks are gushing gore
    To stimulate humidity.

Too few are left who care to tell
How starved men fought and ponies fell;
But "Crook was right," the papers yell,
    To George's great felicity.

On the twenty-fourth of October, 1876, upon officially disbanding the Big Horn and Yellowstone Expedition, General George Crook—the target of so much derision and outright hatred from his soldiers, the object of so much admiration among those he led into battle and forced to keep going until the end of their "horse-meat march"—

addressed himself to his officers and men in General Orders No. 8:

> In the campaign now closed [I have] been obliged to call upon you for much hard service and many sacrifices of personal comfort. At times you have been out of reach of your base of supplies in most inclement weather, and have marched without food and sleep—without shelter. In your engagements you have evinced a high order of discipline and courage; in your marches wonderful powers of endurance; and in your deprivations and hardships patience and fortitude.
>
> Indian warfare is of all warfare the most dangerous, the most trying, and the most thankless. Not recognized by the high authority of the United States Congress as war, it still possesses for you the disadvantages of civilized warfare with all the horrible accompaniments that barbarism can invent and savages can execute. In it you are required to serve without the incentive to promotion or recognition—in truth, without favor or hope of reward.
>
> The people of our sparsely-settled frontier, in whose defense this war is waged, have but little influence with the powerful communities in the East; their representatives have little voice in our national councils; while your savage foes are not only the wards of the nation, supported in idleness, but objects of sympathy with large numbers of people otherwise well informed and discerning.
>
> You may, therefore, congratulate yourselves that in the performance of your military duty you have been on the side of the weak against the strong, and that the few people on the frontier will remember your efforts with gratitude.

All too few in this country, in this day and time, stop in their seventy-mile an hour, sixteen-hour workdays to give thought to those of that dramatic but bygone time . . . those who sacrificed so much.

Both red and white.

TERRY C. JOHNSTON
Slim Buttes, S.D.
September 9, 1994

ABOUT THE AUTHOR

TERRY C. JOHNSTON was born in 1947 on the plains of Kansas, and has lived all his life in the American West. His first novel, *Carry the Wind,* won the Medicine Pipe Bearer's Award from the Western Writers of America, and his subsequent books have appeared on bestseller lists throughout the country. He lives and writes in Big Sky country near Billings, Montana. For a week every July, the author takes readers on his very own "Terry C. Johnston's West: A Novelist's Journey into the Indian Wars"—a HistoryAmerica tour to the famous battlesites and landmarks of the historical West. All those desiring information on taking part in the author's summer tours can write to him at:

TERRY C. JOHNSTON
P. O. Box 50594
Billings, MT 59105